I0652263

THE MOUNTAIN

Matthew C. Lucas

MONTAG

A Montag Press Book
www.montagpress.com
Montag Press
777 Morton Street, Unit B
San Francisco CA 94129 USA

Montag Press, the burning book with the hatchet cover, the skewed word mark and the portrayal of the long-suffering fireman mascot are trademarks of Montag Press.

The sword, pick and hammer symbol is a trademark of Matthew C. Lucas.

Printed & Digitally Originated in the United States of America

10 9 8 7 6 5 4 3 2 1

"And if thou gaze long into an abyss, the abyss will also gaze into thee."

— Nietzsche

PROLOGUE

I N THE MOUNTAIN, in a place high and deep, there once was light.
Along a bridge carved within the Mountain's body, an arcing
granite line held aloft like a spider web glistening in the darkness.
The bridge's light crossed the void of a chasm and touched the Mountain's three realms: from the hidden mines of the Quarter and the
tunneled slums of the Crag on one side, to the high, sunlit valleys and
fields of the Crest on the other. All the peoples of the Mountain called
this bridge the Spine. It was the only link between the realms, the only
way for those who dwelled within the Crag to reach the Crest. And
once, long ago, the way had been lit.

An avenue of statues had stood atop pedestals along the Spine's bal-
ustrades. Tall, daunting alabaster warlords, high priests, kings, thanes, the
heroes who tamed the tunnels of the Mountain, and gods, countless
gods—towering figures of marble raised to mark the people's greatest
feats and fears—in a time before there were clerks to keep records of
such things. Each figure had been graced with a lantern. Lit together,
they scattered the night, a train of flickering flames that had stretched
forth for ages to show the way through the darkness between the realms.

But now the statues were gone. Toppled and dragged away. Their
pedestals remained, but they were empty. Empty, darkened, forgotten. In
an afterthought, faded, tattered flags had been draped where the statues
once stood. They gave no light but proclaimed a symbol instead. A black
emblem set within an amber field. The symbol of the three realms the
bridge still joined. A broadsword, pick, and hammer, crossed and bound
together near the sword's hilt.

One of the flags fluttered off the edge of a cracked pedestal and disappeared into the gulf.

The woman carrying the lantern paid it no mind.

1

Up and down, her metal lamp bobbed. It was twined about a yellow sash that was wrapped much too tightly around her belly. She was middle-aged, sweating, and very flustered, and the light from her lantern's flame was beginning to sputter. A strand of wavy gray hair had tumbled out of a prim knit cap where it curled about a jowly face. The woman's cheeks glowed almost as brightly as the lantern's flame. She glanced over her shoulder and made an exasperated noise: "Hurry up, you three! A clerk is never late."

Lillia, Mava, and Jack didn't move at first. They were slumped over a rail alongside the bridge, looking straight down, transfixed by the yawning blackness beneath them. Pale, thin, of some age between fourteen and sixteen, they were all dressed in drab-colored shirts and trousers that were neat, but poorly fitted. Each wore a yellow sash over their shoulder. They had never been to the Spine before.

"Come on," Lillia tugged at Jack's sleeve, "you're going to get us in trouble."

Jack swatted her hand away.

"Just one more," he said.

Jack hocked from deep in his throat and then spat out into the void. The girls craned their heads to listen. A whisper of cold air wafted by, stirring their hair, bringing a chill.

"Did you hear that?" He wheeled around from the railing.

"Uh-huh," Mava nodded. "I think so."

"Hear what?" Lillia demanded.

"It was like a plunk of water or something. There must be a lake down there."

"No," Lillia shook her head. "You didn't hear anything. You either, Mava. We're thousands of feet up, and it's all rock at the bottom of Cowan's Chasm. Now come on before she misses us."

"How do you know?" Jack had his hands on his sides. His arms and shoulders were starting to fill out, and the wisps of blonde hairs above his mouth could almost be called a moustache.

"I saw it in a map," Lillia replied.

Jack pursed his lips.

"I did," she insisted. "Last week when Madam Teacher took us to the library. There was a map sitting out and I studied it. Very closely."

"Sure you did."

"It was an official map with a clerk's seal. Parchment about this wide," she drew her hands apart in the air to show a document of some considerable size. "And it showed the only water anywhere is the ocean around the Mountain and the lakes up in the Crest. I saw it myself."

"You're such a little liar."

Lillia's face screwed up. She was trying to think of just the right cut to put Jack in his place when an orange lantern light swung in an arc over their heads with a loud metal rattle. It missed them by inches. The woman's voice, harried, out of breath, but still measured, pierced the gloom:

"I am deeply disturbed that my pupils, the future clerks of our Commonwealth, are heedless that they're about to be late to an official function in the Crest."

"Sorry, Madam Teacher," the children replied in unison.

"You were not given special passes so you could dally on a bridge over a hole. I would have thought that would go without saying."

"Yes, Madam."

The teacher's chest was heaving and trickles of sweat ran freely from the folds of her neck. She wiped her arm across her forehead, fixed her hair back beneath her cap, and grasped the closest child, Mava, by the scruff of her shirt. The three children fell in step once more behind the steady clack of their teacher's clogs and the accompanying rattle of her lantern. They hurried over the flagstones of the bridge's road, pausing only to skirt around pieces of broken wagons and crates that littered the causeway.

"No idea how fortunate you are," Madam Teacher spoke as she ran. "Oblivious. Completely oblivious to the honor. Oh, hurry *up*."

As the teacher continued scolding them, Lillia studied her in the swaying glow of the lamp's light. The woman's face was dour and pinched as ever, Lillia thought, but not because she was angry about anything. It was an odd expression that had taken hold of Madam Teacher, a strange new energy animating this person Lillia had spent years scrutinizing. A mood she had never seen before.

For the first time, Madam Teacher seemed excited.

"We're here," the teacher brought them to a halt. "Now listen to me closely. This is a privilege," she pronounced the word meaningfully. "It is a privilege to pass through the Citadel's keeps—and an unheard-of privilege to be granted permission to come into the Crest. I could not have dreamed of such an honor when I was a student."

All three children bowed their heads. Their teacher straightened her sash, which was starting to sag from around her plump waist. She took a deep breath and gestured towards the darkness with a reverent whisper:

"Govern yourselves carefully. We've arrived." Then from the side of her mouth: "And we are being watched."

The children peered ahead. At first, there was nothing at all different to see except perhaps for the bridge's railings, which had given way to barricaded walls. But as their eyes settled, they could begin to make out an outline emerging from the gloom before them. A gray shadow looming within the darkness. As the four of them crept closer, its features came into focus.

A sheer wall of granite adorned with ramparts, and parapets, and turreted towers rose from the bridge to an unseen height. It was a keep, carved from the very stone of the Mountain, impossibly vast, great enough to be its own mountain. The children knew without being told they had reached the Citadel.

There were no lights shining from the battlements, no one came to greet Lillia and her companions. The drawbridge was down as if waiting for them, but it lent no feeling of welcome. The span of black iron led from the end of the bridge into the gated mouth of the Citadel's Inner Keep. Nothing stirred in the gateway. And yet, as their teacher had warned, Lillia felt as if hidden eyes were indeed studying them, watching their movements.

"Come along," the teacher's voice seemed stretched with urgency.

Their footsteps reverberated softly on the drawbridge. They reached a closed set of doors, iron and ancient-looking, but without the smallest blemish of rust or dent. In the lantern's light, fanciful scrollwork could be seen covering their surface, inlaid over a pattern of steel rivets. It made a mesmerizing effect, like a constellation of metal stars shining within a bank of storm clouds. Something graceful, and faraway, and formidable. The words "Thought" and "Peace" seemed to shimmer across each of the doors' faces.

Her hand trembling, Madam Teacher reached for one of the ringed knockers, but then she stopped herself:

"Remember," she said, "we are here for service. Keep your poise. Govern yourselves carefully. Mava, fix your hair. Jack, close your mouth. Now if someone from the Crest should deign to speak to you, just smile brightly, tell them how well cared for you are, and answer quickly: yes, sir, or yes, ma'am. Nothing more. Understand?"

Lillia and her fellow students answered together: "yes, Madam."

She held the knocker a moment longer.

"I expect this function may seem somewhat—disturbing. Since you are children. But it is your duty to bear witness. Your place in my class, your future positions as clerks," she faced Lillia directly now, "or as commissars, could depend on how you discharge your duties today. You will be watched. The Crest is always watching us."

The last door of the Citadel slammed shut behind them. The teacher and her children held their hands before their faces, grimacing from the sudden onslaught of daylight and sound.

When her eyes adjusted, Lillia saw people, hundreds of them, milling outside beneath the afternoon sun of a marketplace. These people laughed freely, seemingly for no reason, as they ate and drank in a plaza of neatly swept daises and stairs. Some were enjoying the shade of budding spruce and acacias. Others bartered in front of storefronts. Peals of mirth, interlaced with the buzz of idle chatter, pleasant arguments, and witty anecdotes seemed to fill every part of the air. They were olive-skinned women and bronze men dressed in a riot of colors, and all of them, old and young, were the most beautiful beings Lillia had ever beheld.

High above them all, a weathered dome stretched forth from the side of the Mountain. It was buttressed by a forest of granite pillars spread across the market square. Lillia tilted her head back to stare up the height of one of the columns. It almost seemed to sway. But at its top, she could make out one of the many windows in the dome, a tiny square set in place to filter bands of sunlight to the plaza for everyone's pleasure. A cool breeze blew down upon her face. It carried with it a swirl of scents she had never experienced before—spices, perfumes, grass, flowers—that mingled with the pleasant sounds of the gathering.

Lillia blinked in wonder. Next to her, Mava was crouched down beneath the shadow of a flower pot trying to hide, while Jack stood on his tiptoes to get a better view of what was happening in the market. A few steps away, Madam Teacher was walking in circles, not going anywhere, just licking her lips and wringing her hands. Several times, the teacher seemed on the verge of begging someone's pardon to ask for directions, only to stay her hand at the last moment.

Lillia shook her head and was about to go help her teacher when she spied a peacock preening itself by a fountain. Sunlight reflected off its silken feathers. The bird was pecking at the ground. And then, as if sensing Lillia's gaze, it spread its tail, becoming a score of eyes that had suddenly opened to train upon Lillia. Watching her.

An older woman approached it from behind, and the bird scuttled off. The woman wore a long yellow cloak draped around her, and she walked straight towards Madam Teacher. As she drew closer, Lillia glimpsed a silver brooch on her shoulder bearing a symbol of a crossed sword, pick, and hammer. The woman's face was tinged with sunburn, but the remnants of a pale coloring lingered around her eyes.

She had been born in the Crag, like them. The woman stretched a smile across her lined face and addressed Madam Teacher as one might coax a lost dog.

"I've been looking for you. You are our guests from the Crag today."

"Yes, Madam Commissar," Madam Teacher answered with obvious relief and gestured for the children to come join her quickly.

"I had expected you sooner."

"The-the small legs," she stammered. "Not used to such a long trek. Our apologies. Our sincere apologies."

Madam Teacher flashed them a hasty look, and each child repeated how sorry they were. Lillia watched as Mava tried to sputter how well fed and cared for she was in the Crag, at which Jack rolled his eyes.

The commissar nodded. She unwound a scroll she carried tucked beneath her arm and read it over while a troop of armored guards brushed past them, the last one guffawing loudly at some jest. The commissar deftly stepped out of their way, never losing sight of the page she was reading. She paused, and then, for the first time, regarded the children. The corners of her mouth drew higher.

"I see here one of your students has been nominated for the Commissariat."

At that, Madam Teacher drew herself up.

"Yes, Madam Commissar. Lillia Tanner. Present yourself, Lillia, there you go. She has earned extraordinary marks in all her tests. And her fidelity is unquestionable."

The commissar leaned ever so slightly forward and narrowed her eyes at Lillia who was still bowed.

"Look at me."

Lillia raised her head. The eager and deferential countenance she had mastered since the first days of her classes appeared reflexively. But an unsettling feeling crawled over Lillia; it was as if she were on the verge of being caught in a lie. The woman said nothing for a long while but studied Lillia closely with her probing, gray eyes.

The commissar spoke quietly, directly to Lillia, as if they were the only two in the market:

"What is the primary role of the clerks and commissars?"

"To administer the guidelines of our Commonwealth. And with the assistance of the wardens, to ensure compliance."

"And what distinguishes the commissar from the clerk?"

"A commissar serves the Commonwealth's needs in the Crest. The clerks work in the Crag among the workers."

"Is that all?"

Lillia studied the commissar's face closely. It betrayed nothing. Lillia thought a moment and made up her mind.

"No, Madam Commissar ... There is something more. That is—I've read that a commissar must not only know the rules promulgated by the Stewards but understand the Stewards' minds when they make the guidelines. The purpose behind the rules. In that way, the commissar can better serve the Stewards."

A twitch, ever so slight, fluttered past the commissar's eyes. It might have been amusement, or perhaps derision. When the commissar spoke again, her voice was only for Lillia. "Some might deem that notion as subversive. Then again, some might argue it does not go far enough ... Your supposition is correct." The commissar straightened herself so that the others could hear:

"A final question. Correct or incorrect: a clerk can never adjust a promulgated guideline for a worker's wages."

"Incorrect," Lillia's answer was automatic.

Mava's mouth dropped at her friend's flubbed response to such an easy question. She started to whisper something, but the commissar cut over her:

"Why incorrect?"

"Because if a guideline contains a discretionary clause, a written direction to encourage thrift or punish slothfulness, then a clerk may withhold wages from a worker. So long as a note is made of it." Lillia knew instinctively what to say next: "And it has happened before. The last time the guilds threatened to strike in the Crag."

The commissar nodded approvingly while Madam Teacher beamed from over her shoulder.

"All perfect responses," she said. "And you have a rare inclination toward lateral thinking."

For some reason, the commissar's tone did not strike Lillia as entirely complimentary, but then the woman set her hand gently on Lillia's shoulder. It felt strong, the fingers rough with calluses. She spoke evenly:

"I was not much older than you when I went to the Commissariat for my instruction. Is that where you would like to go?"

Lillia looked at the ground and then nodded.

"So you would renounce your home and your family? Never have any children of your own? You aspire to be alone for the rest of your days, unwelcome in the Crag, unknown in the Crest, to be beckoned at anyone's will and pleasure?"

"I will go where the Commonwealth directs me and serve as its Stewards command me."

"Another perfect response. An impressive student, Madam Teacher. Just as you reported."

The commissar cut a discrete path through the crowds in the portico, Lillia and her companions from the Crag followed close behind. No one in the market paid them the least attention when they passed; no more than if they had been a flock of sparrows or a group of stray cats meandering across the market grounds. As they dodged and sidestepped their way through the market, Lillia focused on the train of the commissar's yellow cloak and how it shone almost white whenever the woman passed beneath a ray of sunlight. It was the loveliest thing. Lillia's fingers strayed longingly across her small sash of yellow.

At a turn in an avenue, they came to a locked gateway set in the middle of a brick wall. It was a neglected place that everyone else in the market seemed to avoid instinctively. Covering most of the mortar and bricks were pages of weathered handbills that no one had bothered to pull down. They fluttered in a whisper of a breeze. The commissar unlocked the door and motioned for the others to follow her. The hinges groaned as she shut it behind them. On the other side was a long shaded alley. A makeshift slatted roof kept out most of the daylight, and Lillia's eyes had to adjust once again to the return of darkness.

Not that there was much to see. A banner hung limply from a pole. It was a long piece of faded yellow cloth, but the Commonwealth's sword, pick, and hammer were still discernible. Beneath it were a few stools and a long wooden table with a stack of papers on top of it. And in the middle of everything was a cage inside of a wheeled cart.

A man sat hunched inside it, his arms clasped tightly around his knees and his head buried in his chest.

Jack moved his hand toward his mouth, then quickly lowered it before he spoke. "That-that's the one who will be removed?"

"Yes," the commissar nodded. She sat down in a cushioned chair behind the table. "Lillia, why don't you have a look at these documents? You'll need to learn them soon enough."

Lillia made her way around her companions. She passed a small bench with a tray of uneaten food on it. As she went by it, the man inside the cage stirred. Lillia tried to hurry past without looking at him, but her eyes accidentally strayed and she saw him. They stared at one another.

His eyes were gray, like hers.

The man was thin, almost haggard, dressed in rags, with limp black hair that hung to his shoulders. His cheeks and jaw were covered in stubble and an open sore underneath his eye was weeping pus. Dried blood had crusted around his lips. His mouth kept gaping open and shut, and Lillia realized that the man's tongue had been cut out. Holding her gaze, he stared straight at her for a long moment—and then he smiled.

It made Lillia reel.

"Careful," Madam Teacher came over to steady her. "You've done well so far; don't ruin it now."

Lillia took a deep breath and approached the commissar who was meticulously working through the stack of documents, signing one page after another with a gull feather pen. Each piece of paper was covered in flowing, ornate script and bore a variety of wax seals along the edges. The words, "Warrant" and "Guilty" kept appearing in tall, bold letters as the commissar's fingers flipped through the papers. She spoke to Lillia without looking at her, the words a steady cadence alongside the rhythmic scratching of the feather's tip across the paper:

"For any removal, we must review the case file for compliance. Which I have now done. Here at the end of the file, we find the judgment and warrant, as well as the final documents to close out the case. Here's the judgment. Now any judgment pronouncing removal is countersigned by a commissar stationed in the high court, but it is the warrant—right here—issued by the Board of Wardens that authorizes us to carry out that judgment. Which is what we will do today. Here is the order transferring the prisoner to my custody, which I sign here. My acknowledgment of receiving that order. An order disposing of any personal effects back to the Commonwealth—those are always brief. Another acknowledgment. This last one, a final disposition form, we hold until after the removal has been—"

The man in the cage let out a long, groaning sound, but whether it was in pain or anger, or simply to bear witness that he was still alive and could make noise, Lillia could not tell. The commissar continued without a pause:

"Some commissars maintain an old tradition that allowed prisoners to make brief remarks before the procedure. Ostensibly, it was a way of reconciling the adjudged with the Commonwealth before their removal. Whether you wish to do so will be entirely at your discretion, Lillia."

It soon became clear that the man in the cage was indeed trying to speak. He was motioning with his hands, which sent blades of straw and bits of his rags tumbling out, and when no one responded, he banged against the bars as hard as he could. But the effort for attention proved too much. The man fell over in a swoon. He was grasping at his mouth that had begun bleeding freely from where his tongue had been severed.

"As you can see," the commissar closed the top of the inkwell, "I align with the more modern approach. He's had his day in court. Why should our fair Commonwealth indulge any more of his inflammatory words?"

Dusk had fallen. A crowd of nearly two hundred mingled about near a tall wooden stage at the far end of the portico. There was a festive mood in the market. Everyone was talking casually outside in what promised to be a cool and pleasant evening, eating early dinners, drinking wine, a few were making wagers of some sort. Tavern workers were plying tankards and stronger spirits. A straggly looking poet slurred through a recitation of his recent work, something about the futility of aspiration. All the while, the empty stage cast a long shadow over the gathering, including Lillia, Jack, and Mava. The students made themselves inconspicuous, just as they were told to do, huddling in the branches of a potted myrtle tree.

They had been there nearly an hour. Lillia was just beginning to tire of the cramped space and the prickling twigs when, suddenly, the hum of entertainment receded. Scores of faces turned to watch what was happening at the base of the stage. From where they were hiding, Lillia could hear the sound of a cage door creaking open, and shackles rattling. Overhead, a pair of ravens took notice, calling out greedily. The man who was to be removed was being jostled out of his cage, up the steps of the platform, and forced to his knees, where he was bound to a block of granite. Nearby, noting everything that transpired, the commissar sat at a desk.

Jack was teetering on his toes, neck craned. "I can't see!"

He poked his elbow hard into the small of Lillia's back, but she ignored him.

"It isn't fair," said Mava. "I mean, we all got passes."

Madam Teacher was gone, having managed to find the one place near the foot of the stage that was not pressed with men and women, just underneath a gutter spout. Even from a distance, Lillia could see the teacher appeared entranced with the spectacle unfolding onstage, and completely oblivious to her duties. Lillia made a face, wishing the teacher would come back to put her students in line.

"We could all fit up front there together if you moved over," Mava suggested.

Jack opened his mouth as if to argue the point further, but Lillia cut them both off:

"This is where the commissar told each of us to stand, and so this is where we're going to stand."

"Aw, come off of it, Lil—"

"Jack, you're taller than me. Get up on your tiptoes, and then you can see over that limb. Mava, you're probably just going to look away when they do it, anyways."

"I won't."

A man standing beside their tree sighed loudly. He was pot-bellied and middle-aged with greasy, peppery hair that was pulled back and tied in a tail. His voice was high pitched:

"I came to watch a Craggie's removal, not listen to a Craggie's banality."

A pitter of laughter erupted around the children. A woman a few feet behind added: "Gregory, ask if there's room up on the stage for three more."

Lillia's face grew hot. She felt small and wished she could shrink even smaller, down into the cracks of the cobblestones beneath her sandaled feet. She watched her toes curl, but she drew a deep breath and mustered enough courage to address Gregory directly. She knew what propriety required:

"We are so sorry, sir," she said. "We are grateful to be here today. And how well cared for we are in the Crag."

But Gregory's attention had already been drawn to the stage where the commissar was now standing. Her hands were outstretched to the crowd. For one of her stature and age, the commissar's voice had a ringing, authoritative quality to it:

"Ladies and gentlemen of the Crest, I humbly pray you to give heed, draw close, and bear witness to the justice of our Commonwealth. This prisoner stands before us, awaiting execution of a judgment of removal from the Commonwealth. He is called Sam Paul, a resident bound to the Crag. On the third day of spring in the Twelfth Year of the Ninth Plan of the Commonwealth, he was duly tried and convicted of violating the guidelines and regulations of the Crag. Specifically, he was found to be a member of a guild, an unlawful confederation of farmers, who harvested barley in excess of the fair and just allotment set by the Council of Stewards. Thereafter, he and his co-conspirators organized an unauthorized private market to engage in illicit transactions, thereby threatening the peace and equality of—"

She was reading from one of the warrants, Lillia realized, when Gregory remarked to someone next to him, a companion of some sort, just loud enough to interrupt her thoughts:

"Is that still illegal, Marcus? Belonging to a guild?"

Marcus, another husky man of middle years, took a long drink from a goblet. Tiny pink droplets tinged his beard and moustache and sparkled for only a moment before his silk sleeve wiped them from his face. He answered with a stifled belch:

"For some more than others."

"I thought the wardens just looked the other way at the Craggies' little unions?"

Marcus enjoyed another swig, swishing it around in his mouth loudly, and then gave a long, knowing nod.

"They do. Most of the time. So long as the wardens get their fair share of the fruits of everyone's labors. They'll let the guilds train their own people, run a market or two off the books, even meet in secret ... so long as the bribe gets paid. But if you're a guildsman and you don't pay your clerk and warden their cut ... well," he made a stabbing motion to his chest and pretended to punch his head.

"Hm."

"Kind of a shame," Marcus continued, "because the guildsmen are the only ones in the Crag that can make anything halfway decent. Most of my glassware's probably got a guildmark on it, the stuff that's not broken." He drank again, and his words slurred: "Bit vinegary, but it has some life in it. Unlike that one up there, eh? Eh?"

Gregory's voice turned oddly bright, as if he was striving to sound casual. "Ah, that reminds me. I am hosting a debate soiree this weekend for some colleagues and find myself in need of a case or two of wine. What's the best price you'll give an old friend?"

"Bit on the high side, I'm afraid. Madam Acacia's gone and cut her vineyards' production again, so all I've left in stock is this vintage here, which really is the top of the line ..."

Lillia craned her head to hear over the men's chatter, but the commissar had already finished her address and retired to her seat. The woman in yellow stared ahead, silent, her feather pen poised above a document, ready to record, to catalogue, what would happen next.

"Hang on a second," Marcus stopped himself. "Looks like the show's starting."

Marcus drained his cup, and everyone in the crowd, as one, drew a step closer to the stage.

Three more commissars, men dressed from head to toe in yellow—tunics, pants, boots and gloves, and hoods with a narrow slit to see through—appeared from behind a curtain and approached the prisoner. Sam Paul did not stir, did not even look up, until the first of their shadows fell over him, and then he began weeping quietly, his shoulders heaving in spasms. Each one of the hooded men clasped a satin bag of a deep amber that, one by one, they opened.

Mava clasped tightly onto the nape of Lillia's shirt, twisting it around with her fist, pulling at Lillia's neck. Lillia saw the girl's eyelids fluttering as if she were on the verge of fainting. Which would assuredly attract attention.

"Just lean into me," Lillia whispered. "Now stare up at the clouds. It'll look like you're still watching."

"Thank you," Mava mouthed.

The three hooded commissars dropped their bags to a smattering of half-hearted cheers. In their hands, each now wielded an instrument made of ebony and a tarnished silver metal that dimly reflected the fading sunset.

The commissar in the center held a broadsword. To his right, a pick; to his left, a great quarry hammer.

Each one swept apart in a slowly performed motion, like a macabre dance, that ended with all three raising their instruments poised above their heads. Then Madam Commissar stood and read aloud from another warrant, while a breeze stirred the kneeling prisoner's rags. He sobbed once more from his block of stone.

While he wept, Marcus and Gregory haggled over Marcus' wine.

"If there are no porters who can transport the crates to my home," Gregory explained, "why should I have to pay for shipping?"

"I told you because it's out of my hands," Marcus held his palms up as if to prove it. "I have to keep within the Stewards' guideline here and—"

"Oh, don't give me that clerkish gibberish. You're making a fine living."

"It's not just that. I've got to pay my broker here in the Citadel before I can—oh, look, they're finally doing it."

"About time."

The commissar bowed her head to the man carrying the hammer. He stepped forward and yelled from within his hood:

"For the Crag!"

A pause, and then the hammer came down, a slow avalanche of metal crashing silently into the back of Sam Paul's skull. His head wobbled then settled at an unnatural angle. Sam Paul's eyes were wide and lolling. Even from where she stood, Lillia could see the man's nostrils flaring.

"If you can wait until next month," Marcus offered to Gregory, "I can give you three and a quarter a bottle."

"Impossible," Gregory folded his arms. "The debate was scheduled months ago and the topic is pressing: how changing dynamics in the Crag since the recent reformation of the guidelines may have led to manifestations—"

Marcus shrugged his shoulders: "Then four's the best I can do."

"Seriously?"

The next hooded commissar approached. His pick trembled when he hoisted it over his head. An adolescent voice cracked from behind the hood:

"For the Quarter!"

A grunt and the point was buried between Sam Paul's shoulder blades. What was left of the prisoner's rags became soaked in his blood. But the hooded man struggled with the pick. He pulled it back and forth, back and forth, with the end stuck fast in Sam Paul. Finally, the commissar propped his foot onto the execution block, gave it a few tugs, and wrenched it free. A spray of droplets flew out with the pick head so that the commissar had to endure the embarrassment of wiping his boot clean on the stage.

"He must be new," Marcus shook his head. Then, to Gregory: "I can throw in a good bottle of spirits."

Gregory's eyebrow arched. "Not cragfire?"

"I said a good bottle, didn't I?"

"Fine. Ship it all together to the coffee house and send me the bill."

"Done."

The last hooded man strode past the other two and squared his feet behind the twitching body. The commissar did not bother raising his voice, but Lillia could hear him over the strains of conversation:

"For the Crest."

He turned the sword over, its tip honed on the base of the neck. The thrust was swift, almost effortless. An awful, tongueless howl shook Sam Paul's body as the blade pierced all the way down into his torso. The executioner pulled the sword free with a practiced motion and stepped away quietly, while another commissar hurried onto the stage to unbound the dead body and clean the gore. As he worked, a torrent of blood cascaded down the granite block, down to the edge of the wooden planks, and into a gutter where it drained out the spout above where Madam Teacher was standing.

The blood came falling over her like a rain shower. There was a rush of laughter from those nearby, but the teacher scarcely seemed bothered. She plucked the cap from her hair, wrung it out, and then cast it away, letting her crinkled hair down, which elicited even more laughter. Now Lillia could see it plainly: her teacher was in ecstasy.

Lillia turned to her companions. Jack's mouth hung open, his face paler than Lillia had ever seen. Mava was crouched down on the floor with her eyes shut tightly. Just as Lillia suspected, she had never looked.

"I didn't—I-I wish …" Jack began. He was running his fingers through his hair until finally he hid his face behind his hand. He let out a long breath.

Lillia nodded. "That was hard—a hard thing to watch."

It seemed like the appropriate thing to say, and Lillia tried to make it sound comforting. But if she had been asked, and if she had had to answer truthfully, Lillia would have confessed that she felt nothing. Nothing at all. Of course, the man's removal had been unpleasant to watch, as Madam Teacher had warned. But that was as far as it went. An unpleasantry. Her only thoughts now revolved around Madam Commissar. When Lillia considered that woman's calm, ordered assurance, how she had managed the whole affair, how all the papers had been so carefully attended to, the removal had not been that bad at all.

Lillia studied the commissar working high up at her desk. The trim of her yellow cloak never moved as she wrote across a paper, probably that final form she had mentioned back in the alcove. An approved form that would note how a farmer named Sam Paul had been "removed from the Commonwealth," the date and time of day, who had performed the execution, how it had happened.

A stamp. A signature. The commissar folded the last paper, and it was done. The case was closed.

THE CRAG

CHAPTER ONE

"L illia?"

Tom Tanner's whispered breath hung in the stairwell, a little cloud of mist floating in the ether. The darkness before him made no reply. There was only his labored breathing, and the drill of his heart beating in his head, and the tread of his feet plodding on weathered stone.

"Lillia," he repeated, his voice rising.

Tom was winded from the descent and lightheaded, and his legs were beginning to tremble. Despite the cold, a film of sweat beaded across his forehead. He came to a halt, wiped his face, and cupped his hands to call out a third time:

"Girls?"

The sound of his voice fell into the void beneath him, unheard and unanswered.

Tom clenched his jaw for a moment. It was rare for Tom's face to show vexation. He was tired, though, and starting to feel the chill in his knees. It had been a long time since he had made this journey; longer still since he had had to keep such a hurried pace. He was trying to catch up with two children.

Tom was considering whether he ought to just try shouting for them when a noise startled him from a few steps below—a faint shriek, followed by a flurry of tiny, savage squeals. Tom squinted at a movement in the shadows.

Two rats, their muzzles caked with blood, were squaring off over the mottled body of a third. They had clamped their teeth around the corpse, and neither one would let go.

Tom frowned. He drew a breath of frigid air, shook his legs loose, and resumed his trek downward.

All morning long, Tom had been traveling the crumbling artery of rock that wound through the workers' realm of the Crag. There were thousands of these staired avenues scattered throughout the Crag, but this particular run was the longest. Not a true stairwell nor a corridor as such, but an avenue of loosely connected flights, landings, bridges, and broken steps, all of which ran, more or less, up and down to join the three wards of the Crag together. A long time ago, long before Tom had been born, when the tunnels were in better repair, the route had been called Forward Way. But that was under an old Plan, not the current one, so no one knew its name anymore. They were just stairs and tunnels. Decrepit, crumbling steps, no different than all the others in the Crag.

The only light in the stairwells came from metal pots nailed in the walls every hundred feet or so. These were filled, intermittently, with gulleystars—black, rancid smelling mushrooms that grew wild in the Mountain's cracks. When pressed and packed together, a potful would cast an oily, yellow glow not much weaker than a cheap candle's. For many who worked in the Crag, it was the only light they ever saw.

Tom passed beneath one of the glowing pots, a wiry, wavering shadow stealing down an expanse of empty stairs. At the bottom, he turned a corner and descended another flight, and then another, which became a long, winding curve that ended abruptly in a mortared wall and a makeshift doorway. The door was just a rectangle of planks nailed together and held upright on rusted hinges, but there was a picture of blue waves painted on its surface just above a sign with a single word in black. Though Tom could not read the word he knew what it meant.

A wisp of relief broke across his lips.

From the other side, Tom could hear a low murmur of voices. He shouldered the door open and stepped down into a small, windowless waiting room filled with people.

"Girls?"

All at once, there was a loud creak from another doorway opening and slamming shut, a waft of salt air, and a blinding light, followed by a chorus of groans. Tom held up his hands too late to shield his eyes and bumped into a lump of a woman who was slouched on one of the steps. She made a half-hearted open palm swing at Tom's face. "Watch it, you ass."

"Sorry. Lillia? Mava? Where are you?"

Still blinking from the sudden flash of light, Tom could make out the outlines of a small crowd huddled in front of a doorway. As his vision returned, he saw that the score or so of people here were his own kind, cut from the same mold as he. They were all Craggies: thin, ghostly in the light of the room's only gulleystar pot, all dressed in coarse drab, with plain, expressionless faces. Stone people, queued up in a stone waiting room, within a chamber of a stone mountain.

But not a girl among them. Tom worried.

"Beg your pardon," the man next to Tom tapped him on the shoulder. He was very tall, and a pale scar running across his forehead had left his eyebrows permanently raised, as if he were perpetually enraged. But he spoke respectfully:

"Are you with them two sashes that just come through?"

Tom lifted his chin. "Yes. My daughter. And a friend of hers."

"I thought so," the eyebrows raised even higher, almost to the crown of his head, and the man gave a wide, toothless grin. "Could tell right away. Warden's already let them through. Why don't you go on ahead and give a knock, since you're on business with them? Hey, clear a lane down there! The sash's daddy's coming through."

Not everyone in the crowd was inclined to give up their place in line, but another shout from the man and the waiting room reluctantly shuffled itself around to make way for Tom. Tom ignored the glowers and muttered curses and sidled up to the far door. It was heavy and oaken. He rapped three times with his fist.

The door lurched open. The deluge of sunlight was obscured by the helmed head of a bearded, middle-aged man peering inside:

"Not time yet. Back of the line," the helmet growled.

"I'm with them, warden," Tom tried to point over the guard's shoulder. "The sashes. Right there, see?"

A sneer broke across the man's leathery face, but he stole a quick look behind him, just in case. Beyond the doorway past the warden's station, a lone ray of afternoon sun filtered through a haze of smog and fire smoke; it was just enough light to illuminate the hovels and lean-to tents of a seaside market. Built in an open bay of the Mountain's side, where the rocky shoals met the water, a flat, featureless plateau of stone had been raised above the breaking waves to make a place for the labors and trades of the sea. A constant din arose from carts rumbling past, and men and women shouting over each other, and the barely audible peal of distant ships creaking in their berths, and countless gulls calling out noisily from the clouds above. Perhaps half a thousand of the Crag's men and women, cramped together, were carrying on their work.

In the middle of the clamor, two young girls were laughing uproariously at one another.

One was a small, round-faced blond; the other, a gangly adolescent with mouse-colored hair that badly needed combing. Neither was particularly lovely. But they were confident, and that made them stand apart. The short blonde had her hands on her hips. The crowds seemed to bend around her.

Both girls wore a yellow sash over their shoulders.

"See?" Tom pointed again and yelled. "Lillia!"

Neither one responded.

"Lillia, it's me! Over here!"

The guard's head swiveled back and forth. At last, the blond, Lillia, heaved an exaggerated sigh and rolled her eyes. Without saying anything, she waved at the guard for Tom to join her and then resumed her conversation with her friend.

The warden licked a set of chapped lips and nodded:

"Alright, you're vouched for. I'll still need a look at your pass. Sergeant's out on rounds. Might be watching."

"Sure," Tom handed him a wadded paper from his shirt pocket that was weighted down on its corner by a seal. The warden opened and folded it again without looking at it. So long as there was a dab of wax, it was a pass. Tom identified himself:

"Tom Tanner, Industry Caverns, Upper Ward of the Crag."

"Uh-huh, here's your pass back, Tanner. Go on. Rest of you, better have your passes and your fees ready when it's time for your shift. And I better not see a guildmark on any of those baskets, or I promise you I will torch them right here with you inside. So help me, I will."

The guard did not stick out a palm for a bribe, so Tom hurried through the door to join the children. His legs, not used to walking on level ground, throbbed in protest, but he moved briskly, weaving through the market without ever looking anyone in the face. He made his way across a plaza of broken tiles, straw, fish entrails, and pools of seawater that had collected wherever the ground was soft. A few fires smoldered, burning trash that sent waves of foul-smelling soot billowing into the air. Tom's eyes were watering by the time he reached the girls.

He looked down fondly at Lillia, his hands clasped behind his back, and waited patiently.

Lillia did not pause her conversation to greet her father.

"It's so obvious Lynne's just trying to curry up to Madam Teacher. Ever since we got passes to visit the library, she's been jealous. But when we got to the Crest to see a removal. She's seething—*seething*—at us now."

"She certainly is," the taller girl nodded and forced a reedy laugh. Something Lillia had mentioned made Mava frown; she started to wring her hands. It passed quickly, though, and Mava turned her expression back to the rapt attention of an animal hoping to be thrown a scrap of food.

"It's pathetic," Lillia continued. "I mean, when has she ever asked for more accounting work?"

"Never. Nobody ever asks to do extra accounting work, right?"

"I wouldn't go that far. I suppose if all you can aim for is a bursar's position, it might be a good idea. Do the best you can with what you've got."

"That's true."

"We all know Lynne will never have the marks to be a full clerk. She's not like us, Mava."

"No, she certainly isn't."

"And she doesn't have any pull, like Jack."

"Uh-uh," Mava nodded.

The conversation had finally reached a lull. Tom smiled at the girls: "We ready to go see the ship?"

Lillia sighed. "I guess. Since we must. Why Madam Teacher is making us go through with this insipid assignment when we're almost graduated, I have no idea. What is it you need again?"

"What we need," Tom corrected her, "is salt. Two sacks for the tannery."

Lillia winced at being reminded of her family's trade, and Mava had to hide a smile.

"It's on a ship called the *Plentiful*," Tom said. "Not far up the Docks. When we get there, I'll introduce you to the dockmaster. His name's Mr. Overton. He's decent enough. I'm sure he'd be willing to go over how he does his job with a couple of academy ladies. Help you with your reports. I'll show him my papers, pay him the fee, and let you chat while I unload the cargo. Maybe afterwards the captain, Asa, can show you around the ship."

Mava thanked him, while Lillia preened her hair and let out a yawn.

"Stay close to me in this crowd," said Tom, leading the girls from the square. "The ship should be moored by now."

They passed between little gatherings of people that were spread across the square. Clerks weighing nets teeming with fish; a sullen line of dock-workers waiting for their wages while women of all ages dressed in loose, short skirts lingered nearby, throwing their arms and their legs around each man as he got paid; some boys hurling rocks at a pelican. Hovering just over the crowds was a chair built atop a tottering wooden platform. In it a flaccid, balding woman called a lector slouched over to one side, trying to stay awake. She was reading official pamphlets in a voice as loud and grating as a seagull's cackling, and no one paid her the least attention.

As they reached the plaza's end, Lillia spotted a class of workers' children, all in rags and sitting in a ring around a half-blind old man whose clerk's sash was bleached white from years in the sun and salty air. He was a teacher, going over the rudiments of Crag labor:

"—and once you've finished training for your work as ship cleaners, the clerks will see that each of you receives the fruits of your labor. No one can ever exploit you. You'll always have your rights and dignity. Our all for all. Isn't that wonderful? And such good work you'll get to do, scraping barnacles in the nice, outside air, catching rats. So much finer than scrounging gulleystars or growing potatoes on the Farms, you lucky little—Paula, pay attention! You want to go work on the Farms?"

"Sorry, Duncan," Paula sang.

"That's Master Teacher. Now, who remembers what a worker's first duty to the Commonwealth is? We just went over it. Hm? Anyone?"

Lillia made a point to cast a condescending sneer as she walked by. Not towards any of the children, who were beneath her notice. But to be stuck training workers' whelps—it was surely one of the lowest assignments a clerk could bear. Poor old man. She tisked at him and followed her father.

They came into a quay where an even bigger crowd had gathered so that it took the three of them a long while to elbow their way onto the first pier. Lillia was feeling jostled and annoyed by the time they finally reached the water's edge, but as they set foot on the first plank, all three came to a halt. They tilted their heads back and stared.

A massive wrought iron arch, soaring taller than any ship's mast, spanned across the tops of the first two pilings. It was rusted, and its swirling latticework was blunted with bird droppings and spray from the constant crash of waves. But still, it loomed, a shadow of lost splendor from a time before there were clerks and lectors, poised high above the lines of broken wooden docks and the dingy tides of people that they now carried. Tom, Lillia, and Mava stood silent in its presence.

Tom spoke, his voice thick with awe. "Isn't it something? I always like to look at it whenever I come here. Nobody could make this nowadays."

Mava nodded, but something about the arch offended Lillia:

"Why would anyone want to?"

"I don't know," Tom shrugged.

"It's hubris," Lillia said, showing off a word she had recently learned in class. "Look at all that wasted labor, all that iron left to rust, and for what? A giant bird perch. Such hubris."

"I hadn't thought about it that way. I suppose that's a fair point. Still. It is nice looking at. Kind of makes you feel small, but part of something big at the same time—I don't know."

"It was made by the priests, and that's exactly the kind of thing they would have wanted you to think." Lillia tried to soften her tone. "It may be hard for you to grasp, but things like this, these monuments, they're just idols, you see? They were made in the old days to be bowed down to. To exploit you. That was their only function." She cast another disapproving glare at the arch and straightened her sash. "It's the kind of hubris the *dwarves* would wallow in because we let them keep their stupid religious superstitions. But *we* are better than that. No. This doesn't belong here. It should have been thrown into the sea with all the gods. In fact, we shall make a note of it, Mava, so that a committee can see about reclaiming the material."

"Alright," Mava never took her gaze off the shadow above her.

"Come on," said Lillia, "Didn't you say the ship was waiting for us?"

They passed beneath the arch silently, Tom leading the children out onto a crowded highway of weathered timber where their feet joined a steady drum of footsteps. They were elevated high above the ocean, and with each passing wave, they could feel the barnacled posts give way so that the girls nearly lost their balance. It quickly became an amusement, particularly for Mava, and Tom had to remind them not to linger.

They followed the main pier beyond the breaking surf, where it split into smaller docks, which in turn split again, and again, like a splintering tangle that had somehow taken root and spawned in the dark, turgid waters of the ocean. Without pausing, Tom followed a route Lillia knew he must have walked countless times before. The girls lingered behind, resuming their prattle about their school and their classmates.

As they went, a blur of faces passed before them. A team of wharf-men shuffling in a line. A poxed, legless sailor begging for change within a driftwood shelter. Men aboard a fishing boat roaring in laughter as a scrum of shirtless, feral children clawed each other for scraps of fish. Here and there clerks sat propped up in officious looking chairs and benches, most of them sleeping through their shifts. The girls had to hold their sashes to their noses to ward off the stench of bilge that filled the air.

At last, Lillia, Tom, and Mava reached a turn that took them past a long row of barrels, fishing nets, and a pile of empty crates piled up along the pier's edge. Tom scanned the berths and indicated that the ship was up ahead, a small transport with a single mast and a low cabin, already tied off. Scrawled in flaking, uneven yellow letters on her port bow was her name: *Plentiful*.

As soon as they reached the ship's gangplank, Tom knew something was wrong.

A hatch on board burst open. A young woman came racing barefoot out of it and leaped across the plank, straight towards Tom.

"Asa?" Tom held out his hands, not sure what else to do.

The girls gaped from the dock as the woman collapsed into his arms. She was younger than Tom, but only a little, and very sunburnt. Her black hair was matted in knots, and her shirt had been torn at the nape. The side of the woman's face was swelled from a massive purple welt. As he struggled to keep her on her feet, she pulled Tom's head close and the scent of her blood filled Tom's nostrils. When she opened her mouth, she whispered so that only he could hear her words:

"Tanner, is there—is there no help for a worker's daughter?"

Tom went pale. He almost let her drop, but at that moment Asa slipped her hand into his, and he felt a leather pouch being pressed into his palm. It made a soft, metallic clink. Their eyes met. He grimaced, but quickly shoved the pouch into his shirt pocket and hoisted her back up. She had suddenly found her strength again.

A loud curse rang out in the air, and a heavy-set man stormed across the gangplank. The wood groaned beneath his weight. "Where you think you're going, Asa? We're not done yet."

Tom stole a look toward Lillia, hoping she would understand what he had no time to explain: that she absolutely had to keep her mouth shut. Then he drew his lips tight, squared his shoulders, and yelled straight back at the man:

"Who are you?!"

A flock of terns flew off, cackling loudly at the sound of Tom's voice. Lillia let out a gasp, as if she had never heard her father raise his voice before. The man on the plank wavered, but not because Tom had checked him. He was catching his balance. The man's eyes were bloodshot and glassy, and a reek of cragfire, the cheap, tasteless fungal spirit allotted to workers, wafted around him like a cloud.

Tom lowered his voice, though not its menace: "I said, who are you?"

The man swore until he finally managed to get his footing right. He was twice Tom's size, and just as pale, but with a gray, sickly tinge around his cheeks and a bulbous, veined nose. The man's shirt was unbuttoned, and Tom could make out fresh scratches on his neck and sagging chest. He also saw a yellow sash tied like a belt, although it was nearly falling off of him. The man adjusted his clothes and grunted at Tom:

"I'm the dockmaster."

"What?"

"Overton's been replaced," Asa answered, glaring at the man. "This is the new clerk. His name's Craigman … He doesn't know how things work here."

"Oh, I know more than you'd guess, my sweet."

Tom's head was spinning. He silently cursed himself for bringing the children here.

"Look," Tom lowered his voice, trying to sound calm, "I'm just trying to pick up some salt." He reached for his shirt pocket. "I've got papers."

"Don't give a damn about your papers," Craigman belched. He found a small cask that was laying on its side and flipped it over for a chair. An iron whaling hook, bigger than a fist, had been wedged into one of its planks; he jerked the hook free and sat down. "Ship's been impounded. Along with all her cargo." Craigman made a leering glance at Asa and pointed the hook at her. "And her crew. Nothing's leaving here."

"Why?" Tom asked.

Craigman glowered at Tom as if to size him up, but then he answered:

"There's guildmarks all over the crates in the hold," he flapped his hand behind him, tottering on his barrel. "Hell, they're all over the hull. If this little minx isn't in a guild, I'm a Craggie. So I'm impounding this ship and setting a fine on it. Now. In the meantime. You said you need some salt out of the cargo? Might be that a particular sack doesn't have a guildmark on it. Or if it did, I might not be able to see it."

Tom breathed a small sigh of relief. He dropped his voice:

"How much?"

Before Craigman could begin haggling, Lillia's voice broke in a high shrill:

"Don't you dare pay this man *anything*! I know what he's doing. We learned about this in class. He's asking for a bribe. A payment over the guideline for his own profit!" She spun on her heel to face the man; a quaking finger extended. "I'm a sixth-year academy student and admitted to the Commissariat. Show me your guidelines."

"Lillia, no!" Tom hissed.

Craigman's eyes glowed, his face screwed up, and then a great guffaw burst out.

"Who's this little Craggie think she is? Guidelines, ha!"

Lillia sucked in a breath of air. Her fingers clutched her sash. She began sputtering a dozen things at once. She was in an academy, practically a commissar already, and he, a mere dock's clerk. Where were his guidelines? Where were his orders? Was he profiting? And over and over, the threat: she would make a note of him.

Craigman was not listening. His eyes strayed to Asa, who was still standing next to Tom, clutching her shirt tight to her chest. But when Lillia walked out onto the plank, the dockmaster whirled about with an angry shout.

"Where do you think *you're* going?"

"Mava," Lillia's voice was shaking but defiant, "run and find that warden by the gate. Tell him—tell him a commissar has taken control of this, uh, boat, and is placing a clerk under arrest. For bribing."

Mava was rooted where she stood, wide-eyed, like a rodent spooked from a noise; Tom knew the girl would bolt at any moment, but not to fetch a warden.

Tom shouted: "Lillia, get down from there, now! Craigman, please, we-we don't want any trouble. Really. Just tell me how much—"

Craigman chuckled and slurred something that might have been, "C'mere." His weight spilled off the barrel he had been sitting on. He turned clumsily, waving his free hand to keep his balance while his other hand reached for Lillia.

The moment froze before Tom: a cluttered berth, a teetering shack, the boat, the wooden pilings split and covered in white bird droppings. The smell of saltwater and filth was redolent in the air. A wave broke nearby, shining green beneath a break in the clouds. Lillia was standing on a plank, about to say something, her face a mask of indignation.

Suddenly, Lillia's face went blank. The sun peeked through once more, catching a gleam of metal.

The metal hook that Craigman held.

And then it was gone, buried within her belly. Lillia's shirt, her flesh, her sash: all became the same color, red.

CHAPTER TWO

"BUT THIS ALREADY happened."

Lillia's words sounded thick, slurred, and somehow distant, even in her own ears.

She was in a shanty, a cave with a narrow door that connected to a tunnel in the Lower Ward of the Crag. It was her old neighborhood, deep in the Mountain's base. The families here all worked in the bottom tiers of skilled labor—porters, lamplighters, carvers, tanners. Most could read little more than their names on their work orders or recite the slogan that was plastered across the flyers posted on every wall. Lillia could see one of them peeling above the doorway. "OUR ALL FOR ALL," it read.

The whole ward was dingy, and dank, and cold, brutally cold. It had been her family's home before she was admitted to the clerk's academy.

Her gaze fell upon two glowing gulleystar pots hanging from a cord tied around an enormous, creaking iron pipe that jutted through the ceiling. The pipe was a connecting line between the tunnel waterways that had been built long ago by the dwarves and a crumbling fountain outside the Tanners' doorway that gurgled out a few jars of silted water each day. The top lantern glowed steadily, but the bottom one was on the verge of waning out. In the pale light, Lillia could see piles of pig skins in different states of decay, all of them slowly rotting in the slime that dripped from the pipe above. There were some shearing knives in a bucket. A rod was suspended above a pit for hanging the hides after they were cured. Empty urns that reeked of piss. In the center of the room was a pit for cooking.

Lillia realized she was in her room, her old room. It was just a crack in the wall far enough from the leaking water pipe that she could keep a bed relatively dry inside. It was the only place of privacy in their home. The only space where there were no drafts, no pelts, no mice, set aside just for her. Lillia's little wool blanket would be nearby. And the scroll of papers she kept hidden. Everyone seated around the cooking pit on the other side of the wall looked just as she remembered—six years ago.

Mother and Father were arguing. Her older brother, Tim, cowered nearby, working on sewing a leather belt together, practicing the careful stitch lopping his father had been drilling into his fingers all morning. Timothy was pretending to concentrate, but he still looked nervous. Tim was always nervous.

"She's already putting on airs," her mother thrust her chin towards Lillia's room. She was thinner then, Lillia thought. But still stolid with flowing auburn hair and skin as callused as the pelts she was sheering. And she had the same piercing, suspicious gaze wherever she looked. Lillia tried to make a sound to let them know she was in here with them, awake, but it was as if her mother was staring straight through her.

"Every time there's work to be done, real work, I mean, she's suddenly got to practice her letters and study her rules. Letters and rules, letters and rules. It's all I hear from her anymore." Her mother dropped a scraping knife loudly into a bin. "Oh, she'll move a few hides for appearance's sake. But forget soaking them. And shearing? Oh, no, no, no. Lillia hasn't time for *that*. Lillia's studies mustn't be interrupted for *that*. Like she's got her sash already."

"Well," her father's voice was even, "she almost has. She got the best marks in the ward on the first two tests. One more, and she'll be admitted."

The contrast between Tom and Bette Tanner had always struck Lillia. Where her mother would dominate a room with her presence, her father hardly seemed to cast a shadow. He was lean, almost gaunt, with oily blond hair, a slight hunch in his shoulders, and a voice that seldom rose above a murmur. He had a habit, whenever speaking to anyone, of staring directly in their eyes for an uncomfortably long time; only Bette was not put off by it.

"And what then?"

Tom stretched his long arms, locking his fingers behind his head. He watched the pipe in the ceiling for a while before he replied in a way that almost sounded as if he were answering himself:

"She'll get to study. Get to learn things."

"What good'll that do any of us?" Bette picked up another knife only to throw it back into the pail. The noise startled Tim, but he kept working. "Look, if you're thinking that once she becomes a clerk, she'll be able to cull us some favors, that's a bad bet. Just ask the Coopers around the corner. When's the last time their little Anthony came round? He's a clerk now, you know. And when his old man didn't make his quota four months in a row, you think little Anthony lifted a finger to keep him from getting taken up? You think it did Cooper any good in court that he had a brat with a sash?"

"Probably not."

Bette's eyes narrowed, her brow sprouting furrows. She loomed over her husband, her fists in her hips, but he only seemed interested in how the joints in the iron pipe above him were groaning. "And who put this whole academy notion into her head in the first place?"

"That would be me," he turned his head to meet her gaze.

"That would be me," Bette mimicked him. "Of course it was you. Anything for your clever little girl. 'Look how well you did your sums, Lillia!' 'What a clever thing you said to the warden's guard this morning, Lillia!' 'Our little clerk, Lillia.'" Bette wiped her hands across her apron and spat. "You've been puffing her head up since she could talk."

Tom just smiled: "She's a clever child."

"Puffed up and filled with airs. When she wasn't even an allotted baby. We never got a stipend to feed her. Never got anything for her." Bette let out a frustrated sound. "We should've sold her off to the madams when we had the chance. Could've made some money for the trouble of her."

At that, Tom rose. He glanced towards Lillia's room; his face clouded:

"Keep that to yourself," Tom's voice dropped. The gulleystar light cast his features in a dark shadow as he stepped closer towards Bette. "She doesn't need to hear that sort of thing."

But Lillia did hear. Or had heard. She had buried herself in her bed, shutting her eyes, shutting her ears with the blanket wadded around her little hands, anything to make her mother stop talking. A part of her remembered pretending to snore when this had happened. Later, she had cried.

But this time she watched. The light in the room wavered and took a strange turn, like oil spreading across water. Her parents were still fighting. Bette was waving her arms, shouting something, but the sound drew farther away. There was a ringing in the air, like a boat's bell. Now Bette was sobbing:

"—after that, there weren't no others!"

"There's nothing I can do about that."

Her father haltingly reached for Bette, but she hit his hand away. Bette was shaking with anger, Lillia could see, even as her mother's body receded into a haze. The last sheen of her red hair disappeared. Her voice became muffled as if she were talking from behind a heavy door. "You know you're blind to what that girl really is, Tom. She's trouble. She'll turn us out one day. You wait and see, Tom Tanner ..."

A curtain of darkness descended over the room. The cooking pit vanished like a wisp of smoke. Her father and brother went with it. The pipe in the ceiling, her books, her blanket—they were gone now. Only her mother remained, but she too was fading quickly. The image of her tear-stained face was dwindling into memory—and then that was gone, too. But not completely. Lillia could still sense Bette's eyes. They floated beyond the nothingness, probing, searching for Lillia.

From within the blackness, Bette's eyes glowed. Two angry embers became two flames. They sprouted, and twined together, and then stretched themselves to devour the void. A sheet of fire scorched the emptiness until even the memory of Lillia's room, her home, her family had been burned away.

There was only Lillia. Screaming. Screaming because the burning would not stop.

Tom awoke with a muffled cry. His eyes darted in circles. He was in the same chair where he had fallen asleep. It was his daughter's room, and he was sitting by her desk. Her writing quills and her papers were all left exactly where they were supposed to be, neatly stacked, untouched. So that Lillia would know just where everything was when she woke up. A little slate with a chalk message was the only addition. Something the clerk's boy, the one in her class, had left for her a few days ago—Jack, that was his name, Tom remembered.

Lillia's body was still lying in her bed, curled on its side.

"Stop," she moaned in her pillow. "Stop ... looking at me ..." Lillia groaned one more time and then fell back into silence.

Tom reached over, stroked a strand of hair from her face, and let his palm linger on her forehead. He rested it there for only a moment; her skin burned too hot. She had been saying all sorts of odd things in her fevered sleep over the past few days as if she were looking for something and hiding from it at the same time. Tom kept the door shut so that no one would hear her and make a note of it.

But word had already spread. He knew what the neighbors were whispering, the long glances they gave him when he went down to work at the tannery. They were all saying she would die; and then the Tanners would be reassigned, back to the gutter where they came from. So Tom had stopped going to work.

He felt her head again and considered lifting her blanket to check if it was still there.

Of course it is.

The odd protrusion beneath the coverlet rose and fell with Lillia's breathing. Craigman's hook still held fast in his daughter's belly, right where he had stabbed her.

Tom stretched his arms and rubbed at an ache in his neck. The pain felt strangely welcome; it had been the first time he had slept for any length. He rubbed the sleep from his eyes and listened to his daughter's soft, rasping breaths. His daughter—who was dying.

He watched her for a while and Tom's thoughts wandered into reminiscence. Lillia as a baby, studying the letters on a flyer they had used to wipe her face; Lillia as a toddler calling him by his first name (that had always made Tom laugh); Lillia as a young girl poised over a wax tablet, practicing her letters:

"O-U-R-A-L-L- ..."

He would have gladly stayed here, dwelling on her childhood, but the memories of the past three days could not be held at bay.

Since Lillia's accident, he had scoured every house and door of Industry Caverns, their residence in the Upper Ward. Because surely here, in a ward reserved for clerks and clerk students, a real doctor could be hired. There were a few. And Tom had hired every one of them. He had paid these apothecaries, and healers, and chemists, and doctors all his savings, even traded some of his tools. But no one could do anything for Lillia. The hook was still stuck in her stomach. The bleeding had stopped, but now the skin around the hook's barbs had become streaked with flaring purple veins. It had taken on a strange smell, too, like salt in a tanning urn.

Unbidden, the words of the last man he had hired came back to Tom. He had been a squat, bow-legged thing who claimed to have been a ship's surgeon:

"Nothing can be done for her, Tanner," the man had shaken his head as he fingered the copper ring Tom had given him for payment. "It's a whaling hook, and it's set. It ain't coming out—unless you want to tear her innards out with it and give her a quick end."

Tom had roared at the man, picked up a stool, and beat him over the head right there at his doorstep while the neighbors watched. They might report it—would report it, he was fairly certain—the wardens' eyes were everywhere in this part of the Crag. But after that, Tom had given up on doctors. There were no more to be found, and there was nothing left to try. So he would try something else.

His fingers felt for the little leather pouch that he still had hidden underneath his belt. The one Asa had slipped him on the gangplank. The coins inside shifted, the metal scraping lightly together. Instinctively, his grip tightened.

His eyes felt heavy once more. The lids fluttered, then shut, and Tom was asleep again.

Lillia turned in her bed and moaned softly. The noise startled Tom. His eyes blinked open and came to focus on a squat woman with short-cropped auburn hair leaning on the doorway, eyeing him suspiciously. She was slicing an onion.

"Is she finally up?" The woman flicked a sheet of peeling off with her knife.

Tom shook his head at her.

"Thought I heard something."

In the shadow behind Bette, he could see Timothy perched on his tiptoes, peering over her shoulder into Lillia's room. Tom's son, Timothy, a perfect replica of Tom, but with a fuller head of hair and a wider nose, like the boy's mother.

"Just me, Bette," Tom replied. "I fell asleep."

"Uh-huh. Well, while you were sleeping, your man showed up."

"What?" Tom was on his feet.

"He's in the front room," she pointed with her peeling knife, "though he shouldn't be."

"Why didn't you wake me up sooner?"

"This one's a real prize, Tom. How you'll pay his fee, I've no idea."

Bette carried on with her complaining, but Tom was already bumping past her to reach the hallway. His eyes went wide when he saw that the front door of his home was wide open for all to see what was seated in their foyer.

"Bleeding, shitting—," Tom cursed under his breath.

He grabbed his guest by the scruff of a dirt-stained silken kerchief and jerked him upright to get out of the doorway's view. "I thought you would be discrete," Tom closed the door quietly. "Half this tunnel's on the warden's payroll." As if to punctuate the point, he heard a door from across the corridor creaking shut. Tom made an annoyed face and told Tim to fetch a chair. It came just in time for the man to collapse into it.

"Thank you, boy," the man smiled benignly at Timothy. "A blessing will be upon you."

Tim gaped in awe at the stranger. He might have asked the man to do a trick had Tom not brought the boy back to his senses.

"Make yourself useful," Tom snapped at his son. "Go stuff some sheets around the doorway to hide the noise. And keep your ear to the door."

"Yes, Father."

"Give the sign if you hear anyone coming."

Tim paused in mid-step. "You mean the sign for—"

"I do."

The youth nodded at his father. Tom turned to face his guest. Just the sight of this ridiculous looking scarecrow with a ruddy nose, a man obviously roiling in a stupor, left Tom with a sinking feeling in his stomach.

The guest tried to get to his feet.

"Allow me to introduce myself," the man's voice was slurred with drink. "I am the Divine Eli." He stumbled on a chair leg and ended up slumping back down in his seat.

"Divine Eli," Bette's voice dripped with disgust. "As divine as my ass. Don't leave him out of your sight, Tom. I don't want him pissing on any of the furniture you've left us. No, I know. Keep it to myself, you don't have to tell me. I'll leave you to your business."

When she had returned to the kitchen, Tom leaned forward and whispered:

"Did you walk all the way here dressed like *that*?"

Eli ran his hand over his clothes and held his sleeves up as if noticing them for the first time. From head to toe, he was covered in silken rags of purple, crimson, violet, and pink, all stitched together, and all smeared with grease, dirt, and, Tom suspected from the smell, a fair amount of vomit. Eli tapped a slippered foot in a slow rhythm. A train of glitter cascaded with each bounce—and doubtless left a trail that no clerk or warden could be bribed to ignore.

"Wasn't sure you'd have a place for me to change into my work clothes," Eli shrugged. "Anyways, you're the one who asked our friends to find me."

"So I did. But I thought your name was Elliott."

"Eli is my, uhm, priestly name," he smiled. "What the dwarves call me."

It was all Tom could manage to keep from laughing at the man's audacity. Whatever their oddities, whatever may be said of them, no dwarf would ever stoop to greet this fool. But Tom had invited him; and he was still a brother, of sorts. Tom locked his gaze onto the man's bloodshot eyes. He held out his hand and asked:

"Do you have a token for me?"

"We've got to go through that? Oh, fine. Here you go."

Reluctantly, Eli extended his right hand. His fingers trembled in the air between them, but they finally found Tom's and clasped on tightly. They each covered their grip with their free hand, never breaking their stare. One of Eli's eyes was darker than the other, Tom noticed.

"Are we alright, then?" Eli asked after a while.

"Sure," Tom released his grip and sank into a fur-covered couch. He pinched the bridge of his nose. "Look, I'm sorry. I've never done anything like this before. Hired someone for this kind of thing, I mean."

"I hear that a lot," Eli offered a reassuring pat before proceeding into what sounded like a rehearsed speech. "You have nothing to worry about from the Crest. Now it's true, this is *technically* against the law. But not for me. You see, I got a special license to practice, well, *study* religion, if you take my meaning. 'Cause of all my years of porter work in the Dwarf Quarter. I try not to talk much about it, of course. They're a prideful folk. They don't like it that we call 'em dwarves and they sure don't like bein' reminded about the Treaty, an' that the Crest gets to call the tune for what they're allowed to do with their gods. But they'll still share their godly secrets with us. For the right price. And the Crest don't mind if a few of us Craggies dabble in their craft. S'long as we keep our mouths shut and pay for a license. Which I have, if you care to see for yourself," he groped around his breast pocket and produced a worn and folded sheaf of gray papers.

Tom did not take them; there was no need. They were fabricated bunk, as they both knew perfectly well.

Eli leaned forward to share a knowing look. A crooked smile broke through the stubble of his patched and wiry beard, and with it came the pungent waft of balm, the most potent and illegal spirit distilled in hidden holes throughout the Crag. In Eli's mouth, there were the telltale flecks of rotted potato stems and rotting gray teeth that marked a balm drunk Craggie. The man would never live past his middle years. Tom had known dozens like him, none were still alive.

"So I've got papers, you see," Eli leaned back to make himself comfortable.

"You've got papers," Tom agreed.

"And really, what we're doing here is not something as the Crest would even take notice of. Since we're in what you might call a transition. Yes, indeed. Ninth Plan's coming to an end. New years to start counting. Some new stewards'll be taking over. New wardens, too. A whole different direction. It's got all the clerks and commissars scrambling 'round like cockroaches trying to figure out who to latch onto, I can tell you that."

"That's dangerous talk, brother." Tom had heard it before, and in much more detail, but this was not the place to repeat it, and certainly not the time.

"Is it?" Eli shrugged. There was a little serving bowl with old raisins on a stand next to his chair, which Eli dispatched with a single gulp. "My point," he continued, his mouth full, "is the Crest's got more important things to worry about than a little faith healing. So don't worry about anyone noting anything. We're fine, brother. 'Specially in times like these. Last thing the Crest wants is to get the dwarves whipped up about their gods again. They let the small folk hold onto their gods, just not too tightly, see?"

This was bordering on treasonous. Tom rose from his sofa.

"My daughter's in bed in her room. If you're ready."

Eli's mismatched eyes followed him. "So we have a bargain?"

Tom reached beneath his belt for the pouch. The two shook hands, and Tom led a man who claimed to be a priest into his daughter's bed-chamber.

Eli pulled at his collar and shook his shirt. The air was stifling. The little iron stove in the corner of the girl's room must have been burning coal all day (a rare luxury even in Industry Caverns) and the heat it spewed hung like a heavy blanket. The bed at the far end had sheets, nice ones from the look of it. A stand of lit tallow candles was weeping tiny streams of yellow wax. Eli wiped his forehead. His silk cloaks stuck to his skin.

Tom pulled up a chair and motioned for Eli to sit down next to him. Eli fixed a pleasant expression on his face as he cased Tom's possessions. The place was impressive. The ceiling here was a bit lower than in the hallway, but still ample enough that no one needed to hunch. Besides the bed, stove, and candles, there was a rug, a closet, a wooden writing desk that was plain enough in appearance but took up an entire wall, a nicely framed portrait of the Commonwealth's signet, and a bookcase filled with actual books. The chairs all had cushions on them. This family had wealth. Eli made a note of it for later. Putting on a kindly smile, he settled in next to the bed, grateful to be off his feet, and looked over his patient.

He saw a little bulge beneath a pile of blankets, a few sweat-soaked strands of blond hair peeking out from underneath. The lump stirred, twitched slightly, and let out a sigh before falling silent again. Eli wiped the sweat from his face with the back of his sleeve:

"May I?"

Tom nodded.

He pulled the blanket back hesitantly and quickly turned his face in revulsion.

"The smell started right after the fever," said Tom.

"Yes, yes," Eli nodded vigorously, his arm pressed against his nose. He felt his stomach roil and wished very much that he had a drink to settle it. "That—that's to be expected."

"You alright?"

"Just preparing myself. With prayer. Silence now, please."

A drop of sweat fell from Eli's nose and melted into the girl's blanket. He drew a succession of slow breaths and steadied himself by pretending to fret through his pockets. His "pilfer pockets," as he liked to call them, were stuffed with everything he needed for his rituals. Eli sensed a second pair of eyes and spared a glance over his shoulder. In the doorway behind them, the man's wife had reappeared, her arms folded in disapproval. She shook her head but lingered to watch all the same.

"I will need total silence," Eli repeated, "as I invoke the gods for, uh. For, uh."

"Lillia," Tom prompted.

"For Lillia …"

Tom stood silently as Eli drew his arms wide and tilted his head back in supplication. In one hand he now held a piece of stick about as long as his forearm. It was painted in faded stripes of red, yellow, and blue and topped with a rusted tin amulet with a crudely etched picture of an eye on one of its faces. In his other hand, he cupped a pinch of silvery powder. He lifted the bedsheets with the end of his stick and pulled them back with a flourish.

Lillia was naked to the waist and soaked in her sweat. Every one of her ribs protruded through her skin, the bones and flesh all the same dull, lifeless hue, broken only by stippled blotches of crimson veins that spread across her torso. The sprawl radiated like a web, its center a long shard of iron sunk within her body. The hook. Lillia's eyes were shut tight, oblivious to the man performing over her.

"Hear me, oh gods! It is I, your servant, the Divine Eli of the Crag. It is I who call upon you. Hear me now, even as you hear the voices of your other children, my brothers, the dwarves, who have taught me your ways and your prayers. Hear me! Whence I have come from and whither I have traveled, near and far, to beseech you of your bounties on behalf of this child, for whom we come together now, joining our prayers with all who through the ages have ..."

Eli went on and on in this kind of speech, and in a way that somehow seemed practiced yet meandering at the same time. His voice rose and fell in tides of gibberish. There were invocations, and flattery, and a long stream of moaning and wailing about the state of affairs in the Crag and the forgotten friendships between the gods, the dwarves, and men. Once, Eli shuffled on his feet in what Tom reckoned was supposed to be a dance. A little later, he dropped the powder he had been holding into one of the candles by Lillia's bed. The flame fluttered for a moment, turned bright orange, and then quickly returned to normal, at which Eli, by this time huffing and out of breath, proclaimed it to be a portent (though of what kind, good or ill, he remained frustratingly evasive).

Tom found himself riveted to the performance. His eyes flitted between what Eli was doing and whether Lillia was reacting to it. Tom leaned forward at one point when Eli's wand (that was what Tom thought of it as) touched Lillia's eyelids. It pressed them in gently and nothing happened. Tom sighed in disappointment but remained no less spellbound.

Bette, however, grew restless. She had come and gone in the doorway throughout Eli's chanting and gesticulating and had mostly kept to herself except for a few exasperated groans. But it was getting late, and apparently, she could no longer contain herself.

"Is he still carrying on?"

"Bette!"

Eli ignored them both:

"—and blessed Kaley, whose bosoms hold all that is pure, sustaining, and good, and blessed Thonnerix, whose winged gracefulness dispels the odors of the fourteen hells, and handless Nord, and, uh, Amdal, yes—"

"I'm not serving him dinner," Bette raised her voice over Eli's, "if that's what he's hoping for. He's a hired man, not a guest. And we've barely enough for ourselves. Now that you've beggared us."

Eli, who had grown somewhat hoarse, fumbled over what he was saying. He was completely plastered with sweat and growing very pale, as if the effort of maintaining the performance was proving more than he could endure. He stammered on a little longer, licking his lips feverishly, and sank into his chair. "Amdal's blessing, too," he tried to catch his breath but seemed unable to stop himself now. "Nord's blessing—in the Mountain."

"You're ruining this," Tom pointed his finger at Bette. "And you're doing it on purpose."

Bette rolled her eyes. "You're one to be talking about ruin! Who's throwing away our money on this nonsense?"

"On our daughter, you mean?"

"Your little clerk."

"She's your own child, woman."

"Not my only one," Bette's shoulders hunched high, preparing for the fight she had clearly been hoping for. "You have a family besides your precious little clerk. But do you care about *us*? Oh, no. We'll all be sold out of Industry Caverns. It's back to the gutter for the rest of us. And all for your clerk. Who's as good as gone. Look at her. She's gone, Tom. Gone. Just like our money. Such a fool—"

"I am losing touch with the gods," Eli gasped. Tom turned his eyes from his enraged wife toward the priest. The man looked like he was on the verge of collapsing. He clutched at his chest. "The communion—the gods—breaking ... It is—we are in—"

Tom flinched as Bette plunged into a tirade, a pitched fit of uninterrupted yelling that somehow steadily grew louder. She unloaded a store of accusations, her memories and resented intimacies, and all of her husband's wrongdoings.

If Eli had been paying attention, he would have enjoyed himself. He always liked the spectacle of a family burying their teeth into one another, and in this side profession of his, he had witnessed it plenty of times. Occasionally it would offer an angle for him to make a little extra money. But not this time. He could barely hear what Bette was screaming for the thumping in his head:

"—while me and Timmy get the scraps! 'Cause that's all we're worth to you, isn't it? We're scraps. Someone to plug when you're bored and an extra set of hands for the tannery. How's she get so much more than us then? How, I ask you?"

Eli was swaying, unable to contain his motion as Tom sat on his little bench in stone silence next to him, his eyes glazed over.

"Too hot in here—" Eli reached over the bed to steady himself.

No one noticed Lillia stirring in the bed. Her breaths were coming more rapidly. An arm twitched. Her eyelids fluttered, like moths struggling to wrest themselves free from a spider web, but they could not quite open all the way. And then, all at once, her hand burst from beneath a blanket and clasped onto Eli's.

The room fell still.

Lillia's lips quivered, as if she were trying to say something.

"Lillia?" Tom gasped. "Lillia!"

Her fingers locked into Eli's with a strength that stunned the man. Their tips felt like tiny hot pokers, scouring into his palm. Eli's wand tumbled from his hand and hit the bed rail with a clatter. Lillia held him fast. His eyes went wide.

"Let go of me," the girl said, her voice barely audible. "We ... come."

"What are-what are you doing to me," Eli was unable to take his eyes from her. He was panting: "Dark ... So dark." His head spun around madly. "Someone fetch me a candle—a gulleystar, something ... I-I can't see. Oh, no, no! Where am I? Where am I?!"

The room faded into a fog. Eli thought he heard a voice.

Eli almost fell headlong onto the bed, but something caught him. Lillia was holding him upright. Then their hands, the girl's and his, traveled down Lillia's chest, down the curve of her stomach, down to her wound. As one, they pulled the barbed hook free from her side. Plucked the wicked thing out like a splinter. There was no staunch of blood, no bile. Lillia's skin enveloped around the hole, like water pouring into a crack. And now at last Lillia's eyes opened all the way, the veins receded from her face, from her torso. She turned her head to meet Eli's and in a faint voice asked where she was.

"In the Mountain," he whispered without thinking. He drew a hard breath as if something cold had suddenly struck him. His head turned slowly. There was a stirring in the air above him. Up there, in the corner of the ceiling, he would have sworn he saw a shadow moving.

Eli jerked his hand free from Lillia's. His fingers clutched at his eyes in terror, his bottom lip quivered noiselessly.

And then he fled. With Tom crying and clasping his waking daughter, with Bette trembling in her half-vented fury behind him, and the neighbors thrusting their doors open at the commotion that the whole cavern could hear, the Divine Eli fled. His priest's robes flapping madly behind him, he knocked Timothy to the ground and ran as fast as he could down the corridors of Industry Caverns, his empty hands flailing madly about his face, his shrieks echoing long after he had disappeared. In his flight, Eli had left behind his wand, his staff, a few forged papers, a wad of rags, and the pouch of coins Tom had given him.

CHAPTER THREE

Tom sat with his children at the table, quietly devouring a breakfast of boiled mushrooms, radishes, and strips of goat meat laid out in a skillet. The smell of grease filled the air. Tom and Tim ate greedily in their work clothes. Lillia pushed a mushroom around in circles on her plate. Her sash hung from the arm of her chair, almost draping the floor. Bette had gone out for the weekly market day to collect their wages from the clerk and buy whatever food could be found.

Tom held up a piece of paper close to his nose and chewed on a lump of fat. His face was still pink from shaving, and he had combed his hair back, pulling it tight with a piece of string he had found in Eli's belongings.

"So this teacher's note," he said, gulping down the gristle, "it says you can make up your missed work assignment at the Docks by spending a day watching a clerk do an accounting of a goat herd." He spoke in a tone that could have been a question. When no one answered, Tom continued:

"That would be today, by the looks of it. I can see a date here." He turned the paper on its side. "And we'll be going to—what's this name here? Looks like it's Cuh-cuh …"

Lillia leaned across the table to look over her father's shoulder.

"Collin Grounds," she read aloud, "he's a herder in Prosperity Farm." She slumped against the back of her chair and stared at her plate of uneaten food. She looked exhausted already, though it was only morning.

"I knew it started with the cuh-sound," Tom nodded, folding the paper. "Recognized the letter."

"I've met him before," said Tim, wiping his mouth. "Grounds, I mean. Once when I picked up some hides." He paused to stare at his father. "He travels up the Mountain sometimes—you know?"

Tom winced at the boy's poor attempt at subtlety. Tim might as well have just said aloud, "Grounds is a guildsman." Tom gave the boy a quick, curt nod then turned to his daughter:

"And the clerk you'll be watching, Lillia, it's your classmate's father?" Tom asked. "What's that boy's name again?"

"Jack," Lillia replied.

"Nice of him to arrange all this for you," Tom made a gesture with his spoon at the paper. "He seems like a good man, with good prospects. I like him." Jack had been one of the few friends of Lillia's to ask for her when she had been hurt; and the only one to visit since she had been healed, though the boy's visit had lasted no longer than a few muttered words before he skirted back outside to rejoin some friends of his.

Lillia said nothing but rested her face in the cusp of her arm on the table, while Tom and Tim finished the meal in silence.

"We ought to get going," said Tom, rising. "It's a short hike, but you've not done much walking since—well, for a while. This'll do you good. A little fresh air, help you clear your head before you hit the books again. Just what you need to get all better."

"Can I come with you?" Tim asked, jumping to his feet.

Tom glanced at Lillia, bracing for the rant. It would be impossible, she would declare. Tim was not included in the pass Jack had gotten for her. It would be a gross impropriety to impose like that; Tim was not even a rated laborer yet; someone might make a note of it. But Lillia only sat in her chair with her head on her elbow, a vacant expression fixed on her face as her gray eyes flitted between the cracked edge of her plate and the tiny flickering flame of a table lantern. Just as Tom knew he would, Tim took his sister's silence as an opening to press his case:

"I could pitch in and help, too. With the herd. The clerk wouldn't mind that. And since Collins's a traveling friend of ours—"

"—Enough," Tom said. Tim bowed his head and bit his lip, and a strand from his tangled blonde mop of hair fell past his nose. Tom's mouth pursed in thought. He cast a final questioning look at Lillia, but she still had not moved. Finally, Tom shrugged.

"I suppose we can all go."

Tim hopped from his chair and cleared the table, bouncing with excitement. It took some coaxing, but Tom was able to stir Lillia from her lethargy long enough to reach the door. They had only gone a few steps down the tunnel when he noticed something. A pang of worry churned in the pit of his stomach, but Tom kept his voice calm. He turned Lillia around, cracked the door back open, and pointed inside their home toward the table, to Lillia's chair:

"Don't forget your sash," he said.

Lillia found Jack waiting for her and her family in a deserted junction four levels down from Industry Caverns. He greeted her warmly, nodded to Timothy, and, after some hesitation, shook Tom's hand. Then he ushered them toward a warden's post set inside a tunnel wall. The guard, a fat, jaundiced man in mismatched yellow pants and doublet, jumped to attention at the sight of Jack and took his papers with a bow. He made a pretense of counting his companions.

"So it's just two workers, then, sir? And, uh, the sash—er, I should say, academy student with you? Says here her name's Tanner. That's not the girl that, uhm …"

Lillia did not react, but she watched as Jack shot the man a menacing glare.

"Right, you're in a hurry," the guard pushed open a warped wooden beam that barred the corridor. "Our all for all."

"Our all for all," Tom and Tim repeated.

They walked together as a loose group down a wide corridor that led to Prosperity Farms. Tom and Tim kept a good pace in front while Jack and Lillia lingered behind far enough to accord a proper distance between the clerk's students and Crag laborers. The cobbled rock floor slowly gave way to drifts of sand that were littered with countless black balls of dried droppings. A tiny square of gray daylight at the end of the tunnel, framed by a gate, still lay far in the distance. All the gulleystar lanterns here were dark, the mushrooms from the last time anyone had bothered to fill them were shriveled to little more than stems and powder. But there was light enough to make out the faded pictures and lettering of signs dotting the walls. Those who could read were reminded to follow their clerks, make a note of unusual workers, and to give "Our

All for All!" A pungent scent clinging in the air grew stronger the further they walked.

"So are you coming back to class after this?"

It was the first time Jack had spoken to her since meeting the Tanners at the warden's post. The sound brought Lillia out of a daze.

"I suppose," she answered without looking immediately at him. Then, lifting her head, she spoke a little more firmly: "Yes. Yes, I will."

"Mava will be thrilled," he rolled his eyes.

"What do you mean?"

"She's been angling for your commissar appointment ever since you got hurt."

That brought a faint, but bitter laugh out of Lillia.

"Someone's going to get it," Jack said. "Teacher's still got the appointment to give out. Mava says it's going to be her. Not in front of Teacher, but the word's out. And Teacher hasn't told her no."

Lillia halted and faced Jack. He looked taller than she remembered.

"What about you?" she asked. "You could've gone after that spot. Did you?"

Jack shook his head. "Nope. Not me. I'm fine right here."

"Really?"

"Yeah. I like this farm. It's outside, not a lot of people. Work's pretty light. Smell's bad, but, you know, could be worse." He shrugged.

"Can't be worse than a tannery."

"Exactly. We get a good allotment from the Crest, the other clerks don't bother us. My dad's got pull out here. Even the workers like him."

The two walked along in silence for a while, the sounds of their footsteps crunching in the loose gravel. Ahead in the distance, Lillia saw Tim lose his footing for a moment until her father braced his elbow.

"It's the sand," said Jack. "Most Craggies don't know how to walk in it."

"You were scared, weren't you?" Lillia surprised herself as the question seemed to spring out of her, almost on its own.

"What're you talking about?"

"In the Crest. When we saw that man get removed. That scared you."

Jack thrust his hands into his pockets and dropped his chin into his chest. He shot a glance at Lillia, his eyes betrayed annoyance at being reminded of something unpleasant, before he muttered, more to himself:

"Wasn't that scared."

"I wasn't either."

"Really?" Jack stopped and looked at her.

"Yeah."

Jack's next question came slowly. "Did you know—I mean, had you heard how it would happen? What it was going to be like?"

"No."

Jack was staring down the tunnel now, his long arms crossed tightly against his chest. The gate was only a little farther now; the tunnel had filled with light and the scents of saltwater and animals. They could hear the mindless drone of goats bleating in the distance. Tom and Tim were waiting patiently in front of the doorway for them to catch up.

"I mean, I kind of wished I *hadn't* seen it," Jack said after a pause. "It's like—once you've seen a removal—been through it—it stays in your head. I get why the Crest doesn't want us watching them."

Lillia thought for a moment. She felt her face harden. Her mind was racing ahead, like when she was on the verge of solving a particularly difficult computation, and then she released a sudden loud breath:

"No. You don't get it at all."

"Huh?"

"The only reason they don't let us watch is so it *will* stay in our heads. That's what makes a removal different. That's why it's not the same as being taken up to court, or getting lashes, or even doing time in the Tombs. When a worker goes through the Citadel—he just goes away. He disappears. People will gossip, come up with crazy stories about all sorts of horrid things that might have happened to him. You might believe what they say. Or you might not. But you'll never really know. That's the point. Since you don't know what they do in the Crest, you'll keep thinking about it even though there's nothing to think about."

Jack shook his head.

"You're talking strange, Lil. I'd keep that to myself."

"In my head, you mean?"

"Yeah," he laughed uneasily. He clasped a hand behind the back of his neck. "Exactly."

Lillia sat down on a mossy rock to gaze at the surroundings, scarcely noticing the wetness that seeped through her clothes.

Prosperity Farm had no crops or fields. It was nothing more than a wide plateau that spanned like a gash across an otherwise barren and sheltered side of the Mountain. The place was pocked all over by boulders, loose gravel, sand drifts, and crevasses; but it was the color green that gave the place its most prevalent and jarring feature. Miles of leafy, branching lichen covered the rocky surface like a curtain, glistening with tiny water droplets whenever a rare burst of sunlight broke through the clouds. A mist hung over everything, either from the sea half a mile below or the clouds descending from the summit of the Mountain high above, and it made everything cold, and damp, and slick.

She wanted to do nothing but sit still and breathe the air. Even with the smell of manure and rotting vegetation all around, it was fresh air, and her lungs craved all of it she could get. But the deeper she breathed, the more she found it made her head swim. So she sat and tried to clear her senses.

Waves of mist passed aimlessly before her and when it finally lifted, she could see a meandering line of beige in the distance. It seemed to be pulsating. As she brought it into focus, she realized the line was moving closer.

Goats. There must have been hundreds, thousands of them. Wandering with their shepherds to return to the farm's entrance, where she sat. A strange notion came over Lillia that if she concentrated hard enough, she could make this living, moving line draw itself longer, or shorter, turn to the left, or pirouette right. Maybe even fly. Her thoughts were broken by Jack calling her name.

"Hey, where've you been?" He jumped across the tops of two boulders to reach her. He followed Lillia's gaze out into the fog. "They're still about a mile away. But it won't be long. They're moving a lot faster than they look."

Lillia nodded. "Do any of them ever fall off?"

"What, goats? No. Never. Now and then we lose a worker. Like if they're drunk. Or sometimes if a Craggie from another section comes out on new orders, but he doesn't know how to walk the rocks right—that's what we call it, walking the rocks—he might take a spill."

Jack was balancing on one foot now, poised on the edge of a sharp point of granite that jutted out over a drop of forty feet. He was showing off for her, Lillia could tell.

"It takes practice," Jack said, trying to sound casual. "But you could learn how. I could teach you. You have to get up, though. You know?"

Lillia stared at him. Jack hopped back from the edge and crouched low. Lillia could see her tiny reflection in his eyes, her small and distant face, wavering, silent, while a teenage boy's voice dropped low:

"Look, my dad's been waiting for a while. He's not used to that. Not out here. I told him you were winded from the walk, but uh, you need to come and introduce yourself already."

"Okay."

Without asking, Jack clasped Lillia by the elbow and hoisted her up, and then led her across a stretch of rocks, up a gravel path that wound around an outcrop of boulders, until they reached a low-roofed hut built from piled stones. The men working nearby all stopped what they were doing to holler a greeting or a crass joke as Jack went by. Jack laughed with them. They came to a wooden gate, and Lillia felt out of breath once more, so she paused, pretending to survey the area. There was little to see other than the hut, some sacks of feed, and an enormous swath of ground that had been fenced off. A few workers were scattering straw there and filling troughs with water. The door to the hut was open, and Jack led her inside.

It was a wide and windowless room, lit by a fire that burned low inside an iron stove, with a few lanterns propped on top of bookshelves, trunks, and mismatched cabinets. Some pigeons flapped their wings noisily in the rafters near the roof. Jack shut the door behind them, and the warmth that filled the place felt welcoming. In the center of the stone floor, there was a table covered in sheaves of paper and another lantern. Tom and Tim sat next to each other on one side, and both looked visibly relieved when they saw Lillia. Next to them sat an older, wiry man wearing a worker's outfit and heavy boots, smoking a stump of a pipe. At the head of the table, wreathed in smoke, was a heavier version of Jack— blonde, broad-shouldered, but with a looming, solid belly—whose face transformed from an impatient scowl into a wreath of smiles so quickly that Lillia almost missed the former expression. The man ground his thumb into his pipe to put out the smoke.

"Well, are we feeling alright now?" his voice boomed in the empty room. He stood up, pulled out a chair next to him, and waved for Lillia to come and join him.

Lillia's head barely reached the bottom of his chest, so he thrust his hand down to shake hers.

"I'm Blaine," he tried to clasp her hand tenderly, but that was not something he was suited for. Lillia winced in pain. Tom almost shot to his feet, but the man next to him only smiled and clasped Tom's shoulder. Blaine jerked his head in the man's direction:

"This here's Collin Grounds. The crew boss."

"A pleasure, sir," Lillia forced a smile. "Lillia Tanner. Academy student."

Blaine nodded and Collin bowed his head.

"I've heard reports about you," Blaine reached for Collin's pipe, relit his own from it, and handed it back. "A lot of reports. Probably shouldn't be helping you out like this. But Jackie here, he gives you high marks. And in my book, that counts for something."

Lillia smiled broadly, her amusement completely genuine. Jack's cheeks were flushing bright splotches of pink.

"Hah!" Grounds hacked a laugh that sent tendrils of pipe smoke from his nose. "Now you've gone and embarrassed the boy."

"So I have."

The two chuckled, while Tom fidgeted uncomfortably:

"Mr. Ridgemore," he said, "We really do appreciate your help with Lillia's assignment. I'm sure she'll learn a lot from you. And like I said, Tim and I are more than willing to—"

"Oh, we'll put you both to work, not to worry," Blaine cut over Tom, "Collin here's always complaining how he needs more hands in the pen when it's counting time."

"For all the good it does me," Collin took a long pull from his pipe.

"Yeah, well, anything to get an honest day's work out of you. For a change." Blaine hoisted his belt up above his belly and got out of his chair, and everyone in the room immediately followed his example. "So Collin will tell you boys what to do, while Jackie and Lillia help me with the books." Then he pointed at Collin. "Go ahead and put them to work in the back of the pens. Out away from the cliffs, if you know what I mean."

"That I do," Collin nodded.

"You boys don't know how to walk the rocks, and we can't be having any accidents, especially with our young academy student around. So stay in the pen. It's the safest place out there."

Lillia sat riveted behind a desk that had been set up outside of the hut near the animal pen and, although her little stool was unbalanced and uncomfortable, she did not dare to budge. She was trapped where she was, a speck of stillness amid a torrent of movement. Wave after wave of goats seemed to be coming from every direction. They had formed a great, bleating mass, black, beige, spotted, all pushing and pulling in every direction, coming and going in living tides and currents. Here and there, a human handler, hard to tell apart from the animals, would peek above the crowd. These men would scream, always in curses that cut above the din of animals, and when they did, the herd around them would flinch, and then the sweep of a hooked staff would send a dozen or so of the animals scampering in a new direction. And in that way, another little rivulet of goats would flow a few feet closer to the gate. The men were diverting a running, living river—a cup at a time, but they were moving it. At the far end, Lillia could see her brother scurrying about, falling over, failing miserably at his task of tying a shred of white cloth around a squealing goat.

Lillia looked up at Jack's father who was standing with one foot on top of his chair and the other on the desk. He had his hands cupped to his mouth and his voice shot across the pen:

"What the hell are you doing, Tanner?!"

Jack made a face, as he pulled at his father's sleeve. From a chair across the table from Lillia, he had been sorting the clerk's record books, preparing them for the count. "He's never done ranch work before. Probably never even seen a goat, much less spot one that's nursing."

"Well, that's for certain. He hasn't marked a single one yet." Then he yelled again:

"Shit and death, man, are you looking for love out there? Just grab the ones with teats, get a band around the neck, tie a knot, and move on."

Blaine slid back into his seat and took a long pull from a jug of wine, cursing loudly to himself, while Tim continued to flounder among the wandering goats, looking hopelessly lost. The strip of cloth clutched in Tim's fingers fluttered uselessly in the breeze. Tom, at least, had managed to wrestle a small goat to the ground; he had tied a long length of rope around its legs and was pulling it towards Tim, shouting something that Lillia could not quite hear. The rest of the workers were in a frenzy of activity, and far too occupied to lend a hand to useless strangers.

"Dad, shouldn't we get ready?" Jack asked.

Blaine took another drink and shrugged at the boy, who at once thrust a sheet of paper across the table to Lillia.

"Here," Jack started scratching lines across his paper. "So you set up your record as a cross-section. Three columns. It's always going to be three—one for adults, one for kids, and the far-right one is for nursing does. I guess we'll have to leave that one blank for a little longer."

Lillia picked up a crude wooden stylus by her hand, held it as if for the first time, and finally dipped it into the ink well between them. It took her several tries before she could draw her lines. She was focused on making the lines straight and didn't see Jack's eyebrow raised at her.

"You got it?" he asked. Jack's impatience was palpable.

"Yeah. Sorry."

"Okay, as soon as the last goat's penned, the second the gate's shut, we run out there and start the tally. We have to be quick. They'll bust through the fencing if we take too long."

Lillia stared out over the mass of animals. A cloud of dust and hair floated upwards, mixing with the fog from the Mountain. Three-quarters of the herd was inside the pen, and to Lillia, it looked like every inch of space was teeming with pulsating bodies of fur, and hooves, and horns— and eyes. It was strange, how their eyes kept grappling Lillia's attention; she found herself drawn to these creatures and their jarring hazel eyes with the pupils shaped like—like what? The black lines cracked within the amber orbs, it reminded her of something. While she thought, the movement of the herd slowed. A brown and white face peeked through the bottom slats of the gate and regarded her. A second goat joined it. Silent, gazing. How strange that they should be so fixated with her.

Lillia shook her head:

"How-how are we supposed to count them all?"

"The workers will set themselves up in a grid," Jack said. "You holler out to each man, one at a time, and he does a quick count. They know the system. But the goats won't sit still, so the count's only good for a few seconds. That's why I say we've got to be quick. So that we're accurate."

"Accurate enough," Blaine interrupted with a knowing look, "for guidelines. You don't have to be perfect. Don't get the girl hung up too much on precision out there, Jackie," Blaine waved at the herd and turned to Lillia. "We get an allowance, you see, and we got to use it. That's important, too."

But Jack ignored him. His face glowed with excitement, and he scooped his record and stylus pen tight beneath his elbow. "They're almost done. Watch how I do it, Lil; then I'll tell you when to start your count. Are you ready?"

Lillia managed to fold her sheet of paper into quarters, although her fingers were trembling. She got to her feet and felt the ground roiling beneath her. Somehow, she held herself upright. The clamor of goats and shepherds, the musty stench, the dust, the cold, even the smell of Blaine's wine—it all blended into a maelstrom of sensations that made her dizzy. Her mouth pulled tight across her face.

There was a loud, wooden crash followed by the sound of a latch. A cheer from the men. Lillia lurched forward, bumping the table's edge. She was trailing after Jack, who sprinted ahead, yelling over his shoulder, something about how to mark her count of the herd.

They ran to the gate. Jack clambered up the fence and stood on the top plank. But Lillia could only prop herself up just high enough to peek between the uppermost slats.

And there, waiting for her, was the face again. Tawny with dappled white fur, pierced by glowing yellow eyes that were, themselves, pierced by something black and jagged through the center. The goat stared at her, unmoving, even as a mass of bodies surged behind him. His eyes never blinked. An image came to Lillia's mind, so powerful it nearly knocked her to the ground: the sword, pick, and hammer of the Commonwealth. Our all of all. The goat held her gaze.

"Hey," Jack was hollering down at her. "Lillia! Come on! Watch me. I said, watch me!"

"Watch me," she mouthed the words.

Jack was shouting the names of his men. The workers in the pen, one after another, bellowed numbers back to him. Without looking, Jack's pen flew across his paper, ticking off each one's response. One after another, Jack would point and shout at a man, and he would bark something back at Jack. It became almost like a song, a tuneless melody over a chorus of braying animals.

"Watch me," Lillia heard the words repeating in her head. But now it was someone else's voice—a brigade of voices, rolling like an avalanche underneath the Mountain:

"*Me ... We ... we come ... Elon ... We come ...*"

Lillia was falling through the air.

She hit the ground hard on her back, gasping because the breath had been knocked out of her. Shattered planks of wooden fencing fell like hail around her. She blinked and heard from far away, the sounds of men's screams, something between rage and panic, that was quickly drowned by the rumble of hooves. She turned her head and saw Jack on his knees, covering his head, as the whole herd of goats surged, as one body, through the broken gate.

"Pen's been breached! Form a line! Form a line, right here!"

Collin appeared next to Jack and was able to heave one of the broken boards up from the ground and clasp it across his chest to shield Jack from the rush of goats. As he pushed back against the wave, forcing the animals to move around him, Collin roared out orders to the farmhands. Tom and Tim were still at the back of the pen, stuck against the current of the herd's movement. Blaine reached Collin first, lugging a table from the hut. He flipped it over to make a barrier between his boy and the press of goats.

"Get the posts up first!" Collin yelled through his clenched teeth. "Forget the bracings, Andrew—just get the damn posts back up. The *posts!*"

"Jackie, back to the hut," Blaine's voice broke. "Now." Jack's knees wobbled. His father propped him up, threw his arm over his shoulders, and together, they scurried back to the safety of the hut, both dazed and bloodied.

Men were scurrying everywhere, panicked, trying to rebuild a fence in the middle of a tidal wave. And all the while, the brown and white goat stood next to Lillia. While hundreds of others raced by them in a blur, it stood, still and sullen, staring down at her. The stampede raged all around, but in the small sanctuary of the space between them, nothing touched Lillia. Deep in the throng by the fallen gate, Collin stole a glance at Lillia; his eyes narrowed and then he saw it, too.

Not one of the goats would touch her. It was as if she were a canyon. Or a flame.

"*Watch me,*" Lillia thought she heard the words again, drifting away in the air.

Without a sound, the brown goat walked around her to join the others outside.

"Tanner!" Collin was yelling to her father. "Bring that line over here. No, *here!*"

But Tom was making straight for Lillia. Tim stumbled after him.

"Lillia!" she heard her father yell over the din of the stampede. "Stay there! We're coming."

"Tanner, bring me that rope!" Collin said.

"Lillia!"

"*Look!*" One of the men who had been working next to Collin pointed to the edge of the Mountain, beyond the stone hut and the paths that led from the pen. He was frozen, horror-stricken, unable to move the finger that was still outstretched from his hand.

"Get back on that post, Andrew, or I swear—" Collin began, but then he looked behind him and saw it, too. "What—are they—" The color drained from Collin's face; his forehead crinkled. He rasped, struggling to form the word: "—*doing?*"

The goats that had escaped, a crowd of several hundred, were mulling quietly into a winding line that led away from the farm paths and shelter of the Mountain's chasms, out to the edge of a sheer drop. The only sound was their hooves, scraping along the gravel in a steady march. They were queuing toward a cliff.

One by one, the goats were leaping off the edge. They hopped out into the openness beyond the rocks, lingered for a moment in the air above the spray and the fog and the unseen jagged rocks far below, and then each fell, perfectly calm, never flailing or grasping. Each one, a silent plummet. Followed by another. Then another. And another. In perfect order, they were falling to their deaths. In their last moment, each one flared a pale light that extinguished when their bodies splattered against the crashing shoreline below, like falling stars.

"Was there no help …" Andrew started.

He came to his senses when Collin's fist pelted the side of his head. The fence's gate finally rose, and though it was teetering wildly, the hands were able to pitch it upright to make a semblance of a barricade. It was just enough. The remaining goats inside the restored pen slowly settled. Gradually their bleating, and chewing, and nosing at one another returned, as if a flimsy wooden palisade was all that was needed to bring them back to their natural order. As for the men working the ranch of Prosperity Farm, most of them fled the moment it was safe for them to run. All except for Collin.

Lillia felt herself being swept up into her father's arms.

"I-I'm fine," was all she could say to her father's questions. "I'm fine."

But now she was being jostled. Collin stormed headlong into Tom and nearly knocked them both over. The man was drenched with sweat and his face, reddened, dust-covered, flecked with blood—his own mixed with goats'—had a wild look to it. It was the first time Lillia had ever seen her father avoid a man's gaze. Tim stepped between them.

"She did this," Collin spat a trail of pink from his lips. A tooth clinked to the ground. "That girl. I saw it. It was her."

"Did you get hit in the head?" Tom replied. "How could a little girl have done that?"

"It was her!"

"You're the ones who can't keep a gate shut."

Collin started to charge at Tom, but Tim locked his arms around him. Collin roared:

"I'm telling you; it was *her!*"

"Stop it," Tim struggled to hold Collin down; the old man was surprisingly strong for his size. "Grounds, stop it! We're workers' sons, remember? Me, him, you. We-we're all brothers here."

Collin stopped fighting. "So we are," he said at last. He stepped back to let Tim loosen his grasp. Collin wiped his hand through his hair, now plastered in odd angles, and fixed Tom with a penetrating gaze. "I've been around goats my whole life. They're dumb and docile as a Craggie.

What happened out there—the way they all charged—the way they ... they jumped. And then to steer around your girl like that ..."

"What of it?" Tom asked.

"She's as good as noted."

"No."

Collin eyed the three of them.

"Everyone saw what happened, Tanner. Everyone. And them that ran," he motioned back towards the pen, "they're warden's men. They'll talk."

Tom held an arm around Lillia tightly, as if to protect her from the whispers, the rumors, the reports that were already swirling around her. "She's in an academy. She'll be a commissar one day. She's clever."

"She's noted. If she wasn't before, she's marked and noted now." Collin turned, straightened his torn and dirty clothes, and muttered as he left to save what remained of his herd and his livelihood: "I'd cut that clever girl loose if I was you, brother. Or go and hide her if you can. Someplace deep, though."

CHAPTER FOUR

MILES BENEATH PROSPERITY Farm, many flights below Industry Caverns, there was a little tannery hidden in the Mountain's lowest ward. Built along the shore of a hollow cavern lake, the entire tannery was nothing more than a dismal pair of huts, a run of basins and ditches, a lean-to tent used to cover the heaps of animal skins while they cured into leather, and a great pile of clay pots. Tom and Tim had added a few drying racks for oversized pelts, but otherwise, the tannery was just as it had always been for generations. A dank, foul-smelling little factory by a black lake in a cave.

The water of the lake was always calm. A winding maze of tunnels and fissures, miles long, separated the tannery from the rocky shoals of the Crag's outer fingers. Tempests might rage outside. A hurricane could stir the ocean to war against the Mountain's stones. But within the solace of this crack, deep in the roots of the Mountain's base, the water never stirred. It stayed dark and still and quiet.

It was quiet and utterly foul. A stench of stale urine clung to everything in the tannery. Rows of open cisterns were always filled with sewage. The refuse would be churned, strained, and then poured out to drain over rock piles, where the piss mixed with the lake's saltwater to soak into animal skins, which, after a long rotting, would become flimsy leather pelts. The smell made most people ill.

That was partly why the clerks and wardens never came to this place. But also, there was this: the tannery's proprietor, Tom, ran his operation quietly and profitably. Every morning, he would walk the long sets of steps from his home to the tannery, work without resting for twelve hours, and shuffle home for supper and sleep, and then repeat the routine on the morrow. He never got sick, never complained about his quotas. Once a year, he sought out his supervisors and paid them a generous bribe without so much as a word of haggling. And so the tannery had, by and large, been left alone.

It was the only place Tom could think to hide. He had lost track of how many days they had been down here in the huts, the three of them, working their old trade, pretending that nothing was amiss.

Tom plunged an armful of shorn goat hides into a cistern and then heaved them back up. The brackish water streamed down his arms and shoulders, soaking his bare chest. The skins dropped with a wet thud. His son reached for the top hide to start his work of thinning out the pelt with a mortar, but then he paused. Tim fumbled with his tool, bit his bottom lip, and then finally spoke:

"Do you think she'll come back?"

The question seemed to echo in the small space, and it shattered a silence that Tom would have preferred to keep. Tom stopped what he was doing and watched the water drip from his hands. It pooled into puddles around his bare and filthy toes. He took a deep breath and faced Tim.

There sat his son, a cracked stone mortar in one hand, a goatskin pelt clutched in the other, in eager anticipation, as if the boy were about to present it for his approval: *see how well I cured this one, Father?*

"Will she?" Tim repeated.

Tom knew he ought to say something; he hadn't spoken to the boy all day.

"I doubt it," Tom said. His voice sounded harder than he intended.

To his credit, Tim would not let his father see him cry.

"She has lots of cousins," Tom explained, "down in the Farms. Wouldn't cost much to get a clerk to put your mom on a new list, with a new name. Mom will be fine. So long as she keeps to herself."

Tim nodded gravely and went back to his work.

It was the first time anyone had mentioned Bette since they had fled their home in Industry Caverns. Since the day when Tom, Tim, and Lillia had staggered through the front door, dazed and bleeding. In the panic, in the hurry to pack whatever they could carry away, Tom could hardly explain to Bette what had happened to them at Prosperity Farm—how could he, when he couldn't bring himself to believe what they had all seen? Tom must have sounded like a lunatic babbling gibberish about goats, and cliffs, and a guildsman's warning that they were all marked and noted now. He knew she would never believe him. Bette had stood obstinately in the kitchen with her ladle spoon quivering in her grasp, and the moment Lillia's name came out of Tom's mouth, Bette erupted.

The fight had been vicious. Vicious, but fortunately brief.

The front door had been wide open, and the neighbors loitered shamelessly in the hall, not even making a pretense of ignoring the commotion Bette made. That bastard at the end of the hall, Littlepool, was writing everything down on a scroll. Between Bette's blows and screams, Tom had had enough time to stuff a bag full of clothes, some tools, a few of Lillia's papers that were in easy reach, and the pouch of coins, which he wrapped within Lillia's sash and wedged down at the very bottom. Before they left, Tom had stood in the doorway, his sack slung over one shoulder, his other arm wrapped around Lillia. He stared at Bette. In the clutter between them stood Tim, torn between leaving with his father and sister, or staying with his mother. Poor Timothy.

He had made his choice. And now, days later, though the welt on Tim's head that Bette had given him had healed, Tom sensed that the boy was no less torn. The look on Bette's face—not of loss, but betrayal— would surely be haunting him. Tom knew he should say something more to him, anything to ease the burden of what he must be feeling. He took a halting step toward Tim inside the tent. The boy paused in his work and met his eyes. Tom focused on the pelt he was curing.

"That's good work," was all he said, and then he turned around again and let the flap of the tent fall behind him.

Once outside, Tom stretched his shoulders. The muscles in his back and arms were cramped; he had not worked like this since Lillia had started with the academy. He trudged stiffly across the ground, the crunch of pebbles beneath his feet soon giving way to the softer squish of clay. The sound of a tiny wave lapping on the shore could be heard out by the shoals.

She was sitting on the edge of a pool wearing nothing more than a thin shift and absently running the edge of a blade in a strange pattern that had almost worn through the pelt that was spread across her lap. Her back was to him. As he approached, he could see her eyes reflecting the blackness of the lagoon water. Unblinking and inscrutable, they did not move when he greeted her.

"Was getting worried about you. You've been out here all evening. You'll catch a cold."

"Leave me alone."

Tom blew out a long sigh. He pretended to scan the waters and then sat down next to Lillia in the mud as if joining her vigil. Her soft breaths turned to mist around her. The ground felt like a dampened block of ice, making the arthritis in his knees begin to throb. He was struck by the emptiness that had taken hold of her features. If it weren't for the querulous eyebrows and that dimly familiar air of annoyance, Tom might have had no affinity with this girl.

"Sorry we haven't been able to get you back to class yet," he offered. "I know you must be worried. It's just—with all that's happened—"

"I don't care about my class."

Tom blanched in the darkness. "You don't mean that."

"Yes, I do. Madam Teacher, my classmates, they don't know anything. They're all idiots."

"Well. That may be true, by your marks."

"There's nothing for me to learn there. I've no use for them anymore."

Tom thought to himself.

"You know," he said slowly, "I think I can understand why you might feel that way. Take me for instance. I don't much care for the company of clerk-trained tanners, not since I got properly trained up by my master. Nothing wrong with them. But here I've mastered leathercraft, where I can make some real pieces that would last a man his lifetime, but none of them can so much as sew a pouch that won't unravel. It's as if we've nothing to say to one another. We're too different. Not that tanning and learning are the same thing—but, well, what with you being the cleverest, being so far ahead of the others in your class … it might make you feel a little lonely sometimes."

"I'm not lonely," she cut him off. "I wish I was, but I'm not."

Tom fell silent and looked at her. A wind stirred in her hair, brushing the bangs across her face, but she never broke her gaze from the lake. They sat and listened to the water dripping and the scraping noise of Timothy working his pelts from inside the tent until Lillia tilted her head, half-facing her father for the first time:

"Do you know what dreams are?" Her voice was flat.

Tom faltered that it might have had a ring to it, but he shook his head.

"I wouldn't expect you to. They don't even lecture about it in class. Something I came across in the library." She shifted slightly in her seat, oblivious to the squelching mud. "In the old days, before the Overthrow, the priests used to claim that they could see and hear their gods—talk to them. While they were asleep or praying or whatever. Like having a conversation."

Tom made a sour face, as he had been trained to do whenever the subject came up of the priests and their deceits.

"Of course only certain priests could have these dreams," Lillia continued, "you had to achieve a blessed trance, or go on a pilgrimage on the right day, or stare into a bowl of water in just a certain way. And only they knew how to do it, so no one could ever prove whether their dreams were real or made-up. It was all a trick. But no one cared at the time."

"Mm-mm," Tom shook his head.

"But now and then, something strange would happen. Someone would claim to have a dream, and the dream would have nothing to do with cheating people out of their money or getting them to bow down to anything, or anything about the gods at all. They'd see … no, that's not the word. They'd *experience* things, in their sleep, when they were awake. These dreams would never leave them alone. It was almost like the dreams would possess them, and they'd end up going mad. Some of them died. And yet … they loved it. The ones that wrote down these dreams, you could tell. They loved whatever it was that was happening to them."

"What kind of things did they see?" he asked.

Lillia's voice grew cold and stretched. Like an icicle melting the last of its drops on an indifferent earth.

"They would call them black shadows," she said. "Or demons. Dragons. Dark things with golden eyes. They said they whispered and screamed. Or sang songs. They would come from in the Mountain, the shadows … The journals of these priests' dreams, the few there are left, it's like reading …" Lillia's voice trailed off.

Tom stared at her as she sat peering out once more across the waters. He watched the vapor in the air trailing her breaths. The Mountain lake still held her gaze, its surface a seamless, unbroken mirror, with a depth of darkness that almost shone. The hide and tool she had been working with had fallen carelessly to her side. Lillia hugged her knees tight and declared in a tired voice:

"I've been having dreams."

Tom cast a sideways glance back out toward the lake at the brittle shadow still hunched near its shoreline and decided he would waste a little wood to build a fire.

She still hasn't recovered. Not all the way. With all the commotion, how could she? She just needs a good rest. A warm bed and a hot meal, and rest.

His stash of branches was small, but he always laid aside a store of kindling and it did not take him long with a steel ring and flint to get a pyramid of flame ignited on a crop of rocks in front of the tent. Tim had gone out to fetch a sack of salt and would be pleased to return to the warmth. Maybe they could even roast some meat if the boy happened across something while he was out there.

The fire's smoke, sprouting from the sandy ground, wreathed like strands of gray ivy around Tom's face and disappeared into the darkness above. The smell of the burning twigs and the prospect of their first cooked meal in days took hold of Tom's thoughts, sent him into a brief reverie. He never noticed the shadows flitting like embers around the tannery until he heard Tim screaming:

"Father!"

Tom stomped the flames out and snatched up a knife. He was pointing the curved blade at a group of men hurrying towards him. They were warden's guards; he could tell from the spears and helms they carried. A few well-dressed clerks with their yellow sashes tied prominently were close behind. They had Tim bound in ropes with a sword's tip pointed at his throat. Lillia stumbled along next to him, staring blankly.

The man at the head of the group was smiling as if he was an old friend. A sword sheathed in a yellow scabbard was at his side and a captain's epaulets graced his shoulders. He spoke authoritatively, and with a very slight lisp:

"Now, Tanner, there was no need to douse that cheery little fire. There's certainly no need for scrapers. Careful with that, now. Why don't you go ahead and leave that little tool here where it belongs? There's a good fellow. I hope you'll forgive the unannounced intrusion, but we thought it might be time for a chat."

Tom was forced inside his tent and made to sit on a stool across from the captain, who introduced himself as Oliver. With the glow of several more gulleystar pots inside, Tom could better see the man's features more clearly: meticulously combed hair, beard oiled and trimmed, with a slanting, hooked nose that was the only mark against a very handsome face. His suit of clothes was perfectly tailored around his wiry frame. The captain lifted a lilac scented silk handkerchief to his nose and scrunched his eyes.

Oliver chuckled, "no escaping the smell in here either." He took one last whiff of his perfume and then folded the handkerchief away. A stooped and balding clerk stood behind Oliver's shoulder, scowling. The clerk licked the tips of his fingers angrily as he paged through a small stack of papers that, by the look on his face, must have been highly offensive. The three were the only ones allowed in the tent. Tim and Lillia were being taken to separate huts.

Tom clasped his hands together tightly and stared at Oliver's chest. A copper amulet of the Commonwealth hung loosely over his tunic, the sword in the center, the biggest of the three tools, reflecting the pale glow of the gulleystars.

"Now Morgan here will have a few matters to go over with you concerning your tannery's accounts," Oliver began.

"It's a full accounting, actually," Morgan corrected him. "There hasn't been an inventory taken of the Commonwealth's goods here for over five years."

Tom cast his eyes down. "Because the clerk never comes around anymore."

"It's your responsibility to report your work to the Commonwealth, not the other way around."

"Yes, yes," Oliver held a gloved hand up to warn Morgan that he was not at liberty to speak yet; and that Tom would be better served by holding his tongue. "I expect it probably has been quite a while since a clerk has deigned to visit this, uhm, rustic factory." He pinched his nose and made a grimacing smile. "Can't imagine why that would be, eh?"

"Yes, sir," replied Tom. He craned his head to see if he could spot Lillia through the crack in the tent's canvas. There was only darkness outside.

"So the clerks will go over all that in due course. I'm certain you and Morgan can divide, and factor, and multiply, and carry enough ones to get your accounts back in balance. That is not why *I* am here, though, Tom. But I suspect you know that already."

"No, sir. I mean, I don't know why you are here. I've never met you before, sir."

Oliver laughed freely, while Morgan rolled his eyes.

"Well, well. And here I feel I've known you your whole life. Correct me if I'm wrong in any of the particulars. You are Tom—not Thomas—Tanner, born forty-two years ago in the Lower Ward, not quite a Noman since the clerks eventually tracked down your father in this tannery. That was how you received your name, fortunately for you. You had some aptitude with letters, but not enough to warrant further testing. Rated a master in tanning and binding. Managed to avoid being pressed into guard service. Which let me say is a pity, since you look like you had the makings to be a serviceable corporal. Bit too old for that now, I suppose. You've been married twenty years to a gulleystar miner's daughter named Bette. Presently separated. We've already spoken with her, by the way ..." Oliver's eyebrow arched. "You and Bette have two children: Timothy, who has been rated a skilled apprentice in tanning and has no notes of any consequence. And Lillia, who I'm told was earning record marks in her class until a recent incident. There, have I got you right?"

Tom's eyes dropped to the floor. Oliver bent closer, reaching out to Tom's chin, which he nudged for Tom's attention. He was smirking.

"There's a bit more to the profile, I think," Oliver whispered. "Would I find a guildmark or two among some of these finely made leather goods stacked around here? They look exquisite."

Tom shook his head and answered reflexively. "The Commonwealth pays a fair wage for my labor and provides for all our needs."

Oliver leaned back and crossed his arms. "So it does. And that's a right and proper answer. I really don't bother with the guilds, to tell you the truth. I've worked with quite a few guildsmen over the years. Always found them to be an honest and square dealing lot. A tad entrepreneurial perhaps, but there are worse vices in the Mountain."

Morgan made a sound in his throat and spat on the floor.

"Of course, my clerk colleagues probably hold a more conservative view. Still, so long as we are all putting in 'our for all,' what's a few secret handshakes among friends, or a little work on the side when it's asked for?"

Tom said nothing. He kept his feet rooted in a rut on the floor and tried to avoid watching the clerk Morgan too closely, who was sifting through pelts, and going into every bag, box, and drawer in the tent, and noting everything he found on his paper. Oliver ignored him, too.

"I honestly do not care whether you're in a guild, Tom," the captain continued. "Truth is," now he was whispering, "that's not why I'm here either. Unfortunately, I'm here because of Lillia."

"Lillia?"

"Yes. Our Lillia. Remarkable girl. Splendid marks, a recommendation to the Commissariat. We all expected to see her in the Crest eventually. You must be bursting with pride. But, uh, you see—I don't know how to say this, Tom, other than to just say it: the clerks have received some notes about your daughter recently. She was said to be involved in an incident that might be considered improper, perhaps even inflammatory."

"Two incidents," Morgan corrected from behind a cabinet he was about to tip over.

"Kindly allow me to discharge my duties," Oliver's silken voice was now laced with the undercurrent of threat, "and I will extend you the same courtesy." He sighed at Tom. "So, there are two incidents that have been noted. Do you have any idea what they might be?"

Tom's head shook once, very slightly.

"No?"

"I-I wouldn't have any reason to, to—"

"Hm. Ah, well, I assumed wrongly," Oliver started to rise. "If you don't know anything, then I suppose we ought to just speak to the girl directly about—"

Tom reached out to Oliver. His mind was racing. He knew the game Oliver was playing and knew that he had no prospect of winning it.

"The goats just went crazy, sir," he blurted. "Lillia had nothing to do with that."

"You're referring to what happened at Prosperity Farm a few days ago?" Oliver slowly returned to his seat. "Were you there as well?"

Tom nodded that he was.

"Tell me about it."

It felt cold inside, even with the lanterns, and Tom was suddenly aware that his pants and feet were still wet from the lakeshore. He rubbed his feet against his pant legs and gathered his thoughts. Morgan paused in his ransacking of the tent's belongings to write down what Tom would say. Oliver steepled his hands beneath his chin, looking both concerned and a little amused.

As Tom spoke, the clerk's pen scratched across a blank page of paper filling it with lines of tiny, black symbols; a soft, droning rhythm of sound, broken only when he would dip his stylus into a jar of ink. It was strangely mesmerizing to watch his words take form before his eyes. The clerk would only look up to glare at Tom whenever he paused in his story, which was not very often. Three pages, front and back, were filled with perfectly spaced lines when Tom finally finished. The three of them stared at one another in silence inside the tent for a long moment before Oliver clapped his knee.

"Well, that was quite a day for the Tanners, wasn't it? I'll wager you'll never set foot on a farm again. Ha!"

"That's what happened," Tom said, the sound of his voice meek in his ears.

"What bunk!" Morgan's pen nearly punched a hole through the paper. He had been on the verge of erupting by the end of Tom's recounting and now he could no longer contain himself. His sagging neck warbled angrily as he shook his pen in Tom's face. "A completely unacceptable statement of particulars. If I were to close the investigation on this record, they'd take my sash—and rightly so."

"Now, Morgan," Oliver began.

"This man's offered nothing—nothing—to explain how one hundred eighty-four of the Commonwealth's goats escaped their confinement and disappeared from a farm he and his daughter just happened to be visiting under a special pass that, frankly, should never have been issued. And what was your son, who had no pass or leave, even doing there? This whole matter reeks of impropriety." Morgan counted from his fingers. "We have the farm's longtime clerk, Ridgemore, who holds you and your family responsible for this enormous loss of property. Then his son says it was all the fault of a ranch hand, Collin Grounds, who, as it happens, is a known member of the ranchers' guild. We have eight workers that we've been able to locate and eight more stories. And they're all bunk. The animals did not simply get it in their heads to leap off a cliff. They were taken. I'll ask it plainly, Tanner: who stole the goats? Because thus far all of the explanations, yours included, have been sorely wanting."

"I have an explanation for all of this," Oliver laughed. "A simple one you clerks should be familiar with. It's called a *bribe*. A few bottles of cragfire left here, a few coins dropped there, and poof, I can make a thousand goats disappear to you clerks."

Morgan thrust his papers into a scroll case and clanked his inkpot shut, clearly unamused by Oliver's observations.

"Warden, we have no choice but to take this man, his daughter, and his son, up for further administration. We need to press charges and take him to the court."

Tom felt as if he had been punched in the stomach. He could accept that fate for himself, but not her. Not Lillia. His fingers locked together, constricting each other until his knuckles turned white. His chest felt like it would burst.

"You are ahead of yourself once more, Master Clerk," Oliver crossed his legs, the metal of his sword's scabbard jingling an unspoken threat. "I will do nothing of the sort without an order. In the meantime, I must kindly ask you to leave. You are distressing this worker and impeding my investigation."

Morgan's face contorted indignantly, but Oliver had made clear a boundary between them. And though the clerk's cheeks glowed brighter than the gulleystar pots, it was a line he did not cross. He fumed a moment and then stormed out of the tent, muttering over his shoulder that Oliver had better hurry up this "farce of an investigation." Oliver bowed his head courteously and waited a while until he was sure that Morgan was well clear of the place.

Oliver was about to say more when a commotion broke outside. The sound of splashing water was followed by a chorus of yelling. Tom thought he could hear Tim; he might have been crying, asking the same question over and over. But the sound was faint, it came from the far side of the lake.

"The clerks must do their due diligence," Oliver sighed. "But they're just jostling him a little. They won't do any more than that without my leave. He might have a mark or two, but nothing the boy won't bounce back from. But I can see you're worried, Tom. If you'll excuse me for a moment, I will go and check on young Timothy for you."

The warden stood up, motioned for Tom to stay where he was, and left the tent. He was gone for only a few minutes when the noise outside quieted. The tent flaps pulled back open, he strode back inside, made an apologetic smile at Tom, and sat back down with no more compunction than if he was just returning from getting a drink.

"Your boy is fine. But listen, Tanner. I can only help your family while I'm here. If we leave and Morgan applies for an order, he's going to get it. And then, well," Oliver held out his palms. "It will be out of my hands. You know how it goes with orders: *a clerk's pen sets to write; a warden's sword must go and fight.* Makes you wonder which is mightier, eh? Sorry, I know this is no laughing matter for you. But such is life in the Mountain."

Oliver stood and strolled around the floor of the tent. He reached out to touch the wooden post in the middle and then glanced at the surroundings, the scattered debris and overturned boxes, as if taking stock of Tom's destitution.

"I can understand the wish—the need—for a little more than what the Commonwealth provides. It's perfectly natural. And herd animals, they're like gold these days. So whatever's happened to those goats, whoever has them—"

"They really did—"

"—it doesn't matter. It really doesn't. Fine. All the poor goats just up and died. I will believe that, if you like. But I must make the clerks believe it as well. And as you see, they are rather disinclined to do so. Unless you can clear up a much more important matter. The matter at hand, actually."

Tom knew he could not hope to pretend ignorance and keep Oliver here, keep what little leverage he might have. He would have to yield something now.

"What happened at the Docks?" Tom asked.

"What happened *after* the Docks."

For the first time in his conversation with the warden, Tom felt wrong-footed. He listened while Oliver explained that they were already well aware of the "circumstances" that led to Lillia's tragic accident with a fishing hook. That matter was all but closed.

"But this Divine Eli fellow has been making quite a stir lately," Oliver shook his head, then looked at Tom. His gaze lingered as if searching Tom's face, but Tom was genuinely dumb-founded, which, fortunately, Oliver was reading quite clearly.

"You really haven't heard?" he asked Tom. "Ah, but then I suppose you wouldn't, holed up down here. Well, well. Of course, you'll remember that after Lillia's accident, a certain guildsman who styled himself as the Divine Eli came to your home. Please don't deny it, Tom. I have reports, and I have this," he reached into a pocket of his tunic, beneath his Commonwealth emblem, and then he opened his hand.

It held a painted stick with a metal amulet hanging from an end.

"He did come," Tom admitted.

"And he claimed to be a priest."

"Yes."

"And you hired him. To heal Lillia."

Tom's head nodded.

"Ah, well. I suppose I can understand what a father might do out of desperation. For his child. Especially a girl like Lillia. Still, this is a serious matter. It's made a problem for us."

Tom held his face in his hands.

"You see, for the past several days now, this man who had up until now run a nice little confidence scam pretending to be a priest has been slipping in and out of the tenements, proclaiming to every balm drinker, pickpocket, and whore that will listen to him that he *really is a priest* and that he worked a miracle. That he healed your daughter. Your daughter, the elite student who was recommended to the Commissariat. Utterly ridiculous, of course. He's completely mad. But some in the lower rungs in the Crag are beginning to believe his nonsense. They claim—well, neither here nor there what they're saying." Oliver waved his fingers in the air and shook his head. "Suffice to say, we need to get this tamped down. Which would be easy enough, if it weren't for the unfortunately common knowledge that you brought this man to your home just before Lillia's—shall we say—extraordinary recovery from a wound most had thought was going to be mortal."

Tom could feel the warden's probing now, despite the casual ease the man seemed to exude from his chair. His eyes were boring into Tom's. Tom waited in the silence, waited for what he knew was the reason for this entire charade. This man wanted something from Tom, and now he would lay out his demand.

Oliver spoke slowly and very deliberately:

"Thank goodness, Tom. Thank goodness there had never been a need for Eli to come to your home, despite your panic, despite your momentary lapse of reason in hiring him. Thank goodness for Dr. Mosley, that eminent physician in the Crag's infirmary, the one who *actually* saved Lillia's life."

Tom stared at Oliver. The captain reached once more into the folds of his clothing, and this time produced a folded piece of paper. He laid it gently on Tom's knee. It was covered in writing with a blank line at the bottom next to a wax seal of the Commonwealth, which felt surprisingly heavy.

"You'll set things right, Tom, by telling the truth. By telling everyone what really happened with Lillia. You will state that she had had a successful surgery under the care of Dr. Mosley. She was already recuperating when this Eli fellow barged into your home, uninvited and unannounced. He refused to leave until you paid him off. You will denounce him, Tom. That will squelch the rumors. And then everything will go back to the way it was. You and your family will return to Industry Caverns. And Lillia will return to the academy. Under escort, of course. So we can keep an eye on her. It's all been arranged. You'll tell that story when I call on you to do so. In the meantime, you'll sign that paper. It's an affidavit of what *actually* happened."

The paper fluttered slightly on Tom's leg. From his childhood, Tom had always secretly longed to be able to read; he never felt it as keenly as in this moment. There was something there, something beyond whatever all of those scratches of ink on parchment may have meant. It was like a door, hidden somewhere behind the letters, but he could not tell if it was opening or shutting.

"The affidavit's just legal huff-puff," Oliver smiled at Tom's hesitation.

"I don't understand. Why not just take him up?"

Oliver let out a long breath, an annoyed expression temporarily clouding his face.

"You're not in a position to be asking questions, Tanner. But if you must know, this Eli has proven to be a bit more elusive than your typical madman. Apparently, these blasted rumors have spread all the way to the Gutters. We have a delicate balance with the Quarter when it comes to these kinds of matters. Certain channels must be respected. This whole silly affair has rocked the cart at a time when we need stability. Since you asked."

"It's just that—if I say what you want me to say—if I sign this, I'll be putting a knife to my own throat."

"What, with the guilds? I rather doubt you've much to worry about from them; though you would know their business better than I. Oh, I expect it may make things a tad awkward for you, denouncing a fellow guildsman, but only for a little while. I suspect the guilds would just as soon be rid of this headache as well. We can work all of that out. If you help us."

Oliver slipped a quill into Tom's fingers and pointed to the line.

"Make your mark there. And I'll witness it. That's all we need for tonight."

Tom lingered, but only briefly. He ran his fingers through his hair and squinted one last time at the letters. They hovered there on the page, ominous and strange. He clenched his teeth and traced the three letters he knew how to draw right above the line.

"And that is that," Oliver retrieved the paper and patted Tom's knee. Tom felt a slight chill run through him. "Glad to have this business behind us, Tanner. I'll send for you when it's time. Meanwhile, the clerks will give you your instructions."

"But Lillia won't get taken up."

Oliver shook his head and answered warmly:

"We need her. In class, I mean. Girls like that don't sprout up on farms after all. No, it's back to school for her, and back to work for us. Our all for all, and all that."

CHAPTER FIVE

THE SIGN OUTSIDE the classroom door was still there, its painted line so crimped that the letters touched:

OUR ALL FOR ALL.

Lillia stared at the faded words stenciled across what had once been a barrel top. The wood was mostly rotted, and it had been nailed into the wall to cover a crack. She took a deep breath and entered the room.

She had been back for several days, but the chamber that served as her classroom still held only the vague familiarity of a childhood place, remembered more for the impressions it left. It was not that anything was out of place. The square tiles, the slate board on the wall covered with accounting work and figures to memorize, the windowed lantern hanging from the ceiling, the honeycombed wooden shelves for organizing papers, the desks and chairs, they were all in the places she remembered. A poster on each wall extolling the public service of the clerks and commissars, small, poorly drawn pictures of bright-eyed, determined men and women, armed with pens and papers to mold a prosperous future for the Commonwealth. There was the scent of mildew, of burning lamp oil and chalk dust.

The students were as they had been before. Sullen, quiet, and mostly fretful. They all sat in the same places; only Mava had been moved to the front of the room, closer to Madam Teacher, where Lillia used to sit. Mava looked at the others a little more haughtily now, Lillia thought. Madam Teacher wore the same apron and leather belt, her hair pinned tightly beneath her yellow cap, and scarcely acknowledged Lillia's presence. A tiny fragment of Lillia's mind recoiled when she first realized she had lost her teacher's favor, how the woman's upper lip had coiled ever so slightly when Lillia presented her with her return order the Clerk Morgan had written up for her. Lillia was shown her new seat and, following their teacher's cue, none of her classmates spoke to her.

Except for Jack. Her first day back, he had looked at her very seriously and then leaned over to whisper that he wasn't the one who had noted her, that he wasn't a snitch, nor was his father. When he started to ask about her guard escort, Madam Teacher had bustled over between them. Before Lillia could answer, the teacher gave him a swipe with her belt that left his ear swollen and red.

It had taken several days, but eventually Lillia's awkward return to class became a routine of sorts. Lillia would leave her home with the armed escort Oliver had assigned to her, to "monitor her safety." His name was Robert. He was young, plain-looking, and very quiet; aside from the clanking of his weapons, he scarcely made any noise at all. Her father would offer him breakfast and every day he would say the same thing, the only words she ever heard from him: "No, thank you" and then, to her: "Are you ready?" They would walk the route to class each morning, and any worker who happened to be in the tunnels would scurry off or clear a wide space at the sound of Robert's boots and spear shaft. When they reached the classroom, he would stand at attention in an inconspicuous spot in the hallway outside. She would quietly slip into the room, turn in her homework, and find her place in the corner. There she would sit, alone, listening as attentively as she could, which was not very much at all, and counting the time until Robert could walk her back home. The monotony quickly became wearying.

This went on for two weeks. Then one morning during a civics lecture, something Madam Teacher said struck Lillia, and she suddenly felt more aware, more engaged, in a way she had not since returning to class. The teacher had been droning on about the wicked old priests who used to rule everyone in the Mountain until they were finally overthrown, and now everyone was healthy and happy … the usual diatribe. And then the teacher mentioned the three realms. The Crest, the Crag, and the Quarter. To Lillia, it was as if a bright lantern had been thrust into a dusky closet. She found herself leaning forward, staring as if she would clutch every word that the teacher was reading from the enormous book balanced in the folds of her arms.

Oblivious to Lillia's scrutiny, Madam Teacher turned a page, adjusted her weight, and continued her mumbled recitation of the lesson:

"... of that most glorious event, the Overthrow, when we threw down the idols and cast away the thieving priests and all the exploiters into the sea, which culminated in the Treaty with the Dwarven Quarter and the founding of our Commonwealth with its three, united realms. The Crag at the base of the Mountain, the Dwarven Quarter, set deep within, and the Crest above them all. Now," she paused to survey her classroom, "question one: which is the greatest realm?"

It was a trick question, and not a very clever one. Lillia knew the right answer straight away. She also knew, by some awakened instinct inside of her, that that answer was utterly false. It was Jack who thrust his hand up and responded confidently:

"None of them's the greatest, Madam. We're all equal in the Commonwealth. 'Our all for all.'"

Madam Teacher shut the book, looking anything but satisfied.

"That is an utterly lazy response, Jack Ridgemore. Even an untrained worker can parrot 'our all for all.' It's just the slogan for the Ninth Plan, not the answer to any and all queries."

An acne faced girl sitting next to Jack seemed to have suddenly remembered something, and seeing no one else's hand, ventured an answer, a line she must have just recalled:

"'The hammer because it hits hardest; the pick because it digs deepest; the sword because it strikes sharpest.'"

The teacher eyed the girl circumspectly, but then dismissed her offering with a curt flick of the hand:

"That is just a ditty you learned in your first year of class. A catchphrase. Hardly much better than Jack's." She heaved an exasperated sigh at the class. "Gracious. You were selected for this academy because you could not only follow but understand the dictates of the Commonwealth. What does is it *mean* for the realms to be equal?"

The girl's pimples flushed, but she pressed on as if to acquit herself in front of her classmates:

"That we're—that we're all in it together?"

Jack started to snicker, and a pitter of laughter broke out. It was immediately stifled when the teacher fingered the leather cord around her apron that she used for discipline. She shook her head, glowering, but then seeing Mava's raised hand, gestured toward her:

"Yes, Mava."

"Each realm has an equal status, but not an equal role."

"And how is that?"

"It's like—kind of like—they're all parts of the same body, the realms. Each has its own job, and they work together. So, they're equal. Because every part of the body needs the other parts. But their work isn't the same."

Madam Teacher smiled:

"You read that somewhere, didn't you, dear?"

Mava dipped her head modestly and admitted she had, with an apology.

"You mean Lillia read it to you at the library," Jack's whisper was just loud enough for Mava to hear, who spun around and fixed Jack with a venomous look.

"So long as it's the right books," Madam Teacher continued, "it's perfectly acceptable for a student clerk—or commissar—to read beyond their assignments. That's why I extended a library pass to you." She opened her book back up with a creak and flipped through several pages near the end. "That was Judge Surefoot's metaphor, I think."

"Yes, Madam," Mava answered. "I, uhm, saw it in a scroll left out on a library table."

Jack made a face at the back of Mava's head.

"Yes, it's noted here in my manual. So, Judge Surefoot's premise is that we can liken each realm to parts of our bodies. Hands, feet, arms, and so forth. Let's listen to what his Honor wrote." She read aloud from her book, following the page with her finger. Lillia found herself captivated, not with the teacher's monotone narration, but with an idea buried within the reading. Voices she had been hearing in her sleep were coming awake, intruding into her thoughts, speaking alongside the teacher.

"Each realm must work together for the common good," the teacher read, "while, at the same time, respecting the unique and singular identity each realm holds. The residents of the Crag and the Dwarven Quarter perform the physical labor and the technical feats, respectively, which are needed in the Commonwealth's day to day life.

Their worth is measured by their work, and their work provides sustenance and finished resources. But labor without direction is wasted. Worse, it is exploited; as it was when the priests reigned, when there were no boards to govern us, and the workers were left to the whims of luck to earn their food. Thankfully, those days are no more. We have a head for our Commonwealth," and here, the teacher bowed, while the children reflexively copied her, "the Council of Stewards and Board of Wardens, whose eyes are always upon us, who bear the burden of directing our society towards its great and noble future, and whose expertise we may always rely upon. They offer the body both its purpose and its direction. They are its will. And just as the head, while tethered, is physically removed from the workings of the limbs, our leaders reside in the Crest, high atop our Mountain, so that workers and Stewards have sufficient space to fulfill their assigned tasks.

"There is one other vital component to this body of our Commonwealth. A sustaining force through which the limbs and the head can function together. Our Commonwealth's torso is the clerks and commissars. Working with the residents of the Crag (and in solidarity with the Dwarven Quarter's appointed leader), these dutiful men and women mark, and measure, and regulate all that comes to pass in our society's daily life. It is the clerks who focus the Crag's workers on their given tasks, mete out their wages, and assign them their punishments when they do not fulfill their duties. The commissars, in turn, provide their service to the residents of the Crest. Together, the clerks and commissars liberate the Crest of the mundane minutiae that would otherwise bog down the head of our Commonwealth. It is thus the clerks and commissars who bind us all together into a unified whole, a body."

Madam Teacher shut the pages meaningfully, sending a small cloud of dust into the air. She set the book down on her desk.

"Hopefully, you may all share in that great work someday."

The teacher cast a friendly glance towards Mava, but then her face fell. Her eyes narrowed as she noticed Lillia standing by her chair, her thin arm stretched above her head. Every child in the classroom turned around in their chairs, riveted. The teacher's mouth opened and closed for a long moment before she collected herself:

"You—you have a question?"

Lillia's voice sounded strained, as if she was suffering from a cold, but her words were clear, without a trace of a stutter or pause:

"Isn't there more to it?"

"More to what?"

"More to the body."

"The illustration is meant to—"

"The illustration's specious." Madam Teacher glared at her in affronted silence, which Lillia paid no heed to. "Sure, there's limbs and tissues, and a will, but that's not all that makes up a body. A living body, at least. Something has to animate it. Maybe we can't see that, or touch or smell it—or even read about it. Granted. Maybe it remains hidden deep down. But it's a part of the body, too. It has to be."

The children shifted in their seats or put their heads on the table, afraid even to appear that they had heard what Lillia just said. This was inflammatory speech. Madam Teacher took charge:

"I'm not entirely sure of your meaning, Lillia Tanner. But I am sure I don't like the tone of it. Judge Surefoot's Body of the Commonwealth thesis has been thoroughly vetted by experts and modified, where needed, by the Steward of Education. There's complete consensus on it. I would not be heard to disparage it, nor to add any more to it beyond what the Crest's finest thinkers have seen fit. Certainly not with notions of invisible body parts that are there, but not really there."

"That's not what I mean." She had been listening to the teacher, but to something else as well. Something she was trying to recall from her sleep. But now those thoughts were dimming, receding to where they came from, like a tide; and the more she spoke, the faster they slipped away. It was like trying to hold water in the palm of her hand. She was not ready to let them go completely, not yet. There was something important about this. "It's just—it's just he's got it wrong," Lillia pronounced it with the soberness of a heretic proclaiming her belief. "He's missing something, and so he's got it wrong. About us, about the Mountain … It's all wrong."

There was a very long silence, broken only by the sounds of some feet shuffling against the floor, a sniffle, or someone sighing in the way that children do toward one of their own who has become an outcast. At last, Madam Teacher walked to the front of the class, her slippered feet squelching with each step. Lillia watched her remove a specially sealed pamphlet from her drawer. A line of letters on the chalkboard, milk-white in a cloud of slate, floated just above Madam Teacher's capped head, bent in concentration: "*The whole must be greater than the part.*"

The teacher's head shook sadly.

"Boys and girls, we're going to adjourn class early today. Unfortunately, it is my duty to suspend one of your classmates. Lillia Tanner, I must ask you to remain behind while we process the forms. Your return order said nothing about tolerating sedition. The intolerable cannot be tolerated. Certainly not in a classroom."

Lillia leaned on the corner of a support beam in the corridor, closed her eyes for a moment, and caught her breath. The walk to and from her home still winded her. There was a small knot of workers milling around the busy avenue known as Capability Corridor; porters mostly, carrying heavy baskets, jars, pots, and crates bound in their net bags, some waiting in line in front of a pillar with a cracked, rusted pipe end that spewed a steady trickle of water into a basin. The junction and stairwell that would lead to Industry Caverns were still a few more tunnels away. She set out again and caught up with Jack, who had been waiting for her underneath a street sign.

"Her suspension's only good for five days until a senior clerk or a commissar reviews it," said Jack, as they jostled past a group of workers. His yellow sash shone under the gulleystar lamps, as most of the porters pressed themselves up against the side of the walls at their approach. Robert was marching a few paces behind them. "Five days only. That's how it works. And it doesn't cost much to get it denied."

"You know from experience," said Lillia. She was still troubled by whatever had possessed her to argue with Madam Teacher, and over something so trivial. Lillia knew she had the right of it, there was no question of it, but why had that mattered so much? The teacher had been looking for an excuse to suspend her; the form had been filled out ahead of time.

"She tried this same thing on me last term," Jack continued. "Believe me, she's nothing."

"She's a teacher."

"Exactly. She's just a fat, old teacher."

"For a clerk's class."

"Which is still beneath a senior clerk. She can strap us in class, but that's it. She doesn't have the pull to do anything else. Not to me."

"Is that so," Lillia was not paying attention to the conversation anymore.

"I'm not just some worker's whelp who passed a test. I've got pull."

They walked a little further, Jack talking the entire way until Lillia stopped once more to look around the corridor. They had reached a junction with alcoves and stairs leading off in different directions. A tattered yellow banner of the Commonwealth's emblem hung from a terrace that had been boarded up. The place was bustling with workers, clerks, even a few students. In the center, two men were steadying a rickety ladder while another at the top replaced the mushrooms in a gulleystar light post. Lillia watched a woman with a painted face grab a clerk by the hand, laughing, and then they ducked into a darkened hallway together. At the far edge of the crowd, a small commotion broke out, a group of men arguing over who would get to take a stairway first. Robert appeared next to Lillia, almost like a shadow, and followed Lillia's gaze. Without a word, he went over to the arguing workers to investigate.

"This is where I turn," said Lillia. "You probably shouldn't be seen with me anymore."

Jack shrugged. "That's what my father thinks, too."

"He's right."

"You're not going to get taken up," Jack said. "They'd have done it already. You'll lose your commissar commission. But that's a good thing."

"Oh, is it?"

"You were starting to put on airs there for a while, Lil."

A smile broke across Lillia's face, for the first time in days. It felt refreshing, like a cool drink washing through her. But the feeling was gone almost as quickly as it had come.

"So now Mava gets to be the sad old lonely hag stuck up in the Crest," Jack grinned, "she can look down her nose on us all if she wants. Have at it." He made a rude gesture. "Clerks have a hell of a lot more fun than commissars; everyone knows it. You've still got prospects. You've got the marks to pick up an assignment once you graduate, with a little help. You just have to lie low for a few weeks. Wait 'til the term finishes out, pay a fee to pass the test if you need to. Then I can get you set up."

"You've got it all taken care of, huh?"

"Yeah. I do."

Jack spotted a group of boys from another class who were rough-housing underneath a statue and using their sashes like whips. He waved to them. Lillia saw him make sure the boys were looking, and then with a swift motion, he leaned down, close enough that Lillia could smell the must of Prosperity Farm in his hair, feel the warmth of his breath. He brushed his face against Lillia's. She had no idea what he was doing, until after he had finished kissing her, and then she heard the other boys bellow out cheers and laughter. Jack raced over to them, beaming, and Lillia saw him take a coin from one of the older boys.

Lillia watched Jack disappear into a tunnel with his friends, her hands folded above her skirt, wondering why she had not punched him, and why she was as indifferent to his kiss as she was to her suspension. She felt tired and a little confused, but nothing more. She wandered down Capability Corridor to follow a dimly lit flight of stairs that would take her to Industry Caverns. She was so lost in her reflections, Lillia didn't realize that for the first time in days, she was walking alone.

She was nearly halfway down the flight when she heard the sound in the darkness below. Out of the cold black expanse of the arched stairwell, past the last clay gulleystar pot that still had any light left in it, it was the quiet flapping of bare feet on stone. They stopped. Then Lillia heard a man's voice. He was calling up to her:

"Is that you?" he asked.

Her throat went dry. She tried to keep her breaths from gasping, to say something, but the words died inside of her chest. She glanced over her shoulder, expecting Robert to be there. But she was alone, and the corridor that led into this stairwell was three flights above her now. She could never hope to outrun whoever was here with her. The cold stone step she was perched on held her feet.

"Is it really you?" he asked again. His words were slurred, as if he had something stuffed in his mouth. "Lillia."

"Who—" she managed to breathe.

"'S'me," the man said. A few soft steps and he emerged from the blackness into the pale glow of the lamp pot. "Don't you remember me?"

A man in his middle years, naked except for a goatskin loincloth that clung to his distended belly, took a tentative step up the stairs. His skin was hanging in folds. He reeked of caked blood from countless scratches ringing his swollen mouth and eyes. In the gulleystar light, his eyes looked like sockets of a skull. The man's teeth had been shattered; he had done that to himself, somehow Lillia knew it.

She made a frightened noise.

"I healed you," he held out a hand. His jagged fingernails pointed at her chest, and Lillia instinctively fell back a step. "Remember? The hook in your belly. I pulled it out of you. It was—it was a miracle."

"Eli?" she whispered.

He faltered for a moment as if stunned that she had spoken his name aloud. Lillia could not tell if he was slipping on the steps or trying to kneel. His limbs looked so frail. He bowed low, his joints creaking, and buried his face in his hands. "Why did you do this to me?"

"Do—do what?"

"Showed them the way into me. You let them all in. It's like poison. You spread the darkness in the light."

Lillia stared at him. He began babbling and the longer he spoke, the more he fidgeted and shook:

"They never let me rest now. Never. I have to run. Or they'll catch me. All I hear is them chasing me. Always. Not even balm shuts them out. They never rest. Never stop … Never … I-I ought to kill you—for doing this to me."

Lillia could think of nothing else to say but the one question that held her with a mounting sense of panic. It should have struck her as peculiar, but for some reason, she needed to ask him:

"What if you just … stopped running?"

The man fell into a sorrowful laugh that racked his shoulders and became a sob. He was hacking up spittle of phlegm and blood. His fingers curled around his eyes, clutching at them, but then he forced his hands back down to his sides.

"I can't do *that*! They want to kill me. And kill me, and kill me ... forever. You'll find out. They're coming for you, too. I can see them swirling 'round you already."

"Who?"

"The shadows. Your children. Them," he pointed eagerly just above Lillia, and she glanced up only to see a sagging support beam in the fluttering light of a gulleystar pot. "Them," he pressed, "right there. From in the Mountain. Oh, oh! They've caught up—"

The man was crying uncontrollably now, but with no tears. She felt something stirring inside of her; not empathy, but a curiosity. Lillia knelt closer to him. His hands suddenly lurched from his side and clasped around Lillia's wrists in a cold grip.

"You should have done like me. You should have run. *Run!*"

Lillia screamed. She heard the sound of her voice echoing against the walls. Eli's fingers writhed around the skin of her wrists, clawing it apart with his fingernails. Droplets of her blood fell to the stone floor. She screamed again and pulled back so hard that she fell over. For a moment, Eli's panicked face was leering down at her, framed by the beamed ceiling of the stairwell. Then it was thrust aside, and the stairwell burst with noise and movement. Hands, arms, an iron-toed boot, the smells of Eli's stench and moldy leather, voices all shouting at the same time.

"He's slippery." A man cursed.

"Hold him down!" another voice.

Lillia recognized the third voice murmuring in her ear with surprising calm. It was Robert. She felt a strong, gloved hand pulling her up by her elbow.

"Are you alright?" he asked.

Lillia held her wrists, wincing. She looked up at the small crowd of men that now surrounded her. They were all wardens, burly and dangerous looking, but dressed only in hooded cloaks with no armor or any weapons other than sheathed daggers. Even Robert had slipped out of his chainmail. They had stolen down the stairwell silently behind her. Farther down, Eli had been forced to kneel by three wardens who held him by his head and arms. The pile of men surged and it looked as if Eli might still overpower them. Eli was squealing at Lillia to run. A cloaked officer casually strode past Lillia, drew his dagger, and smashed the pommel into Eli's nose. A spray of blood exploded from his face, and the man collapsed unconscious.

"Rather feisty, these zealots," the officer remarked, wiping the handle clean with a handkerchief. One of the guards brought out a thick rope, and Eli's arms and legs were bound fast. A small white cloth floated down to her wrist.

"You'll want to wash that out when you get home," said Robert, "so it doesn't get infected."

"Uhm, thank you," she tied it around her hand.

Robert's face remained expressionless, but he inclined his head.

"So good to see you again, Miss Tanner. I don't know that we were formally introduced when I visited your father's tannery. I am called Oliver."

Oliver's smiling face approached her. He rubbed his hands together and opened his mouth to speak when his eyes fell on her bandage. "I trust you were not hurt?"

"No, sir."

"Thank goodness. You've had quite enough hurts for a child your age, I should think," he winked. Then he sat down on the steps and patted her back.

"Lillia, after this excitement, I'm sure you want nothing more than to get back to your father and brother. How are they, by the way?"

"They're both well," she replied. The room was still spinning before her eyes, and Oliver sounded much further away than he was, but at least she could hold onto the wall now.

"Good, good. Glad to hear that. You've been through quite a scare here. I only have a couple of questions for you, and then you can get back to your family and your homework and forget all about this despicable fellow. Can you answer my questions, child?"

Lillia managed to nod.

"Excellent. We weren't able to reach you in time to hear everything, but did this man ever identify himself to you?"

"Yes."

"What did he say his name was?"

"Eli."

"The same Eli that barged into your home when you were recovering from your surgery?"

"I-I ..."

Oliver's head inched closer to Lillia's and he whispered:

"The one who pretended to be a priest and pretended to heal you?"

"Yes. I mean, he came to our home before."

"Very good. You're doing wonderfully, Lillia. But then that's what we've all come to expect from you. I have only one more question."

"Okay."

"I know it may seem inappropriate to talk about, but I must ask it. And you must answer me as the honest girl that you are. Did this Eli say anything to you, anything at all, about—this may sound ridiculous, I know—about a miracle?"

Lillia's head fell.

"Don't be afraid."

Lillia told the warden what Eli had said. Oliver let out a long sigh, gave Lillia a reassuring grasp on her shoulder, and then stood up.

"Thank you, Lillia. Very well done. So, Robert?"

"Yes, Captain."

"I'll write out a detailed statement later, but in the meantime, you'll need to apply for an order to take this man up for direct violation of Article One. We haven't done one of those in a while, so you'll need to—"

Robert reached inside his cloak.

"Here's the order, sir," he replied. "It's already been processed and executed."

Oliver whistled. "Well, someone was confident that he was going to get his man."

"Yes, sir," was all Robert said. He stood aside as the wardens carried Eli's bound and still unconscious body up the stairwell.

"I tip my hood to you, Lieutenant," said Oliver, pulling his cloak back up over his head to follow them. "We'll make a clean sweep of this yet."

THE QUARTER

CHAPTER SIX

J ACOB STRUGGLED TO marshal his features. For an hour, he had been leaning (there was no place to sit comfortably) against the sculpted wall of a
very old and nearly empty cavern, where he had been forced to endure,
of all things, a song. An interminable hymn that, he had come to
believe, might have been composed for the sole purpose of driving him
mad. It was almost unendurable. Having been born without an ear for
music, he could not have known the song was nearing its finale.

The four who were singing the tune had their eyes closed. Jacob
indulged to roll his in disdain. He drew his yellow cloak around his
shoulders to ward off the cold in the air. A copper medallion emblazoned with the Commonwealth's emblem had tumbled down over this
chest. He discretely tucked it back beneath his shirt.

The slow, somber tune plodded along for a while longer, when suddenly it burst into a run of arpeggios that soared higher and faster, as
if untethered to anything in the world. Then, just as abruptly, the song
stopped. The final notes hung in the air and echoed against the face of a
massive metal door set deep within one of the stone walls. The frame was
covered in dust and the door was held fast by a black lock in its center.
Before the doorway, the four singers stood in a ring with their hands
clasped, their eyes still shut tightly, as if waiting for the power of their
voices to dissipate. Jacob watched from a distance.

The half-blind, lumbering Cragmen of the Mountain called them
dwarves, Jacob and his companions, because they stood no taller than
the bottom of a Crag dweller's chest. But they were the nephil. The
firstborn children of the gods, begotten of fire and stone. Each was
broad-shouldered without a hint of softness around their bellies. Their
faces were smooth and colored in one of the myriad shades of stones
in the Mountain. Their hair was combed and tied, or braided in pleats

long enough that they would have caught the light with a metallic luster, had there been any light. But none of them needed a torch fire or lantern flame. They had not even brought a gulleystar, for the eyes of nephil can see farther in the darkness than they can by the sun or moon's light.

The four in the ring were outfitted in furs and woven woolen tunics, with an array of leather belts slung around their chests and arms. A slew of picks, hammers, handholds, chisels, ropes, and braces hung from their waists, all perfectly arranged and organized. Everything that they carried, from their cloaks to the pieces of flint clicking in their pockets, had been handcrafted and would have passed as a piece of art among the men in the Mountain: a tunic's thread pattern made to resemble a cloud; an axe handle carved in spirals that seemed to have no end; a belt buckle molded to look like a dragon's open maw and forked tongue; even the extra rags stuffed into their backpacks had lines of glimmering metal woven into them. All of it, every inch, had been made with beauty imbued unsparingly, even carelessly.

As silence settled back over the cavern, Jacob ventured to step towards the group. He paused when one of in the ring, the tallest, threw his head back. The tall one's skin was dark and gleaming, like iron ore buried deep in stone. His hair fell to his shoulders in lines of flint. He broke away from the others, and with his eyes still closed, strode a few paces over to a rock column and pressed the side of his face close against its surface. Then he inhaled deeply and opened his mouth wide.

"Great," Jacob said to himself, "another damn song."

It was not a song, but a single note that sounded like the tolling of a massive bell, resonating inside the column until it spread throughout the cavern. It was so deep Jacob could not hear it, but rather felt it reverberating inside of his chest. It tingled at first, and then, as the note stretched on for an impossible length of time, the vibration became painful to endure. Jacob's fingers were too thick to stuff into his ears, so he pressed his hands hard against the sides of his head and crouched down behind a boulder.

Slowly, the singer brought his chin down, his tousled gray hair settled over his shoulders, and the music of his voice softened and then transformed into spoken words. His arms were stretched wide to the others in the ring. "Oh, great and mighty Nord, beneficent and all-knowing, your child Abidan calls upon you with my brethren."

"Hear us," the others chanted in unison.

Jacob stifled an exasperated sigh and walked back by the cavern wall, pretending to check the pack bundles piled there.

"By your leave," Abidan continued, "and at our king's command, we come to delve the bosom of your lands. By your call, we claim the gifts you have wrought for our people. Give us steady hands and strong legs to reach them. Keep far from us the perils of the unknown. Bring us safely home, rich with your blessings. Hear us, as you hear your servant, our priest, the Divine Nicodemus, as we pray: be it so!"

"So mote it be!" the others answered, and then each one held his index finger to his forehead, pointing above. The sign of the gods.

Jacob stepped out from the packs with an unctuous grin. He clapped his hands together and made his voice beam with enthusiasm.

"All finished? Ready to go at last, are we? Terrific!"

Abidan let out a long breath, as if being roused from a deep sleep. He held Jacob with an uncomfortably long gaze, his eyes reflecting some unseen pool of light. Then he smiled.

"You in a hurry?"

Jacob straightened his yellow cloak and the medallion spilled out again. Unable to hide it this time, Jacob pretended to brush an unseen speck of dust from its polished surface. Compared to his companions' gear, the pendant he wore looked crude and cheap. But he clutched it tightly as he tried to meet Abidan's stare.

"I am. Since you ask. Aren't you? It's been years since we've been allowed to delve for metal."

One of the other nephil in the ring barked a loud, mocking cough. "We, he says. As if he'd stoop to digging."

"I mean our people," Jacob said. "Our people haven't dug in these parts of the Mountain since the Treaty. What's that, two, three generations of men that have come and gone since—?"

Abidan raised an eyebrow. "I wouldn't measure much by the fluttering of men's lives—if I were you."

Jacob held out his hands. They were short, stubby, and like the rest of his body, the color of chalk.

"That's not what I meant, either."

"What do you mean, Jacob? It's hard to tell."

The question was one Jacob had heard his entire life, asked a thousand times in a thousand ways, from subtle to brazen. It was always meant as a barb. He could answer almost by instinct and without the least offense, but it began and ended with the conviction Jacob held about his people.

They were fools. He always had to remind himself to speak to them as such.

"All I meant was that it has taken me—or, I should say, us, our people—a very long time to reach this place."

"By my count, less than a twelve-hour march." Abidan winked. "Once we got past that blocked up tunnel near the Gutters."

There were scattered chuckles, and Jacob pretended to be amused by Abidan's jest. He was a thane after all. A petty one from the Gutters. But a thane no less, and a cousin to the king. Someone Jacob would have to suffer, like so many others. Jacob's smile never wavered when he answered:

"The journey may have been short. But the preparation was long and difficult, and more than a little dangerous to my concerns."

"I've no doubt."

"Not that I care about my welfare."

"Of course you do. That's why you're in a hurry to see us off. Sooner we're off, the sooner you can start profiting from what we find, right?"

Jacob watched as the others laughed in their sleeves and whispered into each other's ears. He saw and heard it all clearly, even as he held his eyes steady and stretched his face into a look of mock surprise, to play along.

"Perhaps I have a modest personal stake in our venture's success. But that can't be helped, can it? How could I have managed a warrant for something of this magnitude without some investment of my own? You have no idea what I had to give to wring this out of the Crest. The scum I had to break bread with, the endless line of clerks and guildsmen with their palms out, all waiting for a coin to be dropped, only to turn on you the moment it reaches their pockets. Truth is, this delve has cost me a fortune."

He brought out a vellum scroll with a heavy amber-colored seal on its edge.

Another nephil turned to Jacob. Contempt flashed in his piercing amber eyes; disdain glowed brightly from his cheeks. "He sold his soul for that there scrap of paper."

"Actually, it is a warrant, Suriel," Jacob replied. He paused and studied Suriel for a moment. A scowling face of red quartz, and peppered freckles, and a lump of clay for a nose—pinched and petulant as ever. "It was issued by the Council itself. Directly to me."

"So, you peddled for a paper," Suriel waved his crimson hand dismissively. "Good for you. Sure, it's worth eating and drinking with men and wearing their fetters around your milky neck like a leash. You even smell like them, you know that, Jacob? And for all that, you got a paper. Good bargain."

"This paper is what will open that door. And you will never know how hard I worked to get it."

Suriel stepped closer to Jacob, his belts clattering threateningly, his contempt barely concealed. Jacob felt his muscles tense, but he kept his expression calm and passive.

"What do you know about work, little warden? Are you going to come delve with us in the deep? Get your pale, delicate hands dirty? When we find metal, are you going to coax it out, or make something from it—besides some scheme? No? I thought as much. You talk of work? I'll give you work. Here, carry my pick." Suriel dropped a tool, a small pickaxe, before Jacob, who scrambled to catch it. It fell with a clang on his foot. "Not even good for that!"

Jacob let the laughter roll over him. He stared at the pickaxe on the floor, brushing against his toe, and wondered how such a small thing could break apart the veils of stone that hid the world's deep treasures, how it could shape or shatter, how it could kill.

"Why don't you run back to your masters already?" Suriel's golden eyes narrowed. "You're not wanted here."

Suriel made as if he would tear the scroll from Jacob's hands and rip it to pieces, but a warning glance from Abidan held him in his place. From the midst of the others' scowls, Abidan's face suddenly opened up into a grin that shone like a ray of light in the cave's darkness. He chuckled a deep, booming noise.

"You'll start another war, Suriel. Save your strength for the dig. We've got a long march ahead of us. Shoulder your gear, boys. We delve!"

A cheer went up, and the delvers flew into a flurry of activity. Only Jacob and Abidan stood still, each eyeing the other.

"You are wanted, you know," said Abidan so that only Jacob could hear him, "Nicodemus says this delve will be blessed. My cousin Elon thinks so, too. So, the gods must have made you part of this for a reason. They've given you something special."

Jacob smiled uncertainly at the thane. He had no more use for gods than he did for music, and he was unsure what Abidan could have meant. So, he started to break the seal on the warrant.

"Not that ridiculous paper." Abidan laughed again. "That's not what I'm talking about."

"I don't understand."

Jacob felt an odd sense of trepidation standing beneath the thane's mirthful gaze. The other delvers hoisted their packs and bags and shouldered their tools for the journey ahead of them. Slipping his pack through his arms, Abidan clapped Jacob's shoulder and pointed at the metal door before them. A tiny circle of blackness within its round lock seemed to stare back, like a lidless pupil.

"They gave you the key," he said.

It would be nearing daybreak in the Crest by Jacob's reckoning. Like all his people, he could mark the passing of time by a count, always running, in his head. At this moment, he thought, the streets of Boaz would just be coming to life, the house windows lightened—except the pubs, of course, which would only now become shuttered. There would be a mist clinging to the grass and around the trunks of the little trees, and the sky would silver from the dawn over the Mountain's jagged spires. Dogs and cats that had been out hunting all night in the drains would be returning to their lairs. So, would the last of the revelers, stumbling to find a bed to sleep in. The sun would be peeking through the treetops right about—now.

He had been to the Crest only once, years ago, but he could still picture the rolling meadows, the wide-open parks and squares, the lonely heaths bathed in sunshine and wind. He had relished that brief visit, cherished the sensations. It had been a place of warmth and light.

Here in the cave, it was dark and cold. And perfectly still.

The delving nephil would be twelve, fifteen, miles down the corridor that stretched beyond the open doorway before him. Their clanking gear, their choruses of marching tunes, their laughter, were long gone. Silence had settled over Jacob, wrapped upon him like a blanket. In his mind, he could still hear the last words that Suriel had called out from the yawning darkness of the open doorway:

"See you in a week, warden's boy."

Jacob stared at the door, still ajar, while he sat on the floor with his hands beneath his chin. A gentle breeze slipped through the entrance, carrying a scent of dust and something else, Jacob thought, almost like dried flowers. The hall beyond the doorway looked wondrously carved, with granite and marble tiles covering every inch of the corridor's surface. The door itself had been easy to swing open, though it was three hands thick and hard as diamond. Of all ironies, the barrier that kept his people from leaving the Inner Realm, their country, had been cast by his people. Of course it had; the men could never hold them in otherwise.

The key to the door was subtle. A small, plain cylinder, platinum in color, without a head or bottom, or any obvious markings; it might have been mistaken for a steel dowel. Jacob twirled it absently in his fingers. To pass the time, he held it close before his nose, then slowly drew it back until it was near his ear, at the very edge of his vision. Only then would the key's bitings appear—a maze of lines and angles, each no wider than a hair—and after a fleeting moment, they would vanish from his sight, until he brought it around again. For some reason, watching the engravings appear and disappear brought back to his mind the slow refrain from the hymn Abidan and his team had chanted before the delve:

> For all that might, but never was,
> The stillborn kings, the gods unsung,
> The darkened fires,

The silent lyres,

Let all give thanks for the Curse we sired.

It was more of a dirge than a song, he reflected, but he kept thinking about the final verse, repeating the words over and over to himself. He tried whistling the tune and it came out poorly, which brought Jacob back to his senses. He stood up to brush the cavern silt from his backside. Then he picked up the Crest's warrant, which was now unbound, the seal broken into pieces on the floor. He read the bottom flap of the page once more:

> *… and notwithstanding the Peace and Repose among the diverse realms which the Treaty has long ensured, said economic conditions having been studied, examined, noted, and vetted, and the various subcommittee reports thereof fully considered, the Council of Stewards determines that the issuance of this Warrant violates neither the terms nor the intent of that Treaty. Therefore, this Pass and Warrant is hereby issued to the designated Warden of the Dwarven Quarter with our full faith that he will execute it dutifully. Govern yourself accordingly. Done in Jachin on this, the 54th day of Spring in the Twelfth Year of the Ninth Plan's guidance of the Commonwealth.*

The words were handwritten in ostentatious calligraphy, followed by a hastily scratched notation that ran off the edge of the page:

we remind the warden holding this Warrant that there will be <u>a full accounting</u> at the conclusion of the expedition. A full and complete account

He rolled the page tightly and slipped it inside his pocket.

Let all give thanks for the Curse we sired.

"You're welcome," Jacob said aloud.

Then he walked over to the wall, quietly shut the metal door, and turned the key to lock it again, just as he had been told to do.

The change came over Asher's uncle Abidan suddenly, without warning, like a tunnel collapse.

For three days Abidan's nephew and his fellow delvers had clambered deeper into the Mountain than their people had delved for many years. What began as a sculpted avenue gradually devolved into a carved tunnel held aloft by ancient cypress beams, then a rough one, and finally, what was little more than a long and winding fissure within the heart of the Mountain. For a mile, they were forced to crawl through a hole just wide enough for them to wriggle through on their bellies heaving their packs behind them.

When the tunnel opened up again, Asher heard the sound of dripping water echoing from unseen rivulets and leaks. The floor and ceiling had become riddled with stalactites and stalagmites, smooth, opal colored, with flecks of metal glistening like embers in the darkness. Where they touched together to form a single column, they were called "teeth," which Asher's people always held in reverence. Their picks cut through only what was needed for them to press ahead, and always with a prayer.

Throughout the journey, Abidan had been at the lead, silent and seemingly in good spirits, followed by Suriel, then Asher, and finally, the eldest of their number, a fat and gloomy slate-faced delver called Gad. At first, when the going had been relatively easy, they had reveled in songs and stories and drinking hard cider that Gad, who had thought to bring a keg, begrudgingly shared. Every so often, Abidan would pause to examine a wall or an outcrop of fallen stones, and sometimes, prompted by a silent impulse he never disclosed, his uncle would carve a rune into the stone to mark their return, so lightly that only his people could ever see it. Asher would joke that he was smelling either gold, iron, or shit, and everyone, even Gad, would laugh, and Abidan would smile and tap his nose.

The merriment seemed a distant memory now. They had crossed a small chasm that no one had ever heard of, and ever since had been wandering in a wild place. No hands had ever touched the stones here. The rocks were fiercer, dangerous, and untamed. Abidan led the nephil far into the depths, heedless of marking their passage with any more signs. He rarely spoke.

From the moment they passed into this terrain, Asher sensed that a darkness had taken hold of Abidan. He was sure the others felt it as well, though no one would speak of the change. The delvers found themselves hurrying to keep up with a leader whose only wish, it seemed, was to become lost in this wilderness of the Mountain.

It was late in the day, and they had reached the end of a long crawl when the tunnel abruptly ended with the sheer face of a wall of marl rock. They scampered up over the wall's top, where Suriel set a hook and a rope line, and, one by one, descended the other side. At the bottom, Asher found himself in what, at first, appeared to be a regal hallway. The ground was level here, without a trace of dirt, and the walls on either side were solid slates of polished onyx that stretched for as far as he could see. It seemed impossible, but the place looked as if someone had carved it, recently, from within the Mountain. The passage ran in a perfectly straight line.

The delvers were dumbstruck with wonder. Suriel started to speak, but Asher snapped at him to shut his mouth, and Gad growled his agreement. So only the clink of gear, and the soft thud of boots, and their heavy breathing broke the stillness.

Abidan had not uttered a sound in all this time. Without a word, he began his march again and disappeared into the passage's gaping darkness. The delvers, who were by now tired, aching, hungry, and, in truth, more than a little uneasy with where Abidan was taking them, grumbled. But at Asher's urging, they followed after their leader.

And then something in the shadows of the tunnel changed. Asher and his companions felt it as one. Felt it, even if they could not see or hear anything, or put into words what it was they had sensed. It was as if the stone, the cracks in the floor, the specks of dust lingering in the air, maybe even the darkness itself, all of it had been stirred. The delvers walked practically on top of one another now, as silently as they could. Only Abidan, as if oblivious to the menace that now hung in the air, kept his pace.

"What's his hurry?" Gad spoke under his breath.

Asher glanced at his companions, who looked ready to flee at the first noise.

"Stay here," Asher ordered.

Asher ran ahead, and, catching up to Abidan, took him by the arm. Abidan scarcely noticed him. The black walls and ceiling were growing wider, a few stalactites could be seen, and yet there was no echo at all from their voices.

"Hey, you're keeping a good pace," Asher huffed, "but the rest of us could use a drink and a breather, Uncle. This is—this is a strange place. Maybe we ought to—"

Asher knew immediately that Abidan had not heard a word he said. He kept walking, his pace never slacking. Abidan's dark eyes were fixed, unblinking, on the space before him. His jaw was clenched. For a moment, Asher thought that he looked as if he were ready to strike a blow, or kill someone. Instinctively, Asher recoiled.

"Uncle?"

"I choose—" Abidan's voice was brimming with rage, "—to fight …"

"Fight who? What are you talking about?"

Asher reached out to stop him when Abidan suddenly broke into a run, charging down the corridor, flinging his pack and tools aside.

"I see you!" Abidan roared at the empty air. "I see you all! Here I come!"

"Abidan!" Asher shouted after him, but the sound of his uncle's footsteps was already fading in the passage. Asher called back to the others:

"We've got to go after the thane. Drop your gear."

"What?" Suriel came to a stop and squinted at the darkness ahead of them. He was wheezing and out of breath. "What's got into him?"

Gad came stumbling after him, cursing loudly.

"I don't know," Asher tried to keep his voice calm. "Air's a bit off here. Some funny backdrafts. Might have gotten Abidan's head a little clouded."

The others mumbled; their voices thick with discontent. Asher knew his lie was a weak one. The air was moving alright, but purposely, if that were possible.

"Hey, look up there," Suriel pointed.

"We don't have time—" Asher started to say, but then he caught a glimpse of what Suriel must have seen: "—what is *that*?"

"Look!" Suriel jabbed his finger in the air. "There it goes again! Up there, up by that crop of teeth …"

"There's nothing up there, idiot," Gad glowered without looking. He was bent over, shivering in the cold, and his chest was heaving.

Asher stared at the stalactites and then called out ahead once more. He could no longer hide the panic in his voice:

"Abidan!"

There was no reply. Asher's mouth gaped. His throat tightened, but he was able to shout:

"*Abidan!*"

A long silence. And then Abidan's voice came echoing from out of the void. It was barely a whisper, yet it pierced through the walls, the floor, and the ceiling, and it carried the trace of the same musical note as his song at the doorway:

"*We are in the Mountain.*"

The three stared at one another. Then Asher saw what had been lurking in the air above them.

First, it was a stab of light, a yellow flicker, opening and closing.

Then another joined it, a pair. They moved closer together. They became slits. One of them blinked at the delvers huddled together in the tunnel.

A clatter broke the silence. Gad had dropped his pick. He swore a loud oath, but it might have been a cry. His fingers trembling, Asher clasped at a medal that hung from his neck, an open palm cast from bronze. He grasped it as if it were from an actual arm stretching out to help him.

"Nord ... save me—"

The words of his prayer were choked with fear. The sound of shovels, picks, hammers, all of their gear, raining to the ground, filled the cavern. The delvers were fleeing, scrambling in the tunnel to find the rope line.

Another pair of flaming slits appeared, this time in front of them. Then another. They were blossoming. And now Asher knew what he beheld:

They were eyes.

Hundreds of glowing eyes. Filling all the space in the darkness of the corridor and the shining black onyx of the walls. Growing. Drawing nearer.

"Leave us alone!" Suriel cried.

A shooting pain erupted in his hand as if he had been struck by a blade. Asher was on his knees, crawling wildly to escape whatever it was that chased him, unable to see anything. The rope was gone. His scream was cut short. And then only blackness and Abidan's voice remained, whispering the same melody throughout the passage:

"We are in the Mountain ..."

CHAPTER SEVEN

J ACOB ROCKED ON his toes in front of the bright green door, leaned his head closer to hear if anyone was moving within, and pulled the braided silk chord to ring the bell again. It tingled clear on the other side. Probably silver, he thought, from the sound of it.

He was standing in a grand, marble corridor of the Quarter—or, as its citizens still insisted on calling the place, the Inner Realm. The hall's opulence glowed in the firelight from countless, unnecessary lanterns that hung from gilded chains above him. The flagstone floor was nicely polished, and a line of doorways, each bearing a plaque with a name and address on it, spanned along both walls. A fountain bubbled nearby, and on its curb, beneath some statuary, a pretty nephil maiden played scales on a harp. Jacob smiled at her, but she was lost in her music.

He waited another minute and then knocked.

A woman's voice exploded from the other side of the door: "Can't you take a hint! He isn't here. And if he was, he wouldn't see you."

Jacob heaved a sigh toward the ceiling. The harpist giggled but kept playing.

"Master your features," he said to himself under his breath, "your feelings will follow." Then he called gently to the door:

"Hello?"

"Go away already! You've come to the wrong place."

She was from the Gutters, the realm of piped tunnels and caves that straddled the border between the Crag and the Quarter. He could tell from her accent. Probably a servant. But it would not do to offend her master's household. A pained smile would have to be summoned.

"Madam, I'm afraid you're mistaken. I have an appointment."

The door did not budge.

He examined the arch above the doorway. A prosperous-looking place, by the look of it. The door had its own lantern, with oil and a wick, glowing warmly, a fresh coat of paint, a shiny knob, and a bronze nameplate perfectly centered. It read:

The Divine Nicodemus
14 Elu Corridor
The Old Mines

It was the right doorway. Though it still showed no sign of opening for him.

Jacob knocked again, much louder this time. He stole a glance over at the fountain and saw that the girl had been joined by two nephil boys on the cusp of manhood, both of whom were competing with one another to make her laugh. They were shirtless and strapping, and probably very insolent. Their skin had become a lusty color of granite, drenched with the water they were splashing on each other, as their laughter floated across the corridor. One of them might have said "warden," but Jacob was not sure. Instinctively, he fingered the Commonwealth medallion beneath his shirt.

A spoiled generation, he thought for the thousandth time, coddled and puffed up at the same time, and all because they happened to be the youngest—as if it were some kind of a privilege to be the last born in a dying realm.

"Madam," Jacob now spoke with an air of authority. "Open the door this instant. I have important business with your master."

He could hear her footsteps stomping away.

Jacob clutched his hands into helpless fists. This was absurd. One of the lads at the fountain shook the water from his hair and shouted over to Jacob:

"Hey, there!"

Jacob assumed a pleasant face, gave him a little wave, and promptly pretended he was not there. But the boy was already walking toward him.

"I'm talking to you."

Jacob turned. The one approaching him looked to be at the height of his vigor. His chest, arms, and shoulders were strong and still dripping wet, as was a great mane of red and brown hair that hung below his neck. As taut as a living statute. His companion, who looked much the same, sauntered behind him, while the girl watched from the fountain, hiding her mouth behind her hand.

"And what can I do for you?" Jacob asked.

"Leave."

The other boy laughed.

"I beg your pardon?"

"You're the one who's a warden, aren't you? The one called Jacob?"

He knew there was no point pretending. So, he held his chin high, as if he might be able to look down his nose on these impertinent sprats, despite being a head shorter than either of them.

"I am called Jacob. Who might you be?"

The red-headed one wiped his hands across his face, sending droplets everywhere. He sneered:

"Pagiel. He's Moholi. You're knocking on the wrong door here, warden. You need to leave."

"Well, Masters Pagiel and Moholi, since we're past formalities, and since you're both plain-spoken, I'll speak plainly to you: you ought to mind your own business. I don't appreciate your tone."

"Oh, yeah?" They both took a threatening step towards Jacob.

"Or that condescending look on your faces that is about to be replaced with a more appropriate expression of deference."

"We don't have much respect for wardens and Crag's men," said Pagiel.

"No? Well, at least you ought to respect your elders. Especially elders who know your names, and where you live. And have a very long memory … and who know people you'd rather not."

They hesitated. Moholi stole a nervous glance at Pagiel who was shifting from one foot to the other and blinking very rapidly.

"What if he makes a note—" Maholi started.

"Shut it," Pagiel snapped. "He doesn't know where we live."

"Of course I do, boy. Both of you live in this corridor, in one of these very doorways. That's why you're bathing out here without a towel. The girl, too. That's far too heavy a harp for her to carry very far on her own." Jacob made a point to dip his head in a bow towards the girl, who promptly blushed. "She does seem quite taken with you, Pagiel. Dragging her into trouble hardly seems a fitting way to return a young lady's affection."

Pagiel rubbed his head and glanced back over at the fountain. Jacob let the moment draw itself out.

"As you say, I am a warden, and I'm here on official business. I would rather not have to make notes of who might have threatened me, who their families and companions are, where they live, and so forth. At least, if I don't need to. Perhaps there has simply been some misunderstanding. Perhaps an apology might clear the air."

They both eventually muttered they were sorry, hung their heads, and Jacob was satisfied that their arrogance had been sufficiently neutered. Now he could afford to be a little benevolent. He drew himself up, stepped in between the boys, and hooked his arms through each of their elbows, his face brightening.

"I'm surprised at the two of you," Jacob said very loudly. He started walking briskly toward the fountain. Pagiel and Moholi stumbled to keep up with him. Their heads darted about, wondering what he could be doing, but they followed. Jacob paused when he reached the fountain's edge, and he shook his head:

"What poor manners! To leave a beautiful young lady all alone in this drafty corridor by a pool of water. What if she should fall in? Or require an escort?"

Pagiel and Moholi stammered and looked every bit like the two foolish and soaking wet boys that they were. The girl dropped her head demurely, her cheeks tinted with a warm rosette. Jacob gave each boy a painful pinch.

"In my day, we were taught that a gentleman's first duty is to see to a lady's comfort." Jacob made a sweeping bow, at which the girl tittered. "My dear. I am returning these escorts to your gracious company where they belong. My humble respects, uh, Miss?"

The girl's face was as pink as an opal.

"Sara," she replied with another giggle. A mop of light curls cascaded down to her shoulders. As useless as a doll, Jacob thought to himself, like all the others of the last-born generation. Jacob bowed once more.

"Miss Sara. Please carry on with your music. It was lovely."

"Thank you." She was grinning like an idiot.

He gave a last, meaningful look at the two boys, while Sara picked up her harp. "The thanks are all mine," he said.

Sara had only begun plucking at her instrument when the sound of a creaking door was followed by a shrill whistle. A small shadow of a much older nephil woman standing in the light of the open doorway at 14 Elu Corridor was yelling at Jacob:

"He said I had to let you in."

Her message delivered, she spun on her heel and stormed back into the home. But at least she had left the door open for him.

A scowl was fixed across the woman's basalt face. It pierced through the cloud of steam billowing from her teapot. Jacob held a porcelain cup and saucer up for her to fill, and a stream of scalding brown liquid poured from the pot's spout in a perfect arc into his cup.

"Thank you, Miss, uh?"

She laughed derisively and wiped the spout clean with the corner of a greasy apron. Everything in her features, from her tied up hair to the muscles around her block-shaped chin, looked drawn and tight, and proclaimed her poor lineage. A Gutters nephil to the bone.

"Just 'Miss' to you, warden's man," she answered in a stern voice, as one who was accustomed to being obeyed within her domestic domain. "Go on in. Sit down if you like, but mind you keep your grubby feet off the furniture. And don't you dare touch the food; that's His Divinity's supper, and he's hardly eaten today. I told him he's got to change out of those vestments if he wants his meat, though. So, he'll be with you once he's dressed." Then, under her breath: "and the sooner the better to see you gone." A swinging door to the kitchen closed behind her, and Jacob was alone inside the comfortable and amply furnished entry of the Divine Nicodemus's apartments.

Jacob took a few sips of tea, which left a spicy but pleasant sensation in his mouth and he looked about discretely, as one does when coming into another's home for the first time. The moment he drew past the foyer, Jacob was in awe.

The apartment within was a single great chamber, hewn and care-fully glossed, with soaring geometric archways and marble flooring all around. Jacob wandered in a circle, entranced, breathing in the warm, rich air. At one end of the room were rows of oaken cases, standing almost to the ceiling, all filled with leather-bound books and neatly stacked scrolls. On the side closest to the doorway hung an enormous silver mirror, casting a warbled reflection of Jacob's face. And a stone pedestal was mounted before it. Throughout the room there were hanging lamps, casting a warm, orange glow upon carpets, velvet cur-tains. But it was the collection of statuary that struck the breath from Jacob. Looming men in armor and soaring cloaks, beautiful women, giant falcons, half-beasts, hydras, serpents, owls, and dragons, carved in shimmering marble, quartz, and veined granite. They lined the walls and filled pedestals; some were hidden within alcoves; others were left out on sconces.

They were perfect, these statues; that was the first thought that struck Jacob. As if in answer to Jacob's unspoken question came a friendly, weathered voice:

"They're from the time of the priests."

Jacob spun around. There before him stood Nicodemus, His Divin-ity in person, the only priest the Treaty allowed, wearing a stained house robe. It was an old face that addressed him, worn with thoughtful lines from years of study and set within a canvass as gray and granular, and shifting, as silt. His Divinity was bald now, except for a stubborn wisp of white hair that clung to the back of his head. He was leaning on an expensive-looking cane and smiling graciously. Like the kitchen woman, he was on the small side of their people, thinner in stature. Jacob began to apologize, but Nicodemus cut him off:

"And, yes, in case you were wondering. They are gods. Most of them, anyways."

Jacob swallowed and feared he might look blanched in all this light.

"How—?" he started.

"—did they survive?" Nicodemus absently fingered a nearby war-rior poised to slay a writhing winged snake. "The Overthrow was hardly an organized affair. Wars never are. No matter what the men and their teachers say." He chuckled. "Truth is, men are lazy ... Not that I can blame them for tiring out. Have you ever tried heaving a half-ton piece of stone up a mountainside? Just so you could push it off into the sea?"

Jacob shook his head.

"Hard work. Dangerous, too. And there were a lot of gods in our little Mountain island." He patted the warrior statue's foot like an old friend.

"I thought—I thought all the gods had been thrown into the sea," Jacob's voice quavered, though he tried to hold it steady. The statues' eyes seemed to follow his. He had once read that this roving gaze was a trick only the greatest of the old artisans had ever mastered.

"Not all," Nicodemus replied. "A year into the Overthrow and the wardens still hadn't finished sweeping out the open-air shrines. Much less the temples inside the Mountain. But by then, the novelty was wearing off. Oh, it was good fun at first, watching the gods go splash. But how many times will people cheer for a bit of rock falling in the ocean? It just wasn't worth the effort anymore. That and the porters kept getting killed moving all those statues out to the Crest. I remember seeing this one group go down. Twenty Cragmen, all young and handsome, all decked out in yellow, pulling one of the big ones along the High Road, just as pleased with themselves as if they were heading to a fair. They hoisted the stone up the Mountain's side with ropes, all the way up to the edge of a cliff." Nicodemus whistled low and made a spiraling motion with his finger, smacking it against his other hand. "The god plummeted into the sea, and all twenty of those boys followed him like a chain of daisies. Someone forgot to undo the clasping billet, you see. I forget which god it was. Might have been Nord, come to think of it. There's some irony for you. Anyway, after that, the Crest decided they had toppled enough idols. The rest, they'd just lock up in our Realm. Hide them away, and everyone would go about their business, and eventually, they'd forget there were ever any gods at all. And here they are, poor things. Have a seat."

Nicodemus led them over to a set of plush chairs set beneath a small gilded canopy held up by a wooden screen. With a low table, an ashtray, and a plate of mushrooms, garlic cloves, and poultry waiting on a plate, it felt like an inner room of a pub.

"Smoke?" Nicodemus offered him a pipe.

"No, thank you."

"I hope it doesn't make you too uncomfortable—the gods, I mean, not the smoke." Nicodemus lit a taper from a nearby lantern and was soon billowing clouds of blue and gray pipe smoke around them. It had a sweet aroma to it.

Jacob folded his hands and tried to sound diplomatic:

"I'll confess it is a tad awkward."

"Is it? I'm sorry."

Jacob made one of his practiced gestures, the one that conveyed helplessness and authority at the same time.

"Not that I mind, Nicodemus. I hold your faith—that is, your profession in the highest esteem. I do. Your contributions to our people have been immeasurable. But those," he discretely pointed outside the canopy, "could be seen by some—not me, of course, but those we ought not to offend—as something of a violation of the Commonwealth's First Article. The Crest indulges religion in our Realm only because the Treaty requires them to. It is a delicate understanding we must maintain."

Nicodemus shrugged:

"Why should the Crest care if an old dwarf chooses to live in an old storeroom with a few old gods?"

"You're hardly just an 'old dwarf,' Nicodemus."

"I am to them. Mind if I eat?"

"Not at all."

With no pretense of table manners, Nicodemus plunged into his dinner, tearing the meat from the bone, swallowing mushrooms and potatoes whole, slurping up the juices. He only paused to take a pull from his pipe or let out a belch. When he began to scrape the plate, Nicodemus picked up the conversation again:

"Dwarf," he spat the word out with exaggerated disdain, as he worked to free an annoying piece of gristle from his teeth. "I can still remember when the men called us by our true name, or even 'the holy folk.' Back when they held our people in esteem. Some would touch their foreheads and ask for our blessing."

"We're all equals now," Jacob replied. It was not the first time he had heard this wistful complaint. "Diverse in identity, equal in respect. That's the law of the Commonwealth."

"Hm. Well, you'll note that I forewent blessing this meal—out of respect to the Crest." Nicodemus smiled and wiped his mouth with the back of his sleeve. "Actually," he said, "I was just starving. There. Belly's full. Now I can attend to our business, which is what brings you to visit my humble home."

"Yes," Jacob at once felt more comfortable. "Our business. Well, good news there."

"Did they get off alright?" Nicodemus clasped his hands together tightly.

"Yes. I've just come from the border. Everything's playing out perfectly. Our people have passed the border." Jacob paused to allow the words their full effect. "I said, our people have passed the border. Your sermons worked."

"May Nord keep them safe," Nicodemus bowed. "And give Abidan strength."

"Yes, of course. I suppose that's appropriate. It's a historical accomplishment after all."

Nicodemus studied his companion:

"You're proud of the part you've played in this."

Jacob shook his head.

"No. My work has to remain anonymous in this venture. But ... I won't deny that I'll be pleased, very pleased, with the result—if all goes well."

Nicodemus's eyes lifted until they met with a stone face of a three-headed alabaster goat perched atop a sconce near the ceiling.

"If all goes well," Nicodemus repeated, more to himself. Jacob took it as a question.

"Why shouldn't it? They say the iron and silver were flowing like a river right up until the Overthrow. It may take some time, but the delvers will strike into it again. They'll find it. And then the wealth of the priests will return. Just like you promised the people. But this time, it will flow through *our* hands. Think of it, Nicodemus."

"Oh, I've thought on it—prayed on it—for a long time now." Nicodemus let out a long breath and glanced up at the goat statue again as if expecting a response. It remained frozen in stone, a noiseless bleating. "I've prayed and I've prayed, but I have yet to hear anything. If

I'm honest—and we must always be honest in our supplications to the gods—I don't give a fart whether the delvers find any metal or not. Don't tell that to Elon, obviously."

"Obviously."

"The truth is—"

Nicodemus left the thought hanging, but Jacob picked it up for him:

"—you're hoping the delvers might come across a baby or two out there?"

Nicodemus bowed his head.

"Yes," he admitted. "Seems foolish to say so out loud. But that is my hope."

"Who knows?" Jacob shrugged. "Maybe they will. Maybe when they return, and we're feasting their success, the sight of all that new silver will finally put some children in our women's bellies. The Curse will be broken."

"You make it sound like the Curse was some sort of a bargain," Nicodemus snapped. "No. I've gone along with you in this, Jacob, I've preached the sermons you asked me to, I've stoked up a fire good and hot in Elon's heart, got him to part with his money for this delve—because there's nothing left to try. This Curse ... Our people won't yearn after children forever. They're growing restless."

Jacob raised an eyebrow. Nicodemus did not notice, but continued:

"Just the other day some young fellow—what was his name?—he came to me for counsel. Claimed he had been having dreams—real dreams, mind you—about dragons chasing after a little girl in the dark. And a baby caught in a barrel. And a new goddess that's burning up everything. It was all gibberish, but very vivid."

"Probably a poem he heard somewhere. Or ale. That's quite good for dreaming."

Nicodemus shook his head. "No. What he described to me. The *way* he described it. He professed faith in this goddess, and at the same time, he was terrified of her. I could tell. There was fear behind his eyes. Real fear. But also, conviction. And a kind of—challenge. As if I dare not doubt him. I've not seen such—I don't know how to describe it—fervor, I suppose, in years. Not since the priests were still in the temples."

"Hm."

"This fellow—Gershon! —that was the boy's name—he may very well have heard a true calling. From the gods. I understand he's got a few folks in the Gutters thinking so."

Jacob studied Nicodemus for a long while. The lantern light guttered and cast the old one's face in a contemplative shadow. At last, Jacob spoke very carefully:

"That needs to stop, Nicodemus."

"Oh?"

"I know the Gutters have always been a restless place when it comes to that sort of thing. But we are allowed one priest. One king. One priest. Sanctioned by the Crest's Stewards. That is the Treaty. Our people have one priest to talk to their gods and one king to keep their peace. You hold the privilege of that priesthood, Divinity. The Crest will not tolerate any others."

"Rather presumptive of them."

"Such is life in the Mountain. So long as they're many and we're few."

Nicodemus pinched the bridge of his nose and gazed across his table. He looked past the warden shifting in his guest chair, past the puffs of smoke rising from his pipe like incense before the giant blocks of marble around them, and let out a long sigh.

"We put a stone around our neck the moment Zebulon signed that damned Treaty."

"It's kept us alive."

"It has. So that the Crest men can take everything from us and give us scraps of food and paper in return. Our women are barren. Our men are despondent. Truly a blessed life our people enjoy. Sometimes I wonder if Zebulon shouldn't have ... well, too late now. We'll just have to keep steadfast with the bargain he struck, won't we?" Nicodemus shook his head with a joyless laugh. "Now here you've got me dealing with the men just like Zebulon did. I think that's what troubles me most about this business of ours, Jacob. What if all we're doing will only leave us doubly cursed?"

"Leave the men to me, Divinity. You've done your part. The delvers came forward and Elon's invested. Now rely on me to deal with the men. Oh, the Crest will be adamant that nothing be held back. Elon will be just as stubborn that nothing be yielded. I'll be surprised if the men's guilds don't demand a cut once the silver and iron start flowing again. But I can manage all the pushing and tugging, the outstretched hands. Believe me, once we strike the first vein, once we're celebrating our riches, the costs will seem trifling."

Nicodemus drummed his fingertips across his chest. After a long silence, he picked up his smoldering pipe from the ashtray and with the stump directed Jacob's attention to a tall granite statue behind his chair.

"Recognize him?"

Jacob craned his neck.

"Uhm, no. Sorry."

"That would be Nord, our all-knowing father."

"Really?" Jacob was not at all certain why the old priest was pointing out an idol to him. But he pretended to carefully inspect the statute. It was taller than most of the others and certainly more severe. A bareheaded nephil lord, standing in plate armor, holding a ball in his one hand, his mouth agape.

"I hadn't seen his depiction before," Jacob said after what felt like a suitable amount of time. "Not very pleasant looking for a father figure."

"Nord looks angry because he is in pain. As would you, if your hand had been cut off. See?"

Jacob turned around in his chair again.

"Ah, so it has. How unfortunate."

"Nord is the most blessed of all the gods because of that loss. Your talk about outstretched hands and costs reminded me just now of the mystery of Nord, how he became all-knowing and all-powerful over the other gods. It's the center of our faith and one of my favorite stories. If you'd like to hear it—no?"

"Thank you, Divinity, no. My shortcomings of faith are past fixing. Though I appreciate the offer."

"Are you sure? It's an exceptional myth, even if you don't believe a word of it. Its truth has stood the test of time."

"I'm sure it has, whatever truth is."

This was growing tiresome, all this wasted talk about his people's foolish imaginings and fading glories. Tedious and pointless, like that hymn of Abidan's. Nicodemus fixed Jacob with a searching look and explained:

"Here's a truth for you, Jacob: there is no such thing as a trifling cost. Whatever you would hold dear must be paid for dearly. You hope for silver, I can tell. I hope for—something more valuable. But we'll each have to pay the price for what we want, the real price I mean, eventually." Nicodemus took up his pipe to fill it again and added. "Nothing gets shortchanged in the Mountain."

CHAPTER EIGHT

B Y HIS COUNT, he had a little time to spare before his next appointment. And since his next call would involve some unpleasantness,
and Nicodemus's servant woman had refused to cook him so
much as a slice of potato while he was a guest in the priest's house, Jacob
decided to wander in the neighborhood of Elu Corridor for a bit.

With no real destination in mind other than a place to buy some
supper, he meandered through a warren of wide and traveled avenues
and up a long, spiraling flight of steps, then out into a great hall that was
much larger than it needed to be for the numbers it now held. Perhaps
eighty of his people were out and about trading or working their crafts.
There were small forges, and a band strumming music, and a collection of colorful banners, and a jade-faced storyteller entertaining a half
dozen old-timers by a fireplace, which burned a flame that would shift
and change colors every time the story reached a dramatic twist or turn.
High above the little throng, a great, fluttering tapestry hung from the
ceiling. There was scaffolding all around it, and a crew of weavers was
busily knitting gold, silver, and platinum runes and pictures; most of it
was unfinished. The conversations inside the tunnel, though scattered,
were loud and jovial and somehow intertwined with the noise of the
band's instruments, although none of it was the least bit coordinated. It
all annoyed Jacob, and so he pressed through the square as quickly as he
could. He found the small side doorway he was looking for and slipped
into the shadows of a narrow hallway.

He trudged up another, steeper flight of steps that ended in an arch
that had a faded sign above it. The halls were a little less refined here, the
statues, friezes, and fountains a little less plentiful; the doorways had their
numbers carved into the rock next to them. Here and there, an iron pipe
joint or a metal bend jutted rudely out of a corner, like some unwanted

visitor intruding upon an otherwise pleasant gathering. The denizens
were different here; smaller and warier in their speech and manner. They
did not shun the sight of Jacob's yellow cloak, but nodded at him as he
passed, begrudgingly if not respectfully. There were far fewer loiterers
here, Jacob noted approvingly.

"Welcome back, sir," a sweating burly nephil greeted him. He carried a long chisel, still covered in chalk, and his beige flecked hands were
caked with powder. He wore a matching set of woolen pants and shirt
that were once red, but now almost white with film.

"Good to be back, Okran," Jacob smiled. "How's the pottery
business?"

Okran licked his lips and scanned the tunnel. Jacob appreciated his
caution; this was not a conversation he wanted to be overheard either.

"Better, sir. Gods be praised. Since you've opened up a little trade
with the Crag's guildsmen, at least we've got a few of their folk who will
buy our makes. It's mostly the Crest's tin coins and promises to pay, but
it's better than nothing."

Jacob held a finger to his lips for silence, and Okran sputtered an
apology. Jacob patted Okran on the shoulder and winked.

"Glad to hear it," he said quietly. "Better days ahead for all of us, let's
hope."

"Yes, indeed, sir. I hope so. I do. Uh, still, though. It's mighty tight for
some of us in the Gutters. Me included; truth be told."

Jacob held up his hand again. "You're a plumb and level fellow. I'm
not calling in your debt." Then with another wink, added: "You won't
be taken up just yet."

Okran was visibly relieved. "Much obliged, sir. Very much so. We'll
always keep you in our prayers. Bless you."

"Not at all," and even as Jacob said it, he was computing the com-
pounded interest that he would write in his book tonight. Okran went
on with more thanks, and about the orders he could be filling, the want
of good clay and kilns, and, over and over, how much he was praying for
a return to the days when they could mingle with the Crag's men more
freely. Jacob looked grave and sympathetic, but the pinch in his stomach
was making him impatient.

"—I'll certainly look into all of that, Okran ... listen, is the Copperbottom open for lunch yet?"

"Huh? Oh, I believe so," Okran craned his neck and squinted. "Yep. Looks like Miss Rachel's setting the lamps out now."

"Excellent," he waved a hasty goodbye to Okran, who, still standing in the middle of the tunnel with his chisel in one hand and his index finger pressed to his forehead with the other, called out a blessing upon his lender.

Jacob hustled across the tunnel, through an opening in a mortarless rock wall about the height of his waist, and then crossed a courtyard that ended at a pleasant little porch and red doorway. A few nephil men were waiting around wooden tables, playing cards or dominos and smoking rich tobacco from clay pipes. The drone of their conversations lulled for only a moment when Jacob walked by, but soon the clink of mugs and forks and the bawl of hearty laughter resumed. On a stepstool in front of an open window, a woman was on her tiptoes, reaching up to stop a copper cauldron that was swinging from a chain in the ceiling. Lithe, but with sturdy looking hands, she had long, black hair that flowed freely down her shoulders and caught the light of a taper's flame that was poised between her fingers. She was trying to light a lantern inside the cauldron as it swung by, but having little success, swore a string of colorful curses that sent a group of nearby miners into merriment. She swore at them as well, but not without a little smirk.

"Need a hand?" Jacob offered.

"Hand indeed, you prickless little—oh!"

She nearly fell off her stool. Jacob grasped her by the thigh and steadied her, clutching a handful of skirt. Her leg felt taught and very strong. "Sorry, Jacob," she said stepping down. She was nearly Jacob's height, with a reddish hue to her bronze skin that always reminded Jacob of rust on water pipes. The heady scent of ale and hearth smoke clung to her clothes. She dabbed at the sweat beading on her brow and extinguished the taper. "Didn't know it was you. Quiet down over there!"

The miners clucked to themselves, then lowered their voices to hoarse whispers.

"It's been a while," Jacob observed.

"Yes, that it has."

"My usual booth available?"

"We don't open for another hour. But as it's you …"

She heaved the front door and ushered Jacob inside a warm and empty tavern. Though carved entirely from within the Mountain's stone, the floors and walls were covered in richly grained wood panels. Another copper-colored cauldron, smaller than the one outside, had been nailed up on the wall behind a wide and ample bar. Beneath the cauldron, the words "Copperbottom," and "Rachel, daughter of Liza, Proprietress," were written in flowing bronze letters. A pyramid of bottles covered the bar's top, reflecting tiny diamonds of green, brown, blue, amber, and scarlet lights from a burning fireplace that kept the place well warmed. A flank of goat was turning on a spit over the fire, and the scents of sweet seasoning mingled with ale, mead, and soap from the freshly mopped floors. Jacob felt a warmth rising inside of him. He looked for his favorite booth, the one in the farthest corner with a stuffed seagull presiding on a perch, and the sofas propped against the wall.

Jacob sat down in his usual seat, patted the gull fondly, and ordered a plate of food.

"You spending the night?" she asked. Jacob looked at her closely. "I'm sure you'd prefer the Groat, but I can make a bed for you here."

"I only have time for supper—and a short rest."

She closed her eyes a moment longer than he thought she needed to, but an inviting smile remained on her lips. It was a pretty mouth, Jacob reflected; it almost compensated for a face that was, for nephil women, a bit plain and overly round.

"May I—may I join you?" she asked, and her fingers wandered to Jacob's cheek, stroking his hair back.

"I was hoping you would ask."

He reached into a pocket of his tunic and found a coin, fairly small, but with a hefty thickness, which he laid on the tabletop. It had the Crest's symbol, a sword, emblazoned on it; and it was pure silver. Its image shone in Rachel's dark eyes, then disappeared, as she slipped it into her bosom.

It was the price of keeping a humble tavern in the poorest corner of the Inner Realm stocked with wares, and its patrons fed and happy. The price of Rachel's affection. Such as it was, he reminded himself.

"I'll go and fetch your supper for you now," she leaned over, kissed him, and with a coy tilt of her blouse, quickly turned to head back to the kitchen.

Jacob was alone, enjoying the sounds of the fire crackling in the hearth and the hiss from cooking meat. The dead gull's feathers glowed yellow in the light of a guttering candle, while its eyes, two spheres of polished onyx, stared, unblinking, across the tavern's empty tables and chairs. He could still catch the murmur of the miners outside on the porch, playing their games, trading bits of songs and stories, complaining about the leaking pipes, about him as well, in all likelihood. But here in his booth, in the relative quiet of a bar in the Gutters, Jacob could ignore the jibes. He felt his shoulders relax.

Rachel returned balancing a tray beneath her breasts. She set a small, but sumptuous feast on the table.

Jacob's face beamed with pleasure. The girl's cooking was a kind of art unto itself. The ingredients were nothing different than what could be found at any guild market in the Crag. But Rachel wove them together with the precision and flair of an architect. Pepper perfectly apportioned across mushrooms, soaked in ale. Slivers of beans, spiced just enough to make the inside of his cheeks tingle, but never burn. A honeyed apple carved into the shape of a bee that almost seemed to take flight from his plate. Even the steam coming off the broiled haddock was entrancing. Of all the tedious endeavors his race spent time and labor crafting, food was the one thing Jacob ever felt a real appreciation for. And there was no better artisan of it than Rachel daughter of Liza.

He ate his meal in silence with Rachel, who knew better than to pester Jacob with stilted conversation for the sake of talk. As he chewed, she fixed him with a quiet but very pleasant look from across the booth. Jacob drank down a tankard of her spiced ale, then, when she refilled it, another. A warm, refreshing drowsiness surged like a wave that began deep inside his stomach, spreading to his loins, then, crashing, swept his senses away from behind his temples. The tables, the tavern, the stuffed bird with the gleaming black eyes, everything except Rachel's face, faded into an oily light. The muffled voices outside became a buzz. Jacob teetered from his chair, and this time it was Rachel who steadied him. They stumbled together across the planks of the tavern's floor. Then they were behind the bar, kissing, knocking over a bucket of dirty water and a tray of empty mugs, groping their way into the pantry, a makeshift bed chamber that was hidden in a hallway behind racks of pots.

Once inside the cramped, dark room, they were quick about it; Rachel made sure of that.

Jacob was still untangling his pants from a soaked blanket when Rachel arose, her cheeks still glowing hot. The air lingered with the smell of their lust and the mildew of the leaking pipes in the ceiling.

"No rush, darling," she murmured. She scoured a brush over her head to tease out some matted hair. "You stay and relax as long as you like."

He stretched his pale legs and arms across the mattress. The room was still swaying, but the sense of dizziness was beginning to subside. His toes curled against a silk pillowcase. "Where are you going?"

"Almost opening time. My customers will break down the door if I'm so much as a minute late."

"To hell with them. Let them storm the tavern."

"You want them to find you? In a closet, like this? And since when did you start believing in hell?"

She was smiling down at him, even as she wriggled her naked torso through her skirt and threw an apron on over her blouse. He reached up and pulled her back toward the mattress.

"You've made me a believer," he murmured in her ear. He started to kiss her neck, then her shoulders. "Without you, I am in torment. I'm lost. You're my goddess, Rachel. I worship you."

"It's what's between my legs that you worship," she pushed him away playfully, yet still with plenty of heft. It only aroused Jacob more, but he knew he would not be getting another bout with her. It was, after all, just one coin.

"And what's wrong with that?"

"Nothing at all," she shrugged and finished straightening her clothes. "So, you can take a sleep if you like. Or once you're decent, just head out the back."

Jacob felt a pang.

"I'd better say goodbye to you then. I've got a long journey ahead of me."

She fixed her mouth into a frown.

"Just supper and sex, is it?"

"Supper and sex, the only gods there are."

She shook her head and drew her index finger across her forehead, a perfunctory motion for protection from his blasphemy. "Better watch that kind of talk. I can lay with a godless warden to keep a roof over my head and fuel in my ovens, but then I'm the best cook and barkeeper in the Gutters. There are folks around here who won't tolerate jibes about the gods. Not even when it's in fun."

Jacob regarded her and then thought of something.

"So, have these new preachers I'm hearing about been coming around the Copperbottom?"

"I'm a bedwarmer, not an informant."

He held his hands up. "I'm only asking."

"I know exactly what you're doing." She sat down a moment and fixed Jacob with a level gaze. "The answer is, I wouldn't know. I only ever ask the Divine Nicodemus for his prayers."

"Good. I'm glad, Rachel." He watched her. "I really am. All the same. A bit of advice. If any of these trouble-makers running around the Gutters with their visions, or dreams, or what have you, if any of them should want to hold a meeting in the Copperbottom, or gather together here for a meal—"

"You know how busy it gets here. I can't keep track of everyone I serve a drink to."

"I understand. Just try to stay clear of them if you can. Keep them on the other side of the door. They may get noted if they're not already."

"Who?"

She was feigning, he knew it. Worse, she was scarcely trying. Not that it mattered.

"Their names are Kohath and Merari. And Gershon."

"I'll not so much as give them a thimble of water if they ask, and then I'll curse their mothers for good measure."

"That's my girl."

He drew her close, and she ran her fingers through his hair. She opened her mouth wide for his. Her tongue tasted like honey, like a sweet velvet dessert. Even though it was past opening time for the

Copperbottom and the press against the tavern's front door was growing boisterous, even though Jacob knew he would be late for his next
appointment, he got his second bout with Rachel.

A wind howled across the cliff's edge. It bit sharp and frigid. Where it
stirred from, no one knew, for beyond the cliff was a vast, dark expanse
beyond which none, not even the nephil of the Inner Realm, could see.

The void beyond the cliff had always been called Cowan's Chasm.
A canyon, miles long, that separated the Quarter from the foundations
of the Crest, where no roads, or lights, or signs marked its presence. Few
ever ventured to the place any more. It had a somber, haunted feel about
it. But those who ever came knew at once when they had reached it.

As soon as he trudged his burning legs over the last transom of steps,
the freezing wind hit Jacob's face like a slap in the dark. He pulled the
hood of his cloak down fast around his cheeks. The yellow cloth fluttered uselessly behind him. It was like walking into a gale.

"I'm here," he strained to catch his breath. He had pressed on hard
for most of the day without pausing to eat, through a slog of partly
flooded tunnels, blocked stairways, and a string of corridors that kept
turning back on themselves before he reached the base of the final flight
of stairs that led to the Chasm. He heaved in air that felt like needles
piercing his chest. His legs roared in pain. The glow from his visit to the
Copperbottom was long faded.

"I'm here," Jacob called out again. The wind maintained its piercing
howl. His eyes teared from the blowing dust. "Damn it all—I said I'm here!"

Two Cragmen in studded leather jerkins standing about a hundred
feet away, both turned at the same time. One of them lifted a lantern at
the sound of Jacob's voice. The men clutched what looked like a sack
between them.

"Hey!" The man with the lantern answered. "That you, Jake?" The
lantern waved and clanged wildly. "Over here. Hurry up, it's freezing."

"I'm coming," Jacob scowled.

"Mind the cliff," the other man warned. "Follow Edmund's lantern,
if you can see it."

"Of course I can see it," Jacob muttered under his breath, "you're the ones that are blind as moles."

As he came to the edge of the ring of light, Jacob saw that the two men were shivering and standing several yards back from the edge. At Jacob's approach, they shifted the weight of the load they carried.

It was a young nephil man, beaten unconscious. A thin line of blood dripped from his mouth and spilled down his torn shirt. Jacob walked closer, bent down to examine his face, turned it from one side to another, and grimaced.

"And how am I supposed to ask him any questions in this condition?" he demanded.

"Not our fault," Edmund sniffed. "Meyers read him the warrant, read it real nice to him."

"I did," Meyers nodded.

"But he wasn't having it," said Edmund. He put the lantern down and showed Jacob what looked like a faded scar on the bottom of his chin. "Gave me this when I very gently took him into custody. Real scrapper."

Jacob did not believe a word of it. More than likely, they ambushed the boy in some corner of the Gutters near the Crag; or they just snuck into his home and took him up while he was sleeping.

"Good thing there were two of you then," he sneered. "Here, give him this." Jacob handed over a leather skin of Rachel's ale he brought from the tavern. He had hoped to enjoy it, alone, when he was finished with this business, but the boy needed its medicine now. "Just a mouthful."

The beer slopped down the boy's chin, but most of it made it down his throat. He sputtered and gasped, and the two men let go of him, thinking he might start to retch. Instead, he curled into a ball.

"Bring him over by the edge," Jacob ordered.

"What, we're doing this out there?" Edmund glanced back nervously.

"You have someplace better in mind?"

"It's just—that's awful steep," said Meyers.

"That's why you've got rope. Bring him."

The men grumbled but dragged the young nephil to the edge of the cliff where they dropped him in a heap. The wind stirred his hair. What had been a blonde set of ringlets was tangled and matted brown with dried blood. Most of his face was covered in bruises that emanated from a shattered nose.

"Bind him up tight, but leave plenty of line," Jacob said, his voice quiet.

The nephil let out a pained groan while Meyers and Edmund worked a heavy rope line around his chest and legs. When they finished with the last knot, Jacob kneeled and spoke very softly in his ear.

"Gershon, my boy," his voice sounded soothing, almost sorrowful. "Gershon. I'm so sorry you find yourself in this predicament. Truly I am. Oh, try not to move. Just lie still. Here, a little more ale will ease your pain."

Jacob grabbed the skin of ale from Edmund and brought it to Gershon's lips. He swallowed too greedily and choked on the fiery liquid.

"Go easy on that," Jacob laughed gently, "it's expensive stuff. A bit more? There."

Gershon finally cracked an eye open. His pupil was black, lolling, but it eventually focused on Jacob.

"Where-where . . ." Gershon rasped.

"We are at the Chasm. I'm afraid you've been taken up."

Gershon's eye shut. A tear lingered at its corner, then finally fell where it mixed with the dust and blood.

"Why?" Gershon whispered.

"You really don't know?"

As if in answer, the eye shut tight again. Jacob craned his head around and mouthed to the others to go and find someplace to tie the free end of the rope. Meyers and Edmund grunted and then lumbered off to search in the darkness. When they were far enough away, Jacob spoke under his breath:

"I've sent them away so we can speak freely. But we've only a few moments. You know I am a warden. Which means I can help you."

Gershon's eyes opened in amazement, or disbelief.

"Wh-why would you?" he half-choked.

Jacob tried to look kindly. "For your mother—she was a dear friend once. I've always held her in the highest esteem. I would do this, risk my position, for her sake. To spare her pain. But I must have your cooperation. Your total cooperation."

"I c-can't."

"So, you'd rather break her heart?" Jacob hissed in his ear. "That's what you want? A painful death for you—oh, yes, that's what's coming—and her left to beg. For what?"

Gershon was wracked by a spasm of pain. He managed to cry out two words:

"The dreams."

"Dreams?" Jacob scoffed. "That's what you want to throw your life away for? Dreams can be taken care of with ale. Or money. Or girls. Trust me."

"You-you don't understand."

The boy was talking to him, and rather freely. This might not take long after all. Jacob discretely felt the weight of what was left in his aleskin and held onto the hope that he would not have to waste much more. A good drink of Rachel's brew would be just the thing, he thought. Still, he had to finish this business dutifully, to the end. Jacob heaved an exaggerated sigh.

"Gershon," he said, "without my help, you will fall. You'll die, and your family, your poor mother, will be ruined. I want to help you. It's not too late. I can save you. All you need do is whisper a name into my ear. Just tell me the name."

"I can hear it. Even now … I've never heard it when I was awake before."

Jacob leaned closer, his face almost brushing against Gershon's:

"What do you hear, Gershon?"

"A song. A bell."

"Whose?"

The young man drew a breath and let it out slowly:

"Hers."

Jacob shook his head. Then he stood up, his knees creaking, and he waved at the others to return. Meyers was the first to arrive:

"Found an old, fist-sized iron stake back there, sir. Driven deep. Right in the middle of the ground. It's pretty rusted, but the rope seems to be holding on. Will that work?"

"I'm sure it will," Jacob remarked. "Pick him up."

Gershon whimpered as Meyers hoisted him over his shoulder. Crouching down low so as not to be taken off balance by any sudden gust, Meyers inched closer to the cliff's edge, until a stream of gravel spilled over the side from his footstep, and he would not dare to take another step. Jacob slid around the man's legs until he was directly beneath Gershon's head, so the two could see one another, each upside down to the other.

"I truly am sorry," said Jacob.

"No!" Gershon started to scream, but then his voice was stifled in terror as he was hurled out beyond the cliffside. The boy, the clumped coils of rope, his torn clothes, the splatter of blood flowing from his face, they were all suspended in midair for a moment, held aloft like some terrible sculpture on a pedestal until Gershon plummeted down. He disappeared, and the line that was tied to his body tore against the side of the cliff as it followed him over the edge. A low thump, like the snap of a bowstring, and the rope was taught; and then it swayed from side to side. Only the sound of the wind blowing dust through the air remained.

"Pull him up," Jacob commanded.

"Aw, c'mon—" Edmund started to complain, but Jacob pointedly reminded him of their orders—and their superiors, with whom he was on quite friendly terms—so the two Cragmen began hauling on the rope, hand over hand, grunting, in rhythm.

When Gershon emerged, a fresh gash of crimson stained his right shoulder where he had crashed into the cliff's face. The arm jutted at an odd angle from the elbow where the bone had broken. He was shaking violently.

"I swore—I swore," he struggled to form the words.

Jacob helped him: "What did you swear?"

"Oath. The sect."

"Is that what you call yourselves? Just the sect?"

There was a grain of cleverness in that. Keep a name anodyne, and your neighbors will never wonder what your group believes, or what you may be up to. Nor will your overseers. The boy was trying to speak again:

"We all swore."

"Well, then. Can't have you breaking any oaths." Jacob looked up at Meyers. "Again."

Gershon was thrown over the cliff twice more, but he did not cry out either time. The rope began to fray as Meyers and Edmund pulled him up after the second time.

Jacob brushed Gershon's hair back gently from the pulp that was left of his face. His body was no longer trembling. Only his eyes, which were round and blinking in flurries, showed any movement. Jacob had seen this before. The boy would be dead in an hour, two at the most. The idiot Cragmen had done too much to him before Jacob could start his work.

"Gershon? Gershon? Can you hear me?"

He coughed a spray of bile and blood. "Just—just—take me to the Tombs already."

"Ha!" Edmund scoffed. "Little fellow fancies a stay in the Spine's finest dungeon. Thinks he'll get a nice warm bed and meal beneath the courthouse. As if they'd ever let a filthy little dwarf set foot in there."

"Quiet, you idiot!" Jacob shoved the guards away. Gershon would soon pass the point where he would feel any more pain. He was ready to yield to death, but his body was still refusing to follow the direction. He was poised to give Jacob what he needed now, but the moment would pass quickly.

"Never mind your so-called friends in your sect," Jacob whispered. "What of your mother? Don't you love her?" Another tear somehow escaped from one of Gershon's butchered eyelids. "Of course you do. You're a good son. She always said so. And a good son would see to his mother's protection—if something were to happen to him."

"She ..." was the only word he could speak through his shattered teeth.

"Surely, you've made arrangements for her. A kindly shop steward, a mason, perhaps one of the thanes, someone who will take her in."

"Can't."

"Again."

"No ..."

Gershon was hurtled over the cliff one last time. Jacob pressed himself flat against the ground and crawled up to the very edge to peer over the side. He could see Gershon's body swaying in the void, like a baited line dangling out in the depths of a vast ocean. The Chasm's air hit Jacob's face like a wave of frost. He winced at the coldness.

"Gershon?"

Another moan, weaker and distant this time.

"I can take you up to the Tombs now. Would you like that?"

A long pause, and then a voice, racked in pain, rose from the depth below:
"My lady—"

"I will see that she is taken care of, I promise."

"—help me."

"I will. But first I have to know. Where is she? Where's your mother?"

"Mother?"

"Yes, your mother. Where can I find her?"

"Elon."

Jacob's face drew tight. Gershon was gasping for breath.

Meyers bent over and asked:

"One more, sir?"

Jacob shook his head and slowly stood up. He dusted his clothes off and wandered back toward the pale glow of the men's lantern, lost in his thoughts.

"Well?" Edmund grunted as he walked by. His face was mopped with sweat.

"Cut him loose," Jacob replied.

"Finally."

Edmund found a place where the rope's strands were worn and spindled from being pulled back and forth over the rock's edge. Then he drew a dagger and cut it through. The taut end of the line whipped away into the dark and vanished without a sound. If Gershon knew of his coming fall, whether he held any fear or gratitude for his fate, he kept it to himself. Only the men, Jacob, and a cut off bit of rope tied to an old stake remained now. Their business was finished.

Jacob handed out three copper coins to each of the men. Meyers bobbed his head, while Edmund shoved his into a pouch on his belt. Then Jacob started for the stairway. He was ready for that drink now.

"So, all this bother was over the brat's mom," Edmund clicked his tongue and leered. "She must be a real charmer. Who is she?"

"I have no idea," Jacob answered without looking at him. He started to uncork the aleskin. It was sorely needed now, every drop of beer that was left in it. Jacob rubbed worriedly at his temples and then added: "From everything I'd heard about Gershon, she raised a good boy. Fell in with a bad crowd from the Gutters, but he's still a good boy … And good boys never stray far from their mothers."

CHAPTER NINE

A FORGE SONG SHAPES the air. It binds together the pulse of bellows blowing out their scorched breath, the grunting heave and strain of the workers toiling in the half-light of molten metal, the crackle of fire, the soft hiss of steam. Its melody joins voices, and clinking hammers, tongs and anvils, around the harmony of a furnace, which is at the heart of it all.

Elon, the King of the Inner Realm, leaned back in his chair, letting the sound wash over his senses. A bronze goblet of wine, hardly touched, lay within his reach, as his fingers drummed in time against the table's edge. He was seated on a towering platform made of oak beams overlooking a deep recess in the cavern floor. At the center of the inlet was a furnace that was fed by countless tributaries carved into the stone, each of which carried a vein of bright, flowing magma. A small crowd of nephil raised their voices together. While they sang, they each pulled in unison on an end of chain that was fastened to a hanging system of wenches and pulleys. Slowly, they drew what looked like a small hill of glowing iron from within the furnace's grate. It was like watching a birth.

"Look at that! Will you look at that? Brings back memories, eh?" Elon beamed at his guest. A broad smile creased the corners of his mouth into wrinkles. They looked like merry fissures breaking through a honey-stone façade.

Nicodemus, who had just swallowed a spoonful of piping tuna from his plate, simply grunted. Elon said something more, but the sounds of metal pinging erupted from the work floor as a dozen hammers began beating out the metal's infirmities. Most of his words were drowned in the din. Still, Nicodemus knew, without hearing a thing he said, the king was reminiscing—and in glorious spirits. For a moment, he almost seemed a real king, a king of old, not the vassal to the Crest to which his family had been reduced.

The hammers rang clear and loud, sending waves of sparks through the air like flecks of sunlight, and then, gradually, grew still. A noise rent the air. They were pouring buckets of water over the metal—"giving it a drink," the old-timers called it—to prepare it for the work that would come next. An enormous work that would unleash the skills of a hundred smiths and armorers.

Elon swung around in his chair looking perfectly content.

"Just like you promised, Divinity. I've been blessed."

Nicodemus made the sign of the gods. He brought his finger to the bridge of his nose, pointed at the ceiling, and muttered, "So mote it be." Then he took another bite of the tuna.

"By the gods, just listen to the old songs … Mm. I spent most of my boyhood on that floor, you know. Lugging tools. Fetching buckets. Only when I came of age, grew to my full height, then I got to work the valves." He made a motion with his fingers, like twisting a knob. "You had to get the levels, the mixtures, just right. You'd flood the whole forge with magma if you weren't paying attention. It was hard work. I was the king's son, but I tell you, I never got a lesser load. Or less of a lashing, when it was called for."

"I'm sure," Nicodemus nodded.

"Abidan was the worst," Elon winked. He took a drink of his wine.

"Oh?"

"Gods, yes! He and his little gang of cronies would chase me every chance they could, whenever the masters went on break. If they caught me, if I couldn't fight them off, I got a dunking. In coal slurry. My whole body, clothes and all, stuffed into a barrel of slurry. With my own cousin slamming the lid down hard on top of my very head."

"He didn't."

"He did."

"The spawn," Nicodemus shook his head and chuckled.

"That's not all. When I'd finally wriggle my way out, all drenched and black as a gull's ass, the bastards would start to shout, 'Orc! Orc!' and chase me some more."

"Ha!"

"You laugh. But the forgemen—even old Reuben—would drop whatever they were doing to join the chase and give me a thumping. 'Get the orc!' I can still hear it. I'd beg Samson to save me, beg him to— he's my sworn bodyguard, after all—but he'd just laugh and tell me to toughen up." Elon's face caught the orange light of the melted rock that was flowing in the channels through the forge. He watched the work unfold before him.

"I've been blessed," he said again.

"That you have, Majesty."

They sat awhile, enjoying their private feast, exchanging stories and old jokes. The only interruptions came from the stony voices down in the forge hollering over the bellows and the clink of tools on anvils. Eventually, though, Elon and Nicodemus came to a lull in the pleasantries and Nicodemus could study his host more closely. A stout but graying ruler, too young to remember much of the priests and the temples; yet, too old to be ignorant of what his people had been in those days. And now, no less than when he was a child being chased and whipped across a shop floor, a restless spirit. That was what all this forge work was to Elon, Nicodemus reflected: action for the sake of movement.

"Well, that was a lovely meal," Nicodemus complimented, wiping his mouth with a napkin. "Good food. Good work. Hopefully, good fortune. I'm sure you're making some fine—well, what exactly are you making?"

A mischievous grin spread across Elon.

"A wondrous surprise," he tapped the side of his head. Nicodemus knew better than to press him for details, although he was curious. This went far beyond the modest investment he had coaxed from the king to outfit the delve.

"Well, whatever it is you're making," Nicodemus said, "I'm sure you'll be paid handsomely. Once the silver and gold come pouring in from the delve. Yes, the days ahead hold many blessings for you, Elon. The gods willing, of course."

"The gods willing," Elon repeated. He took a drink and fixed Nicodemus with a serious expression: "Divinity, can I ask you something?"

"Of course, my son."

"In the old days before the Treaty. Were the gods so—so confusing?"

Nicodemus met that with a puzzled look. Elon tried to explain, "I mean were their messages ever, I don't know, gibberish? Or would that be some sin of their messenger? I just don't know."

Elon scooted his chair closer to Elon's.

"Speak plainly."

Elon took another drink of wine and dropped his voice low:

"I have always respected your ministry, Divinity. But—well, it's no secret—I hate the Treaty. I'll never allow that men—*men*, of all creatures—can say who can or can't speak for the gods."

"I agree," Nicodemus whispered.

That seemed to take Elon by surprise.

"I-I would have thought—"

"—many of our folk would think that, too. But none who know me very well. The gods will speak to whomever they wish. And if they choose to converse with an ordained cleric, or a tavern wench, or a king's son tarred in coal slurry—"

"—they're not talking to me."

"My point is, they speak to those of *their* choosing, not ours. Certainly not men's." Nicodemus gave him a long, sideways glance. "Do you suspect the gods are speaking?"

"I—yes." He closed his eyes and nodded. "I believe they are."

"To Merari, Gershon, and Kohath?"

"Yes, Divinity. To them. They don't just preach sermons—no offense, Divinity."

"None taken."

"They have dreams. And prophecies. They've predicted things that come to pass. I think I even saw one of them perform a miracle."

"Tell me about that."

A light gleamed within Elon's eyes. He leaned forward and spoke eagerly.

"When I decided to reopen the forge, there was nothing to build from. The channels had been blocked for years, and the furnace was just a skeleton. Before we could light the first fire, we had to find the valve caps for the magma channels. But they were scattered all over the Realm, and no one knew how to recast them. They were diamond, you know."

"Yes, I remember your father hiding those during the Overthrow, along with his arms. A wise precaution."

"Except Old Storm Eye never bothered to tell anyone where he put them before he up and died. So here I am ready to rebuild, and no one has a clue where any of the damned caps were. We looked everywhere. Tore the Gutters apart. I figured they must have been lost and was about to call off everything when along comes this Merari. This quiet, nameless carpenter comes shuffling into my outer hall one evening just as I was leaving. He looks like his own shadow's spooked him, but what does he hand me? All ten of the missing caps. Found them in his pocket, he said."

"Really?"

"So, he said. Lad takes off his trousers one night, and in the morning, he's got artifacts that my father had buried sixty years before he was born."

"Unbelievable."

"That was a miracle. Surely. Wasn't it?"

"Was it?"

"I think it must have been. Only—"

"—only you can't be sure. Because there's no one left to vet such things."

"I thought, perhaps ... You might?"

Nicodemus took a deep breath, inhaling the scents of ash, and sweat, and sulfur. A cloud of smoke and steam rose to the platform, carrying with it a wave of heat. When it passed, a servant clambered up the wooden steps to refill their goblets. Nicodemus drank deeply. The wine was chilled and refreshing in the stifling air of the forge. The king was watching him expectantly.

So, this was the reason for the invitation to supper.

"You've taken a risk," Nicodemus remarked.

"I have," Elon agreed.

"I can't imagine what it must have cost to rebuild the old forge. And feeding all these workers. All this steel. Good steel, too, from the look of it."

"It cost all my father's fortune," Elon replied evenly, "and then some."

Nicodemus's eyes rounded. Elon was always impetuous, and the prospects of the delve had stirred the king's excitement ever since Nicodemus had planted the idea in his head. But his entire fortune? That was a wager that went far beyond anything Nicodemus had preached.

It was plain Elon would say no more, not here at least.

"I wish you good fortune, then," Nicodemus bowed.

They finished their meal, and a new shift of forge workers, fresh-faced and clean, bustled onto the floor to relieve the ones working the furnace bellows, who were, to a one, flushed red beneath soot, and grime, and sweat. Though certainly exhausted, the crew that had just finished their shift lingered to mingle with their newly arrived colleagues a while, laughing, and griping about their pains, their families, the food they got. There was life in the work down there.

"Divinity?"

"Yes, Majesty?"

Elon drew a deep breath.

"Would you come—to meet some friends of mine?"

Nicodemus slid his hand over Elon's and felt the strength in the king's fingers. The palms were coarse as a smithee's glove. He felt the sharp edge of a gem on a ring. Perhaps it had been his father's. Perhaps it was the last of Elon's treasure. Despite the good food, the wine, the warmth and vitality of the forge, Nicodemus felt nothing but a sense of foreboding.

"Nothing would give me greater pleasure," he lied.

As giddy as a child on his birthday, that was how Elon seemed to Nicodemus as they rushed through the outer hall of Elon's court. A spacious but informal chamber, the hall served as a place where Elon's clerks, guards, and servants, or anyone hoping to present a petition to the king without an appointment, could congregate. It was almost empty now with the stoves along the walls all dimmed and the bronze doors to his inner apartments shut and locked. Elon hurried Nicodemus over to a low doorway in a far wall, passing only one silver-haired fellow who bowed deeply and then returned to contentedly strumming on an old fiddle and talking to himself.

"Sorry about all the secrecy," Elon apologized under his breath for what must have been the fifth time. He slipped a key into the door's lock.

Nicodemus patted him on the shoulder. "I understand," he whispered.

The door swung inward, and the two of them passed into what might have been a narrow service tunnel or a long closet. The place was filled with coal bins, brooms, bracings, and dripping pipes all along the ceiling that ended in what looked like a faded portrait propped on the floor that covered much of the far wall. Elon quickly closed the door behind them and toed his way around all the clutter. He spoke in a normal voice for the first time.

"I am sorry, Divinity," he repeated, "that we can't just sit down and talk out in the open. But, well, some in my court don't think much of the sect, and if anyone saw you with them it would travel beyond my realm. It might even reach, well ..." His voice trailed off.

"I understand completely," Nicodemus assured him. No need to spoil his Majesty's excitement with the reminder that he, the supposed king of his realm, was also a subject of the prying eyes and ears of the Crest.

They had left the platform above the forge with Elon's call for Nicodemus's blessing—and the utterly ridiculous announcement that he, the king, would "now accompany his Divinity home" so that they could join their prayers in Nicodemus's personal sanctuary for the forge's success. A clever touch, even if it was a trifle clumsy in its execution. Since then, they had kept to old, abandoned passages in a very roundabout route to reach this storage room. Nicodemus was grateful for the rare display of discretion on Elon's part. It was as much for Nicodemus's protection as his Majesty's. Though Nicodemus still had no idea where Elon could be taking him.

"Can never find the other point," Elon muttered, scanning the portrait closely. Nicodemus came closer and peered over Elon's shoulder to examine an unfinished picture of Elon's father, Zebulun. Even without all the details, the artist had captured the old king's guarded gaze and his stoic demeanor perfectly on the canvas. Old Storm Eye, they used to call him: as deep, and as inscrutable, as the ocean. Nicodemus noticed that the fore and middle fingers of one of the painting's lowered hands were extended at a slightly odd angle.

"Ah, there it is," said Elon. He reached out, as if to embrace his father's touch, and carefully brushed two of his fingertips against the portrait's. A brief shimmer ran across the canvass, Storm Eye's face rattled silently, and the outline of a square within the painted king's torso emerged and creaked open on a hinge. Part of the wall behind the painting opened with it and revealed a hole. The sweet smell of incense came billowing out of the entrance before them. Elon paused at the threshold:

"This place," he explained quietly, "was the last that my father ever built. He always wanted a sanctuary for his court, but then the Overthrow happened, and he couldn't have it dedicated. When the time's right, I'm going to open it properly. We've set it up as best as anyone could remember how. We tried. I hope it won't, well, offend you."

Nicodemus promised he could not possibly be offended, and followed Elon into a long, low tunnel that ended in a circular room with a great domed ceiling.

For Nicodemus, it was like walking into the past.

"The gods be praised," the words escaped his lips, on their own.

Scores of candles flickered from bronze stands like a constellation of stars. Censers were burning rich spices. In the center was a marble altar, carved with images of his people all around its base, arms lifted, exalting what the table held: which was a goddess. Set high on a pedestal atop the altar and surrounded by fresh flowers and laurels was an alabaster statue of a goddess that Nicodemus had never seen before. She might have been one of their people, or a child of the Cragmen. Whatever subtle craft the sculptor had used to meld the two races into one figure was masterful, and a trifle unsettling.

A small group was huddled around the altar about to begin a hymn when they heard Nicodemus and Elon enter.

"He's come," Elon announced.

A small cheer went up and together they all rushed to greet Nicodemus. He recognized only a few faces, mostly women and no one of any prominence, but he could not get a word out in the commotion. He smiled uncomfortably as the congregation pressed themselves against him, trying to clasp his hand. Whatever heresy they may have fallen under, at least, Nicodemus reflected, they still held the true priesthood in esteem.

"You've come!"

"Praise the Maiden!"

"You've come!"

"Welcome to our sect!"

And over and over: "Your Divinity!"

"Yes, yes, yes," was all Nicodemus could manage to answer. Eventually, the fervor subsided and the little crowd thinned so that Nicodemus could approach the altar—where two boys stood, one wringing his hands, the other with his arms folded across his chest.

Nicodemus stretched his smile a little wider at their sight. From their age, they would have been born just before the Curse had fallen—there were few left in the realm that looked so young. They each wore plain, white woolen clothes, dust speckled around the pant legs and sleeves. Both looked underfed, and tired from the shadows underneath their eyes, the smaller of the two seemed on the verge of exhaustion. Everyone else watched, expectantly, the joy radiating from their faces.

"I'm honored to meet you," said Nicodemus. They glanced at one another, and the smaller of the two, fearing he had not shown the proper decorum, fell to his knees.

"No," Nicodemus laughed, hoisting him back up by the arms. He weighed almost nothing. "We never bow to the priest, only to the god."

"Ye-yes, your Divinity," he stammered.

"And which one are you?"

"Merari, Divinity," he mumbled into his chest.

The other looked straight at Nicodemus: "I'm Kohath."

Nicodemus examined them each with a benign, friendly expression fixed fast, and quickly took their measure. Something about these two troubled him. An air hovering about them, Kohath in particular.

"And where is good Gershon?"

The boys' heads dropped. A hush fell over those gathered; their exuberance momentarily dimmed. It was Elon who answered:

"We've not had word from Gershon for three days."

"But he'll return soon," added someone in the crowd, to which only a few murmured their agreement.

"Let us hope and pray he does," said Nicodemus. "And these must be your mothers who are beaming with so much pride?"

He introduced himself to two white-haired matrons who, when they were not dabbing away tears with handkerchiefs, were indeed smiling brightly. They each held the hand of a third woman, Gershon's mother, who was stooped and disheveled, her face partly veiled by a gray scarf. Nicodemus gently clasped her hand in his and offered a word of comfort, as that seemed the appropriate thing to do. But Gershon's mother would not be comforted until she had her child. She gave one resolute nod and returned to her chair.

Then Nicodemus turned his attention to the goddess. The alabaster reflected sparkles in the light from two paper lanterns that hung from the ceiling above her. Her likeness was striking in its duality: if she was a human girl, she would have been considered lovely; if a nephil, perhaps a little plain, but clever and resilient. It was impossible to tell which she was. There was intelligence in the face, some guile, and also a trace of haughtiness as would befit a goddess. But otherwise, she could have been any girl from any realm in the Mountain. Her hands were clenched in fists, which was unusual for an idol. A broad swath of white silk had been slung over her shoulder like a sash. Nicodemus felt an instinctive aversion to this goddess.

"So," Nicodemus said after a time, "who is she?"

"We don't know her name," Kohath answered tersely, as if the very question were inane. "Her power is beyond naming. Like her virtue. So, we call her Our Maiden. She speaks to us."

Nicodemus stood awhile at The Maiden's feet, breathing deep the incense and flowers and listening to a hymn that a few of the congregants had taken up again. His eyes strayed aimlessly over the statue, and the more he studied her, especially her face, the less he liked her. He was about to turn around when he noticed something on her foot. He leaned closer to the altar's pedestal and saw a faint outline in gray, not a vein in the stone, but from a painting. Though faded and scoured, he could see it on top of her right foot: a sword, pick, and hammer, the seal of the Commonwealth.

"Didn't expect to see one of those."

"Eh?" Elon had wandered next to Nicodemus to see what he had been staring at. "Oh, the damn Crest symbol. My artisan did the best he could there, but, well, the men had been using the stone as some kind of a signpost, if you can believe it. Perfect alabaster all scrawled up in paint. He got everything else brushed out, but that last spot's like a tattoo. I told him just make sure to keep it on her feet then."

"Subversive. I applaud it." Then he asked Merari: "But tell me, how did you come to learn of her?"

Merari stole a nervous glance at Elon.

"It's alright," Elon answered, "he's a priest. Tell him."

The boy nodded, gathered his thoughts, and told Nicodemus of his dreams. His voice was flat, and he kept his eyes downcast, as if he could hardly bring himself to look at Nicodemus when he spoke. He tended to stammer over the recollections that were vague or confusing, which were many. Still, Nicodemus listened closely and, as the telling went on, nearly lost his count of time he became so entranced. Nothing within the sanctuary stirred while Merari gave his testament, except the smoke of the incense or an occasional cough from one of the congregants. When he had finished, Nicodemus sat in silence for a long time, deep in contemplation beneath the shadow of the Maiden. His finger tapped absently against his upper lip. Then he asked for Kohath's story. But he was contemptuous of having to recount "his revelation" to Nicodemus, and so had little to add; though what he did speak of seemed to hold a darker aspect than Merari's telling. At last, Nicodemus spoke, softly so that only the boys could hear him:

"She says nothing else in any of these dreams?"

"She says enough for us to know her," Kohath replied.

Merari trembled. "I-I wish sometimes she would say more—or leave me alone. I call out to her. Beg her. The shadows swirl around and around, but I know that if she leaves, they'll come crashing down on me. I-I try …"

"Go on."

"Sometimes I try to reach out to her. But as soon as I'm about to touch her, she becomes—like a wall."

"What kind of wall is it, Merari?"

"I think—I think it must be a mirror. Because then I just see myself, alone, and the shadows are coming. The mirror flies away. Then I wake up."

Nicodemus turned to Kohath.

"My shadows," he said, rubbing his neck, "they're all dragons. And they bite. The Maiden will burn them away, though."

Merari was nearly as pale as his goddess' statue and shaking all over now. The poor boy was haunted, that was plain.

"Dreams can be confusing, and troubling," Nicodemus said evenly, placing his hand on top of Merari's curled hair to bless him. He left Kohath alone and returned to the altar and the statute of this goddess, all the while feeling the eager stares of the congregants' eyes—particularly Elon's—on his back.

It was a shame. He relished the feel of the place—the memories of the temples it evoked in him—even if he didn't care for the statue it honored. Somehow, Elon had restored the mirror image of what would have been a grand shrine before the Overthrow. The right incense, the pews and chairs set in the style of a forum, even the placement of the tapers was perfect. Perhaps he remembered more from the old days than Nicodemus had suspected.

Nicodemus inhaled a deep breath of the flowery smell and felt a sudden longing for the marble water pedestal in his private chamber, the one that the temple priests had once used for their scrying. Not that he would have known what good the thing could have possibly done here. It was simply a conviction that it might have been wise to show these people a ritual from the old ways. The calm water in the pedestal was said to reveal the gods' desires. Scrying was an elaborate ceremony when done in public, a sound and settled tradition within the established precepts of the old faith.

The true faith, he reminded himself. Which allowed for new deities (that was how the pantheon had once grown to fill the Mountain, after all), but only ones the priests could understand—and name. Nicodemus frowned at what Kohath had told him about this Maiden. Only once, had there ever been an unnamed god in the Mountain; and that brief apostasy had not ended well for anyone.

"All-knowing Father," he mouthed the words so that they could not be heard except by Nord, "give me … discernment."

He did not know what else to ask for. The little congregation in his old king's unfinished sanctuary was still watching him. At last, he turned his back to the altar to face them, opened his eyes and smiled, and held his arms out, as if to embrace them.

"My children," Nicodemus declared in his best sermonizing voice, "I shall pray for you all."

Somehow Elon kept his fingers from clamping fast to turn the valve wheel, but only just. The anticipation of what would happen, what was about to be unleashed, once he turned it had him on the point of bursting. He smiled at the spoked little circle. Such a marvel. That so much power could be restrained by something so small and subtle. A joyful laugh bubbled up at the thought.

Elon was on the forge floor standing underneath a curtain of dangling chains with the back glow of channeled magma casting all who had gathered there in a light reminiscent of a hearth fire. He was smeared from head to toe in soot and sweat, and his teeth shone as bright as pearls. The crew surrounding him looked much the same, though a few had to hold themselves up by hanging onto the chains or leaning against posts. They were all panting, and the forge had been stoked until it felt as hot as a fever.

His thumb brushed across the valve wheel's polished edge, which somehow felt cool to the touch. A churn of molten rock gurgled up as steam. A soft hiss of air breathed out from the bellows. Otherwise, the forge was silent. And pregnant with anticipation.

Like the moment before a child is allowed to tear the wrapping paper from a gift, he thought. Elon could have stretched it on forever, but he knew he should say something before he turned the wheel. They had worked so hard these past weeks; they deserved to see the gift, at long last.

"Well, boys," Elon began. "It's been a warm piece of work, I know. Bet you're eager to see the payoff now, eh?"

There were several murmurs, and even a few good-natured curses, and everyone was nodding their head or pumping a gloved fist high into the air. One of the foremen standing in the rear happened to also be a bodyguard of Elon's. He was tall, older than Elon, but still had a chest as broad as a set of bellows. His name was Samson.

"We got a pool going, Majesty," Samson cupped a hand to his mouth, though his voice was loud enough to fill the entire forge. "Three-to-one odds says it'll explode."

The blacksmith standing next to Samson, Tubalcain, grinned even wider:

"And two-to-one odds that you will."

Elon joined in their laughter.

"Did you bet on me or against me, Samson? No matter, let's hope I can beat all those odds," he grinned. Then he grew serious for a moment.

"Remember, you're still bound by the oath of secrecy when we made this bargain. I'll release you all from it soon, I promise. You can shout across the Realm what we've done here—just not quite yet."

Samson, Tubalcain, and several others brought their forefingers before their faces in the sign of the gods. They had not even whispered to their wives what it was they were working on in Elon's forge; in fact, the women had their own pool going concerning what their husbands were really up to in the Gutters.

Elon bowed his head, hastily mumbling a prayer for success, and when he reached the end, paused. He thought about it only a moment, then making up his mind, whispered:

"In the name of the Maiden, be it so."

No one else heard him, but seeing their king in prayer, they had all bowed their heads or touched amulets they wore to their gods.

Then, his smile gleaming once more, Elon grasped the little valve wheel and turned it hard to the left.

There was a deep, groaning noise, as if the Mountain was letting out a long, tired grunt, and a geyser of steam erupted from one of the channels. Seeing it, Elon quickly worked one of the other controls, and it dissipated as quickly as it came. The magma dimmed its light, the glow fading into little more than a hazy gray light, as all the forge workers watched the channels with mounting excitement.

Then the magma changed the direction it had been flowing.

There was a cheer, but no time for celebrating yet, as Elon leaped from the valve and rushed over to where another cluster of chains hung from the ceiling. Pulling hard on one of them, another grating noise, this one of gears grinding on metal groaned from deep below. Elon leaned his head precariously over a ledge near one of the channels and peered down a long black hole.

A rivulet of orange molten rock was now advancing steadily towards it.

Elon nodded and stood back up. The rest of the forge workers gathered around behind him, and Samson rested his hands on his shoulders. They watched, as inch by inch the flaming liquid advanced closer to the lip of the hole. It was like witnessing the opening bow before a dance, a dance between light and dark, heat and cold. And then, at last, they came together, and another blast of steam and sound burst forth from the pair's joining.

Perfect. Tubalcain, Samson, and the other old-timers all agreed the thing had been done perfectly.

"That's a proper baptism," Tubalcain declared solemnly before he roiled off a volley of curses at all the younger workers who had voiced their agreement but couldn't have possibly lived long enough to have ever seen a forge work being baptized.

"Let's see it," they all urged.

Samson handed Elon a pair of heavy gloves with a nod. It was his right to be the first. Elon stuffed his hands into them and then began pulling down a thick chain with a hook at its end, which he dropped down into the hole. He lowered it further until it felt about the right depth. The metal of the chain links was soon glowing red. Just like he remembered Abidan showing him when he was a child, Elon swung the chain back and forth, back and forth, until the hook on the end had latched. Then, grunting, Elon heaved the chain back up hand over hand.

At first, he couldn't feel anything more than the weight of the hook, and as the chain's links reappeared, a mounting dread crept into Elon's stomach. What if the steel hadn't been cured long enough, or the heat from the magma was too great, or too mild? What if the parts his men had fashioned had all simply—fallen apart? No one had done this kind of work in years. What if he had bankrupted his kingdom—for a melted slab of iron? Only now, at this moment, did Elon come to realize the audacity of his wager.

There was a metallic clank, and all his worry melted away.

"You've got it," Samson yelled. Forgetting himself for a moment, he clapped Elon hard between the shoulders. The forge hands erupted in another cheer.

But when the hook finally reappeared, when what it bore emerged at last from the hole, another silence fell over the entire forge. The bellows went quiet, and even the rumbling of the Mountain's magma steadied. The workers dropped to their knees in reverence. Only Elon and Samson stood before the black metallic shape that loomed over them, the figure of a nephil man suspended on a chain.

A suit of armor, its parts connected and coursing with the Mountain's fire, had been born. A thousand plates of steel woven perfectly together as muscle, sinew, and skin. Within the body, hidden deep, the steam and power of the magma had been bound in a labyrinth of tubes and hoses. The armor pulsated from where it hung. It needed only a helm. But that would come when the Mountain deemed that it was time. Along with many more.

"Your dad," Samson whispered, "and Abidan. They'd be proud. Real proud."

Elon's mouth opened and shut. He no longer felt the scalding heat in the palms of his hands, or the aching in his arms and shoulders from pulling the chain. This was more than joy. Elon wiped a tear from the corner of his eye with his elbow. At last, he nodded.

"I've been blessed."

CHAPTER TEN

J ACOB STOOD BEFORE the gateway of the empty cavern, fighting to control his features. He was perplexed. Perplexed and genuinely frightened, and neither sensation was one he had much experience with. Behind him, Oliver and a troop of men mustered from the Crag waited, muttering among themselves and making more noise than was possibly needed. In the pale glow of the gulleystars they brought, the men would have looked like a simple gang of Crag workers, dressed all in rough aprons, smocks, homespun pants, and draping shirts, with stubble on their faces and dirt on their hands and underneath their fingernails. Even Oliver had left his ridiculous hat at home and replaced it with a simple hood. But the rose color in their cheeks and tanned noses would have given away the lie of their appearance; so, too, would the chainmail they wore beneath those clothes and the long pikes they carried, disguised to look like lantern poles.

"Are you sure this is the right place?"

Oliver was smirking, Jacob could feel it without looking behind him. A couple of his men, his "tunnel rats" as he called them, snickered. Jacob did not answer but scanned the gateway once more. He could almost hear that final, sad note of the delvers' hymn still lingering in the air. His eyes roved over the symmetry of the arch, its jointless arc, the perfectly smoothed and polished stone, but they kept returning to the same place.

The wide and beckoning blackness of the tunnel within.

The iron door was open. Not cracked, or partly pushed in, but thrown open as wide on its hinges as it could swing, as if inviting these newly arrived guests in the cavern to come inside and see what lay in store for them. Jacob pressed his fingers tight around the metal dowel key. Perhaps he had only imagined locking the door before he had returned to the Gutters? Perhaps he had been careless.

He shook his head. No, the gate should have been locked, just as he had left it.

"Because if this is the right place," Oliver continued, "I must say, I'm not impressed with how your people secure your tunnels." He passed his hand back and forth through the open air of the gateway. "I expected more of a barrier. What with the fame of dwarven craftsmanship."

That was met with a round of laughter. Jacob felt his face flush. But he could not allow Oliver, or any of these men, Crest-born or not, to see him flummoxed. Too much was at stake. He let out a quiet breath and looked down at the floor when he caught a glimpse of something. His eyes narrowed, and he crouched down to grasp it.

"It's the right place," he answered at last. Then he turned and showed Oliver what was in his hand.

It was a piece of the seal from the warrant he had opened. Jacob explained what it was, and the two gazed at it for a long while, each pursuing his line of thoughts.

"You're certain you locked it."

"Positive."

Oliver held his nose up at the open gateway, as if sniffing at the air. He clicked his tongue against the roof of his mouth.

"Well. Someone must have gotten here before us," he finally declared. "Someone with a talent for opening locked doors. One of your people?"

"Don't be ridiculous," said Jacob. "They're bound by the Treaty. *My* people do not break our oaths."

"And *my* people do not know how to break your locks," Oliver replied.

Jacob pursed his lips, a sharp retort weighed on his tongue, but then he thought better of it. The wax in his hand felt heavy. He stuffed the shard back into his pocket. He took a few tentative steps beneath the gateway's arch and looked deep into the darkness. Nothing but the floor tiles and columns as far as he could see. He let out his breath, softly so the men wouldn't hear it, and then he went inside.

"Do be careful, now," Oliver called after him.

Jacob ignored him. In the distance, perhaps a hundred yards ahead, he thought he spotted four shapes within the shadow of a wall that were neither rocks nor pillars. He found himself trotting, then running down the long corridor. His feet skidded to a halt, sending up a small cloud of dust.

There, sitting upright against the wall, were Asher, Gad, and Suriel. Fully clothed, their gear neatly clasped to their belts or stowed against the wall, they looked perfectly calm and at rest, as if they were in a deep slumber. Seated slightly apart from them, Abidan sat, cross-legged, with his eyes shut.

A soft, amber glow shone from Abidan's face. His companions, however, were as gray as the stone beneath them. All of them were dead.

Jacob extended his hand toward the light's penumbra about Abidan's head, and feeling no heat, withdrew it. He whispered their names, waited a moment, and stooped down to look more closely at the bodies. Not a mark or a bruise showed how any of them might have died. But they each bore a faint smile. Abidan looked like he might have just heard a joke, while Suriel's insolence had vanished completely; he could wake up any moment in a fine and friendly mood. If he weren't dead.

"I like you much better now," Jacob said to him. He carefully leaned Suriel's body forward so that he could look inside his pack. "Still plenty of food left. And there's some mead in that skin you so carefully hid from the others, I'll bet. Of course there is … So. Care to tell me why you're dead?" Suriel's heavy lips remained frozen, content to keep their secrets. Jacob glanced around. "Or what happened to your thane that he's glowing like a gulleystar? No? Nothing to say? That's not like you at all, Suri. Death's improved your manners tremendously."

Jacob heard a sound behind him. A light bobbed up and down and slowly approached from the entrance. Oliver's sword hilt was banging on his belt and the sound of poles tapped against the floor right behind him, as Oliver and two of his guards almost walked into Jacob.

"Down here, tunnel rats," Jacob sneered and gave them all a good start.

"Oh! Where are you?"

"Right here."

Oliver swung his lamp around in a wide circle, trying to get his bearings, until he noticed Jacob stooped by the wall. Both guards held their gulleystar lamps overhead, and in their glow revealed Jacob kneeling before the corpses.

"Hello, there," Oliver greeted Jacob. "Doesn't look like they got very far. Did they suffocate?"

"In an open, ventilated passage? I doubt it." Jacob snapped Suriel's pack closed and slid it back underneath the body's arm. "They had plenty of stores. There's no sign or smell of any sickness."

Oliver nudged his toe into Gad's side. "This one was a bit of a porker. Maybe too much dwarfish ale did him in. Hey, is that one glowing?"

To Jacob, it was as clear as fire what Abidan was doing, but he responded that if he was, it was very faint. Then Jacob stood back up. The two guards were starting to poke around the place, so Jacob snapped at them to keep still. He could see things the men would miss, and he wanted to examine all there was before they wrecked the tunnel, stumbling about.

Only there was nothing to see.

No footprints, no scrapes on the wall, no sign of why these four delvers had died or how their bodies had come to be returned—for he was sure they had not died here—or when. No sign at all of what—oddity—had befallen Abidan. Jacob was at a loss.

"So," Oliver bent a knee to prop his foot on the wall behind him.

"So."

"A note is—"

"—out of the question."

"Indeed," Oliver agreed. He clicked his tongue. "Indeed, it is. I suppose we ought to, just, proceed as planned. As best as we are able."

Jacob let out a long, frustrated sigh. The contingencies were now spinning worryingly fast and out of control, and multiplying. Oliver had no grasp of half of them, but he did have a point.

"As best as we are able," Jacob nodded. He examined the bodies one last time and cast a long, searching look down the corridor. "Alright, then," he said. "Do it."

"The boys were expecting a fight. Some were hoping for it."

"They'll still be paid."

Oliver nodded slowly and then glanced across his shoulder.

"What about the door?"

"It's—open," Jacob answered absently. "Doesn't matter how. So long as it stays that way."

"Let's hope it does, warden."

Jacob wandered back to the gateway, his hands stuffed in his pockets, fingering the key and the piece of the wax seal. Deep in his thoughts, he vaguely heard the noises of Oliver's men beginning their work behind him—blades ripping into flesh, rocks crushing bones, a hoot and a whistle, peals of laughter. The rest of the guards rushed past him to join the fun. While the men reveled and spread their debris throughout the tunnel, Jacob sat down on the floor beneath the shadow of the open iron door and contemplated its meaning, alone. Then, without another sound, he got up and started for home.

Jacob ran faster to catch up, his medallion bumping up and down against his chest. His thoughts were flying in a hundred scattered directions as he hurried after Elon, Samson, and a new team of nephil delvers through the long and winding corridor. They had not stopped since they set out from the Gutters, but only Jacob seemed to have felt the strain from the long journey.

The week had passed, and the appointed time had come to meet Abidan's delvers at the gateway. Elon had insisted upon coming. They would come upon the gate after the next turn in the passage.

The most important thing, Jacob kept reminding himself, was to convey shock—genuine shock—but without too much emotion. An overflow of sorrow from one widely regarded as having no soul would arouse suspicion. Perhaps like the surprise, he felt when he discovered the gate was still open; that might do as a good reference. Which brought Jacob back to wondering about that gate, and how he would manage Elon once events unfolded. His Majesty could be notoriously volatile. Handling him would be … a challenge.

Jacob was so wrapped in his planning that his features began to follow his feelings. He didn't realize how careworn his face must have looked.

"Why so glum, warden?" Elon had stopped in the middle of the corridor. His hands were in his hips and a ridiculous grin spanned the entirety of his travertine face. "It's me who's lost a pile if this delve's a bust. You'll come out ahead either way, I'm sure. As always."

The others had laughed at all the king's jokes, but this one at Jacob's expense earned the heartiest response yet. Jacob retorted with a forced chuckle and at once returned his face to the expression of bland indulgence he usually carried around Elon. But with the slightest downturn of the corner of his mouth, Jacob shared an unspoken remonstrance—in his cheer, his Majesty was letting slip a hint about their bargain that he ought not to have.

Elon changed the subject.

"Samson," he said, turning to his bodyguard, "I hope you've got enough hands lined up at the forge to work a river of silver."

"I've got the hands. Have you got the space? We bring home much more metal, and we'll need to start stowing all these pretty new, uhm, platters you've got us forging underneath your throne."

That brought an even wider smile to Elon.

"I hope so," he replied. "You can never have enough platters."

They walked on briskly through the last passage, where a chillness in the air greeted their arrival. Though they could all see well enough, it seemed to grow darker the further they went. The passage opened into a cavern of high, looming walls. The gateway was at the far end.

The group came to a halt.

"Hey—" Elon squinted ahead. "Wasn't there supposed to be—?"

His companions were gaping at the wall ahead. Jacob's face went pale.

There was no need for him to feign his reaction; the shock was genuine.

The iron door was gone.

A door that had been the size of a keep's entrance, vanished without a trace, mark, or scratch on any of the smooth border stones or walls around where it once stood. Even the hinges were missing and the holes that should have been drilled deep into the stone were nowhere to be found. It was as if the mightiest gate that had been hung on the day of the Treaty—had never been.

"Wait, it-it was—it was there," Jacob started. "The door was right there. I opened it myself."

"Maybe Abidan got greedy for the metal," Samson tried to joke, but no one would laugh. There was menace in this place.

"Follow me," Elon ordered, and he hurried into the corridor beyond the gate. His men ran after him, and Jacob followed behind, his wits now entirely struck from him. As he passed beneath the arch, a shiver went through his chest. The open void, the emptiness that was in here with them, it felt like—a presence. Jacob shook his head, chiding himself for holding a sentiment he would have ordinarily condemned.

As soon as he crossed the transom, he heard a piercing scream.

It was followed by a roar of curses; someone fell into sobbing.

Jacob crept forward slowly, trying to summon some cogent thought, a plan, an idea, of what he should do, but the hole where the gate had stood had driven out everything from his head. He knew what the others had found; and that these first few minutes would be vital. Jacob drew closer to the sounds of the cries. One of the delvers noticed Jacob's approach and scowled. His bottom lip quivered. All the man could do was point angrily to the ground. As if accusing it.

Jacob's eyes quickly took in the scene, and he knew at once there would be complications.

The men had staged the slaughter badly. It was too much, far too much.

Scattered across the ground, now stained black with their blood, pieces of Suriel, Gad, and Asher had been hacked and set up in a macabre display. Their hands and feet had been cut off and lined up in rows. One of their torsos—it had to be Asher's—had been stripped naked and stuffed inside Gad's gutted body. Nearby, there were pieces of broken tools. A long reaper's blade, a saw, some picks. Samson was holding up a shearing knife close to his nose, a disgusted look on his face. A guild-mark was embossed on every one of the blades, right in the center, like an emblem.

In the midst of one of the puddles of blood sat Elon.

Elon, who moments before had been childlike in his mirth, had collapsed in the slurry of dust and gore. He was shaking violently, unable to speak, perhaps even breathe. His mouth opened again and again but made no sound. Tears mixed with blood were smeared across his face. Clutched in his hands and pressed close against the side of his head, as if an embrace, was the severed head of his cousin. The faint expression of bliss, Jacob noticed, was still there on Abidan, even if that unnatural glow was not. At last, Elon let out a terrible cry. It came bursting forth like lava pouring from the Mountain; once begun, nothing would stop it.

The warden bowed his head.

In the end, that was the only thing that seemed right to do.

In his dream, Abidan was chasing him. Across a cluttered, darkened forge floor that extended farther and farther out the faster he ran, where all the tables, and bellows, and chains, and barrels, were all trying to trip him or slow him down. Abidan's face was contorted with fury. Elon was unable to speak or hear in the dream, but he was certain that his cousin meant to kill him. Elon spun around, holding up his hands, to plead with him to stop. The bloodied, bodiless head of Abidan hurtled toward him from the dark, screaming with silent rage, his eyes burning bright and yellow. His mouth was open as if he would devour Elon, consume him in wrath.

Darkness. But then a light. Soft, white, filling the void.

Elon stirred.

The silk of a pillow brushed against his cheek. His eyes fluttered open, and he awoke.

He was lying in the canopied bed of his chamber, bathed, and dressed in a house robe. All the blankets were twisted in knots around him.

"Sire?" Elon's chamberlain called out tentatively from the doorway and bowed low.

"Jemuel," Elon's tongue felt heavy. Then, to his horror, he realized he had lost his count. "How-how long have I—?"

"One day, twenty-one hours, eleven minutes since, uhm—"

Jemuel's face tightened and he tapped his fingertips nervously together. He was tall, thin, and, most times, patrician in his bearing. At the moment, however, he looked ashen. The chamberlain was stammering to find the appropriate words.

"Since our arrival at the gate," Elon finished for him. The grogginess was quickly dissipating, now that he had his count back. He swung his feet out of bed and motioned for a fresh set of clothes and a tureen. His whole body was covered in a film of sweat.

Elon washed his face and with each plunge of his hands into the bowl it felt like he was soaking himself in the cold bitterness that had gripped his heart. He was snarling by the time he got dressed.

"Your Majesty," Jemuel began haltingly, "we are all so, so very relieved to see you awake—and-and well. It pains me to trouble you at such a time as this. But, uhm—you have a visitor. He's been waiting all morning in your hall, praying for your recovery. Along with much of your court."

"Send him away," Elon snapped. He sunk into the sofa next to his bed.

Jemuel shut his eyes tightly, and then, with a pained expression, opened them again and replied very softly:

"I cannot, Majesty."

"Eh?"

"His Divinity has come—in his office as priest. I cannot turn away the gods' ordained clergy. I beg your forgiveness for this unfortunate impertinence, and will tender my—"

Elon growled and flicked his hand at his chamberlain.

"You're not resigning."

Elon felt another surge of anger on the brink of rolling over him, but he kept it in check. Of course, the priest would come to console. Of course, the king would have to endure it. There were pretty words that had to be spoken at a time like this, and only the priest could say them.

Empty words, like his sermons.

He let out a long breath, gathered himself together, and spoke to Jemuel with the formality expected of a king:

"Show his Divinity in."

Nicodemus stood next to Elon sharing the space and the heavy silence of the bed-chamber. He kept his mouth turned in a frown and let out a succession of heavy, sorrowful breaths. It was the kind of sympathy most of his people appreciated when they had lost one of their beloved—simple, stoic, meaningful. He had found it to be an effective ministry. But with Elon, it was like trying to give comfort to a tethered bull.

"Majesty," the priest finally began. He started to reach out to clasp Elon's forearm, but quickly withdrew his hand. The way Elon's face had flashed, the rage, it was there to see, on the brim about to billow over, as if the lightest, misplaced touch might cause it to burst. Nicodemus sighed. "There are no words."

"No," Elon agreed.

"At this difficult time, when we are beset with grief, and trouble, and confusion, and our sorrows threaten to overwhelm us, we must turn to the gods for comfort."

A bitter laugh burst from behind Elon's clenched teeth:

"Which god should I turn to? The one who ordained this sacred delve in the first place?"

Nicodemus' head dropped. He heard the sound of his words being repeated back to him, but with a vitriol that cut straight to his heart:

"'Our all-knowing father's greatness,'" Elon pretended to be giving a sermon, his voice slowly rising with mocking contempt, "'his power, his very being came from delving. That is how the true treasure is found. By delving. Great Nord now calls us to emulate his example once more. As in the old days, we must delve to rise.' Those were your words."

"I know what I said," Nicodemus replied after a while.

"It was a lie," Elon snarled.

Nicodemus' shoulders slumped. A tense quiet unfolded.

"I've made the arrangements for the delvers," Nicodemus said, his voice soft. "They've been cleaned and dressed. Given silver to hold before the pyre. I thought—well, under these circumstances, with your permission, I thought we should call out to the bones. Bring their remains home ceremoniously, as companions of the gods. It's an old ritual, hasn't been done in years, but it would seem appropriate. It might give comfort to their wives, to our people. If you wish ..."

"Do whatever you want with the bodies. They're dead now."

Waves of anger were now rolling over Elon, fiery, like bellows stoking a furnace. He rose from his sofa and held a finger up at Nicodemus.

"I staked this delve on Nord. This was his idea. Tell me, priest. Where the hell was he when my cousin was slaughtered?"

Nicodemus could say nothing.

"No answer, eh? I don't have one either." Elon began pacing around the room, lurching in sudden changes of direction. "To hell with him," he declared and spun around on his heel as if daring Nord's priest to take offense. "To hell with Nord," Elon said more loudly. "He's no more use to me than he was to Zebulon."

"Elon, I can imagine the depth of pain you must be feeling, but you—"

"Can you? Can you? Because I can't find the bottom to it!"

"In time, you'll—"

"There is no time."

Nicodemus blinked, unsure of Elon's meaning. Elon was standing still now, his hands clenched into fists:

"We were promised safe passage to delve. The men betrayed that promise. They broke their bargain."

"But can we be sure," Nicodemus replied carefully, "who was responsible for this crime?"

"Men were!" Elon nearly bellowed.

"*Which* men, though? There were guildmarks on the weapons that were found in the tunnel, were there not? I'm told the guildsmen are held to be thieves and liars. Perhaps this was simply a robbery. Tragic, yes, but not necessarily treacherous."

Elon rolled his eyes. He was about to unleash the fullness of his wrath when a scurrying noise followed by angry shouts from outside his chamber interrupted him. The door burst open and Jacob came rushing inside, still in his warden's garb (though he had wisely tucked his medallion in a pocket). Jemuel was chasing after him, screeching that his Majesty and his guest could not be disturbed for any reason.

"Majesty," Jacob panted, "I came as soon as I heard you were awake."

"Like a rat to the rot, the Cragmen's pet dwarf comes running," Elon sneered. Jemuel skidded to a halt, apologizing profusely, as he tried to grasp Jacob by the cloth of his neck. Jacob shook him off.

"I've news," Jacob announced loudly, "of your other bargain."

Elon glared at Jacob, at first uncomprehending. Nicodemus joined him.

"Forgive me, Majesty," Jemuel glowered at Jacob. "With all your guards at prayer or in mourning, I should have been more watchful for unwanted visitors—"

"—Leave him," Elon murmured.

Jemuel was taken aback.

"Sire?"

"I said leave him."

Begrudgingly, Jemuel bowed. He paused to give Jacob a full measure of his disdain and then slipped quietly back out of the chamber.

"So?" Elon grunted at Jacob.

Jacob's eyes lingered on Nicodemus who was still as shocked by the warden's unannounced appearance, as he was at Elon's tolerance of it.

"May I speak freely?"

"You mean before the trusted priest of Nord?" Elon flourished his hand. "Of course! Nothing stays hidden from his god, you know."

"Yes, that may be. But, uhm, I trust, Divinity, you'll keep this conversation in confidence? If not from your god, then at least from ears that do not need to hear of it."

Nicodemus inclined his head slightly.

"What's your news, warden?" Elon was growing impatient.

"The guilds had no part in this."

"I know that. Gods, a child could see that scene was staged."

"Yes," said Jacob, "but they may not be entirely without blame."

Now it was Elon's turn to be confused. Slowly, he sunk back down into his sofa, and Nicodemus took a chair next to him. They listened as Jacob spoke.

"While you have mourned, I have made inquiries. The guilds knew nothing about the delve, I'm sure of it. They're afraid, truth be told."

"What, that I'll not be able to keep my promise to them?"

Jacob shook his head slowly.

"That they won't be able to keep theirs to you. Your bargain with the guilds is in jeopardy." Nicodemus nearly spun in his seat, the surprise welling thick in his throat.

"You made a bargain—with *those* men, too? The guilds? Elon, what were you playing at?"

But Elon ignored him.

"I have heard," Jacob continued, "that the guilds' master of masters, or whatever it is he calls himself, was overheard to say in one of their meetings that they will find it difficult—perhaps impossible—to make the payment of your bargain. I've since confirmed it. They don't have the money."

A rumbling sound came out of Elon that were they in an open cavern, might have portended a rockslide. Jacob quickly spoke to intervene:

"I'm sorry, Majesty."

"We had a bargain!" Elon roared. "I *beggared* myself to open that forge!"

"I know you did."

Elon jumped to his feet and kicked his sofa down, shouting down curses upon all the men in the Mountain. Then he stormed across the entire length of his bed-chamber and into his closet, where he threw aside stacks of chests with a loud crash. When he returned, Elon's clothes were rent into shreds, and he was wielding a long trident.

Nicodemus recognized the weapon at once. It was Elon's father's.

The length of the shaft was twice as tall as the king who now held it, and the sheen of the metal, its mirrored surface, shed a faint, glacial glow and somehow made the space inside feel colder than it had been before. Elon's eyes were fixated, and it struck Nicodemus that the king was trying to hear something, though what it could be other than his own frightened breathing, he could not imagine.

"Murder and a broken bargain," Elon declared at last. "There must be vengeance."

"No—" Nicodemus began.

"I suppose you have no choice," Jacob agreed.

Nicodemus turned. He had not expected that at all, not from Jacob.

"When our people learn what has happened to the delvers," Jacob explained to the priest, "and, believe me, they've all already heard this news—they'll demand revenge. And rightly so."

"You-you, of all people, would counsel *war* against the men?"

"No, no, no. Not a war. But I would counsel a strong response—to save any more of our people from being slaughtered. Otherwise, we may as well proclaim to the men, 'come and kill us, we can do you no harm.' It doesn't have to come to war, though, and the response doesn't have to come from us. Listen, Majesty. I have friends in many different places in the Crest. Their stewards have worried about trouble brewing in the Crag for a long time now." He took a step closer to Elon. "If you were to recast the arms you're forging—for them. Remake the armor and weapons for the Crest, then they can rearm their soldiers. And decimate the Crag workers, and their guilds if it comes to it." He came another step closer. "I say, send the wardens your arms, and let them give us justice. You were going to sell your protection to one group of men. If they've broken their bargain, you're free to sell to a different group, the way I see it."

"By the gods' graces," Nicodemus's voice broke, and Elon turned away, "was *that* what you reopened the forge for?"

"Not originally," Jacob replied for him. "But now there's been a change in circumstances …"

Nicodemus threw his arms up in bewilderment.

"Elon, this is madness! Our people have always withheld our craft from the men—and for good reason. Because of their numbers. As long as the men are left with their rusted armor and shoddy blades, we're safe. But they'll put our swords to our throats if you give them the might of your forge."

"Why would the Crest do that, when they need us?" Jacob retorted. "No. You have a rare opportunity here, Majesty. To get paid in silver *and* in vengeance from the same buyer. That kind of a bargain will never come around again."

This was utter madness, Nicodemus wanted to shout. Instead, he tried to invoke his last hope of reaching Elon's sense of reason:

"Your father would never even consider such a course," he warned. "Yes, Zebulon withheld when the men were swarming the Realm. Yes, he sheathed his sword and took a terrible oath to save us all. But he never, *never* trusted the men to whom he made that oath. Not for a moment. You cannot give them the work of our hands. They will defile it and then kill us all with it."

"They will *use* it," Jacob countered, "for what it was meant. Nicodemus speaks of the past. This time is different. This time, the men will fight only their own." Jacob sidled even closer to Elon now, so that he was now between Elon and Nicodemus. "But only if we sell them what they need. The Crest can kill the Crag, and bring our people vengeance. It's possible. I can broker that bargain. If you'll—Majesty?"

Elon had begun to wander away, seemingly losing interest in his guests and their dire conversation. He withdrew to a tall mirror that stood at the end of his bed.

"Elon?" Nicodemus called out.

The king made no reply, but stood there quietly in his torn garments, staring at his image in the mirror. At last, Elon brought his father's trident before his eyes. Then he spoke something softly into the pronged blades, but Nicodemus could not make out his words. He might have been praying, or perhaps he was laughing to himself. But when he turned back to face them, a light shone from behind the dark circles around his eyes, and his voice sounded as ominous as a storm. To Nicodemus, it was as if his old king, the Storm Eye, had returned in the presence of his son.

"You're both wrong," Elon said.

"Majesty—" they started.

"Priest, there will be vengeance. And it won't be brokered, warden. It will come from *our* hands."

"Elon, don't," Nicodemus dropped his head into his palms, "I beg you."

"The Treaty's broken. You hear me, gods! It's done ... I renounce the Oath."

He brought the trident down hard upon the stone floor. Its echo reverberated like a peal of thunder and sent a small shower of sparks into the darkness. Elon's voice flowed after them:

"You were right about one thing, Divinity. You said the delve would ... what was it you said in your sermon? 'Stir us to faith, so the gods would stir again.' You were right. We delved. And now the gods are stirring—new gods. They're speaking from within the Mountain, and I can hear their voice as clear as a bell. We will come with vengeance."

THE CREST

CHAPTER ELEVEN

THE COURT OF Common Corrections was in session and Judge Jonathan Acacia rubbed the bridge of his nose. He was a young man for a judge, though he had always looked old for his age: thin, sallow, a slight hunch in his back from his studies, neither handsome nor plain.

The Court was an outpost within the Mountain that straddled the Crag's farthest border, it was at once a decrepit fort, a depot and warehouse, an occasional marketplace when the Crest allowed, a dungeon, and the only court of justice for all the Crag. Its towered gatehouses and teetering walls barred the only approach to the Spine, the bridge that spanned Cowan's Chasm to the entrance of the Citadel. The fort was like the dingy, snarled end to an otherwise gossamer thread, a line that bound the Crest to its two sister realms. The court's dungeon—the Tombs, most called it—was notorious.

The courthouse inside the walls was nothing more than a wide, windowless hall of mortared stone blocks. The inside had originally been painted yellow, but over the years the walls had turned into a stained, dull beige from the floor to a head's height from countless bodies that had pressed and loitered there. Threshes covered the floor, replaced, more or less regularly, every month. The only light came from pots of gulleystars in the galley and a wrought iron chandelier of candles over the judge's bench at the far end.

Jonathan ran two fingers across his brow to wipe away the sweat. There was no fireplace or hearth in the courtroom; none was needed. For the court was always stuffed with people, too many people, some in chains, all of them unwashed, unkempt, and utterly ignorant of what was happening to them. Bored looking guards in dull yellow jerkins would prod one group out, another in, the blunt ends of halberd staffs showing the way; or, if it was too crowded, a boot would work just as well. All the while, troops of clerks and a smaller contingent of commissars, all garbed in yellow tunics and yellow sashes, bustled about importantly, swarming in front of the judge's bench or back outside to the courtyard, all bearing reams of rolled-up paper like bees carrying nectar through the hive. Over all the activity, a banner of the Commonwealth's sword, hammer, and pick was draped on the wall behind the judge's high wooden chair. Immediately beneath it, faded words etched into the stone loomed ominously; and every man, woman, and child, no matter their age or learning, knew what they said:

OUR ALL FOR ALL.

A stray bang of black hair fell before the judge's face. He found himself tugging at it in frustration. The noise of all the conversations, the groans, the crying babies, angry shouts, and coughing racked in his ears.

"Is there any way they could hold it down?" he muttered to himself. "Just a little." He felt the stubble on his chin and tried to focus. The sour taste from last night's wine refused to leave his tongue, no matter how much he opened his mouth and grimaced.

Nicholas, his chief clerk, discretely slid a pitcher of water with lemon slices and an empty cup beside the judge. Careful to not spill anything on the docket papers, he poured Judge Acacia a drink.

"Thanks," the judge nodded and drained the cup in one draught.

"Certainly, your honor. If I sound the first case, that should bring court to order. At your pleasure, of course."

Nicholas tidied some of the papers around Jonathan's elbow, discretely pulling out the one that would need his attention first, which he smoothed out next to an open inkwell. Fastidious in his every word and motion, this chief clerk, but in the three months since Jonathan began his tenure as a judge, he had learned how smoothly things proceeded if he followed Nicholas' direction.

"Yeah, might as well." Jonathan poured himself another cup of water.

Nicholas slipped down the steps from the judge's bench, past a long table that seated four commissaries, which he bobbed his head towards, then shoved his way through the crowds of clerks, prisoners, guards, and onlookers until he reached a small raised dais in the center of the room. It had an arm rail around three of its sides, and everyone else in the packed courtroom avoided it as if they knew, without being told, that it was not a place for them to stand. He bowed low to Jonathan and the Commonwealth's flag, then straightened himself to his full height and called out in a high-pitched, lisping voice that immediately brought the deafening hum of the crowd down to a more modest murmur.

"The Court of Common Corrections is in session. Judge Jonathan Acacia presiding. Long live our—you there!" he pointed at an old man in shackles and filthy rags who was weeping on the shoulder of a bored-looking woman, who had nowhere else to stand. "Court's in session. Govern yourself at once, or it's back to the Tombs. That's better. Now. We've got a busy docket today, so pay attention. I will call out your cases, one at a time. When you hear your name called, you raise your hand, thus," as if he were showing a child how to behave in class, Nicholas lifted his arm straight into the air, "then you come forward, right up here onto this dais. I will announce your charges. And then, his Honor will ask you the question of whether or not you are guilty of your charges. You may admit your guilt and ask his Honor's leniency, which he may be inclined to give depending on the severity of your crimes. If you do not admit your guilt, the learned Commissar will call witnesses and bring evidence against you that will prove your guilt. His Honor will then likely impose the fullest sentence for your crimes. Govern yourselves accordingly."

The Judge scanned the courtroom. The noise had mostly died down now, and the bailiffs were getting the first defendants on the docket moved toward the front of the courtroom. The faces staring back at him were all properly resigned or withdrawn. Then he noticed a young, olive-skinned woman, very well dressed, who had just entered and was whispering to some of the prisoners as the guards prodded them past. Jonathan glanced at his clerk whose mouth curled into a frown.

Nicholas's voice rang out again. "I see we have with us today our volunteer attorney from the Crest." The woman paused long enough to make a blank face at the clerk but did not otherwise acknowledge him at all. "Welcome back. Counsel is directed to the table up here to the left of the bench, as befits her station—where she will await his Honor's pleasure. She may confer with her clients when his Honor allows it. Would you care to make your appearance for the record, Madam?"

"Miss Temple," she answered tersely and then returned to a hushed and hurried conversation with a shirtless, bedraggled looking man, whose smashed mouth and cheeks left him only able to communicate with crude hand gestures. He was frantically making a swiping motion of some sort with his palms.

"To counsel's table, if you please, Miss Temple." Nicholas gestured at the guard closest to her.

Muttering an apology, the guard took the attorney gently by the elbow and pulled her away from the shirtless man, who groaned and repeated the same enigmatic hand sign with even more fervor.

Nicholas' face pulled into a tight, deferential smile as she passed by. The guard gave her a chair next to a small table that held the day's docket on a single sheet of paper, a wooden stylus, and a bottle of dried black ink. Miss Temple stood perfectly erect and faced Judge Acacia with a defiantly bemused, expression. Then she bowed low and took her seat.

Nicholas scampered from the dais and raced back up the steps to the judge's bench to begin the court's session:

"Prosecuting commissars, make your appearances, please."

All four commissars rose together, adjusted their attire in the same fashion, and said their names, and that they were warranted to represent the Commonwealth of the Crest, Crag, and Quarter. A host of pens began scratching as they introduced themselves, the sashed clerks in their lower stations and tables scribbling down every word that was said.

"May I begin?" Nicholas whispered to Judge Acacia.

He knew the headache would recede once he got into the rhythm. But it would take a few cases to get there. He took a deep breath and nodded.

Nicholas licked the tip of his finger, turned a page in the packet of papers he held, and read in a loud, clear voice:

"Case number nineteen, eighty-four dash six, two, five, one, nine, zero, three; Commonwealth versus Jesse Noman. Jesse Noman of the Lower Ward. Jesse Noman!"

A wide-eyed, teenaged boy wearing a greasy apron and pants that were much too large for him, suddenly remembered who he was and shot his hand up with a shout, "Here, sir!"

A bailiff came over to slap him on the side of the head with a heavy glove.

"Just raise your hand and come forward," Nicholas pointed to the dais. "Unless you are asked a question, we don't need to hear your voice."

Jesse rubbed his temple where a welt was already swelling and shuffled past the glowering men and women to the little dais. To the scrawny boy, it could have been its own mountain, this little stand in the middle of the courtroom, adrift within a sea of pinched, suspicious faces and armed wardens. Somehow, he pulled himself up, shot an anxious look at the bench, and then stared at his feet. Nicholas continued:

"You are charged with violating section four hundred seventy-seven of the Commonwealth Code of Conduct, to wit ..." Nicholas brought the bundle of paper to within an inch of his nose and read more slowly, "... throughout the middle day of each week, you knowingly expropriated the just wages of others' labor in an amount less than ten pence, or an unskilled laborer's half-day of remuneration. Fourteen counts. How do you plead?"

There was a momentary lull in the noise and shuffling of the crowd, as everyone wanted to see how the first case would unfold. But Jesse only rocked from one foot to the other, twirling the bit of rope that held his pants up in his dirty fingers, not able to even blink. Jonathan shook his head, but he had seen this often enough already. When the first case was a first-time defendant, it always took a little prod to get the cart rolling.

"Noman," Jonathan's voice rasped, so he cleared his throat. "Jesse."

The boy jumped at the sound of his name. "Yes-yes, sir. Yes, your Honor?"

"Is this your first time here?"

"In-in- Craggie Court? Y-yes, sir. I never been taken up before."

"So, let me explain, for your benefit and everyone else's," Jonathan began his rehearsed speech, grateful not to have to think for the moment. "The clerk has just read what you've been charged with. You can either say, 'guilty,' and I'll probably let you off pretty light since it doesn't look like you've ever been in trouble before. Or you can say, 'not guilty.' Then we'll have a trial. That doesn't happen very often because most folks are honest and want to do the right thing. But I can give you a trial if you want one. Now. In your case, you're charged with petit theft.

Fourteen times, they're saying, you stole some money." Jonathan paused and looked over the young man quivering in the dais. "You've been working the crowd's pockets on paydays?"

"No, sir!" Jesse's eyes nearly leaped from his face. "Never. I've never picked no one's pockets. All I do midweek is run a domino table off the market—"

"Ah," Jonathan nodded his head. "I see what's happened, then. Who's got this one?" he asked the commissars' table.

One of the commissars, a fierce-looking man with a peppered beard, stood briskly.

"May it please the court," he said, "Commissar Highborough, warranted prosecutor for the Commonwealth."

"Fourteen counts of petit theft for a domino hustler?"

"He's been warned repeatedly, your Honor," Highborough retorted. "He takes up market space that has not been allocated to him. He refuses to apply for permits. And it's a game of chance, your Honor. Which, I submit, is the worst possible exploitation of a worker's labor. We have multiple witnesses."

Jonathan scratched his chin with his knuckle. "I'm sure you do." This was not at all how he wanted to start the docket.

"It's just penny-a-throw dominoes," Jesse pleaded. "It ain't stealing, I promise. As for papers, sir, your Honor, I couldn't afford the sashes' bribe to get a proper table, and nobody said it was—"

"Enough," Judge Acacia warned, and held up a hand to stifle the growing murmurs and cascading laughter around the courtroom. "We've gotten a little off track here. Jesse, what you are doing is technically a violation of the law. Gambling is a form of economic exploitation. You're taking profit off of others, but you're not working for it. So, I could punish you up to fourteen years in the Tombs—"

"No!" Jesse almost fainted, and a sick cheer went up from the crowd behind him.

"Order!" Nicholas rapped a gavel against the edge of the table.

"I said," Jonathan raised his voice, "I *could* punish you up to fourteen years, one for each count. But if you just say, 'guilty,' I'll let you off with a month of re-training and a fine."

"Really?" Jesse was practically reaching out towards Judge Acacia with open hands, as if he had been on the verge of drowning alone in the ocean but had suddenly discovered a line.

"First-time offense, sure. Why not," Jonathan pointed at Nicholas, who had already finished writing out the sentence in a margin on the docket sheet.

"Okay," Jesse nodded, and then, taking a deep breath, admitted: "Guilty."

"But your Honor," Highborough huffed.

"Calling the next case," Jonathan cut him off.

"The Crest wishes to be heard on sentencing."

"It's a kid playing dominoes."

"Respectfully, you cannot mitigate a sentence that far downward for this defendant. Section K of the Rules of Correction limits the Court's discretion to fifty percent of the maximum sentence—here, one year per crime—where a defendant is sentenced in multiple criminal cases. We have fourteen cases here. The lowest possible sentence is seven years. Respectfully, Judge Acacia, we are prepared to take this on appeal in the Crest."

Something about what the commissar said sounded off to Jonathan, and he certainly did not appreciate the remark about an appeal. The courtroom was growing restless, though. This was a horrible case to begin the docket—a penny-ante offense that was only brought because some clerk was not getting a piece of this boy's take in a rigged game of dominoes—as it was rife with complications. They should have started with a battery case: a simple tavern brawl, or a scuffle over a girl. Those always went smoothly. He needed to get the proceedings into a rhythm soon, or else he would be stuck in this chair all morning. He was about to change the sentence when Miss Temple arose:

"May it please the court?"

Jonathan rolled his eyes, even as a smirk unwittingly broke across his mouth.

"Counsel."

"Elaine Temple for Mister Noman. With all due respect to the learned commissar," she said without a trace of sarcasm, though Jonathan knew it was there, "he misreads the rule. Section K's limitation applies to multiple *cases*. Not multiple *counts* within a case. Mister Noman indeed faces fourteen counts of petit theft. But the Commonwealth has chosen to bring only one case against Mister Noman. Therefore, your Honor has complete discretion to mitigate the defendant's sentence accordingly. And," she added, "your Honor's sentence is well within the guidelines given this defendant's otherwise spotless record—as you astutely observed."

Jonathan rifled through the stacks and scrolls Nicholas had so carefully organized but gave up on finding the book he was looking for. So, he pretended to read from something else, which was, in fact, a list of his current clerks' names and duties, gave a satisfied nod, and announced:

"Counsel's argument appears to be well taken. Rule K does indeed speak in terms of cases, and we have here only one case. Noman?"

By now, the boy on the dais was trembling uncontrollably. A sickly pallor had fallen over his cheeks, and he had to hold himself upright with both arms. He squeaked an incoherent noise.

"The Court accepts your plea and sentences you to half-wages for six months and one month of hourly re-training sessions with a clerk to be assigned in due course. You need to find a new trade, young man."

"S-s-sir," his head bobbled.

"Your Honor," Highborough pressed, "may we be heard further?"

"The sentence stands as pronounced," Jonathan growled. As if to emphasize the judge's decision was final, Nicholas dashed an underline beneath his notation on the docket and promptly announced the next case. Highborough closed his eyes dramatically but sat back down, and the morning's docket in the Court of Common Corrections proceeded.

A steady flow of men and women trickled across the dais. Most were basic "shirking" offenses—workers failing to perform their assigned duties, cheating up their wages, or collecting money amongst themselves for unlicensed labor. The Craggies could be quite clever in their dealings to avoid work or a clerk's accounting. But sooner or later they always got too confident (or greedy), and someone would make a note of them. There was also the typical array of balm addicts, many of whom Judge Acacia now knew by name, who always stood out like black-mouthed skeletons, staggering through their short lives in scenes of public debauchery, shirking, battery, or, as often as not, the catch-all offense of "public disruption." Their sheets were always lengthy and monotonous. Some fights. Some picked pockets and burglaries. One or two men who had been "pressed" into service by the wardens, too stupid to know that, though they had the right to object to being forced into guard work, their objection to a properly executed press order was itself a criminal offense. A few unlicensed whores who had somehow managed not to have their throats slit by the Guild of Madams. It was the usual flotsam of society; and, as usual, it would all be channeled into its proper place in the courtroom where it could then be meticulously noted and recorded.

The only curiosity of the morning was a shirking case that involved a group of ranchers who had left a herd of goats on a dangerous ledge outside their farm. Probably so they could slip off for a drink. The poor creatures had all fallen to their deaths, at a not inconsiderable loss of value to the Commonwealth. A rather wild account, according to the commissar, but they—like everyone else—pleaded guilty, and Jonathan ticked through their sentences in a brisk, staccato rhythm. Sometimes Miss Temple would stand and make an argument on behalf of a defendant, asking for lenience, which sometimes, Judge Acacia would indulge. She even urged a few of the poor workers to plead not guilty and have their trial—but none of them ever did.

Through the long morning, the clerks made a record of every charge, every judgment, every utterance in court. Their feathered quills fluttered across a ceaselessly flowing stream of paper. With one line, a man was given ten lashes and a year of re-training; a stamp took back what little food a woman had been allowed to buy that month; a crimped notation chained a girl to a dungeon wall for three months. Names and records, fines and adjustments, scrupulously organized, to be filed away, somewhere, in good order. The crowd slowly thinned until, at last, it was gone, and the clerks and commissars gathered up their papers to prepare for the next day's session. Nicholas called out each of the names from the docket who had not appeared, one last time, then solemnly proclaimed them all fugitives. The court was adjourned, and Jonathan retreated to his chambers without a

word to anyone, intent on nothing but leaving the courtroom as quickly
as he could.

It was very good quality, this batch. The mushroom caps were speckled
scarlet, without a trace of odor, and very hard to find. Redcaps. He had
heard them called that name. They crumbled easily into powder between
Jonathan's fingertips when he pinched them. Just like a gulleystar, a tiny
spark of light would flash when it was pressed.

He dropped the crushed powder into a glass of warmed wine. It
disappeared with only the lightest swirl. His hands were not shaking, not
yet, but all morning he had had to keep opening and closing them to
dull the tingling in his fingertips. He could hold the tremors off a little
longer. He poised the glass close before him, turning it this way and that
so that the wine caught a candle's light at just the right angle. The heart
of the glass now shone like a ruby.

He first learned of redcaps from a balm addict, of all things. A slender, handsome young man—tragic was the impression he had left with
Jonathan—who said something offhand, right before his sentencing. It
had seared into Jonathan's memory:

"I sprinkle them in my drink because it makes the world beautiful."

Such a wild and evocative notion for a dock worker to have ever
grasped. It had piqued Jonathan's curiosity. He had the man brought back
to his chambers afterwards, strictly for questioning, of course; perhaps a
few words could help the fellow turn his life around. That was what a
good judge did.

They shared the drink.

Jonathan smiled faintly at the memory, took a deep draught from
his cup, and the relief washed over him. The haze of beauty descended.

What was his name? Lon? Lane?

Jonathan let his mind drift aimlessly along pleasant, meandering currents of thought.

"At it already?" came a woman's voice from his doorway.

He discretely dropped his fingers and wiped them on the underside
of the table.

"You've driven me to drink, Elaine. Once again."

Elaine glided into his chambers with no more reservation than if she were walking into her own living room. She gave him a chiding look and sat down into a plush cushioned chair across from Jonathan. He started to pour her a glass from his bottle.

"Too early. What do you have to eat?"

He got up to open a cabinet and returned with a tray Nicholas had prepared. It held neatly arranged cheeses and rolled up slices of roasted beef, a bowl of porridge, another bowl of fruits, and a small jar of honey. She leaned across the table, indifferent to her blouse billowing open, plucked a yellow apple from the top of the fruit bowl, and took a loud, succulent bite.

"Hard work defending the cause of the workers?" Jonathan asked.

"Wif vis judge, yeah," she said, her mouth still full. She wiped at a line of juice before it fell from her chin. "Why do you even bother telling them they can plead not guilty? No one in their right mind would ever go to trial. Not when you threaten them all with life sentences or removal if they do."

"It's exactly what the Code says." He pressed his wrists together. "My hands are bound."

"Please," she rolled her eyes, "you're the judge. Some of those people didn't do a damned thing wrong. Some of them might be innocent. If you'd listen to them. Like Judge Cloud used to."

"Former Judge Cloud, you mean."

"True."

"Who now teaches at the Commissariat, for one-third of the pay."

"There are rumors he's being noted there, too," Elaine smiled wistfully then shook her head. She finished the apple in four more bites. Jonathan studied her as he sipped his wine. Her forehead was still beaded with sweat, and her clothes, plastered around her waist and legs, carried the stench of the courtroom. Elaine's face was angular and somewhat plain, but she had a kind of restless vigor in her movement that was not unattractive. She leaned back in her seat and tried to fan herself with her hand.

"I'm surprised you came down to the slums again," said Jonathan. "Don't you have enough to do to keep you busy?"

She made an annoyed gesture. "I can't stand practicing in Jachin. All they do there is file papers. This is a real court. This is practicing law."

"You think so?" His cheeks were surely glowing already, but he took another drink.

"And," she added, "down here I get to appear before the Crest's most promising young jurist. Before he ascends to the Supreme Court and forgets all his friends."

"Thank you for the compliment. But I'm sure that's not why you came."

"You're right, it isn't. Is that lamb?"

"Beef. But it's very fresh. Try some. Not that I mind working with you again, Elaine. I always used to enjoy our little debates in law school. And Judge Cloud raved about you. But I am curious. With everything you have going on, why do you waste time with Craggie criminals? Other than that you're bored."

She devoured a roll:

"What are the three legs of the stool of justice?" she asked.

"Ah, the Judge Surefoot method of teaching law. Answer a question with another question that has no answer or a metaphor that has no meaning. Wonderful pedagogy."

"I'm being serious. It's how I'm answering your question."

"Alright." Jonathan finished his glass. His head felt a little heavy, so he propped it up with his hand, pretending to be deep in thought, and ticked a count on his fingers. "Let's see, I believe they were: social justice, cognitive justice, and economic justice."

"Right. Now, how is it economic justice when some poor worker gets taken up just because he can't pay the clerk a bribe?"

"Depends on who it is. How much pull he has."

"What an awful notion of justice you have, Judge Acacia. If I weren't still hungry, I'd storm out of here and make a note of you."

Jonathan laughed.

"I'm not joking. A judge who disavows the Commonwealth's justice—it's a very serious matter."

"What does that even mean, economic justice? Getting everything you want?"

Elaine only shook her head as Jonathan pressed on:

"Ask ten people that question, and you'll get twenty different answers. Everybody wants everything, and they'll do what they must to get what they want. That's why there are bribes. That's why there are 'poor workers' who get taken up. Either you can get what you want or you can't. Either you have pull or you don't. If you have it—you've got economic justice."

"Such a cynic."

"It's the truth. And thank you."

"That's not a compliment," her nostrils flared slightly, but she kept her voice level and a half-smile never left her lips. "Cynics are very ignorant people, Jonathan. And lazy."

"That sounds like Cloud again."

"It is. And he was right. Cynics can only feign intelligence. That's all their sarcasm and world-weariness is, a disguise for stupidity. Press a cynic and you'll find he doesn't have an original thought at all. Because why bother with the work of striving, or trying, or coming up with ideas? When you can just disparage everyone else's and look smart at the same time? Utterly lazy people, cynics. I have no use for them."

"Well, that hardly seems fair," Jonathan tried to sound like his feelings were hurt, but he was grinning, his head spinning from the wine and the first meaningful conversation he had had in days. "I mean, I may be a cynic, but I work hard at it. Look, you have to allow that it took a little effort for me to hack apart one of Surefoot's three legs of justice.

"No, you fell short there, too. With all due respect, your Honor, your whole argument was flawed from the beginning. You've disproven nothing."

Jonathan looked at her. She leaned forward as if she were sharing a secret:

"Your argument is nothing but relativism, and relativism and cynicism are both worthless crutches. At best, they'll prop you up, but they'll never take you anywhere. Listen," she turned the core of her apple over to show it from different angles, "just because something is hard to describe or hard to put into words, just because we can't say precisely what something means or it might have more than one meaning to different people—it doesn't follow that it has no meaning at all. You can't describe precisely what economic justice is. Fine. How about the feel of sunlight on your face? Or the smell of jasmine? The buzz from wine? Or the taste of this apple? Are those all meaningless nothings, too?"

Jonathan held her gaze, stretching the moment as long as he could, and then he clapped his hands. "Bravo. I'm not sure what any of that has to do with sentencing shirking Craggies, but I will dutifully reconsider my cynical, relativist ethos. And if only to ensure my learned defense counsel returns to prove her argument, I'll concede you've raised—an interesting point."

"It's the truth." She plucked another apple from his plate and took a loud bite.

A tremulous knock made them both turn around together. The door swung open, and Nicholas tumbled inside, blustering an apology for the intrusion. A tall, bronze-skinned man swept past the clerk. His broad shoulders, crisply pressed clothes, and erect bearing proclaimed his professional calling.

"Lieutenant," Jonathan dipped his head and then rose from his seat. His knees knocked a little from the wine. The man's face erupted in a smile:

"Brother!" with one arm, he wrapped Jonathan in a vice-like grasp that was, as always, meant to crush the wind out of him. With the other, he motioned for Elaine to come join him. "If you want to spend the rest of the day locked up in the Tombs, I won't stop you. But you can't have my fiancée."

Elaine's face briefly contorted until it settled upon something between pleasant surprise and a muted restraint. "Michael," she said brightly and sprang to her feet. She took his massive hand in her own, "you've come to save me."

Nicholas was still in a fluster:

"I informed Lieutenant Acacia that your Honor always retires to chambers for lunch before returning to the Crest." He eyed Michael warily and rubbed his arm through a crumpled sleeve. "But he insisted on an immediate entrance, in the most strenuous terms."

"My brother's company is always welcome," Jonathan remarked.

"You look awful, Jon. Spending too much time in Craggie Court." He began helping himself to the platter. "Ugh. And eating too much Craggie food."

"A small price I pay for my service to the Crest. Nothing like the hardships you brave men of the High Guard must endure."

Elaine stifled a laugh.

"Hm," Michael grunted. "Listen, Mother expects us—all of us—at the Amphitheatre for dinner."

"Oh, sod that vile place," Jonathan swore.

"That's what she thought you'd say."

"So, she sent you to fetch me."

"Do we have to go there tonight," Elaine released her hand, pouting. "The theatre is always tedious. I feel drained every time I leave it."

As she spoke, Michael's hand traced down Elaine's spine, and his eyes made a hasty wandering over her body before they alighted with more enthusiasm.

"This is different," he answered proudly. "Tonight, *I'll* be performing. With the High Guard."

Elaine's eyebrows tilted, a trace of apprehension passing across her brow. But Michael only smiled to himself. He patted her shoulder reassuringly:

"Don't worry. You'll have diversions. Mother will have Boaz's finest women there for you to chat with."

"Who will I chat with?" asked Jonathan.

"The women, who else!" Michael laughed. "Dr. Karl's coming, too. And that whole little troop of philosophers Mother likes to keep at hand. Both of you will have plenty of entertainment if what's happening on stage isn't to your liking."

"I don't know what your soldiers plan on doing, but the company in our box sounds awful," Jonathan said jokingly, yet in a way that still was clear he meant it. "Look, I hadn't even made up my mind whether I was coming home or not. I detest the walk to Boaz, and Elaine's right about the theatre's lectures—yours excluded, of course."

"Tonight will be no lecture," said Michael. He had a grin now, moronic, as subtle as his grip.

"Hm. I just want to pass a quiet night in my rooms in the Citadel."

"Sorry. Mother's orders." Then Michael stood at his full height, towering between Elaine and Jonathan. He took them each around the waist, like manacles. "We're all her prisoners tonight."

CHAPTER TWELVE

IN A SLATE COURTYARD before a barred gatehouse, Jonathan gazed disinterestedly at the flurry of activity that was finally settling down.
A long train of wagons had finally been whipped into a semblance
of order, as dozens of shirtless porters raced back and forth between the
stockyards, moving the remnants of a small mountain of crates, baskets, jars,
glasses, and bundles to where they belonged. They were racing to finish
their loads in time.

A swarm of particularly burly clerks, yellow-sashed and pink-faced,
swarmed about, screaming over all the noise. The clerks hit, kicked, and
swore at the workers, threatening to dock their wages, withhold their
cragfire or, when that didn't spur sufficient effort, make a note of them
for shirking.

Every day this caravan sojourned out from the walls that guarded
the Court of Common Corrections to cross the bridge over Cowan's
Chasm. The carts had to be single-file, for the Spine was only wide
enough for one wagon and its carters. In a long, lumbering line, the
porters carried their loads across the Spine to the Citadel. It took over
an hour at a trot.

Once they reached the Citadel's Inner Keep, a brigade of commissars would unload every box of food, cask of ale, thread of cloth—all
the fruits of the Crag's labors—to be measured, weighed, cataloged, and,
eventually, distributed to the people of the Crest. Then emptied, the
porters would return their carts to the stockyards of the Court to be
refilled the next day. This great exodus had been a daily ritual for as long
as anyone could remember, perhaps even before the Commonwealth's
beginning, if that were possible. One by one, the loaded carts would
slowly disappear into the dark, save only a cluster of smaller wagons left
behind to be sent on to the Quarter for the dwarves' allotment.

A few court bailiffs and commissars always accompanied the caravan when it set out, to guard the wares, but also because no one who lived in the Crest ever spent a moment longer in the Crag's court than was required. The judge, of course, could come and go as he pleased with a full retinue of guards. Most of the court's judges had always left the court for the Crest well before the caravan's departure. But Judge Acacia was peculiar in this regard. He preferred to travel in the midst of the caravan on his daily journey between the court and the Crest despite the slow and ponderous pace. No one had ever asked him why. If the question ever were asked, Jonathan offered a vaguely official pretext along the line of, "solidarity with our workers," or some other nonsense. In truth, on the first day of his appointment to the court, Jonathan had once walked this bridge, alone, in the dark. He had never done so again.

He sat in a covered wagon, staring blankly at the sweat-soaked backs of the six men who pulled it. It was as comfortable as such a conveyance could be with two rows of cushions, lacquered paneling, a lilac censer to cover the stench from the outside, and a small lantern that hung close to the roof and was always in danger of bumping against the passengers' heads. Its light jostled as the wagon pulled ahead, changing the features of Elaine's face from shadow to light, then back to shadow. She sat across from him and was studying a paper intently.

"I thought you said riding in this thing helped you get more work done," she said, breaking Jonathan's reverie. He watched her bring the paper close to her nose, straining to read the words until she gave up and folded it away. "I can't see anything in here."

"You get used to it in time," he replied. The swaying motion of the wagon felt relaxing. He let out a yawn.

"It's so loud," she shook her head.

"A bit," he agreed.

He listened to the rumble of wheels, the creaking wood, and plodding feet, and scores of men grunting and swearing at one another. Anywhere else, he would have had to stuff his ears with cotton, but out here atop the Spine, the press of noise and men was something of a comfort to him, though he seldom reflected on it.

There was a terrible cracking sound from far ahead, like a tree trunk being rent by lightning, followed by a roar of voices. Jonathan and Elaine

craned to look over the porters from their seats. The men were muttering among themselves, obviously displeased.

"Well, we got pretty far before the first hold-up," Jonathan observed.
"Hopefully, my brother will take charge. If he has the porters whipped,
we might miss the Amphitheatre yet."

"That's a terrible thing to say," she glanced nervously out into the
darkness. "Still. I do hope they hurry up. I don't like being stuck out
here." Her gaze lingered beyond the bridge. She gave a shudder that did
not come from any chill. "It's so—oppressive."

It was a phenomenon that always disturbed Jonathan as well. How
the darkness out beyond the bridge seemed to gather like a cloud the
moment one was beyond the view of the court's gatehouse. As if their
trudge across this slender expanse of stone were nothing but a spectacle
before a hidden audience, just out of sight, who was watching everything
in rapt silence. He sometimes caught himself wondering what would
happen if he just called out to them …

Jonathan was debating whether to try to explain any of this to
Elaine, when Michael's ruddy, glowering face appeared by the wagon.
He leaned inside, and Jonathan could feel the heat from his forehead.

"These people are cretins, and they move like snails."

"They're carrying quite a load," Jonathan explained.

"Nonsense," he darted around the wagon to strike one of the porters
who had taken advantage of the delay to sneak a drink of water. The
man cowered over, dropping his flask to the floor. Michael returned to
the wagon, huffing. "One of the lead cart's axles broke. And they're all
just dawdling around it!"

"Something like this happens every time," Jonathan waved a hand.
"Leave it to the clerks to sort out."

"I'll get it sorted out right now," he growled and disappeared in the
throng ahead, shoving his way through.

"Michael—" Jonathan called out, but he was already gone. "He'll
only make things worse."

"Mm."

Elaine was staring out of the wagon, her attention seemingly fixated
upon the gaping void beyond the orbit of the lanterns and torches of
the caravan. Jonathan followed her gaze. The lanes of pale, yellow light

spilling from the cart's lantern seemed to bend wherever they strayed beyond the bridge's railings. Light, sound, thought, it was all being pulled into that ocean of nothingness that surrounded them. Oblivion, just past this little window.

"Elaine," Jonathan started, "what do you think—"

His words were cut short by a tremendous crash, much louder than the first, followed by a horrific scream and a cascade of angry voices. Someone was crying, a man. Elaine gave a start and turned to Jonathan, who was already getting up.

"Stay, stay," Michael reappeared and ushered his brother back to his seat. "I've taken care of it. We're moving out again." He was flushed and breathing heavily and looked very satisfied with himself. Dangerously so, was Jonathan's immediate impression. "You six!" Michael scowled at the wagon's porters. "Can't you see the caravan's moving? Back to it—unless you want to see the bottom of the Chasm, too."

Slowly they pulled forward. The cart soon fell into the familiar rattle and sway, as Michael walked alongside, chatting away at Elaine, who obliged him with a faint smile and nod every so often. The sullen glances the porters stole over their shoulders and their venomous mutterings were beneath his notice. Michael's laughter rang loud, almost defiant, out from the bridge's stone roadway. The darkness swallowed it, too.

The caravan resumed its ponderous trek, and although Jonathan was certain they had at least another half of a mile before them, the first empty pedestals that adorned the end of the bridge appeared almost at once. The familiar yellow banners of the Commonwealth marked the final stretch, a widened, hundred-yard span that led to the Citadel, the fortress carved into the side of the Mountain, which guarded the Crest's border. A half-smile came to Jonathan's face as he spied the twinkling lights that peeked through the arrow slits and windows of the Citadel's Inner Keep, which guarded the Crag side of the stronghold. As they drew closer, they saw that the portcullis was already up and the iron gates opened, awaiting the caravan's arrival.

A welcome din of sounds and smells came pouring out, along with scores of stern-faced commissars, who pulled a line of empty wagons behind them. With feather pens and rolls of papers, they took charge of the caravan's clerks, checking notes, writing orders and receipts, directing the packed freight from one caravan to be loaded onto the waiting wagons of the other. They mingled in a frenetic, if not steady course, like sojourning ants pulling one mound down, a grain at a time, to create a new one.

Despite all the bustle surrounding them, Jonathan and Elaine managed to clamber down from the covered wagon and follow Michael into the Inner Keep. Clerks, commissars, and exhausted porters dove to get out of his way. Michael barreled past the salutes of the Citadel's gate guards with nothing more than a cursory grunt with Elaine flailing behind in his grasp. Jonathan rubbed an ache in his lower back from sitting so long and walked a stiff, but brisk pace to keep up with them.

The teeth of the portcullis loomed high and ominous above him, seemingly swaying it was so vast; the thing always gave Jonathan a moment of worry whenever he walked beneath it, a vague sense that one day someone would be drunk enough or stupid enough to let the whole mass of jagged steel come crashing down to the stone. Michael and Elaine disappeared into a long, arched tunnel that spanned through the Citadel's Inner and Outer Keeps, and on to the outside world. Michael was obviously in a hurry, which only made Jonathan want to tarry.

The smell came first, as it always did, and it brought a smile to Jonathan, despite the pain in his back and the gloom of the tunnel. It was the scent of fresh air. Of leaves, grasses, and flowers. And of water. Real water. Not the fetid, lifeless pools that percolate through cracks beneath the earth or slosh along in iron pipes, but water that runs free, wherever it wishes, beneath the open sky. It has a scent all its own. Jonathan breathed it in deeply. He walked on and instinctively shielded his eyes as the first daylight doused his face. It had a golden hue; the sun would be setting.

A little way further up the sloping tunnel and at last he emerged into the granite expanse of the Citadel's courtyard. There was a cool evening breeze blowing in from the east, and the crickets had just begun to take up the first of their night's songs. A few commissars were sweeping the tiles around a bubbling fountain and greeted Jonathan with a courteous, "your Honor." He nodded at them but recognized no one else around.

Elaine and Michael had already disappeared among the little crowd that still lingered around the courtyard's steps and porticoes. The market stalls were closing. The stage in the center of the plaza was empty and dark. The first torches were being lit to open the reading rooms, coffee houses, theaters, and taverns. Jonathan scanned the crowd once more, now that his eyes had adjusted to the light, and when he was sure there was no one here he knew, he drew his cloak tight over his head and walked quickly toward a dark alley sheltered between a towering warehouse and a villa where commissars were housed.

He had just enough time. The apothecary's sign was out, the door already open.

He had not made it three steps into the alley when he happened to glance up from the curb and nearly plowed headfirst into a massive body.

"There you are!" Michael boomed. "We were just circling back to find you."

Elaine stood close behind him and cast Jonathan a quizzical look. Jonathan pretended to adjust his hood and wiped his face.

"Sorry," he turned about in a circle, furtively, as if trying to get his bearings. "Must have gotten lost."

"You don't look well," Elaine said and put her hand to his forehead. "You're as cold as a fish."

"Too much time in the Crag," Michael clapped his brother on the shoulder. "Come on, the High Road is back the other way. We've got a good three-mile walk to Boaz, and the show will start soon." He looked back at his brother as if noticing something for the first time. "Should I call a cart for you?"

Jonathan gathered himself as one resigned to perform some unpleasant duty, but managed to make himself sound good-natured:

"Thank you both, I'm fine. Really. Too much time underground, like you say. That's all." He ran his hand through his hair which was now damp with sweat and fashioned a tight smile. "Better get started. Mustn't keep Mother waiting."

The High Road. A travertine artery that sprang from the Citadel's Outer Keep, it wended through the domed courtyard, past a run of foothills and neighboring villages, and on into the green valleys of the Mountain, tying together the Crest's three principal centers—the Citadel, the City of Boaz, and miles above, atop a plateau perennially hidden within a curtain of clouds, the Crest's capital, Jachin. Built long before the Overthrow, the road was a cleverly designed connection of stone byways, bridges, and lifts held together by hundreds of soaring flights of stairs. It had weathered the shoes and sandals of millions of travelers, wars and blizzards, hurricanes that deluged the side of the Mountain, and drought summers when the roadway's stones became so hot, commissars could cook eggs on the sidewalks. It had endured. Though if one bothered to stoop down and look at it closely, the missing tiles, the worn, discolored railings, the cracks stretching across the mortar, were becoming plainer and plainer with every passing season.

It was evening, and the little clusters of travelers along the High Road leaving the Citadel were talking and laughing merrily among themselves. Dozens of tiny sparrows flitted close behind them, hoping to steal a crumb of biscuit or cake that might happen to fall. Tall cedar trees lined either side of the roadway, straight as sentinels, casting lines of gray shadow across the way. Beyond their boughs were wide, rolling hills, what had once been pastures and farmlands, now overgrown and fallow. There was a teetering shell of a barn, a line of rotted fence posts drowning in ivy. The houses along the way were in no better repair, hamlets of moldy stone buildings with roofs missing shingles, soot-covered chimneys, and shutterless windows.

The air was cool, the sky had turned magenta, and just above the rustling weeds and wildflowers, fireflies danced about like tiny flurries of falling stars, a spectacle that drew no one's notice.

Jonathan tried not to lag, but a sharp ache was pressing inside his temples, and it made each of his footfalls feel like the thump of a hammer driving a nail into his head. His mouth was dry, and a bad taste kept belching from his stomach. His hand lingered toward his pocket; it took some effort to restrain it from plunging after what the pocket held. Unaware of his brother's discomfort, Michael was droning on:

"I don't know why we couldn't do this on a monthly or even a weekly basis. I've talked to my captain about it. He's friends with one of the Board Wardens. There is no reason why we couldn't just commute every one of those prisoners to the High Guard. But supposedly, the Stewards on the sub-council of justice won't approve it," he grimaced back at Jonathan, as if he were personally responsible for this obstacle of bureaucracy, before he continued: "we could get valuable training out of those Craggies, but instead they're all to be thrown away. Total waste of material. All because of legal nonsense."

Elaine, whose long legs glided easily alongside Michael's march, threw her head around and smiled sadly at Jonathan.

"That's not at all fair. Jonathan can no more change the law than you can question orders."

Michael's face screwed up in thought:

"Is that true, Jon? You've no pull with the justice under-stewards?"

Jonathan held his hands out helplessly, then yanked them back at the sight of his trembling fingers.

"I'm still on the bottom rung of my ladder," he answered.

Michael stopped on the road to regard his brother. It was as if he were being inspected, Jonathan thought, his brother's eyes probing him, somewhat disapprovingly, from top to bottom. A group of young men who had been trailing behind joked about blocking the High Road. They had been passing an amphora of wine freely since leaving the Citadel, but when they noticed Michael's uniform and the sword that hung from his side, they quieted down and parted around them. When they had gone, Michael grunted:

"Well, everyone has to start somewhere." And then, a little more benignly: "I had to do my share of night watches and drunk house guard, too. When I first got out of the academy. You won't be stuck in the Crag forever. We'll make sure of it."

"Such the protector," Elaine squeezed Michael's arm, and the pain stirred inside Jonathan's bowels once more, although, as he studied her more closely, it seemed there was hardly any fondness in Elaine's touch, or in her expression. She faced Jonathan now, and, as if sensing his thoughts, laughed out loud in an exaggerated fashion: "Not that Judge Acacia needs a helping hand with his judicial career. Top of his class, prestigious internship with the right subcommittee, published scholarship in the right journals. He's doing all the right things. Just like you are. He'll end up a Steward in Jachin, right beside his brother, the future Warden."

If there was the faintest note of reproach in her voice, only Jonathan detected it. From the other side of a hill ahead, a bawl of laughter carried across the evening air. The drunken boys from earlier, probably sharing some private jape. It prompted Michael to remember they were still running late. They began walking once more as the first stars appeared above them. Michael led them at a trot and picked up his earlier trail of conversation:

"What's really galling about this prisoner thing," he gestured with his free hand toward Jonathan, "is that in my line of work, there aren't that many opportunities to distinguish yourself. We need every fight we can get."

Jonathan was struggling to keep up with their pace. "What about your drills," he huffed. "Or all those parades you keep dragging us out to."

Michael waved at him. "That's all performance. Like when they bring up a Craggie to execute outside the Citadel instead of just slitting his throat in the Tombs. It's good entertainment for you civilians, but it doesn't mean a thing to the Wardens."

"Really?" Jonathan breathed.

"You think high step marching in formation has a blasted thing to do with actual warfare?"

"Hadn't thought of it," Jonathan acknowledged.

He pretended to listen as Michael recounted the latest theories of combat training, a speech that sounded vaguely familiar to Jonathan, enough so that he knew when he would need to express some obligatory response and when he could safely let his attention wander. His gaze drifted toward Elaine. Her outline was mostly hidden in shade, but Jonathan could still make out her features in between the trees. The click of her sandals matched her betrothed's step for step, but she scarcely bothered with a pretense of interest in anything Michael was saying. They went up a steady climb in the cobbled walkway, pausing only to pick their way around a washed-out drainage culvert. At last, they reached a junction of sorts, where the cedars stopped growing and two cracked sets of stairs veered up separate paths. The closest one spanned more toward the left. It was steep but only held a few landings before it ended beneath a lit archway at the outskirts of a town. The right one wound along a gentle hillside through wild brush for as far as one could see until it disappeared in the horizon. The first set of stairs was marked by a quartz obelisk and a lamppost that lit one of its faces with an orange, wavering hue. Four, enormous block letters, "BOAZ," spanned from the top to its pedestal base.

"We'll just get there in time," Michael glanced at the sky and then charged up the first stairs without once looking back. Elaine started after him but paused mid-step.

"So, are you going to make it?"

"Eventually." Jonathan was bent over at the waist, catching his breath. He searched in vain for a bench or a chair, but the only seat he could find was a boulder half shrouded in briars that was well off the roadway. He doubted he could reach it before he collapsed.

"You used to be in better shape. What's happened to you, Jonathan?"

"I became a lawyer," he answered. "Just you wait. Too much time in a courtroom wrecks your health."

"Or too much wine."

Jonathan's fingers clenched in a fist. He nearly snarled, but then he saw her, much closer now, on the step just above him, the fading glow of dusk brushing her cheeks. She was smiling in a teasing way, but with a sincerity in her voice that touched him immediately.

"And what's that supposed to mean?" he asked.

"A bottle with every lunch? Not that I'm one to judge. But that much wine—especially the swill that gets smuggled through the Citadel—it can't be good for you."

Jonathan's mouth gaped:

"How on earth—"

"Oh, I have my little birds, just like your mother. You'd be surprised what we women can find out about our men."

"These birds, do they have yellow bellies?"

"No, you don't," Elaine laughed, and this time, it had a fruity, joyful ring to it. "Go and catch your own birds. I won't help you with any clues."

From high above, a party's raucous sounds broke the silence that fell over them. The murmurings of a town coming to life. The lamppost light glowed brighter as the last of the sunlight retreated behind the horizon.

"Come on," she said, "before your brother calls out the watch. If we hurry, there might be some decent vintage left. Maybe an Acacia Midcrest. Anything to help get us through this horrible show. At least for once you won't have to drink alone." She held out a hand. "Climb up with me, I'll help you."

"I'd rather climb alone."

He had meant it as a joke, but it came out harsh, almost bitter. Elaine blinked twice:

"Suit yourself."

She turned and disappeared up the stairs, climbing all four landings without a pause, all the way to the illuminated balustrade at the hilltop, which led into Boaz.

Jonathan was alone, at last.

Although he did not feel it. A dingy moon, waxing near full, looked down on him like a tired, lidless eye. The monotonous drone of crickets rose in a crescendo, striving to overcome the mounting noise of the city's revelers. Nearby, a watchdog barked. But only one voice, his own, whispered to him. One glass of warm wine, it assured him, just one with the lightest sprinkle, was all he would need for the night. Nothing more. Jonathan felt inside his pocket, felt the comforting presence he had brought with him, and braced for the climb and the night ahead.

"*Up we go.*"

Whether he had spoken aloud or merely thought to himself, it was impossible to say.

CHAPTER THIRTEEN

"**D**EAR, YOU LOOK ghastly. Sit."
The woman had finally spoken to Jonathan, more of an assessment than a greeting. Her heavy lids blinked at him from within the lavender folds of a chair's headrest. She pointed to an empty cushion next to Elaine and at once forgot all about him.

"Hello, Mother," he leaned past Elaine and kissed the air around his mother's cheek.

"Regina and I were so worried you might not make it," Elaine said coolly. She glared at him for a long moment, but then patted the seat and bade him to join her.

They were inside his family's private box high in the amphitheatre gallery. In the space behind the front row, where Regina and Elaine sat, a small gathering of fashionable looking men and women, all regulars of Regina's patronage and accustomed to enjoying her wines, maneuvered about a table of food illuminated by an enormous brass candelabra. The box's audience was all the same pallor and obesity as Jonathan's mother and seldom ventured beyond the orbit of Regina's seat, while a collection of commissar servants ran between the theatre's kitchens and the box to keep everyone's wine glasses full and the dishes on the table heaped high. The crowd, though small, was noisy. They had greeted Jonathan's arrival respectfully, if not warmly, and at once resumed in their talk, a debate of some sort, which always seemed directed towards Regina and Elaine more than each other.

Jonathan slumped into his seat. Even in their family's box, the cushions were stained and threadbare around the edges. The coarse stitching rubbed against the back of his legs, but it was a relief to be sitting down. He wiped his brow with a napkin and glanced over the railing.

The crowd was small in the amphitheatre tonight. Most of the audience seats were empty. In the arena, a ring of torches showed a tall, shrewish looking woman with magenta stained hair. The warm-up act, she was some kind of a lecturer who was earnestly reciting her dissertation on societal criticism (or perhaps it was critical societalism, Jonathan couldn't tell); throughout the woman's performance, she was throwing her arms around in wild rings, screeching until she had nearly gone hoarse, and seemingly unaware that no one in attendance was paying attention to a word she said. The torches were at least a nice diversion, sending shimmers of heat and a faint scent of charcoal into the air.

"A glass, if you please," Jonathan said when one of the commissars happened by.

"Where have you been?" Elaine hissed into his ear, never breaking a practiced, amused expression. She traded a pleasantry with an older woman, who asked after her uncle, then continued out of the side of her mouth. "You've no idea how insufferable this has been. Dr. Karl is deep in his cups, and he's in a lecturing mood."

"Let's follow his lead then. The cups, I mean, not the lecture."

"I'm sure you'll catch him fast enough. You don't dawdle when it comes to wine. Seriously, did you stop somewhere on the way?"

Jonathan almost winced, for that was precisely what he had done. Instead, he made a plaintive gesture:

"It was a hard climb."

He craned his head over the back of his seat to search for the commissar but saw instead a man of close to Jonathan's age, returning from the table with a plate heaped with stuffed quails. Thinking Jonathan had turned to greet him, he smiled broadly:

"Your honor," the man gushed, lifting a goblet of wine he had balanced in his other hand, "welcome to the fray."

"Oh, hello, Gregory," Jonathan nodded.

Elaine let out a vexed sigh, but the man plopped, unheeded, into the chair directly behind Jonathan and Elaine, close enough that they could smell the garlic on his breath. His hair and beard were oily, and he spoke quickly, with a trace of a lisp, and with the obvious intent of being heard by everyone:

"We've been discussing with your esteemed mother and future sister-in-law, the Stewards' deliberations in Jachin. All unofficially, of course," he patted Elaine's shoulder. "Everyone agrees the Tenth Plan for the Commonwealth will be announced any day—but I'm sure Miss Temple knows that better than any of us. The gossip is pouring out now. Everyone's astir. I, for one, suspect the Stewards are deliberately fanning rumors."

A corpulent man next to Regina stood up quickly. He was pink-faced and teetering from his girth, but he cut over Gregory with near-perfect precision in his speech:

"You're quite right to say you, for one, Gregory. You're the only one who would think anything so daft."

"It is a perfectly reasonable supposition, Karl."

"Doctor Karl," Regina gently scolded Gregory.

Dr. Karl folded two flabby arms across his chest and thanked Regina. Gregory blushed, but pressed his point:

"Sorry, Madame. I simply meant to convey my conviction that sweeping changes are likely afoot in this new Plan. And if so, it would make perfect sense for the Stewards to ease those transitions into the Commonwealth as gradually as possible. Plant the thought first, then implement it. I suggested as much in my report last year on demography trends."

"No one but your little coffee house comrades reads your damned papers," Dr. Karl retorted. This was met with a smattering of laughter. His cheeks now burning bright, Gregory scowled into his plate and ripped off a quail wing, while Dr. Karl hectored the box:

"The Stewards have started none of these rumors because there will be no sweeping changes. The forthcoming Plan will make *adjustments*," he drew out the word for almost an entire breath. "Thoughtful, incremental adjustments. A new guideline here. A revision to an old one there. Some studies will be ordered, undertaken by suitably credentialed boards. It will be technical, and it will be incremental, of that we can be assured. Probably take the better part of a month just to finish reading it once it's out. That is how progress works. I should know. I've been through two of these Plans since I came of age and had the privilege of once serving on a study committee in Jachin. There's always a mill of gossip just before a new Plan is announced. The Seventh was particularly clamorous, I remember. It's all just chatter, though. The

Stewards will let the experts exercise their expertise, and we'll have a new, thoughtful, *modest* Plan to guide the Commonwealth."

Dr. Karl resumed his seat, apparently satisfied that the topic was decided.

"With a sufficient allocation of resources to maintain the Crest," someone nearby added.

"Of course," Dr. Karl snapped. "That goes without saying. But allocation adjustments," he declared firmly, "will be the full sweep of any so-called sweeping reform. You can mark my words."

No one did, for the conversation had already turned to something else. Jonathan's wine came just in time. No sooner had he taken the goblet from the servant's tray, when Gregory sidled himself in between Jonathan and Elaine, bleating into Jonathan's ear like they were fast friends. Jonathan tried his best not to flinch, steadying himself with a long draught from his cup. At least, he reflected, the wine was good—though it needed one thing more.

"I beg your pardon," Elaine began, but Gregory ignored her:

"Alright, perhaps sweeping was a bit strong of a word," Gregory murmured to them both, "but that Karl's puffed on so much, no one else can be heard. He's a doctor and all, but still." Gregory glared across the box and licked his lips, hungrily, it seemed to Jonathan. "His reports get no more notice than mine." He mimicked Dr. Karl's voice under his breath: "'Privilege to serve on a study committee.' What stuff! Neglected to mention they disbanded the study before it was even half-finished and sacked him from his post. Don't you believe for a moment he's not still smarting from *that* slight. Ah, well. Miss Temple, I'm sure you and your mother-in-law can discern whose word is worth recommending—who's up and coming, and who's an old scroll—after the Plan has been officially published, of course."

His talk had come out in a torrent, almost breathlessly. Jonathan watched Elaine pretend to listen to Gregory as patiently as anyone could. But the gush of unrelenting namedropping must have seemed interminable, for Elaine's face tightened, like twine on the verge of snapping.

Thankfully, Regina came to her rescue. She tapped Elaine on the shoulder:

"All this talk about the Stewards reminds me that I neglected to ask you: how is your dear uncle, the Steward of Maritime Resources?"

Her reply was instantaneous and rehearsed:

"His duties these days keep him busy. We've not seen or spoken with him for months, though our family misses him terribly."

"He does his duty for the Commonwealth," Regina nodded solemnly and gave her what might have been a sympathetic touch on the knee, "and his family must dutifully suffer his absence. My late husband was a liaison to the Council, and I hardly saw him for years at a time. I fear it will be much the same when you marry my Michael."

"I am certain it will, Mother," Elaine replied.

Jonathan smiled inwardly. For Elaine to call her "Mother" in public, and in the hearing of all these tongue-wagging parvenus, would surely please Regina. As much as the old woman could be pleased.

At that moment, a shrill, wavering note sounded from the arena. A hush fell over the entire theatre; within the Acacias' box, the commissars discretely dimmed several of the candles and covered the serving trays of food. The lecturer with the colored hair made a hasty retreat as an acne faced boy marched solemnly out into the middle of the floor, his sandaled feet kicking small clouds of dust into the air with each step. He was garbed in a red and yellow checkered tunic. He puffed his cheeks out and blew another note into a dented brass horn that draped his shoulder. Then he spun around on his heel and retreated a few steps.

A thin severe-looking woman, dressed only in a thespian's hooded cape, took the trumpeter's place and held the theatre's patrons with her gaze. Her features were framed ominously in the torchlight. She threw her hood back, held her hands aloft, and proclaimed:

"Ladies and gentlemen! On behalf of the dramatists, orators, and understudies of the Dew Street Amphitheatre, welcome. I am Janet, director of productions. Tonight, we are honored to yield our humble stage in service to the Commonwealth. I give you … the High Guard of Boaz."

On cue, the sounds of ropes and pulleys lifted a dark, hidden curtain from the far end of the arena. More light poured inside, and from within its aura, a troop of armored silhouettes emerged.

"Quickstep, fall in!"

It was Michael's voice. A thunderous tramp of metal and feet made the theatre seats rattle, as a row of fourteen men came rushing toward the center of the arena, kicking their boots high into the air in something between a dance and a high step march. Michael was at the head. The soldiers strutted about the ring of torches, coming in and out of formations, and saluted the theatre's audience, who took that as a cue to clap a polite applause. The line eventually verged toward the middle, straight toward Janet, but at the last moment broke into two, which ran in separate arcs before halting at attention. A low fog of chalky dust hovered just above the ground. Each line faced the other in grim silence, a silence that stretched out, on and on, when suddenly, as one, the shafts of their spears thumped the ground. More scattered applause; even Regina tapped the back of her hand lightly against the other.

The High Guard of Boaz stood erect and as still as statutes in two lines of red and yellow. Their cloaks hung almost to the floor. Helms topped with peacock feathers covered their faces, except for Michael's, whose helmet had a raised visor, a mark of his officer's commission. At a glance, they were resplendent. But if one looked closely at any of them for very long, the torches revealed scores of little blemishes that, try as they might, could not be concealed: specks of rust on mismatched breastplates, a halberd head on a spear shaft, a stubborn dent along a shield's edge, a belt that was too long, booting that matched no one else's. Michael took one step forward, his sword's scabbard clanging against a set of scalloped greaves, and called out:

"High Guard, Seventh Company, present arms!"

The men responded in unison with another tamp of their spears:

"Our all for all!"

While the audience was fixated upon the spectacle, for that was the feel of all the promenading and display, Jonathan's fingers had slid slowly, imperceptibly, into a hidden pocket of his shirt. The knotted string of a tiny velvet purse unwound, as if on its own. He stole a glance in Gregory and Elaine's direction, but Gregory was busily devouring a leg bone, while Elaine stared straight ahead, staring and gritting her teeth as the director resumed her presentation. The purse opened. He felt the smoothness inside until his fingertips brushed against something soft and coarse. No one saw his thumb and forefinger pinching together, a warm spark flashing, hidden beneath the cloth. Janet's voice rose:

"—to these brave men who have pledged their lives to keep our border secure, and to their stalwart leader, Boaz's very own Lieutenant Michael Acacia," she swept her head low toward the box, and Regina, from her chair, deigned to dip her chin. "We show them our thanks and solidarity by bearing witness tonight. Tonight, we will see the fruits of their martial studies before our very eyes. A most deadly exercise to sharpen the acumen of our soldiers."

Another group of shadows appeared from behind the curtain, but these forms were stooped, shuffling, and made no sound at all, except for the clink of chain links that bound them all together. They held their hands to their foreheads, the brightness and noise overcoming their senses. Commissars on either side of the line shoved them forward with barbed truncheons and whips. One of the commissars dropped a pile of wooden clubs and sticks on the ground.

Jonathan held his hand within his pocket, his bottom lip quivering.

The chained men were prisoners from the Tombs. All were covered in rags, hollow-looking, and plagued with, what Jonathan recognized, were the blackened mouths of balm addicts. But the sight of one crouching on the periphery took Jonathan by surprise.

The prisoner's face, though wracked from want, was as striking as Jonathan remembered. No more than twenty years old. With a high, almost intelligent brow and piercing eyes. The dockworker. The one who had shown him the splendor that redcaps brought to the world.

He was still beautiful.

And here he was, alive, with those same flashing gray eyes, shaking uncontrollably, holding his knees together with his slender wrists, a puddle of urine spreading beneath his feet. Without realizing it, Jonathan started to rise, but he caught himself before anyone in the box had noticed. He felt his body trembling, like the man on the stage below. Jonathan's eyes darted about guiltily, as he wriggled his back as far as he could into his cushion. But he wanted to stand, to shout the man's name. The name he had once whispered on a sofa that had been much too small for them both. The name he now remembered.

Liam.

"I sprinkle them in my drink because it makes the world beautiful."

A fingertip gently touched the top of Jonathan's knuckles. He jerked his hand away.

"What's the matter?" Elaine whispered.

"Nothing," he rasped. "Nothing. I just—it's nothing. I'm fine."

He tried to smile at Elaine, but her worried expression only hardened.

"These individuals," Janet continued, all the while eyeing the shackled prisoners warily, "residents of the Crag, have been convicted of terrible crimes. They have all been deemed a danger to our Commonwealth. Yet, in the benevolence of the Board of Wardens, they have had their sentences commuted. There is but one cost left for them to pay ..." Janet paused to let the words sink in, as she now regarded the audience with a crooked smile. "By sparring with the Seventh Company, these men can render service to the Commonwealth, redeem themselves of their crimes, and regain their dignity. Armed with these dangerous instruments, they shall fight our High Guard for your entertainment. Tonight, in this arena. Ladies and gentlemen, I give you the Commonwealth's justice!"

Janet hastened from the arena, her actor's cape billowing behind her like a wavering shadow, as the commissars unlocked the men's chains. Their fetters dropped to the ground in a clatter. The noise reverberated across the theatre's walls.

And then they simply stood there.

For what felt like an unending time, nothing happened. The men in rags stretched or crouched, rubbed their wrists, shifted from one foot to the other, wiped their noses, scratched the back of their heads. One even started to bury his feet in the sand. They were, one and all, doing whatever they could to avoid noticing the two lines of armored guards pointing spears at them. The pile of dangerous instruments they had been given to defend themselves still lay where it had been dropped, equally unnoticed. It was remarkable the lengths they went to pretend the soldiers standing at attention around them were not there. Remarkable and growing increasingly awkward. After a while, even the guards grew restless.

One of the gallery's patrons could no longer stifle her laughter. In the box, several of the onlookers began muttering.

"Should someone bang a gong or something?" someone offered, which was met with both laughs and disapproving scowls, especially from Regina.

At last, Michael took it on himself to break the inertia. He drew his sword, and the sound of the blade running from its scabbard immediately riveted everyone's attention.

"Ah, here we go," said Dr. Karl, sounding pleased. He squinted his eyes. "Fine looking blade, Regina."

"I'm sure it is," she agreed, her face buried completely in her cup.

In the arena, Michael walked, almost leisurely, towards the closest man to him. He barked the order:

"Choose a weapon."

Liam's gray eyes rounded when Michael's shadow fell over him. He looked up, trembling. Michael motioned for him to reach for one of the clubs, but the dockworker only stared back at him. Michael waited a moment longer, and then the pommel of his sword floated above his head, even as the blade's point descended to train upon its mark. Each man froze in the other's gaze, neither speaking, neither moving, the breadth of a world in the closeness between them.

It was surprising how quietly the sword thrust through Liam's neck. Only a gasp from the gallery marked its passing. The body slumped backward, drenched from a shower of blood that spurted from where his larynx had been—and, even then, Jonathan felt with an ache, he looked so very handsome in how guilelessly he moved. Michael steadied a boot on Liam's chest, and, after a few pulls, was able to retrieve his sword.

At that moment, in the theatre box, while he watched Liam's life ebbing away, Jonathan's hand emerged from the velvet pouch and passed over his cup which was now balanced upon the space of cushioning between his legs. Liam's blood soaked into the ground; the powder fell into Jonathan's wine. Jonathan flicked his fingers lightly, swished the wine inside his cup, and chanced to look over next to him. Elaine was staring straight ahead, unblinking, her face frightfully pale in the diminished light, while Gregory was nodding at the arena approvingly. Jonathan felt a weight falling from his shoulders, one he had not realized had been there. No one had noticed what he had done.

"That was well executed," Gregory whispered.

"Wha-what?" Jonathan's head spun around; the color drained from his cheeks.

"Your brother's blow just now. I've seen my share of removals, and he's clearly well studied."

"Oh."

Gregory stifled a belch, arose, and repaired to the banquet table, despite its closure, to make himself another plate.

Michael's excursion had been all that was needed for the training to begin in earnest. The prisoners now looked at their captors squarely, the terror no longer avoidable. Some grunts and hand gestures from the guards, and then they formed a queue not far from Liam's corpse. They stood in line to choose from the small pile of broken poles, branches, old axles, and odd-shaped mallets, and then wandered off in different directions about the arena's ring. Wherever they went, the wooden instruments they picked up for weapons hung limply from their fingers. Like sullen children made to clutch at toys they never wanted.

The show went much more smoothly after that.

Michael shouted more orders, and his guards broke ranks and fell upon the prisoners in what, from the gilded theatre box, looked much like a vignette of loosely organized butchery. A few prisoners tried to run away, most simply held their hands before their faces, three swung their clubs against the guards' shields to the delight of the crowd. But they all died quickly enough, with much the same gasp when the blow came.

Except one. A young and wiry red-haired boy, bare-chested, threw his broken axe handle away to seize on a better weapon, the long line of manacles the commissars had left in the arena. He was swinging a chain in a wide circle, holding off his opponent, when Gregory returned to his seat chewing a mouth full of food:

"I'm curious, Miss Temple, what your thoughts would be on this exercise as a manifestation of unification."

Elaine had completely blanched, and Jonathan sensed that the closeness of this greasy, overly familiar man with a bit of gristle stuck to the hair of his moustache, only made her feel the worse.

"Unification?" the word fell out of Elaine.

"Yes."

"I-It's ... difficult to watch."

She was struggling to catch her breath. In the arena below, a teen-aged boy swinging a piece of chain over his head screamed helplessly as men clad in mail closed around him. A tear formed in the corner of Elaine's eye, and she wiped it away furiously.

"Do you wish to leave—" Jonathan began softly, but she bit her lip and jerked her head once, refusing to turn her attention from the arena.

Seeing her, Jonathan felt a sudden urge to give her his cup, to share what he had, and ease her discomfort. He had nearly slid it into her clenched hands, but something stopped him. Something about the chain this Craggie child was thrashing around. Its arc made a kind of boundary around him within the arena, a line that could not be crossed, not without peril. There was a boundary here, too. Jonathan would not cross it. So instead, he drained his cup's contents at once in a hurried swallow. Gregory's voice retreated into a dim reflection of sound; his shape became a shadow:

"Have you never been to a public removal before? Ah, then I'm sure this must seem distressing."

Elaine said nothing but continued watching. Jonathan shut his eyes and steadied himself in his seat, while the staccato buzzing of Gregory's voice rolled over him:

"As his honor is well aware, prisoners under these sentences are usually removed by commissars, if they haven't already died of their own accord while incarcerated. But here we see them in our very own amphitheatre, working together, with our people. It's a small, but no less extraordinary development."

"They're being slaughtered by the High Guard," Elaine said, her voice sounding blank.

"But that's the point, you see? Instead of serving their sentences all boarded up in their own realm, they're here," he waved at the arena, "serving it in the Crest. Sharing a stage—with the High Guard, of all things. It's a working model of the theory. Aric will be positively livid that he could not be here to see this. But perhaps you haven't heard about the latest studies—on unification."

"Unification," she repeated.

"Between the realms. It's something on the cutting edge in my particular field, and its development has begun to span into others, or it will soon enough—I dare say, even into the law. We've got a small circle of young, up-and-coming scholars here in Boaz who are pursuing this notion—I'm not sure I fully agree with them, mind you, but it certainly deserves discussion—that some small, incremental level of interaction between the realms, a limited union of sorts, while still respecting the diverse identities and boundaries, may be beneficial. Some would go further still. It is, as I said, cutting edge. We've not yet been invited into any notable forum to debate the merits of the idea or work out its qualities. So, it remains unsanctioned and, well, rather theoretical, I suppose."

A line of guards, as one, locked their shields together and plowed into the red-haired boy at a sprint. His chain whipped across the face of their shields, and then he was lifted off of his feet and driven into the far wall of the arena. His teeth clenched, and he let out another cry, as the guards crouched and pushed, and cursed at him to die already. The sound of his ribs cracking jolted everyone in the amphitheatre. He squealed and slumped to his knees. And then, to everyone's astonishment, the boy began reaching for the chain that had fallen from his hand. One of the guards who had rushed him stepped closer, kicked it aside, and raised his sword so that its point was just above the back of the boy's neck. A grunt, and then he thrust the sword into his flesh. The guard lost his balance and staggered to the ground. His blade had broken at the hilt.

"An unfortunate malfunction of equipment," Dr. Karl tisked when the crowd in the box stopped groaning. "The lieutenant should note it."

"Indeed," Regina shook her head. Then, she leaned over and took Jonathan's elbow. "Make a note for Michael. One of his men's equipment has apparently malfunctioned. I believe it was a dagger of some sort."

Through the gathering haze around him, Jonathan managed to answer:

"Alright, Mother."

Elaine bowed her head.

"Miss Temple," said Gregory in an unctuous whisper, "I hope you won't find this presumptuous, but, uhm, I suspect you might share some of my friends' philosophical inclinations. In terms of this new theory. At least, you may find their ideas intriguing. As one who has a professional interest in the Crag."

She raised her head to look at him. Even in the stupor that had fallen over him, Jonathan could almost sense the furrow forming on her brow, the indignant tilt of her eyebrow:

"And what do you presume to know of my interests?" she demanded.

Gregory held up his palms.

"If I have spoken out of turn, I pray for your forgiveness. Only—well, you must have realized your frequent excursions into the Crag's court would be noted?"

"I-I hadn't. Did you say noted?"

"And commended," he smiled, "at least among the more enlightened thinkers here in Boaz. Many of whom I count as friends."

Elaine said nothing.

"They'd be astonished if I brought you," Gregory continued, "or I should say honored—we would all be most honored if you would deign to join one of our discussions. The debate is lively, and the fare is always good. We meet each week at the coffee house." He leaned closer now. From behind the smile, he breathed conspiratorially: "We call ourselves the Solidarity Guild—isn't that just scrumptious?"

In the arena, Jonathan watched the High Guard resume their formations, their heads held a little higher, their high kicking steps a little less choreographed now that the floor was strewn with corpses. He saw Michael, his helm cast aside, beaming at Elaine, or perhaps he was beaming at Mother. With a flourish, Michael dipped his forefinger into the blood that stained the tip of his sword and saluted the Acacias' box with a bow.

While his brother adulated in the theatre's growing applause, a sweet, blissful sleep descended over Jonathan. The last thing he remembered was hearing Elaine turn to Gregory and ask a question:

"What's this theory called again?"

CHAPTER FOURTEEN

THE LIGHT WAS unrelenting; it pressed its presence into Jonathan's vision no matter how tightly he clenched his eyelids. A moan escaped from the back of his throat. He slid his tongue along the roof of his mouth, which felt like gravel, as he pulled the end of a bedspread over his face. Someone must have thrown the curtains open wide. Wherever Jonathan twisted, he was inundated with the noon sun pouring mercilessly over him.

He had no memory of how he had gotten here. But he knew, even without opening his eyes, where he was. His old bedroom. The blend of scents he remembered from his childhood, parchment and lantern oil, jasmine blooming on their vines outside the window, and that old rug with the faded seal of the Crest's court, they were what had first awakened him. He blinked in the sunlight, and the throbbing in his temples grew into a steady drum.

Stiff and pale, like two spindly twigs falling from a tree, his legs dropped and hit the floor. He staggered a pace, caught himself, and reached for the table he knew was somewhere close by. A washbasin clinked when he bumped into the table's edge, sending a splash of water over its sides.

"Shit."

His breath felt hot, almost barbed, inside his raw throat. He must have vomited at some point in the night. Jonathan leaned over the water and plunged his face fully into the porcelain. He lifted his head and let the tiny rivulets of cool water trickle back down his nose, his mouth, the stubble on his face. He rubbed his eyes to take stock of himself in a bronze mirror that hung just above the table.

Terror clenched his chest, a scream caught in his throat.

Jonathan's arms flailed as he fell hard to the floor. He was scrambling, his feet lashing out to push him away. He kicked and hit a table leg, causing it to wobble. He clutched his hands before his mouth and watched the washbasin teeter and then smash to pieces on the ground. Slowly, he lifted his gaze back to the mirror.

A spider as long as his forefinger sat perched atop the mirror's gilded frame. Its body was shiny, yellow, and black.

"Go away!" he hissed between his teeth. "Go—*away!*"

A long, front leg slowly extended from its body and slid forward across the metal's surface as if caressing the mirror. Jonathan felt his heart hammering in his ears. The horrible thing was staring at him. As if pondering what to do with him.

"Please ..."

As suddenly as it had appeared, the spider turned about, scampered up the wall, and vanished into a crack near the ceiling.

Jonathan lay on the floor, splayed and panting, his face now drenched in sweat instead of the basin water. No matter how hard he tried, he could not break his attention from the spider's hole. Its eyes were upon him, he was sure of it, stalking him as if he were a fly caught in a web. But when his breathing finally calmed, and the silence drew out longer and longer upon itself, he ventured to sit upright. The shards of the bowl were scattered within a puddle, some of them holding droplets that caught the sun's light. Jonathan cursed at himself.

"It is nothing. Nothing but a stupid, harmless insect. Nothing."

He made a defiant glance towards the mirror, as if daring the thing to show itself again, now that he had recovered his senses, but the spider did not return. One last look at the crack, and then Jonathan picked himself up, dressed, and descended the stairs.

In the great room, shafts of sunlight from high windows cast a sweeping terrazzo floor in blinding whiteness. When his eyes adjusted, he saw his mother, sitting at a long, covered table with the remains of a meal well picked over. She was writing her correspondence. A pheasant feather bobbed in her hand across a long sheet of paper, then paused at his approach:

"I heard a noise upstairs," she said without looking up.

"Sorry. I, uh, saw something."

"What was it?"

Jonathan clenched his jaw.

"A spider."

"Sounded like you broke my good porcelain. A sandal would have worked just as well."

"Sorry, Mother. I'll replace it."

"I doubt it. Porcelain's impossible to find these days. Sit down. There's breakfast left over."

He found a chair across the table from her and made a pretense of picking at an egg that had gone cold with a fork. He poured himself a cup of lukewarm tea and drank it while his mother continued writing. The only sound between them was the scratch of her quill across paper, the clink of his cup and saucer, and a noisy crow squawking outside. At last, she put the feather down, blotted her writing, neatly folded the paper, and let out an exaggerated sigh.

"These negotiations will have no end. All these legalities over a marriage contract. You lawyers have turned matrimony into an ordeal." She made the observation in a tone that seemed to hold Jonathan partly to blame.

"Elaine's uncle has some demands, does he?"

"The man wants a ransom—an absolute ransom—on our accounts, our properties, our vineyard stocks. Which would be exorbitance enough, but then there are all of these 'particulars,' is what he keeps calling them," his mother could not conceal the cynical smile that quivered across her lips. "This latest one now is they wish for Elaine to maintain her family name of Temple after the marriage, for her as well as any children that may issue. Which of course requires us to agree upon a lengthy document."

Jonathan was intrigued.

"What does Michael think of that?"

"Who cares what he thinks?"

"Well, what do you think then? It would mean there would be no more Acacias."

She narrowed her eyes and chewed on the feather end of her quill before she replied.

"It is neither here nor there. If she wants to strut about as a Temple with a litter of Temples in tow, fine. So long as her uncle provides what I require in Jachin—at a more reasonable price. If I get that, I could care less what she calls herself."

"It is a rather unique name. In this day and age, I mean. I'm surprised they've held on to it for so long."

"Don't be. They relish it," she gave the document she had just finished a meaningful tap, "why else go through the trouble with all this? Oh, they pretend to be demure about it, to be embarrassed by their connection to the old regime, as they call it. But it was a high connection, you see. And they want to make sure no one forgets it. All they have to trade is their connections, and this steward uncle of Elaine's holds onto every one of them as tightly as a merchant. No, I was expecting this."

Jonathan sipped his tea. His mother stared at him a moment and brusquely changed the subject:

"You're drinking too much."

"It's such lovely tea, though," Jonathan tried to joke.

"Of wine," she answered.

"I had one cup last night."

"And it put you in a stupor."

"I must not have been feeling well." He could hear his voice rising, becoming defensive. "I've been suffering from headaches lately. It's because of my work. I'm below ground for days at a time, surrounded by criminals—"

"Where you drink a bottle of our Midcrest Vineyard every evening. Sometimes two."

Jonathan was stunned for a moment, but quickly recovered:

"Which I water down. I always water it down. Did your little sources tell you that? And I never drink during court. It affects no one but me."

"People are beginning to whisper. So, it affects me."

She studied him closely, then tilted her chin back and let her eyelids flutter close. The folds of her neck rose and fell in a deep, contemplative sigh:

"Your father was the same, for a time. When he was first building his trade in wines. Whole cases of bottles disappeared down that man's gullet. Every night at that wretched Oak and Crow pub. Customer calls, he

would claim. They always ended with him staggering home, as red and
fat as a pufferfish," she shook her head, "or sometimes he'd just sleep on
the pub floor. Utterly disgraceful. But that all stopped once his license
came through." She now leaned forward across the table, her fingers
steepled, and spoke very carefully. It was, Jonathan reflected, how she
used to look when she would lay down a punishment. He felt his stomach begin to knot. "When your father procured the exclusive right to
the vineyards, we put a stop to all the drinking nonsense at once, and he
promptly began to govern himself with composure. He knew. Whatever
the Commonwealth gives, it can take away."

Jonathan could not hold his mother's hardened stare any longer.
His eyes fell to studying his hands, clenching and unclenching a pewter
spoon.

"Your judgeship came about, in part, because of your achievements,
in part because of the unfortunate rumors surrounding your predecessor,
and, in part, because of the favorable word I was able to secure for you
from my many acquaintances. It was no small feat, all those parts coming
together."

"I know," he groused.

"No. You don't. If you did, you wouldn't hazard your position so
carelessly." She leaned back in her chair, leaving Jonathan to shift uncomfortably in his.

"You don't understand. It–it's been hard. The court. The dirt, the
smell. All those people."

His face fell into his hands. It was vexing, to still feel so daunted by
this woman; and to still crave for scraps of her favor, like a mewling lap
dog. Jonathan grit his teeth and swallowed. As if sensing his thoughts,
Regina relented, if only ever so slightly. She talked aloud, more to herself
than to her son.

"I'm sure the Crag's court is a ghastly place. One's nerves would be
tried. The mind would grow weary from all those wretched people. Yes,
one must find a way to cope … You need a hobby. That's it. Some diversion more suitable than the cups. A girl perhaps? No. You're very much
your father's son in that regard as well." She thought a while, and then
set her hands on the table, her mind made up: "You will work on a book,
Jonathan. That should sufficiently occupy your energies."

"I've already written one."

"You have?"

"Yes. No one ever read it."

"Then write one people will read."

"I—" he started, but his words fell into the tablecloth, and he rested his chin in his hands, a blank, sullen look settling over him. Regina smiled.

"It's settled. We'll turn these wagging tongues into praise, as we turn your mind towards more noble pursuits. You will drink less and begin writing an eminently respectable tome—something to do with the law, I suppose. That shall be how you manage the hardship of your current commission from now on. I'll wait a suitable length of time before I begin passing remarks about your project. Say a month." Regina studied her son for a moment, as if surprised that he had not already produced a book for her review. Then she returned to her letters and finished her meal in silence while Jonathan, her child, sat quietly, alone in his thoughts.

He wandered through the streets of Boaz engrossed in a running conversation with himself. It was mid-afternoon now, the air was cool for the season, but he left his shirt collar open carelessly. His feet shuffled across the pavement, down one alley then another, beneath the shadows of the city's buildings, paying no heed to where he was going, but occasionally bumping into people.

"You fool … completely careless of you to—" Jonathan chided himself.

"Who're you calling careless, you little ass?" a fat merchant blurted back at him. A cluster of receipts fluttered around his feet. "You knocked into me."

"Huh? Oh, sorry. Sorry."

"Now I've got to start all over …"

Jonathan hurried around the man and resumed his walking and his fretting. He had been talking to himself ever since he had left his family's house. Scolding himself, mostly.

"Of course, people would start noting it. They're not blind, and you've been careless. So utterly careless." He stopped beneath a signpost and scanned and surroundings to make sure no one was looking his way. Men and women came and went, no one taking notice of him, and yet Jonathan had this sense, this mounting anxiety, that they all knew what he had been doing these past months. They were talking about him or would be soon. They knew because he had scarcely tried to hide it. He punched his fist hard into his hand. It was not in defiance, but a kind of surrender.

"It's gotten ahead of me. I should've caught it sooner, but now it's gotten ahead. One glass. It needs to be a single glass at a time—with a pinch of seasoning. But no more than one glass. From now on."

He inhaled a deep breath, let it out. Then he closed his eyes and did it again, letting the briskness take over inside his chest, to loosen the tightness. His thoughts slowly settled. For the first time, perhaps in days, Jonathan felt a genuine ease washing over his senses without the aid of wine. It was liberating, and yet still lucid. He became more aware of his surroundings. The people milling about seemed less severe, less inclined to watchfulness. Their conversations sounded pleasant. A group of children squealed excitedly, splashing one another in a fountain beneath a ring of statues, their nannies dutifully ignoring them. The sculpted faces that watched their play were bleached white from the sun, and the bronze picks, and swords, and hammers they held high in the air had long ago rusted into patina. He tilted his head back to see past the tops of the buildings, to the wooded face of the Mountain above. Verdant green climbed and faded into gray then disappeared in a bright array of clouds that clung to the precipices, like a coronet reflecting its luster down upon the city—his city.

"Hello again, sir," came a friendly voice behind him.

Jonathan turned, expecting to find a lawyer or perhaps a commissar. His bemused expression turned to surprise when he saw who it was.

A thin, and very kindly looking old man wearing a faded cloth apron was waving to him from his storefront.

"It's Harold, the apothecarist," the man said. "You came in last evening. How is the headache?"

"Hm? Oh—better, thank you."

"Excellent, excellent," he clapped his hands. "If I may be so bold, you look much improved."

"Thanks to your cure."

"Gingerroot and cayenne," Harold winked. "As a tonic, there is simply no better."

They chatted amiably, and Harold, who seldom had customers or company, insisted that Jonathan come inside again for a visit. In the pleasantness of his present mood, Jonathan answered brightly and followed the apothecary through a swinging, shuttered door. He turned in a half-circle, remembering, only dimly, the crowded shelves and overrun tables of the cramped, dusty room. It was like recalling a scene from a dream.

While Harold went to fetch some tea, Jonathan searched for someplace to sit down. Everywhere he turned, there were cases, cabinets, pots, and jars, all covered in papers and labels. Everything was placed on top of something else, it seemed, with one slender aisle on the floor that allowed for a passage through. By an amphora lay a beige cat, which almost blended into the pile of vellum it had turned into a bed. It lifted its head, blinked its pale eyes once at him, and went back to its nap. At last, Jonathan found a stool that he managed to pry out from behind a curio just as Harold returned.

"Here we are," Harold said, handing Jonathan a cracked cup of steaming brown water. He settled himself on the amphora as if it were a perfectly natural place for anyone to sit.

They drank and talked about the goings-on in town, the rumors of the Stewards' new Plan, and Harold's musings about all his customers who had died in the past few years. The apothecarist was from one of those unnamed villages off the High Road a little further down the Mountain, a place he spoke of wistfully. His life savings had gone into purchasing this long, cluttered hole in the wall near the central square of Boaz. As he talked, the cat kept snoring softly, completely unperturbed by Harold's habit of stroking the fur from the back of its head over its eyes. But after a while, Jonathan sensed that Harold was struggling to broach something, something he very much wanted to talk about, but that he feared could prove unpleasant. When Harold had slurped the last of his tea, he finally got around to it.

"I am very much obliged to you, spending so much time entertaining a lonely old man."

"It's been a delight."

"You're too kind. That you are … You know," Harold said, lifting his finger thoughtfully, "I, uhm, was a bit puzzled by your other purchase last night."

Jonathan raised his eyebrows.

"Redcap is an unusual item to carry, for an apothecary. The only reason I had any at all was because it had been a part of the back stock when I purchased the business, oh, some six years ago. Always thought it an oddity. Would have gotten around to dumping it, but, well," he shrugged and gestured at the store's surroundings, "I never have the heart to get rid of things."

Jonathan focused intently on drinking from his cup.

"Everything has a use eventually," he replied from behind its brim.

"Yes, sir," Harold nodded vigorously, nearly dropping his saucer. "Indeed, I've always held that to be true. It's what drew me to studying plants as a boy, all the things that can be done with them. Everything does have its use. But, uh …"

"Yes?"

"Well, that's just it, sir. The speckled gulleystar, that's its proper name, it doesn't really—have much of a use, that is. At least, not up here. It'll glow like any other gulleystar, I suppose, but then, that's not something we would ever need in the Crest. Not when we've got torches, and candles, and lanterns, and all … Truth is, sir, it's something of a, uhm—of a poison. Alcohol dilutes the toxin to a degree; water less so. But if one were to ever accidentally ingest it, it would kill a man straight away."

"I certainly do not intend to eat them!" Jonathan laughed, perhaps a bit too loudly.

"No, no," Harold shook his head. "Of course not, sir. I didn't mean to imply you would. It's just. Technically, speckled gulleystar's supposed to be registered. It's that deadly. So, uhm." Harold fell into a fit of clearing his throat and petting the poor cat with a nervous energy that would have had any other animal howling in protest. Jonathan clasped his hands together and dropped his voice.

"You wish to know what I bought them for, is that it?"

A look of relief washed over Harold's face.

"Yes, sir. I'm very sorry for the impertinence, but yes. I was shock—er, surprised, I should say, that someone wanted the horrid stuff, and I was certainly glad to get rid of it. But it's been weighing on my mind ever since. Then I happened to see you again today, and well ..." His voice trailed off.

"I understand, Harold. It's a simple explanation. Have you ever worked in the Citadel?"

"The Citadel?" Harold's eyes went wide. "No-no, sir. I've never had leave to go there. You mean that you—"

"I work there, yes. A minor administrative post. But one that entails a great deal of reading."

"My goodness."

It was plain from Harold's reaction that working within the Citadel was as exotic a notion as working within the moon. He looked at Jonathan with something between awe and trepidation.

"I spend the better part of each month in there," Jonathan explained, "where, unlike here, it is rather dark and we always find ourselves in short supply of all those candles, lampposts, and torches you noted."

"I see, sir. I think I do. That must be hard on the eyes."

"It is. I shall probably go blind one day." Jonathan had to stop himself from saying more, for he was on the verge of laughing. But then Harold, who still seemed bothered, scratched at a wisp of his silver hair and posed a question that caught Jonathan off guard.

"But why the speckleds? It's an awfully rare species. And there's ample plenty of the plain grays to be had in the Crag, which'll glow when pressed. Wouldn't the grays serve your purpose just as well?"

"You would think they would," Jonathan answered slowly, his eyes flitting around the clutter of the room. When his gaze fell on a toppled pile of yellowing inventory papers, an answer occurred to him. "But have you ever tried to read by the light of an ordinary gulleystar?"

"No, sir, I've not had leave to do that either."

"I have. Turns out they glow almost the same color as our paper. Which completely washes out any lettering. You might as well stare at a blank page than try to read anything by them. The speckled, on the other hand, gives a nice, warm scarlet light. Steady as a candle. And the words are clear as day. I can read an entire report by the light of one of those fine mushrooms."

"I had no idea, sir." Harold seemed genuinely impressed. "My, my. That is clever."

Jonathan dipped his head.

"A simple solution to a simple problem. So long as I always keep a few handy." He patted the little bag he carried with him. "I must return to work tomorrow and had run completely out of my supply. That is before my headache brought me to your fine dispensary. So, you helped me twice over, Harold."

At that, Harold positively beamed. He tapped his fingers as if applauding. The cat stirred, shook itself awake, and stretched.

"My, my," Harold said again, his head now bobbing with his amazement. "It's just as you say, sir. Everything has a use. So it does."

The dawn came on gray, and heavy, and overcast, which suited Jonathan's mood. He stood at the transom of an open doorway to his mother's house, as tired as when he had gone to bed, and stared out across the gravel road for his cart to arrive. A mist hovered above the grass lawn. The air had a crisp edge to it, and the cicadas were buzzing noisily. He rubbed his temples and adjusted the satchel his mother had hoisted on him when he had made his goodbye. It held a glass vial of expensive ink, a cluster of quills, and an entire ream of blank paper. It felt heavy on his shoulder.

Next to him, Michael was leaning against a pillar. He was freshly shaved, but dressed in one of his more casual uniforms since his parade attire still needed laundering after the performance at the amphitheatre. Michael looked bored and had hardly spoken to Jonathan.

He's only here to keep an eye on me.

A momentary cloud break allowed a feeble hint of daylight to fall over them, but it was gone as quickly as it had come. That might be the last he would see for days, Jonathan mused. His fingers were beginning to twitch, so he pressed them again to the sides of his head, while Michael stretched his arms in front of him and let out a loud yawn.

"Are they ever going to get here?"

Jonathan made an ambivalent noise. He drew his magistrate's cloak farther over his shoulders against the chill and glared at Michael.

"Are you going to follow me back to my court chair?"

"Hey, I only hired your cart. After I get you loaded, you're on your own."

Only, Jonathan knew, he would not be—not really. Mother had surely made arrangements to have him watched for the whole journey back to the Crag. She had her eye on him now; that was what their little breakfast meeting yesterday had been all about. Her eye and, as evidenced by how quickly and quietly he was being shunted back to the Crag, her finger as well.

"What if I want to be on my own now?"

Michael shook his head.

"Can't do it."

"Of course not," Jonathan sighed. There were so many pointed, terrible things he wanted to shout into Michael's vacuous face just then. He could raise such a scene that the old woman would have to emerge from her lair. He thought on it briefly, but in the end, decided it was not worth it. It would never be worth it.

"Mother's orders," he said to himself.

"Mother's orders," Michael agreed.

Jonathan watched a lone, gray rabbit sit upright from within a clump of ivy. It sniffed the air and then bounded off, disappearing into a silvery mist that was beginning to dissipate. It would turn into a warm day; he could already tell.

"Where's Elaine?" Jonathan asked.

"Some coffeehouse. Didn't get enough of the entourage at the theatre, I guess. So now she's having breakfast with them."

That drew Jonathan's attention from his headache. He looked over at Michael.

"Who's she meeting with?"

Michael made an annoyed wave. "The usual climbers: Gregory, Aric. She said some other names, but I wasn't paying attention. Oh, wait. She did mention somebody you'd know. That loopy old codger you replaced on the court, the one who got himself stuck in the Commissariat."

"Judge Cloud?"

"Whatever his name. Elaine said he was going to be there. Maybe she wanted to laugh at him before he gets taken up."

That was strange. For Judge Cloud, with all his past troubles, to be out and about in public was reckless; not at all in keeping with the deliberate, soft-spoken scholar Jonathan recalled. Former officials out of favor were often taken up, especially right before a new Plan for the Commonwealth is announced. There was ample precedent for that sort of thing. Surely, he would know that. Jonathan wanted to press his brother further, but it was clear to him that Michael had already grown bored with the line of conversation.

"Can you—can you tell Elaine good-bye for me? I don't think she was expecting me to leave until this evening."

"Sure, whatever."

Their attention was broken at the sound of a small cart's wooden wheels crunching across the gravel roadway.

It was a crude, two-wheel cart, the kind that a connected commissar could let out for extra money when he was off duty. A colorless, underfed ox was yoked to its front, and as it pulled closer, Jonathan recognized the driver. He was a bald, heavyset man in his fifties who did odd jobs for his mother and seldom spoke a word. The man was cracking a long switch across the beast's shoulders every few steps. The cart came to a halt, and without a word, the commissar slid down, pulled out a step, and motioned for Jonathan to climb up onto a rickety bench behind his seat. As he got settled, Jonathan watched Michael drop a handful of coins into the man's palm—more than the trip should have cost—and then the man hoisted himself effortlessly back up over the rail and gave the ox a hard switch. As if in reply, a loud, wet snort sprayed from the animal's nose, the cart lurched forward, and they bumped down the road, a much faster pace than Jonathan thought was entirely safe.

Jonathan looked back only once. The sprawling house, the porch, the ivy-covered columns, the rolling lawn—his home—drew farther away. Michael had already gone inside. When the cart reached a pine tree wood that bordered his mother's land, a light rain fell. The driver paused to open a small wooden locker beneath his seat where he kept a bundle of oiled parkas. Jonathan refused, at which the man simply shrugged, slipped his own over his head, and set out once more, taking, what seemed to Jonathan, to be an out of the way route through the foothills. He was steering wide to avoid the streets of Boaz, Jonathan realized.

They wended for miles, up and down sloping runs, through wild heather and weeded meadows where no one had lived or worked for years. The cart slogged in the mud past collapsed cottages and overgrown fences. Soon Jonathan was soaked to the skin and shivering. When they reached the top of a particularly steep knoll, he could just make out an outcrop of buildings through the storm. It was the very edge of the city. He stared at the building's lights and wondered whether any of them might be that coffeehouse where Elaine and Judge Cloud were gathered.

"I think I would have liked that," he muttered to himself.

The more he thought on it, the more the idea of passing a morning with company, with Elaine especially, at a table with bread and a hot drink, seemed like a pleasant prospect. Before they had gone much farther, Jonathan ventured to ask the driver if he knew of a coffeehouse where they could stop, just to warm themselves of course, but the man did no more than glance over his shoulder to shake his head. He whipped the poor ox into a trot, and Jonathan could only watch the lights dwindle and fade in the distance. He squinted his eyes as heavier droplets fell. They stung against his face.

The gray storm swallowed the last of Boaz's buildings, and Jonathan wondered whether at that moment, perhaps in that very house, if the people he was thinking about were gathered around a roaring hearth. He imagined they would be sipping chocolate and making eloquent speeches about lofty ideals, while a brilliant former judge sat upon a cushion at the head of their table and spoke the truth about the horrid conditions in the Crag, and the need to elevate its mistreated residents. Judge Acacia sat upon his wet and splintered bench in silence, while a cart pulled his Honor, most unwillingly, back into the Mountain.

Chapter Fifteen

J ONATHAN SHIFTED IN his chair and felt the numbing throb in his feet
begin to ease. He stretched his legs, and in doing so brushed up against
something on his desk, which sent a ream of pages tumbling into his lap.
"Blast it all," Nicholas swore under his breath. Then, quickly com-
posing himself, "I beg your pardon, your Honor."

Poor Nicholas, normally indefatigable in the courtroom, had been
running all day between clerks, files, defendants, bailiffs, and the bench,
trying to keep pace with the backlogged cases and Jonathan's rulings. His
hair was thoroughly tousled and all of his fingers stained with ink. Without the least heed to Jonathan, he leaned across the judge's chair, reached
between Jonathan's legs, and bunched up all of the scattered paper.

"Sorry," Jonathan grunted.

"Next case," Nicholas called out, as he flattened one of the pages
on the table. "Case number nineteen, eighty-six, dash oh, oh, three, one,
one, forty; Commonwealth versus Adele Grimes of the Lower Quarter.
Charged with three counts of unlicensed fornication, three counts of
unlicensed bartering, one felony count of spreading a communicable
disease—where is this woman Grimes?"

A bailiff emerged from a gray, murmuring crowd that was still milling about in the gallery and tiptoed up to the podium in the center of
the courtroom. He dipped his head toward Jonathan and replied:

"Looks like the woman had an accident in the guardroom."

Accident indeed. "When will she be well enough to appear?" Jonathan asked.

The guard grew skittish, pursing his lips. "Believe she's dead, sir."

"Case closed then," Nicholas scratched through his page, and a set of
clerks hunched over a long row of tables in front of the bench did the
same. "That's the last of the backlogs," he murmured to Jonathan.

They had worked through the day without a break. Elaine had been in court for most of the morning, hammering away at every point and turn for the good of all the raggers, herdsmen, scullery cooks, and dock workers that had been rounded up into court; and to Jonathan's annoyed bemusement, she managed to somehow slow down an already ponderous docket. But by noon, she had to catch her cart back to Boaz, and without a lawyer to prolong the proceedings for the defendants, the Court of Common Corrections was finally beginning to make some progress in the day's docket.

It was very late in the afternoon, and they were about to tackle the final run of cases scheduled for the day. Jonathan was as weary as he had ever felt on the bench. Though he was glad they were nearing an end, he found that he was already missing Elaine's clever imaginings. The last case she had argued, in particular, where with a straight face she likened balm addiction to "a disease"—no different than a cold or gout—still had Jonathan smiling to himself.

He turned to Nicholas to call the next case when he noticed the clerk was transfixed by something on the docket sheet. His little eyes darted back and forth and then froze.

"Blast their incompetence!"

"Nicholas?"

"My apologies, your Honor. My profuse, *sincere* apologies. Blast it all! This should have been brought to our immediate attention before we even began." His face was pinched in anger and he shouted down to the clerks, hissing at them to look at the top of page seventy-three. "Someone's going to get noted for this."

While Nicholas sent the clerks into a panic, Jonathan craned his head to look at his docket sheet. Just above his clerk's gray-speckled thumb, he saw a case's style:

Commonwealth versus Elliott Porter

It was followed by a strange series of notations Jonathan had never seen before. Even the charge was foreign. Next to the case number, it simply noted, "A-I."

"We'll need to clear the front transept, and bring in a second scribe for publication, "Nicholas was barking orders and at the same time, trying to explain to Jonathan.

"It's a high-profile case. Should've been called first, before the backlog. Commonwealth's counsel's been waiting."

"Can't we at least take a moment to—?"

"—impossible," Nicholas shook his head firmly. Before Jonathan could press him further, his clerk was running down the steps of the bench and over to the commissars' tables where he spotted a man sitting with his back against the wall in a plain black cloak and a beige set of expensive clothes. In all the mayhem of court, Jonathan had not noticed him. The man's face was tanned and wore a bored expression, but he acknowledged Nicholas' profuse supplications with a condescending smirk. He rose from his seat and followed Nicholas over to the podium, where Nicholas held his hands to his mouth and shouted:

"Oyez, oyez! Ladies and gentlemen. Men and women. Harken and hear me. Give heed, draw close, and bear witness to the justice of our Commonwealth. The Court of Common Corrections is now in session, the Honorable Judge Jonathan Acacia, presiding …"

It was the formal invocation for court. The only time Jonathan had ever heard Nicholas use it before was on his first day presiding as a judge. Despite his headache and fatigue, Jonathan felt his pulse begin to quicken. Nicholas introduced the dark-cloaked gentleman, a Solomon Waters, C.C., and then called the case of Commonwealth versus Elliott Porter.

Jonathan glanced down at the scribbled notes on his docket page once more, still trying to make sense of them, when Waters addressed him in a deep, soothing voice.

"May it please the Court?"

"Yes, counsel. I'll confess, I'm at a bit of a loss. Apparently, we owe you an apology for keeping you waiting—"

"Not at all, Judge Acacia," the man smiled easily, and the oil in his combed hair gave a warm sheen that seemed to set him apart from the drab faces that surrounded him. "I'll confess, your honor," he said as if he were sharing some friendly secret, only the two of them could hear, "I was quite looking forward to the day when I would have the occasion to present a case before you—though I had assumed that would be in Jachin. But these things have a way of working out for the best."

"You've come all the way from Jachin for this Porter case?"

"Correct. I am honored to serve as counsel for the Commonwealth in this matter." He cleared his throat. "Since the Crest has not prosecuted an Article One case in nearly a decade, may I assume, your honor, that this is the first such case you would have encountered?"

It ran against his instinct to admit such a thing in open court, but Jonathan had no idea what this lawyer was talking about.

"Quite understandable," Waters assured him. "Fortunately, they have become a rare event in the peace and prosperity of our modern society. But, alas, they do still arise from time to time." He unwound a set of carefully bound scrolls, glanced at them only briefly, and continued, never once taking his eyes off of Jonathan. "Elliott Porter, also known as," and here he coughed, as if the alias name had stuck in his throat, "also known as, the Divine Eli, has been charged with a direct violation of Article One of our Commonwealth. 'There is no god, and none shall be proclaimed.' This man has publicly proclaimed faith in deities and incited others to do the same. His inflammatory speech has disturbed the safety and peace of the Crag. To wit ..."

Jonathan listened as the Commonwealth's Counsel recited, in meticulous, forceful detail, a story that, to Jonathan, sounded like nothing more than a creative porter's scam of a family with a sick girl. This Eli apparently pretended he was a priest. Which would have been laughable in itself, but then he proceeded to "cast a spell" to heal a child's fever, after worming a few coins out of the father. The only things at all noteworthy were that the girl was in an academy and she later recovered from her illness, probably owing to the natural hardiness of Crag children. Yet, Waters was laying out a presentation that would have been worthy of a case of high treason. The Crest prayed that the man be removed "in due form," a phrase Jonathan had never heard before. Waters finally reached a conclusion and turned towards the gallery.

"Excellent, I see we have the defendant present."

It was the first time Jonathan had ever been shocked at the sight of a litigant in his courtroom. The skeletal limbs, the eyes settled deep in the hollows of a skull, the open wounds, the rags and chains, were no different than countless other prisoners who had been brought up from the Tombs. But something in this man seemed to wear these conditions with no more care than a set of clothes. As if he might cast off his battered body whenever the mood suited him. He tilted his head up, revealing a radial of scars around his cheeks and eyes, and looked straight at Jonathan. They were mismatched, the eyes, which made the man's appearance all the more jarring.

It took a moment for Jonathan to remember what he was doing. He faltered, then began his colloquy about a plea, guilt or innocence, trial or mercy, the potential severity of punishment if he went to trial, although in truth, he had no idea what the sentence could be, or even what this man's crime was. The defendant only stared at him with mild disinterest, when Waters cleared his throat once again.

"Forgive me, your Honor. I should have mentioned this before. But in an Article One case, there must be a public trial. I understand that is not the custom in most Common Corrections cases, but the defendant here cannot plead for the Court's leniency. You must hear the Commonwealth's case and then declare his guilt."

Jonathan found Nicholas's attention, who very subtly inclined his head to confirm that what the lawyer had just said was both correct and inarguable.

"Well. I suppose we'll enter a not guilty plea and, uh, proceed accordingly."

Waters straightened the clasp of his cloak, placed his fingertips along the edges of the podium, and with a long, poignant pause, began his case against Eli.

He first called a haughty looking Crag officer who Jonathan had seen in court from time to time to testify. Oliver was his name, and he seemed familiar—overly familiar—with the workings of the court. Jonathan began to write notes for himself, but the man's recollections simply repeated much of what Jonathan had already heard. The defendant had heard about a sick child named Tanner, barged into her home claiming he could "heal" her in exchange for money, somehow she got better, and then the man became unhinged by the belief that he had been responsible for a miracle. A few weeks ago, the defendant ran into the girl and accosted her. In Oliver's decade of service to the Commonwealth, he had learned to spot the trouble-makers, and he could say, with complete certainty, Eli was one of them. Oliver was certain the Court would adjudge him harshly.

"Where's the girl and the father?" Jonathan asked him, looking around. No one matching their description remained in the gallery.

"Your Honor," Waters answered apologetically, "despite Captain Oliver's best efforts, most of the girl's family is presently in absentia."

"Really?"

Oliver replied with an almost sing-song flippancy:

"It happens on occasion," he confessed, "the Craggies have ears like the rest of us, and sometimes they hear whispers when they're about to be taken up. It's an enormous realm. And the checkpoints are not always manned as closely as we would like. We catch up with them eventually, but, uhm—well, this Tom Tanner, that's the girl's father, he's a bit of a wily one. Known guildsman, Tanner. The defendant too, actually."

"I see."

"Fortunately," Waters continued, "Captain Oliver took the precaution of obtaining the father's affidavit before the man absconded. If I may present it to the Court?"

Nicholas delivered a rolled, weather-stained paper to the bench. Jonathan broke a small wax seal, unfolded it, and read the affidavit of Tom Tanner. It was a document that, judging by the hand that had written it, and the scratched, pinched signature at the bottom, had been drawn up by someone other than Tom Tanner.

"He can write his own name?"

"Indeed he can," Oliver said. "I watched him sign it myself. Didn't need a bit of help. He's quite resourceful for a Craggie."

"And not very fond of the defendant, apparently," Jonathan mused, as he read over the affidavit once more. "I was always under the impression that guildsmen were more brotherly than this. I don't suppose this Dr. Mosley is here, either."

"The importance of his work," Waters replied, "prohibits him straying so far from his assigned patients. But I am told that the doctor would confirm that he treated the Tanner girl for a common infection and that she made a full recovery under his care. We do have one witness from the family."

Waters glanced behind him and then motioned impatiently at a woman sitting in the corner to come and join him on the podium. She was squat, unkempt, and visibly shaking. When she was not wiping her hands on a soiled apron, she was pulling at an end of her peppery red hair that otherwise would have covered pocks in her cheeks. She must have carried an odor, because at her approach, Waters crinkled his nose in disgust. The lawyer spoke quickly, severely, obviously intent on getting the examination over with:

"State your name to the Court."

She looked up, a canyon of space between them, and tried to smile sheepishly at Jonathan. But then her bottom lip quivered until her mouth simply fell agape.

"Bette Tanner, sir," she finally managed.

"Bette Tanner, your Honor," Waters growled.

"S-sorry. I mean, sorry, your Honor."

"Not me. Never mind. To whom are you married?"

"No one now."

The lawyer blew out a harsh breath, and Bette must have recognized that she had answered the question wrongly. She tried to correct herself, her body slouching from the effort:

"I mean to say, sir, that officially, like on the roles, Tom Tanner's probably my husband. But I've not seen him or my Timmy for weeks."

"Tom Tanner is your husband, is what you mean," said Waters.

"Y-yes."

"And Lillia is your daughter?"

"I birthed her. Yes. Timmy is my little boy."

"We are not concerned with your son. Do you recognize this man down here?"

Her head darted nervously as if the mere sight of this man might petrify her, and then she nodded.

"Who is he?"

"That's the one who came to our home, back when we lived up in Industry Caverns. He claimed to be a priest."

"Tell us what you recall."

Jonathan found himself leaning forward as this Crag woman, who had once lived in a nice apartment, but now had to pick crops from a shack, stumbled through her story. He was certain she was being truthful; the woman was too stupid for guile. But as she went on, something bothered Jonathan. He kept looking down at the affidavit, and many of the details she remembered flatly contradicted what the father had said. No doubt, the woman was bitter with her husband, and she loathed her daughter for some reason. The inconsistencies would not have troubled Jonathan, only they concerned things that neither she nor her husband would have had any reason to lie about. If they were lies, they were pointless lies, with no possible purpose or motive. When she came to a pause, Jonathan interrupted her.

"And at what point was Dr. Mosley called?"

She stared back at him.

"Dr. Mosley, sir?"

"Yes, the man your husband hired to treat Lillia. The man who healed her. When did he arrive?"

"I-uh, don't know, uhm. We got her a doctor?" Bette's voice fell. Her head now swiveled between Jonathan and the lawyer looming above her, a man who looked as if he might strike her in the face at any moment. Waters' face grew taut, then the serenity returned when he addressed Jonathan:

"Your Honor, the witness' nerves are strained. The events themselves were likely distressing. I suspect at the time she was incapacitated with worry, so her husband simply brought the doctor on his own."

"Was that what happened?"

"I don't—" she looked imploringly towards Waters before answering, "A doctor? —I mean, it must have been as he says, sir. Whatever he says is what happened."

At that moment, a revelation came to Jonathan. His gaze had alighted on the tapestries hanging in the courtroom, the Commonwealth's flags spread wide to cover the stained walls, and it struck him then how much they resembled curtains on a stage. The whole courtroom was a theatre. The clerks, the lawyers, the bored, lounging bailiffs, the prisoners, and, yes, the judge, they were all playing their parts and saying their lines in a tedious play, here in an amphitheater, a drama that no one was watching. Only Bette had missed her cue.

Jonathan knew then that this woman and her family were condemned. As this defendant would be soon. He would have dwelled on

that thought longer had the lawyer not given another one of his obse-
quious coughs.

"Your Honor, the Commonwealth will excuse the witness at this
time and conclude by calling the defendant, Elliott Porter."

"Bring him forward," Nicholas hissed, prompting one of the bailiffs
to usher Eli closer to the bench. His gaze never broke from Jonathan's,
even when Waters began questioning him. The man made no response,
no indication that he had even heard the Commonwealth's counsel's
accusations, no matter how soaring or how damning they were. Do you
worship gods? Do you claim to be a priest? Who else is with you? You
bragged that you had healed this girl by magic, didn't you? Do you deny
that your inflammatory words have harmed your fellow residents? That
you are a threat to the Commonwealth? Waters had worked himself into
a fever of indignation. His nostrils were flaring:

"Even now, your cabal of god-worshipers spreads your lies across the
Crag, like a cancer, will you not deny it, Porter? You stand charged of a
capital crime. His Honor has the power to remove you in due form from
the community of our Commonwealth. Have you nothing to say, man?"

The silence was broken only by the sounds of some feet scuffling and
a few murmurs in the gallery. Waters was about to continue, but Jonathan
held up his hand. Something in this man's unwavering stare troubled
Jonathan; it was not at all like the other madmen he had judged. There
was a lucidity lying beneath the surface here, Jonathan could almost feel
it.

"Eli," Jonathan said, "I know you can hear me. And I know you can
speak. If you don't answer counsel's questions, I will have to find you
guilty. You'll be condemned to die, like he says. But I also have the power
to save you, if you speak."

At that, Waters let out a muffled gasp, but then quickly composed
himself, deliberately smoothing his shirt and trousers. He was watching
Jonathan warily now. And then Eli opened his mouth. His voice was a
rasp, like a man who had been hunted, but somehow everyone inside
heard it clearly:

"You can't save me," he said softly, "The girl—her darkness, it's …
spreading everywhere now. You can't save anything."

Now Waters was beaming. He gave a wink at Jonathan, impressed by what they had done, as if, together, as lawyer and judge, they had conspired to finally wring an utterance from this wicked man.

"Well done, your Honor," Waters gushed. "A most excellent— a most compelling—point. The Court extends the flower of justice's mercy, and this zealot stomps upon it. His silence has been nothing but scorn. Let the record reflect the defendant refused the Court's offer of leniency. The Commonwealth rests, confident that the Court will judge this man's crimes, and his obvious contempt for this Court, most justly."

Jonathan was irritated. That was not what he had been after, at all. He pinched the bridge of his nose and looked down from the bench. Eli stood below him, still unmoving, his eyes twinkling in the glow of gulleystar pots and the few tallow candles that were still flaming. He was, it seemed, both acutely aware of and utterly indifferent to the fact that his life hung in Jonathan's hands.

Who was this man? An utterly unremarkable Craggie. A porter. He had no record, hardly any notes. Innocuous as a gulleystar. As faultless as one, too. But one that had to be pressed. The Crest demanded it and awaited only one word from Jonathan, the word of justice's demand. The time had come.

Jonathan delivered his line.

Eli studied his hands. Gnarled, gray, they smelled like turned milk. The fingernails had fallen off. These bones were once my fingers, he thought impassively.

Two shadows were coming into focus, one wide, the other tall, standing in silhouette against the torch-lit portal of his holding cell. A mail-clad fist clamped onto his shoulder and hoisted him up with a jerk. The manacles on his forearms were unlocked and replaced by a set of smaller shackles, the ones he had worn in that big courtroom.

"Time to go, Porter," grunted the larger shadow.

That would be Tye, Eli could tell from the voice—and the smell of cragfire. The other one would have to be Rod, the boy.

Eli stood slowly. Under the weight of the chains, it took him a while to cross the distance of the cell's floor. He had to shuffle around the naked body of a stout, middle-aged Crag woman splayed on the ground, her hands still bound behind her, her gray and auburn hair soaked in her blood. The woman had been twitching in painful throes when they brought him back here from the courtroom. That was hours ago, and now she was dead. She had been a tanner, one of the guards had mentioned. Eli closed his eyes as he passed by her.

Tye and Rod, for once, were not cursing him, or hurrying him along, and their roughness was subdued, half-hearted. They led him down a dim and narrow hall of the Tombs. There were only a few cells here, and they were quiet, though Eli could feel pale, haunted eyes following his movement. From within one of them, Eli saw a lone hand extending past the bars, open as if beckoning for his attention. It slowly drew into a form with a single, jagged index finger pointing upward; it was brought to a forehead that was shrouded in the darkness. Eli stared blankly at the cell. From within, a voice whispered:

"Remember me, Porter. When you've reached the gods …"

"What's that?" Tye bellowed. His spear came crashing down hard against the iron bars, splitting the hand into a bloody spray. The prisoner curled on the ground, howling in pain.

"Now clean it up." Tye threw the man a rag that had been hanging from a peg. He spun on his heel and gave Eli a light thump to move him along.

"That better be spotless when I get back," Tye called over his shoulder, "or you'll get the same for your other hand. Anyone else want to make a sign of the gods? Maybe hold a little prayer circle? Offer sacrifice? Come on, now." He glowered at each cell door. "There's plenty of room for more at the Falls." The sound of water dripping echoed from somewhere, and the prisoner with the broken hand muffled his sobs. The other guard standing over Eli tried to sound menacing, but his adolescent voice cracked.

"Don't look like you've got any takers."

Tye tisked and shook his head. "No, it don't, Rod. Just us then."

The corridor moved by; a trance of gray pierced by shafts of light from the few torches lining the walls. At last, they reached the final door, a black iron sheet thrust into an arch chiseled into the Mountainside. It seemed only vaguely familiar; so much time had passed since Eli had first come through. He remembered staring over his shoulder as it slammed shut, like a coffin lid, he had thought with horror. And now it was opening again. Tye fumbled with the lock and then gave the door a shove.

"We've got to dress you in due form, Porter," Tye said, motioning to a chair with clothes on it. The shackles came off, they stripped Eli, and a cheap, scratchy garment was tied around his waist so that his chest and lower legs were bare.

"Get the cable," Tye ordered.

Rod reached over Eli's head for a heavy rope, as thick as a ship's line, which was wound around a hook on the wall. He looped it once about Eli's neck and pulled it so tight Eli was sputtering for air.

"Don't strangle him, you idiot," Tye gave Rod a drub on the head. The line loosened, and Eli drew a painful breath. "You off one of these, even if it's an accident—even if it's a *real* accident—and the clerks will have you flayed, boy. Porter, lift your head."

Eli did as he was commanded and watched as a set of hairy knuckles flecked with dirt stretched a black cloth to cover his eyes. It would be the last thing Eli ever saw.

They had walked for hours, maybe days. One step, then another, then another. His feet no longer feeling the rock beneath him. At first, it had been dark, a darkness so encompassing, it seeped through Eli's blindfold, as something felt, not seen. Other than their footsteps, the guards' booted and his barefoot, it had been a quiet journey. Buried deep within that silence, though, Eli could still hear the voices. Not the jailers' prattle, the voices in the darkness. He smiled to himself.

Because today, for the first time, the voices were not screaming. They were singing. Softly. A somber melody, a kind of song where he could make out his name in some of the distant strains. It was pretty. Almost as if, he thought, the shadows were finally ready to make a peace with him.

Or maybe it's me who's ready?

He found it a pleasant conundrum to mull over. Despite his shackles and his battered health and what he suspected was soon going to be a painful fate, Eli felt relief like none he had ever known.

He was still wondering at this change in the voices when his guards came to a halt. Men came and talked brusquely, the singing in the dark faded into a kind of postlude and was gone. There was the grate of a metal door swinging open, an onslaught of sound, real sound that made his ears ring, and then Eli felt fresh air upon his face.

They were outside, on the Mountain. He took a few halting steps. Warmth penetrated every inch of Eli's skin. A rushing noise, like gouts of water coursing through pipes on the verge of bursting, accompanied each gust of wind. Eli sneezed, his nose roiling from the strange smells, and Rod broke the guards' silence by bursting out laughing. Then they set out walking again.

They traveled along a roadway that wended them around in bends, up and down flights of stairs, over hills and bridges. All the way, the cable around Eli's neck pulled him along steadily, while Tye and Rod talked in hurried snatches of conversation whenever there was no one else around. Eli stumbled where the cracks had grown wide enough that they had to jump. Sometimes Eli could hear the horrified gasps and whispers of people that they passed on the way. Only one addressed them.

"What are you doing here? Where are you taking this man?" the young woman's voice demanded.

Eli could hear Tye patting down his pockets, hurriedly searching for something, as he stammered:

"Th-this one's been convicted in Craggie Court, ma'am. We're taking him to be removed in due form. I've got the papers here somewheres, ma'am. Ah-hah, that's them. Right here. See?"

A long pause.

The woman's breathing grew louder, then it calmed.

She was next to him now, talking quietly in his ear. He could smell cinnamon in her breath:

"Would you like a drink?" she asked.

"Yes."

A clay jar was brought to his lips, and sweet, cool wine trickled down his throat, a taste Eli remembered, once, from long ago. He licked the moistness from his lips.

"Take this, for him," she said to Tye.

"Yes, ma'am. Begging your pardon, ma'am, but we were just wondering which stairs we take here. To get to the Falls. This first one going up to Boaz looks steep, but I'd dearly love to—"

"—you take the second set, beyond. Do not set foot in Boaz."

Rod and Tye sounded dejected. A painful snap came from the rope, and Eli was walking once more. Now he was being pulled up a hillside. After a mile or so, the stone and gravel road gradually gave way to trampled grass, then weeds, and then briars, which cut deep into Eli's feet. In places, they could no longer walk, but the jailers could not remove his blindfold, so they had to hoist and shove him blindly over a muddy path that grew wilder and wilder the farther they went. The warmth and light of the day were fading, the air grew damp, and the wind picked up into a howl that bit through what tatters remained of Eli's rag. His legs were shaking uncontrollably, but somehow, he managed the final reach, and they came to another halt.

Rod blinked in wonder at the sight before him. It was an overhang built of old flagstones and columns, set high on the Mountain, so high that he could see the whole expanse of the Ocean and the tiny strands of white that marked the waves coming in to shore. Wisps of cloud floated by, tantalizingly out of reach. The horizon beyond seemed to have no end.

The one building that still stood on the overhang was decrepit, though. It looked much like an old office might, one that had never been built with a roof or walls. The fluted pillars near its center held a thin decorative ring of stone and a few peeling wooden slats to shield the worst of the elements. The flooring ran twenty feet until it reached an abrupt end where, instead of a wall or window, there was only an empty sky. Arcing out farther from one part of the rock's edge, a thin walkway stretched forth like a plank. There was a crude plaster statute of a staring owl set atop a poorly hewn pedestal, some bins filled with papers weighted down with any stone that happened to be at hand, and a wooden desk where there sat a bald man with a hooked nose looking much like a vulture. He was perched in a chair, dressed in a commissar's tunic, and scribbling through a ream of papers when he stopped, glanced up from his work, and squinted at the newcomers with two tiny black eyes.

"Who is this?" he demanded.

Rod was winded from the climb and he knew his bulkier, older companion would be feeling the trek even more deeply. But he dared not answer the commissar's question. Not while the man held a pen, like a drawn sword, ready to cut a note and take down his name.

Better leave it to Tye; he was, after all, the senior guard.

The commissar growled at the silence:

"Come, come! Surely one of you knows the name of your charge?"

At that, Tye drew himself upright. Rod watched as Tye set down the jar the woman on the road had handed him, wiped his forehead, and held out his folded paper for the commissar, who did not bother to rise from his chair but snapped for Tye to bring it over to him. The commissar's eyes scanned across the parchment and then he slowly rose to dissect the charge that had been brought before him.

"The prisoner will respond to the questions of the Crest's commissar, does he understand?"

The man's words rolled away into the wind. Eli tried to pay attention, to focus, only because the man's voice seemed so earnest in its insistence that Eli should have to listen to it. The voice repeated the question.

"... does he understand?"

Does he understand?

Such a grating, self-imposing query. Coming from this man, the question almost felt like a splinter—no, the *remembrance* of a splinter. Eli said nothing and stared into his blindfold.

A silence had welled up within Eli; the voices in the dark had remained quiet, and for some reason, Eli found that more troubling than anything else in the world. He had finally begun to grasp what it was they had been trying to tell him. It had been something deep and lovely. There was beauty in the cacophony, by surrendering to it. He knew that now. The shadows had much more to tell him, and he had so much more to learn.

But they were still. He yearned for them to sing, to speak again, just a word.

All Eli could hear was the commissar. His stupid question, his flat, pointless words, no different than the cackling seagull that was flying over them. The commissar sounded angry now.

"I said, the prisoner ..."

Was that what this man thought of Eli? A prisoner? There was something droll in that notion. It almost brought a smile to Eli.

Rod glanced at his silent prisoner, then back to the commissar, who sighed and motioned for Tye to come closer. The heavy guard was still doubled over from the climb, and his cheeks were glowing bright and pink, but he obeyed.

"This happens on occasion," the commissar explained, "so I will require you to answer for him."

"Uhm. Alright, sir. I'll do my best."

"The record will reflect the prisoner is in adequate health and mental acuity to understand this proceeding. Having refused to give answers, the prisoner's guard will respond to the required colloquy for him. What is his name?"

"Uhm, Eli, sir," Tye replied. "Elliott, I should say."

"Last name?"

"Porter."

"That's his occupation as well?"

"Believe so. He's a guildsman, sir."

"That will be noted."

As the clerk spoke, his pen danced across a sheet of paper so that he was both writing and conversing at the same time. The clerk's gaze never broke from Eli. "What was the primary place of residence?"

"Uh, says here ... the Crag, Hopeful Shanties, Middle Ward."

"Does the prisoner know why he is here?"

Tye's mouth opened and shut. He glanced over at Rod, who could not surmise an answer (and would not have offered one even if he could). Rod knew enough of clerks and commissars to recognize a question that would only be answered with a note. He let his gaze wander this way and that, anywhere but the commissar's desk, until at last it landed on the plaster owl statue, which he pretended to study very closely.

The commissar leveled his cold glare upon Tye. His index finger passed across the tip of his tongue and folded back a corner of a page that was about to take flight in the wind. Then the commissar's face stretched into something that might have passed for disappointment. Finally, he spoke:

"There has been a failure of duty here, guards. I expected as much." The commissar rose from his seat, his knees creaking loudly. With his faded yellow coat and pants fluttering, and his arms spindled over his desk, he might have been a thorny shrub that had taken root on the mountainside. A long finger looped into a buttonhole and curled round hard. He raised his profile and let out a long sigh. "This is a failure of the clerks of the court ..."

Rod blew a sigh of relief; whatever this failure could be, it was not their fault, and they were not going to be the ones written up for it.

"... This prisoner has not been reeducated. He has not recanted of his superstitions. He's probably not even aware of the gravity of the crime he has committed. We have failed him and the Commonwealth. How unfortunate. Let us discharge our final duty to the Commonwealth with more diligence." The commissar stretched the document Tye had handed to him across his desk, signed the bottom, and read aloud in a formal voice:

"To Elliott Porter, who calls himself the Divine Eli, a denizen of the Commonwealth, bound to the Crag. You have been duly tried and convicted of violating the First Article of the Commonwealth: there is no god, and none shall be proclaimed." He paused in his reading to address Eli directly. "Now, what does that mean? It is the first of our three articles, after all—certainly the most particularized. Why do we execute removal for its infraction? I shall explain. In all the Mountain, in our common life, there are only two things that are real: resources—all that we can see and touch—and the will, our will, to put resources to use. Resources and will. Nothing else exists. So that which cannot be seen, or which is not the will of the people, cannot be real. Do you follow me thus far?"

A damp lock of hair brushed across the bottom of Eli's nose, and the commissar continued.

"So, the very idea of an unseen, untouchable being separate and apart from our resources and our will, is patently false. It is also insidious. Because the notion that anything apart from this Mountain has a will of its own, directing our affairs is, in truth, nothing more than a projection of one's *own* will onto others ... That is the crime, Porter. Your crime. Your inflammatory speech would elevate your will, the will of one, insignificant man, over the will of the many. You have no right to make such a claim upon us. Any more than did the priests."

Like a professor whose lecture was finally concluding, the commissar let out a long breath, shook his head sadly, and resumed reading from his paper, the final paragraph:

"The Court of Common Corrections having found you guilty, and having sentenced you to removal from the bosom and community of the Commonwealth in due form, I, Signal Velarius, Chief Deputy Commissar stationed at the Falls, affirm that this is a true and correct warrant of removal—" without missing a breath, he signed his name again— "and have witnessed the same on this, the eighty-seventh day of spring in the Twelfth Year of the Ninth Plan of the Commonwealth. All forms are in good order and execution of the Court's warrant shall issue forthwith. Our all for all."

"Our all for all," Tye and Eli mumbled in response.

"Well go on," the commissar prompted Tye, who was gaping at him for direction. "Remove the prisoner. Right out there." He pointed toward the edge of the overhang, where the Mountain ended and the sky began. The mortared stone plank leading out from the floor looked minuscule and very fragile.

Tye swallowed so hard that Rod could hear the hard, wet sound from the older man's throat. And then, to Rod's horror, the next thing he heard was Tye ordering him to do the removal himself. It was a senior guard's direct order, issued in the presence of a commissar. Rod whined and sputtered like a frightened child, but between the dual threat of the commissar's note and a blow from Tye's fist, he could no longer hide from doing his duty.

Eli felt the rope around his neck being untied and lifted over his head. A shove in the middle of his back was followed by Rod's quivering voice:

"C'mon, already. Get this over with."

He was being nudged forward. The wind stirred again. The seagull called out. Some pebbles slid out from beneath Eli's foot and cascaded down, landing on nothing and without a sound. Eli knew then what would happen. He knew he would fall.

"Although not technically required by law," the commissar called out from his desk, "there is a custom in which prisoners may say a few final words before their removal—it will have no bearing on your sentence, mind you—but perhaps, now that you realize the severity of your crime, you might wish to reconcile yourself to the Commonwealth. Before you are expelled from her bosom."

Eli stood silently.

He still could not see anything but the blackness of the cloth across his face, but he had a sense that something was waiting for him far below in the Ocean. If he could have lifted his blindfold, if his eyes were better and he had time to study what lay near the rocks at the foot of the Mountain beneath him, he might have been able to make out the pieces of a broken statue. Enormous and fragmented, the stones lay strewn among the rocks and the crashing waves. Half of a woman's granite face, a bit of sculpted robe, a horn, and a lone arm, extending high above the lapping waters, covered in grime, with an outstretched hand that seemed to beckon. Eli's covered eyes saw none of this but somehow knew that it was there.

Eli closed his eyes tight beneath the blindfold, and the cold, the pain in his body, the beating of his heart, were gone. The wind became a whisper, so familiar it could have been his mother's. And then, without realizing it, Eli stretched out his arms into an embrace.

He was weightless. The air was roaring, singing, laughing past his ears. The statue's face drew closer; the corner of its mouth became a smile. Eli's arms, his fingers were like the wings of the gull, wide enough to catch the air and carry him away, even as he plummeted toward the Ocean, to the outstretched stone palm of a forgotten goddess.

THE CRAG

CHAPTER SIXTEEN

A WHITE PALM: PALE, almost translucent, the skin cracked where it stretched between the fingers. Dull, faded blisters marred its surface. Her palm.

Lillia's eyes blinked at it. She was staring at her outstretched hand, spread wide before her eyes, lost in the nether between waking and dreaming. It was a place she dwelled more often than not lately. She remembered falling ... tumbling head over feet down into a darkness that seemed to have no end, and that had a mind of its own.

That mind had mocked her for her fear. She knew she could stand up to the dark, wrestle it, force this malevolence to submit to her, to her will; but she was terrified of falling, and that had only made her fall faster in the plummet of her waking dream. Just a scared, wretched girl, condemned to hurtle down a bottomless hole because she was scared and wretched. A surge of self-loathing flushed in her cheeks. The darkness reveled at it. Voices, not her own, taunted her confusion.

Her fingers curled into a fist. Lillia was climbing now, and slowly her senses registered her surroundings, corporal sensations returning in progression, one at a time. Cold, hard, dark (real darkness), damp. Her thoughts coalesced, taking harder shape, and as they formed something solid, the voices in the shadows were slowly walled away.

But not completely. Not here. Lillia had never been this deep inside the Crag before.

She propped herself wearily on her elbows. She was in a hollow far from the tannery, a place where there were no corridors, or pipes, or people. Hidden by a tumbled pile of boulders, the space was just wide enough for her father, brother, and Lillia to spread out, but only she could stand upright inside. A lone rock column hung from the middle of the ceiling and provided a steady drip of milky looking water. Tom had

led them straight to this obscure hole, he didn't even need to search for
the entrance. Perhaps it was a place from his childhood. If that was the
case, she could never ask him about it.

But where were they? How long had they been here? Lillia forced
her mind to concentrate on those questions. They had fled the tannery
four days earlier. Or was it five? How many times had Tom gone out
since then? Measuring time in the deep was impossible. Supposedly the
dwarves had the skill, she had read that once, but she was not a dwarf.

Useless. This was not working. The sounds inside her head were
growing restless again as if stirred by her effort to reorient herself into a
place and time. So, she stopped up her ears and trained her thoughts on
remembering.

The tannery: she had been trying her hand at working the shears,
which hurt terribly; Tom came rushing in, his arms full of packs and
tools, his face dripping in sweat, panic just beneath the surface; he was
telling Tim to go and fetch his coat now; heavy boots squelching around
the lakeshore, men yelling; the smell of burnt wood and animal skins; the
tannery in flames; a blaze of yellow reflecting against the waters, stabbing
the darkness. The fire had transfixed her, a struggle between the darkness
of the cave and the light from the burning tents and hides, the shadows
fleeing before the flames—or were they embracing? —that was what she
had been trying to figure out when she was whisked into a corridor, her
father's hand clamped hard around her waist. The memories riled one of
the voices, made it angry. Lillia clenched her jaws.

"Be quiet," she whispered. "You aren't real. I only want to hear real
things."

When Lillia opened her eyes again the voices receded. She could still
feel their presence in her mind, like scurrying behind a gossamer curtain
that was drawn close to her thoughts; they were whispering secret plots
among themselves, waiting for the cue when the veil would lift again
and they could come out.

"Quiet," she repeated.

"What'd you say?" Tim's face appeared from around a corner of the
rock.

Lillia drew up with a start:

"Nothing, I ... I—I just—it's nothing."

"Didn't sleep well?"

Lillia rolled her neck. The weight of her head felt as if it had doubled. Her eyelids were sinking on their own, falling shut; she forced them open.

"Yeah," she nodded and yawned. "That's what it is."

Tim was holding what looked like a grated, metal egg-holder which hung from a delicate chain he had wrapped around his wrist. A trinket that passed for jewelry in the Crag. A faint glow from a single gulleystar pressed inside of it warbled whenever Tim's hand moved. In the light, she could see he also held a ladle. It was strange, Lillia thought to herself, the things he had thought to grab as they fled their home: they were all Mother's knick-knacks.

"Do you think we can go out yet?" Lillia asked.

"Dad's still checking. Should be back soon. You, uh, want some porridge?"

"I'm not hungry."

Tim's face fell, and Lillia could at once sense his disappointment in the silence.

"Unless you made it," she added. "That's different."

"I did. And it's definitely different."

"Just a little bit, okay?"

Tim was already bustling to the other end of the hollow to fetch a pewter bowl and spoon that he had at the ready. He set it down before her, his simple, hopeful smile shining in the gulleystar's glow. Lillia looked down into a bowl filled to the brim with steaming grayness and perfectly cubed chunks of darker grayness. She wasn't hungry, but the soup was not half bad. She took another sip.

"Mmm. That's even better than Mom—I mean, it's the best I've ever had. How'd you make this?"

"Got the stock over there," he pointed towards the dripping stalactite, "pinch of salt, potato skin I found in Dad's bag. Caught a couple of rats, and there you have it."

"It's good."

"The secret is how it's cooked. Since all we've got is Dad's lantern, it's got to cook real slow."

"It's called a simmer."

"Yeah. Somehow it makes it taste better, I think."

He pulled out a second spoon, and together they finished the bowl, the chinking of their cutlery and Tim's slurping the only sounds that passed between them. Tim cleaned the dish, and then they sat down next to one another to wait for their father. Something in the silence pressed upon them a sense that it ought not to be disturbed. When they spoke, it was quickly, quietly, and always initiated by Tim.

But at last, after what seemed like hours, they heard their father returning, his soft, careful footsteps followed by the sound of rocks being moved back into place to cover the entrance. He clambered inside, stooping to keep from bumping his head, and helped himself to the bowl of porridge Tim had left out for him. "We have to go," Tom announced the moment he had finished eating.

"Where?" Tim wiped one of the bowls clean with a piece of rag.

Lillia watched Tom scan the room. He stole a quick look over his shoulder, as if someone might have followed him inside, and then he rubbed at the stubble around his cheeks. Tom spoke, as if to himself:

"Find, hide, move."

"Yeah, but where to?" Tim repeated.

Tom's face was blank; he seemed lost in thought.

"First," he answered carefully, "the tannery."

The stench had changed. The fires had gone cold, their embers disappeared, the ashes were beginning to scatter, but the presence of smoke—lingering, burning, choking smoke—now filled every crack and corner of the darkened tannery. An acrid smell, omnipresent, it had swallowed all the tannery's familiar scents and reeks. Tom made his way to the lake's edge, sniffed the strange air like a small, wary animal, and skirted out upon an open plain.

Find, hide, move.

Something had reawakened in Tom. An instinct from when he was a boy, one that had been lying quiet, asleep for years, but, as if it had only been dozing, was no less honed or sharpened. He huddled beneath a small berm on the shoreline to listen. The silence, at least, was reassuring, though it did little to calm his worry.

The idea of coming back to the tannery was one that bordered between shrewdness and madness. But, then, that was the very calculation that made the risk of returning worthwhile. It all depended on the wardens following the sensible notion that no Craggie in his right mind would return to his razed and raided home. If they followed that logic, the wardens would not waste posting guards in a burned-out camp, not when they could otherwise be out looking for their flushed quarry.

Tom could take the chance. His instinct told him it was worth the risk, because if he could find what he had left behind, then he could hide for as long as he needed, perhaps even fix whatever had gone wrong that had gotten them all noted and marked.

If it was still there ...

The lakeshore ended, and Tom crouched down to let out a small breath of relief. The black waters lapped up gently along the sand behind him. He scanned the ground one more time and then Tom doubled back in a long, winding curve across the tannery, his feet kicking up small clouds of ash with each running step. In the dark, he sometimes tripped on debris; so many things had been strewn out of place, lying in places where they were not supposed to be.

A light breeze stirred and a flapping sound broke Tom's momentary fixation with the sight. The tent was not far away now. It was teetering on two poles; he could see it now. If anyone was trying to keep watch from a hiding place, they would be inside. He dashed for its entrance.

The smell of burnt wood was even stronger inside. It made Tom's nose crinkle, and he had to stifle a sneeze. His eyes watering, he edged past the tumbled over furnishings, letting his fingers trace over an upturned desk that nearly fell apart at his touch. Everything had been burned or smashed to pieces. His hides, his leathers, his tools and dishes, the cupboard where they stored their food, even most of the tent's canvass. Tom poked absently at a skeletal remnant of metal that might have been a winch or a storing hook, he could no longer tell. They would have to make do with what they had escaped with.

Still, though ...

An afterthought came to Tom. He crept into the back of the tent and rummaged around what had been Lillia's bed. Dust. Silt. Soot covered twigs (they might have been styluses). Tom spotted a corner hidden in the dirt beneath the burnt clasp of a support beam and felt a little surge of excitement. Pulling gently, so as not to break its binding, Tom pulled out a book, one of Lillia's class texts. It was singed all around its edges and the binding was barely holding together, but somehow it had survived the flames. A tiny, pewter canister, an ink holder, fell out from its pages. He clutched them both close to his chest.

He was dawdling. Tom shook himself as if he were waking up from a short nap. Time to fetch what he had come for. It would be nearby (if it was still there), perhaps a hundred yards or so out from the tent, not far from where he had hidden the children.

He left through the back of the tent and snuck across the ground, running and yet holding his breath at the same. The closer he got, the more he felt his stomach tighten. His head pivoted all around.

There was nothing out here. An indentation in the dirt, some indistinguishable lumps just beyond it, the trenches, the latrine, Tim's fool head bobbing up, practically out in the open ... Where was it? He kept from groaning aloud, but then, at last, Tom spied what he had been searching for.

The shadows of two earthen jars, each nearly as tall as a man, were lying on their side. They had been toppled over, and the one closest to him was smashed to pieces. The ground beneath it was drenched from the bleach the jar had once held. But the other one was intact. As Tom had hoped.

He tapped at the jar, which still sounded half full. Then he pressed down onto the ground, letting the muddy soot soak through his shirt, as he tried to slide his arm as far as he could past the jar's opening. The fumes were still powerful, and the bleach burned his skin, as he knew it would. His face tightened. Tom's fingers scraped and fumbled around; their tips felt as if they were being seared to the bones. But at last, he touched something metallic in the liquid and heard a clinking sound from inside the jar.

"Got you," he breathed through his clenched teeth.

One by one, Tom plucked out thirty coins. They gleamed bright, even in the blackness of the tannery. He wrapped them up carefully in a piece of rag he had brought with him in his pocket. The hair on his forearm was gone, and his fingers were pruned and bleeding. But he had the coins, the small fortune that the guildswoman had slipped into his hands the day Lillia was almost murdered. A simple tanner could never spend them, not even in a guild market, not without getting noted. Silver was too rare and precious for a Craggie like Tom to hand off as money. But there were other palms in the Mountain, greater than his, that could.

And if a few of those palms need to be filled ...

Tim hissed at him from the latrine:

"Dad, what are you doing?"

Tom shook his head, annoyed, and waved at the boy to stay put.

"I saw you reaching around in the urns," Tim said as Tom slid down to rejoin them in the ditch.

"Hold your voice down." Tom hid his bleeding hand in his pocket and tried to muffle the coins.

"Sorry. We were just wondering what you were looking for out there."

"Lillia," Tom said, ignoring him, "look what I've brought you."

From beneath his shirt, he produced the book and ink holder he had found in the tent. Lillia stared incomprehensively at them. He slipped them into her hands. The book's pages were all curled at the corners. Without a word, Lillia tucked it under her arm.

"So where should we start?" Tim broke the silence that followed.

"Start what?" Tom asked heavily.

"Cleaning up. The tannery. Isn't that why we came back? We can set up again now that the wardens got what they were after. Right?"

Tom simply blinked at the boy, unable to believe what he had just been asked. He spoke slowly, drawing his words out like points on a shearing knife:

"Son. You can't possibly be that stupid. If you are, you're as good as done for." He watched the boy stammer and turn red before he continued, careful to keep his voice at a murmur: "You really think we can come back here? When we've all been marked?"

"Wha-why? I didn't know we were—we were marked. I thought they just wanted to catch that crazy porter. I didn't—"

"—think? No, you didn't. The porter," Tom shook his head in disbelief. "They torched the whole tannery to find somebody they had already caught?"

"Maybe they wanted to make sure we weren't hiding any of the porter's friends," Tim said, sounding helpless. "It was just a shakedown. They do that to the guilds sometimes. It always blows over, though. That doesn't mean we're marked. Does it?"

"They came to kill us," Tom locked onto his son's eyes that were now beginning to brim with tears. Tim gasped, but Tom continued: "This isn't going to blow over. Think about it. Before the raid, a whole troop of wardens, and clerks, even a captain, they all came out here to question us, why?"

"I didn't tell them anything," Tim responded. "Nothing. Not even when my nose got broke."

"Because they weren't trying to get anything out of you. If the wardens wanted you to talk, they'd have done a lot more than just thump you in the face, wouldn't you think?"

It was clear from Tim's dejection that that thought had never occurred to him.

"You have to learn to read things, boy; otherwise, you're not going to make it. I got us out before that raid because I could read what was about to happen."

"The teachers never taught me letters."

"This is a different kind of reading. You have to read what's happening around you, what people are doing, why they're doing it. When the Crest wants to take a man up, like that porter and his friends, they keep it quiet, and then they do it quick. But when they want to make a clean sweep of things, they come out in numbers, and they keep coming back—until whatever needs to go is gone. That's what's happening to us, Tim. They're trying to sweep something away, and we're caught up in it."

"Wha—why?"

"How should I know?" Tom snapped.

Weariness and an accompanying irritability were beginning to take hold of Tom; he could not remember the last time he had slept and was starting to feel bleary.

"Will we ever be able to—?" Tim started.

"That's what I've been trying to sort out," Tom cut him off. "There might be a way, eventually. But meantime, we've got to keep moving." He looked down at Lillia, who seemed distracted by something outside. He glanced in the direction she was staring but only saw darkness. "I don't know what's to be done about the academy," he said to her, "what with everything that's happened and your teacher suspending you."

Lillia nodded. "My friend thinks Madam Teacher's nothing to worry about. That she could be fixed."

"Is that Jack who said that?"

"Yes. But he can be stupid sometimes."

Tom pushed his hair back to think.

"We'll sort all that out, too." It came out almost as an apology. "I promise."

She simply shrugged, as if it were not a bother either way, and for some reason that was profoundly painful for Tom. So, he turned his attention back to the present.

Where to go. It had been simpler when he was a boy; he had been alone then, nameless and beneath anyone's notice. His only purpose had been to scavenge and hide. There were plenty of cracks and holes in the Crag to hide in, plenty of things to steal. If you were alone.

But where to go with these two? It was Tim who ventured the idea.

"What about the Farms? It's a big place. They always need hands. That's where Mom went when she wanted to—you know. Get away."

There was Tim's real motive, Tom was sure. The boy hoped to see his mother again. Which, of course, was out of the question. There were problems with the Farms—it was a low place filled with low people, and in some corners, it could be dangerous, especially for girls. It would be a far walk, almost as far as the Docks … But it was a sound plan, the most viable one they had. With the coins, Tom could make it work. His thoughts settled, his instinct affirming his son's idea.

Tim's muddied face gazed back at Tom. He had wiped away his tears. His beard was starting to thicken, Tom noticed.

Tom regarded his son another moment, and then he nodded.

For days Lillia and what remained of her family moved by running—always running—whenever the tunnels were empty, and only in places where the gulleystar lamps had gone dark, or a broken pipe had flooded the floor, or a ceiling had caved in. If her father found a good hole where they could cover up, they stopped. Eating, sleeping, relieving themselves, everything other than running became relegated to the cracks and crevasses Tom happened across.

The route they followed (if that was what it was) circled and meandered up and down a seemingly endless succession of stairwells and old, abandoned tunnels, none of which Lillia had ever seen before. Tom was always at the head, the tiny orange flame of his lantern bobbing quietly in the darkness, with Lillia trying her best to follow the sudden bursts of sprinting down hallways or darting around corners. Tim came lumbering behind in the rear, louder than his father or sister, usually because he was bumping into things or complaining how hungry he was. A few of the stairwells looked familiar to Lillia, as if she might have come this way once before, but most of the corridors looked strange and very old.

Every part of Lillia's body ached. Her shoulders felt like they might snap beneath the weight of the satchel she carried and the ridiculous book her father had made her bring along. Exhaustion seeped into her bones. And yet, despite the weariness, she felt more awake than she had in weeks. Lillia was beginning to grasp things again. The voices and the dreams were in retreat; still there, but growing fainter. Like a fog that was finally beginning to lift. The closer they drew towards the Mountain's outside—for that was where they were heading—the more she felt like her old self.

She welcomed the change, for however long it would last.

It was inevitable. Sooner or later, they were bound to come across other people. The Crag was vast, true, with miles of caverns, but it held the foremost share of the Mountain's men and women.

One day, the Tanners came to a halt before an enormous pillar that had collapsed across the floor of the corridor they were crossing. Lillia was helping her brother clamber over the top of the fallen column when they noticed their father had frozen in place on the ground beneath them. His legs were spread wide and his finger extended in silent warning at his children, commanding them to hold still.

"Why are we—?" Tim began.

There was a thin yelp, and Tom's shearing knife came out from his belt just as three shadows lunged at him from behind a piece of fluted capstone.

Lillia tried to comprehend what was happening—there were three filthy Crag boys, about Tim's age, beating at her father with clubs—but it was as if she were watching from someplace high in the clouds, so far removed from the earth that the movements had become stilled. Like pictures in one of her books, the pages turning slowly.

Her father was lashing at the boys with his knife, he was trying to cut the largest one. One of them dropped his club. Now they were all locked together, four wild animals tearing at one another. Lillia turned and saw Tim gaping down, still riveted in his climb, struggling to summon the courage to do something. Lillia returned to her senses, and time began to move in its ordinary course again:

"Help him!" she cried at her brother.

Tim licked his lips. He looked at her and then at his father, and with a high-pitched squeal, plunged into the melee. He grappled with the first boy who had attacked their father, heaving himself up on the boy's back in an awkward attempt to pin him to the ground. Despite Tim's weight, the boy still held a sinewy arm in a chokehold around Tom's throat.

"Let him go!" Tim shouted.

Tim managed to peel the boy's arm from his father's neck, just enough so that Tom could escape. And the moment he did, Tom spun back around and plunged his knife hard into the boy's stomach. All the way to the handle. He pulled it out and did it again, and again, until Tom's hand was slick with blood. After the fourth stab, as if it had been mutually agreed beforehand, the fight ended. The other two boys dropped their sticks and fled in different directions down the tunnel, leaving their companion on the floor.

Tom slumped down next to him to catch his breath. Tim stood transfixed, his face as gray as the stone in the walls. Lillia slid down from the pillar and inched toward her father, who was still watching the boy's body impassively. A pool of blood had spread across the ground. The boy's chest was heaving in spasms and his pale eyes were fixed, unblinking, as if something in the ceiling had captured the final moments of his attention. He let out a garbled gasp.

With the calm precision of a man who had practiced cutting flesh for many years, Tom brought the knife's blade across the boy's throat, and with a single sure stroke, ended his life. Then he wiped the blade and his hand clean on a piece of the boy's shirt that was still dry.

Lillia stared at her father unable to speak.

"Come on," Tom's voice sounded tired. "Might as well walk in the open now."

The sound of his voice was like a splash of water pouring over Lillia's head. The shock of the encounter dissipated. She felt her feet moving beneath her once more.

Tom paid the corpse no more attention than he would if it had been a goat's hide, but Lillia tiptoed around the body of the dead Craggie boy. She wanted to force herself not to look down, to catch up to her father and pretend she had not seen what he had just done, but her eyes strayed as if of their own will, to meet the boys'. Gray eyes, like hers, staring up into nothing. Whatever light they had held was gone. A shadow passed between them, startling Lillia for a moment, and then it too vanished. From then on, Lillia kept a little farther behind her father, with her brother by her side.

But now Tom was walking in his regular gait. The days of dashing and hiding had ended, it seemed. Tom no longer watched the shadows or stopped to listen in the air. The hall widened as they went farther down, and soon they found themselves bathed in the light of gulleystar pots strung from rusted, metal wires all along the tunnel ceiling. For a mile, the dimly lit boulevard in the Mountain descended, and with each step, the air grew warmer so that their clothes soon stuck to their skin.

They were close now, perhaps another hundred yards or so. Tom would have liked to halt here for a bit, think about what their best approach might be, but he was interrupted by a cluster of people approaching from the tunnel ahead.

It was a cadre of "raggers," old widows who made their living trading bits of cloth, metal, carved stone, or whatever else they could find or steal. Tom groaned to himself and quickly doused his lantern, but they must have spotted it, for soon Tom found himself surrounded by four crones, pressing close, pawing at his clothes:

"We've got wares to trade for that lantern of yours."

"C'mon, make a fair offer for it."

"It's probably broken, ain't it. We can trade, though. No clerks around."

"Have a look at the wares. Some of 'em got guildmarks."

"Something pretty for your pretty little missus?"

Tom shoved past the women without breaking his stride. They grumbled and cursed him, but, knowing their place, accepted the rebuff and withdrew into the shadows.

Gradually, more and more Craggies appeared in the tunnel. They were all hunched over and wearing the same assortment of workers' clothes; some carried tools, others baskets, all of them looked sullen and suspicious. Some of the younger men leered at Lillia, but otherwise, no one took any notice of the wiry, middle-aged man and his two children. The noise of muttered conversations was everywhere. The throng was surprisingly dense for a relatively unused tunnel.

Tom felt uneasy. There was no market out here, no intersections nearby, no homes, or fountains, or workplaces that he could see. He scanned the collection of faces around him. These were all workers, but none of them seemed surprised at how crowded the tunnel was becoming. When Tom noticed a group of men with gardening hoes beginning to form into a queue, he stopped the children and pulled them close to the wall.

"It's a checkpoint," he whispered.

"I don't have a pass," Tim replied, as if his father had forgotten such an obvious point.

"None of us do," Lillia scolded her brother. Then, to her father: "Can we get around it? Take some other way to the Farms?"

Tom craned his head slightly, trying not to appear like he was casing their surroundings.

"No. That last landing, there were only two stairways. One goes to the Docks, the other to the Farms. There's nothing in between except the market cavern, which doesn't take you anywhere. No, this is the only way. If we still want to try for the Farms."

As he said it, for the first time, Tom found himself questioning whether it had been a wise decision after all. But before the thought could take hold, his instinct welled up in an affront, pushed it aside. A second guess will cost a man his life more often than save it. He had made up his mind. There would be no turning back from this path.

Tom's hand went to his pocket to feel the weight of the pouch hidden within it. An edge from a round coin pressed into his fingertip.

"Not out here," he said to himself.

"Huh?" Tim asked.

"The problem is," Tom continued, "there's too many people about now. I can get what we need from a clerk, but I've got to get him alone. There's going to be four, maybe five clerks at a checkpoint like this. Wardens, too."

They stood pressed against the wall, watching the noisy crowd begin to eddy towards the back of the tunnel. At the far end, Lillia could just make out a Commonwealth banner, the point where everyone seemed to be converging. The echo of clerks, shouting to organize, and sort, and order their charges rose above the angry mutterings of the workers in response. Lillia slipped off the satchel she had slung over her and opened it up. She pulled a stained and wrinkled yellow sash out from the bottom.

"That won't work," Tom shook his head. "They'll have a note to be looking for an academy girl with two men."

"So, they'll be looking for an academy sash," she answered. Tom watched her pull the cloth over her chest, smooth it across her stomach and then tie it, three times, around her waist. "Not a clerk with a writ of passage."

The realization, and the audacity, of her plan, came to him as she drew herself up taller. Lillia fixed her hair and moved her mouth, her cheeks, and her eyebrows into a haughty visage. For a brief moment, it was like seeing his daughter reborn, the way she had been before the accident at the dock.

"I just need a minute to write something up," she said. Out came her old textbook. Lillia carefully tore one of its back pages free from the binding. Then she popped open the ink holder and using the prong of a fork, wrote hurriedly on the dusty floor—a meticulous, severe script emerged across the blank paper.

"What a clever girl you are," Tom whispered down to her.

CHAPTER SEVENTEEN

HERE WAS A scattering of farms across the Crag. Soggy patches of earth nestled deep within stony cracks and fissures where the wind and rain, through long years, had wheedled through the Mountain's skin to fester. Like boils of fertility. They were cramped, musky places. Places where workers, under the watchful eyes of clerks, could raise goats or grow barley; a plot of arable dirt for onions or radishes; some patches of open ground to cage hens. They were always given names to tell them apart, like Prosperity Harvest, Bountiful Barleys, Overlook Ranch.

The Farms were different. No one had ever bothered naming the place, because it needed no description. A worker always spoke the word in a way that inferred its singularity, its enormity. It was said the Farms were the stomach of the Crag. Lillia had read that somewhere once. Its crops fed the whole Mountain.

Standing at the top of the last landing of steps, looking out across the Farms beneath her, she felt like a speck.

A vast hollow stretched forth from the bottom of the stairs out into the Mountain's periphery, a mile away. It was a ward in itself, one that had been carved and hewn into one perfect, elongated cube. Across its height, a grid of square holes ran the entire length of the ceiling, sending shafts of light and fresh air to mingle with the soil below. All along the walls, giant iron pipes thrummed with the sound of water moving back and forth.

Wedged between her father and brother, Lillia stood on her tiptoes, squinting to see how far the Farms reached. After a long while of staring, she could just make out the mouth of a cave at the end. It was barred by stalactites and something else—pillars, she thought most likely—probably to buttress the ceiling. Bars of sunlight broke through the spaces between them. For beyond the cave's entrance was the open sky and the whisper of waves that would have been crashing hundreds of feet below.

As she peered ahead, Lillia became distracted by a noise, tiny and strange. A pair of finches, cheeping from some hiding place. They suddenly burst from a hole in the wall above Tom's head and made a dashed flight for the far end of the cavern. She watched as the birds flew farther and farther away, becoming smaller, until they melted into a flock that was swooping in and out among the stalactites, a directionless cloud flitting between the world within and without. The sight of the birds, their wings flashing in the sun so far beyond her reach, brought a pang to her for some reason.

This had all been made, she reflected. Once, long ago, places like this had been made. Lillia leaned against a wall, letting the smooth, cold surface support the burden of her tiny frame.

Her attention wandered to the floor, which seemed to undulate. There were hundreds, maybe thousands, of hands down below, scratching the ground beneath them, heaving carts around, tending an endless succession of rows of green. Every hundred yards or so, a raised chair for a lector's seat broke the monotony. If one watched long enough, a dab of yellow, a clerk, would bustle with self-importance over to a cluster of workers, who would break up only to reform as soon as the clerk had gone again. She could have stood here, just breathing the air for days, but Tom broke the silence:

"We need to go," he said, "try to blend in while we look around."

The children followed their father down the stairs. Within a few steps, a welling heat had them enveloped, like a mantle that had been flung upon their shoulders. Tom wiped his face, his eyes stinging, and set foot on the Farms' rich soil.

It was loose, but not like the silt of the tunnels. This was brown earth. Deep, spongy, filled with life. He looked out across the tilled rows that seemed to stretch endlessly before him. Sprouting from every inch of the raised soil were clusters of flat, spade-shaped leaves.

Potato plants, fanning out in ordered columns, some were little more than shoots, others looked ready to burst from their fullness. Tom watched a roaming group of workers pull a few out, clear some little stones, and then hoe the dirt back into place. It was the same everywhere he turned. The labor here looked to be as repetitious as the landscape.

No one was paying much attention to their presence. Still, Lillia could sense a glance occasionally lingering on her, as if she were a tool that had been left out for the wrong kind of work. They could not simply keep standing in place without someone noticing.

"Try to look like you're working," Tom said out of the side of his mouth, "'til I find a clerk to deal with."

Tim and Tom stooped over and began fidgeting with some of the plant leaves, sifting piles of dirt from one side to another, scraping holes with their hands and filling them back in, the sorts of things that made a show of hard, focused work but accomplished nothing at all. It had its effect, though. By all appearances, they were two unobtrusive farmhands, dutifully playing their small part within the rhythm and movement of the Farms.

Lillia, however, found herself at a loss. In the close confines of a classroom, with the teacher constantly surveilling the students, it was impossible to *pretend* to be engaged in work. One either completed the assignment, correctly, or else one got strapped. She had never learned this skill. She felt conspicuous. At last, Lillia haltingly bent over and pulled at a stalk that looked like it might have been out of place. It came up hard, a tangle of white roots wriggling from a malformed clump, that sent clumps of dirt all over Lillia's frontside.

"What're you doin'?" an old woman's voice from the row behind her chastised. "Those ain't due for harvest yet. Not for another four moons, at least."

Lillia turned around sheepishly and muttered an apology. The woman was covered in brown that was smeared across a withered forehead, bulbous nose, and sagging cheeks; brown stains colored every inch of her clothes and went down to her legs and bare feet—two wide, callused stumps that looked like they might have been potatoes themselves. She set down a canvas sack to glare at Lillia.

"Are you slow or somethin'?"

The woman was squinting at her now.

"What?"

"Put it back."

"Oh."

Lillia dropped the plant back into the hole, but she must have done something wrong because the woman heaved an exasperated sigh. Tom stepped over a row of plants to stand next to Lillia.

"She yours?" the woman pointed at Lillia.

"She's new here," Tom explained. "I'm trying to find a place for her."

The woman hacked, which seemed to pass for laughter.

"Even idiots gotta work, I suppose. Better take her to the new clerk. Hear he's an idiot, too. Probably put her on the roll for a turn with her." The woman started to leave.

"Where's this new clerk?"

"Where they always shunt the new sashes," the woman snarled over her shoulder. "In the countin' house."

The counting-house was at the end of a short tunnel that veered off from the Farms, not far from where the Tanners had first arrived. A crudely made room filled with clay silos built into the floor, it apparently had been added long after the Farms had been completed, without any attempt of assimilating the architecture that it joined. The room served its function, though. It was wide and very high. A rickety platform had been erected at the far end high enough above the silos that it had to be reached by a set of wooden steps. The only light inside came from gulleystars.

At the moment, two things filled the counting-house, packed it so tight there was almost no air left to breathe: potatoes and people. There were potatoes piled in small mountains inside the silos, potatoes spilling out of cracks and crevasses, potatoes rolling around on the floor, mashed into a greasy pulp by an endless line of workers pressed against one another in a crowded line, all bent over from lugging still more potatoes that bulged in sacks slung over their shoulders. They were standing in a queue, waiting. The food they had brought would be packed by porters into crates and shipped off in caravans to feed the people of the Crest and the dwarves of the Quarter. Tomorrow they would fill it up again. But in the meantime, the hands were waiting to receive their allotment, the fruits for all this labor.

Every so often, the line would shamble a few steps forward, wait a long while, move another step, wait a little longer. Lillia's father and brother stood on either side of her. She would lean against her father when her legs grew tired, but they hardly spoke to one another. Tom had his hands tucked inside his pockets. Tim gawked at everyone around them, no doubt amazed at the sight of so many people in one place. At some point, a scuffle broke out not far behind the Tanners. Two men—a fat porter covered in boils and a very drunken farmhand—beat each other bloody while the only warden standing guard on the platform watched them from above with a bored expression on his face. Aside from the fight, it was fairly quiet for such a crowded place. A few grumbled mutterings here and there, but what was there to talk about? It was as hot as a fever and just as uncomfortable; wasting breath on conversation only made it worse.

Lillia stared at the backs of all the people ahead of her, then stood on her tiptoes to get a better look at how far away they were. The last silo was behind them, and now they would be going up the steps, up to the platform, first to the check-in desk with the guard who, so far, had not bothered to check anyone, then to the clerk's desk, and finally the ladder and cordoned passage that led back out to the Farms.

The clerk's desk would be the true challenge. Lillia risked another glance up at the platform.

He had cut his hair shorter. That was why he looked different now. Lillia wiped her forearm across her face, spreading the sweat into her eyes, and focused harder.

It was definitely him. She watched the clerk poring over his record book upon his raised wooden deck, a still newish looking sash hanging lackadaisically around his waist. She registered nothing more than the familiarity of recognition. Even that felt distant, as if from another life.

The line pushed ahead three more steps. Three steps closer to the clerk.

"Dad?" Tim whispered.

"Hm."

"I think that clerk's—"

"It's him," Tom cut him off in a way that made it clear to Tim not to say anything more about it. Tim chewed his fingernails thoughtfully, as he watched the figure at the clerk's desk turning the pages of his enormous book frenetically, then digging through a worker's sack of potatoes, apparently dissatisfied with whatever the worker had just told him.

"Well, that's something," Tim remarked.

"Maybe."

Tom's hand moved imperceptibly. He had finally managed to wriggle one of the silver coins out of the pouch that was tied to the inside of his pocket without anyone noticing. He tucked the metal tightly into the palm of his hand but kept his face a perfectly impassive mask. The people in front inched forward. They climbed up the first two steps of the platform's stairs. Tom pretended to yawn.

Step after step, they slowly ascended the stairs. The wood groaned beneath the weight of all the waiting workers, and every time the line moved, the whole stairway would sway a fraction of an inch, enough to catch off balance anyone who had not kept their feet spread apart. The Tanners stepped onto the platform, which felt only slightly firmer, with Tom leading the way to the warden's desk, his hand ready to slip the silver to the guard if it came to it. As they got closer, Tom saw a white-haired, jaundiced looking guard with sad, pink eyes and a habit of constantly sniffing. He seemed remarkably indifferent to the queue before him, fingering the shaft of his spear, or spinning a tin coin on the top of his table, or fidgeting with the order of some moldy papers that he never read.

Tom smiled inwardly. The guard was passing his shift doing nothing more than keeping his eyes open, waiting out the time until his watch was over and he could sneak off to a tavern. This might be manageable after all. They moved past his table without the least notice, and Tom kept the coin out of sight.

The clerk's table was directly ahead of them. And now he could hear the boy's voice clearly for the first time.

"There's no way your count's right," the clerk kept looking from the floor to the woman standing before him. She was not much older than he, but already had a hump in her shoulder from working in the fields. "Look here, per—well, whatever regulation this is—it says, standard-issue sacks carry," he was struggling to read from his book, examine the contents of three sacks that were half-opened on the floor by her feet, and suitably intimidate the woman with his glare, all at the same time, but not succeeding at any one of them, "the standard-issue sack carries 'not less than one hundred three, and not more than one hundred forty-four standard weight yields, unless one of the following exceptions apply …'" His eyes hurriedly scanned a pinched column of writing that followed for the rest of the page.

The woman simply shrugged her shoulders. She answered him in a tone that was perfectly pitched between deference and, bubbling close underneath, rank insolence:

"You can check 'em yourself, sir," she gestured at her feet. "I don't know nothing 'bout your standard sacks; these here were what I could find an' stitch together. But I counted 'em twice before I got in line. To make sure. Three hundred thirty-six, with not a blemish on any one of 'em. But check 'em if you like, sir. I stand by my work."

"Oh, I'll check them," the clerk growled back at her, "Soon as we're done with the tally, I'm going to count these myself. If I find you're inflating your count, it won't just be a note. I'll make sure they take you up to court."

"Yes, sir. I don't doubt that, sir. But it's three hundred thirty-six to the one."

A metal lockbox was flung open, and the clerk counted out six flat, tin coins. Tom knew without seeing them what they were: a cluster of grapes on one side, the Commonwealth's seal on the other. The only kind of grape a low worker could ever hope to see. Tinners. Worthless Crag coins to buy scraps in the Crag's empty markets.

The woman swept them up but did not budge from where she stood.

"Well?" The clerk demanded.

"Thirty-six is on the rounding up side of a fifty-count, I believe, sir."

"Are you serious?"

"It's the proper wage, sir. What I'm entitled to for the fruits-uh-muh-labor," she said the phrase in a practiced, singular expression, as she had learned it as a child. "Yes, sir. Rounding up's the proper wage."

Some of the workers behind Tom muttered support for the woman. The boy turned a bright shade of pink but finally slapped a seventh coin hard on the table. She dipped her head, whether in thanks to the clerk or to acknowledge her little triumph, it was impossible to tell.

And now Tom was next. The clerk was busy writing in his record book, scowling but focused on whatever it was he was recording. Tom would wait, give the boy time to collect himself before he said anything to him. He would have to remind the boy who they were, and at the same time, show the silver without anyone else seeing it. Tom could do it, but it would all depend on the first impression. The clerk blotted his writing, sprinkled a pinch of sand on the paper, and flipped the page of his book back.

"Next," he said.

Tom drew a deep breath and started to walk toward the desk when Lillia stepped in front of him and calmly addressed the clerk in a quiet, steady voice:

"Hello, Jack," she said.

Jack's face tilted up at the sound of his name. His blue eyes were tinged with yellow and a little bloodshot. He looked older than he had before, grayer in the face. He stared blankly at Lillia for a moment, then the bottom of his mouth fell:

"Lillia?" he breathed, and he could not conceal the delight that shone from his expression. It quickly passed, though. His mouth recoiled into a tight even line. He leaned forward to whisper to her:

"What are you doing here?"

Tom shifted his feet. The story he had concocted, a plausible tale of why the three of them had left the tannery without a pass, was going to be a complicated one to tell. "If we could have a moment of your time—"

"We're trying to find a place to hide," Lillia said. "We need your help."

"No, what she means—" Tom gently ushered her back behind him "—that is, what we're looking for is an unassigned position on the Farms. To get on the roll."

Jack turned from Lillia to Tom, to Tim, and then back to Lillia. He was baffled.

"Sir," Tom tried to sound reassuring, "I can explain if you can spare just a little bit of time."

Jack regarded Tom warily, and for a moment Tom was worried the boy might call the guard over. As it turned out, Jack did call out to the guard:

"Hold them up."

The guard glared at Jack incomprehensively, but when Jack repeated himself, the guard rolled his eyes, muttered something under his breath, and slowly got up from his bench.

"Alright," the guard drawled lazily, "back it up, back it up down there." He picked up his spear and turned it on its side, using the shaft to shuttle the press of workers a few steps back down the stairs, out of earshot from the clerk. "I said back up! There's plenty of room down there."

The workers in line complained half-heartedly, but they all knew what a bribe looked like; whatever the added inconvenience, they would accept it, so long as the clerk would be quick about it.

Jack stood up. His eyes narrowed at Lillia and his voice trembled:

"Why should I help you? Because of helping your stupid family, my dad got audited. And I got stuck down here!"

"I'm sorry that happened," Lillia replied.

"Sorry? Sorry?" Jack thumped the top of the table with his fist, sending an empty inkwell careening over the side. "Teacher was *laughing* when she gave me my commission—everyone laughed at me! I'm nothing but a shitty bursar now. Stuck in this hole. My dad can't get me out because he's in trouble, too. He might get taken up. And it's all because of *you*! Why should I help any of you?"

Lillia dropped her head, but Tom leveled the boy with a steady gaze. Jack's shoulders were rising up and down and he was breathing heavily, but Tom locked onto him, forcing him to give attention:

"Here's why," Tom said calmly.

The time had come for his explanation. Without a word and without ever taking his eyes off of Jack's, Tom opened his palm and carefully placed a coin of pure silver on top of Jack's papers. A faded profile, a woman's, was etched on its surface, a spangle of stars and letters that were impossible to read hovering above her brow. It glowed like a flame and illuminated every inch of the young clerk's face, the awe—and the greed—plain to see.

The lector took a long drink from his wineskin, settled back into his platform chair, which creaked from the weight, and let out a belch loud enough that all the workers tending the quarter-acre patch near the counting-house could hear it. The Tanners were among them, spread about beneath the shadow of his chair, an overcast day lighting their work of pulling and baling weed grass that had sprouted along the potato trenches in the weeks since their arrival. The lector's nose and cheeks were already tinged pink and a wreath of smoke from a pipe hung about his head like a fog. Although well into his second skin of ale, he could still read aloud in a piercing, sonorous baritone that most of the farm-hands enjoyed hearing. His name was Victor. Tom bundled a small bale of grass blades together for the porters to pick up later—the weeds here would be used as feed for the other farms and ranches. Victor flipped the page of the morning's announcements over and resumed his monologue:

"… a truly exceptional harvest, glorious, historic, exceeding all quotas, thanks, of course, to the Stewards' careful study and expertise. Serendipitous times, my friends. Serendipitous. Page eleven. Important news on this page, fellow workers—very important news—so the Crest requires redoubled attention for the following announcement, as we continue to exceed our quotas. Recent reports of violent incidents occurring near the Gutters are being thoroughly investigated by our most doughty wardens. The criminals responsible for these appalling attacks are being brought to justice, even as your humble lector speaks. Thanks to our brave men and women of the warden's guard, our security is ensured. In an abundance of caution, however, workers with passes to the Gutters, particularly Unity Corridor, or any tunnel nearing the Dwarven Quarter are encouraged to travel in groups, to check in with your reporting clerk immediately upon your arrival and departure, and to complete your assigned work as quickly as possible, and return home. If you see or hear anything suspicious concerning these recent incidents, you are obliged to report it immediately to your clerk, under penalty of prosecution. If you notice something, note it. Our all for all."

He paused to take another drink, while Tom, Tim, and several other workers muttered back: "Our all for all."

"Let me just add, as your long-serving lector," Victor set his dispatch aside for a moment and leaned forward, his voice dropping lower, "I will make myself available to talk further about this critical page of our report, and in further detail, with anyone interested at this evening's bonfire." He said this in a meaningful way, cleared his throat, and was about to continue when Jack's voice cracked across the fields from the entrance of the counting-house:

"Lillia!"

"Oh," Victor could not hide his grin as he scanned the plot to find Lillia. "Tanner. You're being summoned. Again."

Lillia let out a groan. The small bag she had been carrying drooped to the ground. A single malformed potato rolled out and touched against her big toe, as if it had always belonged there, a part of her. Her feet, like her hair, her face, and her fingers, were completely caked in a slurry of silt and sweat. Drab and brown, she was like all the others on the Farms now, a walking body of dirt, trained to dig in the dirt. Lillia kicked the potato away. One of the women hoeing a trench nearby hooted:

"Twice in the same morning? You'll be squirting out your own taters pretty soon. Little blonde ones."

Lillia scowled at the crone.

"Nothin' wrong with being a clerk's woman," another bent old woman behind her declared. There was a hint of experience behind what she said. "Gets you in from the fields."

"If you do it right, it does," the first woman agreed. "But this one's still out here. And her daddy and brother, too. Must not be doin' her inside job very proper."

The second woman tisked and shook her head knowingly:

"It does take a little more than just lying on your back." She said this to Lillia as if she were imparting a kind of sisterly wisdom.

Lillia held her breath and tightened her stomach so that her cheeks would blush, while the other workers around her snickered as she trudged past. Her father dutifully pretended she was not there at all. Victor began reading from his dispatch again. Only Tim dared to look up from his weeding to give Lillia the slightest bob of his head.

Jack's voice called out again:

"Lillia Tanner! Report at once!"

"Better pick up the pace, Tanner," Victor prompted. He flipped his paper over: "Page twelve ..."

"Aye, hurry, dear," the first woman yelled to Lillia's back. "Run and get some more seed!"

Guffaws of laughter echoed across the track of muddy farm troughs.

"Be quiet," Lillia groused over her shoulder, in an effort to sound cross. She could care less what any of these workers thought about her, but she knew she needed to play a part if only to get along. It was becoming tedious, though.

The counting-house was empty for the moment. Jack was alone seated at his desk and poring over a long roll of paper that tumbled from his tabletop to the floor. He was sweating (he was always sweating it seemed) and looking particularly worried. A crude candelabra overrun by dripping wax and an untouched plate of food were the only other things on the table. Lillia quietly closed and locked the door behind her. The smell of tilled plants and lingering must from all the workers clung to the air in the counting-house, no matter how empty it was. It was a scent Lillia despised with renewed vehemence every time it struck her nostrils.

"What do you need now?" she demanded.

Jack looked at her. She was at his shoulder, skimming the work in his report, and had already spotted multiple errors.

"I still don't get it," he groaned. "Why do I have to subtract all of these wages from here," he thrust an ink-stained finger at one column, "if I'm just going to add them back again over here," he tapped another set of numbers on another page.

Lillia pinched the bridge of her nose. Even from a cursory glance, she could tell the sets of numbers would never match.

"Because you're accounting," she explained. "You have to reconcile the costs on your rolls with your receipt of the week's wages from the Crest. See, this part of the crop went to the Crest, this part to the Quarter, and that little number there was for the workers. They sent you that number of coins for wages. So now you have to balance it all."

"But I already counted the coins they gave me when I paid them out."

"Not this again. Jack, I've explained this, what, five times already? Accounting is not the same as tallying. In accounting you have to keep adding and subtracting until you end up with zero—the whole point of accounting is to end up with nothing."

"And I still say that's stupid. And pointless. Who cares about zeroes?"

"Fine," Lillia was in no mood to have this argument again. "It's pointless. But your report requires it."

Jack's head hung, and his shoulders rounded in what might have been the beginning of a stoop. He was rolling his quill absently along the desk's edge, his eyes never focusing on anything in front of him. It took all of Lillia's restraint to keep from asking him how he ever managed to graduate from the academy. After a long while, he looked up at her again:

"I'm never going to figure this out."

She was standing just behind him, trying to make sense of his computations, and a strand of her hair fell from behind her shoulder and brushed across his face. She sat down onto a bench next to him:

"No, you're probably not," she agreed.

"So, could uhm—could you just do it for me?"

She had been waiting for the question for days now and had her response ready. She repeated her words exactly the way Jack had sounded when they first arrived at the counting-house:

"Why should I help you?"

It caught him off guard, and he stammered at first.

"Well. What do you mean, why? Because—" he bit his lower lip and glanced around the empty room. For some reason, he still dropped his voice. "Look, I-I gave your family a room, put you on the rolls. You've got a place now."

"You did that for a piece of silver," she replied evenly. "Which you'll probably use to get reassigned out of the Farms. If you can ever get your accounts straightened out."

"I—" Jack sputtered as if he wanted to say something, but he gave up. He let out a long breath and sank his head into his folded arms. She had simply spoken aloud what they both already knew. He heaved another sigh across his forearms.

"If I can get reassigned. Get another post someplace else ... I could— I could take you with me."

"And then I can truly be your woman?" she laughed sardonically. "We'll make it official, so it won't just be a rumor anymore?" In response to Jack's puzzled expression, she explained: "You've been having your way with me for days in here. According to the hands."

Something in the way he suddenly sprang up out of his lethargy, how his eyes widened hungrily, Lillia could sense he was surprised by this news; surprised, and somewhat pleased.

"They-they think you're my woman? They're really saying that?"

"Yes."

For just a moment, a smile cracked the corner of Jack's mouth. He turned his attention to his food and began devouring the cold, oily potato quarters and radishes that had been lingering on his plate, a clumsy attempt to hide the blush spreading across his face. Lillia studied him, thought for a moment, and then asked:

"Would you like that?"

His fork paused, hovering over his plate:

"What?"

"For me to be your woman?"

She was sitting on her hands, neither pulling away nor drawing closer to him. Sweat dripped from Jack's nose onto his plate. He wiped his face with his hand and ran his fingers through his cropped hair, more from habit from when he had worn his hair longer.

"I—I wouldn't. I'd have to think about that. I mean, you're not a clerk—not a real clerk. You're noted. I don't know how that would look—I mean, if we were open about it. But, uh, we could still … I wouldn't mind. If you wouldn't."

He licked his lips and, without once looking at Lillia, brought the palm of his hand across Lillia's thigh, then rested it on top of her bare knee. His fingers clenched gently, hesitantly at first, then a little more firmly, like a spider feeling the first sensation of prey caught in its web. Lillia's back stiffened. But she remained where she was, unmoving, perplexed that she could feel such revulsion at this boy's touch, and yet still submissive to it. If only he would look at her, she thought.

Jack was trying to straddle one of his legs over hers. He bumped the desk, knocking over his papers. His eyes shut tight, he opened his mouth wide for her.

"No."

"Wha-why?" Jack blinked.

She studied him, this boy she had known most of her life, now on the cusp of his manhood. He had a handsome enough face. With a little luck, his fortunes might return to some level of his father's. He would be amiable, then, perhaps even pleasant to talk to, someday if ...

Suddenly, an image came to Lillia, as startling as it was unbidden. Jack's face receded, and instead, she saw a goat's. Like the ones from Prosperity Farm. Gaping dumbly out from behind a fence, feigning to speak to her. A sash wrapping tight around his neck.

That was all Jack would ever be. An animal, passing his life from pen to pen, in a herd.

"No," she said, her voice beginning to rise.

He slumped back in his chair, struck by some force within Lillia's glare. She stood up and straightened her smock. A tear brimmed in her eye, and she wiped it away angrily:

"I'm not going to be your woman. And I'm not going to do your clerk's work, your thinking, for you." She straightened her shoulders and remembered threads of distant refrains, rote mantras she had memorized long ago, only now, realizing what they meant. She recited from one of them dutifully: "The Commonwealth has assigned me to farm labor. Not clerk's work. I'm entitled to the fruits of my labor."

Jack stared at her in disbelief. He started to get up.

"Don't," she warned.

His eyes smoldered, but he stayed in his chair:

"You think you're better than me? You're just a worker's whelp."

"I am."

"I could have your guildsman father taken up, your whole Craggie family thrown in the Tombs if I wanted to."

"You're not that cruel, Jack. Or that stupid."

Jack laughed at her:

"You don't think I've got the pull?"

"To have us taken up? I suppose the wardens would get around to a note from you, eventually. But workers can make notes, too. And testify. You took our bribe, Jack. Now you're stuck with us."

"My father—"

"—also took bribes. And look where you've wound up."

The first sounds of the workers lining up outside of the counting-house broke the long silence between them. Jack was trembling, but whether from embarrassment or rage, Lillia could not tell. His back was hunched, his jaws clenched tightly, and a vein throbbed near his temple. The candlelight showed the first line cracking his forehead and dark circles growing underneath his eyes. A foreshadow of a bitter, middle-aged man.

"Get out," he whispered at last. "I don't need you. Don't want you. Get out! Go be a ragger. Go wallow in the dirt. I hope the hands bend you over at the bonfires, in front of your father. I hope you get chopped to pieces like those porters in the Gutters."

"Jack—"

"Get out!"

His voice filled the empty storeroom. He kicked over the bench and let out a cry. Lillia hurried out the back doorway into the tunnels that led to the safety of the Farms' tilled dirt, without looking back.

As she left Lillia could hear a boy in a yellow sash weeping bitterly to himself.

Chapter Eighteen

LAMES LICKED THE sides of the pillars along the grotto's entrance. A wall of fires, twinkling like gemstones lost in the dark. They spewed black, putrid clouds that rose in columns alongside the mighty stalactites and stone beams that marked the Farm's boundary. Waves of sparks would lift up every so often, only to be swatted back down by the wind and rain beating in from outside the Mountain. Spray and smoke. Inhaled then exhaled between the stalactite teeth of a cave's mouth, the admixture of hundreds of bonfires and the ocean's salted winds. The Mountain's Breath, some called it. Far away, torpid ocean waves crashed against the rocks in unceasing, mindless rhythm—indifferent to names, to fires, to shouts and screams from the workers gathered in huddled knots.

It was a festival of sorts. Every new moon, all the Farms' hands and porters gathered up the bales of weeds, diseased potatoes, gulleystars that had lost their glow, and any other trash lying about and heaped it all into pyramided piles that were spaced across the length of the cave mouth. One after another, the accumulated refuse of the Farms was then lit in great pyres. Ostensibly, the bonfires were assigned work, needed to keep the Farms clean, but over the years an understanding had developed. The fires became the sanctioned source of revelry the clerks allowed to the Farms' hands, a scheduled, orderly release of pressure and steam to keep the Farms' working parts operative. Open drunkenness, fighting, fornication were indulged for one night each month. Invariably, when the ashes were cleared the next morning, a few dead bodies would turn up, and someone would have to make a note of it in a report; but the loss of life was always more than compensated nine moons later with a fresh birthing of a new crop of squealing, ruddy-faced whelps. As part of the implicit bargain that had evolved, the clerks and wardens seldom attended a bonfire, at least in their official capacity.

This was the first bonfire for Lillia and her family. As if by instinct, they had congregated with the hands that worked their little plot near the counting-house. A small cooking fire lit the faces of the men and women, still smeared with soil from the day's work. They spoke to one another gruffly but in good humor, in the shared, coarse language of those whose lives are spent toiling together. Tom and Tim blended with the other hands seamlessly, as if they had lived and worked on the Farms their whole lives.

Tim had met a girl the day before yesterday. She was a simple-looking moonfaced creature about Lillia's age, whose only notable features, from what Lillia could tell, were an easily bewildered nature and a missing front tooth. Her brother was trying to make the girl laugh by imitating the warden in the counting-house and having a small measure of success. Pretending to suddenly awaken, Tim stumbled, and a frothy splash from his mug of beer sloshed down his front, which elicited howls of laughter from the other hands. For his part, Tom's attention appeared to be divided between a conversation he was having with two men, his son's capering, and Lillia. Lillia could see the worry in his eyes whenever they came back to her.

The only time Tom seemed to stir was when a jug of balm was passed around the fire. Tim glanced at the toothless girl for a moment, perhaps wondering whether she would be impressed if he could stomach the drink, but Tom calmly wrenched the jug from the boy to pass it along to an old woman sitting next to him.

"You can't even handle your ale," Tom pointed at his son's dripping shirt and gave him a playful thump on the head.

Everyone snickered and Tim blushed in the firelight. The woman thanked Tom for the balm and drank the jug dry, the girl tittered until she let out a snort, and now Tim's face glowed with its own light, as a fatuous grin spread across his mouth.

Lillia watched them impassively.

She was sitting cross-legged on a flat rock, removed from the others, and now and then found her gaze pulled toward the sky above the sea, beyond the mouth of the cave. The stars were blotted out from the smoke, and for some reason, that bothered her. She shivered at a frigid wind that penetrated through the warmth of the bonfires. For a moment, the stench of burning trash, and rats cooking on spits yielded to the salted scent of the ocean. Lillia drew her shirt tighter over her shoulders. Between the searing heat of the fires and the bitter winds that kept whipping in from the storm, there was no warm middle ground to be found. Lillia preferred the cold.

Sitting aloof, she was the first to see Victor arrive. The lector's portly legs were staggering in the darkness between the fires, and he called out for a hand.

Lillia slid off her rock and found the man easily. He was deep in his drink from the smell of it, but he still spoke as smoothly, and in the same quaintly educated accent, as if he were in his lector's chair reading the day's reports. Leaning the better portion of his weight against her slender shoulder, he thanked Lillia:

"I am in your debt, my dear."

"Not at all, for I am at your service."

Victor halted in his steps:

"Why, Tanner," he declared, "I've never heard such fine manners at a bonfire. And from such a young thing, too." From within his bloodshot, wavering eyes, she could sense a penetrating scrutiny that at once made her feel uncomfortable.

"I-I heard a clerk talk like that once," she said.

"Ah. Just saying it as you heard it, I suppose." He craned his neck to make a good, close study of her before he whispered in her ear: "Best not to repeat everything we hear, my dear … Unless, of course, it's to me."

He gave her a friendly wink and followed her over to the fire. The moment Victor walked into the light, he spread his arms wide:

"My friends! Your humble lector has arrived!"

He was greeted with a round of hearty cheers, as all the workers stood up at once. A steaming bowl of stew—thick and brown with vegetables and a piece of meat—was pushed into his hands, along with a mug of ale that had been specially set aside. A dozen conversations erupted around him all at once:

"What's the news?"

"Are we ever going to get bread in the market?"

"C'mon, you know there's none to be had. What about meat? Used to be a man could buy a shank if he knew a guildsman."

"Have they announced the new Plan from the Crest?"

"Are they raising the wage for farmers?"

"Forget farmers! What about the porters?"

"My sister, Claire. She lives on the outskirts of the Gutters. Have you heard any word of her?"

Somehow, Victor recalled every one of his interrogators by name (and even asked for their children) and replied to every one of their queries with—"Oh, there's news, alright." "We're still hopeful some of the grain from the Crest will trickle down our way." "Goat meat would be most welcome, that it would …"—and shared a friendly clap and the same easy familiarity with every one of the farmhands gathered around the fire. They were all soon smiling.

Victor sat down on a makeshift bench to pick at his bowl and then, after a deep draught, declared that this was, without a doubt, the best beer of any fire he had been to that night. Far better than the harvesters', who, Victor warned, were already getting a little rambunctious—the ladies might want to keep an open eye should they venture out. Then, the pleased grin still plastered on his broad face, he straightened his shirt and cleared his throat politely, as if to signify he was now ready to conduct some sort of business.

"My friends," Victor said warmly, "as always, I am happy to share with you all what little I hear from time to time as I receive my dispatches. If anyone would care to bend an ear?"

His eyebrows tilted up very slightly, and without a word, several men formed a queue in front of him. Victor set his bowl down before him, as each man, one after another, dropped one of the coins from their wages into the lector's outstretched palm. Tom was the last in line, and when he paid his tinner, Victor raised a finger and gave him a meaningful glance.

Lillia crept a little closer, just behind her brother and the toothless girl, who was now resting her hand on top of Tim's. From between their shoulders, Lillia watched the lector share what he had brought with him.

Victor set his hands on his knees and held the crowd in his gaze. Then, in a deep, gravelly voice not much louder than the crackling fire, Victor whispered to the little gathering what the "real news" was in the Crag, his eyes flashing in the fire's light:

"First," he announced, "though they be few, the good tidings. That bumper harvest of fish we've been reporting on is real. There's cod in the waters for a change. No knowing how long it will last, but it's making for some good stew," he held up his bowl in a salute to whoever did the cooking, "so stock up on what you can at the market next week. No other cave-ins or tunnel collapses to report besides what you've heard already. Docks are still holding together, somehow, and the clerks aren't pressing ships like they were a month ago. Still no Plan out of the Crest, which means no reshuffling of the clerks for the time being. Our little Jackie's staying put a while longer, if that counts as good news to any of you."

There were a few ill-mannered cat-calls directed towards Lillia. Tim started to stand up, his hands clenching into fists, but Lillia touched him gently on the back to tell him not to make a scene. Victor ignored the noise and continued:

"Unfortunately, that's all the good news I have for you. Now, for the bad ... The Gutters."

"What's happened now?" asked one of the older women.

"Worse than what's being reported in our dispatches. Much worse. All of you have heard the whispers, I'm sure. Headless bodies turning up in out-of-the-way holes along Unity Corridor. Pools of blood underneath the pipes. Lately, there's been strange sightings, very strange—and here, let me caution, I cannot confirm these particular rumors—but there's been a lot of talk of, uhm, of small, black ... demons. That's the word I hear most—demons, pouring out of the holes between the Gutters and the Crag. With fiery eyes and swords, if you can believe it."

Lillia felt a chill run down her spine. The wind beyond the fire moaned, sending a gust of smoke near her. Some of the hands were scoffing at Victor's tale. It sounded more like some balm drinker's nightmare.

"I only repeat what I have heard," Victor shrugged. "But not everything I hear comes from workers and balm drinkers," he tapped his ear. "As for the bodies ... I've seen one myself. Oh, yes. A sweeper I have had dealings with for many years. Left the poor old timer's head perched on top of a street sign along Inclusion Corridor, just as cross looking in death as he ever was in life—though, I doubt any of you would look too pleased if your body had been cut out from under you and your face gnawed up by the rats. You can scoff at the rumors, count them all up to drink, but I saw that sweeper's severed noggin with my own eyes, and it was as real as any of you sitting here."

Victor broke off from his news telling to stifle a belch, then he continued:

"Bad as all that seems, it's prologuery compared to what happened a week ago." He paused again to ensure he had everyone's rapt attention. "For the first time," he said darkly, "a clerk got it. Offed him while he was working at his station. The wardens tried to cover it up quietly, but it was his chamber cleaners who first found the body, and too many people heard their screams before the guards could sweep them up. They say they found the sash spread across his tallying desk, cold as a stone, with his hands cut off. And in his tally book, written in his blood, two words. *We come.*

"Well, the wardens weren't giving a warm fart when it was Craggies getting culled—but a clerk? That's a blow that hits too close. It brought them out in force. A dozen guards, strong ones, spears sharp, head to toe in leather and mail. They made a clean sweep of Unity Corridor—ran out every living man, woman, and child, swept their homes, shut down every guild market. Took up scores of folk. Some of them were good folk, too. And then … *they* got it. The wardens, I mean. The whole lot of them," he snapped a finger, "taken out. Hacked up to pieces. No bloody words this time, but some folk who were near where it happened, they said they heard a gong or a bell, and then an awful voice that said—" Victor cupped his hands to his mouth and made a deep, booming sound, "—'we come, we come.' That was just how it sounded. Shook the very stones from the walls. Last thing those poor bastards probably heard," he let out a loud burp this time and shook his head. "It's strange tidings, my friends. Very strange. But that's as I've heard it."

It was silent around the cooking fire. The only sounds came from the distant reverie of the other bonfires and the passing breezes.

"Who-who's behind this?" One of the men next to her father asked.

Victor leaned closer, his face as orange as the fire beneath him:

"Officially? Take your pick. At first, it was escaped prisoners from the Tombs, then it was the guilds—it always has to be the guilds' fault somehow—but some of the first bodies that turned up were known guildsmen. So, then it became a faction of 'subversives,' whatever that means. Who knows? Next, they'll probably try to blame the lectors, eh?"

Victor let loose a long, hacking laugh that sent him rocking to one side. When he finished, he wiped a tear from his eye and continued:

"Those are the official accounts, and, let's just say, they're a tad inconsistent. Now, *unofficially* . . ." Victor paused and arched an eyebrow, "I've talked to a couple of friends who are in the know. They're whispering—and I, for one, think they might be onto something—that this is the dwarves' work. They say the dwarves have been stirred up, and they're back to fighting again. Wouldn't be the first time."

That was met with a smattered rumbling of disapproval. Victor held out his hands.

"It's still speculation, I only tell you as I heard it. The truth, my friends, is that nobody is sure who's behind this. The sashes and the wardens are as baffled as they are frightened, and that is saying something. Meanwhile, there's more fights, more gongs, more bodies piling up on our side of the Gutters. What does this mean for us?" He shrugged again in answer to his own question. "Your concerned lector would say simply this: don't go anywhere near the Gutters, my friends. Stay as close to the outside of the Mountain as you can. And let's all hope these troubles stay far from us."

The farmers around the campfire nodded and murmured in agreement, while Tim brought his arm protectively around his girl's shoulders. Victor finished his beer, asked for another fill, and turned his talk to other happenings in the Crag that were a little less dire.

For three more mugs, the gossip never stopped. Victor only paused for breath or drink, until, at last, the time had come for the private correspondence, and the lector called over one or two of the hands at a time—which was followed by more payments of coins. One of the hands Victor motioned for was Tom. Lillia watched the lector whisper something to her father that only the two of them could hear. Her father's face went pale, only for a moment, though, and then he simply nodded and sat back down.

While the others talked, Lillia's attention kept wandering back to the soot-stained night sky beyond the cave. Something about the lector's story, and its mention of demons, agitated what had been becalmed; and memories (if one can make memories within dreams) that were not forgotten, but had, at least, settled beneath her thoughts, were now beginning to froth near the surface again. It was no good trying to push them back down; like stirring away bubbles from a boiling kettle. The dark shapes, the voices, were writhing outside, whispering again. *We come ... We are in the Mountain ...*

Victor had to repeat himself to Lillia:

"I said, Miss Tanner—would you be so good as to bring over some of those old gulleystars behind you? The fire's about to die."

"Huh? Oh. Oh, of course." Lillia looked around her feet until she spotted the pile he had pointed to and picked up an armful. They were cold and some had a moist, slimy film around them. She tried her best to hold them all together in her grasp as she made her way over to the fire, but one slipped from between the crook of her elbow and onto Victor's lap when she drew past him.

"Hey, look at this now," said Victor, his smile brimming wide again. He brought the little mushroom close to his nose. "I believe that's a red-cap, Tanner. It surely is. Look at the spots. They're good luck—goodness knows, we could use a little of that." He set the pod down in front of her toes. Unsure, Lillia looked about her for help, and Victor prompted her:

"Go on and give it a stomp."

Gingerly, as if it were something living, Lillia lifted her heel and slowly pressed her weight down on top of the mushroom. It held its form and dug into her foot with a sharp pang until it finally snapped. A flash of red light, brighter than the fire's, burst from the ground beneath Lillia. So bright, for an instant, she could glimpse the bones within her foot, her arteries and vessels, her blood flowing inside her body. A flash from a fallen star. The spectacle was over, there was a smattering of applause, and Victor smiled and congratulated Lillia on the good fortune she had found.

But in the cold night air, Lillia acknowledged none of it. As the sparks rose from the fuel she cast on the fire, she felt only the clamoring of the darkness, stirring once more.

A gray haze of smog hung over the predawn air when Tom shut the door of their hovel behind him. An acrid stench from the bonfires still lingered. The soil felt hard, almost frozen beneath the carpet of silver mist that covered the Farms' ground. He scanned his surroundings, brought the hood of his cloak over his face, and crept away, a small shadow moving noiselessly in the fog of a vast, open field. He lingered only a moment by the lector's platform, as if uncertain of something, and then made his way to the stairs that led out of the Farms.

Shuffling feet, some coughing and hacking, scattered curses, the sounds of the few farmhands who held market day passes reverberated within the stone stairwell. Tom melded with them, trudging up the winding steps into the Mountain. As they climbed, more joined them from other caves and corridors. Gradually, they became a lumbering crowd, moving like a herd in the narrow stairwell, through checkpoints manned by half-asleep wardens, workers from all around the Lower Crag all heading to the same cavern, to the market. The press of people was now shoulder to shoulder, good cover that Tom welcomed instinctively. He tried to gather his thoughts, to prepare himself.

Victor's hoarse whisper was still in his ear from the night before:

"Your token, your words … In the next market."

Tom had been summoned.

It had not come as a complete surprise. He had taken his precautions; like any careful animal, he had hidden away what could be hidden whenever he could. They had kept quiet. But the old saying was true:

Press a gulleystar, make it shine,
Once it's lit, nowhere to hide.

Tom swiveled his head toward a rusted pot on the tunnel wall filled with gulleystars casting their oily, yellow glow over the workers. Threads of light slipping out from the pot's holes for everyone to see. There could be no hiding Lillia, not for long, at least. Too many notes, too much glow about her. Perhaps about him, as well. He had been there at Prosperity Farm, too; and it was his signature on that warden's paper, denouncing a brother. It was inevitable they would be found. He knew that, had known it from the moment they fled the tannery.

Tom went over his plan once more, what he would say, what he would not, what he might say, and when, if it came to it. At least he had had time to prepare, for which he silently thanked the lector.

The air felt sticky from the press of bodies. Bump, shuffle, a few steps, another bump—a slow, mindless movement that lasted perhaps an hour—then the crowd suddenly lunged forward and the ground leveled. A warden threatened everyone to hold still, then barked at them to keep moving. He had arrived at the market cavern.

It spanned hundreds of yards in a perfect oval that had long ago been carved within the Mountain. The sounds of conversation, wagons being pulled, a few crackling fires, all flowed freely, echoing from a ceiling so high it vanished within the darkness. Once, it must have been a truly grand place. There were marble flagstones here and there, probably laid down in the days of the priests, which in places were still perfectly joined, the dulled splendor hinting at some broken mosaic. And all along the walls, empty sconces and broken pedestals spanned in rows and columns that someone had half-heartedly tried to cover up with threadbare Commonwealth bunting or fill with crude imitations of the statues that once stood there: workers wielding hammers, workers bearing overflowing sacks of wheat, workers rising from the ground, grim, serene, all hollow plaster and chipped apart. What rubble was left from the place's origin had been piled, forgotten, or worked around in strange ways, like the marble elbow of a statue that now served as a brace for a clerk's desk. Old emblems and busts of shields were tabletops. What had once been a massive granite obelisk was now festooned with bits of wood and stretched pieces of hide skin, dangling all up and down its sides like leeches. The signs bore crude drawings and arrows to show where in the market one could find food, utensils, clothes, cragfire, medicines, and, wherever there was a red-painted oval, women.

Tom wandered, pretending to examine some of the stalls, all the while keeping an eye up. The people shopping were all dour and their talk with the stall sellers—who were low rated clerks—was terse and devoid of any real haggling. Tom made his way over to a table with a canopy that was a little removed from the rest of the stalls and situated himself on a rise in the ground that offered a good vantage of the market. His face expressionless, he fell in line behind two, stooped women, both clearly raggers, poking at what was on offer here:

"Look at this, Clementa," the one with a kerchief tied around her hairless scalp sneered at her companion, "just look at what four tinners buys you now."

Clementa tisked and shook her head. "Them's the most piss poor lookin' carrots I've laid eyes on in a market. Wonder why anyone bothered pullin' the things."

"Just last month, I could break a tinner in half and get twice as much. And better carrots, too."

"So you could," Clementa nodded vigorously, "you surely could."

"Someone might make a note, I think."

A sweating, obese clerk, who had been studiously ignoring them, now roused from her stool. She rolled her eyes and heaved a deep breath, either from annoyance or the effort of shifting her girth. A faded, wrinkled sash disappeared in her bosom.

"Either pay out your coins or move along."

"But these prices—"

"—have been set by the Stewards' boards. They're within the guidelines."

Clementa and the kerchief harrumphed for a while, and the bald woman's voice rose:

"I wonder how much of your guidelines is making its way to someone's pocket."

"Might be something to make a note of," Clementa agreed.

If they thought that would get a rise from the clerk, they were quickly disappointed. The woman heaved out a small scroll, unwound it, and pointed to a crowded column that ended in a wax seal.

"Right there. Set by the experts."

"Experts, indeed!" the kerchiefed one turned to Tom, as if to enlist him in her cause, but he had suddenly found a need to retie his sandals. She prattled on a little longer, but soon changed her tack to a more pleading tone:

"Look, we're all honest women here. You're probably a mother, like Clementa and me. These prices—who can pay them? I ask you, Madam Clerk? All the fish got bought up already. Now there's not so much as a plate of food to be had for less than half your week's wages."

The clerk simply shrugged and wound the scroll back up. "You were paid a proper wage for the fruits of your labor. This here is the proper price for carrots. Four tins. According to the stewards' experts."

"But who can pay that?"

"Not my affair."

"Well, then," her voice dropped, "I guess you'll just drive us all to deal with the guilds. They'll have another market soon enough. Might have to meet on the sly, but 'least they have some wares to sell."

"An' *they'll* offer a fair price," Clementa added.

Another sigh from the clerk. She lifted a pudgy hand to her lips and raised a nasal bellow:

"Warden here!"

Off the two raggers scuttled, cursing the clerk the entire way, and Tom noticed, as they disappeared into the mill of the crowd, that Clementa had managed to slip one of the carrots into her skirt. His mouth crinkled into a smile. The clerk sat back on her stool with a grunt, now firmly intent on ignoring Tom and anyone else who would deign to bother her at the stall. Still, just in case a guard might answer her summons, Tom thought it best to find another place to resume his watch.

He only made it about a dozen paces. When he turned a corner, a hand suddenly reached out from a fissure in the wall and clamped hard on his shoulder. Tom froze in midstep, rooted to the ground like a stone. He did not dare to move or make a sound; because now everything would depend on his seeming, on his being, calm and composed. Over the din of the market, he heard only the whispering of a voice from the darkness:

"Brother, can you spare a token?"

CHAPTER NINETEEN

TOM TURNED SLOWLY. He forced his face to resemble something expectant, friendly, ignoring the pounding in his chest. From the shadows, he saw only a shaded figure, its face hidden within a hood, with its hand extended towards him. Hoping his palm would not feel sweaty, Tom took it firmly. The other hand slid over their grip to keep the token they shared concealed. The man's fingers were surprisingly smooth.

Tom caught a glimpse into the hood and could make out the bearded chin and nose of a man around Tim's age. No more than a couple of years older perhaps, but a fully made guildsman from the grip he gave Tom. The man murmured his name, Evan, and three more shadows emerged from the darkness within the wall and surrounded Tom.

"This way, Tanner," one of them nudged him toward the crack.

He was turned sideways to fit into the opening, and with the young man before him and the others behind, Tom was forced into a tight, black, cold space between two jagged stone walls. It was like scaling the side of a mountain. They shimmied through the cramped space for what must have been a quarter of a mile, the walls scraping against Tom's shoulder blades and, in one place, gashing his cheek, until, at last, they emerged into a hollow that gradually opened up into what looked to be a diminutive imitation of the marketplace cavern they had left behind. In its center, a few tallow candles burned low, shedding light on a small gathering. They were engaged in quiet conversations, exchanging coins and parcels, writing up ledgers. The talk hushed the moment Tom entered. A lockbox was slammed shut.

A tall and lean built woman appeared out of the darkness and walked straight toward Tom. From head to toe, the woman was enveloped in seal skins tied close to the joints of her body, her only features a pair of dark, intent eyes. She carried a spear against her shoulder that was made from a long wooden staff with a fillet knife bound at the hilt.

She would be the sergeant at arms, Tom knew, a fighter who safeguarded guild meetings from intruders and eavesdroppers. Tom didn't recognize this one, but she was coming to test him.

"Who comes here?" the sergeant demanded.

Inwardly, Tom swore to himself. He tried to sound nonchalant:

"I've already given my token; do we really need to—"

"Your words, Tanner. Who comes here?"

There was a note of menace there, Tom detected. It had been a long time since he had repeated the words. Tom took a deep breath and searched his memory.

"A brother bearing light in the Mountain."

"Where have you come from?"

"From the base."

"Where are you traveling?"

"To the dark of the summit."

"By what means?"

"By ship."

"Her name?"

"The *Solidarity*."

As soon as he had answered, Tom knew he had gotten something wrong. There were scattered groans across the cavern, and now the woman was gripping her spear with both hands, leveling the point of the knife straight at his chest. Tom tried to inch away, but Evan pushed him right back until the sergeant's blade hovered just above the neckline of Tom's shirt.

"What was her name?" the sergeant repeated.

Tom's mind went blank. He clenched his teeth, and his eyes darted all about, searching the surroundings, trying to find something to spur his memory. He repeated the lines to himself, mouthing the words quietly, but when he got to the ship, he could not coax the right word out.

"Now!" she demanded.

"It-it's the ... the ... shit."

An image from the docks, the metal archway over the entrance, suddenly flashed before his consciousness, and somehow the word flowed after it:

"The Symbol."

They each let out a sigh of relief. The spear lowered, and the woman shook her head.

"Trying to get yourself killed, Tanner? That wouldn't do your little girl much good, would it?"

Tom wiped a line of sweat from his forehead. "Sorry."

"Been a while," she muttered before she returned to her post by the crack in the wall.

"Yes," Tom agreed. "It has."

The men that had followed him from the market cavern led Tom over to join the rest of the guildsmen gathered around the candles. Tom recognized a few of them, but when he tried to acknowledge anyone, he was answered by a downturned face, or simply a scowl. There was an empty stool, and Tom was about to sit in it when Evan once again clasped him by the shoulder. He patted down Tom's clothes. Tom raised his hands and tried to sound indignant:

"Is this how guildsmen greet brothers now?"

A silver-haired man, dressed in thick, flowing black clothes, arose from his chair, slowly and deliberately, and, only after every inch of Tom's body and clothing had been searched, shooed Evan away. He had an aquiline nose, a neatly cropped beard, and eyes the color of marble. He gave Tom an apologetic smile and brought a handkerchief from his pocket to dab the scrape on Tom's cheek.

"Brother Tanner, it has been a long time since you've joined us. Too long. We hardly recognized you, as perhaps you've gathered. You are well?"

Tom took his seat stiffly, folding his hands across his lap, as if the twenty or so men and women in a ring staring at him warily were not to be noticed.

"All things considered, I am."

"Good. Good," he pressed his hands together. "It has been such a very long time, you probably don't know who I am. Master Samuel, head of Potters, Coopers, and Boxmakers. I've been elected presiding master of our Guild of Guilds."

"Such as it is," someone hissed just loudly enough to be heard.

Samuel ignored the jibe and joined Tom on his bench.

"Do you know why you've been summoned?"

There it was, straight to the point, the question that would begin the dance Tom was about to perform:

"I believe I do," he answered.

"Fucking right, you do," a burly, tattooed man hovering behind Samuel growled. The man's face was dappled in flaming, pink splotches that twined with jade and black-painted lines drawn in a paltry effort to conceal the disease wasting over him. He hissed, and Tom could see his rotted teeth beset with flakes in his gums. "You're a traitor and a thief. And now you've been caught!"

Samuel lifted a hand, the passivity in his features interrupted only fleetingly:

"I am presiding, Master Elwin. The porters will be heard in due course. As we agreed. Now. Brother Tanner, tell me. Why are you here?"

"Because one of his porters," Tom gestured towards Elwin, "got taken up on account of attacking my girl. I'm sorry that that happened. I really am, but—"

Tom was speaking as mildly as he could, but the tinder smoldering behind Elwin's eyes suddenly leaped into flames. He sprang from his chair, knocking over those next to him. The splotches covering his nose and forehead were burning bright—from the balm, Tom thought as he scurried backward. He may have been half-sotted from drink, but Elwin was still built like a block, and he could move swiftly for one his size; he waded through the men and women between them, groping for Tom's throat.

"I'll make you sorry!" Elwin shouted, sending spittle into Tom's face.

The guildsmen who had accompanied Tom quickly formed a wedge around him. Everyone was yelling at once, some with Elwin, a few against him. Two of the guildsmen managed to grasp Elwin's arms and, with a great deal of struggle, hold him in place. The bench Tom had been sitting on a moment ago was broken, its plank split down the middle.

"They're cracking our skulls because of that traitor and his little sash!" Elwin spat. His lip curled angrily, and now Tom could see the flecks of potato clearly in the man's teeth. He had just finished drinking, in all likelihood. "They've brought the whole garrison down on us!"

"Masters, brethren!" Samuel spread his arms. "Comport yourself, Master of Porters. I said, comport yourself! Sister sergeant, your help is needed—"

"Don't bother," Elwin growled, pulling himself upright. He was breathing heavily, scorching those around him with the fumes of balm. Elwin straightened his ripped shirt collar and leveled everyone in the room with a contemptuous glare. "I'm done with this lot. Sam, if your little Guild of Guilds wants to talk, and vote, and comport with each other's asses, fine. I'll have no part of it. You know the porters' position. What it is we want. If we don't get what we want today," his eyes fixed on Tom's, "well, now we know where to find you, *brother.*"

Elwin murmured something into a woman's ear before he stormed out of the cavern by a doorway in the far wall, the anger in the air lingering long after the sound of the door slammed shut behind him. Tom crouched down and tried to turn his bench upright again. It fell apart in splinters.

Samuel sniffed and pulled at his collar. "Master Elwin has not been himself lately."

"You can't blame him," said the woman Elwin had spoken to. She was younger than Tom, with broad shoulders and a face lined and scoured from hard work, but brimming with intensity. "Nothing's been right for our guild, not since his daughter got our Eli taken up. We're getting pressed on all sides."

"Pressed porters, dead porters, porters running off," her friend next to her muttered into her hands. "Joanna's right. It's been nothing but hard times."

Tom listened, but more than that, he watched. The faces around him, the wariness behind the glares, the way each one was looking to someone else to break some unspoken indecision.

"This is what I've been summoned for?" Tom asked. "To answer for what the wardens are doing to the porters?"

"No," Joanna hissed, "for what you did to Eli."

"The man went running through the halls of the Industry Caverns dressed up like a priest, waving a wand around, and drunk on balm. He attacked my only daughter. He was a lunatic. He was bound to get—"

"Enough of this," Samuel held up his hand.

"How dare you talk that way about Eli," Joanna pointed a finger at Tom's chest. "When it was your daughter who drove him over the Falls. Just like she drove those goats off Prosperity Farm—oh yes, we've all heard that story, too. She's cursed. Eli warned us about her. 'Watch for her,' he said. 'Lillia. The one who scatters darkness with light. Who carries toil in her hand?' She's brought down this curse from the Gutters, too, I'll wager."

"I said *enough!*" Samuel's voice cracked.

Joanna's words rang in Tom's ears.

Eli warned us about her.

Joanna curled a pair of filth covered knees into her chest, glaring at Tom and oblivious to Samuel raising his voice at her. Samuel was exasperated, Tom could sense it, as if some nuisance he had thought should have gone away by now was drawing all of his resources. Samuel spun in a half-circle to ensure he had everyone's attention. Yet, it was Joanna that Tom found himself watching most closely.

"I made it clear," Samuel declared, "very clear, that these beliefs—these sentiments—what have you—the sort of thing that's been swirling about as of late … it can have no place in the work of the guilds. We have enough problems."

Now Samuel turned to face Tom fully.

"As do you, Tanner. You find yourself windward in a storm, as the sailors might say, concerning your family's involvement with our late Brother Eli. Attend to it however you see fit. But that is not—I say again—*not* our concern at the present."

"It isn't?"

"No. You've been summoned because of what happened at the Docks."

"The-the Docks?" Tom ran his hand through his hair and stared at Samuel, a perfect mask of perplexity.

"Yes."

"You're talking about Lillia's accident?"

"I'm talking about the ship. Were you or were you not approached by the *Plentiful*'s captain?"

Tom pursed his lips and scratched at his chin. Samuel leaned closer:

"Her name was Asa. She was a—"

"—a guild sister, yes," Tom nodded, as if suddenly recalling the detail. "Sorry. That day was so confused—Lillia nearly died. Yes, Captain Asa approached me. But it was—no, I remember … She was in distress."

"She gave you the signal?"

"Not all of it. She couldn't. There was a clerk right behind her. He had impounded the boat, I think. She looked hurt. Or scared. It's hard to remember."

"Listen, Tanner. This is vitally important. Did Asa hand you anything?"

"Like what?"

"Just answer me," Samuel glared intently at Tom. "Did she try to give anything to you? Ask you to hold something? Slip something into your pocket? Tell you to come and fetch something. Anything at all?"

It was an honest question. The man had no idea.

A momentary pause and Tom shook his head.

"No. No, she started her signal from the plank. And then the clerk was there and took her up. I'm sorry."

Samuel slumped down, his shoulders deflating. He rubbed at his beard worriedly, but never once took his eyes from Tom's. Glancing around, Tom could see in the flickering glow that most of the guildsmen had their faces buried in their hands. One of the men leaned over and started to whisper into Samuel's ear, but he waved him away angrily, motioning for Evan's attention.

"Master?" Evan drew himself up.

"Your search, it was—thorough?"

"We went over every inch of the place and dug all around it. Only thing of value was an old book that looked like it belongs to his girl. He doesn't have it."

So, the guilds had come to their home. Probably in the middle of a shift, Tom thought. There would be plenty of light, with ample time to set things back in their place afterward, and nobody was likely to stumble across them while they worked. Evan was right, they had been thorough. Tom had not noticed so much as a fold in the blankets that was out of place. But, then, they could have ransacked the hovel for all he cared.

You can't hide anything in your home, not if you want it to stay hidden; that was one of the first lessons Tom had learned as a boy.

Samuel let out a curse, followed by a volley of shouts that echoed in the closeness of the cavern. "It's lost!" was the refrain repeated most. Some were demanding that Samuel step down; some shouting to arm themselves; a few were pleading for solidarity, to come together, but their voices were drowned.

They were all afraid. Tom stood unmoving from his spot, while the meeting he had been summoned for, it seemed, broke up of its own accord. Men were slipping out through the crack in the wall Tom had come through. Those who remained were buzzing around Samuel, who now found himself surrounded and peppered with questions he did not at all seem keen to answer.

As for Tom, he had already been forgotten. He waited for what felt like a suitable amount of time, but when no one said anything more to him, he decided he could safely make his exit as well.

The sergeant at arms was leaning against the cavern wall in the shadows near the crack. She looked wryly at Tom when he approached, then shook her masked head at all the commotion behind him.

"Leaving already, Tanner? The meeting's just getting interesting."

"I figured it was over, since—well." He motioned behind him. "Should I stay, sergeant?"

"No. They're done with you, I think. Truth is, they're just done."

Tom looked over his shoulder once more and dropped his voice low: "What's happened with this Asa?"

The sergeant gazed into his face, her black eyes probing, as if testing them for something. Her knife's blade caught a flash of candlelight as she moved her spear over to another shoulder.

"She's dead," she said at last.

"I-I'm sorry to hear that. It sounds like she was carrying something important."

"You could say that ... She had all of our money."

"What?"

"Her ship, the *Plentiful*, it was carrying a bag of pure silver. Everything the guilds could scrape together. It was supposed to buy us protection."

"Protection from what?"

The sergeant leaned forward, her eyes narrowing. Beneath the seal furs she wore as protection, she blended seamlessly with the color of the hides. Yet, the camouflage could not conceal her fear.

"From whatever it is that's coming," she told him.

Frozen shards of granite hovered in the air, tantalizingly close. Hundreds, thousands of them, in endless rows, floating upon nothingness. Upon each surface, flecks of metal reflected some unseen light. A teasing hint of luster. There they were. Pieces of the Mountain's riches, spread out before her, enticing her, there for her to grab. The way Jack had grabbed her father's silver coin. To have, to hold. A longing ache welled up within Lillia.

But every time she reached out her hand to grasp one of the pieces, it became smoke. Again, and again, she lunged after the silvered stones, and each one would disappear, just as her fingertips were about to brush upon them. She was spinning around furiously, trying to seize just one with her hands stretched wide.

She could knock them down by kicking at them—yes, that would work!

Only now her legs would not move. They felt just as strong as ever, but for some reason, she could not lift her feet. Not so much as a twitch.

This was absurd. She was perfectly able to move her legs, she could fly like a seabird if she wished. The only thing binding her legs were— her legs. The stones, the silver—she had to have that silver—her own body was conspiring against her, thwarting her.

A shard floated within inches of her face; the metallic pieces so close she could almost taste them with her tongue. The silver pieces became the shape of a face, one with many eyes. It began mocking her, opening its mouth to embrace hers, even as it was on the verge of scurrying away. She moistened her lips and spread her jaws as wide as she could, but it was like trying to bite her own teeth. Lillia clamped down hard, cutting the side of her tongue, and tasted blood.

Then all the stones, as one, went dim, as if someone had suddenly doused a lantern. They crumbled into dust that hung motionlessly before her, suspended like a cloud on a windless day. Slowly, the dust and detritus gathered together, swirling, and became a pillar of smoke, a tether joining a bottomless floor to an endless height. It twisted violently, faster and faster. She was trapped within it, her hair flying about her face. Lillia held her breath, her eyes shut tight. Ash, dust, vapor, pebbles, a maelstrom flew about her with a deafening roar, blinding her sight.

She couldn't breathe. The pain, the crushing pressure—it was too much; her chest heaved in spasms. Lillia's mouth gaped open once more, flooding her lungs with the stinging stench of burning trash. Her tongue, her cheeks, her mouth were full of scalding sand. She spat, but it only made it worse, and a horrible awareness dawned upon her that this smoke, and dust, and debris, it was not blowing aimlessly around her; it was joining, deliberately, a million bits of rock and dirt bound together by a common purpose. To force their way into her body.

She screamed.

"*Is she alright?*"

It was the girl's voice. A man grunted something, and then she started tittering. Lillia tried to call for help, but the sound was strangled.

"*Lil?*" the man called to her.

Lillia jolted upright from her bed, panting wildly. The air came in deep gulps; cool air, tinged with the earthy smell of the Farms outside. Despite the pain it brought in her chest, she welcomed each breath. Her bedroom lurched, and a tingling sensation enveloped her fingers and feet. She felt her forehead. The skin was clammy and damp. Lillia held out a hand for the wall to steady herself.

A trickle of loose sand fell from her touch. No whirling wind, no tornado. It was staying on the ground, where it belonged; a thin line of gray on a dingy blanket.

The dizziness was beginning to pass when the sackcloth curtain that separated her bedroom was gingerly drawn back a few inches. Her brother's face emerged, framed by the tiny glow of their mother's gulleystar lamp.

"Hey—is everything alright?"

"Fine," a pained expression passed over Lillia, but when she looked up at Tim, she tried to smile. "I'm fine."

"It's just that—we could hear you. Enid was worried."

Hearing her name, Enid appeared over Tim's shoulder. Her hair was as tangled as Lillia's, although assuredly not because of a bad dream. She lingered behind Tim expressionlessly, hiding in the periphery of the hovel's common room just beyond Tim's light. Her eyes were wide, vacant, as they always seemed to be. Wiry, fatuous, like any other goat's.

Enid, the girl without a front tooth, was Tim's woman now. Ever since that first bonfire. Tim had been staggering from his ale, and Enid had helped him find his way home, even after he had vomited his supper. Their laughter rang across the Farms. Once inside the room, she never left his side.

"We'll leave them to it," her father had whispered to Lillia that night. "I'll find you another bed."

Lillia shook her head and sat down next to her father, and together they spent that night on a chair outside their hovel's doorway, Lillia watching the twinkling bonfires, Tom smoking a pipe he had scrounged, a strange, contemplative look on his face. Without a word, he put his arm around her as if to keep her warm, though Lillia had not felt all that cold. And that was how Enid had joined their family.

"I really am alright," Lillia tried to smile at Tim and then began making her bed, silently wishing they would both just go away, even if it was for more lovemaking. But Tim lingered in the doorway with a worried look:

"It's happening again, like before, isn't it?"

"I told you, I am fine," Lillia replied, her voice becoming shrill. A silence hung between them until Enid offered in a faint voice:

"I'll make us something to eat."

It was part of what had become an understanding between them, Enid's role in the home: she cleaned, gathered gulleystars when they were needed, helped Tim with his quotas, and, now, prepared the family meals. Their fare had been better when Timothy had done the cooking, but that was something no one talked about yet. Lillia tried to tell her not to bother, but Enid was already stoking the fire in the common room's hearth, eager to make herself useful. Tim hung on Lillia's curtain, shirtless, smoothing the cowlicks of his hair.

"I thought the dreams," he pronounced the word as if it were from a foreign language, "the strange things you were seeing, I thought that had stopped—when we got here."

"It did. I mean, it has."

Tim studied his sister.

"Has that clerk been bothering you again?"

Tim refused to call Jack by name. Lillia kept straightening her bedsheets.

"Not really," she replied.

In truth, since that day in the counting-house, Jack had scarcely acknowledged her. He was mortified, but whether it was because she had refused his advance or his demand for her to do his accounting, it was hard to say. Most likely it was both. They no longer spoke, or even looked at each other, but a courier began bringing her his tally sheets at the end of each day with the same note:

"Do it. Or leave."

Four words in Jack's pinched handwriting, but they said much in their brevity. She would do his tally sheets, but from her home; the accounting, though, he would just have to struggle through on his own. Probably by bribing the clerk that did the audits. Jack kept their coin; she kept her family's place on the Farms. And they would each pretend the other did not exist. Another understanding. A tacit truce. A bribe.

It occurred to Lillia that much of the Mountain's life seemed to revolve around bribes. They were as ubiquitous as gulleystars, yet they were a topic Madam Teacher had only once ever mentioned aloud in class, and with a long, vicious string of invective, as if a bribe were the vilest form of treason one could commit against the Commonwealth. Clerks and workers were removed in the most horrendous fashion for taking bribes, and rightly so; the teacher had pointed at each one of her students individually to drive the point home. The very idea of a bribe had seemed unthinkable to Lillia then, terrifying. Now she found herself wondering whether anyone had ever worked together outside the bond of bribery. As if all of life's undertakings were nothing more than an accumulation of silent, secret understandings. All transacted and paid for.

Tim broke through Lillia's reflections:

"Do we—I mean, Father's friends—do they need to pay a call on this clerk?" He stood a little taller and flexed his shoulders, as if he would like nothing better than to take care of this himself. "I could get the word to a guildsman that—"

"Don't be a fool, Timothy," Lillia hissed. She lowered her voice so that Enid would not overhear them: "Father's in trouble with the guilds already. Isn't that obvious?"

From her brother's expression, it was not—at least, not to him. He bunched his lips in thought, his face oscillating between befuddlement and anger.

"All-all he said was he had to answer a summons. A quick meeting, that's all it is."

"Listen to me, Tim. I don't know what has happened. But you stay clear of the guildsmen until Father says otherwise."

"They're our brothers."

"Who'd slit your throats for a coin. Just stay away from them."

Tim blinked at her and shifted awkwardly in the doorway. From the common room, it sounded like Enid was working to fill a kettle with water but spilling most of it onto the floor.

"I was only trying to help you," he muttered, as he turned to leave.

They were cleaning up after Enid's meal when they heard the commotion outside. Tim cracked open the door and Lillia saw dozens of hands, all running in the same direction, talking excitedly, every one of them carrying empty sacks, bags, chests, buckets, anything that could be used for holding.

A shipment had arrived.

Wagon loads of potato seed for the next season's planting, days behind schedule, but here at last. With no forewarning, the clerks were measuring out allotments to everyone with a sack. They heard the news from one of the women that worked their plot. She was breathless from trotting as fast as her stumpy legs could carry her and, as soon as she had shared what she had heard, she quickly disappeared around the lector's stand.

Their father had told them all to wait together inside for his return, but the prospect of missing an allotment that might not come around again for months seemed too much for Tim. Had Father known a shipment was arriving, he would have wanted them to go and get their claim. So off he ran out the door, charging after the excited throng, with Enid trailing after him. Annoyed at his impulsiveness, Lillia raced after the two of them, if only to keep everyone together.

They were soon pressed from all sides in a bustling crowd of farmhands, everyone hollering and shoving to push forward. It had begun as a line but quickly devolved into a mob. But Tim plodded through the throng until the clerk's table came into view ahead. A line of sashed men and women, sweating profusely, checking off names from one list, writing up allotments on another. There was plenty of seed left. A gap appeared, and Tim started to move closer when Enid froze in place and grabbed Tim's hand.

"What's wrong?" Tim asked her.

The people around them cursed loudly to keep moving, but Enid ignored them. She bowed her head low, pulled on Tim's arm so hard he nearly fell over, and led the three of them off to the side, out of the line. She slipped behind a wooden barricade that served to mark a trash heap and crouched low.

It had been little more than a week since the last bonfire, but already the garbage was piled higher than Tim's forehead, a steaming mass with an awful stench. Lillia felt her stomach roiling. Enid's face was pale, her round eyes wider than Lillia had ever seen them before. She kept looking beyond the trash, as if searching for something within the crowd.

"What're you doing?" Tim demanded.

"I-I saw a man up ahead. At the clerk's desk. Watching us."

Timothy glanced through the crowd but saw nothing other than the mass of farmers getting their allotments. "What of it?"

"He's not one of us."

Tim thought she was being ridiculous, but Lillia could sense the danger reflected in Enid's face. The girl tried to edge away.

"This is silly," Tim shook his head, "we're getting back in line."

"Tim, wait," said Lillia. "Enid's been here longer than we have. We should listen to her. Enid? What did this man look like?"

Enid cowered behind Tim's back. Her eyes were glazed with fright:

"He-he's got a porter's smock like he's one of the wagon men, but he's all clean underneath, you can tell. His hair's too nice. He's not a Craggy. Not a clerk, neither."

"What was he doing?"

"Just standing there, behind the clerks' chairs. He was looking right at you, Tim, and that's when I saw him smile. We need to go."

She tugged at Tim's shirt for him to follow her, to someplace farther away. But Timothy would not move.

"What's wrong with a porter smiling at me?"

"Tim, please!" Enid was pleading. "He's not a porter. We need to go."

"Listen, why don't we just head back home," said Lillia.

"Yes, yes," Enid agreed. Then suddenly her spine stiffened. She held a finger to her lips, which were now white and bloodless.

Over the noise of the crowd, from the other side of the wooden partition, Lillia could hear the sounds of booted footsteps walking by. The steps paused and then drew closer. She never saw whose they were though, because at that moment, Enid heaved Tim into the mound of trash, headfirst, and pulled Lillia in behind him. Like a mole, Enid was burrowing deep into the filth, forcing Tim and Lillia to go deeper and deeper behind her. It was horrible; and yet, they both followed her, blindly, trusting the instinct that was driving Enid's flight.

Lillia's clothes were soon soaked, and she felt hotter than she had since her fever. She tried to hold her breath. There was more than just trash and potatoes in this pile; it also served as a latrine. Foulness dripped down her shirt, over her nose, between her fingers, until at last, it burst into her lungs.

Her stomach lurched like an animal bursting from a cage. Lillia vomited all over herself. Next to her, Enid whispered for them to hush, to hold still. Another wave of nausea, followed by a spell of dry heaving, and now Lillia could hear a faintly familiar voice outside, a man's, who spoke with a haughty, lisping ring of authority:

"I could have sworn they ducked around this way."

"Are you sure it was them, Captain?" asked another.

"Of course it was them," he snapped. "I do not forget faces."

Lillia could feel her brother beginning to quake next to her. He was on the cusp of losing his stomach, too, it seemed. She gently touched his arm to calm him down. One of the voices spoke again:

"We could do a sweep?"

The first man laughed.

"Corporal, have you enough men to quell the riot that will ensue when we start turning away all these hands and flipping over their hovels? No? I thought not. We shall have to find them another way."

"What about their clerk?"

"Which one? There's as many clerks down here as there are Craggies. If we start taking up clerks, word will race 'round like wildfire. Mustn't flush our quarry again. Uch, why is it every place this matter has led me must smell like a toilet?" The man laughed again, without mirth. "I suppose it's better than being stationed in the Gutters."

"You're right there, sir," the corporal agreed.

It was quiet for a long while. Something tickled at Lillia's toes, cockroaches, most likely, and every muscle in her foot clenched with revulsion. She shut her eyes and tried to focus all her concentration on what the men were saying. But the captain spoke only once more before they walked away:

"An idea occurs to me. These bonfires I've heard so much about, perhaps they might serve our purpose just as well as our impromptu seed disbursement."

"That could work, sir. It very well could. All the hands come out for the fires, and they're nice and spread out. And with all the debauching and drinking, no one would pay any mind if the pickup turned into a scuffle."

"Alive, Corporal. I remind you; I need the father alive. I've a question or two now concerning some of his associates."

"Yes, sir. We'll make sure that one's still breathing—so he can talk."

"How long until the next bonfire?"

"It's by the new moon, sir, as I understand it."

"Well, well," the captain sniffed. "That's a bit of a wait. But I suppose it's the best we can do. Perhaps we'll get lucky and bump into him sooner. Hopefully, he doesn't slip away again. This Tanner's a slippery fellow ..."

CHAPTER TWENTY

I T WAS WELL past midnight, and Lillia was tossing in her sleep, mumbling senselessly. Another one of those dreams, Tom thought sadly.

"Lemme—lemme go," she breathed. Her eyes fluttered from behind the lids but stayed shut. Tom nudged her gently:

"Lillia."

"Don't hurt me," she murmured.

"Get up, Lillia," Tom whispered.

"Father?"

Her eyes came open. Two troubled, gray orbs, reflecting a gulleystar's glow. Tom could make out his reflection within them. A tired, careworn man with a sack and a bedroll slung over his stooped shoulders. He smiled sadly:

"I'm here. But we have to leave. I've got your things packed already."

Lillia hoisted herself up from the bed. Her hair was disheveled and her bleary eyes widened as she scanned the room. Tom had already cleared the place. Lillia's few possessions were stowed in the middle of the common room, ready to be shouldered. Tom helped her into a clean set of clothes and continued:

"Your brother already told me what happened yesterday. I'm so glad—" he paused and closed his eyes, "—it's a good thing you hid when Enid told you to. That was the right thing to do. Here, this should help cut the last of the smell from that garbage." He sprinkled some clear liquid over her hands. "Keep it out of your eyes."

Lillia's face pinched. "Isn't this—balm?"

"Mm-hm. Don't forget your hair. That was foul stuff you were rolling around in. We don't want to attract attention."

At first, she held her hands out far from her body, as if the very touch of balm might be poisonous. But cautiously, she started to sniff the air

300

and noticed that, for the first time, the lingering stink that had soaked into her palms and fingertips was gone. Lillia looked up at her father.

"Everything has a use," he shrugged. "Come on, you can finish while we walk."

Wiping the sleep from her eyes with her shoulder, Lillia followed Tom into the common room where Tim and Enid were waiting, each holding a small backpack before them. Pots, pans, forks, and knives were all dangling from cloth rings and belt loops. Next to Tom, they looked exactly like a group of peddlers. The hearth had gone cold, the gulleystar lamps emptied, and the few pieces of cutlery, pots, and pans that had been in their kitchen were put away save a little bowl with some porridge left over in it. Enid picked it up and handed it to Lillia, who sipped at it uncertainly.

"Where-where are we going?" Lillia whispered.

Tim was shifting from one foot to the other, while Enid absently twirled the nape of her shirt with her finger. Tom quietly cracked the door open a little wider before he answered:

"The market. It's risky, but if we make it early enough, we can buy passes, good ones with wax, so we can move wherever we need to."

Tom had everyone do a final sweep of the hovel to make sure they had left nothing behind that might betray where they were heading, and then he reached for the door. He paused, fixating on his fingers clamped around the knotted end of a rope that served as their door latch. In the glimmer of a gulleystar lantern, the shadows between his knuckles looked like gray indentions in stone-colored flesh. An old set of hands now, Tom thought. Strong from years of use, but slower, nearer to the verge of faltering. He let out a long breath and slowly turned his head.

There was his family. Watching him, waiting for him to lead them away from danger. His son, a taller, broader—and dimmer—reflection of Tom in his youth; touching the boy's arm, a Craggie girl, as plain and unremarkable as the dirt beneath their feet, but resourceful and wary, a good match for Tim; and Lillia. She looked tired again. He felt the same.

Tom shut his eyes. If he hadn't been taught all his life that there were no gods, that there never were gods, that if there ever had been gods, they were irredeemably wicked and cruel—had he known better—he might have offered one of them a prayer right now. He very nearly did.

Despite the Commonwealth's training and the hardness of his small existence, somehow, as he stood there with his hand resting upon the door,
a kind of prayer stirred within Tom Tanner. It came about in its own
way and without his even realizing it. The most ancient and natural of
prayers: Tom prayed to keep his family safe.

Then he opened the door, and the Tanner family left the Farms
behind them.

The last time she had walked a flight of stairs was over a month ago in
their flight from the tannery. While Lillia's arms and hands had grown
taut from picking potatoes, her legs were still soft. She rubbed at the
aching muscles, trying to worry out the knots that were forming while
keeping up with the others. Enid, Tim, and Tom loped far ahead up the
stairwell, taking two stairs at a time in the cracked dimly lit passage. Lillia
reached a sloped and moss-covered landing where she stopped to catch
her breath. Her head was feeling dizzy.

"C'mon, Lil," Tim whispered to her from the darkness above.

It was colder in here, now that they were removed from the earth
and verdant growth of plants. Lillia shivered beneath her coat and bundles and tried, for the hundredth time, to find a more comfortable position for her pack's straps. Fortunately, they had only run across a few
travelers in the narrow stairwell.

Tim called out to her again to hurry. With a grimace, Lillia resumed
her climb, now using her hands to help hoist her legs up each of the
stairs.

A twinkling yellow light from a gulleystar lantern revealed
another landing a little further up, where a small gathering of workers was loitering around a clerk's table. There was a narrow-eyed,
suspicious woman in a frayed yellow sash seated behind a small
mound of papers with her feet propped up on an overturned box,
listening to whatever Lillia's father was murmuring to her from the
side of his mouth. Without moving, or even acknowledging that he
had spoken to her, the woman jerked a thumb at Tom, who quickly
ushered Tim and Enid around the table.

"Her, too," Tom said a little louder. He waved for Lillia to join them.

The clerk only grunted, moved a sheet of paper from one side of the table to the other, and then barked at everyone else to get their papers ready for presentment.

Lillia was winded by the time she reached the landing, but before she could get her bearings, her father was scuttling her through the crowd and into the market chamber. The sight of the place drew what little breath she had left in her chest.

With its lanterns freshly filled and lit, the former grandeur of the market cavern could not be concealed, as if the mold and disrepair that now prevailed were only temporary, a veneer that could be wiped away any moment. It was broad and high and filled with the most evocative ruins. Broken pieces of statuary, shattered mosaics, carved pillars, they reminded Lillia of that iron lattice that had loomed over the wharf at the Docks. The one that had been built by the priests. She sensed a kind of cunning within these old works, now, a thoughtfulness weaved into their being, although she still could not comprehend what their use or meaning could possibly be. She was hardly paying attention to her father, her gaze captured by a cluster of flickering shadows beneath a rusted grate: rats scampering out from the pipes.

"Are you listening?" Tom's pale eyes broke into Lillia's view. They were rimmed with pink, she noticed.

"Sorry. What did you say?"

"I have to do this business alone. Stay close to Tim and Enid. Blend with the crowd. Look busy. Don't talk unless you're spoken to. Don't let your brother ... just make sure he keeps an eye on you as well as Enid. You understand what I'm telling you?"

"Of course."

Tom nodded. Then he stooped down so that only Lillia could hear him.

"I need you to hold this for me. Just for a little bit."

She felt the weight of a worn leather pouch being pressed into her palm, the movement of metal within it, and her eyes rounded. She mouthed a question to him:

"Why?"

"Never hold things for too long. If you try—they only end up getting taken from you. No one can take what you're not holding onto."

He stood at his full height again, and Lillia tucked the pouch away into a pocket. Tom regarded her silently a moment longer and then quickly turned to say goodbye to Tim and Enid. He left the three of them beneath a hand-painted sign of "Our All for All" and glanced back only once before he disappeared around a pillar.

Tom kept close to the columns, walking purposely, as if he knew exactly where he was heading, all the while searching the faces around him to find the man the sash at the gate had described. It would be a poxed, oily-looking man with a flat nose, probably loitering around beer barrels. He would answer to the name "Sharp." At least the name was somewhat familiar to Tom.

The market crowd was already beginning to gather inside. He needed to find Sharp and get this business finished quickly. The faces surrounding him were all surly, tired, and increasingly frustrated. He passed by a pottery stand, some empty tables with clerks asleep behind them, another stand selling pots and jars, a painted woman offering herself to Tom before he quickened his pace and brushed past her, more empty tables. There was nothing for sale, he noted. Then Tom spotted them. A small, tottering pyramid of leaking barrels stacked behind a fallen column, just beyond the clerks' line of sight.

Tom clambered over the stone and found a group of men sitting cross-legged on the floor, throwing dice. One of the men was on his feet, red-faced, and cursing loudly.

"That's the fifth nine-throw you've gotten, Sharp! Let's have a look at those dice—"

Sitting at the head of the group, a long, sallow man looked up. His face was marred by holes and splotches of purple and a nose that spread almost to his cheeks. Somehow, despite the deformities, he could manage an expression of maligned innocence. Sharp sighed and tossed two granite cubes up to the other man, who brought them to within an inch of a bulbous nose, squinting closely, as if the dice were trying to foist a lie over him.

"They're clean dice, Porterman," one of the men in the gathering said, flexing his arms. "Checked 'em myself."

"You don't wait until you're down fifty tinners to make an accusation like that," added another.

Porterman stammered:

"It-it's just that-that the dice, they—"

"—are perfectly square and level," Sharp said in a sad, reedy voice. "I hope the same can be said of your credit, Porterman."

Porterman was trembling he was so angry, or it might have been from fear. He stumped his feet, and blubbered, and rubbed at the dice nervously until his fingertips were nearly bleeding. The rest of the group only glared at him. A single, incensed peep chortled in the back of Porterman's throat, but he finally threw the dice and a brass-colored coin at Sharp's feet before he stormed off and then broke into a sprint.

Several of the men groused loudly. Unless it was pure brass, the coin was too small to cover the debt; and Porterman's rudeness should have earned him a beating. But Sharp picked up the coin without bothering to look at it, announced it was time for a drink, and the matter was forgotten as the players went to fill their mugs. Only then did Sharp acknowledge Tom's arrival.

"Come to join the fun?" he held out a hand.

Tom took it but shook his head.

"I'm trying to find some papers."

"Oh? I used to be in that line of work."

"So I've heard."

Sharp stopped mid-step and looked at Tom quizzically for the briefest instant before he put his arm around Tom's waist in what was meant to look like a friendly gesture; but from the probing hands, Tom knew he was being patted down. A search for weapons. He had expected as much.

"What did you hear?" Sharp asked when he had finished.

Farmhands, Tom soon learned upon his arrival at the Farms, passed most of their hard lives by gossiping about other people. So it was that Tom had heard Sharp's name long before today. He was once a clerk on the Farms, one with a small amount of pull, but who had had his sash taken from him. Flat-nosed, oily-looking babies seemed to sprout from Farm women wherever he was assigned. And the women's men had a habit of disappearing. Notorious, but without ever drawing too much attention to himself, Sharp dwelled in the sliver of space that bridged the clerks, the wardens, the Craggies, and the guilds. Few had ever remained there for very long before they were taken up or killed but Sharp had somehow managed to last.

"I heard that some friends of yours wear sashes," Tom answered.

"One or two might," the wracked face made a half-smile, "but I wouldn't call them friends. Let's walk over this way. Tell me what you're after …"

Tom would have preferred to stay behind the column, or anyplace that was sheltered, but it was clear that Sharp wanted to conduct his business away from any prying ears. They made their way out into the market, which was now humming with the noise of a bustling crowd and Tom instinctively pulled up his hood. The two of them talked in hushed tones, and only in snatches, but the business was quickly concluded. The only point that caused any pause was when Tom told him he needed all four passes that day.

Sharp hid his surprise well, merely raising an eyebrow at such an onerous request—before he doubled the price. Tom agreed—he had no choice, as Sharp must have surely surmised—and the two soon parted ways. They would meet at the barrels when the announcement was made that the market was closing. The dissipating crowds would offer good cover for their exchange.

Tom stuck his hands into his empty pockets. A piece of dirt still clung to the cloth, freshly dug from when he had retrieved the coins from underneath the lector's stand. Tom flicked the dirt away and smiled inwardly. A good thing he had left the purse with Lillia. It would only cost him two of the coins to cover the price of the passes, and buy Sharp's protection in the market, as well. Had Sharp known how much he carried—well, Tom would probably not be walking anywhere. All they would need to do now is lie low and stay out of sight until the market closed.

Tom let the flow of the crowd carry him along, eventually wending back towards the place he had left the children, which was now overrun with raggers trying to divert any passersby that would give them a moment's attention. Tom looked around, scanning the press of people, hoping to catch a glimpse of Tim's blonde head above the others.

"Ooh, there's another one," one of the raggers was pointing frantically to the ground near Tom's feet. Something squealed, and Tom saw that another ragger had pounced on top of an enormous rat, which was flailing about helplessly as she held it up by the tail.

"Nice catch!" the first one said. "So big and meaty to be out in the open. But now you've got to split it, Bea, since I's the one that spotted it—"

"Not on your life!" Bea spat. "Go catch your own. There's plenty running 'bout the market today."

Tom quickly got out of the way, as Bea and the other ragger soon came to blows, much to the delight of those standing around them. He left the cheers and taunts of the onlookers behind him, while two women pummeled one another over the spoils of a captured rat. Tom made a wide arc, keeping in the shadows wherever he could, towards the back walls of the market, farther from the tiled floors to where the rocks were cracked and split in narrow fissures. The place where Evan had stopped him to bring him before the guilds.

Tom drew a deep breath and examined his surroundings. It was still nearly empty in this far corner. That fat clerk selling carrots was in the same spot as before; Tom could make her out, even from a distance. She was talking with a warden, shaking her head in ignorance. No, there were two wardens. One of them turned, and Tom could see his profile, a groomed beard punctuated by a long, clever nose.

He recognized the man at once, and when he did, all the blood drained from Tom's face.

"We've already been round this way, twice," Tim complained. Lillia could sense that he was as tired as she was from waking early and having to amble around on his feet after the long hike up the stairs. His mood was likely not helped by the press of bodies constantly pushing and shoving around him. His stomach let out a long growl.

"There's meat cooking somewhere." Tim sniffed at the air, "I can smell it."

"If there is, it's the wardens' and it won't be for sale," Enid answered quietly. She looked behind her at Lillia, but Lillia had not said a word since their father had left. She kept up, barely, her face growing paler and paler, her clasped hands never coming out from beneath her shirt.

The three of them had been bumping along together for a long while, hands clasped, trying to stay together inside the same throng of people while watching for their father. It was a pointless meander, a tour of empty stalls and picked over tables; Tim more than once asked aloud why they even bothered to have a market. Which was a fair question. But hundreds had come, and still more were being let in, presenting their passes (or their bribes) to the gate clerk, all following the same vain pursuit. Scouring for the last scraps of commodities to trade for the fruits of their labors, like sheep nosing about a barren pasture for any overlooked sprigs of grass. The smells and sounds of so many workers moving in a herd from one place to another only made Tim feel more drained and vexed.

"A warden might sell us a plate, maybe for the right price—" Enid drew in a breath as if to speak, but Tim stopped himself before she could say anything. "I know, I know. We're supposed to blend in." Timothy clasped his free arm around his rumbling stomach. "Can we at least try over there?"

"Where?" Enid asked.

"Up that little mound. See that table with the big, fat clerk and a picture of a carrot. We haven't been by there yet. We'll just see if she has any food left," Tim continued. "Then come right back here."

Lillia missed a step and nearly fell over.

"Lil?" Tim came back to help her.

"I'm fine." She bent over and tried to breathe more deeply. "Fine …"

Tim said something more, but now his mouth was moving wordlessly. Lillia recognized the formations his lips were making, something about "carrots," but there was no sound in any of his words. Her brother's voice, along with all the talk and clamor of the crowd, was blending together, somehow slowing down and melding into a jumbled slurry.

It was like in her dreams. Lillia shook her head, tried to snap herself back. They were in the market. She told herself that again and again, unconvincingly. All she could feel now was her father's pouch in her hands—where had all these coins come from? —and a vague sensation that the ground was trembling. Lillia looked down, trying to focus, to gather her thoughts. A line of furry shapes was scampering across the floor. Shadows in flight. The larger ones were being snatched up.

"C'mon, you'll feel better once you eat," Tim took Lillia by the shoulder and led her and Enid out of the crowd, up the gentle slope of the paved floor towards the clerk's table, straight towards the set of eyes that had been searching for them yesterday.

Tom hunched low to the ground and darted around an empty wooden table straddling two low boulders. He set his pack down as quietly as he could behind one of the rocks, never letting his eyes stray from the clerk's desks by the fissures. A small brush fire was burning low inside of a metal bucket nearby one of the tables, its light melding with the gulleystar lamps, and Tom could see the two figures now. The pudgy clerk, sitting more upright in her chair than Tom would have thought possible, and next to her, almost shrouded in the darkness, a man dressed to look like a Crag warden—who was nothing of the sort.

Captain Oliver was uniformed like any other Crag guard, his epaulets probably tucked away in his dresser, but even shadowed and from a distance, his bearing set him apart. He could mingle about in the Crag, wear the rough spun clothes, probably talk like any other worker, but he remained separate: a man in the Crag, but not of it.

Tom shifted over to get a better view of the market while staying hidden from the captain's view. Groups of workers bobbed about their business, migrating from place to place in a dour, directionless flow of motion. Muffled noise carried across the cavernous room. Tom squinted, but he still saw no sign of his children.

He did, however, sense something in the air. It was a tension, a nervous energy, and it seemed to be swelling. Tom craned his head back towards the clerk's desk just in time to catch sight of Oliver walking, quickly and purposely, down towards the crowd. Two guards scrambled after him. Tom followed the direction the captain was headed, into the mass of men and women, and then he saw them.

Two wisps of blond, divided by a head of earth-colored hair, walking away from where Tom was hidden. The tallest, Tim was unknowingly leading them straight towards Oliver.

"No, no," Tom hissed. "Stay in the crowd. The crowd!"

Oliver had spotted Tim and Lillia. There could be no doubt. He was going to cut them off. Tom watched the captain wade through a circle of raggers, his hand making for the handle of a sword. Heedless of being seen, Tom stood upright and cupped his hands to his mouth:

"Go back! Go back, you idiot!"

A few pinched faces and some angry curses were the only replies he got. Tim would never hear him over all this noise, not from this distance. Tom raced around the table, leaving his pack behind, and dove headlong into the mass of people.

It was like trying to swim against an ocean current. The weight of hundreds of elbows and shoulders pushed against him. They seemed to bar his movement no matter which way he turned. He lost sight of Lillia.

"Move!" Tom yelled.

"Watch it!" a one-eyed man glowered at him and raised a rusted lantern.

"I've got to get by," said Tom. "Let me by."

"What's the hurry?" a younger man behind him joked.

"Got to get to her ..."

Tom's mind was racing. He was getting turned around, becoming disoriented. Tom cupped his hands to his mouth and shouted:

"Lillia!"

To the left, a small break in the crowd opened. Tom lunged for it. He found a large broken porter's crate and clambered up its side to try to gain a vantage over all the heads.

There. Only a little farther. Past that circle of raggers, there was Tim's back, still turned away. Enid was clinging to his arm with Lillia trailing behind. Tom shouted Tim's name. How could the boy not have heard him? Oliver was only steps away from them. The captain was opening his mouth to hale Tim. Tom could see the glint of his blade between the bodies.

And Lillia.

There was a brief parting in the press of people when Lillia happened to turn around. She saw her father standing on his tiptoes on a piece of a box, screaming wildly at her. Their eyes met, and Tom froze in horror.

Her face was glowing, as brightly as a bonfire.

"Oh, Lillia," Tom breathed.

At that moment, a gust of wind swirled across the stalls and tables of the market and then disappeared into the darkness above. It was as if the very air of the market had suddenly been inhaled, drawn back into the lungs of the Mountain.

Everything stopped. The crowd within the cavern looked up, blinking in silent wonder.

And then the market was rent apart.

A sound, unlike any heard in the Crag for more than a century, rumbled deep from within the stones. It grew, the ground quaking, dust and pebbles falling freely from the ceiling, until, at last, it emerged fully, a booming, metallic resonance that seemed to shake—and then reshape—the whole world around it.

It was a bell. One that rung so deeply it could only be felt, and its sounding was everywhere at once.

Tom toppled over from the crate. As he fell to the floor, he saw Oliver dropping to his knees, plugging his ears with his fingers, his sword falling to the ground. The blade shuddered from the drop; it should have made a terrible clang, but Tom heard nothing but the bell. Those below him were bent over or swooning or waving in the air, as if they could shoo away the terrible noise. Tom struggled to one knee and saw that only Lillia remained on her feet, seemingly unaware that the Mountain was being brought down around them all.

Tom tried to call out to her, but his breath had been knocked out of him.

The bell rang once more.

With the second tolling, the darkness around the cavern walls moved. There was a stirring from within the cracks, and then they took shape. Dozens of shadows coalescing around the rocks suddenly spewed forth with a cry that was almost as deep and as horrifying as the bell's:

"*We come!*"

The shadows descended like rivulets of black water, flowing down the flagstones into the crowd. They were figures, perhaps forty in all. Each was covered from head to toe in plates of steel armor. Spikes, spears, pole-axes, swords, and maces bristled from their gauntlets. With each step, each movement, came a clank of metal and a gush of steam from their joints, sounds that were both ominous and graceful at the same time.

Tom was too stunned to do anything but watch as the shadows drew down into the market. They could not have stood above Tom's chest, and they had a slight, slender build, almost like older children, but their stature only made them seem more deadly, more cunning. When the first of them reached the stalls, he could begin to see their features more clearly. The sight of their helms sent a fresh jolt of dread into Tom.

Every inch of the figures' heads—even the eyes—were covered in a seamless sculpture of metal, broken only by slits of onyx. Nothing like the crude bowls of metal the wardens sometimes donned when they bothered to arm themselves, these were fearsome, fitted masks, each one different, each depicting a nightmarish face: a dragon, a wolf, a demon, a spider, a leviathan, a serpent, death's head. Leading them all was one, taller and darker than the others, wielding a trident. His mask showed a storm in movement, swirling clouds that seemed to float along the metal's surface, a bolt of forked lightning seared across the helm's face.

"We come," his voice boomed.

His trident struck the first blow. A clerk, as old and frail as a scarecrow, held his hands before his face, and never saw the blades skewer him through his bowels. He collapsed in a heap, with a contortion of shock and pain forever frozen on his countenance. With that one swipe, the dread that held everyone in its clutch, the panic that had been strung so tightly across the market that it felt like a presence of its own, was unleashed at once.

As if the Mountain had exhaled another breath, this time as a scream.

The workers in the market were fleeing in terror, crying, shouting, pushing over tables and chairs, and anything else in their path to get away. Tom tumbled over backward, as a lector's platform came crashing down on top of him. He got back to his hands and knees somehow, but his vision was blurred from something stinging in his eyes. His blood, he recognized with an oddly calm detachment. He rubbed his face with the back of his hand and blinked.

Another clerk fell, this one run through from behind with a pike. The armored shadows were weaving into the panicked mob now, lashing out with their weapons, as if to clear a path. A score of bodies lay under their feet already, only a few had breath enough to groan their way into death.

Not Lillia, though.

Where was she? Tom staggered behind the demolished stall. He felt sick for some reason and went to his knees, heaving. His ears were ringing and the entire market felt like it was listing away from him. But he forced himself not to blackout. From his hiding place, he watched what unfolded, as silent snatches of scenes that flashed before him:

A girl—no, a young woman—wailing, clutching the blood-soaked body of another woman to her chest—it was the whore who had tried to get his attention earlier. In her grief she did not see the eagle-masked figure hovering above her, lifting a morning star mace.

A clutch of wardens and clerks frantically stuffed coins into sacks, throwing away their lockboxes into the stampeding crowd. One was tossing armfuls of paper into a fire, which was attracting the attention of one of the armored shadows.

Two of the men who had been playing dice with Sharp were holding Porterman, the man who had tried to welch on his gambling debt, against a stone pillar. One was pummeling him with a crowbar until one of the shadows approached and the men scattered in different directions. The raider wore the mask of a rat, which glanced at Porterman, struggling to hold himself up. As if an afterthought, the rat thrust a spear into Porterman's gut before rejoining its companions.

At the far end of the market, a crew of fishermen, trapped in their booth, were making a desperate stand. Two had spread a trawling net between them and, running madly down an aisle, somehow managed to capture one of the armored warriors within the webbed ropes. With a feeble cry, the rest of the fishermen piled on top of the net to bring the raider down with their weight. But their fishhooks and filleting knives sparked helplessly against their prey's armor. There was a great burst of steam, and a silver cloud covered the men. When it cleared, the captured warrior was standing at his full height, the net now in tatters, the fishermen, burned and bloodied, crawling away, to be slaughtered, one by one.

Nearby, the carrot stall was in flames, its clerk's enormous corpse roasting on top of the pile.

And then Tom saw Timothy. Wedged in the middle of a throng that was stuck between the lanes of pillars. In their panic, the clerks, and wardens, and workers who had been in the market's main avenue were caught on top of one another, all trying to flee to the market's entrance. They were trampling over the tables, and one another, and clogging their only hope of escape. A stone signpost still stood in the middle of the avenue, blocking any hope of movement, the words, "Our All for All" hovering overhead in mock encouragement. Three masked figures—a sea hawk, a shark, and a madman's face—marched purposefully towards the back of the crowd and leveled their spears.

Tom stood up. He could see Tim's tall form, those gangly arms of his, waving wildly. He was yelling, trying to barrel through with Enid in tow, but like everyone else, unable to move more than a foot or two. Tim whipped his head around and happened to catch sight of his father, holding himself up on a stall's desk. A faint trace of hope broke across the boy's terror-stricken face, and he mouthed something, what looked like pleading.

"Son," Tom whispered.

Tim was waving at him—maybe for help, maybe for him to stay back, Tom could not tell—and then the men behind Tim all fell forward at once, the shafts of spears thrusting through their chests from behind. Tim went down hard with them. He was trying to shield something.

Tom's throat clenched. He wanted to scream, to fight, to run over there. He wanted to, but couldn't.

Lillia was not in the avenue. He had to find Lillia.

That thought brought Tom back to his senses. He took a halting step, started to stumble, then caught himself. Sounds returned to his ears, the moans and screams, the hissing, thumping boots, the crackling flames.

"Lillia," he sputtered.

A woman holding a rag to her forehead bumped past him. He lurched forward and was nearly toppled over by a troop of wardens running the opposite way. The last of them skidded to a halt and grasped Tom by the throat.

"Tanner," Oliver snarled.

The meticulous hair and beard were now disheveled, the sardonic face wild with fury, but Tom vaguely recognized, as if from a distant memory, who it was. There was blood on Oliver's sword. Tom tugged fleetingly at Oliver's hand and tried to keep moving, to search for Lillia. Oliver took Tom by the shirt, hurled him back behind the stall, and forced him to his knees. The point of his sword was at Tom's throat.

"What has she to do with this?" the captain demanded.

Tom only blinked at him. He tried to get up.

"Tell me!" Oliver drubbed the side of Tom's head with the hilt of his sword. "Tell me, or I will cut your daughter into quarters—before your eyes."

"Lillia?"

Oliver crouched down close to Tom. The debris only partly concealed them from the slaughter and mayhem, but Oliver had somehow regained his calm demeanor, though he spoke briskly.

"They were only supposed to strike Craggies in the Gutters. Why have they come here? Why are they killing clerks? And why do they—" he struggled a moment to find the right word, "—why do they yield to a Craggie girl? Speak quickly."

It was all jumbled nonsense what Oliver was saying. Tom tried to make some sense of it, to put the pieces Oliver had thrust before him into place, but nothing would fit. He was half unconscious and could barely form a thought. Oliver was growing impatient. The sword's tip pressed harder into Tom's larynx.

"Disorder follows your daughter like a shadow. Here is disorder," he motioned behind him, "and—what do you know? —here she is." He brought his face to within an inch of Tom's. "They *bow* to her. Why? What has she to do with the dwarves?"

Tom's mind emptied. Why was Oliver going on about dwarves? The ringing noise swirling between Tom's temples grew louder; it was all he could focus upon, and he felt his limbs sagging, as if from a heavy weight. He started to sink. Oliver swore and turned his grip around on his sword's handle, readying to plunge it through Tom's throat.

Suddenly, what was left of the stall they had been hiding behind was smashed to splinters. The end of a flail clanked against the bits of wood that remained. A braying, metal goat's head loomed through a cloud of smoke. Oliver saw it just in time to duck. A spiked metal bar at the end of a chain whistled through the space where Oliver's head had been a moment before. The warden rolled over on his side, lunged at the figure, and brought his sword up to parry another blow.

"Bastards!" Oliver yelled at it and swung his blade in a wide arc, forcing his enemy back. "You don't belong here. You've gone too far. Get back to the Quarter!"

Tom fell backward, his head reeling. The warden and the warrior struck at one another furiously, the clash of steel ringing loud, piercing through the marketplace. It was like watching a man trying to give battle to a wisp of smoke, the goat-helmed warrior moved so swiftly and silently. They traded blows, feinted, each trying to flank the other. Somehow Oliver held his own. But he was soon gasping for air, the captain's shoulders sagging from the weight of his sword, which had only once dented his opponent's breastplate. And the other showed no sign of slowing. Oliver kept pressing, though, forcing his opponent to parry his blows, so that the warrior could never bring his flail into a full swing. Oliver kept it up for as long as he could, and then the point of his sword touched the ground. The warden was nearing the end of his strength. Oliver made as if he was going to lunge to his left, but it was a weak ruse. When his blade finally came around to the other side, the warrior slapped it aside easily with his gauntlet. A shower of sparks flew from the glancing blow.

"Dwarf ... bastard," Oliver huffed.

A small hiss blew out of the helm's façade, a strange, musical sound almost like a flute, and then the spiked flail was whirling in a deadly blur over the goat's curled horns. The air thrummed from the noise of the chain. Oliver wiped his eyes with his shirt sleeve, glowered at the approaching warrior, and spat.

Instinct took hold of Tom.

I'll be next ... Fight.

Without fully knowing what he would do with it, Tom grabbed a plank of broken wood from the ground and rushed toward the goat-headed warrior's back. When he was just within reach, Tom heaved the board straight into the air, as high and as hard as he could. There was a tremendous crash as the hungry chains of the flail wrapped around wood instead of flesh, followed by an explosion of splinters. Tom careened to the ground. The flail was ripped from the warrior's grasp, and then, he too toppled over. Tom heard a voice cursing from within the helm:

"*Damned Cragman.*"

Tom pulled himself back up to his feet.

Now move.

He staggered a few paces, then broke into a run. Bending low for cover, Tom stumbled out into the remains of the marketplace.

The smell of ash and blood filled his nostrils. Every stall and table was immersed in fire, sending a cloud of scalding, black smoke into the cavern's heights. It was slowly filling the market, and with it, an ominous quiet had begun to settle.

Tom called out Lillia's name, then fell into a hacking fit. He clambered towards the market's main avenue. The place was littered with bodies; the dead were the only people left, it seemed. But far ahead through the haze, near the edge of the cavern wall, Tom saw movement. He ran toward it.

Tom's eyes were watering, and it was almost impossible to make headway through the debris, but somehow, he stayed on his feet. Corpses covered every inch of floor between the pillars and the signpost. Sightless faces, dozens of them, staring into nothingness, forever joined together in a terrible embrace. Tom tried not to step on any of them, tried not to look—not until he found Lillia. But he could not help but see: a clerk splayed across the squared base of a column; her neck nearly cleaved all the way through. Beneath her, on the ground, a brazen rat was already picking at another corpse, pulling a tuft of blonde hair with its muzzle.

Timothy's body.

And beneath him, curled up like a child, Enid's.

A single sob wracked Tom's body, he dropped the bit of plank he had been holding, but quickly caught himself. His instinct could be pitiless when it needed to be.

No time. Lillia. Move.

There was still some motion over by the cavern's edge. Within the cracks and crevasses, Tom noticed a light.

Tears rimming his eyes, Tom waded forward. Amid a flaming carrot stall, within the darkness of the cavern and the smoke and embers, he could make out Lillia's diminutive figure shining white within the darkness. He rubbed his eyes with the back of his sleeve to make sure he was seeing right.

Before her, the warriors' leader, the one with the storm cloud helm—was kneeling. His trident was laid on the ground between the two of them. Behind the kneeling figure, the rest of the armored shadows formed into lines. They were withdrawing, pulling back into the stones that had seemingly given birth to them. Tom watched, as the kneeling figure brought a steel gauntlet to his mask and held it there in salute.

Lillia was gone.

Tom had rubbed his eyes again, and at that moment she had disappeared.

The last warrior rose to his feet, picked up his trident, and with a bow slipped away, back to the shadows in the Mountain.

In the Mountain ...

... in a place high and deep, a tiny light fell through the dark. Just a glint, a spark of white, plummeting through a void that seemingly had no bottom. Strands of hair shimmered in its wake. A torn, soiled sash of yellow flapped noisily with it. Within the falling ember, wriggling as if in a cocoon, was a girl named Lillia.

She pinched her eyes in the wall of roaring wind that broke before her face.

At first, she had screamed. Early on, when she was certain that the bottom was coming. When she feared the jagged spires, or rocks, or the lake of ice, or magma, whatever it was that waited at the bottom. When it came, it would dash her body to pieces. It would hurt, and it would kill her. The anticipation had almost driven her mad. She had cried, and yelled, and beat her chest with her fists. She tore her hair. At one point, she remembered shrieking into the emptiness, pleading, "kill me already!" The bottom was coming, it would appear any moment, and when it did, that would be her end.

Only ... Lillia kept falling.

The endless array of black air, replacing itself, rolled on, and on. Never hastening, never slowing. No matter where she looked, it stayed the same. Wind and dark. Repeating. Interminable, irrational, impossible.

It took a very long time, long past when her voice had become hoarse from crying, and the last of her tears had disappeared into the nether, but Lillia had, at last, become accustomed to falling, so much so that it almost—almost—doused her terror of the bottom. Somehow, with time, she had grown used to it. She would fall. Every so often a thought would stray back to wondering when the surface would strike her, and how ineffably excruciating it would be, and she would tense, reflexively. But the air continued rushing past her ears, wiping away the tears from her cheeks, while her weightless arms kept hanging suspended at her sides. She would fall forever, it seemed.

Which was, of course, impossible. That nagging troubled Lillia.

She searched her memory for what must have been the hundredth time but drew nothing more than the fragments she already had uncovered. She had been in the Mountain, in a place with solidity. It was real. She remembered a long and tiled cavern. A market. Crowded, bustling with food stalls and people. Her brother was there, he and his woman. Her father, too. And Lillia. They were all points on a solid plane that had been measured and laid out. One that was bounded by a shape and a firm distance. It had breadth and height, and an ending. Like the Mountain.

"There is no room for the infinite in the Mountain," she said. "It's … impossible."

Like this falling.

Lillia shook her head and made up her mind:

Wake up. Just … wake up already.

That was the only possible conclusion. She was sleeping. And this freefall through nothingness, this darkness, the penumbra of light about her, the whispering noise in her ears, her skirts flapping about her face, the dryness in her mouth, everything she was experiencing, was nothing more than another vexing, meaningless *dream*. That phenomenon of restless sleep, that stirring of detritus thoughts, that hoax the priests once proclaimed as deific "vision"—that was where she now found herself.

She was asleep and dreaming. Nothing more. And all she needed to do … was wake up.

Lillia spread her arms wide, embracing the void, and fell, and fell, and considered the matter over, how to bring consciousness into a place locked with shadows, until the endlessness of her falling and thinking became a kind of sleep in itself.

THE QUARTER

CHAPTER TWENTY-ONE

THE DIVINE NICODEMUS stood to the fullest height of his small stature, his lined face cringing at the sanctuary's ceiling. His arms were outstretched over the top of a marble altar. Outstretched and quivering. The polished globe and staff Nicodemus clutched in each of his hands were made of solid steel and weighed nearly three stones. And his servant had taken it upon herself to festoon the sleeves of his ceremonial robes with a generous weight of polished opals. Every muscle in his Divinity's shoulders was throbbing. Nicodemus wanted nothing more in all the world than to let these ridiculous props fall to the ground, tear off his robes, and soak in a warm bath.

But this was a benediction, the blessing of the people. Only a priest could bestow it. And Nicodemus was the only priest left in the Mountain. He swallowed hard and looked down from the dais.

In the old days, before the Commonwealth had all but banned his people's faith, King Elon's sanctuary would never have been used for a ceremony like this. It was a small octagonal chamber, set behind the king's throne room, meant as a place for quiet reflection, where a king could make his prayers. But like everything the nephil of the Inner Realm built, it had been wonderfully made. The half-dome ceiling was cunningly painted in gold leaf and ringed by twelve quartz pillars that were carved and decorated to look like writhing storm clouds. A subtle homage to Elon's late father, old Storm Eye, the king who had first commissioned the sanctuary's construction. There were banners and burning censers. Cushioned aisles had recently been installed, as well as a priest's throne. All very proper. In the center of the sanctuary, the focal point of the radius was this dais, and this beautiful altar … and two gods. Two idols, cramped next to each other, sat atop the marble's surface, as if competing for space.

Nicodemus grit his teeth to hide the strain of keeping his silt-colored face impassive. It was hard to speak the words, but he wormed them out:

"May the Maiden to whom this sanctuary is dedicated hear us."

From the front aisles some of the gathered nephil answered in a chorus: "Hear us!"

The only thing more annoying than his tired muscles, Nicodemus decided, was the goddess he was having to share his prayers with. The idol that loomed on his left, and that seemed to cloak the whole dais in its shadow, was a tall piece of alabaster sculpted into an insolent looking girl, too graceful to be human, too plain to be nephil. The Maiden, they called her. A young woman no one could even name who had somehow captured the faith of the poorest nephil in the Gutters, and now, it seemed, of King Elon himself. Nicodemus was one of the very few nephil who could truthfully claim that he knew Elon's father Zebulon, Old Storm Eye. For all his famed impassivity, the late king would have thundered in rage if he had seen the goddess his son had placed in his sanctuary.

And yet, as Nicodemus gazed upon the congregation packed in the sanctuary, he had to admit to himself, he had never seen such genuine … faith. True, most of the congregants, the ones in the back who kept the old gods, were appropriately stern, standing in silent rapt attention—this was, after all, a funeral. They looked just as they should. But in the front rows were the Maiden's disciples; poor, shabby nephil with little more in the world than what they carried in their pockets. They were swaying with their hands open, dancing in what space they could find, their eyes shut in rapture. All basking in the glow of their faith.

To Nicodemus, as to most of the others gathered there for this occasion, it was a bit unseemly. But Elon was there among the Maiden's disciples, still fitted in his armor's chainmail, along with several of his warriors. The king stretched his hands before his chest, his head lowered, and mouthed a silent supplication to his new goddess. Even from the altar, Nicodemus could see the change in the king's honey-colored face. He almost looked serene.

A candle guttered on Nicodemus' right and brought his attention back to the ceremony, back to the true god that was in this sanctuary. He stretched his thin lips into a smile and glanced at the idol on his right.

"And most blessed Nord," Nicodemus raised his voice as he tried to stretch his arms wider, "all-knowing, our father and protector, the giver of peace, we pray you to hear us."

This time the response was louder and joined by more voices:

"Hear us!"

Nicodemus silently prayed for his god—the true God, he thought to himself—to grant a moment more of strength, to make it through the needles stabbing across his arms and back. Nicodemus tilted his chin back and concluded the blessing:

"Give us the grace of your divine presence—presences. Bestow blessings upon us now. So mote it be!"

"Be it so!"

Nicodemus's arms came down with a flop, and a sense of relief immediately washed over him. From an alcove, a musician began strumming a minor chord on a lyre, the prelude of an old hymn, which was soon picked up by a flute and then a bagpiper. Nicodemus smiled inwardly. The lyrist was a perceptive fellow, he must have sensed the simmering division in his audience: he had chosen a psalm to all the gods of the Mountain.

When the first verse began, everyone, young and old, lifted their voices together. To Nicodemus, it was a distantly familiar sound, the singing of a temple joined together in praise of the divine, but it evoked in him little more than the vaguest sense of sentiment. It was the familiarity he was fond of. It reminded him of the days before the Overthrow, which had been better days than these. He tried to hum along in his faltering tenor for a few measures as he set the staff and orb before Nord's feet. A censer of incense hung from a silver chain, which he lit and, true to the old ritual, began his slow circumscription around the altar. A step, a clank from the waving silver censer, another step, another wave, he kept in rhythm with the hymn and, and as he lumbered in a circle before his congregants, dressed from head to toe in a riot of colors and huffing for air, he could not temper the mounting sense of self-awareness that came over him.

Was this a ritual ... or just a recital?

The same vexing question, always the same. Whenever Nicodemus performed as a priest, no matter the venue or the occasion, this mine-run of doubts would always plague him. Were the gods watching, or listening? Were the gods even here? If they were, why should they care about his prayers? Nicodemus squeezed his eyes shut tight, and when he opened them, he caught another glimpse of Elon, the king's hands now raised high above a smile of perfect contentment. If only he could lose himself that way, he thought ruefully. The way Elon, it seemed, had come to learn ...

But no sooner had that idea begun to form, the scrutiny of his learning rose with indignation to strangle it:

You old fool. Yearning to feel young again, that's all. Get back to your duty.

Nicodemus strode to the head of the altar, doused the censer, and lifted his hands once more.

"Now that we have sanctified this congregation and this space and made ourselves ready, let us join together to call our beloved home. Come forth, our brothers! Come forth Gad, Suriel, Asher, and Abidan! Come forth!"

In one voice, they called out:

"Come forth!"

Their echoes faded, and a cold silence fell over the congregation. A hovering fog of silvery incense smoke hung in the air before the altar, washing out Nicodemus's face. He stretched the moment as long as he could, until, at last, he could detect some of the older nephil in the back rows were growing impatient. He took a deep breath and made a mournful grimace. His voice was firm, filling the temple, but quivered with an effect of emotion.

"My brothers and sisters," Nicodemus' proclamation rang in his ears, "we have called, but no one answers. We have welcomed, but no one comes. We have opened our hearts for company, but our hearts remain empty. Because those we love have gone forth from the Mountain. As an ordained priest, I declare unto you that our brothers, Gad, Suriel, Asher, and Abidan, who fell in battle and delving, have joined the fellowship of the gods. May their memory always remain sweet to us and spur us each to walk the road which they have traveled. May we meet again with our brothers in the halls of Nord—" His cadence was broken by murmuring in the front rows, so he hastily added "—and by the cool fountains of the Maiden's dazzling light. Indeed, may we dwell forever in *all* of the gods' eternal palaces, where neither rust nor worm shall ever dint that perfect splendor which our sainted friends now share. Where there is perfect peace and harmony, and no more suffering of any kind. Where the blessed ring of children's laughter can be heard again. May our sainted brothers intercede to lift our Curse. And bestow a child unto our people once more."

Many in the gathering brought their index fingers to their foreheads in blessing.

"And now," Nicodemus concluded by stretching his ringed finger high into the air, where for a moment it glimmered like a beacon through the smoke, "though we are filled with sadness, let us honor their memory by honoring their remains. Here, in this hallowed place beneath the eyes of the gods, we give honor to our delvers … Bring home their bones."

From the alcove, the bagpiper took up a silver bell, which he rang three times. A door was thrown open, and every head turned toward the sound. A figure emerged from the darkened entrance, and a gasp went across the temple. Several of the women broke down into tears. An older nephil, statuesque in her grace and elegance, wearing a long, onyx gown, stepped onto a carpeted aisle that led to the dais. Her shoulders were slightly stooped, whether from age, or grief, or the weight she now carried before her on a silk pillow, yet it somehow made her seem all the more erect. She held her chin defiantly, even as teardrops trickled down her alabaster cheeks, down upon what she now carried on the pillow clutched to her chest.

The charred skull of Gad, moistened by his mother's tears.

Behind her came two more. Borne by younger women, practically maidens, unable to restrain their grief, the wives of Suriel and Asher brought their husbands' blackened skulls across the aisle of the sanctuary. They faltered in several places, and Suriel's wife nearly dropped the awful weight she carried before she could steady herself again.

And then, lingering at the end of this gruesome train, a last woman draped all in black shuffled forward. Abidan's widow was veiled and shuddering. She carried Abidan's skull on a dark purple pillow clutched in slate-gray hands with a steady, purposeful gait. At first glance, Nicodemus thought the thane's head might have been lit within by some candle or taper. But, no, it must have been a trick of the light inside the sanctuary. She, too, made the long walk up the aisle, and when she passed Elon, the king quickly swiped his hand across his eyes to hide his brimming tears.

As they processed, many of the women in the congregation quietly tisked that a ceremony could be so cruel to put grieving widows through such an ordeal. The men stared ahead stoically. For no one was permitted to touch the women until they had passed the sanctified remains they carried into the hands of Nicodemus, the priest.

He met the widows at the bottom of the dais. Each was bowed, and drained, and though, like all nephil, their coloring was as varied as the rocks of the Mountain, each woman looked drained of her natural color, deathly pale.

It really is an awful ritual for the bearers.

Nicodemus's long face would have shared a grim, silent condolence if any of these bereaved women could have looked up, but that was too much. So, he took their pillows, one at a time, relieving them of the burden of this spectacle, while the sanctuary's benefactor, Elon, after kneeling before them, led them each back to seats of honor. There they collapsed, arms linked together, and the silence was first shattered with an awful wailing: Asher's wife screeching his name over and over. They wept together, the four of them, never letting each other go, even as their families surrounded them, but none would be comforted.

Nicodemus took the pillows up before the altar, grimacing through the aches of climbing steps after standing for such a long time. Before he set them down, he stole a final glance to examine the four newest proclaimed saints of his people.

Four brown lumps flecked with scorch marks. The middle, the heaviest, had to be Gad's head. Nicodemus could almost see the thick, plodding face sneering back at him. Probably complaining about something, thought Nicodemus; the thing looked displeased, even for a skull. The two smaller skulls flanking Gad's were indistinguishable except the one on the right, which bore a deep rut where the forehead had been smashed in. Last of all, Abidan, and now Nicodemus could swear the severed head was shedding a light apart from the altar's illumination. The thane almost felt—warm.

Once arrayed on the altar, he studied them more closely, these new holy relics. Nicodemus mouthed a prayer and tried to empty his mind of its tangle of thoughts. He would be open in this sacred space, ready for the gods' message.

He waited. He listened. He heard someone cough, a set of feet scraping the ground, a chair creaking.

But Nicodemus heard no voice. He saw no vision within any of the skulls. Just round, empty bits of stone. And now it was beginning to feel stuffy up here at the altar. He let out the breath he had been holding, and it came out as the tired, resigned sigh that it was.

Time to close this. Time for ale.

Tenderly, Nicodemus elevated each skull to the top of the polished slab of veined marble, lit four new tapers as he proclaimed their names aloud, and finished the ritual. Almost flawlessly, he thought approvingly to himself. All things considered, Nicodemus was proud of himself for completing a ritual that had not been performed since the boyhood days of Old Storm Eye himself.

Storm Eye. Nicodemus found himself thinking more and more on Elon's father lately. He would have railed against this new faith of the Maiden. Likely he would have whipped Elon's back skinless if he knew his son had taken to it. But would he have nevertheless condoned this ceremony? If the priest had indulged it for the sake of the people, so would the king. He had been a shrewd one, Storm Eye. Nicodemus knew, intimately, the many indignities Storm Eye had to bear during his lifetime; he could withstand a few more.

His sanctuary hallowed to the old gods was being intruded with the cult of a new one whose grasp was growing stronger by the day. If in some high place, the old king was grousing, he was drowned out by a new hymn to the Maiden that dozens of his people, and his only son, now took up.

They had always feasted well in Elon's hall. It was a point of pride in Elon's family, the platters heaped as high as a peak, the sumptuous recipes, the rare wines, the froth-covered chilled lagers, the long pageantry of art and music that would be unveiled for the first time throughout the meal's numberless courses. Elon's father, old Storm Eye, was one of the most sullen and saturnine rulers ever to sit the throne of the nephil, but when he held a feast, he gave his guests the finest of his kingdom's cellars. The merriment of his table had been legendary.

Those memories were nagging King Elon, as he frowned at his throne room. Elon was as prideful as any of his forebears, so he found it hard to face the fact that the delvers' funereal feast was shaping up to be such a subdued affair. It was putting him in a sour mood.

The festivities had all the veneers of a royal banquet. The smells of roasting meats, of beers, and liqueurs, and strong, spiced wines still floated freely along the air. Though unneeded, the hearth fire was roaring, joining its warmth and light with sconces that flittered like stars across the great stone gallery. Tables, richly clothed and adorned with trinkets and shining stones for the guests, packed every inch of the floor.

But few of the tables were filled. The laughter (there would always be some laughter so long as there was wine) was scattered, and in some quarters, it sounded a tad forced to Elon's ear. A band of violins and flutes played a newly composed and contemplative minuet; it was complex, layered with harmonies and counterrhythms, and the musicians played it well, but few nephil, it seemed, were paying any attention to them.

From his ornate chair at the high table, Elon saw and heard all of this. He rested his chin on his fingers and narrowed his eyes. The factions were all there, as plain as cracks in mortar. Perhaps as dangerous. Nearest the high table were his household, accompanied by the sect of the Maiden's followers and their families. A gulf of empty aisles and chairs, and then, in the far end of the throne room, close to the doors, four of his thanes had clustered together: auburn-haired Reuben, tall Simeon, smiling Benjamin (Elon had always enjoyed Ben's company, but his old friend would not even look at him now), and Phannias. His nephil lords all seemed cagey, agitated—the few that had bothered coming. They had brought cousins and children from their households, but most of their seats were filled with chamberlains and pages. Each thane was dressed in slightly different garb, depending on which part of the Inner Realm they haled from, but they all shared the same wariness, a palpable uneasiness that Elon could feel from afar.

Elon shifted in his seat and glanced over at his throne. As was only right, an enormous, satin pillow had been stretched across the armrests for his most revered attendants. In the center of the cushion, the newly consecrated skulls of Abidan, Gad, Suriel, and Asher presided over the festivity.

Elon rose and lifted a silver tankard.

"A toast," he said. At once, everyone in the hall thrust back their chairs and lifted glasses, cups, and mugs. "To our hallowed guests," he bowed toward the throne and was answered with a murmur of blessings and clinking cups. The chairs shuffled back into place, and the conversations resumed where they had left off.

Nicodemus was seated next to him, still in his robes, and had thus far, managed to finish through two courses without spilling any food on himself. The priest set a boiled egg to the side of his plate, leaned close so that he could gain Elon's full attention, and whispered:

"A touching gesture, Majesty. But that's the fourth toast you've given them. I think that's probably ample."

Elon only grunted and took another drink. The ale was strong, but it did little to cheer his mood. He watched as the priest made a pretense of examining the gathered guests, as if it were the first time he had deigned to notice them.

"Fairly good showing," Nicodemus said at last, "under the circumstances."

"Missing six, by my count. And I don't see Eliazer."

"His gout's flared up. I prayed over him myself."

"That's a thane's excuse for ignoring his king's invitation? I scoured the larders bare for this feast."

Nicodemus let out a long sigh.

"The largest thanedoms are here, and that's what matters."

Elon clutched his fork tightly and scraped its prongs across his empty plate. Then, aware of the outward showing, he hastily set the fork back down. "It's an affront."

Nicodemus's mouth drew tight. "I would not—" he started, but held his tongue.

A line of roasted lamb shanks was brought out, still sizzling, carried on poles by four servants. The flutes launched into a popular tavern medley in the vain hope of encouraging a sing-along among the tables. Nicodemus made a contemplative expression, then spoke again with an almost wistful note:

"Such a rare occasion to have all—er, so many—of the thanes together in one hall. With events ... such as they are, it would be a shame if there were no discourse."

Elon felt his knuckles whitening around the handle of his table knife. "They can come up and pay their respects."

"True. They could. But they are here as your guests. Isn't it the host who must do the mingling?"

Elon mulled the priest's admonition—for that was what it was, despite his usual, buttery manners. He listened to the music limp along, but with no one answering the chorus, it finally faltered. The flutists were either ready to give up on the medley or were simply growing hungry for meat that was rapidly disappearing. The last refrain of the song fell away and Elon abruptly rose from his chair. Nicodemus looked up at him in genuine surprise.

Elon's face twisted into a snarl. "What are you waiting for? I'll need a witness, won't I? For all the welcoming words I've got to spew out."

Nicodemus scrambled after the king, smiling. They wove through the closest tables first, where his guests from the Gutters had gathered. His fellow believers, the sect of the Maiden, were thrilled to greet their host. However dour his mood might have been, he made himself the very picture of the warm and friendly benefactor among his subjects. Laughter and grins all around. Private toasts, for he had filled his tankard just before coming down. Hugs between dear friends. But after all the greetings, the inquiries about health and relations, the expressions of surprise, or joy, or sorrow, as befitting the news, and—with these folk—exchanges of blessings from the Maiden, Elon could no longer delay his thanes. As tactfully as he could, he made his way over to the far tables. To the thanes who were, to a man, watching him with stony silence.

As Elon peeled away from the last of his friends to cross the rows of empty tables for the crowd at the far edge of his hall, he had to pause. There was one who sat alone in the expanse between the two groups of guests, between the sect of the Maiden and Elon's thanes. A small, pinched nephil in yellow clothes with dark cunning eyes that glinted from a face as pallid as chalk. Elon could not, with any pretense of manners, pretend to ignore him. Not when he jumped to his feet at Elon's approach.

"Your Majesty," the nephil bowed, "thank you for your most generous invitation. The food and drink are delicious and rare, the entertainment a wondrous affair, and the talk of the tables—" he faltered at this point of the guest's traditional greeting. Elon knew it would have been hard for anyone, even him, to describe a ring of empty seats as "all merry and fair."

Elon dipped his head, murmuring something about being welcomed here.

"Your Divinity," Jacob bowed again.

"Jacob," Nicodemus answered.

Jacob was well into his tankards, it seemed, for up close, Elon noticed a rare, ruddy glow peeking through the warden's normally sallow cheeks. Anyone else, Elon thought, would have been mortified to have to sit alone at a great feast, but not Jacob. Some self-amusement, like a private joke, seemed to keep him perfectly at ease and content to be the solitary guest at a table for twenty, picking apart a plate of ribs with no company around him. The warden laced a hand across Elon and Nicodemus's shoulders, drawing them closer, and whispered:

"I assume you've come down to make the rounds with your devoted thanes. Or perhaps it's time for another toast?"

Nicodemus' answer was curt.

"His Majesty is giving greeting to all his guests. Yourself included."

"Yes, yes. Greetings. I've been listening to these guests of yours, Majesty—they're a bit mutinous. And not exactly keeping their conversations to themselves. The cauldron's good and stirred. If you will indulge a word of counsel?"

It was all Elon could do to restrain himself from thumping this oily, besotted warden on the head. It was Jacob, along with Nicodemus, who had counseled Elon to trust the Crest men, outfit a delve, and send three of his finest delvers and his cousin, Abidan, to their deaths. It was he who had promoted the cause that had led to so many of his recent troubles. Elon glanced at Nicodemus, who was scowling and fingering the tassels of his robes, looking every bit as complicit as Jacob. For a fleeting moment, Elon felt tempted to grasp them each by the scruff of their necks and smash their scheming skulls together. But, no. That would be poor manners, too. Without hiding his disdain, Elon stooped down closer to the warden's waiting mouth.

"Just listen to them," was all Jacob said.

Elon regarded Jacob closely. He craned his neck slightly at which Jacob gave a brief and emphatic nod. And then without another word, Jacob resumed his seat and continued his meal, as if he were giving leave to the king to go and mingle with his other guests. As Elon pondered the diminutive warden's curious advice, he noticed Nicodemus, blinking with the same puzzlement. Jacob glanced up, smiled at the priest, and gestured at a chair.

"Care to join me, Divinity, while his Majesty makes the rounds? There's room at my table."

"I-I can't," Nicodemus answered, "His Majesty's asked for me to be by his side."

Jacob shrugged, then stuffed a fork full of pork crackling into his mouth.

"Stay close to the king, then," he said, chewing loudly. "But we should talk again soon, Divinity."

"Yes," Nicodemus answered.

Elon turned his back on the warden without a parting word, leaving Nicodemus to catch up after him. By the time Elon reached the guests at the far tables, most of them were already on their feet. The four thanes were the last to stand.

One by one, they stepped forward and bowed to their king. The eldest leveled Elon with a steady glare, another assumed a pleasant face, though even to a stranger, it was plainly insincere, the other two looked as if they would rather be in Elon's burning hearth than in his hall as a guest. Elon greeted each one solemnly, but cordially, in the order of their age:

"My loyal lords," he tried his best to smile. "Reuben, Thane of the Granite Reach. Simeon, Thane of the Old Mines. Phannias, Thane of the New Mines. Benjamin, Thane of the Chasm Passes."

"Hail, Elon," they answered together, "son of Zebulon, King of the Inner Realm.

On noticing Nicodemus's arrival, Elon added:

"The Divine Nicodemus, son of Gurion."

The four made the sign of the gods and Nicodemus greeted each of them warmly. But after Nicodemus had wished each thane a long life and blessings, an awkward silence fell over the gathering. The sound of a log crashing into the embers of a fireplace brought Phannias around.

"Uh, your Majesty," he began, "your food and drink—"

Elon held his hand up. "Please, Phan. I've been drowned in pleasantries already. You're here at my invitation, you've honored my sanctuary and my hall, and for that, I thank you all. Now I've come to you. You have words for me, I think. Speak freely. I'll hear what you have to say."

Reuben seized the moment at once. His skin, like his hair, blazed a deep, rusty hue in the firelight that seemed to set his eyes aglow. He was older than Elon, almost as old as Storm Eye would have been, but he still cut a tall and menacing figure. A rich cloak of gold and black stripes hung almost to the floor from his broad shoulders. His nostrils flared when he spoke.

"A war, Elon? Was that what you were after all along? To finally wage the battle your father shied away from?"

"What Reuben means—" said Phannias, beginning to look uncomfortable.

"I don't need help understanding Reuben," Elon replied, his voice even. "He speaks plain enough. Always has."

Reuben was breathing hard and the lines in his face were stretched tight. He drew his cloak back behind him and continued:

"We've known each other too long to mince words. So, I'll just say it: you've used us poorly here, from beginning to end. We gave you our iron, gave you smiths, even tools for this foolhardy delve you concocted with that damned warden. Just look how that's turned out," he jerked his thumb toward Elon's high table, where the sightless eyes of the four delvers' skulls watched over the feast. "Your poor cousin. Your people. Robbed and dead. All because of your foolish bargain. And yet we still supported your right to seek vengeance against the men. Vengeance, though. That was what you said. A life for a life. That's vengeance. You've gone miles deeper than that. You slaughtered *scores*, Elon—men, women, children, their clerks, their wardens, guildsmen—out in the middle of the Crag, for all to see. And now we hear you're mustering for *another* raid? By the gods, this isn't vengeance. It's a war. That is how we—how they—have seen it."

"I guess it might seem that way," Elon shrugged.

"You don't deny it?"

"That I'm heeding my Lady's call? No. I don't deny it."

Reuben swore loudly and was soon joined by most of the attendants around him. The tables thumped from all the fists and cutlery pounding against their tops. Reuben had to raise his voice to be heard:

"That damned sect of yours! If your aim was to drag us all into a war we never wanted, for a goddess we don't believe in, then you've failed. Do'ye hear? We will not rally. Not for you. And damned sure not for her. Listen to me, Elon. The men will starve you out. Fall on you in swarms. They'll drop your courtiers from gallows while they make you watch. They'll burn you all in oil, like they did in the Overthrow.

"All of that will fall on you, though. Not any of us. It's your head that'll roll, not ours … I'll make sure of that." He lowered his voice, as if sharing a secret, though everyone in the room could hear him. "You're not the only one who can get word to the men. They'll know who their real enemy is. Fight your own war, Elon. You'll stand alone, for as long as you'll stand."

Elon held the tips of his fingers to his lips and stared disinterestedly at the faces before him. "You have any more to say, Reuben?"

"Yes. Since you ask. This new goddess—Lunacy, I call her. We have no use for her, either. We've tolerated this-this sect, this *cult* of yours, even though it's an affront to the true gods." He turned and leveled Nicodemus with an icy gaze. "Why you've let this heresy spread throughout the Gutters is beyond my understanding, Divinity."

"My lord," Nicodemus replied charily, "I have made my position on this clear already. It is not for me to decide whom the gods embrace as their own. Only to declare it, and only when they've made it their pleasure to be known. I continue to pray and to scry for their direction in this matter."

Reuben rolled his eyes:

"We don't need your prayers; we need your support! Fine. You don't want to take a position. Your affair. But this bitch you pray to isn't getting past the Gutters, Elon, I can tell you that. Keep your Maiden here. Keep her apostles away from our realms. We don't want them."

Elon looked at the other thanes, frowning:

"Are you all of one mind with Reuben here?"

Phannias and Benjamin stared at the ground. Only Simeon, who was never one to shy from speaking for himself, faced Elon squarely:

"Majesty," he said, "it's a dire day when I find myself agreeing with Reuben. But he's right about one thing. You're setting us against the gods." Turning to the older thane, Simeon grimaced: "You might have put it a little more respectful. He's still your king."

"I said what had to be said," Reuben sniffed.

"For what it's worth," Simeon continued in what, no doubt, was meant to be a kindly tone, "I came because you called me here. I'm still yours to command in all things ... Just not against the gods."

Phannias, always eager to latch onto anything conciliatory, readily agreed and even started to offer an apology on behalf of all the thanes, but Elon cut him off. He felt a thunder roiling deep in his breast.

"I said to speak freely, that I'd listen to you," he said, "and I have. Quite an earful, too. I've been cursed, threatened, called a fool, apologized to, and had my goddess blasphemed all in the same evening. In my own hall, no less. Truly, a feast like no other. Nicodemus, you'll bear witness that I endured all these sleights with good grace. I'm such a good host, you see?"

"Majesty," Nicodemus interceded, "perhaps we should all retire to your private chambers—"

"What I have to say," Elon cut over him, and the throne room at once grew still, "I'll say so that everyone with ears can hear it." He turned with a flourish so that his whole kingdom could hear him. "My most beloved, most loyal lords, everything you *gave* me, everything, was paid for with my silver. Your iron, your workers, your gear, I paid for it all. Will you deny it?"

Elon glared at the thanes, one by one, but they stood where they were, still and sullen.

"If I've measured my vengeance from a longer cord than others would," he continued, "well, it's mine to measure, isn't it? I'll pay that cost, too, when the time comes. Even if it means a war, even if I'll have to wage it by myself. I'm prepared to pay whatever the cost, you see. My faith is not a cult, Reuben. Our Lady the Maiden is—real. So real." Elon had to swallow hard, for at the thought of his goddess, he could feel tears on the verge of choking his speech. He thrust his sleeve across his nose. "She has spoken to Kohath and Merari. They hear her voice. And I-I've been in her presence. Down in the men's market, after I fought for her—I-I saw … standing just as close to me as you are now, Reuben. She shone bright light down there in the men's hole. Just before she vanished. A holy light. She was—beautiful."

The thanes grumbled more loudly, and some were wondering aloud whether their king had lost his senses. But with the thought of the Maiden now fixed before him, Elon would not be daunted:

"I know you think I'm going mad, and maybe I am. But you know what I say to that? I embrace the madness! She's real! Our Lady is real!"

A shout from the sect's tables answered him:

"So mote it be!"

Elon's eyes were wide and unblinking, yet he was oblivious to the discord he had unleashed in his throne room. Angry shouts echoed from the walls. Reuben and his retainers were roaring across the chamber to drown out the noise of "the heretics," while the other thanes hastily gathered their nephil together to leave. Nicodemus looked like he might faint, and somehow, the damned warden had wheedled his way into the conversation, grinning like an idiot. Elon saw and heard all of this happening around him, but he gave it no more acknowledgment, no more credence, than if it were all a passing breeze. Here for a moment, then gone.

The certitude of what he had seen—what he knew—to be the truth, was like a shield against these benighted fools. He heard his voice cutting above the din:

"Our Lady is real!" he bellowed. "She has called out to us from the Crag. And we will come!"

"Candle wax?!"

Nicodemus's servant came storming around the corner and into his private apartment. She was flailing his ceremonial robes above her head like a flag, and as soon as she had reached his chair, she dropped the bejeweled outfit with a dramatic flair on top of an end table next to him. Nicodemus offered a polite cough in acknowledgment of his servant's histrionics, hoping it would mollify whatever it was that was bothering the woman, but alas, the entrance was only a prelude to the rant she had in store for her master.

"D'ye have any idea what wax does to silk thread? How it sticks to the seams? Do you?"

It was not a question Nicodemus had ever contemplated. He had no wish to do so now. Nicodemus wriggled his bottom in his favorite armchair and continued to stare into a small, still pool of water at the bottom of a marble basin he had been leaning over for the better part of the past hour. He found himself longing for a smoke from his pipe in the ashtray next to the basin. The embers had long since extinguished. Nicodemus held his gaze steady, to show he was still at work, and pretended to ignore the procession of heaving sighs and foot-scraping his servant unleashed. The woman was relentless when it came to domestic trifles. There would be no peace until she had had her say.

It took all his effort, but Nicodemus kept his eyes from rolling as he raised them to face his servant's. She had her fists dug into her hips:

"They're ruined."

Nicodemus flashed a tight but pleasant smile. "What's ruined?"

"Your best robes," she spat each word slowly, like an accusation. As if to ensure Nicodemus realized the magnitude of his transgression, she grabbed a fistful of the cloth and shoved it before his nose. "Ruined. See?"

"I'm sure you'll think of something."

"Just look at this," she pointed to a lump of gray wax the size of her thumb. "How in the hell did you get *candle wax* in your armpits?"

"Hm? Oh," he glanced at the clothing and shrugged. "Must've been from the funeral. I had to holds my arms up for an unbearably long time. And there were a lot of candles."

An apologetic expression fluttered across his face, and, hoping that would end her harangue, and perhaps prompt her to leave him alone, he even went so far as to mutter he was sorry before he returned his attention to the basin. He heard the old nephil plop down into a satin cushion next to him, where she launched into a long string of complaints about the unending burdens of keeping his Divinity and his house in order. She only paused when her knee brushed against a pile of books on the floor, which were all open to different pages.

"And I'm not cleaning this up," she jerked a defiant thumb at the books, "these robes'll take me the rest of the day."

"Mm."

There was only the smallest dot of light burning in the darkness from a hanging censer, though, as nephil, they could see as fine with or without it. Other than Nicodemus and the servant's breathing, the room was still. The marble idols in Nicodemus's apartment stood their cold, silent vigil above a canopy overhead. Nord was there, too, having returned from his sojourn to Elon's temple no worse for the wear and rejoined his place with his comrades. The servant woman studied the heap of robes, while Nicodemus continued his forced reverie in the water basin.

"If I can't wash it out," she said to herself, "I suppose I could just sew a garnet over it. Make it look like the wax is a part of a pattern. That'd only hide it from afar, though. How you manage these messes, I do not know." She heaved one last sigh to punctuate the final extent of her disgust. Then, dropping the cloth again, she got up from her seat and wandered behind Nicodemus. He felt her warm breath on his neck as she peered over his shoulder into the blessed waters.

"What are you doing in here anyway?" she asked.

"Scrying."

In the water's reflection, Nicodemus watched her tilt her head this way and that at different angles. She pulled at some stray silver hairs from her side and tucked them back into the knot behind her head.

"What're you supposed to see in this thing?"

If he had been perfectly honest, he would have replied, 'a bothersome housekeeper and a tired, old priest.' It was on the tip of his tongue. But that was much too close to vulgarity for it to be said aloud in front of a servant. Too close to being a confession, as well. So instead, he answered just as he had been taught, long ago in a temple by a priest he had once very much admired:

"The scry will show us whatever the gods choose to reveal to us."

"Oh." She bent over to look closer, heedless that she was butting him aside. "How's it do that?"

Nicodemus clenched his teeth. Fortunately, being the good priest that he was, he had another answer at the ready:

"We are instructed to search without by searching within, then peering beyond."

She stared blankly at him with no more comprehension than the stone statues that surrounded them.

"It means," he continued, "that when we look with our heart, our thoughts, and our eyes together, we can perhaps see what the gods would have us see."

"Oh." She squinted at the bowl. "Just looks like water if you ask me."

That was what it looked like to Nicodemus, too. What it had always looked like. A puddle in a fancy bowl. His reflection staring back at him. A few more lines over the years, a little more sadness on its surface. And nothing but water underneath.

"It also helps me think," he added.

"Cooking suits me better for that." She stuffed his stained robes unceremoniously under her arm and made to leave. "I'll be at the fountain outside. Scrubbing. It'll take me the whole afternoon. Your lunch's in the larder. Middle shelf, the platter with the cover on it."

"Mm-hm."

"Don't know how much longer you'll be at this, but if the mutton goes cold, I'll not be responsible, and there's no more to be had. You need anything before I go?"

Nicodemus's breath sent a very slight ripple across the water that caused his reflection to waiver. His features were wiped blank, blending with the darkness behind him. He watched it a long while, waiting for his image to return, but the dark in the water seemed reluctant to yield what it had taken. He clutched the cool alabaster bowl, his fingers coiling around its edge, and stared hard. There was nothing to see. His hand went into his pocket and felt the edge of a note, a reply message, he had received just that morning. He let out a long breath.

"No, thank you," he answered.

The clack of her wooden clogs against the tile floor faded, then disappeared. After the front door slammed shut, he returned to the scrying bowl and gazed at the reflection that had just returned from its reprieve, as tired and weathered as it ever was. His Divinity examined the sad gray eyes reflecting at him, took their measure with the inscrutable ruler of his conscience, and sighed:

"No one but me in there."

CHAPTER TWENTY-TWO

THE NOISE OF water was everywhere. Dripping into pools, running in rivulets through cracks on the ground, hissing as steam leaking from miles of ancient, groaning iron pipes in the walls, and sometimes, from the depths of the cavern, as a deep metallic plunk. Fog had settled inside the cramped tunnel. The air was close, moist, and uncomfortably warm.

Rachel pulled at her blouse sticking to her breasts. Lockets of black hair were plastered down her forehead and neck. She crouched underneath a massive pipe joint that hung down from the tunnel ceiling, careful to avoid its scalding surface, and stepped into the clearing. It was a small, open chamber where there were relatively few pipes or gauges and a floor of mildewed flagstones. She squinted, trying to pierce through the blanket of mist that clung to the air when she heard someone's heavy trod drawing closer from within the fog.

"Damn these broken pipes!" the figure swore. "Can't see the blasted floor for all these leaks."

It was one of Rachel's people, a nephil dressed in the simpler style of one born and raised in the Gutters. He carried a load of stuffed sacks over his shoulders and cradled within his arms and appeared to be struggling with the bulk.

"Okran," Rachel called out.

Okran froze midstep and dropped two of the sacks with a heavy thump. "Miss Rachel?"

"Of course it's Miss Rachel," she replied. Her appearance seemed to surprise Okran. "Couldn't you get a porter?"

Okran set down the rest of his load and leaned against the wall to catch his breath. He wiped his brow with his hand, smearing the sweat and grit around, and shook his head.

"No porter'd dare set foot here now, ma'am. You shouldn't have come out this way alone. Crag's practically 'round the corner."

"This is still our realm."

"That may be," he shrugged. "But I had to dodge some pretty rough customers 'bout a mile back that-a-way. Hard thing, running for your life when you're weighed down with taters."

"Just rest then."

He sat down cross-legged on the floor, while Rachel searched until she came across an old metallic box cover bolted into the floor that looked a little drier than anything else. She sat on it and offered Okran a drink from a rabbit skin bag she had brought with her, which he took with thanks. The skin had been filled from the bottom of one of Rachel's last kegs, but it was one of the better brews. She had been saving it for later, for a special friend. Okran deserved it, though. She watched as droplets of amber beer slid down his neck. The look of relief and gratitude on his face brought a smile to her lips.

"I needed that, ma'am. I truly did."

Rachel looked at all the heavy sacks on the floor with some apprehension.

"I thought the men in the guilds were still working with us. None of them would help you with this?"

"Especially none of them," Okran put a finger to the side of his nose. "Not with the troubles the way they are. Which is unfortunate, as the guildsmen were about the only ones you could hope to trust. S'far as you can trust any of 'em. To be honest, ma'am, the only men that'll deal with us now are not men as you'd want anywhere in our realm. Gods but it's hot here."

"Have another drink."

"Thank you."

Okran finished what was in the skin and stretched his shoulders. As he did so, Rachel took stock of what he had brought. Most of the sacks were filled with potatoes, but one held a random assortment of vegetables that still smelled fresh. It was surely a feat for him to have carried all this weight all the way from the Crag. Even so, to a tavern keeper, it was a paltry amount of food. A few suppers at most, if the crowds stayed small and were not overly hungry. She reached into one of her blouse's inner pockets and produced four copper coins for him, and then she picked up two of the heavier sacks.

"Now, I'll carry those, ma'am," Okran said. "Don't you even think of lifting those heavy bags. Mum'd slap me silly if I allowed that. I brought 'em all this far, I can make it a few more tunnels. Just enjoying a breather after that wonderful ale."

Rachel thought she could manage on her own if she made three or four trips, but she knew better than to argue with the man, so she told him thanks and that she hoped he had made a nice profit.

"Well," Okran turned away and started tidying up the bundle of bags, "I do appreciate your business, Miss Rachel, I truly do. See, everything in the pottery works has been dead a long time now, and I'm not saying 'dead' as a figure of speech. The whole works is empty. And since my creditor's called in his debt—" he jingled her coins into a small pouch he had, "—maybe this'll buy me some time. 'Til things turn around."

Something occurred to Rachel. She paused Okran in his work:

"How did you pay the men for all this food?"

Okran's face, ordinarily beige and brown veined, flushed a pink so bright it cast a glowing tinge to the silver mist around him. He jumped to his feet and began hurriedly hoisting the sacks back up until one spilled over. A dozen lopsided gray potatoes rolled across the floor. One fell into a hole.

"Okran?" Rachel pressed him. "How did you pay?"

His shoulders sagged and he let out a long, defeated breath. The words nearly choked in his throat:

"My tools."

Rachel let out a slight gasp.

"I weren't using them anyway," Okran added quickly, "not since the kilns went cold. And it was all I had to trade. Who knows? Maybe some Craggie fellow'll make something useful with them."

"Okran, those were your *tools*. The men won't know how to work them. Any more than a goat. You traded away something—" she paused to find the right word, "—something beautiful."

"I've got to eat. And pay my debts. Tool won't do me any good if I get taken up."

Rachel nodded sadly. From the darkness over their heads, a long hiss escaped from a cylinder, which sent down a steady rain of mist. She reached in her pocket and found two more coins.

"Here," she held them out. Okran's back stiffened straight.

"You've already paid our bargained price."

"Just take it."

"No," he shook his head firmly. "No, ma'am. I don't want your charity."

"It's not from me. This is from the Maiden's sect. We're supposed to share with those who help us."

Okran scratched the back of his hair. His hand went around his neck, feeling for a necklace, and then he brought out an amulet. It was an old bronze thing, covered in green patina, but the image of a hand, Nord's hand, was still unmistakable.

"But I pray to the wise old god," he explained.

"You go right on praying to him," Rachel pressed the coins into Okran's palm. "Meantime, you've got to eat."

It was evening at the Copperbottom tavern, at the brief lull between the supper crowd and the more raucous (and plentiful) drinking crowd. Rachel was on the porch outside, heaving the last of the sacks into a nearly empty shed. She shoved them back on the upper shelves, thought a moment, and then threw some old blankets over them that had been folded in a corner. She frowned that such a precaution had even occurred to her.

"Evening, Miss Rachel."

She spun around and broke into a smile at the sight of an elderly couple that had patronized the Copperbottom for the same meal every ten days for as long as Rachel could remember. They were just leaving, about to set out for the long walk home to their home in the Granite Reach.

"Evening, Mr. Peleth. Mrs. Peleth. Arthritis flaring up, dear?"

"What, this?" the old man hoisted a carved, ebony cane over his head with mock vigor, "I only carry this for protection."

Mrs. Peleth, a squat, sharp-nosed nephil woman, with a wide, friendly charcoal-colored face, withdrew her arm from his long enough to slap him playfully before she slid her hand back through his elbow again. It was clearly a frequently practiced motion.

"He's as stiff as granite. I'm talking about your knees, you old pervert," she rolled her eyes at his cackling and slapped him a little harder. "I told him, we ought to stop by the Pipes since we're already here in the Gutters. All that hot steam would loosen his joints, give him some relief from the pain, but does he listen to me?"

"No, he does not." Mr. Peleth grinned in defiance.

"I'll get you there yet."

"I'm sure you will," Rachel said, then hesitated, "only ... Mrs. Peleth, you might want to save the Pipes for another time. I just came from there."

Mrs. Peleth tilted forward and spoke softly:

"Troubles gotten there, too?"

"I heard there's some—some bad folk about."

The woman's mouth drew a little tighter and she made a terse nod.

"This too shall pass. Nord'll save us." Then turning to her husband, "Well, you old goat. You'll get your way for now. But soon as things get tidied up around the Pipes, you are going there for some remedy."

Her husband let out a loud, plaintive, goat's bray.

"Bah!"

Rachel watched the Peleths shuffle away down the tunnel, laughing and arguing with each other until they had disappeared. She closed the shed and made her way underneath the hanging copper cauldron into the tavern's entrance, where she waded through a changing tide of customers in the doorway. The fiddler who occasionally played for tin pennies was there in the corner, tuning his instrument and, to Rachel, looking a bit underfed. Pipe smoke was already filling the room, settling like a cloud on the ceiling. Her hired hands were bringing out the first trays filled with mugs of ale for the evening patrons who were all pressing close to the bar. Something in the clinking of the pewter didn't sound right to her.

"Make a lane," Rachel said, her voice loud and sharp. Several bemused miners stepped aside to give Rachel room.

"Thank you, dears," she smiled and deftly weaved around the keg barrel at the end of the bar table. Rachel grasped one of her servers by the elbow:

"Those mugs," she said, without breaking her smile, "sound half full."

The old barkeep blinked and shifted from one foot to the other.

"Keg's almost empty, ma'am. It'll never last—"

"In my house, the beer flows over the brim. Fill them. To the top."

"Yes'um."

She let him go, fixed her hair, and went to work. It kept her moving at a fevered pace, but it was a labor she had always loved, one she could lose herself in. At a long table, she took a dozen orders and joked with some of her old familiars. At a booth, she refilled a tankard. As she swept from one corner of the tavern to the other, she cleaned the countless little messes, and passed out napkins, and was almost lost in the wonderful bustle, but when she reached a corner a snatch of conversation brought her to a halt:

"—and they never found so much as a damned vein," a squat delver with a hard, quartz chin said, his voice low.

"Sad," his table companion responded.

"Butchered for a scrap of paper. Elon's cousin, too. What those bastards did to him—mm-mm."

"Yep. Sad."

"We'll pay 'em back, though," the delver stoked his chin up with pride. "Elon's lads are marchin' again—"

"Nord save the poor fools."

"The Maiden hold them fast, you mean."

"I mean what I mean."

Rachel saw the telltale signs of a tavern brawl about to erupt: feet scraping the floor, fists clenching, drinks hurriedly being gulped to fortify courage. The delver slurred his words and jammed a finger into his companion's chest:

"They're fighting for the light. Not some fat, old priest's crippled god that never—"

Rachel decided to interrupt:

"You're in a bar, boys, remember? If you want to talk theology, see the priest."

"If only we had one," the delver growled under his breath.

"Drink up," Rachel grabbed their mugs and topped them off. "On me."

They let out a cheer and blessed her name. And amid the noise, Rachel's attention was drawn to a silent, hooded figure sitting in the shadow of the keg, who seemed to be studying her. He didn't look familiar.

"You'll never get your drink order in over here," she teased him.

"Who said I was thirsty?" the fellow said, chuckling softly.

Rachel nearly jumped from the startle but recovered herself quickly enough to discretely yank the stranger back behind the table before anyone else noticed. He didn't resist but kept laughing softly to himself as she pushed him by the shoulders into the backroom pantry. She slammed the door behind her:

"What are you *doing* here?" Rachel's heart was still pounding in her head. "Have you lost your mind?"

"Is this what passes for hospitality at the Copperbottom these days?" Jacob drew his hood back to reveal a mocking grin. "I get better treatment at the Groat. Or were you just eager to, uhm," he pointedly stared at the turned-down mattress in the corner of the room, "give me a more private greeting? It's so hard to tell with women. Fickle creatures."

"It was stupid of you to come here. If any of my folk recognize you, they'll string you up. You don't know how things are—"

"Oh, I've got a very good notion of how things are simmering in the Gutters. Notice, I traveled incognito."

He held out a well-stitched cloak that was, on closer look, covered in subtle floral designs that shimmered whenever the cloth was rumpled. To anyone in the Gutters, he would have looked like a traveling poet or a poor actor from the Chasm Passes. It fit him well enough, though, with the hood back, one was left with the immediate impression that the clothes and the wearer were never meant for each other.

"You look ridiculous," she said.

"I was trying to impress you."

Rachel shut her eyes to gather herself. The murmurs of the tavern outside turned into song. The fiddler was beginning his first set.

"Why are you here?" she asked, pinching the bridge of her nose.

"Why does anyone come to a tavern? For food. For drink. Maybe for love. No? I'll settle for two of the three, then."

"I'm almost out of food."

"I know."

"We're scraping the bottom of the keg for plain ale."

"I know that, too. Just a small plate. And the tiniest cup of beer you have. That's all the hospitality I'm asking for my farewell supper."

She grit her teeth, but still managed to sound pleasant:

"Farewell, my ass. Wait here."

Rachel left him in the pantry with the mops and brooms and the assortment of clutter that had seemed to multiply since the last time they had been in there together. Back in the tavern, the din of the sing-along was almost deafening, but it did nothing to dispel her troubled thoughts. She must have looked dark indeed, for her bartenders gave her an especially wide berth as she ladled a bowl of porridge and slammed it on a tray. When she returned to the closet, she found that Jacob had set two wobbly bar stools before a little carrier tray that he had propped on top of an overturned bucket. He was straightening a piece of cheesecloth to cover his makeshift table.

Rachel found the sight of Jacob trying his hand at setting a table oddly endearing, but immediately brushed the sentiment aside. He was still the warden.

"Here," she set down the bowl of porridge and what was, truly, the smallest mug of beer she had.

"Won't you join me?"

"I don't have time."

"But I've brought payment for my food—and your time."

"I can't. You saw the crowd out there. They can't drink your coins."

"No coins this time. I've got something much more valuable for you, Rachel."

Jacob flashed her a meaningful look and reached into his pants pocket. This was ridiculous, Rachel thought. If all he needed was a whore for the night, he knew where they could be found. She had a tavern to run. Rachel was about to walk out on him when he brought out a collection of small velvet pouches all bound together. She squinted at them uncertainly.

"Go ahead," he prompted, "open them."

The song outside was reaching a raucous chorus. Rachel extended her hand and let him slip the payment into her palm. The sacks felt smooth against her skin, smooth and surprisingly heavy. She pulled a silk cord and all of them opened as one.

A heady smell wafted up and Rachel felt her face grow warm, a feeling of delight was roiling in her chest.

"How did you—?" she started.

"You're not my only friend, Rachel," he laughed. "Though you're certainly my favorite."

She brought her nose down into the open bags and inhaled deeply. The scents of brewing yeast, hops, sweets and spices—oak, nectar, fruits, and peppers—and malts, filled Rachel's nostrils. Her eyes lolled. She felt Jacob folding her fingers around the pouches. His voice whispered to her:

"Take it."

She wanted to tell him no, to leave. Only she couldn't. The scents lingered, even after she had pulled the drawstrings tight. She felt the warmth tingling like a fire. Outside, the muffled strains of a violin and a crowd of miners' rough voices carried on. But all Rachel could think of was the prospect of making something good with what this man had just handed to her. The thought of brewing—and then of serving what she would create—would not leave her. The feeling was blossoming and turning into desire. Then yearning. With the briefest glance, she as much as confessed all of this to Jacob, who seemed to know exactly what to say:

"I'll get a barrel for you."

Rachel pointed to the door.

"In the hall," she said. She began clearing the room. "There's a little barley left next to it."

She watched him open the door and grope about the piled junk until he came across a small wooden keg filled with water. He rolled it back, then returned with a heavy sack of grain. While he had been fetching the barrel and barley, Rachel gathered together an assortment of ladles, spoons, measuring cups, piping, and, in the center, Jacob's sacks of ingredients.

"It's all here," she giggled. "Even sage? I haven't brewed with sage for months. Jacob, how did you ever—"

"—no questions, my dear. Do we have a bargain?"

She felt her head nodding vigorously, on its own volition.

"Excellent. Go ahead and get started, if you like. I'll watch. I always enjoy watching you work."

At first glance she's rather plain, Jacob thought to himself for what must have been the hundredth time. Even for a Gutters nephil. He smiled pleasantly at the greedy smirk stretched across Rachel's face.

Plain and utterly incapable of mastering her features.

She happened to glance up from her brewing work as he studied her. "Almost done," she teased. Then added coyly: "I mean with the beer."

He usually found the banter of women's innuendo tiresome, but for Rachel, he could play along. He winked back at her and watched as she poured a succession of powders and mixtures into a wide oaken barrel. She reached up, felt for a faucet on one of the overhead pipes, and a line of crystal trickled down in a soft, steady stream. The barrel filled slowly. Jacob withdrew to the bed and leaned his back against the wall. As she stirred the mixture with a churn, Rachel hummed to herself; although Jacob had little love for music, he found the tune not at all unpleasant.

It was the sturdiness of her womanhood he admired, Jacob decided. The way she exerted a strength that was still somehow caressing. She churned gallons of brew in a vortex with a heavy rod. There was something inexplicably attractive in her work. Twice, Rachel paused from stirring to tilt her head up and face Jacob, and the sight of her filled his chest with a flare of longing. Yet, he obeyed her command to be patient. Jacob simply smiled and watched, the din of the tavern blending into whatever song or hymn it was she was humming. At last, she reached a point where her stirring came to a pause. She reached for the first of the spices Jacob had given her.

Rachel stretched her hand over the surface of the water to drop it in, and something peculiar happened.

Her fingers seemed to be moving ponderously, like a moth struggling to break its wings free from a cocoon. When at last they were extended and her palm had opened, the sage she was holding, the powder that should have tumbled into the keg, seemed to—linger. As if it were reluctant to follow gravity's bidding and fall from her hand. Jacob stared in disbelief until, after what felt like minutes, the spice finally trickled down to the barrel. But it came granule by granule, drifting in a line like snowflakes. Jacob shook his head, unsure if he was seeing right, and was surprised that Rachel seemed to be completely disinterested in what was happening. That was when he noticed that Rachel hadn't moved in all this time. It was as if she had been frozen, the two strands of dark hair plastered to her cheek, the earthy half-smile etched in place, her arm left out, her hand facing down.

Jacob felt a strange sensation—it was not quite fear, though it quickened his pulse and brought a chill to the surface of his skin. His senses came into sharp focus. He noticed the music outside had fallen; it was only a distant murmur now. And though he knew nothing about the art, the tune seemed to be lumbering to a halt, until finally all that was left was a single note. Voices and violin rang together with Rachel's sustained hum into a single, low drawn pitch.

A grain of Jacob's sage struck the surface of Rachel's water. It hit with the clap of a bell.

"Rachel?"

"Patience," she teased him. "I'm almost finished."

Jacob drew a sharp breath. The music outside was playing again, its frenzied pace, some sort of a reel perhaps. Rachel was hovering around the edge of the keg, as she had been before, moving lustily and whipping the brew into a froth with her stirrer.

"Are you alright?" she asked without looking up.

"Yes, I—" he didn't know how to explain himself. He wiped at his forehead with his hand. "The beer you gave me—must've gone to my head. Better now."

Rachel squinted her eyes at him for a moment, then shrugged.

"Sometimes the leavings in a keg's bottom have a punch. Just you wait. In nine months, this batch will be ready. Then I'll serve you something divine … There. All done."

She thrust the lid of the keg down, sealed it tight, and sidled next to Jacob on the bed.

"Thank you," he said.

Rachel's dress came off easily.

Though she should have been exhausted from all her work, Rachel came upon him with no less vigor. Jacob fumbled with his unfamiliar clothes, so she helped him peel them away. Once they were beneath the sheet, Rachel was on top of him, writhing, pressing him hard into the mattress.

The reel in the tavern played on.

Jacob was left gasping for air. Her body slid effortlessly off his, her arm left draping across his chest.

"Magnificent," Jacob breathed. "Truly. I felt that down in my toes."

"Mmm," she purred in his ear.

Jacob shut his eyes contentedly. When he opened them again, he saw Rachel's gaze had never wandered from the keg barrel near his head.

He thought he might doze for a few minutes in her arms, but the vexing noise from the singing outside was already intruding on his senses. He sat up, reached across her breasts for the mug of beer she had brought, and finished it off with a single gulp. Its warmth tingled, it brought a flush to his cheeks, but whatever had happened before, however, time seemed to have stood still, it was not from the punch of this tavern ale.

Jacob rose slowly from the bed and wriggled his pants back on.

"I don't know how I'll survive without your hospitality, Rachel," he said to her.

Rachel turned over and shook her head:

"You can't. That's why I'll see you again in a few weeks."

"No," he made his best effort to sound sad. "I'm afraid not. This will be my last goodbye."

He finished getting dressed, and sat back down on the edge of the bed, and stared into her face. Something about the way he had spoken sounded off to him, like an overwrought actor mimicking someone else's part. Rachel, however, seemed genuinely perplexed:

"You-you're going away? For good?"

"I am. A few loose ends to tie up. I've got to clear out my place at the Groat. Then it's goodbye to the Gutters. Farewell to the Realm."

"*What?*"

Jacob couldn't help but laugh.

"What about the—" Rachel began.

"Haven't you heard?" Jacob smiled. "The Treaty's broken. Thanks to Elon, we can all go wherever we like now. Sorry. I probably shouldn't jest like that."

The confusion spreading across Rachel's simple face, the shades of conflicting emotions, or surprise—and the trace of relief that kept springing to the forefront—was, to Jacob, as plain as reading a warrant. Above all, he knew she would be shocked. The very idea of any nephil, even a warden like Jacob, living outside their people's realm would have seemed preposterous. Like leaving the Mountain.

At last, her features settled.

"Where will you go?"

"Oh. Someplace quiet. Where there's space. Someplace I can enjoy a nice meal and not be inundated with gods, and poets, and noise," he waved his hand at the music outside as if it were a pesky fly in the air. Then an old memory came unbidden to Jacob. "I heard about this old cottage a few miles from the Citadel. Out in the middle of a field with no roads or any neighbors. Nothing around for miles. Nothing."

"But you can't—you can't *live* in the Crest. It's impossible."

"Some of the most regarded men of the Mountain pass their whole lives there. Quite comfortably, I'm told."

"You're not a man."

"Our people think I am," Jacob laughed again. "They're always saying so. Mostly behind my back, of course. Maybe they're right."

"You're joking, Jacob. I don't believe you."

"I'm serious. I have the means. All I need is a pass. Then I'll go and live in the sunlight."

Rachel shuddered beneath the bedsheet.

"But why? Why in the world would you want to live out there?"

Jacob leaned closer to Rachel and took her hands in his. There were still grains of spice powder and chaff stuck to the calluses of her palms. A lock of her hair curled down the bridge of her nose; it was as black as her eyes, which were flitting between Jacob and the keg behind him. She had no desire for him, he knew that. The lump welled up in his throat all the same.

She was beautiful.

He made up his mind, mastered his features, and whispered:

"Rachel, I've probably shared too many of my thoughts with you. But for your sake, I will tell you one more thing—it's about the troubles. Just listen. Apparently, there was a plan put in motion that was supposed to—"

At that moment Rachel's dark eyes suddenly went wide, as the air around them was rent by the noise of a great, chiming bell. The floor quaked, and a mop and bucket fell over with a crash. The walls were rattling from the sound of tramping boots, and clanking armor, and the whoosh of steam that accompanied their every step, drawing closer and closer. The bell rang once more, and a voice, both faint and powerful, cried out from the tavern's porch:

"*We come! We come—at the Maiden's call, we come!*"

A burst of shouts, cheers, stamping feet—and a smaller volley of curses—erupted from within the tavern.

"So, they're on the march again," Jacob frowned.

Rachel was already getting dressed, and without realizing it, made a sign of the gods and prayed:

"May the Maiden hold them fast."

Jacob's mouth drew tight, but he said nothing.

The sounds of marching faded away, and Rachel was rushing out of the doorway, throwing her clothes on as she ran out into what sounded like a brawl erupting near one of the tavern doors. Shouts of "Nord" were drowned by those for the Maiden—Rachel's new goddess. Something crashed against the wall, a chair breaking, and Rachel was bellowing at the top of her lungs. In her haste, she completely forgot about Jacob.

"May she keep you safe as well," Jacob sighed.

He got up, his empty beer mug dangling from his grasp. Without knowing why Jacob lingered for a moment by the keg. He ran a finger across its surface. It gave off an earthy smell already, which brought back visions of Rachel: her smile as she had stirred its contents; her body straddling his; the feel of her palms. He thought of the spices he had brought that were now stirring within the fullness of the cask. Amidst all the commotion outside, Jacob felt a curious sense of longing to remain here in this dingy pantry, to see what she—what they—had made. But he could only spare one more furtive glance, and then Jacob left the Copperbottom the way he always did, through the backway, for the last time.

CHAPTER TWENTY-THREE

THEY CAMPED IN a cavern, sitting in patches of open ground between the cave's "teeth," which were large, numerous, and glittering with minerals in the narrow joints between hanging stalactites and rising stalagmites. Moisture fell in sheets from hidden, broken pipes that spanned the ceiling. The water trickled down beneath grooves of their black armor, leaving the warriors soaked and shivering. Mostly, the nephil were milling about, trying to keep dry or eat a little something before they took up their march again. They were only fourteen in number.

Samson frowned at the sight of Elon's "army."

Paltry. Not even a sortie.

The old, broad-chested veteran noticed a shadow crouching near his feet. He looked like he might be praying.

Samson dropped a wineskin into the unexpected grasp of a young, haunted nephil man. The lad was white as sand, and the skin on his face was drawn too tight for his eyes, which had a nervous tick of blinking rapidly when he was spoken to. Samson did not like the look of him.

"Here, drink up."

"I, uh—" the nephil's gaze darted between the skin and Samson. "I don't want any."

"What?"

"I don't drink."

Samson's eyes narrowed. He was the king's bodyguard, and he had offered his wineskin to a boy so young he probably still pissed himself, and the boy had declined his offer. If the little runt weren't one of Elon's pets, Samson would have boxed his ears and broken his nose for giving such offense.

"What's your name, boy?" Samson's question came out a low growl.

"Kohath."

"Where you from?"

"The Gutters."

"Figures." Samson shifted in the weight of his armor so that he was directly in front of Kohath, looming over him. He pointed to the wineskin that Kohath still held in his lap. "Look here, Kohath Gutterling. The only reason a man doesn't drink is because he doesn't trust himself. And a man that doesn't trust himself can't be trusted. That's a problem if you and me are going into battle together. Ever fought Cragmen before?"

Kohath shook his head slowly.

"I have," Samson counted his mailed fingers, "the Docks, the Last Temple War—both sides of that one, come to think of it—the Overthrow, right up 'til Storm Eye signed the damned Treaty. And now with Elon. Been on every one of these raids. Isn't a veteran in the Realm who's dinted his blade on Cragmen's skulls as much as old Samson. If there's one thing I know about fighting, it's this: you drink before you battle. 'Specially your first time. So, drink."

"You don't understand, I can't." Kohath's voice sounded as pinched as his features. His gaunt limbs squirmed within the mail and bolted plates of his armor. He looked like a skeleton trying to escape a metallic coffin. "I took a vow to the Maiden."

"Oh, gods. Another lunatic." Samson spat on the ground. "So, you're in Elon's little sect of girl worshipers, too? Now I know I can't trust you."

It was Kohath's turn to look affronted. His eyelids fluttered angrily and he started to rise, but almost fell over from the unfamiliar bulk of his armor. An angry hiss of steam escaped from one of his polyene joints and Kohath's arms went flailing to right himself. Samson reached out and steadied him.

"Don't fight it," Samson chided, "the armor will move with you as long as you don't fight it."

Kohath stood and glared at Samson.

"You blasphemed our Lady the Maiden."

Samson chuckled, which only seemed to make Kohath more incensed:

"This is a holy quest. We come at the Maiden's call, and you dare—"

"Save your sermons," Samson held up his hands, "I'm not in your little group of skirt chasers. I'm only here because my king told me to come." He chuckled to himself. "That's not true. I probably would've joined up even if he had told me not to. I always did love battles, Nord save me. There's just nothing like better than some good, old wholesome violence to make you feel alive."

A helmed figure approached them from behind a stalagmite. Its metal boots crunched against the stone floor until it came to a halt. Kohath turned around and Samson smiled. The figure's mask on its helmet showed a swirling storm cloud with onyx lightning splayed across the visor.

"Hey, Elon," Samson absently held up a hand in salute.

The storm cloud mask lifted, the metal moving like clouds parting for the sun, and there was Elon's face, plainly annoyed.

"What's going on?"

Kohath stammered that Samson was an apostate, but fell back into silence at the sight of Elon.

"I'm only having fun with the boy," Samson shrugged.

"He's no boy," Elon replied.

"No warrior, either. Lad's never borne arms before."

The corners of Elon's mouth fell into a frown, but he turned to Kohath:

"I want you in the rear of the line when we set out again. You'll be safer there."

"B-but I might not see her then," Kohath said. "I've got to see her with my eyes. Like you have, Majesty. Her words to me were clear: If we come to her in the darkness, she will come upon us with the light. Her summons to me—"

"The rear," Elon cut over him. "If there's any fighting, that's going to be the safest place."

"Majesty, please, I beg you—"

"We're moving out. Now."

Samson got to his feet with a loud clank, while Kohath stood mutely behind him. Samson noticed Elon trying his best to soften his tone:

"I've glimpsed her," he said to Kohath. "But you and Merari, you're the only ones who can hear her. Now that Gershon's gone. You're our prophets. You said our Lady called you to come to her in the Crag. I trust you heard her right. So, it's up to me to bring you safely to her."

Kohath's head drooped. Elon clapped his gauntlet on his shoulder, which made Kohath wince.

"Some of the believers were going to sing before we enter the Crag tunnel," Elon pointed with his chin behind him. "They could use a blessing, Divinity."

Kohath blinked at the king and muttered:

"As you wish, Majesty."

He trundled between the cave's teeth, holding on to the rocks to keep his balance until he found a circle of warriors holding hands before a gaping tunnel. When Kohath was beyond earshot, Samson shook his head:

"*Divinity*, Elon? Better not let your thanes hear you call him that. You'll have an outright mutiny in your realm, and then there won't be any more raids."

"This will be the last raid," Elon said. Samson had to strain to hear his king.

"For him," he pointed towards Kohath, "it better be. That one's got no business marching."

"The Maiden called to him in a dream. She wants her believers to come to her."

Samson swallowed the curse that was welling up in his throat and instead, simply shrugged. "Well. Got to do what he's got to do then. But I thought there were two of them, these, uh, priests of your goddess."

"Merari wouldn't make it down a flight of steps. So, he's keeping a vigil. He'll be praying for us."

Samson grunted, neither approvingly nor disapprovingly, not wanting to voice the opinion he held of Merari's vigil. He watched his king from the corner of his eye. Elon was studying the same meager force Samson had earlier and looking just as displeased with it. The king ground his teeth:

"If only the thanes would come around."

"They won't. Not for your Maiden, at least."

"Doesn't leave us with much of an army."

"No, it doesn't."

"They're blind," Elon said. "Blind and stupid, and they don't even know it. If they'd just see her light, open their eyes as I have, then they'd see her. Then they'd come. They'd all be begging to take up her banner."

Samson bit his lower lip, but said nothing, while Elon's gaze carried across the cavern, to where the circle of believers was now chanting a hymn. Kohath's hands were lifted high, his head tilted back. He was babbling something they couldn't hear. Elon let out a sigh.

"Maybe it's nothing to do with the Maiden. Maybe it's just me they won't follow. I don't know." He took the wineskin Kohath had left, unwound its top and took a long pull, then handed it back to Samson who did the same. "I thought when the Cragmen killed our delvers. When they broke the Treaty, I thought ... surely ... I don't know."

Samson took another drink and looked at his king.

All these years, and he's still chasing make-believe. Like a boy.

But at least Elon was a boy with fire in his chest. A surge of fondness welled up in Samson. It was a hard thing to squelch a child's fantasy, so Samson trod on it as softly as he could:

"You thought everyone would rally to the king, no matter who his god is, just for the chance to fight at his side. Your halls would be stuffed with spears and banners. We'd sing the old war songs and you'd lead the charge, and there would be a great war, and the Cragmen would plead for mercy, and the Curse would be broken. Then you'd have a son and he'd puff up with pride whenever they sang about how his old man, Elon the Great, stormed the Crag to avenge his people—and no one would ever whisper about your father's Treaty anymore. The forge would overflow with steel. Everything would be all covered in silver like it was in the old days. Was that maybe what you were thinking?"

The king stared straight ahead while Samson talked. A wave of mist fell from the ceiling and covered his features.

"'Course it was," Samson continued, "I've known you since your mum—may she feast with Nord forever—birthed you out sideways. Seen you learn to walk, learn to work a forge, how to wield a blade, seen you grow up to be a king. You're as good as any that ever wore a crown in our realm; in fact, a good bit better than most of them. I'm proud to fight with you. But I've got to tell you, Elon, and I mean this with nothing but love and respect. You should've been a poet."

That brought a smile to Elon's lips.

"Oh?"

Samson mimicked how a bard, one with very little sense of tune or timing, might sing an ode,

"The wicked Cragmen smote his friends,
Now Elon's wrath will never end.
Will he take us all to hell and back?
To the bottom of the Chasm's black?
Or will the Maiden curb this spree?
We come, whichever way it be."

Elon was looking at his bodyguard thoughtfully:

"Did you just make that up?"

"More or less."

It was a milder take on a popular, and very lurid, limerick that was circulating in the Inner Realm; the original version concluded with Elon's wrath being assuaged, but only when his Maiden's "moaning on her back."

"We come, whichever way it be," Elon said, "I think I like that."

"That's the poet in you. No offense."

"None taken."

"Not that there's anything wrong with songs and poems, or chasing after goddesses and glory. That's what we're made to do. It's good to have a vision, and great to be on a quest. So long as you can still see what's there in front of your face. Your dad, old Storm Eye, he may have had his faults, but he never lost sight of what was plain."

Elon turned to Samson:

"Go on, then. What's plain that I'm not seeing?"

Samson drew so close that he could smell Elon's musk. He tried to stretch a jovial smile over the hard truth he had to tell his king:

"It wouldn't matter if the thanes had come. If we emptied all the Realm and stuck a spear in every last one of our people's hands, there wouldn't be enough of us to keep this fight up for more than a few months. Not now that the men are fighting back. Hell, there weren't near enough of us in your dad's day, and we were still having babies back then. Unless your Maiden goddess can make more of us, and find food to feed us, we'll be done for—soon enough, one way or another."

They stood in the cavern in silence for a while, listening to the sounds of the water falling and their camp breaking. The nephil were packing their stores away, stomping out fires, sharing a final drink. The conversations were all hushed, nervous, and far too few.

"This will be the last raid. If we find the Maiden—when we find her, you'll protect Kohath."

"I'm oath sworn to you, Majesty, not a Gutterling."

"And I'm sworn to the Maiden now. Kohath's one of her priests. He's come at her call. I want him guarded so he can find her."

"Well, then, I'll just have to watch out for the both of you," Samson grunted as he leaned down to pick up his helm. Its visor was a spider's head, dotted with orbs for eyeholes. Its crest was topped with a golden, severed hand, the symbol of Samson's god. He touched one of its outstretched fingers: "Nord save me."

Merari shuddered beneath a tasseled blanket. Golden balls of thread dangled from its corners, sparkling in the room's pale glow. The cloth felt smooth, luxurious against his skin, something he would have prized were he back home with Mother. He had always liked soft, velvet things, but Mother could never afford the material. His clothes were worsted wool. This was something rare and special. The lord chamberlain himself had brought it in, dropped it in his lap with a dire warning not to get anything on it. It was a king's blanket.

But it didn't keep out the cold.

Merari's teeth chattered. He wrapped the blanket tighter around his narrow shoulders and stamped his feet. The sounds of his leather soles slapping against a granite tile echoed from within Elon's sanctuary. His eyes darted about, fearful of the noise, until, as if against their will, they were drawn towards the statue again. The statue of the Maiden, his goddess.

There she stood. The stone artifice of a divine presence. An unblinking and uncaring deity, just as Merari saw her in his dreams. The censers and candles that surrounded the high altar were all cold and dark, and yet there was this faint shimmering, a glow that seemed to refract the light from an outside source all along the statue's white alabaster surface.

Merari watched it closely. He knew it was nothing but lifeless rock that stood upon that pedestal. A representation, an image, of the goddess it portrayed. It could not stir. His eyes were playing tricks. If one stared too long at a stitch in cloth or a pattern in a painting, it would start to vibrate. That was why her fists seemed to be twitching.

Merari shook his head at his foolishness, and the knot in his throat loosened a fraction of an inch. He searched around for the jar of water that Jemuel, the chamberlain, had left for him. When his fingers came around its handle, though, the jar began to tremble. He feared he might drop it. Such a clatter that would make—the thought of it sent another shiver through Merari's body. Better to suffer the thirst than risk the noise. Something about keeping quiet and still made him feel safer.

He should get back to his praying, he chided himself. That was why he was here, why he had sworn to keep a vigil. That was what the Maiden would have of him. And yet, the very idea of praying left him feeling weak and deflated. An exhaustion he had borne like a porter's weight pressed down hard.

I'm so tired.

Tired of dreams, tired of hymns, tired of prayers. They never seemed to end, and they never left him any peace. Prayers especially. It was like taking medicine: something he had to endure, had to swallow down, no matter how much it made him wretch. Merari's stomach churned in protest.

Which, he knew, meant he should get back to praying. Mother had always taught him: "*What you like least, should be the first you meet.*"

Merari let out a long sigh. Time to take his medicine. He began to pray:

"Oh, divine Maiden, most blessed goddess, hear your prophet's prayer: hold us fast ..." Merari settled into one of the pews and murmured as softly as he could. "Preserve us, protect us, be our guiding light. Preserve us, protect us, be our guiding light ..."

His words fell like the measured drip of water in a cave, slow, rhythmic, finding their way into cracks and crevasses.

"Preserve us, protect us ..."

After a time, Merari felt himself following their course. He was trickling down into the still coldness of the sanctuary, a fall that seemed as gentle as a breeze, though he would find no end to it. A wandering of his soul. Somewhere between the void and the firmament. Merari's eyes felt heavy, they fluttered, but he kept them open. He wanted to stay here, cuddled in this soft velvet blanket.

The dreams began.

Merari's eyes rounded. He felt his heart hammering in his chest.

This was new. Never had his dreams ventured beyond his sleep. Their memories might linger for days, but the dreams themselves, the shadows and the dragons, had never strayed past the boundaries of his sleeping.

But they were coming to him now. Here, in Elon's sanctuary. He could see the dark shapes, sense them, hovering above the Maiden's head. Whirling shadows, like a storm cloud gathering above the altar, distantly calling to each other in a language that seemed both foreign and hauntingly familiar. The statue's hair seemed to be moving with them, as if stirred by their wind. Her hands were open.

Panic seized Merari. His limbs refused his command to move. He blinked hard, forced himself to take deep breaths, to trick himself into waking up.

I must be asleep. I must be.

Instinctively, his hands clenched around the blanket's tassels; he could feel the metallic threads digging into his palms.

It was all real. And it was happening before him.

"Hold us fast," he whispered.

Tears trickled from the corners of Merari's shut eyes. There was a great rush of wind. In the darkness, he saw an image of a girl—no, it was the Maiden—shining like a guttering lamp, plummeting through the darkness. Her hair was tousled from her fall. She was glancing about her with an annoyed expression, and when her gaze passed Merari, she snapped:

"Wake up already."

There was nothing melodic or beautiful about her voice. She sounded like Mother whenever Merari had overslept.

"So-so mote it be," he trembled.

When Merari opened his eyes again, he was alone. The pews, the air, the altar were all empty again. There was only the statue of the Maiden, hands clasped tightly once more, glowering across her empty sanctuary.

He was alone, though Merari no longer felt it.

"He's gone mad," Nicodemus stirred a cup of lukewarm tea absently, "completely insane, like all the rest of them."

The priest tried to stretch his aching legs. He was in a cramped booth seated across from Jacob in an inn called the Goat's Groat. Calling the place an inn was a charitable indulgence. More of a cave, and a seedy one at that, the Groat was situated on the farthest edge of the Granite Reach, within sight of Cowan's Chasm, a waystation of sorts along the meandering caravan route that connected the Inner Realm to the fort of the Court of Common Corrections. The place catered to no one, it seemed, except Jacob, a comatose old nephil woman, and a squat bar-keep, who, after showing them their table, occupied his time by wiping a filthy rag across the same pewter platter in an unceasing circle. The smell of vinegar clung to everything inside. There were a few private rooms, such as where they were sitting, a long and empty communal table by a pit where a fire had burned already out, and a rickety flight of stairs that led down into a cellar and the inn's rooms.

Nicodemus knew it was the closest place Jacob had to a home.

"I probably shouldn't say such things too loud," Nicodemus lowered his voice. He looked behind him, but the inn was still empty.

Jacob laid a hand on Nicodemus' forearm but withdrew it before speaking. "Don't worry no one ever listens here. I make sure of that. I'd offer you supper, but there's none to be had."

"Already ate. I figured the walk here would take a while."

"The Groat is a bit out of the way. But that's why I've remained a loyal patron. That and the lively company."

Nicodemus was too occupied with his worries to acknowledge Jacob's little jest.

"It also has a lovely view of the Chasm from the back porch," Jacob added, "I can show you later if you'd like."

"Gods, no," Nicodemus shuddered. "I don't know how you can sleep within sight of that thing."

"I find it peaceful."

"Peaceful as the abyss."

"Precisely."

Nicodemus shook his head. The thought of the gaping void just beyond the inn's walls, a great, yawning mass of nothingness, separated from his seat by a few plastered walls and the width of a ledge made Nicodemus feel exposed, threatened. He wanted to change the subject.

"Now he claims to have seen her, you know," Nicodemus said under his breath. "Elon has. This goddess of his."

"So I heard. He was rather public about it at the feast."

"You should hear what he says in private. It wasn't a dream. Wasn't a vision. No. He says he *saw* her, in real life. Back when they raided the men's marketplace—which was utter folly, as I warned him again and again—he claims she appeared to him in the flesh. What the priests used to call a revelation. Between the stalls in the men's cave, a shining girl stood before him, blinked a couple of times, and blessed him, for whatever reason."

"You don't sound convinced."

Nicodemus rolled his eyes.

"Madness. I put it to his Majesty. Just what, I asked, would a goddess be doing in a ransacked marketplace of Cragmen? I mean, that's a rather unusual place for a new deity of our people to reveal herself."

"I doubt that ever crossed his mind."

"'I saw what I saw,' is what he told me. Those were his very words."

Jacob took a sip from a tankard.

"Well, there's no arguing with that," he said, stifling a belch.

"No reasoning with it, either."

Slowly, a grin spread across Jacob' face, his eyebrows tilted in mock triumph, and he lifted his tankard:

"We've finally found a common enemy, Divinity. His name is faith."

"Stop it."

"And you're right, there's no reasoning with him. Which has been my complaint about religion all along."

"Put down that damned cup. I'm still a priest."

"Sorry, sorry. I'm so numb to jests, I forget they can give offense."

Nicodemus waved his hand dismissively. "True faith doesn't blind you to the world, it illuminates it. Makes you more attuned to it. That's how true faith works."

"Mm-hm," Jacob shrugged. "Well, by that measure, our beloved king has lost the true faith. Because he is utterly blind to what's going on around him."

"You mean how the food's all disappearing."

"That would be foremost, yes. Although I don't think even Elon will be able to ignore that for much longer. Hunger has a way of butting to the front of the line of priorities."

"Oh, but the Maiden will provide," Nicodemus made a face, and Jacob did not try to stifle his chuckle.

"That sounds like young Kohath," Jacob said.

"I heard those very words from Elon himself. Before he set out on this latest raid of his. Though you're right. He probably heard it from one of those little brats. This Maiden. If I ever meet her, I'll slap her. She's been nothing but trouble. All she does is stir up passions, make our people mad. Nothing like Nord. He gave guidance for our spirits: valor, truthfulness, beauty, yes—but ordered beauty."

"Ordered beauty? Is that what cost him a hand? Pretty poor trade if you ask me. Sorry. I can't help myself."

"The Myth of Nord is no laughing matter, but since you brought it up—"

"No, no, Divinity. I do apologize. I promise, no more jests."

"Hm."

Jacob's attention seemed to be drawn to a movement outside of their private room. The tavern keeper, perhaps having grown tired of smearing grease across the same platter, had pulled out a broom and was sweeping the planks of the wooden floor. It was a slow, ponderous motion and succeeded only in moving dust from one side of the bar to the other. Nicodemus followed Jacob's gaze and watched the old man for a time. He looked frail, stooped over on the warped handle of a push broom, grunting from the effort of each push, not paying the least attention to anything else. Something occurred to Nicodemus, and he turned back to Jacob:

"When was the last time he ate anything?"

"His stores ran out a week ago. I was able to get a tin of jerky to him yesterday. That will be it, though. There's nothing more to be had."

Reflexively, Nicodemus made the sign of the gods and mouthed a blessing, but stopped himself. The gesture felt oddly hallow. He asked the warden:

"How can we persuade the Crag to share their food again?"

A laugh burst out of Jacob, and even the tavern keeper paused in his work to scowl at them.

"Are *you* jesting now, Divinity? We've just slaughtered hundreds of their people. One can understand if they're feeling a tad disinclined to keep feeding us, Treaty or not."

"They struck us first, our delvers," Nicodemus started to mutter, though he knew how pathetic it must have sounded.

"Does it matter what started it? Would it change anything? Could you sit down and reason with the Cragmen, now, after all that has happened? Tell them this was all just some terrible and unfortunate misunderstanding—because our zealous king took a robbery to be the start of a holy war. So, let's just all forget about your butchered families, now, and let bygones be bygones, and go back to trading again … Honestly, Nicodemus. Weren't you around for the Overthrow? Once blood is spilled, it can only flow faster—until it is stopped. That's the way these things have always run their course."

They sat in silence in the booth, Nicodemus brooding in his thoughts, Jacob studying him. At last, Nicodemus broached what he had come out here to ask:

"I appreciate your meeting with me on such short notice."

"No need to apologize for the haste; I'm a bit hurried myself. I'm glad your note reached me when it did, and I'm glad to get to meet with you once more."

"You will keep this in strict confidence?"

"Of course, Divinity."

"I'm only thinking of our people, and preserving our true faith."

"That's why you were chosen as priest."

Nicodemus ignored the way Jacob had emphasized "chosen" and continued: "As one who is charged with our people's spiritual welfare, and who is under the firm and prayerful conviction that our people have little hope in prevailing in this, uhm, conflict ..."

Jacob did not even pause but nodded his head in somber agreement.

"That being so," now Nicodemus chose his words very carefully. "I am asking for your—counsel." He drew himself close to Jacob and whispered. "Of all our people, only you, perhaps, truly know the hearts of men. Could another—another thane, one with a suitably level head ... could he not, perhaps ... strike a truce with the men? A new treaty. On his own?"

Jacob closed his eyes, then slowly opened them:

"Some of them are trying already ... but you know that. Let's be candid, Nicodemus. What you're asking is whether you should throw your lot in with Reuben and cut our heretical king loose to the men."

Nicodemus felt his cheeks grow warm. He shifted in his chair and he was on the verge of protesting, but Jacob gestured that it was unnecessary:

"I'd have thought you a fool if you hadn't reached out to me on this matter, Divinity. I'm glad you did. I only wish I had better counsel to give you."

"So, you think ... Reuben?"

But Jacob only shook his head again.

"No. The truth is, it won't matter who you align yourself with. No one in the Crest will deal with any of our thanes. Reuben will learn this for himself soon enough. Truth is, the Stewards, the ones who could put a stop to all this, they wouldn't know a thane from a ditch digger, and would have no more reason to trust one over the other. As far as the Crest's concerned, if our king broke the Treaty, our people broke the Treaty."

It was about what Nicodemus had expected to hear, what instinctively he already knew. Still, there had to be other possibilities.

"What about in the Crag? There must be someone there who could—?"

"When you bargain with a man, you talk to his head, not his fists. The Crag's wardens have mustered, they're pressing every fit man they come across and blockading all the tunnels into the Gutters. Our caravan route," he motioned over his shoulder behind him, "has been shut down. Nothing is going to pass between our realms now. Not without a fight. And if any Cragman is caught trying to trade with a nephil—thane or otherwise—well, the clerks aren't bothering with notes or the court anymore. It's a summary execution; pretty grisly from what I hear. They're quite intent on starving us out. No. I don't see how the Crag can be reined in without the Crest, and the Crest is being conspicuously quiet about our troubles. I'm afraid we're all stuck in this war Elon started."

The finality in Jacob's voice made Nicodemus shudder. He felt himself wishing the warden would make another damn joke.

"The guilds," Nicodemus started, "they still hold some sway in the Crag, don't they? You know those men. Could you not—?"

"The guilds are broken." Jacob paused, a look of uncertainty temporarily fleeting across his chalk features, as if he were unsure how much more he ought to say before he made up his mind. "Since we are speaking in confidence, I can tell you plainly. Elon's made a particular enemy of the guilds. Though he's probably more in the right in that affair. They broke a bargain with me—with us, I should say—which might have … Well, no sense dwelling on what might have been. The guilds can't help us either."

Nicodemus' cup rattled against the saucer. He glanced down at the droplets he had spilled and saw that his fingers were shaking. He began rearranging the contents on his part of the table. As if by wiping up spilled tea, and stacking wooden napkin rings in a column, and clearing away loose salt, and folding a dirty linen to hide its stains, he could preserve a slice of order in the chaos that was befalling his realm. Nicodemus paused to stare into the cold, gray tea left in his cup. Outside their booth, the sound of a push broom came to a halt, the silence followed by a collection of low grunts, and a chair creaking loudly as the tavern keeper's exhausted body came to rest. The quiet of the man's presence disturbed Nicodemus as much as anything else he had heard.

"So then," Nicodemus said at last, "there's nothing to be done. Nothing we can do."

He could feel Jacob's hard and pitiless stare.

"Nothing to do but starve," the warden answered. "Or fight, if you wish. Or flee, if you can."

CHAPTER TWENTY-FOUR

ACHEL SMILED NERVOUSLY and tried to wipe some of the grease stains sprawled across her apron. She should have left it at the tavern, but there was no hiding the grubby thing now. She was being made to feel keenly aware of her appearance. Before a closed doorway, the king's chamberlain, Jemuel, gazed at her with the intensity of one studying a mildly interesting insect, deliberating whether or not to squash it.

"I only want to check on his Divinity," she tried to explain.

"Master Merari, you mean," Jemuel corrected her at once, leaving little doubt about his personal regard for Merari or their goddess. He tilted his dimpled chin so that he had to look down, even more steeply than before, over Rachel. He was a tall, severe-looking nephil, with an aquiline nose that shimmered with pyrite and high cheekbones as round and beige as boulders. Rachel tried to meet his condescending gaze with a plaintive expression.

"Yes, Merari. He's not been well for some time."

"On that, at least," Jemuel said, his voice acid, "we are in complete agreement."

"The poor dear hasn't had a proper sleep in months, and now that Elon—er, His Majesty—has him keeping this vigil all day and night, well, we're all worried about him."

Jemuel's long nose sniffed.

"I have been tasked with looking after Master Merari, while he keeps this," Jemuel cleared his throat, "vigil. I may not relish the duty, but you can be assured that the boy's welfare and comfort are my utmost concern."

Rachel felt assured of nothing other than Jemuel's disdain. She pressed her hands together in a gesture of prayer to implore the tall chamberlain:

"My lord, please. All I want to do is pass on a kind word from his mother. She's sick with worry about him. She hasn't seen him, hasn't heard from him since he started his vigil. I left her crying at my tavern. I know that he's supposed to remain secluded, but if I could just get a peek—"

"That is out of the question," Jemuel shook his head emphatically. "His Majesty's instructions were absolutely clear. No one is to enter His Majesty's sanctuary or disturb His Majesty's guest. No one but the King himself, his chamberlain, and His Divinity Nicodemus," Jemuel brought his index finger to the middle of his forehead, "our true high priest, are permitted to enter His Majesty's private sanctuary during this, uhm, undertaking. Master Merari's vigil is," Jemuel pursed his lips, as if he were searching for just the right derision, "an indulged intrusion. One which I trust will be singular. It certainly was not meant to open His Majesty's private temple to all and sundry."

"No, no, I wouldn't—"

"Good evening, Miss."

"Please—"

"Madam, in spite of your station and lack of any recommendation, I granted you an interview, only because His Majesty would have assuredly insisted such extraordinary courtesy be extended to one, such as yourself, who shares his, uhm, views. You've now passed the limits of that courtesy." Then, in what was meant to convey a pretense of kindness, Jemuel added: "The boy is fine. He is fed regularly, watered, clothed, and looks as well as when he came here. If you like, you may tell his mother that I have personally vouched for his condition. That should suffice for her."

Rachel would have said more, but what would be the point? Elon was gone. So were Kohath and all the other believers in Elon's court, the few that there were. Tavern maids, widowed mothers, and Gutterlings were what remained of the Maiden's sect. The sundry. Gutters nephil, like her, who were all miles beneath the notice of a lord chamberlain who was now spinning on his heel to return to his royal apartments. Jemuel turned the iron ring of the door and pushed it open.

For a moment, Rachel toyed with the idea of wedging her foot in the jam and racing past him. She was faster than the stiff old servant, probably stronger. She could make it inside, run about until she found Merari for herself or one of the king's guards caught up with her. It was a fleeting idea, born of worry, one that her better sense quickly dismissed out of hand. But she had to do something.

When the door swung shut again, Rachel drew a deep breath and bellowed so loudly she could hear the fading echo of her voice, even after Jemuel had winced and slammed the door shut in her face:

"Your Mama loves you, Divinity. And our Lady's holding us all!"

Jacob was wearing his warden's uniform, freshly laundered, with his Commonwealth medallion, polished and shined and hanging prominently over his chest. A leather sack was slung over his shoulder for his documents, his money, and some personal protection, while the two trunks that held all of his otherworldly possessions came up from behind. For the occasion, he had hired a porter. He had no choice, though it had been no easy task finding one.

Jacob glanced over his shoulder to keep a wary eye on the man. The porter had a habit of lingering behind him ever since they started out from the Goat's Groat Inn, although that might have been from all the weight he was pulling on his old rickshaw. The porter was tall, even for a Cragman, but very thin, and everything about him seemed stretched: the sinews in his arms and legs, the skin across his face, even the greasy strands of flaxen hair that covered his narrow head were pulled as tight as a bowstring into a knot. A round gulleystar lantern dangled from his belt to light his way. He said his name was Gareth. Jacob knew him to be a guildsman.

Their agreement had been a costly one. Before they had set foot from the Groat, Jacob had to hand over three brass coins, a flagon of mead, and a hundred Crag tinners (which were worth little enough but still had to be scrounged). Another three brass coins would be due on their arrival. And despite the heavy price, the bargain remained precarious. If in their journey they happened upon any other wagons that might be out smuggling, or so much as caught a glimpse of a clerk's station, the whole bargain was concluded: Gareth would keep his payment and take his leave of Jacob right then and there.

An understandable condition, given the times. Although Jacob could have pointed out they had nothing to fear from clerks. Jacob was just as much a warden as he was a nephil. But no matter. He had gotten a porter. And now he was on his way.

Jacob and Gareth had traveled together for over an hour now, picking their way over rutted troughs and broken roads alongside Cowan's Chasm. To their left, the ground sloped down for several yards before it ended at the Chasm's ledge and the looming void beyond it. On their right, a sheer rock wall rose high above them. There were no signposts, but both warden and porter knew the way well enough. It was the caravan route, a path that, from time immemorial, had brought the food of the Crag to the thanedoms of the Inner Realm. It would end when they reached the outer bailey of the Court of Common Corrections.

The caravan route. In better times, they would have come across other porters like Gareth, hauling their wares between the Granite Reach and the Crag. But now the worn pathway was eerily quiet. And, to Jacob's surprise, already falling into disrepair. The great sheets of rugged quartz that had marked the roadway's surface were broken in places where loose silt, lichen, and wild gulleystar mushrooms had begun to sprout. It made for a slow going.

"Hoo, but it's cold out here," Gareth shuddered and chuckled to himself. "Wished the guilds hadn't made me sell my cloak. Sure could use it right about now."

For a man who claimed to be deathly afraid of being seen with a dwarf, Gareth had proved himself annoyingly chatty. The porter was trying to keep his voice low, but only a Cragman would have thought it quiet. Over the clatter of his cart's wooden wheels, Gareth kept starting lines of conversation, most of which Jacob had not cared to pick up.

"Not that I complained at the time, mind you," Gareth continued. He gave the rickshaw a heave to get it over an especially deep rut. "You know, you join a guild and that kind of thing's just understood to be part of the bargain. We say 'our all for all,' too—it's just a different 'our.'"

"Uh-huh," Jacob grunted tersely.

"But it was a big ask they made on us. A mighty big ask. I got shaken down for my cloak, a bronze handle, 'bout the size of my hand, a silver-coated pin, an' fifty tinners. Everything I had. Gone. I'll never see it again. Not with these troubles we're having. Sure was glad to get your business."

Jacob could feel the man's greedy eyes boring into his back. Instinctively, he slowed his pace to let Gareth draw closer. Something in what the porter said had finally piqued Jacob's interest:

"Why, exactly, did your guild demand all your savings from you?"

"Oh, I probably ought not say," Gareth rubbed at the stubble on his chin.

"Your affair," Jacob shrugged and motioned for him to continue walking.

They carried on their trek in relative silence for a while, until Gareth, who clearly could not endure holding gossip in the quiet, began talking to himself:

"Then again … since it's pretty stale news. I suppose it'd be alright. You said you're leaving anyways, right?"

"My affair," Jacob replied.

"Sure, sure. Didn't mean to pry. But I suppose there's no harm in telling you now. Even the lectors are talkin' about it."

"Yes?"

Gareth's voice became a hoarse whisper:

"We were raising money to buy off your people."

"You don't say."

"It's what I heard from Victor, and he hears everything. Someone found out there was trouble coming, and that's why the guilds made a call on the brothers and sisters. To buy us all protection. Only something happened to the money before it got paid to the dwarves."

Something happened, indeed.

Fortunately, the Cragman couldn't see the derisive face Jacob made in the dark. Most likely that money was lining the guild masters' pockets. All of whom had conveniently scuttled off into hiding ever since Elon began his raids. The wealth of the guilds gathered up only to be blown away in a breeze of avarice. Jacob simply tisked what a shame it was to have lost that fortune.

"Yeah," Gareth agreed. "Mighty shame. 'Specially since the protection we needed turned out to be from you people."

"There's blood on everyone's hands now."

"True enough," Gareth nodded. The rickshaw warbled and he had to stop to keep it from tipping over. "I could care less, tell you the truth. Whatever's got you dwarves all riled, it's not my fight. I keep my head low and on my shoulders, as they say. The only time Gareth pokes up is for the right opportunity. Your business, for example."

"Indeed."

While the porter waxed on about all the problems in the Mountain, they made their way along the Chasm, Jacob followed by the gangly, chattering porter and his yellow-glowing lantern bobbing in the dark. The air became warmer, and soon they arrived at a place where the ridge narrowed so that Gareth, who could not tell that the ledge was still at least twenty feet away, was pressing his body against the face of the rock wall for support. The rickshaw slowed to a crawl. Soon enough, though, they turned around a bend and the way opened wide once more and began a stretch straight ahead into a long, slow rise. In the far distance, Jacob could make out the faint flickers of torchlight and smoke shimmering in the air. Probably the parapets of the gatehouse, he reckoned. It would be a mile before Gareth's weak eyes could make them out, though.

As the path leveled and became easier to walk, Gareth began talking even more rapidly, mostly about money, a topic that he always seemed to return to. He marched along, his whispered chatter almost sounding nervous, and all the while the gatehouse drew closer. Jacob could make out the outlines of the walls now, the keep, the warehouses, a tottering cylinder that was once a lookout tower. And jutting out far into the Chasm behind the gatehouse, a long, narrow line that emerged from within the darkness, gray and slender. The Spine. Anchored to the crude fortress of the men, the bridge was like a chain that held together this world and the one that lay beyond the darkness, the world outside—the Crest. How was it possible Gareth couldn't see any of this, Jacob wondered.

It was the sound of a faraway murmur of voices around the guardhouse that finally brought Gareth to a halt.

The porter spoke, his voice quiet. "Hold up now. I heard something there, that I did."

"Are you certain?"

"Yes, sir. I am. Sharpest eyes and ears in the Lower Ward, right here. In fact," he squinted hard and pretended to spy something. From the direction he was staring, Jacob knew he could only have been looking at an outcrop of fallen boulders. "I do believe we've arrived at your destination. Yep. There's one of the gatehouses there."

Jacob glanced ahead, also feigning to notice for the first time what he had been staring at for nearly an hour, and agreed with Gareth. The porter rolled the rickshaw over from the wall a few paces and fumbled with a brake on its wheel for what seemed an unnecessarily long time. When he had finished, he took a few steps farther out, closer towards the ledge of the Chasm, and gestured for Jacob to join him.

"So," he said, "I'm just going to leave your trunks here, where they'll be nice and easy for your next porter to spot when you come back for them."

"That's fine. I can manage from here on my own."

Jacob watched the man closely. He was dodging his head about, scanning the area to see if anyone else was around, and licking his lips. He sounded choked when he spoke again:

"You sure? I'll, uh, unload it all for you, if you like. After we've settled up."

Jacob kept his eyes locked on Gareth the entire time, as he pulled his sack from over his shoulder, opened it up, and reached inside. His hand grasped something long and heavy.

"That-uh, that's where you keep your money?" Gareth's tongue darted out from his lips. In the glow of the gulleystar, his face reminded Jacob of a long and sallow lizard. The Cragman's hands rubbed together, and Jacob could see he was hiding a broken shard of wood from the rickshaw, a sort of crude shiv, probably hidden behind the wheel.

"Mm-hm," Jacob's grasp tightened around what he had found in his sack.

"There a lot of it?"

"Why do you ask?"

The shiv came out into plain view. Gareth pointed it at Jacob's chest.

"How 'bout we just have a look at what you have in that sack, little fellow." He took a step closer. "C'mon, let's have it."

Jacob smiled and answered pleasantly:

"Your affair."

The man never saw the arc of the blade. Even after it had plunged into his stomach, he seemed utterly befuddled by what had happened. A long, curved dagger with a wondrous, ornamented hilt protruded from Gareth's thin belly. The whole length of the blade, Jacob knew, had been sharpened to a razor's edge. It was buried between Gareth's ribs, almost to the handle. Jacob gave the dagger a hard twist.

A wheezing noise escaped from Gareth's mouth. His chin dipped, and with an oddly perplexed gaze, he watched the front of his shirt become soaked with blood. The porter's eyes roved in disbelief, but they kept returning to the dagger's handle sticking out of his stomach. At last, he looked at Jacob. There was, Jacob sensed, a slightly offended expression in the porter's face now. The Cragman fell over to the ground with a grunt, sputtering for air. Jacob crouched next to him.

"If you please," Jacob whispered in his ear, "keep clear of the ledge. That dagger was made in Elon's forge. It's quite valuable. I'd hate to lose it."

Gareth croaked a noise that might have been the start of a word, but then his body wracked with pain, and the sound was cut off. He was on his side, curled around his wound, and shaking violently.

The bothersome man would take a while to die, and, true to himself to the end, he was plenty noisy about it. But by the time Jacob unloaded his trunks from the rickshaw and pushed the cart over the side of the Chasm, Gareth had finally stopped his gasping. The light in his eyes was gone. Jacob retrieved his dagger and wiped it clean on the porter's sleeve. A few kicks to get him rolling, then a good hard shove, and Gareth the guildsman porter was plummeting down into the Chasm, quiet at last.

Samson could hear the Cragmen now, scurrying like mice behind the boulders, darting through the crevasses and side tunnels, while trying to stay hidden. One of them staggered within his sight for a moment before ducking back into a crack in the wall.

Stupid, clumsy beast.

The line of nephil warriors came to a halt. Samson tramped forward to speak with the cloud-helmed figure at the head.

Samson turned to him and whispered. "Should I give 'em a scare?"

"Might as well." Elon sounded bored, or tired. It was hard to tell with the king's visor down, but the flatness in Elon's voice troubled Samson. "They already know we're here. Make it quick, and get back to Kohath."

"Aye," Samson strode toward the edge of the tunnel, chuckling to himself.

It was a wild place they were in, an old Crag fissure that, Samson knew, would have once funneled magma from the heart of the Mountain out into the ocean. There were no gateways, no roads or beams, no signs. Picks and shovels had never touched the rock here, which made it perfect for Samson's purpose.

While his companions formed a perimeter, Samson stooped down low to the ground near one of the walls. A small geyser of steam hissed from the steel poleyns that protected his knees, and then he pressed his ear against the cold stone. He only had to listen for a moment. He got down on his hands and began sniffing at a hole that was scarcely larger than a pin's head. Samson pinched one of his eyes shut and peered into it.

Ah, there you are ...

It would be invisible to Cragmen; in truth, it was nothing that could be seen at all, so much as sensed. But for those of Samson's kind, for the nephil of the Inner Realm, it was as plain as gold once it was found. And if one knew where to look, these things were no harder to find than coins in a fountain.

One of the Mountain's arteries.

"Aye, you'll do," Samson grunted to himself.

He pulled off his gauntlets and dug inside a pouch for a tiny brass gong he carried. An iron nail hung from a wire attached to its frame. A smile broke across Samson's face as he gently struck the metallic disk and waved it in a circle just above the hole he had found. No one else heard the sound, but they craned their ears all the same. Then, as an afterthought, Samson leaned into the rock and whispered into it, before he stomped back to rejoin his companions.

"Get ready to see 'em run," he grinned.

The other nephil watched in expectation. Slowly, a deep stirring emanated from the place in the wall where Samson had struck the little

gong. Vibrations at first, they gradually coalesced into a swirl of movement and sound, a deep ringing whirlwind that began rippling through
the stone, spreading farther and farther out. Like an avalanche, but one
within the Mountain's rock, the wave gathered minerals and elements
before it, carrying their force along in a long, inexorable wave. Louder
it rang, until the far walls started to shake. Samson could hear the reverberations in the outer tunnels.

What finally emerged was a resounding cacophony: a mighty bell
followed by a terrible voice booming:

"*We come.*"

A few of the warriors jeered at the frightened noises of the Cragmen,
but most stood in grim silence with their weapons and shields at the ready.
Samson was about to share a curse or two with Elon, but he could sense
the king was in no mood for jest. There had been a glimmer of hope in
the king's face when Samson had struck the artery, but it had already faded,
along with the noise. Samson clapped his visor back down, and Elon gave
the order to pick up the march again. As the tramp of steel boots filed by,
the king lingered to speak with Kohath. The seasoned bodyguard knew
exactly the right distance to trail the two of them: far enough behind to be
discrete, but close enough to be at hand, and within hearing.

"Where are your greaves, your helm?" he heard Elon hiss.

Nearly a third of Kohath's armor was missing, and the boy still
seemed to stagger from the weight.

"I can't walk with all that stuff," he answered. "Ariel's carrying them
for me."

The Gutterling's hair stuck to his skull with sweat. Unless Elon
could find someone to carry him, the rest of the armor would come off
within another mile, Samson was certain of it. A dark look came over
Elon's face. He shot a nod toward Samson.

"Stay close to Samson," Elon said.

Kohath craned his head around and made a sour face. He raised
his voice so that there could be no doubt Elon's bodyguard would
overhear him:

"Why did the unbeliever tap that artery?"

"It frightens the men," Elon replied automatically.

"It's a silly thing to do."

"I suppose … maybe it is," Elon's voice trailed.

Samson half-smiled from behind his visor and shook his head. What might seem silly, what might appear like frivolity, can be as necessary as food, or sleep, or drink on a battlefield. For men who can't caper, can't fight. Warriors knew this in their bones, but how could it be explained in a way that a dainty Gutterling who feared blood and battle could ever understand? Elon did his best to make the point plain to Kohath:

"It's good for the men."

"We are on a holy quest," Kohath said.

Elon seemed to study the boy closely as they walked. Samson could see that Kohath was sweating again already, even though their pace was a little faster than a stroll. A question that must have been nagging at the back of Elon's mind finally reared itself.

"Divinity?" Elon began.

Kohath was still pleased to be called by the honorific as he drew himself up a little taller:

"Yes, my son?"

Samson felt his cheeks flush from embarrassment for his king. It was one thing for Nicodemus, Elon's father's confessor, to call the king 'my son'; quite another to hear it from a fatherless, Gutterling boy, one of the last born since the Curse, and—the realization was now fully settled in Samson's mind—a boy who had not a strand of common sense for anything beyond the cult of his damned fool Maiden goddess.

"Your dreams," Elon said quietly, "from the Maiden—are they-are they ever going to be—something we'll see? For ourselves?"

Kohath paused for a moment of thought before he answered:

"Gershon always saw her the way I did. When we'd wake up, we'd both start talking about what we had just seen, and it was like both of us had just returned from the same place. Like he had been there right next to me the whole time. Sometimes we'd complete each other's sentences when we'd talk about what we had been dreaming. It was fun back then. I miss him."

Kohath shuffled around a stone, nearly tripping over it, then continued:

"Merari's dreams were darker, though. He would always be crying when he woke up. As if all he could see was the Maiden's shadow. I doubt anyone would want to see what he sees in his visions."

Samson knew that was not at all what Elon had meant. The king took a deep breath and asked Kohath the hard, blunt question—what he should have asked before they set foot in the Crag:

"You—you're certain the Maiden called you here?"

That caused Kohath to miss a step. He came down on his knees, and Elon paused to pick him back up, while the rest of the line marched ahead of them down the tunnel. Samson came to a halt, pretending to make adjustments to the valves in his armor. He darted a glance and saw Kohath's eyes burning bright from within the shadows of his face.

"I'm completely certain of it," his voice cracked. "And you should be, too."

Elon said nothing, and Kohath continued:

"For the past week, I've been hearing her, seeing her. Maybe not like you did—not yet. But my dreams are just as real as what you saw in the men's market. More real. In my dream, she-she was falling. Through the darkness. She was angry, and then she reached out and-and … touched me." Kohath's hands were clasped together, as if he were trying to hold onto something. His eyes fluttered, then closed, and then he recited the same story, in the same sing-song intonation, Samson had already endured a dozen times since they set out on this raid: "Our Lady stretched her arms forth from the falling darkness. In one hand she held a basket, like what the Cragmen carry their food in. In the other, a bag filled with blessings. She showed them to me, and then she spoke her command. She said, 'wake up.'"

As Kohath spoke, Samson was mouthing the words from inside his helm and rolling his eyes.

"Her meaning," Kohath declared, "her command, could not have been any clearer. The time has come to awaken the nephil and join our Lady the Maiden who is bringing light to the dark of the Crag."

Elon scratched beneath his chin:

"If you say so."

The three nephil walked in silence a while, their boots tramping the cold ground and echoing against the tunnel's walls, a slower pace than Samson would have liked to catch up with the rest of their men. He could still make out his warriors in the distance; they had paused at an outcrop of boulders to wait for the king. Kohath's sermonizing seemed to have tapped a temporary surge of vigor. The boy was staring ahead defiantly, the glow of his self-assured conviction radiating from his uncovered head as he marched alongside Elon. It didn't last long, though. A hundred yards more, and Kohath had to stop:

"I can't carry all this weight," he said with a huff. He was gulping down air, bent at his waist, and trying to find a way to rub at a cramp in his belly. Kohath fixed Elon with a haughty, unconcerned look of assurance that Samson instantly recognized for what it was: the little coward was exhausted. Perhaps sensing Samson's thoughts, Kohath's eyes fell to the ground and he mumbled: "I have no need of it, anyways. The Maiden will protect us."

Kohath stripped off the buckles and hoses that connected the remains of his armor. Small clouds of silver mist rose from the metal joints, and they fell to the floor in a loud clatter. When he had shed the last piece, Kohath stretched his aching legs and arms.

"Put it back on," said Elon.

"No," Kohath replied petulantly.

Samson tried to come to Elon's aid. He drew a step closer and spoke with all the kindness he could muster:

"Listen to his Majesty, Kohath. The Cragmen are on our trail. They're comin' for us. Their blades may be crude, but there's a lot of 'em, and they'll still cut your flesh if you don't have protection. Do as he says, put it back on."

"The Maiden's protection is all the armor I need."

Elon's face turned bright pink. Samson almost pitied him. The boy had just cast his forge's finest set of arms into the dirt with no more care than a change of undergarments. If it had been anyone else, Elon would have had him scourged, maybe even cut off his hands. When Elon answered Kohath, it was through clenched teeth:

"Did you ever think, Kohath, that perhaps the Maiden's protection—is lying right there, in my armor? Look at it."

Reluctantly, Kohath glanced at the plates he had taken off. Elon's voice rumbled low, like distant thunder:

"Here's a king's set of arms for your quest. And a troop of warriors for your safe escort. It's all been handed to you."

"I—"

"—hadn't thought of it? Of course you hadn't. You've enjoyed my patronage for months without a word of thanks. Why should you appreciate this gift any more than the others I've given you?"

Kohath blinked at Elon with his mouth agape, while Samson did his best to keep from laughing. The effort proved too much, though, for not only was the sight of this spoiled, Gutterling snit comical, but it was refreshing to hear his king speak like a king to him. Almost like he had remembered his old self again, for a moment. Samson let out a snort.

"Put the armor back on, Kohath," Elon said. "Now. Before the Cragmen stumble over it—"

"Elon," Samson cut over him. "Y'hear that?"

The three nephil slowly turned around and peered into the darkness behind them. Nothing stirred, but far in the distance, past where they could see, the scurrying of the men's feet and their gruff voices were beginning to return. Like rats scampering behind the walls. Whatever fright Samson had given them had been short-lived.

"We need to catch up to our folk," said Elon.

"Aye," Samson agreed.

But Kohath only stared at the suit of armor. The steel plates, wondrously covered in a maze of etchings, pipes, and braces that all interlocked seamlessly, sat where he had dropped them, as out of place in this dank, dirty cavern as a beautiful portrait hung inside a sewer. Kohath sneered at it. The boy seemed to resent it for some reason, but Samson could not for the life of him imagine why.

"Here, I'll help you," Samson said to break the silence. He clapped the boy on the shoulder and picked up the first piece of armor. "Lemme see if I adjust the sabaton valves, whether that doesn't make it a little easier going for you."

A wretched look passed over Kohath's face. But in the end, he swallowed, muttered something under his breath, crouched next to Samson, and did as he was told.

Merari came up with a gasp. His breaths were short, his heart pounding in his head, as if he had just finished running a race. Yet his flesh felt as cold as a crypt. He wiped a film of sweat from his forehead and shuddered in the dark sanctuary. An ache throbbed up and down his hip.

He had fallen asleep on one of the wooden pews, still wrapped in the blanket Jemuel had thrown at him. His head peeked over the seatback cautiously. The temple door was shut, locked, and quiet.

He was still alone in his vigil—though he didn't feel it. The words of the prayer at once came back to his lips. From instinct, he began murmuring:

"Preserve us, protect us, be our guiding light. Preserve us, protect us, be our guiding light ..."

Merari uttered the little prayer with no less fervency than he had before fell asleep. If anything, he turned it into a plea, one bordering on panic. Merari's feet scraped against the granite floor anxiously. His knuckles were soon white from clasping his hands together. The sound of his voice fell flat; it sounded tiny and out of place.

"Preserve us, protect us ..."

Had he slept? Or was he sleeping now? Merari tried to take account of where he was, what he sensed. His eyes were open. He could see the familiar clutter of the sanctuary—the altar on the dais, the rows of pews, the tapestries adorning the temple transept's walls, some empty vases, carpets, a water jug and basin. There was a chill in the air that sharpened the ache in his joints. A whirl of air currents was crisscrossing above the nave. He could hear it all too clearly.

He was awake then; he had to be. One never heard sounds in dreams. But then, he was sure he had been awake when the last dream had come.

The dream ...

It had been terrifying—though he could only recall scraps of it now. Sitting in the pew, trying to form a memory of it, stoked a blank and shapeless fear that churned deep in Merari's stomach.

What was it?

Something to do with the shadows. A furtive glance toward the statue of the Maiden's feet confirmed that much. There had been something—off—in the shade of objects, in the dark's hiding places from the sanctuary's meager light. It had *moved*, in ways it ought not. Like this damned freezing wind that never seemed to cease blowing in here.

This stupid vigil. I should've just gone to the Crag with Kohath and Elon.

Merari sighed and felt sorry for himself. The boundary between waking and sleeping had become hopelessly blurred ever since he began his vigil, as if the line were slowly being wiped away, with no hope of redrawing it. If he had been asleep (or was still), it brought no refreshment. He was more exhausted than he had ever felt.

Merari jumped at a sound. His eyes rounded and he tilted his head back slowly. Another air current had stirred one of the velvet hangings in the sanctuary. Black and azure, it depicted a serpent against a starry night sky. Its coils seemed to move from the motion of the breeze.

The fabric fluttered hard, and Merari felt the last of the blood in his face draining. He could not wrench his eyes from the sigil on the banner. Like watching a dragon, a real one, about to take flight. He shook his head hard, and it was a tapestry again. There were no shadows other than the usual ones.

He turned to offer thanks to the idol of his goddess.

Something had changed.

Her face was somehow—darker. And one of the hands were open. He was certain of it. The lithe fingers that had been clenched in defiance were unraveling, almost like a spider's legs, so slowly you could not detect the motion, but he knew it was happening nonetheless. The words of his prayer choked within his neck.

A change came over the air; something was growing unsettled.

At last, Merari managed to make a sound. Only a breath, a whispered plea:

"Save me …"

No one answered. There was only Merari and his waking Maiden, locked together in the fastness of an empty sanctuary. He returned to his prayer:

"Preserve me, protect me …"

The cloth slung around the statue's shoulder shimmered. Like moonlight in a rippling pool. But glowing so white it hurt to gaze upon it directly.

The shadows above the dais stirred. Merari's breath stopped. He remembered now. The waking dream was returning. He lifted his head slowly and stared at her face in horror, powerless to turn away.

From up high, a thin wisp of black smoke slid from her lips with the motion of a thing trying to be born. It swirled before her face absently for a while and then curled around her head, like a crown. The smoke hung in its regal place, growing, gathering form, oscillating between shapes: a crown, a mushroom, a mountain top, a goat's head, a dragon, a crown again ...

Merari fell backward out of the pew and landed hard. He spun around, knocking his knee against the wood, but he didn't feel it. He was screaming, trying to scramble for the door, but his feet slid out from under him, refusing to move.

"Jemuel," he croaked. "Please ... help me ..."

The air froze in his chest. The temple doorway seemed to fall away. He would never reach the wall. Merari wept. He threw his fists against the floor helplessly, crying out for someone to help, but no one heard him.

Another sound. This one like a breath. Merari turned to face the altar, and now the tears flowed freely, staining his face.

"I-I never wanted any of this," his voice broke. "Leave me alone!"

The darkness from the dreams, the visions that had haunted him in his sleep all these months, was finally coming forth. Awakening.

The Maiden was stirring.

She stood in awesome might before him, wreathed in a darkness that was somehow suffused within her light's weight and being. Smoke was writhing all about her covered head, like a living crown of tangled, blackened thorns. It reached out for Merari.

"Leave me—*alone!*" he screamed. "Please. Go away!"

It came closer.

"Mother!"

In reply, Merari heard a whisper so piercing it struck him deaf as it resonated inside his head. He was curled on the floor of the temple, crying uncontrollably, and all he could feel were the echoes of thousands of voices, crying with him:

"*We come ...*"

CHAPTER TWENTY-FIVE

THE ARROW WHISKED through the air silently and landed with a loud clatter against a sheet of dolomite in the cavern wall. The iron head ricocheted, setting off a small spark before the head careened off from the arrow's shaft. Samson, Kohath, and an old friend of Samson's named Nathan watched the crude thing splinter. The volley, such as it was, of the Cragmen's missiles had been intermittent up until a little while ago. By Samson's count, they had been firing an arrow a minute for the past hour of the march. It hadn't slowed the steady banter of conversation and story-trading between Samson and his friend.

"Can they even see what they're shooting at?" Nathan asked Samson. His visor, a visage of a horned nephil wracked in pain, was latched upon his helmet, revealing in its place, a much more composed and hornless, sand-colored face, a few years younger than Samson's, but far older than Kohath's. Samson shook his head.

"Nope, Nathan. They can't see a damned thing." He watched another white spark from an arrowhead fall impotently within an outcropping of boulders. "Doesn't mean they won't ever land a hit, though. Even a blind mouse'll find a hole eventually."

Nathan veered over a few steps from where they were walking, hunched down, and picked up what was left of a shattered wooden shaft. The wood had been warped even before it broke and the string that had held the metal arrowhead in place was fraying and unwinding. Nathan considered it with barely concealed disgust and tossed it aside. Another arrow landed well behind them.

"Should we bother forming ranks?" he asked.

"Nah," Samson shrugged. Then, with a smirk, he added more loudly, "not when the Gutterlings' Maiden's got us all safe and sound."

As always, Kohath was trailing a few feet behind and, as usual, bent over and out of breath. His armor hissed awkwardly from his movements. Despite his king's command, Kohath had his helmet cradled in his arm. His face was drenched. He looked up and sneered at Samson all the same. Samson came over to him and clapped him hard on the shoulder:

"So," he pretended to peer in several directions at once. "Any sign of her yet?"

"She ... will come ... when she ... comes."

"Typical woman," Samson laughed. "Just like my wife whenever we're in a hurry to get someplace." He made a mocking, high-pitched tone: "'I'll be ready when I'm ready.' Oh, don't get all flustered there, young Divinity. I'm only havin' fun with you."

"You blaspheme," Kohath spat between breaths.

"Sure I do. All the time. Nord doesn't mind it." Samson touched an emblem of his faith, the open palm of the All-Father Nord, that was blazoned on the top of his helm. Nathan followed his gesture, tapping a hidden bracelet that hung from his shield hand. "Way I see it, the gods need a little goosing from time to time. Don't you think, Nat?"

"A little pinch of blasphemy here and there's alright. So long as you remember your place."

"Sure. We still got to know our place. But the gods like it when we can josh with 'em. It's like that sermon Nicodemus once told about when the first high priest of Nord who got drunk—remember that one?"

"Aaron was his name," Nathan said, "as I recollect."

"That's the one. How's that story go again, Nat?"

"His Divinity, Aaron, had become a tad tipsy one time at the Festival of Ores. In his merriment, Aaron called up to Nord and asked the god to clap if he was enjoying the music. Asked Nord—" Nathan started to chuckle, "the god who lost his hand—to *clap*."

"Oh, that's rich," Samson slapped the side of his knee.

"Yes, indeed. Nord had a good laugh over that one, according to Nicodemus's telling. He gave old Aaron a blessing. A pair of dice that would tell the future."

"There you go," Samson spread his gauntlets to Kohath to conclude his point. "The gods want us to tease 'em a little. I mean, if you love someone, you have to joke with them now and then, right?"

Kohath, though many decades his junior, glared at Samson as if he were an impertinent child in need of a whipping. He answered Samson indignantly:

"I would never deign to joke with my Lady. And I love her with all my heart, and mind, and strength."

Samson fixed Kohath with his gaze. The old warrior's bushy eyebrows fluttered momentarily; for the first time, he felt a genuine curiosity about the boy. Another arrow landed against the rocks in the darkness. "Do you love her? Why?"

The question must have come as a complete surprise to Kohath, like being asked why something falls when it's dropped. He stammered for a moment:

"Wh-Why? Do I love—the Lady?"

"Yeah."

Kohath blinked angrily at Samson's forthright expression before he launched into a diatribe. The old warrior was a simple soul; he could comprehend only every third or fourth word the Gutterling nephil was spewing, but he could read in between them that he had pricked a raw, tender wound. The boy had never thought to ask the question, much less figure out its answer.

"Our most blessed Lady," Kohath spat, "is the harbinger of all light and goodness. She's perfection. Ineffable. The way to heaven. If you've been in her presence, as I have, if you had eyes to see her, you'd fall to your knees. You'd follow her call to your last breath. You'd renounce your miserable life just for the chance to clutch the trail of her robes. Like I have done. There is no greater love than to lay down your life for the unknown."

Samson studied the boy, who was white with indignancy and trembling so hard the breastplate of his armor rattled. No point poking the lad any longer, Samson decided. Besides, it's poor sport to make fun of an idiot.

"Whatever," Samson turned his attention to adjusting the scabbard on his belt.

But Kohath, apparently hoping to vindicate himself, pressed on: "Whatever, indeed. Why else," he gestured behind him, "would I be slogging down here in the Cragmen's sewers with the likes of you if it weren't for love and devotion. I've come into the bowels of hell to find the one, true goddess. I—"

Samson paused and let out a loud guffaw that shook his whole torso and sent clouds of steam hissing from a dozen different joints in his armor. "Oh, dear gods, stop already, Gutterling. You may be shitting your loincloth, but this ain't *the bowels of hell*. Though I'll allow, there is a stink down here—"

"—I believe," Nathan said, smiling, "the boy was trying to wield a poetic license."

"Well," replied Samson, "if he was, he went and drove his point off a cliff. I mean, there's just no comparing Elon's little tussle down here with any of the old battles we've had to fight in the Crag. You take Old Storm Eye's campaign to root out that cult, the one that was runnin' crazy down on the Docks right before the Overthrow. I ever tell you about that fight?"

"You have," Nathan sighed, "many times."

"Ship to ship. Yardarm to yardarm. Burning pitch rainin' down from catapults above you, sharks swarmin' around in the water below you. Now, *that* was hell."

"So you've said. More than once."

"Worse than anything else that happened in the Overthrow, in my opinion."

"Oh, come on, Sam, not this again …"

As Kohath stood, awkward and flummoxed in his ponderous suit of armor, Samson and Nathan broke into a familiar argument, one that was akin to the timeless debate between all soldiers who had ever served in different wars: who had it worse? As nephil, this particular dispute had decades of standing, so that Nathan and Samson could each pick up the other's points as freely as their own. Only the distant murmur of a man's voice cursing loudly in the darkness brought the debate to an early close.

Nathan tilted his head at the sound and looked about him.

"We'll just have to agree to disagree," he said, pulling a gourd free from his pack. He took a long draw and added: "We're falling behind."

"It takes time to search for true love in hell," Samson said. "Here, let me have a pull of that. Mine's out."

While Samson shared a drink with his companion, Kohath looked fretfully behind in the dark, towards where they had heard the voice. He fidgeted with the short sword that hung from a scabbard on his belt. Samson could tell from the smooth sheen that glimmered from the buckling, Kohath had never drawn the blade. And he could see in the boy's eyes, he was growing frightened.

"Not time to worry yet." Samson belched and fixed the placement of Kohath's sword back to where it belonged. "But Nat's right, we need to pick up the pace and catch up with our people. Listen, Gutterling. As long as you keep 'em spread out, Cragmen aren't dangerous. One or two of them alone are no more than a pester; they can't do a damn thing to you," he gave a friendly thump on Kohath's breastplate, "not even to a skinny, teetotaling Gutterling. It's only when the men herd up that you've got a problem. So that's what we've got to make sure they *don't* do."

Kohath peered into the cavern's recesses at all the tall shadows flitting about far behind the rocks. He swallowed hard and nodded.

"I'll watch the right flank," Samson continued, "where all these arrows seem to be coming from. Nat'll keep an eye on our left. You," he pointed to Kohath, "you watch our rear. If you see the men starting to bunch up behind us, holler out, and me or Nathan'll break 'em up. All you got to do, Kohath, is walk, look behind you now and then, and watch. Understand?"

Two arrows flew over their heads from behind a bluff of shattered stalagmites. Samson thrust his spider-visaged helm back over his head, while Nathan dropped his horned visor. They set out at a brisk pace to rejoin the nephil, with Kohath clambering alongside. The clumsy little snit kept stumbling from the effort of keeping up and at the same time keeping a lookout. Hopefully, Samson thought, he was watching for the Cragmen, not for his false goddess.

"Who," the word fell hoarsely from Nicodemus's mouth, "who—could have done this?"

He had spoken the question more to himself, but Jemuel, his only companion in the sanctuary, shook his head vigorously. The chamberlain's entire body was trembling beneath a wrinkled chamber robe that, in his haste, he had tied around himself inside out. His hair was a silvered, disheveled mess, and his face haggard.

"I-I-I swear, your Divinity. The door was locked and the chamber sealed."

"While you slept," Nicodemus added.

"It was the boy's vigil, not mine," Jemuel said. Nicodemus saw the chamberlain's knees quake, and for a moment he feared the man might teeter over on top of him. Instead, Jemuel reached out for a railing, slid himself down into a pew, and groaned softly in his hands, completely abandoning his customary decorum.

Nicodemus drew a long breath and scanned the sanctuary again, hoping he might notice something out of place: a flagstone askew, an upturned corner of carpet, a wall hanging removed, perhaps a tapestry in a new place—some tiny alteration from the last time he had been in the king's private temple. But it looked just as it had before; the only difference he could discern was the placement of the Maiden's statute, who now found herself alone on the dais since Nord had been returned to Nicodemus' private apartment. He pinched the bridge of his silted nose:

"Who else had access?"

"No one, Divinity," Jemuel lifted his head to show his solemnity. "Only two keys were ever made for the inner door. The king and I are the two nephil who hold them. Here is the one," he held out a slender, platinum-colored cylinder covered with a scrawl of intricate etchings. "His Majesty, may Nord protect him, has the other."

"I see."

Nicodemus grit his teeth and plopped himself down in the pew next to the chamberlain. Everything Jemuel had explained sounded trustworthy and right, and proper—and impossible to reconcile. He looked up at the idol on the altar and frowned. The smug insolence in that pinched, alabaster face felt palpable down here in the pews; it was certainly apropos, Nicodemus thought to himself sourly. This would-be goddess seemed to revel in the consternation she created. Heedless of the impropriety, Nicodemus reached across Jemuel for a bottle of wine on top of a pedestal that was supposed to be reserved as an offering to the Maiden. He popped the cork, cast a brief, defiant glance toward the dais, and felt the guilty satisfaction of a trivial show of disdain for this goddess.

The wine was better than any he had tasted for some time. After a good draught from the bottle, Nicodemus spoke the question that had been troubling him since his servant had woken him with Jemuel's urgent summons.

"Does anyone else know—about what happened here?"

"No one, Divinity. I sought your aid the moment I-I ...."

Jemuel's shoulders lurched with a sob. For a nephil who had always comported himself with decorum, his crying was, Nicodemus reflected, genuinely pathetic. It almost made Nicodemus feel sorry for him. But this was no time for comforting words:

"Let's delve to the core of the matter, Jemuel: your master ordered a vigil. It was supposed to last three days with no interruptions. You were charged with bringing food and drink, and to see that nothing disturbed Merari in his prayers. So, what brought you barging into his vigil in the middle of the night?"

Jemuel's tear-stained face shot back up from where he had buried his head, the terror in his eyes now doubled.

"Surely ... surely y-your Divinity isn't suggesting that-that *I* had something to-to—"

"Of course not, Jemuel. You're as harmless as a gulleystar. But something must have gotten your attention."

When he had caught his breath again, Jemuel answered.

"I-I heard ... I thought I heard ... what I thought sounded like ... someone screaming. I rushed to be of aid, as quickly as I could. I must have been too late. Oh, the gods will punish me surely, Divinity."

Nicodemus considered the chamberlain's words while Jemuel sniffed into a handkerchief.

"And you told no one else?" Nicodemus said. "Not even the guards in the throne room?"

Jemuel's head wobbled from side to side, and he fell back into another fit of crying.

"Good," Nicodemus sighed with relief. "Very good."

Nicodemus hoisted himself up from his seat. His knees creaked in protest, and his back, still desiring the comfort of his bed, went into spasms, making him wince with pain. He brought his index finger to his forehead and, still trying to avoid the countenance of this incomprehensible goddess, slowly walked up the steps of her dais.

Nicodemus did not pray. He simply thought. Of course, Jemuel would never know the difference. Fortunately, out of respect, the chamberlain quieted himself so that Nicodemus could meditate in relative silence. He found himself wandering slowly about the carpeted aisle, weaving around censers and pews, his path gradually leading him to the steps of the dais, then to the altar. When he had climbed the last step, Nicodemus stared hard at what he knew, what he was certain—with a depth he had never felt before—was the handwork of the gods.

Merari's dead body was lying atop the altar. Like a sacrifice.

The boy almost looked asleep, a blanket tucked in around his chest, as if by some loving mother, and were it not for the fact that he felt as cold and still as the stone beneath him, one might have suspected he was on the verge of waking any moment from a very restful nap. Merari's arms were at his side above the blanket, and his palms were facing up. Whatever he might have held, his hands were now empty. A most serene expression was fixed upon the boy's face.

Nicodemus studied him. In the end, at least, the little prophet finally found some peace.

But there was a deeper meaning here. Merari's corpse, his hands, his placement, macabre and transcendent in this sanctified space, carried the hallmarks of a divine message. Nicodemus knew it in his bones, though he could not begin to speculate what it might be. It was like hearing a distant call, or an echo, where only the very last of the garbled words made any sense. Which only reinforced Nicodemus' belief, his conviction, that what he was now bearing witness to came from the gods.

That thought sent a thrill through the pit of his stomach. It warmed him like wine.

The gods have spoken—spoken—to me ...

But whatever it was they were saying left him utterly baffled. As quickly as it had come over him, the joy of his revelation dimmed. The petty annoyances of the present moment returned. How fleeting, the feeling of communion. It had already become suffused with the weariness of being an old nephil kept up in the middle of the night. Nicodemus exhaled a long breath and turned to face the chamberlain.

"Jemuel," he said with what he hoped was a kindly smile, "you've always been known as a trustworthy servant and a clearheaded fellow."

Jemuel's hooked nose sniffed in acknowledgment:

"I like to think I've earned such a reputation, thank you, Divinity."

"You know what will happen when word of this gets out."

There was a long silence. Nicodemus crept down the dais, the sounds of his slippers falling softly on the marble steps. As he drew close to Jemuel's pew, the chamberlain answered, his voice soft and strained.

"That was why I asked for your Divinity's aid."

"Elon, his sect, the Gutterlings that worship this goddess—they'll all think their prophet was murdered ... by you, by a guard, by one of the thanes, it won't matter. They'll say Merari was slaughtered while he prayed to Elon's goddess for Elon's quest."

"I swear on my life, Divinity," Jemuel held his hand to his chest, "my life—I did not touch the boy. I'll swear to Nord—"

"Save your oaths," Nicodemus waved his hand, "I already told you, it doesn't matter who did this. Only that the deed was done." He let out another sigh. "You and I both know how it will unfold. There will be the rage. The accusations. Remonstrations. Each side will proclaim the other as heretics. And then the blood will flow. Our people will be at each other's throats. And the Cragmen won't need to bother killing any more of us. We'll oblige them. With our own holy civil war."

"That is—my fear as well, Divinity," Jemuel answered.

Nicodemus thought to himself for a while. He looked at Merari's body one more time and then spared a final glance up at the statue that towered over him. Still puffed up with pride—still causing trouble. The samite cloth hung limply from one of her narrow shoulders. It looked like it might have been recently embroidered.

"Did you know," Nicodemus heard his voice suddenly brighten as he mused aloud, "that my mother was an excellent weaver?"

Jemuel could only stare dumbly at Nicodemus. Poor, stiff-necked fellow, Nicodemus thought wryly. Probably thinks I've lost my count and my senses. Even now, though, the chamberlain's manners did not fail him:

"Is–is that so?"

"It's true. She was a master, in her way."

Nicodemus reached for the sanctified wine bottle again and took another pull. Jemuel was plainly at his wit's end, for he could only manage a faint nod.

"How–how very charming."

"I never had much talent for weaving myself," Nicodemus continued. "The gods know, she tried her best to teach me the rudiments. But I still remember one of her lessons. The best tapestries, she used to say, the ones of real intricacy and lasting beauty—'the goodest grit,' was how she would have put it—they're always the most fragile. So sometimes, she said, you might have to stretch a thread, or cut a line short—or bring in a whole different fabric—to hold the tapestry together. To keep it from unraveling ... Do you follow my meaning?"

The chamberlain blinked at Nicodemus. Nicodemus took him by the shoulder and brought his head to within inches of his.

"We've got to hold this realm together, chamberlain. You and I. Or our people will tear themselves apart. Listen very carefully ... Tonight, we are going to weave in a new thread to our fraying faith."

Samson peered down both lengths of the cavern, first to his left, then his right. Elon and the nephil were at least a quarter of a mile away and drawing farther and faster from them with every passing minute, while the Cragmen on his right kept creeping closer. Samson could see them plainly: tall, gray shadows lumbering between the columns and stalactites, like vermin sniffing in the dark for a carcass.

They may be blind, but they had caught the scent. His hands tightened around the handle of his morning star mace.

"Give him the signal," Samson grunted to Nathan.

Nathan shot him a quizzical look:

"We'll be showing ourselves to the men."

"Do it."

Nathan grimaced and muttered under his breath but obeyed the old warrior's command. While Samson kept watch, Nathan scampered up the base of a nearby broken pillar. Once he had found a sturdy piece of ledge, he set down his shield and unlatched a small, nautilus shaped rondel, a plate that hung from his armor's left shoulder. It came off with a chirp of steam. From atop the pillar's base, Nathan crouched to one knee and brought the rondel to his mouth. He puckered his lips and blew hard into a tiny aperture in the center of the metallic spiral.

A high-pitched whistle pierced the air. The noise was followed by a whoosh of wind and a golden shower of sparks that slowly rose from Nathan's rondel. As he blew, the flecks of amber light grew larger and formed a cloud that slowly took shape.

A glowing orb hovered in the space of the cavern. Three times, the sphere pulsated and changed its color—first gold, the color of the heavens, then iron, for the Mountain, and last, scarlet, blood. The nephil knew the flair's sequence as a signal of distress, that peril was at hand. Fortunately, the Cragmen were ignorant of its meaning. Samson could hear them scampering for cover and squealing to one another with fright.

Nathan clambered down the pillar, his armor rattling and hissing with the urgency of his movements. Samson held his hand up to his eyebrows to shield his eyes from the fading orb's light from his vision and peered down the cavern again. Elon's nephil had halted near a small cave-in of fallen stones lying between them. He couldn't be sure, but Samson thought they had caught the attention of one of Elon's rearguards.

There. He could see the armored nephil clearly now, standing on top of a boulder, waving a flag at him.

"They saw the flair," Samson announced.

"Yep. There's Elon," Nathan pointed into the distant dark, "he's thumping somebody, looks like. Must not be too happy."

An arrow whisked over the nephils' heads. It chipped a piece of bordering off the pillar Nathan had climbed to send the signal.

Samson and Nathan both turned around.

"Looks like they saw it, too," Nathan said. "They've finally got a mark on us."

"You think?"

A small volley of iron-tipped arrows came crashing down around the pillar, sending pebbles scattering about the two nephil. Neither warrior bothered moving.

"Look at the Cragmen's shots," Nathan gestured at the broken arrows lying on the floor. "They're trained on us."

Another wave of arrows fell. One missed Samson by no more than a hand's span.

"So they have," Samson agreed. He tightened a strap around a greave and patted the spikes of his mace head. "Might be time to bash a few of their heads in, keep 'em from bunching up."

Nathan nodded, but something in his companion's quiet bothered Samson. No one would ever accuse Nathan of being shy in battle, but his old friend seemed bothered, almost reticent about the prospect of combat.

"Hey, at least Elon sees them, too," Samson tried to sound bright. "I suspect that's why he's all hot and bothered. Probably trying to reset his lines."

"They'll strike the right of his rear," Nathan observed.

A grim smile broke across Samson's face as he pointed the weapon behind them:

"I'd give it about another hour before they make a go of it, but you're right. That's where the fight's going to be."

"Where's the kid?"

"Still flat on his ass and sucking wind. Just behind those teeth."

"Maybe we'd better go fetch him."

Faith not tested is not faith. It is only when faith has been hammered, and scoured, when it has been bent like a blade in a forge, and burnt to cinders, when troubles scourge it beyond all recognition, then, only then, does it arise into its full flourishing as faith. Faith unbreakable, unchangeable. Where the dross and slag of doubts have been beaten into pure, unalloyed faith.

Sitting in the dust of the cavern beneath an overhead of stalactites, Kohath ruminated on that old canard. Every nephil of every faith learned it at his mother's knee. Even the so-called priest, Nicodemus (may he one day repent and see the Maiden's light), preached it in his sermons. Faith must be tested. The gods love us when they test us. It was the kind of thing one said to children whenever they scraped a knee, or lost a toy, or needed comforting—back when there were children to comfort ...

He shivered from the cold. His sweat had long since drenched the clothing beneath the steel of the infernal suit of armor, and it left his skin clammy and withered. His legs would not move, they felt as heavy as old stones cracked from ice and fire. He would have rubbed the nettling pinpricks in his calves, but the damned armor was in the way. Kohath tried to force his stubbed fingers past a run of hoses and belts between a joint, but they protested with a wheezing groan from within the armor. The joint snapped shut, pinching his fingers.

This contraption, Kohath was convinced, this metal skeleton he was made to wear, it despised him. The loathing was mutual.

Kohath thought he glimpsed a brief flicker of light in the distance and rubbed his eyes, and it was gone. There was nothing but the air, the stones, and the emptiness that bound them together.

"I am being tested," he closed his eyes and tried to return his reflections to the Maiden. Her holy burning flame. Would he follow her call down into the unknown, into the gloom? Would he endure the company of these unbelievers? Would he bear the burden of this metal cilice? It was testing, all part of his testing.

"Preserve us, protect us, be our guiding light. Preserve us, protect us ... "

But a nagging question, the one he had always had about faith, kept intruding into his prayers:

If you have no doubts, what are you left with? Is it faith, or something else? To believe without doubt is ... to know.

"Shrive yourself," Kohath said. He knew he was tired, and cold, and hungry, and uncomfortable, and lonely. Ample afflictions, they would try anyone's faith. But he could have borne them all, carried them on his shoulders as lightly as a scarf, if only ... The truth, the one that plagued Kohath worse than this itch, was that he longed to know that which he only believed.

A metallic clank and a hiss of steam announced the presence of one of his companions. The unbeliever, Nathan, was sliding between a crop of thin, moonmilk columns. He made his way toward Kohath.

"Hey," Nathan called to him.

"Hello."

"See anything?"

"I thought . . ." Kohath started, but then pressed his lips back together. Had he seen a guttering fire earlier? He was no longer sure. Kohath rubbed and blinked his eyes. His hesitation brought Nathan's hand to the handle of a double-headed battleaxe that was looped around his belt.

"You think they may be bunching up back here?" Nathan asked. Without waiting for a response, he leaned past Kohath to scan the length of the cavern. "Hard to tell. Looks like there's some Mountain smog stuck in the air. All the ventilation is probably shot to pieces. Filthy place."

"I haven't seen men," Kohath said, "but I did see … I thought I saw … maybe it was a flame. Or something else."

Nathan relaxed. "Well, if it's a fire, that's to be expected. The Cragmen can't put one foot in front of the other down here without a torch, a lantern, and a candle to guide them. How many did you see?"

"One. I think."

"It's a Cragman, then. Poor bastard's probably lost."

Nathan leaned against a wide stalagmite and faced Kohath. He had his visor lifted, and Kohath could sense behind the semblance of casualness, something was bothering the nephil. The fog from his breath clouded in the air as he spoke:

"Listen, there's going to be a fight soon. The men are starting to herd on our other flank. We need to catch up with Elon." Nathan bent down and stared into Kohath's eyes. "Can you make it?"

"Of course. I was just—just finishing a prayer."

"Say one for me," Nathan winked. He snapped his visor down. His voice sounded deeper, and hollow from within the helm. "So mote it be, and hurry up."

As Nathan marched away, Kohath returned his attention to the darkness behind him. A gray opaqueness had fallen over most of the cavern a few hundred yards back, like an oily curtain coming down upon a stage. Nathan may have been right; perhaps it was nothing more than Mountain smog from a magma flow, or steam escaping a broken pipe.

There it was again. The light. He could see it plainly, and it was no lantern or torch. A single, white flame stabbed the darkness for just a moment, then disappeared in a shower of embers. Kohath struggled to lift himself off the ground.

"My ... my Lady?"

Could it have been her? Was she now, finally, beginning to show herself to him, to the Divine Kohath—not as a dream, but a revelation? Like Elon?

He stared into the darkness and waited. A minute passed. He wished it, willed it, to come back. The itch in his leg became unbearable.

"I don't know," Kohath breathed aloud his confession.

Kohath said another short prayer and tried to gauge his balance on the uneven ground. His legs were still numb and every step he took felt like knives serrating his feet. With a grimace, he started limping—away from Nathan and towards the light.

"Preserve us, protect us, be our guiding light," he murmured under his breath. "Preserve us, protect us, be our guiding light."

The flame reemerged. It was a searing light blazing through what looked like billowing clouds of black smoke. Black smoke like in his dreams. Rumbling closer. The fire was so bright he couldn't look directly at it.

"My Lady," he choked.

A miasma of smog was drawing towards him as steadily as an avalanche. It shook the ground in its wake. Near its base, hovering a few feet above the ground, burned a smoldering white flame. There were voices, gruff and angry, hissing at one another from within the cloud.

"It is you," Kohath blinked back tears.

An acrid, stinging smell engulfed him as the cloud drew past, but Kohath breathed deeply of the stench and laughed. His helmet, his gauntlets fell to the ground.

"It's *you!*"

A waft of silver sparks burst from inside the fire and showered to the ground nearby. Kohath was shouting, screaming, his ecstasy overtaking him:

"My Lady! My Lady! Look over here! Nathan, Samson! She's come at last! She's come to see *me!* Look, you heathens, look at her and despair!"

Kohath dropped to his knees on the frozen ground, weeping, his arms outstretched in an embrace. The last doubt had been banished from his breast.

Nathan and Samson jolted upright at the noise. Samson's mouth stretched taut:

"I thought you said the back was clear?"

"It was," Nathan snapped. "Nothing behind us but Kohath and some magma fog."

"C'mon."

His morning star mace was unslung and in his hands, and his armor's valves and bucklings roared with action, as Samson raced down the cavern. Nathan was next to him with his battleaxe readied. From behind the lunatic's visage of Nathan's visor, Samson could sense his companion's trepidation. He felt it, too.

They soon reached the outcrop of teeth where Kohath should have been resting and watching.

"Damnation!" Samson cursed.

There was no sign of the Gutterling anywhere.

"He was right here," Nathan waved a steel fist and accidentally struck the narrow stretch of column where a stalactite and stalagmite met. Flecks of white rock went flying. The sacred pillar, the holy tooth the nephil revered, was shattered. Samson let out a groan, and Nathan made a sputtering noise from within his helm. His shoulders slumped. It was an unfortunate, even sacrilegious, mishap on Nathan's part, but there was no time to ask the gods for forgiveness. Hopefully, they would understand.

"Look there," Samson pointed to a set of footsteps in the silt. They were leading away. "He's backtracking. And he's still in his armor."

"We can catch him before they do," Nathan finished Samson's thought.

They were sprinting through the wide cavern, retracing Kohath's tracks, running as fast as their armor would carry them past wild crevasses, piles of loose rubble, and broken slates, but when they rounded a turn, the nephil came skidding to a halt.

A wall of soot and vapor was rolling in the air before them, about to overtake them both. Though it was thick as pitch, they could see, and hear, what lay hidden within the fog.

Cragmen, hundreds of them.

They had rags tied about their faces and held their sleeves before their eyes. They were armed with clubs, broken spears, axes, pitchforks, and sickles and staggering forward with the foulness. It was a mob, unformed, without rank or file; no one held a standard, no captain seemed to be leading them—and yet ... the whole mass of men was moving intently. Keeping within the smog that billowed around them.

Samson's fingers tightened around his mace's grip.

"Run and warn Elon," he hissed at Nathan. "The archers were a feint. They'll flank him if he doesn't reset his line. Run swift and tell the king!"

"Nord help us," Nathan's voice quivered. He was gaping at the mass of smoke and bodies before him. "What about you?"

"*Run*, you damned spawn!"

Samson plowed headlong into the smoke. The spiked ball of his mace flashed like a falling star, an arc of light that was quickly snuffed out. He heard his friend shout his name once more. Samson spared a glance over his shoulder and silently thanked Nord that Nathan did as he was bidden. He saw the back of the nephil's armor scrambling away to warn the king of what was coming.

The haze seared Samson's lungs the moment he entered it. He was soon hacking and coughed and reflexively tried to wipe at his burning eyes, but in his armor, all he could do was blink away the tears. It hardly mattered; his sight went no farther than a few feet in any direction. Even blinded, though, the source of this black, stinking cloud soon became plain.

It was a furnace. The men had torn out an ancient iron furnace, as old as the Overthrow by the look of it, and had it to four of the biggest carts they probably could muster. Wagons, furnace, and fuel plodded forward together on creaking, rusted wheels. They were feeding the oven with trash, and tinder, and old gulleystars—to make a smokescreen. As Samson watched, a young girl ran up to the largest of the carts and dumped an armful of mushrooms into the furnace's fire. It flared into sparks before sending up another waft of sickening dark smog.

Samson could not help but admire the ingenuity.

So, they've evened the fight by blinding us all. The Gutterling's sure to be lost.

As it turned out, Samson was prescient. He searched blindly for Kohath in the stench and scrum, hunched over and hiding behind rocks whenever he could, but he quickly realized only an impossible stroke of luck or a god's help would bring him to the boy. The fog of commotion—and the furnace—had him completely enveloped and as sightless as a Cragman.

It was dizzying. All around him was smoke, and shouts, and chaos. And hordes of men. Dressed in tattered cloth and fragments of leather skins, with scarves and rags covering their faces, the smell of their fear, and rage, wafting strong alongside the burning trash. They moved about in knots and clusters, first one way then another, like a lumbering herd of wild animals constantly being spooked in different directions.

Yet, not completely wild. As Samson crept down the cavern, he caught a hidden glimpse of the same look in many of their faces, whether they were running past him, or shrieking at the shadows, or working to keep the carts moving. There was fear in their eyes, and anger, but also a grim determination. Like in the Overthrow, Samson reflected.

He came upon a cluster of Cragmen, but before he could duck behind a nearby boulder, one of them spotted him.

"Here's one!" The fool was leaping up and down, waving a lantern, and pointing hysterically.

Samson swung his mace to keep the man and his companions at bay and ran by them as quickly as he could, keeping his head down, hoping he might stumble across the boy before the hue and cry brought the rest of the Cragmen down upon him.

So many men. Samson had never beheld such a number. A lull from the belching smoke brought them all into sight for a moment. An army, a real army, living creature in the Mountain had come together as one.

"Dwarf! Dwarf!"

The shouts echoed everywhere around him now.

"Kohath!" Samson hissed.

A group of dirty yellow uniforms spotted Samson and began shouting and gesturing fervently. A crowd was tightening around him.

"Here he is!" one of the men shouted. "Hey! Trawlers! We've got another one over here!"

Samson glanced around him. Another break in the smoke revealed he was completely hemmed in on all sides now.

Nothing for it then.

Samson brandished his weapon and roared a challenge, hoping to frighten them so he could make a dash and get away. A few scurried off, he could hear their weapons falling to the ground, but most remained. One, in particular, a flat-nosed brute with an iron cap and a frayed leather brigandine took a step forward. He leveled a spear and pointed it at Samson. Through the orbs of his helm, Samson could see the man scowling at him.

"So, you want to feel a spider's bite?" Samson gloated.

An angry hiss of steam erupted from the bottom of Samson's helmet, shrouding the horrible visage in a silver mist. Samson drew a step closer. The man's spear quivered, but to his credit, he held his ground. The others, though, held back. Samson thought if he could make quick work of the brute, the rest of the crowd might scatter.

He made a feint as if he would thrust right but then swung his mace hard at the other side. But his opponent was already retreating, and the blow sailed through the fog. Twice more Samson tried to hit him, and twice the man scampered backward just beyond the reach of the spiked mace.

"Why are you running, little bug? Scared of my fangs?"

Samson stabbed at him, and this time the morningstar tore a hole in the leather near his belly. Not enough to draw blood, but close. Samson gripped the handle with both hands and raised it over his head to charge. The man backed up against the wheel of one of their carts. There was no room for him to maneuver now, though, if he tried, he could have made a break for either side—a coin flip that he might escape, but a chance. Yet, the man would not take it. Samson saw him swallow hard, his pale, bloodshot eyes darting in the smoke.

"I've got you," Samson drew closer to him.

The man flinched, then thrust his spear blindly in front of him. It broke like a twig against Samson's breastplate. A mask of dumb, dirt-smeared panic came over his opponent's face. Then, just as quickly, it fell away. The corner of his mouth curled into a wicked smile.

"No," the man grunted. "We got you."

The world turned upside down. Samson's feet, his legs, were hoisted hard up over his head.

"What the …?"

Samson bellowed loudly, flailing his morning star. But his struggling, his every motion, was now completely impotent. He couldn't turn around or get his feet underneath him again. Something bound him. A crushing weight had Samson pressed down hard against the ground and wrapped his limbs tight and close to his body.

Like being caught in a web.

The sensation brought back a distant memory from his childhood, one he had not thought about for years: his father, wrestling with him in the living room, pinning him on his back. It was fun, but the rough and tumble play had been too much for little Samson, and his arm got hurt. He felt the sting in his shoulder, a pain that had lied dormant for decades, welling up. He grit his teeth and screamed. Voices assailed him:

"Caught 'im!"

"Got another one!"

"Dwarf bastard!"

"This way—no *this* way! Bring him over here!"

He was moving, being dragged across the floor, but the terrible weight still bore down on top of him so that he couldn't bring himself upright or move more than a few inches. By hunching his shoulders and jerking his neck, he was finally able to adjust his helmet to see out of one of its eye orbs.

There was a pattern of webbing of coarse stained ropes stretched all around him. Like what the Crag's fishermen used on their boats. He was caught in a net. Dozens of hands were holding blankets and planks on top of him to keep him from striking, while others pulled at the net's end. The mass of them, Samson, and all the men pressing and pulling made it impossible to move. Samson turned his head a little more and bumped into something next to him.

Kohath's head.

The idiot had left his helmet off. What little skin that clung to his face was charred, bubbling, the smoke still writhing from the wounds.

"Gutterling?"

A sickening smell of burnt flesh and blood filled his nostrils as Kohath exhaled:

"Muh ... mah La-ee ..."

Samson felt some of the weight around him relax. He turned and through the smoke, saw pairs of shadows, their hands bundled up with rags, carrying long, clay jars from the furnace towards the net. Smoking oil sloshed out of the jar tops with each step where it bubbled and steamed on the ground. Samson heard the crisp, authoritative voice of a man, one he knew, without introduction, to be a leader:

"Right over here, now. This way. Form a line and be careful with those. Carefully! Now. Madam Teacher, you look eager to be first, so let's have the two of you step up to the edge here. Very good. I know it's heavy, but one strong heave up and an ever so slight tilt forward is all you need to get a good pour going. Mind the splash, though. Let's start with the new one they've just caught, this one dressed as a spider. Aim your pour right there—in the space between the breastplate and gardbrace. Just under the little fellow's armpit, you see it? Carefully now. On three ..."

Samson braced himself and clenched his mouth as tight as he could, for he would be thrice-damned and castrated before he gave the Cragmen the satisfaction of hearing him cry out. His back arched in readiness, the old childhood wound flared again, and then Samson felt Kohath stir within the netting.

"One ..."

The young nephil's voice rasped, wracked in pain, but with no less conviction:

"Pre-zuv us, pro-tec us, be-be—"

"... two ..."

Samson fixed his gaze on his companion in the net. The stump of Kohath's bloodied tongue was probing around his mouth, as if searching for the lips that had been charred off. His body began convulsing at the smell of burning tar that filled the air. He tried to speak again, but he could not summon any more words.

It was not the comrade he would have chosen to fall with, but at least his heart was in the right place. Samson finished the prayer, in his own way:

"Nord take our souls. And damn our foes."

THE CREST

Chapter Twenty-Six

"V IOLENCE," THE FAT gentleman declared firmly, "is a symptom of misallocated resources. The animal response when a worker believes he has been deprived of the just fruits of his labors."

He paused, his eyes wandering across the small audience gathered within the coffee house's lounge, where, in Elaine's estimation, they lingered a trifle overlong on her bosom. Instinctively, she drew her wrap over her shoulders and covered her bodice. The concoction of smells inside the room, of beans, honey, tea, and tobacco, filled the air of the cramped space.

"Irrational perhaps," the gentleman continued with a smirk, "but perfectly natural—and in keeping with the culture of the Crag's population, which we must, of course, respect for what it is. We should not be at all surprised by rumors of fighting in the Crag. Or to learn that religion has found some resurgent interest among the lower strata of workers. They're close cousins, after all, faith and violence, the firstborn in the family of subjugation."

His thick, flaccid mouth opened as if it was so pleased with the droll allusion it had just wrought, the gaucheness of repeating one's line twice in a debate might, for once, be indulged. They quivered for a moment, moist with anticipation. But in the end, decorum appeared to hold its sway upon the gentleman. His lips settled and allowed the silence to draw an audible contrast, suitable enough to mark the poignancy of the thought that had been expressed. His head dipped into what was obviously a practiced mien of contemplation before he twirled a nonchalant hand in the air:

"Oh, I expect we shall hear all sorts of wild stories during this time of transition, while we await a new Plan from the Board of Stewards.

There is misallocation in the people's lives and labors. But inefficiency, ladies and gentlemen, is the sum and substance of that problem. Fix the misallocations and the rich diversity that has nurtured our Commonwealth will continue to flourish. And that is precisely what our Stewards have done. For I am informed," he paused, inclined an eyebrow, and dropped his voice, so that those in the back tables would have to strain to hear him, "by very close sources, that the Tenth Plan … is complete."

Skeptical murmurs bubbled throughout the crowd. It was a rather bold assertion for the fellow to make, Elaine reflected, what with one of the steward's nieces sitting right before him. In the chair next to hers, Gregory made it a point to snort until the speaker had no choice but to acknowledge the impertinence with an arch expression. When the room had finally settled, the gentleman flashed the briefest smile towards Elaine and continued:

"Why, then, would we cast the fruits of our Stewards' work aside and destroy the diversity and good order of our Commonwealth's realms? Why would we pay heed to these radical, divisive shouts for unification?" His voice sank into disdain, "For I ask you: how does one unify that which is inherently separate without destroying that which makes us separate? No. This whole notion of unification is a fancifully dressed rubric for annihilation, as my opponent here must surely concede."

The gentleman dabbed his brow with a napkin near at hand and sat back down into his wooden chair, causing it to creak loudly, the indication that he had, at last, finished his turn. He looked exceedingly pleased with himself.

Elaine followed the dozens of heads in the coffee shop that swiveled to see what the man who sat opposite of the gentleman would do. Where the one who had just finished his diatribe was corpulent, almost obese, oily in complexion, and richly attired in the latest fashion from Jachin, his opponent was slender, dressed in the humble yellow academic gown of a teacher (which he was), with a high, kindly forehead that ended in a trimmed mane of white, wavy hair. Though well into his sixties, the thin man sat perfectly erect against his chair back with his hands folded neatly before him. The two were separated by a small table covered in linen, an arrangement of flowers, and a molding of an owl bearing the Commonwealth's seal on its feathered chest. A brief ray of afternoon sunlight reflected through the room's beveled windows, piercing the pipe smoke and steam from pots of brewing coffee and tea, and settled upon the teacher, casting his face in a serene glow. It illuminated a handbill that advertised the day's debate:

Our All for All?
Who and to Whom?
Is UNIFICATION the Answer?

The teacher remained in his chair, seemingly oblivious to the sunshine, the handbill's enigmatics, the stuffiness of the room, or the throng's impatience. Other than the occasional throat being cleared, or the clink of a cup being stirred, everyone inside waited for his reply with rapt attention. At last, he rose to his feet in the slow, deliberate gait of an elder whose bones held more wisdom than strength.

"Doctor Karl," the teacher addressed the heavy gentleman, his words coming soft and perfectly measured, "I believe you recited Professor Engels' rejoinder just now in your summation. I am certain of it, for I remember when Engels first cast that little dart at me years ago at the University Commons." He paused as if to indulge in the recollection. "'Unification means annihilation,' was how he turned the phrase. You asked me to concede that little barb. I pray your pardon, but I won't. Instead, I'll give you the same reply today as I gave him then ..." The teacher cleared his throat and spoke breezily. "A point built 'round a rhyme, is no point at all, most of the time."

The coffee house room burst into laughter, Gregory so much that he chortled his drink through his nostrils. A wave of applause erupted at the foil. Elaine felt her cheeks growing warm, and a smile starting to curl.

"Well said, your honor," Gregory slapped his knee and jostled Elaine. "Well said!"

Karl was sputtering to make himself heard over the noise. His face had turned a bright hue of pink:

"Is that how you handled arguments when you were a judge? With limericks? No wonder they removed you from the bench."

It was a rude remark that was immediately met with opprobrium. It was as if some clear, but unspoken boundary of civility had been blatantly crossed, and everyone inside wanted to make certain Karl knew they were offended by the transgression—everyone, it seemed, except Cloud. He reached down, took a small sip of tea from his cup, and set it back on its saucer, a picture of passivity. When the commotion finally settled, he continued, now talking more softly so that several in the back began hushing one another to catch what he was about to say.

"Your argument against unification rests on some oft-stated observations about the nature of populations. Your specialty of study, as it happens, so I might as well concede the grounds that I must. First, you noted that no two creatures born are exactly alike. That is true. Second, you remarked that individuals who are more alike than distinct will tend, out of comfort or habit or necessity, to congregate with one another into distinct groups. Also a true statement. Over time, the common features that each group shares will be replicated, generation after self-ostracizing generation, until what began as bundling of uniquely aligned characteristics, calcifies into culture, ossifies into nativism, which must lead, inevitably, into schism. A third truth. Thus, the argument runs, all are born different, form groups together that reinforce their differences, and must, therefore, remain different—and separate. The grouping of populations follows their natural ordering."

"Inevitably!" Karl declared.

"So it would seem."

"Which means there can be no unification," Karl thumped the tablecloth to emphasize the point. "The Crag, the Crest, the Dwarven Quarter cannot be unified without destroying the very diversity that makes them separate. Any more than a head can join with a hand without becoming a hand."

"And I would concede the point: they each hold differences ascribed by nature."

The mild acknowledgment seemed to take Karl by surprise.

"You would? So you—so you've conceded my point. Well, then. This was a rather easy argument to win! I suspect your friends here may be disappointed, though."

Karl grasped at a coffee cup and pumped it into the air in a mock toast, which only managed to slop liquid onto his wrist.

"I've conceded your *point*," Cloud corrected him, "not your conclusion." He began stroking the bottom of a beardless chin and gazing up at the ceiling to collect his thoughts. It did not take him long. "An illustration: let us consider for a moment these two here, who find themselves packed so tightly next to one another."

He gestured at Elaine and Gregory seated before him. Gregory straightened his back, obviously pleased to be made the center of attention, while Elaine held the former judge's gaze with a quizzical look.

"Here we have two different residents of the Crest with whom I have a passing familiarity. How do they differ? One is male, one female. One dark brunette, one I'd call a sandy blonde. One slight of build, the other—forgive me, Gregory—a tad heavy." Gregory did not seem to mind in the least but positively beamed that Cloud had mentioned him by name. "One a lawyer from Jachin, one a, uhm," he paused to find the polite term, "a freelance scholar here in Boaz. One is younger than the other. Let's see, what else distinguishes them?"

Karl waved his hand impatiently at Cloud. "I know them both, too, and could probably list a hundred distinguishing features between them."

A faint smirk broke across Cloud's mouth.

"So now it is you who have conceded my point."

"What point is that?" Karl demanded.

"They are different—but *not* destroying each other." The old teacher pointed straight at Elaine and Gregory. "Why, just look at our exemplars. How different they are, and yet how close they find themselves. An uncomfortable sitting, perhaps, but we'd be hard-pressed to say their proximity puts them in any danger of annihilation."

Uncomfortable was an understatement, Elaine thought to herself. Gregory was taking up far more than the space of his chair, and his breath still wreaked from whatever he had just eaten. He was nodding enthusiastically, as Karl wagged his finger across the table.

"Come, come, Cloud. That is sophistry. I'll concede that trivial differences do not account for much. But when it comes to what matters, the important features, our diverse realms remain apart. Just as surely as the toes of my foot stay down there, while the fingers of my hand stay up here," he wriggled several ringed fingers.

"Ah, there it is again," Cloud chuckled. "That old Judge Surefoot metaphor. The one that has everyone on the Mountain being some body part or other because of our so-called natural roles. We're the head up here in the Crest who do the thinking, the Crag's the limbs who work, the Quarter is the beating heart or something like that. I suppose the commissars must be the liver for all the drinking they do." He paused at the laughter.

"The problem with Surefoot's thesis is he assumed, just as you do, Dr. Karl, that certain diverse traits *may* prove intractably separating, but he gave us no guide to discern *which* ones are so. This trait matters; that one doesn't. Why? Because I have said so! The tautology runs amok. Let us strip away the falsity of his assumption to lay the real question bare so that the truth can finally emerge ... Could it be there are no inherent differences between the peoples of our Mountain that could not be bridged by our far more overarching *commonalities*?"

He had to pause, for as he completed his sentence, most of those who had been sitting rose to their feet in loud, approving applause. Cloud stood impassively as the clapping washed over him, while Karl simply scowled at everyone in the coffeehouse. When it subsided somewhat, he continued:

"I believe the answer is yes—hear me, please—and that answer derives both from logic and the proof of experience. My own experience, in particular. Believe me, the women and men of the Crag are no different than you or me."

"Oh, come now," Karl rolled his eyes.

"Not in the least. Whether or not we are willing to speak about this commonality publicly, the issue is being thrust upon us. You brush the troubles in the Crag aside as mere incidents of misallocated resources. That is a dangerous misapprehension, Doctor. If you are wrong about your thesis—and I think you are—if we are keeping apart that which, by its nature, would be joined ... then violence becomes the logical recourse for its resolution. Fighting becomes a surrogate for the unity the peoples must have. That condition cannot 'be fixed' by throwing a few more loaves of bread or worthless bits of metal at it. The Stewards will find themselves fanning a flame that sweeps over the whole Mountain."

Cloud had just stepped, boldly, beyond the realm of acceptable discussion, even for a debate. The jowls of the doctor's cheeks quivered, unable to form anything more coherent than to repeat "inflammatory" and "must be noted." But he was isolated in his outrage. With the door of forbidden discourse now opened wide, the little coffee shop buzzed with excitement, with energy that lifted Cloud's stature above his diminutive posture, eclipsing Karl's. As if drawing from it, Cloud stood taller. His voice was tiring from strain, but it jolted across the room, his eyes lit with certitude.

"There is nothing inflammatory about unification, ladies and gentlemen. Nothing to fear from it. The Crest, the Crag, and the Quarter are one already. Hands, hearts, heads, call them what you like. The realms are only separate if we squint our eyes so tightly, we no longer see the broader whole—the body—of which each one is a part. That is what unification will be. An opening of the eyes."

A great cheer erupted that nearly knocked Karl from his seat. Elaine was jostled hard from behind. Everyone gathered in the coffeehouse was stomping and shouting together. Drinks were spilled, chairs fell over, calls for "unification," and "Our all for all" resounded.

The debate, such as it was, was over.

When Elaine happened to glimpse over behind the bar where the drinks were served, she noticed Dr. Karl making a hasty exit through a rear door, his whole head glowing bright as a red candle. While in the center of the clamor, surrounded by a throng of earnest young men and women pressing him in from all sides, and all talking at once, Cloud sat quietly in his chair with a scholar's slight stoop and a habit of squinting at whoever was speaking to him. Gregory was, of course, near the center of all this, taking up the most space and the most volume.

"A clarion call," Gregory said, gushing, "to those who have ears. And I, for one, have heard it for a long time now. As a founding member of the Solidarity Guild, I've stood fast at the vanguard of his Honor's movement. Come what may from the Crest, unification is my dream. Like his Honor's. Our guild will be heard. The Dr. Karls up in Jachin can run, they can try to drown us out, they can ignore the evidence, but they can't stop up their ears forever. No, I tell you. The Stewards will acknowledge this important work. Unification will feature in the new

Plan; you can count on it. And I—we—shall be a part of it. I couldn't be prouder to stand with you today, Judge Cloud. And with Miss Temple," he tried to slide an arm around her shoulder, which Elaine deftly avoided, "who has once again graced our gathering with her attendance. Such an excellent event!"

"I'm most grateful for your efforts organizing today's talk," Cloud replied mildly over the din of cheering, "and for the esteemed company." He bowed to Elaine, and she smiled in return.

"But listen," a serious, long-faced woman interjected, "we can't rest on this laurel. This is one front of the larger struggle, the real issue—economic, cognitive, and social justice."

Another echoed her:

"Yes, there's work to be done!"

Gregory's mouth screwed up:

"There's always work to be done. That goes without saying. That is why I am hosting a post-debate conference at the Oak and Crow in honor of his Honor," Gregory tittered at the play on words he had stumbled upon, "it will be a working dinner. A brief repast to refresh our intellects after this afternoon's labor, we can compare notes, and then get to it. Someone will need to prepare a transcription of this momentous debate, I would think—"

"Let's take the debate to Jachin now!" a woman shouted over him.

"Which debate?"

"About the injustice in the Crag that the Stewards have ignored. Open up the Tombs!"

"Hear, hear!"

"No, keep the focus narrow. Unification in the Commonwealth!"

"Hold on—" Gregory began.

"They're the same thing."

"You're all missing the point," a pale, doughy faced man in a red and blue tunic that was much too large for him raised his voice and shoved his way around a table to explain just what he thought needed to be done, which involved making tracts and handbills at a printing venture he had some connection with. "We have to organize," he explained.

And so, a wave of students, commentators, aspiring orators—"thinkers," as most of them referred to themselves—began bumping against one another to seize the center of attention, which now only nominally included Cloud. They all spoke freely, and loudly, over one another, and though they would never allow him more than a word to respond to any of the things they declared, they refused to let the poor fellow retreat to a more comfortable setting.

It went on this way for more than an hour. A gangly, greasy-haired girl wearing a commissar student's sash wove in and out among the crowd to refill everyone's drinks and ask for food orders, but otherwise, no one could move inside the coffeehouse, it was packed so tightly with bodies, and with noise. Only Elaine, who made her way over to a stool in the one piece of open space at the bar, withdrew. She watched all the jostling and speech-making with passing interest for a while but soon grew bored. She saw Cloud let slip a noticeable yawn. For his part, the coffee shop owner's patience expired.

"That's it then," the owner lifted himself high on a barstool and cupped his hands to his mouth. "Alright everyone, that concludes this afternoon's debate." He waved off the chorus of boos and complaints. "His Honor's all tired out. Can't you tell? And you've gone past your rented time. If you want to stay—and order something from the menu—you're welcome to stay. Otherwise, off you go!"

With a considerable amount of grumbling, the crowd reluctantly dispersed. Cloud mouthed a silent "thank you" to the shop owner and slipped around the bar, where the owner and his commissar servant were waiting by the back door. Gregory tried to follow after the judge but was blocked by a press of people heading in the opposite direction.

"This takes you out back to a private alley," the owner whispered to the visibly relieved Cloud. "Mava here will take care of you, walk you to wherever you're heading." He leered down at the serving girl. "Then you come straight back here—to help me clean up."

"I'm in your debt," Cloud said. His thin, silver hair looked tousled, and the first beads of sweat had broken along the top of his scalp. "Miss Temple, I'd welcome your company, as well. Unless you're already engaged."

"Really?" Elaine was taken somewhat by surprise at the offer. She felt a tiny thrill turn in her chest. "Of course, your Honor."

"Come on around, Miss," the owner waved at her. "Hey! I said you people need to clear out already! Do I have to call out the High Guard?"

Cloud took Elaine's hand with a chivalrous grasp that did not seem at all out of place despite the awkward setting. She was grinning as the owner hurried them through the doorway. The door slammed shut, followed by the metallic sound of a latch locking into place, and the three of them, Cloud, Elaine, and the young commissar Mava found themselves in the dusky confine of a cobblestone alleyway running between two rows of buildings. The muffled noise of the crowd in the coffeehouse, now spilling out into the street on the other side of the building, was the only sound in the place. A cat crept out from the shadow of a stack of crates to investigate who it was but slunk away silently when it saw that no one carried any plates or saucers.

"Quite a debate, Judge," Elaine said to break the quiet.

"That it was, that it was. Mava, dear?"

"Ye-yes, sir."

The girl nearly jumped at being addressed. Her thin, trembling hands began gathering her yellow academy sash, tying it and re-tying it around her waist.

"You're rated to be a menial, as I recollect. How is your apprenticeship going?"

"I-I ... I please the owner. I think."

"Ah."

Mava was staring at her murky reflection in a dirty pool of rainwater. Elaine could see a blush crossed her cheeks, although it might have been the remnants of a sunburn.

"You've got a test tomorrow, I believe?" Judge Cloud inquired.

"Yes, sir," she answered without looking at him. "Geography of Boaz."

"Well, you'll never learn Boaz in a dingy alleyway. Better hurry back to the library while it's still open and study your maps. Don't worry about the rest of your shift. I'll send a note to your master."

Mava lifted her face to the commissar teacher, the expression of relief unmistakable. She thanked him and raced off down the alley, as fast as she could run, her footsteps falling as silently as the cat's. Cloud watched her disappear: "Poor dear. That one would probably have been better off remaining in the Crag."

"Not quite good enough to be unified with the Crest?"

Cloud's lips curled into a sad smile.

"Or the Crest's not quite good enough for her."

Elaine was on the verge of quipping something in reply but instead settled on walking alongside the former judge in silence. A brisk wind pushed them along, picked up the scattered leaves and loose papers and trash littering the ground in the back alley, and reconfigured the mess into new piles. Elaine drew her wrap tighter.

"I appreciate your tearing yourself away," he continued after a time, "from the party, I mean. A most engaging assortment of individuals."

She laughed aloud, sending the curls of her hair shaking around her neck. "They're absurd."

"That they are."

"I've been listening to their blathering about unity for weeks now. All their talk about solidarity and not one of them has ever set foot inside the Crag."

"They've not had the benefit of our experience."

"Exactly. I'd like to see one of them sit through a docket call in the Court of Common Corrections. They'd probably faint. And they call themselves a guild?" She laughed again. "Idiots wouldn't know a guild-mark from a birthmark."

The judge let out an indulgent sigh. "You mustn't judge them too harshly. They're children. Play-acting like they have a cause. And causes are such fun to have. Especially when they don't cost you anything. So what if they haven't any notion of what they're talking about? It's still a worthy cause, despite the idiocy of its proponents."

She stopped in the middle of the street beneath the shadow of a tattered sign that had been strung between the buildings. It was from a parade years ago, and the graying letters were briefly illuminated against an auburn backdrop of setting sunlight. "We Alone Guard the Common Good," it proclaimed.

"You believe in their movement?"

"In a way, yes. I'll probably join their little guild meeting at the Oak and Crow. Bring a little order to the children's fervor. Later, though. After a proper meal. I can't abide pub food. I had thought, I had hoped … seeing you this afternoon … Well, I had the spark of a hope that my favorite defense attorney might help me with some adult supervision of a worthy cause. Indirectly, of course."

Elaine looked at him and found herself wondering, not for the first time, whether he had been handsome when he was her age. She decided he probably was. She smiled and touched his elbow:

"I came to hear you, Judge. I never thought I'd get the chance again. After what they did to you, you know, I would have thought ..."

A gray eyebrow was arching inquiringly:

"Wondering what your dear uncle, or your future mother-in-law, will think?"

"You're already noted, Judge. With your history, they wouldn't hesitate to take you up again. Doesn't that—worry you?"

"Not really. As you say, it's not the first time I've shared an unpopular thought about the Crag. Nor will it be the last. But at least I'm not alone in my opinions." He made a searching, sideways glance at Elaine. "How is my successor doing in the Court of Common Corrections? You've been making some appearances down there of late, I hear?"

"Objection," Elaine replied. "Compound question. And leading."

Cloud laughed.

"Alright, sustained. In part. The first inquiry was fair, though. What is your opinion of our young Judge Acacia?"

Elaine thought to herself before she replied:

"He is," she began, "an interesting man. Intelligent—very intelligent. But guarded. And moody. But he's always been like that. Even in law school, he always had this look like he had just eaten something sour. He's got an Acacia's ambition, but he's not a climber. Not really. I sometimes wonder if he's actually related to Michael."

"I meant how is he as a jurist."

"Oh," Elaine held a hand to her cheek to hide the flush she felt in her face. "Overall, I'd say fair but unimaginative. A little on the lighter side when it comes to sentencing. But still well within guidelines. Only ... every now and then he surprises you with a ruling that almost makes you think Judge Cloud was back on the bench."

"He'd better watch out then," Cloud joked, "or he'll find himself replacing me again. I could have the same successor for my court teaching in my stead in the Commissariat. Wouldn't that be an irony?"

Elaine came to a halt and took Cloud's arm a little more firmly:

"I hope not. For both of your sakes. Your Honor, I wish you'd— you'd be a little more careful with what you say in public ... There are worse places than the Commissariat you could end up."

Cloud leaned forward, a pleasant resignation seeming to shine in the dusk, and now Elaine found herself wondering what this man could have done, what he could have accomplished when the Commonwealth was a younger place. The realization came upon her with a shiver from the cold: he could have been a Steward himself, once. A very different kind of Steward.

"Whatever they will do to me, they will do," he replied. "If I end up teaching clerks how to read regulations or add up their columns, well, so be it. One reaches a certain age, Elaine, and one finds that one's views about what really matters ... matures. I've found an irreducible premise in my life. I would see it through to its logical consequences."

From anyone else, she would have scoffed at such pretension. "Come what may from the Crest," was the kind of hubris Gregory and his ilk bandied about, and no one ever believed it. But with Cloud, there was a sincerity, and a humility, that Elaine could only acknowledge and admire. She walked close to the judge, enjoying his presence, and their conversation turned to lighter subjects, about Elaine mostly, her family, her upcoming wedding, her practice in Jachin, her future, the same things she had always enjoyed sharing with Judge Cloud after court.

A commissar who had come out to light the first lanterns in the alley bobbed her head as she went by them, but Elaine and Cloud took their time ambling across the remaining length of the alleyway, neither one in a hurry to reach the town again.

CHAPTER TWENTY-SEVEN

E LAINE AWOKE, BASKED for a moment in the midmorning sun that enveloped her body, and propped herself upright against the headboard of Michael's bed. A jagged slat of oak, it felt hard, angular, so she sank back into her down pillow. Her hand reached out for the end of the sheets to cover her chest as she looked around for her fiancée.

He was standing at the far end of the room, as if at attention before a tall mirror built into a dressing chest of drawers. Though partially hidden behind the furniture, she could see him fully in the mirror. It was an odd, wavering reflection he cast from where Elaine lay. Michael was already dressed. As if sensing her eyes upon him, he smiled at his image:

"Enjoying the view?"

Michael rolled his shoulders back and angled himself so that he was almost, but not quite, facing her. It was a splendid outfit he had on, sewn from the finest bolt of gloss black woolen cloth with dark yellow flashings and chevrons on its sleeves. The Commonwealth signet on its breast, Elaine happened to know (because she had picked up the clothes for him in town) carried an oval guildmark cleverly woven into the embroidered hammer's handle. Its presence assured her it was worth the inflated price that Michael's mother had paid for it; and it added a nice, subversive touch. A uniform of the best materials, tailored by a master. Michael looked ridiculous in it.

"I've never seen a High Guard uniform quite like it," she finally said.

"Tactical design. For underground action. For the new assignment. I'll wear it for the formal procession out of Boaz."

He began primping and pulling at his sleeves, which made a plume tucked into a buttonhole bob up and down. Elaine was at once struck by a vivid image of a pond duck preening its feathers. Michael began explaining his new uniform's uses, the practical advantages of its

reinforced stitching, numerous pockets, and generous padding—neces-
sities for mountainous warfare—how the cost was more than justified,
whatever Mother had paid. All Elaine could think of was a quacking
sound. She stretched and let out an exaggerated yawn to keep from
giggling.

"You seem pleased at the prospect of slumming in the Citadel," she
remarked. "It's practically the Crag's keep, you know."

"Mm-hm."

"I mean it must seem a step down, for a soldier who's chasing after a
post in Jachin. The only things to chase in the Citadel are the keep girls."

Elaine leveled him with a disarming and, had he been paying any
real attention, very candid smile. Michael only turned around to view
his backside in the mirror.

"Nice try," he said. "I'm in too good of a mood to be lured with
your teasing." He paused and angled his head long enough to send a
meaningful glance. "Not that I minded being lured earlier."

Her smile remained, frozen just as it was.

"Actually," he continued, "the Citadel's a perfect posting. What
with all that's happening on the other side of the Spine. It could land
me in Jachin that much sooner. I'm lucky this just fell into my lap the
way it did."

"Oh."

"You see, if the problems in the Crag need martial attention, I'll be
right there in the Inner Keep. Ready to fight. In *real* combat. That kind
of opportunity will never come around again. If things play out the way
I hope, this post could put me on a fast-track. No matter what, it will
build my resume. I've got the training credentials already; I just need to
document a few instances of quantifiable metrics that will show ..."

He went on for a while, saying precisely what Elaine would have
expected, and it all sounded the same: *quack-cluck, quack-cluck, quack-cluck*.
She listened for as long as she could stand it, and finally interrupted him
if only to change the subject to keep from laughing aloud:

"And you'll be closer to your brother. That will be nice."

"Hm? Oh, yes."

"Has he written lately?"

"Mother would know," Michael shrugged.

"I've only had one letter from him since the last time I was in court. I suppose he's busy with work. Or found someone else to occupy his time."

"Well, it's not a girl. He doesn't have a taste for them." Michael was focused intently on the mirror, searching for the best placement of his sword scabbard. "As you say, he's probably just busy."

Elaine frowned. The last letter she had from Jonathan came yesterday, and it bordered on histrionic. He wanted her to come at once, begged her to suffer the short journey across the Spine. If she did not have time to argue any cases, she could at least break the crushing monotony of his docket with a social call. He needed educated company, some reprieve from the dreariness of the Crag, the banality of the place, "so dreary, so tiresome, so pointless …"

For two pages, front and back, the letter went on and on like this. Every sentence in the cramped scrawl had ended with a comment, alarmingly unsubtle for Jonathan, that she ought to bring a few bottles of wine with her, because there were none to be found in the Crag, and he missed the pleasant taste so much.

Of course, there was no wine in the Crag.

Grapes only grow in the Crest in Regina's vineyards, and Regina had paid off all her vintners and bribed all the smugglers who had ever sent bottles across the Spine. Not a drop of wine would reach the Crag.

The whispers that the Honorable Jonathan Acacia was shaping up to be a drunkard, like his father—rumors which probably had some truth to them, Elaine allowed—had been put to a swift and decisive end, thanks to Regina's little blockade. Elaine could not violate the injunction Regina had fashioned, not without permanently breaching her future mother-in-law's trust and complicating the wedding negotiations. Elaine had written Jonathan back, a vague apology that the wedding plans kept her in Boaz, but that as soon as they were finished, she was looking forward to arguing before him once more.

Michael was facing her fully now. "Are you alright?"

She came out of her worry and resumed a pleasant look once more.

"Just still waking up. So, do you think it could come to fighting in the Crag?"

"I hope so."

Elaine rose from the bed, plucked her clothes from off the floor, and got dressed. It may have been that she had not had breakfast yet or that a flurry of tiny vexations had come over her first thing in the morning, which was a bothersome way to start any day, but Elaine was already cross. The sarcasm came welling up:

"I'm sure all those Crag workers have earned a good slaughtering," she said a bit louder than she had intended, "whatever it is they've done."

Michael raised an eyebrow.

"I mean when you hack them to pieces, it's sure to be for the good of the Commonwealth."

A condescending smirk and Michael finally left his mirror to sidle next to Elaine and put an arm around her waist. He smelled of lilac.

"I don't enjoy the prospect of violence, if that's what's troubling you."

The image of him, running a sword through that boy in the Amphitheatre, the focused intensity that had been drawn across Michael's face, came back to Elaine in that instant.

"You don't?" she asked him.

"Of course not," Michael frowned. "Who would want to hurt Craggies? It's like killing cows. But that is part of my duty. I know it may sound terrible. I'm sure your friend Cloud would say I'm a monster—"

"—No, he would say your actions are monstrous. He wouldn't call you a monster. Judge Cloud never attacked a person, only his thinking."

"Whatever. Such is life in the Mountain ... You'd have to be a soldier to understand."

"Understand what, Michael?"

Now it was Michael's turn to appear annoyed. His arm dropped to his side. He muttered how it was hard to explain, his duty, the responsibility, the exceedingly narrow windows through which one must pursue the higher promotions. It was his profession, after all. Then Michael brightened and recited for Elaine a line from a text he had been required to memorize in his first week of the High Guard's academy, in a course on social military theory.

"Violence," Michael said, "is the expression of force, and force is the wellspring of all order."

Elaine studied him closely. She could see past the flowing uniform, the oiled hair and freshly shaven face, the hair trimmed to perfection, the eyes that were so well apportioned, settled, and empty. She could also see the truth woven within this thread of logic he had just presented to her; and, in the breadth of the same instant, she found its appalling end. Elaine murmured it aloud:

"So … violence is order."

"Right!" Michael beamed. "Now you've got it. That's just the way to think of it."

Ten dull, cloudless days passed in Boaz, and the weather went from warm to sultry. The stones of the central square drank their fill of relentless sunlight, while a haze of pollen, unable to escape out of the breezeless avenues, settled over the air. Everything, the streets, the shops, the carts and crates, the statues, even the animals, wore the same film of yellow, dusty, sweat-soaked grit. A simmering stew kept stirred by a frenetic movement of people outside.

It made Elaine feel as restless as a child.

To pass the time, she followed Cloud and that ridiculous "guild" of Gregory's about town. For the heat would not slow Cloud's newfound following in the least.

After the success of the soiree at the coffeehouse with Dr. Karl, Cloud, at Gregory's urging, embarked on a speaking tour about unification throughout Boaz. Two, sometimes three lectures a day (always lectures; no one else dared debate him again), at the Amphitheatre, the Commissariat's lecture hall, the coffeehouse (there were several appearances there), the Oak and Crow tavern, and once on a dais in front of a public fountain. The last made for a pleasantly evocative scene, Elaine had thought, the humble teacher and former judge sharing his sagacity with the sound of cascading water as a backdrop.

Gregory and his growing clutch of followers were close at hand wherever Cloud appeared, to chant and applaud madly while he spoke, and then to "organize" the movement of their Solidarity Guild afterward. Which seemed to always entail drinking, usually Acacia wine. Some of the organizers had recently taken to wearing clothes that were, ostensibly, fashioned after workers' smocks and hats. It was meant to be a

symbol of their solidarity, their desire to unify, with their brethren workers. To one, like Elaine, who had spent time in the Crag and spoken with
Crag workers, the garb was a preposterous imitation: too well made and
far too clean to bear anything more than a superficial resemblance to
what was worn in the Crag. Still, whether because of Gregory's group
or despite it, the crowds that gathered for Cloud's lectures were growing
steadily.

It was mid-morning in the center of Boaz, and Elaine could feel her
shirt sticking to her back. The heat coming off the terrazzo burned through
the bottoms of her sandals, so she started to walk quickly, doing her best to
avoid the little knots of people loitering in the shade of every porch and
public shop. As soon as she came to the cobbled square, Elaine saw that
the coffeehouse was astir. The building was full to the point of overflowing with buzzing patrons, many of them, she saw, wearing those ridiculous
smocks. An older commissar, already tottering from drink, was trying to
clear the gutters outside of what looked like an avalanche of wadded paper.
He was trying to stuff them, without much success, underneath his arms,
while another commissar, a shrewd looking woman, made a pretense of
doing the same work. Elaine was certain the little yellow-sashed fox was
making notes of the people coming and going in the coffeehouse in a
book made to appear like a work form. Elaine dipped her head low and
picked up her pace.

A few people might have called out to her as she passed, but Elaine
made it to the other side of the square, grateful that no one had stopped
her. A meager breeze stirred the air just enough to pick up a dust-
covered, crumpled handbill and send it tumbling past Elaine, where it
brushed against her shoulder. Not knowing why, she caught it and read
the thing.

It was covered with the most pretentiously bold and flowing lettering and purported to be a statement of "*The Guild of Unified, Independent,
and Learned Denizens, in Solidarity with the Guilds of the Crag.*" What followed was a cramped, columned rendering of ninety-five "*Propositions,*"
that Elaine knew, by the fourth word she read, had been concocted by
Gregory. Her eyes quickly scanned down towards the bottom of the
page, which promised that the Stewards' consideration of these modest propositions would "*advance the Common Good of the Commonwealth,*"

retard the Sclerosis [why ever would anyone capitalize that?] *that has taken hold over the Crest that the Slavish devotion to ostensible respect for the diversity between the Realms has engendered while assuring the Social Justice of an equitable apportionment of resources that the Stewards' forthcoming Plan must necessarily ...*"

Elaine blew an exasperated breath from her lips, crushed the paper into a ball, and let it drop to the ground.

"Beg your pardon, ma'am," an old man's voice addressed her gently.

Elaine paused midstep. The voice's owner was standing before a shop and wearing a dampened apron that hung loosely around his waist. A brush and a bucket of filthy water were on the sidewalk next to him. Someone had painted the word, "UNITE," across his storefront, which he had scrubbed into a long drab smear that mingled with a film of pollen. At present, he was balancing an armful of yellowed papers beneath his chin. The man addressed Elaine in something between a warm invitation and an apology:

"Could I, please, trouble you to pick that back up? I intend to burn it in my shop, but I fear I'll have a spill if I bend over to get it myself."

"Oh, of course." Elaine stooped to retrieve the paper.

"Thank you kindly."

"Are you the apothecary?" she asked.

"I am. My name is Harold, and I'm pleased to be at Madam's service."

She might have corrected him to call her "Miss," but he was already hurrying back to his door, trying to hold it open for her with his foot and very nearly falling over. Elaine went inside, wiping the dirt and grime from her sandals on a threadbare floor mat, and carefully stepped along the only path there was through the clutter of tables, shelving, and wooden cases. Instinctively, she found herself hunching over, as if the teetering piles of jars, bottles, and scraps of paper that surrounded her might come careening down at any moment. At the end of the pathway, a collection of amphoras had been put on their side to reveal a fireplace where a pile of small papers, leaves, and pollen was smoldering, making the already close space unbearably warm. A tawny cat snoring softly on top of the fireplace's hearth did not appear to mind the stuffiness.

"Thank you so much," Harold said, coming up behind her. He had taken off his apron and was carrying the papers he had picked up in a bag now. He began to toss handbill after handbill into the fire. Elaine watched the tiny blazes thoughtfully, the propositions turning into ashes.

"So much handbilling," he shook his head, "and all the commotion these days! How these people are getting licenses for it all is beyond me. But that's not my concern. I'm just trying to keep a clean store for my customers." Harold gave the cat a scratch behind the ears "where do you hale from, Madam?"

"Elaine Temple. I'm from Jachin."

"Oh!" Harold brushed the wrinkles from his shirt and try, without any success, to smooth his hair. Elaine immediately regretted having made the kind old man feel his status. "I should never have imposed on you. I do apologize—"

"Not at all," Elaine smiled warmly and looked around her surroundings as if nothing pleased her more than the sight of piled haberdashery. "If you hadn't asked for my help, I might not have discovered this charming apothecary."

Harold blushed at the compliment:

"May I ask what brings a fine lady from Jachin to our humble city?"

"I'll be joining my fiancée in the Citadel," she replied.

"My!" Harold could not conceal his surprise that a reputable lady would have to venture into a place as disreputable as the Citadel.

In truth, her joining Michael had never been a topic of discussion. Neither had written the other since the day, a week ago, when he led his company of guards in a promenade through Boaz and down the High Road to his new post in the Citadel's Inner Keep. Whether she chose to stay in Boaz, or return to Jachin, or find a bed with him in the Inner Keep was a matter of mutual indifference for Michael and for Elaine.

She had made up her mind yesterday when she noticed the money he had left her was beginning to dwindle. Asking Regina for a loan was out of the question, not while her uncle was still engaged in the nuptial negotiations. Michael would advance her funds. And since she would be in the Citadel already, there was no reason she couldn't make a quick jaunt over the Spine to court. It had been weeks since she had heard from Jonathan …

"While I'm there," Elaine continued, "we might have occasion to visit the Court of Common Corrections."

Harold's bottom lip quivered, he swallowed hard, but quickly recollected himself.

"I'm sure you must have very important business that would take you *there*," he spoke in such a way that left no room to doubt his desire for her to change the subject.

"Oh, it's just that—"

But he held up his hand to stop her, visibly anxious not to learn any more than he ought.

"If Madam has a pass," he said, "that's all I would need to know. Though I … I would *wonder* that a lady should ever set foot in such a dangerous place, I really would."

"I've been there before and I am quite capable of ensuring my safety," she replied. Seeing Harold's discomfort, she tried to sound more ingratiating. "I do appreciate your concern. Now that I think about it, perhaps you could provide me with some help. The last time I traveled to the court, something about the return trip left me feeling—out of sorts. I didn't care for it at all."

"I shouldn't be surprised!" He shuddered. "All the airs you'd be subjected to in the Crag. Consumption, grippe, ague, catalepsy, the flux. An apothecary's nightmare."

"I was hoping you might have a medicine or a tonic."

"There's not a course I could prescribe that'd ward off all of the noxious vapors they have down there."

It was no use trying to explain, Elaine realized, and it was plain that Harold was growing wary of Elaine's business. He tisked, and apologized, and muttered how he had never been asked, never dreamed he would be asked, to prescribe anything relating to the Crag. He would very much prefer to leave that place, and its residents, entirely to their own affairs, all this recent commotion about "unification" notwithstanding.

"I've nothing to do with that group," she said. "I simply need a sedative, to help me sleep through the trip."

"Oh. Well. If that's all you need … Let me see what I can do."

He disappeared for a while within a cluster of shelves, leaving Elaine to ponder the fire and the sleeping cat. It was more of a lark, the idea she might visit Jonathan—perhaps take a few more serious cases on while she was there. A passing fancy, yet she found herself smiling whenever she thought of the prospect. Her arrival would surely raise his spirits. Hers as well, perhaps.

The snoring cat on the hearth sputtered, then twitched its paws, stretched, yawned, and fell back asleep again. Harold returned with a palm-sized parcel tied in a string. He already appeared a little less apprehensive.

"There's two heaping pinches of valerian here, ma'am. Stir it all well in water and swallow on an empty stomach. You should have a nice, comfortable rest. Or as comfortable as you can be, given the environment."

Elaine thanked him and handed the apothecary his money. The clink of coins brought back even more of his prior openness, a trait that, like his inclination to avoid being disagreeable, seemed to come naturally to the fellow.

"You know," Harold said, bringing his finger to his chin, "now that I think on it, I had another customer not that long ago who said he was on his way to the Citadel."

"Really?"

"Yes. It struck me as very queer at the time, but he had business down there, too, apparently. Pleasant fellow, though too much on the thin side if he were to ask me. The gentleman required a particular incandescent, so he could do his reading, he said."

"What was his name?"

"Don't recall that he ever gave it to me," Harold shook his head to himself. "But he reminded me of some very good advice I heard as a boy—"

Before the apothecary could finish his thought, Harold and Elaine both turned at the same moment. They fell silent at the noise of distant rumbling coming from outside. It was the peal of thunder, little more than a murmur, rolling towards them out of the east. The cat picked up its head, shook itself, and clambered down from where it was perched, disappearing in the shadows of the apothecary.

"Finally," Harold beamed. "A little rain! Maybe now some of this trash will get cleared away."

The mist fell in gentle, rolling waves, a light sprinkle that washed across the courtyard outside the Court of Common Corrections. It was a rare, though not unheard of, event in the climes near Cowans Chasm. Every few months or so, a gust of air would billow up from the void beneath the Spine bridge and carry a cloud of moisture, and the residents of the fortress would be treated to something like a rain shower, here, inside their darkened cavern. A cool misting, enough to shroud the gulleystar lamps, and leave a few puddles behind, and make everything slippery. These "storms," as they were called, were usually greeted with squeals of delight from the handful of children who would take it as an excuse to abandon their tasks and play, while the older carters and porters would fall into arguments over when, precisely, was the last storm. They were the closest thing to a holiday most of the denizens of the courtyard would ever have. Most times.

Elaine tilted her head back and let the moisture fall across her face. She blinked the wetness from her eyelashes, but then she frowned. The faces shadowed in the amber glow of gulleystars of the courtyard were all dire, the men's gruff voices hushed; no one laughed or spoke above a whisper, so that silence hung like a weight within the cloud. For some reason, no one welcomed this "storm." If anything, the sudden appearance of weather in the Mountain had charged an already ominous air with even more foreboding.

Elaine scanned the courtyard. There were towers of forgotten crates everywhere she looked, piled in no semblance of order across the cobblestone grounds all the way to the outer walls. Food and wares had been piling up for days, and no one knew where any of it was supposed to be delivered, what should be withheld, or what was to be done with the remains. Just yesterday, a group of clerks had fallen into a fistfight over whose records were in better order. While the caravan carts, the few that were still permitted to move, now proceeded at a crawl. The whole courtyard was in shambles. And now it was being doused with rain.

Elaine was so fixated upon the strange sensation of rain falling inside a cavern, she didn't notice that Jonathan had joined her on the back porch of the courthouse.

"That last defendant," he quipped, drawing his magistrate's hood over his thinning hair, "might take this as a sign from the gods. Of some sort. Perhaps they heard her prayers after all."

Elaine tried to keep from grimacing. It was a sarcastic jibe about a glazier Jonathan had just sentenced to the Tombs. She had been a sad, lonely old woman who did nothing more than harbor an even sadder, lonelier ragger who had once been heard to profess her faith in prayer. The glazier, despite having found solace in the ragger's friendship, promptly denounced the ragger in court, so that she would spend only six months in prison for her offense. Such was the Commonwealth's magnanimity.

"There's still plenty of superstition down here," she answered, "despite the Commonwealth's training."

"Yes, yes," Jonathan waved a dismissive hand, "your 'superstition's not the same as religion' defense. If they weren't synonyms, and if your client's roommate hadn't been caught proselytizing, I might have agreed with you and dismissed the charge. Don't look so vexed. Six months was the absolute bottom under the law."

"She'll be dead in a week," Elaine avoided Jonathan's eyes.

Jonathan said nothing, as Elaine watched the porters and carters laboring in the half-lit grounds, moving a stack of boxes from one side of the courtyard to the other.

"Ah, it looks like the storm is breaking," Jonathan said, his voice brightening. "Shall we make a run for your cart?"

The cloud of mist that had suddenly wafted up had indeed begun to dissipate, the droplets subsided, and Jonathan hurried Elaine from the porch, across a stretch of open cobblestones to where her private carriage waited. A bailiff ran out a few steps behind them, hollering to the workers in the way to clear a lane.

Whether it was from the sudden exercise, or the subsidence of the dampness, by the time she reached the carriage, Elaine felt a little better.

"Your charge is here, carters," Jonathan announced when they reached the side of the four-wheeled covered cart. From the sturdy build and polished lacquer and the ox hitched to its front, it was so obviously a Crest conveyance that all the other carters had instinctively left it a wide berth. Two men appeared from within, swung down a wooden step, and opened the door for Elaine.

Elaine took Jonathan's hand.

"Sorry I got upset about the glazier."

"You're a zealous advocate."

"And you're an impressive jurist." Elaine shook her hair, sending a spray of droplets around her. She found herself smiling at the sight of the stooped, bookish magistrate, sopping wet and still holding her hand. "You made some brilliant rulings this morning, Judge Acacia."

"The ones that went your way, you mean?"

"I said 'some,' didn't I? No, in all seriousness. I was very impressed. It's nice to have the old Jonathan back."

Jonathan bowed and met her smile with a self-deprecating roll of his shoulders.

"I have you to thank."

"Oh?"

"You valiantly ignored my pleas for wine."

Elaine bit the bottom of her lip, unsure whether this was gratitude, or sarcasm, or recrimination. It was so hard to sift through what the man's japes were meant to mean. He could be absolutely enigmatic at times. As if sensing her uncertainty, Jonathan gave her fingers a friendly squeeze as he helped her into the carriage seat.

"I'm being sincere. It had gotten a tad ... out of hand. Being in my cups. But now, with my head clear and my book to work on ... I am finding my muse."

Elaine leaned out from the window of the cart. Her dress bunched underneath her chin and sopped up the line of moisture clinging to the sill. She brushed at it without breaking his gaze:

"I'm glad. I so prefer sober Jonathan over sotted Jonathan."

"I think I'm coming around to him as well ... Still a cynic, mind you."

"We'll work on that next."

A line of men bearing iron-bound caskets on their bare shoulders came to a halt immediately behind Elaine's carriage where they drifted about in a directionless circle. At the rear, two clerks were screaming over one another, each ordering the porters to advance in opposite directions. Elaine made a face:

"It's certainly gotten lively here lately."

"Oh, the fort's an utter mess. There's been some sort of trouble out by the Gutters. Fighting apparently. No one knows who's doing what about it." Jonathan shook the sleeves of his robe dry. "What with every-one on pins and needles about the new Plan—it's helter-skelter for those of us who find themselves stuck on this side of the Spine." He sighed. "Sure you can't stay for another docket? There's no knowing what you'll miss down here."

One of the porters in the rear was bawling at a woman in a sash as she wrote a note on him in a furious scrawl. The rest of the group watched mutely, blocking anyone else from getting around them. Jona-than's bailiffs were doing their best to sort out the mess, but the murmurs were becoming increasingly irate.

"Your mother has summoned me," Elaine replied with mock gravity.

"Ah. Dear Mother. And the never-ending nuptials to negotiate. Well, we'd better get you on your way then. My best to her and to Michael. No need for a kiss to give to them; we Acacias never share affection with each other. At least you'll enjoy a respite from this bedlam in my little corner of the Crag. I can envy you for that. Goodbye, Elaine."

Jonathan shut the door for her and tapped the roof to let the carters know to pull forward. A flick of a whip and the ox soon had the carriage on its way.

She held her hand out of the window to wave farewell. As she watched, Jonathan's figure gradually diminished into the muddied blur of the courtyard, a hazy shadow, then it was gone. Blended into the gloom of the Crag. She reached in her pocket for the phial she had brought from the apothecary, took a long draught of sedative, rested her head against a cushion, and slowly slipped into sleep.

Regina rose stiffly from her seat, an irritated expression piercing through her attempt to appear congenial. Standing behind her, a middle-aged man in a commissar's yellow cloak was packing up a satchel of papers, an inkpot, and a stick of wax that was still smoking at one end.

"Elaine, so good to see you," Regina extended a cold, wrinkled hand, which Elaine dutifully grasped in her own. "Sit, have a glass of wine. I'm sure you could use refreshment after your journey."

"Thank you," Elaine replied.

The commissar asked if he could be of any further service, and Regina curtly shooed him off. As Elaine settled in her chair, she caught the man stealing a fleeting glimpse at her. She recognized him from somewhere—a prior proceeding at court. A notary, that's what he was. Before he disappeared, she saw him smirk in a way that struck Elaine as both overly familiar and somewhat distasteful.

Now alone, Regina and Elaine could exchange the requisite pleasantries. It wasn't an unpleasant tedium, both women's table banter being well-honed. The topic of Elaine's long absence—she had not seen Regina since the Amphitheatre—was carefully avoided. With nothing more than a prolonged sip from her glass, Regina conveyed to Elaine that she knew, understood entirely, the reason why Elaine had declined to see her.

Which gave Elaine a small sense of relief. Elaine's pretexts, her excuses, and apologies, as thin as they were, for avoiding Regina were at her uncle's command, who, in the only letter he had sent Elaine in months, commanded her in no uncertain terms to avoid Regina while he worked through the final points of the marriage negotiations. But Regina's invitation yesterday—hand-delivered to her while she was delivering closing arguments in the Crag's court—had been even more succinct:

"My dear, you are to come at once to my home. Tomorrow after lunch. No excuses. Your uncle sends his regards."

So here she was. Sitting at a table, drinking wine with the richest woman in Boaz, who might or might not become her future mother-in-law.

"What shall we toast to?" Regina asked, pressing the flesh of her fingertips together. She reached across the table to refill Elaine's glass in an exaggerated gesture of service.

"More rain?" Elaine offered.

"Oh, I was thinking something more momentous." She paused as if to collect her thoughts, and Elaine noticed an unusual glimmer stirring within Regina's dark eyes. Her glass extended, lifted high above the table, and she announced:

"To Michael Acacia and Elaine Temple. A long life of happiness, together—in Jachin."

Their glasses clinked, and Elaine took a suitable draught, all the while watching Regina with some puzzlement. It seemed Regina could contain herself no longer. She began producing a set of papers, scores of pages, filled with flowing handwriting Elaine recognized from legal documents and piled them on the tabletop before her plate. Everywhere on the papers, Elaine saw, the formal font the commissar scribes carefully prepared had been scratched through, interlineated, handwritten over, erased, and re-written with crimped lines jutting out at precarious angles. The documents were shuffled through, and Regina found what she had been looking for. With an air of solemnity, she carefully laid it in front of Elaine.

It was the concluding paragraphs for all enforceable contracts in the Crest, and it ended with Regina's name and Elaine's uncle's. There were two, circular wax seals: one amber, the color of a Steward; the other, just affixed, was red and still glistening. The scripted letters, "and shall govern themselves accordingly," were curled like a snake poised to strike adjacent to the signers' marks.

"Your uncle is a hard negotiator," Regina remarked in a way that did not strike Elaine as very complimentary. "As is befitting, given the treasure you are," she added quickly.

Elaine dipped her head demurely and thanked Regina, who continued:

"I am a hard negotiator, too."

"Then—it's finished."

A placid smile spread across Regina's face:

"They are finalizing the documents now," she said and took Elaine's hands in hers. Her skin felt cold, dry, like the papers that were scattered all around. "We shall solemnize the matter in the Citadel. And then you'll be married."

Elaine gazed down at her fingers, joined together with Regina's. Or trapped, it was hard to tell. She realized her mother-in-law was waiting for her to say something.

"I'm so thrilled," Elaine remarked, looking up at last.

"As are we. The positions in Jachin sound most prominent."

"Positions?"

Regina gave her a wry look. "For both of my sons. Michael's will commence once his assignment in the Inner Keep is complete. Two or three years at the most, I'm assured. Jonathan's will follow once he finishes some matter he has in that Crag court. The details there were rather hard to follow. There's some level of confidence involved, but my lawyers assure me the promise is enforceable. A seat on the bench in Jachin awaits him."

"So, who do I marry first, Jonathan or Michael?"

Regina let out an exasperated sniff:

"You are only marrying Michael. How could you possibly—oh. Oh. You were being clever."

"Forgive me, Mother. My uncle often says I'm glib. But it's only with those I love."

"Not at all. I had forgotten about your sense of humor. Though Jonathan has mentioned it to me before. It is unusual, I'll allow, the bargain we have finally reached. But it was the only way to solve the problem."

"What problem was that?"

"I have two sons," Regina explained, "but there's only one of you. That was why the negotiating took so long. And why I paid—I shudder to think how much it's been—two attorneys to draw up this mountain of documents."

It had never occurred to Elaine that Regina would also try to secure an appointment for Jonathan through her match with Michael. But it was an obvious aim. There were, after all, only so many available young ladies who carried connections enough for the Acacias' notice; and Jonathan seemed unlikely to pursue the few there were. Regina must have paid a fortune.

"I'm sure both of your sons will be eager to assume their new roles in Jachin," Elaine said.

"So will I."

Regina let out a long breath and loosened the silk shawl that was clasped about her neck. She drained her glass in a single gulp, and when she set it down, the faintest glow of pink broke across her pallid cheeks:

"I need a holiday. My vineyards, Jachin, anyplace but here."

"I should think you would," Elaine gestured at the contract papers.

"Oh, it's not just that. There's all this commotion in Boaz lately, this pot-stirring, and from people who ought to know better. Just the other day, I found one of these," she pointed angrily at a folded handbill at the far end of the table, which Elaine recognized from the town center, "it was pilfered into my mail. My mail! Ninety-five propositions for the new Plan. The temerity. As if the Stewards needed advising from a bunch of freeloaders. No, don't read it, my dear, it's filled with the most odious, inflammatory nonsense. It will only make you angry. I should like some respite from all of this for a nice, long while."

"Michael and I would be honored to host you in Jachin once we're settled." It was, of course, the appropriate thing to say.

"The honor would mine," Regina gave her a pat. "And now that I've finished with the business of your marriage—the money will be yours. And your uncle's. I am sure you will want to thank him when you see him again."

"I don't know if I'll be able to."

"Oh, you'll see him soon enough, I think. With all the back-and-forth he and I have had lately, I gather that the Stewards must have finally finished the new Plan. Probably making some final modifications, and then it will be released, and everything will return to normal."

CHAPTER TWENTY-EIGHT

LAINE WATCHED A sweating, portly man standing on top of a table desk with his hands cupped to his mouth. Despite the scrap of scarf he had tied around the bottom of his face, she could make out the angry hue of purple in his cheeks. He sounded winded and hoarse from shouting, and the outfit he wore was caked with mud. He was perched near a balustrade at the top of the flight of stairs on the edge of Boaz, surrounded by a hundred or so marchers who had congregated at the landing. The stairway led down to the High Road, which seemed to be the crowd's eventual destination.

It was mid-afternoon and uncomfortably muggy. At the moment, the man was flapping his arms about in a square-shaped garment that made him look very much like a limp, beige sail. He was also shouting, Elaine could hear his voice over the murmur of his companions, who, wearing similar garb, seemed to be ignoring him. There was an angry buzz of voices that oscillated between arguments, cheers, chants, and speeches that no one—at times, not even the speakers—were listening to. From what Elaine could gather, they were going to march down the High Road ... to someplace, that much they agreed upon, to present their views ... to someone, someone of suitable authority, whoever that might be.

Apart from the marchers, separated by the propriety of some yards of space and the pretense that they were not truly paying attention to the boisterous crowd of masked youngsters dressed like harlequins, or trying to hear any of their speeches or read their homemade signs, a score of Boaz's citizens watched the spectacle. For that was what it was. And though they should not have indulged what was an unlicensed, unsanctioned mob, the gapers' curiosity had gotten the better of their sense.

Elaine, along with Regina, having rented a cart that morning to shop for linens in town, found themselves among the onlookers. Regina tried to lift her bulk from her seat, bumped her head against the covering, and glared at the throng mingling around the balustrade:

"Blaine," she addressed the commissar teamster who was driving their wagon. "Bring us a bit closer to the portico—I'd like to smell the jasmine blooming by that lattice over there."

"Yes'm," he hid his smirk and stirred the donkeys to pull them a few yards closer to the crowd. As the animals' hooves squelched through the mud, Elaine could hear the makings of a ragged chant:

"*Hear their voice! Hear their voice!*" But not everyone in the crowd seemed to agree with that choice of slogan, so the chant soon evolved into, "*Let them free!*" which, by the time Regina's cart had come to a stop, became "*Leave them be!*"

Regina shook her head in disgust:

"I don't recognize any of those persons. Thank goodness."

"No," Elaine agreed. "You wouldn't."

"They couldn't possibly have credentials for this."

"I'm sure they don't. They've not been appointed to anything."

"Then what business do they have out here making all this ruckus?"

"If I understand their position," Elaine tried to assume her lawyerly manner, if only to keep from laughing at the absurdity of the sight before them, "they feel this is the most suitable way, the only way, to get the Stewards' attention. To have their views considered."

"By foisting their views upon us? By accosting us with divisive, inflammatory speeches? We shouldn't have to bear such verbal assaults."

"Well. We could always just—leave. Or ignore them."

Regina sniffed at the notion but said nothing. They sat in their cart in silence, the two ladies and their driver, each striving to catch the strains of yelling and conversation that carried over from the crowd. The donkeys hitched to the cart swished their tails, more interested in the tufts of grass peeking through the muddy ground.

The scarfed man dressed in a sail was still balanced on top of a table. He was waving a poster of some sort with a hand-drawn Commonwealth's emblem on it that was flanked on either side by the words, "UNITE" and "GUILD." In the flurry of activity, it was hard to discern, but he looked familiar.

"And what does that sign say, the one that girl is carrying?" Regina broke the silence and pointed, "down near the front, she looks like a commissar, of all things. I can't make it out."

Elaine squinted:

"It says, 'We Serve Unity—To Make the Crag and Crest Truly Free.'"

That set off a flurry of escalating hisses and exhalations, culminating with Regina leaning out of the carriage window to raise her voice, as if she were addressing the whole gathering from within her curtained, cushioned bench. Elaine was shocked; until this moment, she had never seen the woman display an emotion. The driver spun around on his bench to eagerly nod his agreement with Regina's vehemence.

"What stuff!" Regina spat. "What do any of you know of service. I've sacrificed a husband and two sons who have devoted their lives in service to the Commonwealth—"

Her voice cracked from strain, she coughed and gave up the effort. Regina sat back in her chair, fluttering a handkerchief to cool her temper. No one, it seemed, had noticed her hectoring.

"Honestly," she continued once she had recovered herself, "I've got a good mind to send a note straightaway to your uncle, and—" she froze, dropped her handkerchief in her lap, and leaned forward. Elaine saw the displeased expression that had resided over her features turn into venom. "Is that," Regina whispered through her clenched teeth, "*Gregory* flapping his hands about in that ridiculous outfit on top of that clerk's desk? It looks just like him."

Elaine already knew that it was. The idiot had unwrapped the scarf from his face so that he could mop the sweat away. He would already be noted. Elaine had to bite her tongue to keep from laughing aloud.

"I can't tell," she pretended to squint very closely. "He does look similar."

"If anyone of my circle is a part of this-this-this—" Regina stammered for a suitably pejorative word, "this *rabble*, well, they won't remain in my circle any longer."

"I'll go and find out," Elaine said, sliding down from the wagon.

"What? Oh, my dear, you mustn't. What if you're seen? Let the appropriate channels deal with this. There are commissars for this kind of thing."

Grateful to be out of the carriage, and feeling a trifle giddy, Elaine flashed a bright smile back at her soon to be mother-in-law:

"I'll be very careful, Mother. Just a quick look, and I'll come right back." Before Regina could say anything more, Elaine gave a wave and raced to join the throng of people. A few chanting marchers at the periphery paused to glare at her appearance. Elaine heard a few sneers of "bourgeoisie" and "troglodyte" but paid it no mind, as she elbowed her way into what felt like an inconspicuous place for a crowd—somewhere not quite in the middle, but far enough in that she could blend with the bodies around her.

The heat, and worse, the smell from all the pressed bodies was nauseating. The latter struck her as something between must, sweat, and spilled wine. It was hard to see much past the shoulders and heads in her vicinity, but a few scenes struck her: a bearded teenager in a commissar's robe and a woman Elaine thought she recognized as a librarian scarcely concealed within the folds of a Commonwealth flag, their legs entwined, very close to coupling, if they were not already; two sisters slurring curses in each other's faces, over what, it was impossible to tell; a middle-aged woman defiantly reading a poem about the plight in the Crag that only "the noble, native Craggie," she claimed, could bear witness to; a good many vapid faces, simply seeking direction. Many throughout the crowd contented themselves with beating on bucket drums, shouting slogans, drinking (a great deal of that was going around), cracking jokes, and everywhere Elaine looked, circulating papers. Handbills, palm cards, posters, signs, bundled scrolls, the pages were floating across the gathering like falling leaves, to be left on the ground trampled and unread. The supply of paper must have been inexhaustible.

"What are we waiting for?!" a girl who had called Elaine a troglodyte suddenly screeched. "To the Mountain! Let's march!"

"No, we need to wait for Judge Cloud!"

"Our movement waits for no one!"

A few people bustled into one another, as if they might start the long descent down the steps, but the bulk of those gathered remained in a loitering mood. Someone else responded that they ought to be heading to Jachin instead since that was where the Stewards were. That idea was answered with an equal mixture of applause and derision. From the clerk's desk, Gregory waved his scarf in the air for attention:

"Brothers, sisters, enough of this!"

Gregory had never sounded so rasp—or looked so pleased, Elaine thought. Despite his sullied appearance, the man seemed positively elated, standing up there on a platform on his tip-toes. He had given up his attempt to rewrap his scarf into a suitable mask but covered his head with another grotesque imitation of Crag clothing, what was meant to be a rancher's brimmed hat. Elaine drew the hem of her cloak over her hair so that there was no danger he would recognize her.

"We have already resolved, the Guild has already voted—" Gregory started.

"To hell with your little clique," an old man shouted over him.

"—we have *decided*—by the leaders of all of the diverse factions represented here—that we are going to march on the Citadel. No, we will *not* open that for debate again. The Citadel. That's where we are going."

"That'll show 'em!"

"Yes. And when we arrive, I will personally present the ninety-five propositions to—"

"—Ninety-nine!"

"Ninety—*five*," Gregory articulated warningly, "which have been thoroughly discussed, drawn up, approved, and sealed." He waved a bound bundle of papers that, if only by virtue of the fact they had not been discarded on the ground, retained an aura of significance. "I shall present and publish our letter, once I'm admitted before a suitably credentialed official of the Citadel." He looked around him with a satisfied expression. "They will have to accept it. Look at the solidarity I have with this entire collective of thinkers—and, of course, all of the workers, as well."

He tried to continue his address, but then another argument broke out over who should introduce who to whom once they reached the Citadel, whether the propositions were, in form, a letter, a communique, or a demarche, by what right Gregory had taken it on himself to assume the role of spokesman, and whether that was even what he was.

Elaine let out a yawn. She had hoped she might catch a glimpse of Judge Cloud, but no … this would have been too much, even for a man of his patience. No doubt he would have given a suitable excuse for his absence from what, he would have known, would devolve into a carnival. As indeed it already had.

Nothing these people said was truly inflammatory, or subversive, or divisive—ridiculous, yes, but nothing more than that. A farce, even if she was the only one who saw it for the silly diversion it was.

These people were simply bored.

And now Elaine found she was growing bored, too.

She glanced around at the motley collection one last time, shared with them a sardonic half-smile, and then made her way back to Regina's wagon, and what, she knew, would be an onslaught of inquiries feigned to be affronted.

The High Road was beset with mire caked across its pavers, a slurry of dust, grime, standing puddles of rainwater, briars, and mud. In the places where the gutters had become choked with weeds, tiny tempests of mosquitoes hovered through the air like black clouds, the only clouds to be seen. Neither the sun's relentless blaze nor the shining orange dragonflies that occasionally darted through their swarms would chase the insects away. They were gorging on a slow-moving feast.

Gregory slapped the back of his pinkened neck and swore to himself. Like what remained of his entourage, he was sullen, dusted, overexerted, and thoroughly bug-bitten. But he tried to sound heartening as he called out over his shoulder:

"Not much farther now."

There was only a small grumbling in reply. The Solidarity Guild, the thirty or so who had not abandoned the march already, tramped on beneath the merciless sun and plague of mosquitoes.

The stairway to Boaz was now in the gray of the horizon behind them. The Great Dome before the Citadel's Outer Keep was only beginning to come into view up ahead. The rows of cedar trees that bounded either side of the roadway offered the ragged line of marchers little shade, for the sun was only starting to descend from its afternoon peak.

In truth, only a few miles separated Boaz and the Citadel, and, were it not for the stifling weather and the mudslides, it would have been a manageable walk across fairly level ground and an occasional bridge. But so few of these coffeehouse thinkers were accustomed to exercise that the exertion, combined with the many discomforts, proved more than their mettle. The chanting had long since come to an end. So, too, the kettle drums and all the heavier signs they had brought with them were gone, discarded along the roadside in the wildflowers.

Gregory held a brisk pace, though, still at the lead of the band, plastered with sweat, his eyes set firmly on the road ahead. A lichen-covered mile marker peeked between a patch of dandelions, and he grinned in triumph.

"Last mile," he said. "Hold out those signs now, for all to see."

It was an odd request. Since the time they had left the fork in the road at Boaz, they had only come across one other person, a partly lame, mostly drunken old commissar, trying to goad an even lamer, older ox, across the High Road to get it to a slaughterhouse. The entire mob accosted the poor fellow with pamphlets, urging, demanding, that he join their march; but he had no leave, he cried, and, thinking they might make a note of him, he staggered off into the foothills, leaving his ox to graze contentedly among the wildflowers. They met one else until they reached the Citadel's outskirts. Still, a few posters were unfurled.

The road began a steady, winding slope downward straight into the Mountainside looming before them, as the dome grew more prominent. They came across a small village of brick houses clustered around a byway, where Gregory met an innkeeper who was only too eager to sell his cheapest vintages at the richest prices. He paid out the last of the coins he had collected before setting out, and the marchers' spirits received a momentary lift. Inside a stuffy common room, amphorae were drained, charred steaks were devoured, and, slowly, the chants of "Unity" and "Our all for all," stirred once more.

Gregory took advantage of a private room to remove his soiled "worker" garb and change into a better suit of clothes, also procured thanks to the resourceful innkeeper. It pained him, Gregory explained, but he needed to don an elite's attire now that the prospect of gaining an elite audience—a real audience—was drawing nearer.

By the time the Solidarity Guild took its leave, a crescent moon was peeking over the shingled rooftops of the hamlet, the first stars were emerging around its radius, and an evening breeze had begun to stir. The marchers, now refreshed and congratulating themselves on the hardships they had endured for the sake of solidarity, were ready to press their case. The posters and flags—those they still had with them—unfurled once more, the little crowd walked the remaining half-mile into the outer plaza of the Citadel, and took up a new chant:

"Listen, listen, here we come,
Hold the Plan—our time has come!"

Gregory glided a few feet ahead of everyone, admiring the tall pillars that held the open dome aloft, all the while practicing what would be his introductory speech to whichever official he first came across.

He came to a jarring halt when he stubbed his toe on a terrazzo step. A stray cloud had covered the moonlight and briefly set the entire plaza in darkness. As Gregory rubbed his foot, he noticed, for the first time, that none of the lamp posts were lit.

"Someone's missed his job, there ought to be a note made."

None of the marchers had thought to bring along lanterns or torches, of course. Gregory's head swiveled about, and then another curious observation came to his attention.

All the daises, the porticos, the great stage in its center of the plaza, and every one of the sundry little alleys and throughways they had passed, were all deserted. A few cats slinked about the edge of the shadows, an occasional breeze stirred the leaves of the trees overhead, but otherwise, the entire plaza was wrapped in stillness.

The small crowd stood gaping at the empty square, the buzz of wine leaving the group with a pleasant if now slightly unsettled feeling.

"No matter," Gregory said. "I planned for this very contingency. I know just the place to go. Come, my friends!"

He led the marchers across a broad, dimly illuminated plaza. Storefront signs creaked in the wind, the only other sound beside their feet shuffling uncertainly over the terrazzo. They wound their way through a snaking alley that ended in the bailey of the Outer Keep. The façade of the fortress was framed by the Mountainside behind it, a sheet of moss-covered rock that jutted straight into the air. It was the barrier fixed between the Crest and the Crag and Quarter, and, as befitting its proximity to the other realms, was a place seldom traveled. Gregory stretched a pleased expression on his face and looked up at the battlements.

The Citadel's windows and archers' slits were veiled in blackness and not a light could be seen anywhere in the great gatehouse. The portcullis was up, but the doors within were closed and locked.

The group from Boaz stared at the silent fortress and by now the realization had settled over them: they had taken a stage without an audience.

For a long while, no one said a word. They listened to chirping insects, and the mindlessly repetitive racket of one sleepless mockingbird, and a soft, eerie moan from the wind blowing through the apertures of the Great Dome above.

Gregory felt uneasy. But the prospect of losing his following, now that he had one, was one he could not bear. He took the matter in hand:

"Friends," he said, "it seems the Citadel has closed a bit earlier than usual today. But no matter! Our voices will still be heard—even if we have to wake the powers that be to listen!"

Gregory paused expectantly, but hearing only a smattering of unenthused claps, he spun on his heel and floated up the steps to the doorway, doing his best to ensure that the coattails from his new outfit bobbed importantly behind his purposeful strides. He went straight towards the crumbling archway of the Citadel's Outer Keep.

There he found two seamless blocks of what was probably the last ironwood on all the Mountain. Doors, twenty feet high, made of finely grained wood from a tree that had been extinct for over a century. He had once heard they had been gifted from the dwarves, long ago, when the first priests came to power. True to their namesake, the doors' wood was as strong as tempered steel and held a dull, metallic luster. Gregory had never been so close to them before. Though it was nearly pitch black beneath the arch, he detected a strange, phosphorescent glow emanating from the wood. It shed enough light for him to make out gothic etchings, as ancient as the timbers, carved into the ironwood's grain to bestow a name upon each door, just above their rings:

On the left, Truth; its companion on the right, Dread.

Gregory leaned his face closer, sniffing, and thought he could sense a ring of scorch marks and dents—scars from the Overthrow, he suspected—the only blemishes that marred an otherwise perfect surface.

Gregory felt small in the doors' presence. It was a fleeting sensation and one that he did not like in the least. It made him hasten his performance.

With a ceremonious flourish, he reached into his coat and unraveled the document he had borne next to his breast since the journey from Boaz. He presented it to his companions with the gravest solemnity. Then he broke its seal with a loud rip, and began the speech he had memorized with a clipped, thundering voice that, he was certain, sounded most authoritative:

"Out of service to the Commonwealth and from a desire to enlighten it, I, Gregory Gables, Master of Arts and independent lecturer at Boaz, intend to defend the following propositions and to dispute on them at any place. Therefore, I ask that those who cannot be present and dispute with me orally shall do so in their absence by letter. In the name of my Guild, and all those in solidarity therewith, and on behalf of all of the workers we deign to serve, I hereby deliver said propositions unto the Citadel."

He reached again into his breast pocket, and a gasp arose from the small crowd, which brought a delighted grin to Gregory's lips. This final touch, he had thought up at the inn, in case no one of suitable prestige could be found. In his other hand, he now held aloft a hammer and a nail. He thought a moment, made up his mind that Truth would be more apropos for the demonstration, and brought the document and the nail to the wood's surface. The door felt frigid against his palms, but he managed not to flinch, as he lined up the top of the nail with the head of his hammer.

The hammer rang out nine times. The cling of metal echoed loudly from whatever lay beyond the doorway, captivating everyone with the haunting, bell-like reverberations it made. On the tenth swing, Gregory missed the head and struck his thumb, and everything he held tumbled to the ground. No sooner had he crumpled down to gather what he had dropped, but the ring to the right-hand door turned a fraction of an inch. Gregory could hear a lock and brace being worked from the other side, and as he struggled to get back to his feet, Dread swung inward.

A tall, sensible-looking gentleman stood in a glow of torchlight.

He had a high forehead of combed brown hair and was dressed plainly, though with ample sense of good refinement. The only adornment on his person was a token that hung from a necklace he wore about his open neck. It was a golden seal of the Commonwealth that Gregory recognized in an instant as one of only thirty-two in all the Crest. An armed party of wardens and High Guard soldiers, all dressed in black, stood a short distance in the corridor behind him, but the man held his arms out wide with welcome.

"Master Gables, my good fellow," he said, regarding Gregory closely, and then, as if suddenly noticing a mob of people, he added: "I should say, my good people. I'm pleased to be at your service."

Gregory's mouth fell open. Behind him, the marchers stood mutely, their banners sagging in the dust. Gregory tried to gather his thoughts, but he stammered, clutching his papers close to his chest, as if for protection. The man smiled at Gregory in a way that was both singularly disarming and disorienting in the same instance.

"Forgive me," the man continued, now only addressing Gregory, "I should introduce myself."

"S-Steward Temple," Gregory said, sputtering over his words. "An-an honor, sir. An *honor*. No idea—" Gregory dropped everything once more to thrust out his hand, which the steward took in his own with the lightest clasp.

"The honor is mine," Temple replied. "How fortunate I had business in the Citadel. Now I get to meet you in person." Then, his smile broadening, he addressed the gathering. "We've heard of your concerns and your movement. Your channels have been rather unorthodox, but we hear you wish to proffer some novel ideas for our Plan. We are intrigued." He regarded the document that had tumbled from Gregory's hands. "May I?"

At that moment, from that simple request, Gregory experienced the ineffable sense of rapture of having his work acknowledged by one who, above all else that could be said of him, truly mattered. A Steward had asked for his writing, Gregory's writing—he had stooped down to retrieve it himself, and now, he was *reading* it.

In the orange glow of his men's torches, Temple's lips moved, ever so slightly, as his eyes flickered back and forth in the dim light. They were hazel eyes. Gregory watched them hungrily. Once, Temple let out a muffled cough, which, Gregory was certain, was in response to the forty-third proposition, one he had drafted personally. It sounded like a favorable cough.

Temple refolded the paper and handed it to one of his attendants, the concentration in his face replaced by his pleasant aspect once more:

"My, my. Ninety-five propositions. A veritable bouquet of ideas."

The attendant let out a chuckle, but a sharp glance from the Steward conveyed this was no time to jest.

"And your group," Temple continued, "you seek to—how did you put it? —'advance the common good of the Commonwealth,' by presenting us with all these ideas. My, my, indeed." He clicked his tongue thoughtfully and then broached what appeared to be a more delicate matter: "I can't help but observe that it has always been the Stewards' policy to discourage provocative discourse about our planning. We would prefer to dampen the public clamor that surrounds our deliberations, as much as we can, so that—"

"Absolutely, absolutely," Gregory held his hands out imploringly, "we meant nothing improper, good Steward, nothing untoward whatsoever. Farthest thing from our minds. Wouldn't dream of disturbing that sound policy." All of the speeches, the turns of phrase he had memorized during his walk on the High Road had tumbled out of his head, and Gregory simply could not cobble any of them back together. But he was desperate to hold onto this man's presence, whatever it would take. "No one has more respect for the need to maintain unencumbered deliberations over one's work than me. The experts need room to be experts. Absolutely. I would never—"

"Allow me to finish, Master Gables," Temple smiled. "It is, as I said, an old policy of ours, which we keep for the sake of good order. But there is another, equally important policy we hold. If I may quote it?"

"But of course! By all means!"

The Steward dipped his head.

"Letting a hundred flowers blossom and a hundred schools of thought contend is the policy for promoting progress and a flourishing culture in our Commonwealth."

Gregory nearly gasped. Not only would the Steward hear their presentation, but the propositions would be considered—on an equal footing—in their deliberations. What else could he have meant? Gregory's thoughts turned to Dr. Karl, and oh, how he wished that pufferfish were here to witness this triumph. The paper, Gregory's paper, there in the Steward's thoughtful grasp, on the verge of being considered, perhaps even cited. His chin tilted up, and he spoke in a slightly choked voice:

"That has always been my sentiment, as well, Steward."

Temple took Gregory by the elbow. "We will take counsel with you," he said, "and with your group. Come inside out of the night air. All of you. It's late, I know, but our work is important. We must discuss these proposals of yours and give them the consideration they deserve. You will all have a part to play in the Tenth Plan."

There was a spontaneous cheer that pierced the night air, as the marchers, now brimming with excitement at what was about to transpire, rushed past the Outer Keep's transom. They held their heads high, a hurried babble of slogans, and conversations, and plots passing noisily among them. The High Guard and the wardens cleared a lane in the corridor for their passage, ignoring the condescending glares some in the crowd cast in their direction, and followed them quietly at a respectful distance from behind. Gregory was at the lead, arm in arm with Steward Temple, talking rapidly, his voice fading down the stone halls as the party disappeared within the Citadel.

One, however, had lingered behind in the shadows.

A young man in a black and yellow uniform, a feather perfectly angled from a buttonhole and a fine sword hanging from his belt, craned his head to listen down the corridor. When the last of their noise had faded, he checked the plaza outside. And seeing no one about, he pulled hard on the edges of Truth and Dread to close them both shut. It usually took two to move the wood's weight, but Lieutenant Acacia was strapping enough to manage the weight on his own. He paused to catch his breath, then he turned the bolt of an iron lock and all was quiet outside the Citadel once more.

CHAPTER TWENTY-NINE

THE FIRST WAVE of sickness always hit Jonathan the hardest. A foul belch welled up from the bottom of his stomach and made him wince. He had to swallow, hard, the vomit scalding his throat.

It would pass soon enough, though. It always did. This was how good medicine was supposed to work, he reminded himself. Any apothecary would tell you: the harder the medicine, the better the cure.

Jonathan slouched in his chair, a half-empty glass of water clutched tightly in his hand, and shut his eyes. It made no difference. His chamber was in near-perfect darkness. Only the lingering sparks of crimson shimmering behind his fingers in the water shed a faint glow of light about him, like from falling stars. The last traces of the redcaps dissolving into water.

Water.

Such a readily apparent solution, in hindsight. It had been born out of desperation—necessity really. Mother had been true to her word: there had not been a drop of wine to be had in the Crag since his return. Not even the smugglers peddling the vintners' dross to the other side of the Spine had dared to cross Regina.

With no wine, Jonathan could not partake of his redcaps. Without that dilution, they were poison; that was what that old dolt in Boaz, the one that had sold him this trove of redcaps, had warned. All those wonderful spices just sitting in his bag, wanting to be drunk, and he couldn't have so much as a sliver because there was no wine. Jonathan had only a very dim recollection of his first days back at court. It had been intolerable.

Ah, but when a situation truly becomes intolerable—one will not tolerate it. One will find a resolution.

The resolution for Jonathan presented itself quite by accident. He gave his glass a little swish, causing the light within it to burst brighter for a moment as he reflected on that day.

It had been near the end of a long docket. They had all been long since his return. The commissars were prosecuting every infraction to the hilt, bent on filling up the Tombs, apparently, and there were never enough clerks or bailiffs to help with the work. Jonathan was still on the bench late one evening, shaking badly. He could barely stay in his chair. It felt as if spiders were crawling underneath his skin. He dimly remembered being on the verge of screaming, when Nicholas—that conscientious, fastidious, eavesdropping clerk of his—brought over a pitcher of water.

"A cool drink will calm this malady, Your Honor."

Water.

A clay pitcher, bleeding droplets through its surface, catching the light of his candle on the bench. It was like seeing it for the first time for what it was. The noise and grime of the court hallways, the weeping and shouts from the defendants, the tremors, they all receded in an instant.

That was the first time Jonathan heard the voice. His voice. Still, calm, not unlike his own, and just as plain as if he had thought something aloud to himself:

"*Try it.*" It had told him.

Jonathan did. A single redcap, pinched beneath the table of his bench, slipped easily into the glass without a trace.

It had been even better than he could have dreamed. Very different, of course. But better.

In water, the redcaps brought new sensations, new vistas to his consciousness. He felt sharpened. The way things touched, their scents, in particular. True, his stomach was never quite right, and his courtroom now seemed to be shining more lanterns and candles than was necessary. But there was no more of the sluggish stupor that the wine always saddled upon him. On the whole, it was a much-improved experience. Like what it would be to enjoy the companionship of a handsome worker for a time, and then one day dress him in livery from the Crest and carry on a lengthy talk about politics. Something already delightful made more so from the novelty of a different point of view and a fresh way of experiencing it.

Jonathan took another sip and leaned back in his chair. His stomach gurgled loudly, then slowly settled. A familiar, mellowing aura settled over him, and his thoughts turned into pleasant whispers, an amusing conversation ensuing with himself within his head, one that varied in its topics but always inclined toward Jonathan's comfort. It made him feel almost … at peace.

The reverie was interrupted when Jonathan's chamber door creaked open. His hand went up to shield his face from the sounds and brightness of the courtroom outside. Against the light, Jonathan could see Nicholas' silhouette stealing inside. Dangling from one of his hands, he had a lantern that gave off a buttery glow from candle stumps.

The clerk knew his way around the chamber, even in the dark. He announced his presence by clearing his throat.

The lantern candles flickered, sending a little cloud of gray smoke into the blackness above him, but there was only the sound of the clerk's labored breathing. So he coughed.

"Not feeling well, Nick?" Jonathan's voice broke through the darkness.

"I'm quite well, thank you, your Honor. I pray you'll forgive the intrusion. I do strive to respect the sanctity of the judges' chambers, to afford you the utmost privacy and allow you to prepare for your upcoming dockets."

It was a baldly false statement, almost laughable. Nicholas practically lived in Jonathan's chambers and all but dictated the Court of Common Corrections' docket. When he wasn't writing notes to Regina. Feeling genial, Jonathan decided to have a little fun with him:

"What, Cloud never invited you back here for an after-work drink?"

It had been meant as the lightest of teases, which of course Nicholas would feel with the utmost severity.

"I never took such liberty. His Honor's—singular—views about our stations notwithstanding, I always declined his Honor's gracious invitations, for propriety's sake."

Jonathan leaned into the glow of the small lantern, which shed a light and warmth at an intensity he found disagreeable. He withdrew a few inches and smiled.

"You missed out then. Cloud's table was supposedly quite lively. Much more so than mine."

"The reason I've come—"

"I was working on my book just now," Jonathan tapped at a heavy leather-bound tome near his chair. "Writing, writing, writing, that's all I do. I've never had such inspiration. It's as if I'm dictating. Keeps me so busy I don't have time for food—or drink—anymore. Mother was quite right about this occupation."

The final comment hit home, Jonathan could tell. Just as he meant it to. If anyone could have gotten a bottle of wine through the little blockade his mother had managed to erect, it would have been his clerk. But, then, who had been reporting his affairs to Mother, sending her notes, in the first place?

Nicholas looked increasingly uncomfortable. Something in Jonathan's present mood delighted in watching the shifty little man biting at his bottom lip.

"Your Honor," he said at last, "I have a message for you."

"Let's hear it."

"It is sealed in a letter. I was instructed to deliver it to your hand."

Jonathan's gaze fell on the carefully folded envelope the clerk held within the lantern's light.

"By whom?"

"Solomon Waters."

Something in the name had a familiar ring to it, but Jonathan could not quite place it; Nicholas came to his aid, speaking quickly and quietly:

"He is the Commonwealth's Counsel that prosecuted that Article One case before your Honor last term. He has another case before your Honor. And he personally handed this to me, just now, to deliver to your hand after we adjourned."

Jonathan took the paper. It felt heavy, the envelope bent from the weight of an amber wax seal with the Crest's sword emblazoned across its middle surrounded by the scales of justice.

"I will leave you to your affairs," Nicholas said, bowing. Then, before he left, he ventured to add in a low, meaningful tone:

"You might find the courtyard somewhat disagreeable. Perhaps it would be best to take the back way to the Guidepost."

It must have been days since Jonathan had set foot outside his court-room or chamber. He pried his private door to the courtyard open and a stench of garbage hit him squarely, knocking his breath away. Outside, the carefully pyramided crates of food and wares that ordinarily awaited the caravan to the Citadel or the Dwarven Quarter had been leveled into foothills of slowly rotting garbage.

A burning mound smoldered near the doorway separated only by a brown, brackish trench of water. Instead of the shouted orders from clerks to workers, now there were only a half dozen or so mute guards, a collection of farmers who looked as bewildered as they were out of place, and a lone, stooped man in an ill-fitting yellow sash who swept the flagstones every so often before jotting something down on a crumpled scrap of paper he held in his hand.

Strangest of all, though, there were oxen mulling about. Jonathan had never seen an ox in the Crag, and the animals' presence among the disarray of the courtyard was peculiarly jarring. Some were hitched to caravan carts, while others were roaming about untethered, searching in vain for grass in the cracks along the stone floor. The poor beasts were braying wildly, white froth dripping from their mouths. Jonathan found himself staring at them. They never brought burden animals down into the Crag; they were too valuable, too needed in the Crest, and the work-ers would only end up killing them for the meat. Besides, moving things around was what porters were for.

Jonathan gripped the message tight in his hand, the seal now broken and paper unfolded, and set out at a brisk walk in search of a building on the far side of the courtyard. He held his sleeve up to his nose, but the fetid smell would not be assuaged. Jonathan hoisted the ends of his magistrate's robe a little higher off the ground to keep them from getting stained. As he did so, his eyes fell to the message he was holding.

"... *immediately and at once to the Fruits.*"

The message had ended with what could only be read as a com-mand. The conclusion was unusual in at least three respects, Jonathan reflected: its tone, its redundancy, and its insistence.

He walked briskly to the end of his building, crossed a courtyard and an open alleyway, and then, after making his way around several piles of refuse, came to a long, low roofed house with a prominently placed yellow sign bearing a Commonwealth seal.

It was called the Fruits, a modest establishment the clerks frequented for various purposes: to trade assignments, get a drink or a companion, complain about their work out of earshot of their superiors—something between a tavern, an inn, and a work hall. Nicholas had some interest in the place, Jonathan recalled vaguely.

It was beneath Jonathan's station to be here, but the message had left no room to doubt the venue. He paused only a moment at the doorway, then ventured into the clerks' building.

The hall inside, like the courtyard without, was nearly empty. The air was dim and smoky, though not as foul-smelling. A crude chandelier filled with gulleystars and a hearth with a small fire provided the room's light—a superfluous quantity of it, Jonathan grimaced as he stepped further in the room. Three clerks were passed out, propped on top of a common table littered with overturned bottles and greasy plates, while a whore from the Crag worked at picking their pockets. When Jonathan entered, the girl bolted upright and gazed at him with the wariness of a cornered animal.

"Uh, Miss," Jonathan began haltingly, "I was, uhm, looking for some people." At that moment, he realized he had never before spoken with a worker directly. Not without the intercession of a troop of bailiffs or clerks about him.

She was a ruddy-faced girl of maybe twenty years, her dyed hair hanging in uncombed strands, and her eyes never seeming to blink. He found the attempt of talking to her disorienting. He tried to explain himself, all the while wishing one of the drunken clerks would stir, realize the predicament, and act as an intermediary. Her eyes narrowed.

"Everyone's gone," she answered at last.

"Oh. Where to?"

The girl's mouth turned into what was meant to be an inviting smile. She was missing several teeth, however, and an old scar kept her mouth at a crooked angle.

"Does it matter?" She took a bold step closer, and let the edge of her blouse fall from her shoulder. Her shirt was a patchwork of different shades of yellow that she must have stitched together from old clerks' sashes. "I'm still here," she continued in a purring voice. "Come over by the fire. You look like you need some warming up …"

"No." It came out as a squeak. "I-I-I couldn't."

Jonathan's revulsion must have been plain because at once the girl resumed her prior wariness.

"You don't belong here," she glowered.

"Sorry."

Had he just apologized? To a whore from the Crag? Jonathan shook his head to try to regain his senses. He was on the verge of taking a draught from the little bottle of redcap water he had with him—it was a bit early, but he felt its need already—when someone entered the hall from a back room.

"Jez, haven't you plied these people enough?"

She glared down at the speaker who, though she did not stand very tall herself, was well beneath her chest.

Jonathan's eyes went wide.

Before him stood a dwarf. As impossible as that seemed—and part of him simply refused to accept what was plain before his eyes—there he was. With fair skin, liquid eyes filled with color, a man no taller than a child but with the air of someone ancient, what else could it be? He wore a warden's uniform, a perfect miniature of a guard captain's, and a Commonwealth emblem hung about his neck, and none of that detracted from the brilliance of his bearing. Like an ideal of some sort, in its embodiment. The dwarf (that word, dwarf; such a base thing to call them, Jonathan thought) shooed the girl out of the hall, while Jonathan stared at him.

"I thought I might find you down here." The dwarf spoke softly, while discretely checking each of the patrons at the table was indeed unconscious. Satisfied, he stuck his hand up for Jonathan's and said a little more forcefully. "I am Jacob, the Warden of the Quarter." He waited a suitable length of time, but when Jonathan failed to respond, he pressed on. "You, of course, need no introduction, your Honor. It's a pleasure to meet you, Judge Acacia.

"What-what are you—?"

"Doing here? That's a long and unfortunate story. I'm trying to leave. But this bothersome war seems to have held up my pass."

"War?"

Jonathan could feel the incredulity sparkling from the fellow's eyes.

"The fighting between my people and yours," Jacob explained slowly. "Well, there's also some back-and-forth going on amongst the Crag folk, too. Wardens taking a crack at uppity clerks, a fair number of guildsmen having a go at wardens who leaned too hard on them. Scores are being settled out there. Mostly, though, it is becoming a war between the Crag and the nephil—or I should say, the people of the Quarter, my people, who, I must confess, are entirely deserving of the attention."

"Is that why I'm here?"

He smiled at Jonathan enigmatically.

"No. You're here for a court proceeding."

The back chamber of the Fruits tavern was a round, dusty room with a low ceiling and a lingering smell of hops and soap. The shelves were mostly bare, the mops and brooms tucked away in an alcove, and the remaining kegs covered with linens to lend the place a more formal air than what a storeroom (which is what it was) would ordinarily engender. A writing table and a few chairs around had been set out on a carpet. At the table, Solomon Waters and a lone clerk, her hand poised to write down whatever would be said, were the only ones seated. In the shadows of the wall behind them, a small figure in chains stirred, but kept itself hidden. Upon Jonathan's entrance, the clerk and lawyer rose at once, and Jacob locked the door behind them.

"Judge Acacia," Waters said, "I hadn't hoped to see you again so soon. Thank you for joining us."

He looked as Jonathan remembered him from before. Prim, serious, every hair perfectly aligned. But Jonathan was unable to break his gaze from the prisoner in the shadows.

"Your message implied I had no choice," Jonathan answered, careful to hide his growing apprehension.

Waters laughed.

"I pray for your forgiveness, your Honor. I would never have presumed to, uhm, well—let's just get it out in the open: that note was dictated by my superior. It was given to me to sign in his stead, though it pained me to do so."

As Commonwealth's Counsel, Waters' only superior would be the Steward of Justice. Waters waited a moment as Jonathan considered the significance of the subtle ruse behind the delivery of his summons. A steward had his eye on Jonathan but did not wish to have it known yet. A courtship of sorts had been commenced.

"Please, sit, your Honor," Waters continued. Then, gesturing towards the wall behind him: "Don't be troubled by this individual. We'll attend to him shortly. In the meantime, I assure you, the good warden here has his charge well in hand."

Jacob's face revealed nothing. Wary and a little flummoxed, Jonathan did as he was bidden and sank into a cushioned chair.

"Your honor," Waters began, "your performance in the Article One trial last term—the one involving that porter—left quite an impression. A most favorable impression, and upon the right people."

For some reason, Jonathan had always found it awkward as a judge to hear his rulings praised. It felt particularly odd to thank a lawyer for anonymous compliments, but he did so all the same.

"Such matters require acumen and temperament," Waters continued, "but more importantly, they must be handled with a certain—delicacy. Not everyone holds that particular talent, but it has been noted in you. You are, if you'll permit the colloquialism, the right man for this kind of work."

Jonathan thanked him again. The prisoner chained to the wall began crying softly, which everyone at the table, except Jonathan, seemed intent on ignoring, until finally, Jacob got up from his chair to attend to him. A few angry hisses, all from Jacob, the last ending menacingly with "… what you owe me paid in full," and the prisoner fell silent.

"So," Waters pressed on as if nothing had happened, "I'm not at all surprised to learn that another high-profile case would reach your bench. Not surprised in the least. A truly rare opportunity for advancement, should you accept the charge. And here it is."

Jonathan glanced around at his surroundings, unsure of what Waters could mean. A nod from the Commonwealth's Counsel and the clerk took notes, her quill pen jotting down lines as the lawyer spoke.

"We are here in the matter of the Commonwealth versus Conspirators One through Fifty-five, a sealed indictment having been filed this morning pursuant to Article Two of the Commonwealth. Solomon Waters serves as Commonwealth's Counsel. The matter has been referred to the Honorable Jonathan Acacia, who, upon acceptance of this referral, shall be the presiding magistrate."

"What's going on?" Jonathan asked.

Waters smiled.

"A trial."

Jacob returned to the light of the table, now accompanied by the chained prisoner, the links of manacles around his wrists clinking softly as he shuffled forward. He was a dwarf, like Jacob, though nearly a head taller and somewhat older. Darker, too; his flesh reminded Jonathan of a sandstone veined with graphite. His clothes, though flecked with chalk, dust, and clay, showed through a wondrous pastel pattern that caught the light, an emerald light, from within his bloodshot eyes. His cheeks were swollen, and an unbandaged gash was still bleeding from his chin. His blood, like his skin, Jonathan saw, looked flecked with iron shavings.

"I've only a brief opening statement," said Waters. "May it please the court?"

"Uhm." Jonathan watched a droplet of blood trickle down from the dwarf's chin and land on the table. It strained to be heard, but the tiny sound invoked the memory of the first pour of wine going into a chalice.

"Of course, your Honor accepts the appointment?"

Jonathan hesitated. He shut his eyes to rub the bridge of his nose and think, to slow the whirlwind that was raging inside his head. Without knowing it, Jonathan started to bring his bottle out.

"*All will be well.*"

The voice echoed behind his temples. Jonathan swallowed and nodded faintly, slipping the bottle back into his pocket, and when he opened his eyes, he could see that Waters appeared satisfied with the response. The lawyer drew himself up to his full height in his chair and launched into his oratory, his baritone voice striking in its rapid cadence:

"We come before your Honor on a grave matter. The very order of our Commonwealth is under assault. Troubles have beset the realm of the Crag as the workers await guidance and direction from a new Plan.

And amid this unfortunate disorder, which will soon be put to rest, subversive elements have been conspiring between the realms. They seek to capitalize on the present tensions to meet their aims. What are those aims? The destruction of our distinct realms. The overthrow of the order that has sustained us all. It falls to this Court—we dare not bring these insurgents into Jachin—to preserve the foundation of Article Two: 'There is no turmoil, and none shall be sustained.' That is the sacred charge in the matter before us."

Jonathan blinked. The opening statement had already ended. Waters paused to allow the clerk to flip over her paper, while he scratched at a hangnail. The two dwarves stood silently, the one in chains gritting his teeth anxiously. At that moment, Jonathan became keenly aware that this trial with the Commonwealth's Counsel would be no different than the one before. He was being led; and the inner voice was telling him to follow along, for now. But to where?

"Ready?" Waters asked the clerk. He returned to a more relaxed, informal tone, as he addressed Jonathan directly. "So, the defendants will be presented tomorrow and the formal charges against them will be read in the ordinary course in open court. I don't anticipate the trial will take us past the lunch hour. The reason we have convened this preliminary hearing—that is how the record will refer to it, don't worry—is because of the *highly* delicate testimony your Honor must consider from this witness. In the present climate, we simply could not guarantee his safety or, indeed, yours, if he were to appear in public. Things being as they are. Hence, the alternative venue," he gestured at the room, "and the closed proceeding."

Jacob gave the chained dwarf a light shove from behind, and he stepped forward placing himself directly between Waters and Jonathan.

"State your name," Waters said to him.

"It-it's Okran," he muttered.

"You reside in the Dwarven Quarter."

"The Gutters, sir."

"You are a witness in this court proceeding," Waters explained, "which means I will ask you some questions, and you will answer them before his Honor. Your testimony requires a promise from you to tell the truth. Do you so promise?"

The blood flushed in Okran's cheeks, and for the first time, a vigor shone from behind his face. His mouth quivered angrily at Jacob. "You didn't say anything about making an *oath* to the men. I won't do it. No matter how much I owe you. We gave them an oath once, and look what it cost—"

"—Allow me, counselor," Jacob interrupted. He fixed a wax smile at his companion and explained in the measured voice of one trying to calm a petulant child. "Okran, he doesn't want an oath before the gods. He doesn't even want a bargain, though he calls it a promise. This is something different. He's just asking if your words are plumb and level."

Okran wiped at his chin, spreading the blood on his face into a crimson smear, and looked at the warden abjectly:

"Are they?"

Jacob met his eyes with a placid expression.

"So long as you tell him what you must, they are. And you fulfill your bargain with me."

Okran slowly turned his head to face Waters.

"My words are plumb and level," he grunted.

"Alright," Waters said. "The record will reflect the witness' testimony was suitably qualified. Now, how did it come about that you are here this evening?"

"I got taken up," he raised his bound wrists to indicate Jacob, "by my warden."

"That's not what he means," Jacob warned.

"S-Sorry."

Waters' patience was thinning. "Listen carefully to the question. How did you come here?"

"It's the first question," Jacob prompted.

"Oh." Okran struggled to gather his recollection, then began a halting soliloquy: "I've turned myself in to my warden's custodial to report a conspiring that I was unwittingly made privity upon."

"What is that conspiracy?"

"Some of my people in the Gutters have joined up with Cragmen to commit treasonish and sed-eesh-us acts of violence to disturb the order of the Commonwealth. They've drawn others in from the Crest, as well."

"That's a serious charge, Okran."

Not knowing what he was expected to say to that, Okran resigned to shifting from one foot to the other.

"Is there more?" Waters prompted.

"Uh …"

Jacob leaned closer and mouthed something in his ear, at which Okran nodded, "right, this same group from the Gutters is also un-deverring to spread religion in the Crag, to get everyone to worship their Maiden."

"How do you know this?"

"I-uh-frequent one of their meeting places, a tavern. The Copper-bottom. They talk about their plans all the time in there. They call them-selves the sect. I should have reported it sooner, like Jacob said."

"Your honor," Jacob added, "I can vouch for what he says, as I'm intimately familiar with this tavern. It's been a hotbed of unrest since a new cult took root in the Gutters. The Commonwealth's sanctioned priest has tried his level best to stamp them out and keep our people within the terms of our Treaty, but without success. They want to upend everything in the Quarter. It seems now they've set their sights beyond our realm as well."

Jonathan regarded the two dwarves standing before him, both so comely and so very different, and found himself wondering where their true connection might lie—for the story he was being told was, as every-one in the room knew well, a complete farce. The full of it would never come out, Jonathan realized. Jacob asked Waters if that was all he needed, and the lawyer made a curt nod.

"You may go."

Jacob lingered a moment. It appeared that he was about to broach something further with Waters, but the lawyer snapped that "it would be taken care of," and that, very clearly, was to be the end of it.

His jaws clenched, Jacob led Okran away, and the two dwarves disap-peared softly into the shadows behind the stacks of barrels and through a service doorway that would take them into an empty back alley behind the Fruits. When they had gone, Waters gave the clerk her leave, as well. The proceeding had concluded as brusquely as it had begun. Jonathan lingered in his seat.

"You're doing splendidly," Waters beamed. He gathered up his papers.

"Thanks, but—I haven't heard anything about an actual defendant. Or a crime. What does any of this have to do with this trial tomorrow?"

"A prelude," Waters assured him, "a necessary one. So that you will have a full flavor for what is at stake. Like I said, we could never have brought those two into an open court. The guards would have ripped them apart. As it is, they'll have to take care not to be seen. Though that shouldn't pose a problem; they are a slight and sneaky race."

"The younger one, that—" it was on the tip of Jonathan's tongue to say "is so lovely," but he caught himself. "The one that's called Jacob. He is an actual warden?"

"He is," Waters nodded. He brought the last of a batch of papers underneath his arm. "Or was. Apparently, he's something of a man without a realm at the moment. For the time being, he's living in this tavern in confidence, under some kind of subterfuge or other. Odd little fellow. I'm sure he'll find suitable accommodation when this is all sorted out."

"Then—that's it?"

"For tonight, yes." Waters tied a cord around a parchment to emphasize the conclusion. "We've made arrangements for your docket tomorrow. You won't be bothered by any other matter. Indeed, this may be your last case on the Court of Common Corrections—Justice Acacia."

Jacob stuffed the cotton wads further in his ears. He was crouching in the corner of a tiny closet behind his trunk trying to drown out the din of lovemaking in the bedroom outside. The grunting reached a crescendo, the girl's headboard was smacking against the wall. He would have prayed, if he knew how, to any god that would bring a quicker ending to this.

"They mate like livestock," Jacob muttered to himself. He shifted to relieve the ache in his knees.

There was a heavy thud, then a long pause, followed by a peal of laughter from the girl. The clerk that had paid for her slurred a curse, something about how small the bed was for what she cost, but she only laughed harder. Eventually, they calmed down, their voices faded into a murmur, and Jacob decided it was safe to remove the cotton. The man was settling his account with her.

"I swear I had twelve tinners in my pocket when I came in," he complained. His words came out thick, as if he had only recently come out of a stupor, which he had. "I got only seven now."

"Must've lost track of your drinking," she replied.

Or had his pocket picked over while sprawled out in a stupor in the common room, Jacob thought to himself. The girl could be clever in some respects. She never robbed a man completely; so he could never be sure if he had been robbed.

"I'll take your seven," she continued, "and we'll say you owe me three more."

The floorboards creaked as the clerk stumbled about the room, mumbling angrily to the air. He was looking around the place, swearing loudly that he knew exactly how much he drank and how much he had. He must have dropped his coins. The man was on his knees, scratching around the floor and slowly coming closer to the closet.

For a moment, Jacob feared the clerk might barge inside. And if he started picking through the clutter, he would come across an uncommonly ornate and sturdy trunk in the corner, and behind it … Jacob fingered the handle of his dagger but left it sheathed. If it came to that—the contingencies could turn into a cave-in very quickly. The clerk was right outside the door now. Jacob could smell the acrid stench of balm about him.

"Hey, look here," the girl called out. "I found your coins. Under the bed. Must've shaken 'em loose. Probably when I ripped those pants off." She giggled coyly, and the man seemed to accept that that must have been the case. Jacob let out a quiet sigh of relief.

He listened to the clink of worthless metal being counted out. A few parting words between them to schedule his next tryst (they coincided with the porters' payday, apparently) and the clerk took his leave.

It fell quiet. Jacob waited for her to let him out, as they had agreed. She was taking her time about it, but at last, he heard her feet shuffle softly across the floor, and the closet door opened.

She was holding a gulleystar lamp, but the beige light could not wash out the bursting red that flushed from her cheeks. They would remain that way for hours, Jacob knew.

"That was close," she muttered. There was a hint of an accusation, Jacob detected, in the way she said it.

"It was," Jacob agreed. He got to his feet and stepped out from behind the trunk. "You handled the situation perfectly, Jez."

"I lost money because of you."

"You mean you had to give back the money you stole from him earlier?"

"It was my money."

Jacob stretched and walked out into the room. The place was a windowless, wood-framed box, part of an enclosed, second-floor platform that had been built in more prosperous times atop the clerk's tavern to provide another row of private rooms. Hers was the smallest, at the end of the hall. It held a bed with some woolen blankets, two tables, chairs, and a collection of garish, threadbare drapes that were supposed to convey a sense of luxury. The walls behind them were unevenly plastered, and whatever the original paint color may have been was lost to a monotone gray of dust, grime, and cobwebs. Its salient feature, for Jacob, was that it had a relatively ample closet he could stay inside. He had been living here for more than a week.

Unbidden, Jacob made himself comfortable on the bed. Jez's clothes were still in a lump on the ground; she had not bothered dressing, and Jacob had scarcely noticed. It was how she often went about, and he was no more unaccustomed to it now than he was when he first became her tenant.

"I'm out five tinners," she said again.

"I've more than paid for any incidental expenses."

Jez squinted derisively at him but made no reply. Jacob glanced at the far table where there was usually a plate of food from the inn, carefully portioned in half. There was nothing left on the plate tonight but a lone scrap of grizzle. She slipped a stained blouse back on over her head and noticed him looking at the food.

"No dinner for you," she said firmly. "Not after what you cost me."

It was not worth the trouble of an argument. Jacob took the strip of fat from the plate and began chewing on it. Ox meat, badly burnt. He took another bite and worked on it a while, as the girl picked up around the room and continued complaining about what he had cost her. Another rant. Something else he had become used to from her.

He called her Jezebel because she reminded him vaguely of a girl from the Gutters in much the same occupation, and because she had never given him anything else to call her. Names for her were easily discarded, like clothing.

Like the Crest's promises.

Sitting there, devouring the leavings from this nagging whore's plate, the realization came over Jacob once again, the same apprehension he had felt when he first passed through the gatehouse and found the courtyard overrun with angry mobs and frightened clerks. He had kept hidden—it was easy for his kind to do with the dark-blind men—but his friends, it seemed, the ones with clout, had all vanished without leaving any word for him. There were no passes, no notes or papers, no payments for the faithful warden of the Quarter.

He had been forgotten. The way that lawyer had so casually dismissed him confirmed his suspicion. Jezebel, it seemed, was the only connection he could hope to prevail upon.

The courtyard was becoming an increasingly dangerous place for Jacob to move about; he needed shelter, food, and, most important, secrecy and silence, while he got his affairs in order. But he was running out of time. Jezebel could be trusted (so long as she was not pressed), but Jacob's purse was half as heavy now that he had her as a landlord. And all he had procured was a temporary leasehold in a precarious sanctuary. Should he try the Citadel once more? And risk the Spine? Or admit defeat and return to the Inner Realm, while the caravan route was still empty and relatively safe for his kind to travel. He had come so far, moved so many pieces into just the right place, he was so tantalizingly close to the Crest …

"Where'd you say you're going again?" Jezebel's growling intruded on his thoughts. Jacob forced a smile.

"I didn't. But since you ask, I'm waiting for a house. Which I'm told will be as lovely as it is secluded."

She was hardly paying attention to him, stuffing soiled linen underneath the bedframe, obviously still irritated about the coins she had had to sacrifice to keep her tenant hidden.

"How much longer?"

It was not the first time the question had come up. The term of his stay had been a point of ambiguity that Jezebel had been harping on with more and more frequency lately.

"The pass should come down any day now," he replied, sliding off the bed.

"You said that yesterday. And the day before."

"And it was no less true then. I'm especially hopeful now, though. Now that I've furnished the powers-that-be what they needed, I think—"

"Your hope don't get me my tinners back."

"I told you—"

Neither of them heard the returning footsteps of the clerk, who, without bothering to knock, shoved the bedroom door wide open. He had his palm held out and a vexed expression on his face.

"Hey, these aren't my coins," the clerk was shaking his head, "I get mine straight from the bursars, and these here are fakes. See how they bend—"

He froze, midstep, his face drained of color. The clerk was, Jacob saw, in his late fifties, unshaven, and trembling from the shock at what was before him. He was also enormously fat. Which meant he would die loudly, and it would be impossible to conceal the body. Jacob's head swiveled from Jezebel to the clerk, then back to Jezebel, and at that moment, the girl had found her escape, which, with the smallest flicker of her eyelash, Jacob read as if she had told him aloud what it would be.

The bargain was off. She mimicked a look of stark terror; her cheeks were still blushed from sex as she pretended to quake.

"Help me! He's got a knife! Help!"

"Dwarf—" a hiss of air came out of the clerk's purpling jowls. His coins fell with a clatter.

Jacob pursed his lips: "Damn."

There was no time to fetch the trunk. Jacob barreled past the clerk and, though much slighter, only just managed to squeeze through the doorway. Jezebel took up the cry again, a piercing screech, which prompted the cowering clerk to finally find his voice. In the time it took Jacob to reach the stairway, the whole tavern had erupted in commotion with the shouts reverberating in his ears:

"Dwarf! Dwarf! In the Fruits! Guards! Wardens! Clerks! Arm yourselves! There's a *dwarf* in here! *Kill it!*"

CHAPTER THIRTY

WATERS HAD BEEN true to his word about the docket. Jonathan entered an emptied courtroom. Two bailiffs, Nicholas, and the clerk from the night before were the only ones in the gallery. They all stood as Nicholas announced in his prim and practiced manner that the court was now in session. Waters had somehow managed a fresh bath, Jonathan noticed, the water was still glistening from his hair. The lawyer dipped his head.

No one spoke but everyone remained on their feet staring at Jonathan as he took his chair. The silence, something Jonathan would ordinarily relish, somehow amplified the singularities of all the ambient noises: Jonathan's steps approaching the bench, the shuffling of his chair, one of the guards clearing his throat, a quill pen being gently laid on the table; it was all much too loud. He squinted in the brightness of the candles on his desk until his eyes adjusted.

There was only one paper. He stared at the page, crammed with tiny lines of writing all emanating from an embossed seal. It registered nothing to him but a curious invocation of a spider's web. His fingers traced along its ink lines.

"May it please the court?" Waters smiled.

Jonathan looked up. He had not slept last night or the night before, and he had not had his first-morning taste of redcaps yet. A dull ache was spreading across his forehead. His speech, like his thoughts, came heavy.

"Sure," he twirled his finger around in a circle.

Waters gathered the hems of his counselor's robe together, folding them across his arms in a sage-like pose, and then slowly strode to the center of the courtroom. The bailiffs, who had never seen anyone from the Crest and had no one to guard, leaned on their spears gaping with their mouths hanging open. The lawyer flicked a finger in his clerk's

direction, and the little group was joined in the companionship of dicta-
tion, her pen marking down Waters' remarks:

"We are in continued proceedings in these consolidated cases. The
Commonwealth issued its opening statement last night and will not
belabor the Court's patience for very long. The cases before the Court
are going to be self-evident. You'll note there is no specific Code of
Conduct section mentioned in the indictment before your Honor. Each
of the fifty-five defendants is being charged with a direct violation of
Article Two."

"Wait, before you start. I had a question about that. I mean, we all
memorized it as children, but all Article Two says is that there's not supposed to be turmoil in the Commonwealth. So how does one actually
violate Article Two?"

Waters gave him a knowing look, then resumed his solemn affect:

"By causing turmoil."

"But that makes—"

"The evidence," he continued, "will make it plain. When considered
in its totality, and with what is at stake, we're certain the Court will find
each defendant guilty—and sentence each one to removal."

Jonathan shook his head. From its bizarre inception, this proceeding seemed bent on colliding with everything he had ever learned and
practiced. The Code of Conduct was supposed to be didactic, precisely
defined and measured, so that it could be followed. This "charge" the
Commonwealth's Counsel was bringing was like accusing a man of not
behaving himself.

"Go ahead," he murmured at last.

Waters nodded at Nicholas, who announced the name of the case in
the same grave intonation one might pronounce at a funeral:

"Commonwealth versus Defendant number one, Kristopher Gulch."

The sound of a loud, creaking hinge barging open gave Jonathan a
slight start. The prisoner was not being brought up from the cellar that
led down into the Tombs but through the front door of the courthouse.
He had never seen such a thing before. What was more, the prisoner had
his hands bound in front of him, and with soft rope, not shackles.

The man's dress was bizarre, something like a smock thrown over a
dusted blue and red tunic. He had a long nose that dipped sharply down,

and his coloring might have been considered somewhat pallid in the Crest, but would never pass for anyone from the Crag. The bailiff escorting him, Jonathan noticed, was just as baffled by the prisoner. The old guard kept whispering and bobbing his head to try to lead him where he was supposed to go without ever touching him. The other bailiffs followed the lead. None of the usual curses or truncheons, their brief interactions bringing the man to the witness stand held the deference of faithful servants:

"Right up here, sir, and watch your step," the guard who brought him in said and then quickly withdrew.

The defendant, Gulch, had no idea how well he had been treated. The man was quivering and cowed with fright and looked dimly familiar to Jonathan.

"State your name," Waters commanded.

Gulch nearly fell over from the fright. The lawyer asked again, but when it was clear the man could not respond, he tried a different tack:

"You are Kris Gulch, correct?"

That brought some of his senses back to him. His head stopped darting about long enough to nod an affirmation.

"You're a printer in Boaz by occupation," Waters continued.

"Y-y-yes. Y-yes, sir. I print papers."

Waters' eyes narrowed. He leaned forward as if he were a predator poised to strike at a wounded animal.

"So you do. On the witness stand's table, right there in front of you, do you see those papers?"

Gulch's eyes bulged, but slowly, as if a terrible realization was beginning to creep over him.

"Do you see them?"

His face fell.

"You printed those papers, didn't you?"

"L-let me explain, sir—"

"The question, Gulch, was, did you print those papers?"

"Yes, but—"

"In fact, your shop printed hundreds of those."

"Yes, Gregory said—"

"What are those papers called?"

Gulch heaved forward and let out a low wail. Waters did not relent. The lawyer held up a set of papers, similar to those on the stand, and read aloud, in a sweepingly derisive fashion:

"Ninety-five propositions ... to—purportedly—advance the common good of the Commonwealth, retard the—oh, this is just vile writing—sclerosis—that has taken hold over the Crest that the slavish devotion—such hubris! —to ostensible respect for the diversity ... Your Honor, I cannot stomach any more of this. Your clerk has a copy that you may read at your leisure if you deem it necessary."

Turning back to the defendant, Waters pressed him with a rapid-fire of questions, which quickly broke the poor fellow down into sobs. He, Gulch, was a member of this Guild. They had surreptitiously scattered hundreds of these documents across Boaz. Held unlicensed rallies. Harassed and bothered the populace with their notions. Traveled, as a mob no less, without leave to the Citadel. It was all true, he could not deny any of it.

Gulch gathered just enough fortitude to face Judge Acacia, his eyes rimmed in red with a trail of snot hanging from that nose of his:

"All this was Gregory and Aric's idea, and that old judge's! I don't care about Craggies. I-I was just trying to make a little money—"

"Enough!" Waters brought the open palm of his hand down on his table and the defendant fell quiet. He shrunk before the lawyer's withering gaze and before he could stutter another sound, Waters dismissed him. To the Tombs.

"Oh, dear," Jonathan heard Nicholas mutter.

Gulch had fainted. The bailiffs had to overcome their aversion to touching him because it took the three of them to carry the printer from the Crest away from the witness stand. And so, the next case was called.

That became the morning's routine. The bailiffs returned with more defendants, one after the other, a succession of the most comically dressed, and abjectly terrified, artistes from Boaz Jonathan had ever seen gathered together. Some he knew by name, others by reputation. Men and women, none over the age of forty. They were writers and poets, librarians, out of work scholars, and self-proclaimed activists and advocates, unimaginative in every respect and endeavor, who Jonathan would often see loitering in the coffeehouse or outside the library when he was in Boaz. The kind that would never find an audience beyond the circle of their commiseration. Yet, here they were, the center of attention.

Their crime, from what Jonathan could gather, was to have taken Judge Cloud's inane speeches literally. Crag and Crest ought to intermingle more, become more unified. That seemed to be the prevailing theme they had all swallowed and regurgitated.

As if any of them knew a thing about the Crag or what its people needed.

Their little movement called themselves a Guild, which made Jonathan audibly scoff when he first heard it. Throughout Boaz, they had made speeches, dressed themselves up like what they thought workers would look like, circulated pamphlets and petitions about unifying with their "brethren" in the Crag, held meetings, a great many meetings, went on a march—it sounded like a peacock's month of merrymaking. Standing before the Court, they cried, or accused one another, or simply confessed (to whatever it was Waters wanted), and all of them ended their case with pleas for Jonathan's mercy. By the eighth defendant, Jonathan had grown bored with the spectacle.

The cases ran on into the lunch hour, and although Jonathan did not at all miss the repast, Waters became self-conscious of how much time he had taken. He grimaced, reading through his notes, made a quick count on his fingers, and then, appearing satisfied with himself once more, announced to Jonathan:

"I'm pleased to report, we have reached the final defendant—and the penultimate witness. We should rest shortly, your Honor, with the deepest appreciation for the Court's indulgence, unless you wish to recess?"

"Let's finish this," Jonathan replied. He was tired, and the prospect of a redcap in a fresh, cold draught had been foremost in his thoughts for the past five defendants.

"Very well. The Commonwealth versus Defendant number Fiftyfive. We call Gregory Gables to answer to the charge of violating Article Two of the Commonwealth."

Jonathan kept his face steady, as he watched Gregory saunter through the courtroom gallery, his familiar portly gait hindered somewhat by the bailiff escorting him and the rope bindings that kept his arms before his belly. He was moving at a hurried clip, and Jonathan, despite his long experience concealing his facial features while on the bench, simply could not help the murmur that rolled under his breath:

"Idiot."

Before Waters could begin, Gregory rushed to the front of the witness stand, knocking all the papers to the ground. He propped himself on top of the podium, as if he would launch his bulk onto the bench and into Jonathan's arms. A look of relief was breaking across his face and a torrent of words came gushing out:

"Oh, thank goodness, thank goodness, a *friend*. Jonathan, there's been a terrible misunderstanding—"

"You address the court," Waters warned him, "as Your Honor, or Judge Acacia."

"Eh? I'll have you know this is the son of a *dear* friend of mine. Regina Acacia ring a bell? I don't know what's gone wrong here, but Jonathan, you have to clear it up. Steward Temple and I were talking in the Citadel—we were! —and it was so wonderful and lively. All about the latest scholarship. And as we're talking about a relatively minor theory my colleagues have been debating, he excuses himself for some refreshment, just for a moment he assured me, and the next thing I know—your brother is binding my hands!" He thrust the flabby, pale lumps of his rope-tied wrists into the air for Jonathan to bear witness. "You can imagine my shock! One moment I'm in the Citadel at a table with a Steward, and the next I'm under arrest. And your brother refuses to say a word. I hold nothing against him. As I said, this simply has to be some misunderstanding. You'll help me. Of course you will. Just a note to your dear Mother and I'm sure we can clear up whatever is—"

One of the bailiffs came up from behind and laid his gloved hand gently on Gregory's shoulder. That little gesture, and the respectful, but no less gruff, throat clearing that accompanied it, quieted Gregory in an instant.

"That is quite enough of that," Waters said. "You are here to answer for your crimes, not prevail upon the past hospitality of His Honor's family."

Gregory's mouth opened again indignantly, but this time he said nothing; his eyes, however, brimmed with tears. Still, he refused to acknowledge the lawyer, but gazed steadily, imploringly, at Jonathan.

On some level, Jonathan felt sorry for the man. He had always been looked down upon, even contemptuously, among Mother's followers. Worse, he had never realized it. Jonathan's face remained set.

"Proceed, counselor," he said.

"You are Gregory Gables?" Waters' voice was now a clipped bark.

"I-I am." Gregory worked his hands around to adjust his coat around his shoulders, an attempt to regain a semblance of his prior composure.

"The proponent of this subversive document?"

While Gregory had been talking, Nicholas had gathered together the papers that had fallen, discretely slipped an exhibit, the ninety-five propositions, back onto the stand, and silently stole back to his place beside Jonathan at the bench.

"Well . . ." Gregory stammered for a moment. "That was-that was a collaborative effort amongst a cross-section of thinkers, developing a thesis that Judge Cloud first advanced—"

"I don't see Judge Cloud's name anywhere on this document. Your name, however, appears at the bottom—right here—the most prominent signature, above the reference, Master of the Guild of Solidarity."

"A-uhm, scholastic pseudonym."

"Which you attempted to nail to the door of the Outer Keep, defacing a landmark of the Commonwealth."

"I was—I was just trying to-to knock—be heard."

Waters read through the propositions, skipping to the more inflammatory ones, which, by now, Jonathan had already memorized: free movement of goods and labor, free markets, free associations, free discourse without censure or censors, that would span the whole of a unified collective ... "'Number Sixty ... We serve unity to make the Crag and Crest truly free, by all means available to us,' that is what you've written." The words came out venomously in the lawyer's reading. "Free," Waters concluded, "to be exploited. And united in the destruction of our unique identities." Waters raised his free hand, curled it into a fist, and struck the document with the vehemence of a man challenged to a duel. "By all means available? This is rank rebellion, Gables!"

"No, no, no," Gregory gave a nervous chuckle, "you have to understand these are all merely academic theories, ideas. Our discussions were a way to foster a debate, create an atmosphere of transparency. We present them in the most provocative terms—but only for the sake of a provocative *debate*. It was all just talk. That's all we were ever after. Ask Steward Temple—"

"Just talk, you say? As if the wounds you inflicted were any less grievous because the weapon you used happened to be *words*?" Waters arced the whole of his back upright, his dark eyes shining. "How many men and women were subjugated by the priests' talk, how many lives exploited, back when everyone said and did whatever they wished to one another. You would have us regress into savagery—"

The pulsing in Jonathan's head had reached a threshold. He cut over the Commonwealth's Counsel.

"This is sounding more like argument," Jonathan warned, pinching the bridge of his nose, "which I thought you said had concluded."

"Forgive me, your Honor," Waters' nostrils were flaring. He paused to recompose himself and fix his hair, all the while his eyes darting across a set of notes he held. His clerk took advantage to stretch her aching fingers. It was a short reprieve.

"Only one or two more questions. You've no credentials, do you Gables?"

"I hold a Master of Arts," he responded, somewhat incensed.

"I mean a true credential. You're not recognized as an expert on anything, are you."

Gregory tried to hold his chin high, his fleshy lips wobbling from the tension of holding his tears in check. He could not respond.

"So, without credential or permit, you held rallies, organized speeches, and led a march, during which this so-called guild of yours repeatedly accosted the innocent people of Boaz with your inflammatory rhetoric—"

"—it was Judge Cloud's thesis—"

"—who was conspicuously absent from this march, just as he was from your document—"

"—all I wanted was for someone to read my writing," the first drips of moisture were finally streaming down Gregory's cheeks. The lawyer let the silence stretch.

"I'd say," Waters' words were low and steeled, "that in that respect at least, you succeeded."

The inference was so blunt, even Gregory could not miss it. Waters sat down. Gregory rubbed his sleeve across his nose, and, as absurd as it was, made one final, fleeting attempt at cordiality with Jonathan:

"Jon—Judge … My old friend. You see how silly this is. You'll help me. I know you will."

Watching him, clinging to the pretense that it was just the two of them, that they were fast companions together in Jonathan's mother's box at the Amphitheatre, or the public room of a tavern, or anyplace other than a courthouse, in any circumstance other than a criminal case, the morsel of pity that remained in Jonathan vanished. Whatever happened to this man, whatever his verdict, Jonathan knew he would never see Gregory again. He would be removed. At least he could bring a merciful end to Gregory's delusion.

"I've heard enough," Jonathan declared, his voice flat. "The Commonwealth can excuse this witness."

Unsure what had just transpired, Gregory balked with confusion, his expressions vacillating like a flickering candle. But as the bailiff led him away, his face suddenly alighted. As if his curt dismissal had signified that Jonathan would come to his rescue. The poor, deluded idiot wept with gratitude:

"Oh, thank you, thank you, your dear, brooding boy. Jon—your Honor! Thank you! You'll have this cleared up in no time, and then we'll all have a great laugh over this at the next play, won't we? Won't we, Jonathan …"

He was still sputtering as the door to the Tombs slammed shut over his head. The sound sent a wave of dull pain down Jonathan's neck. He happened to glance down and was surprised to find he had been scribbling around the margins of the indictment. Without knowing it, he had made a drawing. He shuddered and crumpled the paper before anyone saw it.

"Your Honor," Waters had a watchful look beneath his politeness. "If I may, this has been an exhausting case. We can recess before the final witness."

"No," Jonathan snapped. "We will finish this—now."

Another bow.

"The Commonwealth calls as its final witness against Defendants one through fifty-five, the Commissariat's Master Cloud."

The courthouse door swung inward and a thin shadow slunk across the transom.

Judge Cloud.

The scholar with his academic's gown fluttering from his narrow shoulders, striving to put on an air of resolute self-assurance, his mild-mannered face inspecting the gallery as if seeing the dingy walls and faded Commonwealth tapestries for the first time; it almost masked the shame that Jonathan detected within his eyes. A former judge who had once openly proclaimed from this bench that he could never convict another Crag worker of a Crest crime. It should probably have been a surprise, Jonathan mused, seeing him as a witness for this farce of a trial. But it wasn't.

Cloud made his way, unescorted, to the witness stand, and before he had uttered a word, Jonathan knew why he was here; on some level, he knew all along that Cloud would be here. Cloud had come to bury the knife so deeply in these fools' throats that it could not possibly be withdrawn. Defendants who were accused of nothing more than bandying about a hodge-podge of slogans he himself had probably coined. Elaine would have been horrified, probably broken, by the betrayal. But not Jonathan.

Whatever else one may say against them, cynics are seldom surprised.

"So nice to see you, your Honor," Jonathan greeted him as if Cloud were an unexpected guest at a dinner party. The man inclined his head demurely and muttered some pleasantry. His eyes drifted towards Waters.

"Your Honor," the lawyer said to Jonathan, "if I may, for the record, introduce Master Cloud's credentials?"

"No need," Jonathan replied, never breaking his gaze with Cloud, "a former judge of this Court, a master in the Commissariat, author of the definitive book on cognitive justice, degrees in—how many doctorates do you hold? Eight, nine? Judge Cloud's credentials are impeccable. How could the Court not accept his testimony? I'm sure the questions you have for him, and his answers, will lead us far along the path to truth and justice."

The sarcasm struck Cloud visibly, just as Jonathan intended. Cloud started to open his mouth, then shut it again. The clerk's pen scrawled across her page and came to a pause. Finally, he spoke aloud, but his voice sounded faint in the emptiness of the gallery:

"Mister Waters, Judge Acacia, if it's all the same, can I just say what I have to say? Without all the procedures. It's no one here but us."

"And the record," Jonathan gestured at the clerk, "mustn't forget the record. But I have no objection to hearing what you've come to tell me without the bother of questions-and-answers. Mister Waters, you may stand down. At your pleasure—your Honor."

Cloud's thin face stretched with strain. Without realizing it, he had assumed the contemplative posture of delivering a lecture, angling his head with his eyes half shut, grasping the top of the witness stand with a deep exhalation. What followed was, by the esteemed orator's standards, a mediocre performance:

"Your Honor is aware of my former views, my theory that is now popularly known as unification. I won't bother with all that here, just— well, I've written all that I care to on that topic." He shrugged nonchalantly, as if discarding what had been his life's work and scholarship took no more effort than offing a wet cloak after a rainstorm.

"I take it you now no longer hold those views?" Jonathan propped his chin in his hand.

"No. Upon mature reflection, I've come to embrace the received wisdom that has perpetrated—that is, perpetuated—good order for the Commonwealth for nine plans. The distinctions, the, uhm, diverse identities of our different realms and subrealms, that's what defines us. Gives us our roles. Good order."

"Our all for all."

"Yes, precisely."

"I've just heard from a number of defendants who seem to have had the same revelation. Unity's not all it was cracked up to be, apparently."

"Yes, well ..." Cloud faltered and his face fell into a darker shade of gray. He seemed to have difficulty swallowing, and when he finally resumed talking, a decided hoarseness had taken hold of his voice. "I'm, uh, afraid it's worse than that. I'm ashamed that any view I once held could have contributed to the present, uh, situation. I must try to make amends here ..." He drew a deep breath, closed his eyes once more, and then plowed into a rehearsed narrative. As he hurried through it, Jonathan could see Waters' eyes darting between the bench and the witness stand; twice, he caught the lawyer mouthing the words of Cloud's speech along with him:

"For the past several months, I have been assisting Commonwealth's Counsel Waters and others in a criminal investigation. One in which I was asked to openly espouse my formerly held views in order to draw out subversive elements that, the Board of Wardens had learned, were stirring trouble in Boaz. They call themselves the Guild of Solidarity, a title that purposely alludes to the unlawful confederations of the Crag's trade guilds. And they are your fifty-five defendants, your Honor. I was part of this group's inner circle and can attest to their crimes. They pose a clear and present threat to the peaceful co-existence we have in our Commonwealth."

Jonathan leaned his weight forward and extended one of his fingers to conceal the smirk that was spreading across his mouth. For the first time, the headache was receding.

"These defendants," Cloud continued, "have made numerous contacts with workers and tradesmen in the Crag, mostly known guildsmen, but also certain low-stationed clerks and even a few wardens. These two groups formed an alliance together. Together, they then made common cause with an unsanctioned religious sect in the Dwarven Quarter. This triumvirate of dissidents from the Crest, Crag, and Quarter hope to overrun the Citadel—and, eventually, the Crest itself—in order to impose their tyranny of leaderless, directionless slavery upon the whole Mountain, while enriching their leaders. They also hope to reestablish religion as an integral part of their new society, a religion that is so pernicious, even the majority of dwarves do not countenance it. Thus, various aims, but one common thread: a secret pact between confederates bent on rebellion throughout the realms. Their conspiracy has already fomented trouble and insurrection throughout the Crag and the Quarter, which has led to open warfare in certain areas …"

Cloud paused, seeing Jonathan bow his forehead into his hands. He was struggling to curb his laughter so that no one in the courtroom would hear it.

The utter preposterousness of the story! To have gone to all this trouble; even dragging in those two fair dwarves from the Quarter to lend it a patina of plausibility to this so-called conspiracy. And now former Judge Cloud, of all people, to deliver the closing argument. Brilliance. It could have been a play or a bad novel. He never would have ascribed such creative flair to the Stewards' lawyers.

"Please …" Jonathan waved at him, stifling the chuckle, "continue."

"Er, as I was saying, open warfare in certain areas, most notably the Gutters, which, in turn, has led to a grievous loss of Commonwealth property and life. The caravan's been stymied to a quarter of its former production. This was by design, as alluded to in the sixtieth proposition this guild has circulated, which reads—"

"I'm quite familiar with number sixty by now, thank you."

"Yes. Well. To conclude … to conclude … Well—I believe I've said what I must."

The master's shoulders slumped, as if finishing this monologue had only laid a heavier burden on him than the one he already bore. He was shaking his head, but in response to what, Jonathan could not tell. A wicked idea came to Jonathan from some inner prompting and, now laughing to himself, he could not resist asking:

"Tell me one thing, Cloud …" Jonathan leaned back in his chair, and he spoke breezily, without a care for the quizzical expressions that spread across everyone in the gallery, "as a former judge of this Court, if you were faced with this evidence and these charges … how would you have ruled?"

A terrible look came over Cloud. He started to waiver, and a part of Jonathan regretted debasing the man, more than he had done already. It was, however, a fair question, no matter how deeply it cut.

"Once, I would have …"

"I'm sorry, I can't hear you."

Cloud's face dropped and, at last, the scholar's mask fell with it. A lined, empty skull with vacant eyes stared back at Jonathan:

"I would do … what I had to do. For our all." He shut his eyes, perhaps so that he would not have to bear witness to what he was saying. "I would find every one of these defendants guilty of violating Article Two. And order them removed from the bosom and community of the Commonwealth."

"I see."

Jonathan surveyed the scene before him. The bored bailiffs sneaking whispered conversations in the far corner of the gallery. Nicholas standing beside him, watching Jonathan from the corner of his eyes. Solomon Waters had left counsel's table. He was nodding confidently and whispering something to Cloud who looked as if he were on the verge of collapsing. Almost unnoticed at her rickety table nearby, Jonathan watched the lawyer's clerk continue in her work, going back over her papers to jot down corrections, scratching out misspelled words—making the record perfect. A frumpy middle-aged chronicler of all that was and is, keeper of the great immutable transcript, the record, whose life and volume would go on, and on, long after everyone in this courtroom passed to dust. She licked the edge of the page, flipped it back over to where she had been before, and glanced toward the bench, waiting for the next words to capture in the snare of her quill. Jonathan gave her ten:

"The Court will be in recess to consider its judgment."

Jonathan was in uncommonly fine spirits when he pinched the redcap into the glass of water that awaited him in his private chamber. It was dark inside except for a lone candle burned down to the nub. The outer door was shut. His feet propped up on the table, Jonathan sipped his drink and absently glanced over the exhibits before him, still laughing softly to himself.

"Number eighty-five ... every worker and resident of the Commonwealth has an equal right to the economic, social and cultural rights indispensable for his or her dignity and the free development of his or her personality ... So they want to subsidize even more coffeehouse scholars? Just who's supposed to feed all this personality development, I wonder?"

He shook his head and drank down half the glass. The room brightened even more, and he noticed that Nicholas had slipped a document onto his table at some point during the trial. It was a judgment, filled out in every particular and carefully inscribed to include all fifty-five defendants, with the Court's seal already affixed. He had even written, in his inimitably prim writing, the word "GUILTY" by a blank space that awaited Jonathan's signature. Jonathan stared at the straight, spindly line above his name and title, and something about it bothered him. He set the document aside, picked up the book he had been working on, his book, now nearly two-thirds finished he reckoned, and opened it. A little free writing might clear his head before he tackled the case.

The diversion was interrupted by a prefatory knock at the door, followed by the creak of its opening.

Someone was entering his private chamber, unbidden.

"That was a nice touch at the end, Waters," Jonathan remarked, hiding the edge of annoyance that he felt. "With Judge Cloud, I mean."

"Thank you, your Honor." The lawyer stumbled about in the dark to find a chair and, again without invitation, sat down across from Jonathan. "He was quite eager to provide his assistance."

"The Commissariat will require a new instructor soon, I take it?"

Waters had the temerity to wink at Jonathan. "Well, we may require a magistrate or two in Boaz—what with all the sedition that's afoot. Cloud would seem to be a qualified candidate for one of those positions."

"That he would." Jonathan shut his eyes so that the lawyer would not detect his disdain. He finished his glass and wiped his mouth. "And Jacob and Okran, those fellows from the Quarter ... I had never met anyone from their realm before. Remarkable creatures."

"Don't let the size fool you. They're dangerous. All that passion, that religion. They're clever enough when it comes to making things, and no one's better at fixing the pipes, but they've been giving us plenty of problems lately. It's a matter the Crest can no longer ignore."

"No, I'd say you've given it foremost attention. And you've built an unassailable case that fifty-five of Boaz's worst parvenus have behaved like asses."

It was the first and only time Jonathan ever heard the Commonwealth's Counsel laugh aloud.

"Off the record ..." he said, grinning. "I'll allow these defendants, individually, do not pose the most serious of threats to the Commonwealth."

"They're absurd."

"On their own, yes." Waters leaned closer to convey a more serious note. "But the groups they are coordinating with—these workers, these zealots in the Quarter, they're not to be trifled with. There is armed conflict in the Gutters."

"I thought the line on all that was transition pains. Run of the mill disruption as we ease into a new plan. That's what the lectors have been telling the workers."

Waters fixed Jonathan with a long, searching gaze. The candle guttered then flared, briefly illuminating the spread of papers that lay in the space between them. At last, the lawyer spoke:

"The Tenth Plan has been completed."

Jonathan looked at him. Waters tapped his finger on the judgment on the table and continued:

"This is part of the Plan."

"I see."

They both looked at the document, the wax of the seal glistening orange in the candlelight.

"So, once you sign it, your work here will be done. We can have you packed up this evening—"

"I'm reading over it now," Jonathan replied. "And if the judgment is right in form and substance, I'll enter it."

Waters caught the hint and rose from his seat, bowing. He gave his respects and left Jonathan, alone, to finish his work.

"I do look forward to working with you again soon, your Honor," Waters paused in the doorway, "in Jachin."

As soon as the door had shut, a mounting vexation took hold of Jonathan. The skin on his wrists itched for some reason, as if something were crawling within. He glanced around the table and happened to catch sight of a minuscule spider, black with yellow legs, probing its way from the wooden crest of Waters' chair down to its arm. Jonathan's chest tightened until the thing had vanished again, and in the aftermath, the strangest memory flashed before Jonathan, obscure but no less vivid.

It was an image of that porter, the religious one Waters had tried earlier, standing resolutely before him. For some reason, he could now envision the man's clawed face in far more detail than he had ever recollected seeing it. Jonathan tried to clear his head.

The quiet voice came to him:

"*You have a problem here.*"

"I do," Jonathan agreed, "I've been offered a bribe. The Commonwealth's Counsel calls it an opportunity, which it is. But it's also a bribe.

They want me to make a ruling. An asinine, indefensible, unjust ruling that will kill fifty-five men and women whom the Crest wants killed. They need me to fill out the paperwork."

"*Have you considered the gains and the costs?*"

"Fairly straightforward, aren't they? Waters as much as said it: I'll get a seat on the Supreme Court. As part of the Tenth Plan. And my cost?" Jonathan's attention wandered. The candle at his table had finally extinguished. He closed his eyes in thought, struggling to place the apprehension he felt, a nameless, intuitive discomfort, within an articulate line of reason.

"The costs ..."

He honestly did not care a whit whether any of those cretins lived or died; and while he hoped Okran and Jacob could be spared, their fates were out of his hands here. Surely, this bribe had to cost him—something? Surely. There was something wrong, something he would lose, unique to himself, but the more he tried to grasp at its nature, the more the inculcations of his childhood rose up in revolt:

"Article Three: there is no right, only will; and none, but our all's, shall be allayed."

That was it, then. Some vestige of morality, a stubborn refusal to submit to the present demands of the collective, that was all this hesitation was. So, if the bribe truly cost him nothing ...

"*What you think is gain may be cost.*"

"How–how's that?"

"*Why the Supreme Court? Why Jachin?*"

"Because. It's ..." Jonathan—the part of Jonathan that was responding to the voice—hesitated, thought about the question more closely, a question that never occurred to him, and was ashamed at the only response he could find, an excuse that sounded paltry the moment Jonathan spoke it aloud: "It's just–it's just better."

"*Is it?*"

Here was an idea Jonathan had never pondered. Was it better? What was in Jachin? Nicer quarters, to be sure, more interesting cases perhaps. But it was also filled with people, most of whom he would probably detest. People like Gregory and his ilk. And worse. The kind that would watch him, that would titter at his every misstatement or if he ever so much as made an inflection that was out of place, the kind who would smile indulgingly whenever his gaze lingered too long upon a handsome man—and then excoriate him the moment he was out of earshot.

Michael would be there, eventually. And Mother. Regina's unblinking eyes always on him. Making sure he wore the mantle of Justice Acacia in just the proper fashion. Watching what he ate … what he drank.

The voice continued, its calm logic taking a firm hold over Jonathan, tightening like a noose:

"*In Jachin there is light. Awful, stinging light. It will shine on you everywhere, following your every movement, showing your every thought. You'll never escape it. Here in the Crag, you have the dark. A blanket to cover you up. A friend. You have solace—from all of them. No one is watching you here. We can do as we like in the dark.*"

"Up there, I would be …"

"*… a slave. Truly, you would.*"

It was like a revelation. A point so sublime, and yet so obvious, he wondered how he could have ever missed it. What he had been offered was a cell. A titled, esteemed prison. A shudder came over him.

His redcaps. Would all those prying eyes learn of his taste? What would happen to him when they did? What would happen to them?

"No!"

Jonathan was trembling. The echo, if that was what it was, resounded in his head. He looked down at his fingers, white-knobbed and clutched with fright. Beneath them lay the judgment, still beckoning for his answer. The very touch of the paper made him recoil.

Somehow Jonathan forced his left hand to steady itself long enough to take up the pen his clerk had provided. He missed the inkwell the first time, but then got the metal tip into the jar and was able to hastily add something, his judgment, into the tiny space he had been left for him. Before the scripted word "GUILTY," Jonathan scrawled the word, "not," and the wave of relief sent him, almost instantly, into a deep, restful slumber.

THE CRAG

CHAPTER THIRTY-ONE

H E HAD LOST track of the days. Not that they mattered anymore. Nothing mattered. Only to run, find, and hide. Movement and concealment. That was all there was, all there ever would be. Like before.

Tom looked over his shoulder and gripped at his stomach to keep it from rumbling too loudly. He was not so long without food that his strength would fail him if it came to a fight—but the lethargy would be setting on soon, he knew. The lightness in the head, the tingling in the fingers that made you slow, made you drop things that you needed to hold. He needed to find something to eat.

His clothes were in rags, and his hair had become a wild tangle. A scruff of beard covered most of Tom's face, a mask sprouting over the mask that had settled upon his mud-stained features. His eyes roved constantly now, watching for threats that were everywhere.

Another glance down the tunnel's length to make certain no one had followed him, then he turned to his side and shoved himself into a crack in the rock wall. As thin as Tom had become, the stone surface still scraped his skin as he wriggled further and further in. He made one last lurch and broke through the crevasse into a low, narrow grotto.

An old hiding place. From before, back when he …

A thought was struggling to form, unbidden, so he killed it before it could lay hold of him. He came here for a purpose. Focus on that, and that alone, and keep moving. His cold fingers fumbled around in his pocket. A chain bracelet with a hinged, grated orb that dangled from its end; he opened it up and pinched half of a gulleystar mushroom inside of it. A small yellow light flickered, and when it had steadied, Tom set the miniature lantern down on a stone and searched the floor. The bracelet was the only thing he had had time to take from—Tom winced and pressed his eyes shut tight.

"Not now," he said to himself, somewhat surprised by the edge in his voice. "Not yet."

Grim thoughts could be shaved away, like scraping the leavings from a hide, so long as you kept your focus sharp. Tom summoned a different memory, a very old one, trying to recall where the hiding place would be. He strained to keep it before him, the image of this place as it was when he was a child. He could almost see it. The grotto's floor, a bean-shaped oval of pebbles, fine dust, and sand, and pungent with the smell of rat droppings, was slowly becoming familiar again. It had been much warmer back when he was a boy, that was what had drawn him here. It seemed bigger then. Tom's gaze drifted toward the far wall and he saw that the lone steam pipe that had once shared its heat had turned into a crumpled skeleton of brown rust. Tom approached it and then began sifting through the dirt underneath with his hands.

Like ashes. Like in the market …

He shook his head hard. He could hold that memory at bay a little longer.

A small cloud of dust hovered above the indentation in the ground that was gradually forming. He waded through more silt, using his hands like spades, searching for a layer of clay that was once there, but the loose soil kept sliding back in. He had to move his hands much faster to keep the hole from collapsing on itself. Then one of his fingers brushed against something smooth. A piece of paper. One of many, neatly folded and still spaced exactly as he had buried them.

Bit by bit, like shards of pottery, he brought them out of the hole until he had formed the better part of a small document. It was all in fragments but still preserved enough that it fit together. Near its top were his name and a clerk's signature alongside a stamp. Tom could make out faded stenciling, what was left of a report he had once memorized with the help of a kindly lector:

"… *who presents above-average aptitude for language and written communications,*" Tom pretended to read along the page as he spoke the words aloud, "*and satisfactory performance with rudimentary mathematics. However, with insufficient records to confirm parentage, health, or disposition, per Guideline*

10(a)(iii), this assessor must recommend placement in skilled labor in any available classification. Entered 20th day of summer, 5th Year, 7th Plan."

He was on his knees, smiling at the recollection of the pride he had felt when the lector read it to him, the way she had whistled at how impressive a report like that was, especially for a foundling boy who never had any tutoring. Why, there would have been no telling where he might have gone if he had had a little help, the lector had winked at Tom and gave him a warm pat on the shoulder. "I might have had to bow and tip my bonnet to you," she had laughed.

A memory burst in his mind like floodwater. At its crest, came a voice:

"They bow to her ... What has she to do with the dwarves?"

Tom could hear him, as plain as his heartbeat thumping in his head. Captain Oliver's lisping fury and the deep, dreadful gong of a bell. The grotto receded, and now all Tom could see was the market, as if he were trapped there again. The stalls in flames. The bodies stacked on top of one another like cordwood. Smoke. Warriors in the shadows—no, warriors that were shadows. They were dwarves.

And one had knelt before Lillia.

Lillia.

The tears came on their own, unstaunched. Every thought became a dart. One after another, in merciless succession, they struck him down.

"Lillia."

His hand crumpled a fragment of the paper. His stomach growled. He rubbed his fingers in his eyes, smearing his tears together with the grime, and, heedless that he was sobbing uncontrollably, Tom went on with his work, digging in the dirt, searching for things he had laid away and hidden when he was a child.

He floated through empty corridors and passages of the Lower Ward, a ghost hovering between the remembered habits of his past and a present that seemed to hold only a tenuous grasp on him. Mold covered stairwells fell beneath his feet, crossing signs of old neighborhoods, lampposts flickering, fading into obscurity with no one coming to refill them, a dusty fountain, a shattered Commonwealth seal crumbled across the ground where it had fallen. Images presenting themselves in no particular order and with no real recognition. A waking sleep. Tom was scouring in the shadows, searching.

There were fewer people out now than before. Fellow specters going through the motions of their lives. Some tilled on the Farms, others wandered in circles, weeping softly to themselves. Sometimes a clerk would dart around a corner, as fast and frightened as a mouse bolting for its hole. Once, Tom heard sounds in the distance—of a bell, then screams, and then some kind of fighting. The ground quaked, and Tom had fled.

He floated through the Crag, hiding in the spaces between the tunnels and the untamed cracks of the Mountain, running, hiding, scavenging, and all the while searching. A kind of wandering vigil.

He would never find Lillia.

Part of Tom knew that and accepted it, an immutable fact that he calmly acknowledged, akin to knowing he would never see the Crest, or walk on the moon. A deeper part of him railed against it, violently. Somehow, he held the two in equipoise.

A plan had taken hold of him instinctively and completely. He would keep looking for her. He would never stop looking. If the fires had died out in the market, he would go back there and start his search. He had to be careful, very careful, but he would see for himself—with his own eyes—even if he had to turn over every inch of the Lower Ward.

Tom carried a sheering knife he had dug up from his old hiding grotto. Each hour that he passed was like another stroke from the blade. A cut, a scrape, more detritus cast away, layer by layer. Until what was left for Tom was a vision that had become suspended in his every moment, a single thought that propelled him through the Lower Ward's labyrinths. Its very clarity sustained him.

He remembered an armored warrior, no taller than a child, on his knees. Wreathed in flames. Lillia was shining like a star before him, her light bending around its silhouette like a spout of water.

"*They bow to her ...*"

The light disappeared. The darkness retreated after it. The memory of Lillia had passed.

Tom turned a corner and pressed himself against the wall as a troop of guards passing the far end of the corridor disappeared. The stairwell to the market was nearby. He would count to five hundred, he decided, more than long enough to make sure the wardens would not circle back on him. And then … he would climb to the marketplace.

As he waited, his fingertips scraped against the cold surface of the rock. They found a void where he brushed upon something spongy. Lichen as soft as fur, and within it, a cluster of mushrooms sprouting. There must have been moisture leaking somewhere behind the wall, Tom thought. A burst pipe perhaps. He pinched and brought out a handful of the mushrooms.

Flesh-colored, with thick rounded heads, the kind that could be eaten. He was about to pop the bunch in his mouth when he noticed one near the bottom of his palm that stood out from all the others.

It looked like a lump of charcoal with red splotches. Tom picked the gulleystar out and twirled it before his eyes, studying it, a strange compulsion coming over him. He wondered what would happen if he ate it, if it were different than an ordinary gulleystar, which would turn your stomach. There was something lustrous about the way the red flecks almost seemed to glow, even without being pressed. And then another memory came to him.

At the Farms. Lillia talking with the lector by the bonfire. At the lector's urging, she had crushed a redcap just like this one beneath her little foot, for luck.

A sad smile broke across Tom's haggard face.

He bent over and carefully placed the redcap on the floor beneath his heel. He put all his weight over the foot until he heard the mushroom crack. There was a tiny red flare of light in the empty tunnel that died as quickly as it flashed.

He had his luck now. It was time to look for Lillia.

The smell of burnt wood and refuse clung to the air at the market's entrance. Twining shoots of gray smoke still rose in the distance, but the ashes had begun to settle. White and gray flakes covered the flagstones and the broken debris, a snowy blanket that concealed nothing under-neath it. A few gulleystar lampposts had enough life in them to reveal what was left of the wreckage in a haunting light. Every bit of the mas-sive oval cavern was broken or burnt. A small cloud of ashes briefly stirred and then scattered into a flurry from a breeze. It sparkled for a moment in the dim light by the doorway before it disappeared. Tom frowned at it.

He would have preferred darkness. The broken stalls, the overturned crates, some of the larger pillars, could offer cover, but there were gaps, wide-open squares, and crossroads in the marketplace, that were still well lit. He could be seen. From the look of it, the gulleystars probably had another three, four days left in them. It would be better to wait until they had all faded out. But by then, the scavengers would have the place overrun; and the guards would be sure to follow.

Tom crouched low and craned his ear. In the distance, he could hear feet scurrying, a plank being shifted aside.

So, people were already beginning to return. The allure of unguarded food and goods had overcome whatever fear still emanated from the massacre in this place.

The far end, Tom reminded himself. That was the place to start. To see if she was ...

Tom took a deep breath and stepped out onto a terrazzo shelf that marked the outskirt of the market. The acrid scent filled his nostrils, the smell of cinders and bodies. He crept heel to toe keeping as close as he could to the walls and ruins, a furtive shadow flitting in the peripheral company of great shadows. Sometimes Tom would catch a glimpse of a rat; they, too, had returned at the prospect of an easy feast. Otherwise, the market was as still as a tomb.

He came to a lit lamppost that loomed from the midst of the wreck-age of a lector's chair, and he had to stop. Flickering bright within a shattered pane of glass high above the ground, there was no way to get around its yellow light. In the glow of the gulleystars, he could see a crossroad, a wide and open space that ended in the market's obelisk, now thoroughly scorched and naked of the signs that once festooned its surface. It was a dark, silent sentinel, the next closest hiding place before he could reach the back of the market, where the carrot stall had stood.

Tom surveyed the space. Corpses were lying where they had fallen, hundreds of them, indistinct forms covered in the same shroud of ash tinged with a dull golden glow from the lamp's light.

Tim would be out there, among the dead. This was about the place where he fell.

Tom's mouth grew tight.

Later. Right now, I'm here for Lillia.

He bent low and dashed across the road, trying to keep his footfalls from making any sound. The air burnt his lungs, and Tom had to swallow hard to keep from coughing aloud. As the granite monument drew closer, he saw a semicircle of crates piled high on the far side of the obelisk that looked like a place he could stop and hide. Tom raced through the light, past debris and bodies, and jumped over the crate closest to the obelisk. His foot rolled underneath him on the uneven floor, and he cried out, not from pain, but in surprise.

Four hooded figures, sitting cross-legged and facing each other, looked up at him.

They were gaunt, hollow-eyed, and seemed to be gazing through his body, as if his intrusion were not the slightest concern. The closest one—Tom could not tell if it was a man or a woman within the shadow of its hood—asked him in a distant, empty voice:

"Have you come to join our vigil?"

"Your—?" Tom's head spun around to see if anyone else was about. He stooped down and rubbed his ankle. The four figures sat passively, neither welcoming nor rebuffing Tom's presence. There was no danger he could sense in any of them; even beneath the bulky sackcloth cloaks they wore, Tom could see that all four were as frail as the mounds of ashes they sat upon.

"What are you doing here?" Tom asked.

"We come."

Tom blinked. The figure who addressed him continued:

"We come at the blessed one's call, he who fell and rose again. Our prophet."

"Your—what?"

"Our prophet," the figure repeated, and the others drew back their hoods and lifted their faces so that they could bring their forefingers to the bridge of their noses. They were all women, raggers by the look of them, and when the light caught ahold of their eyes, Tom could see that they had gone lunatic.

"He called us in our dreams," she continued as if singing a melody, "to come to this place to stand guard. Over there," she flicked a knobbed finger in the direction of the far end of the market. "That's where the darkness will return. So we come—to battle it. Are you going to join our fight?"

Tom's thoughts were a swirl.

"I–I'm just looking for food," Tom lied. "Do you know if there's any left?"

"Our prophet's words are the true food of life." Her companions intoned after her:

"His sacrifice our one true defense. He shall save us from the hidden ones. Be it so."

Tom glanced past the raggers. There was some movement in the distance near what looked like it could have been one of the food stalls. The place would be swarming with every hungry body in the Lower Ward before much longer. Tom started to get up:

"You'll forget you saw me," he warned, "if you want to live long enough to see whatever you're waiting for."

"Our prophet told us there is only one true death," the first woman declared, "the death of being bound in the dark. With Lillia."

Tom's feet rooted to the ground; his knees buckled. Hearing the sound of Lillia's name spoken aloud by this madwoman drove every thought from his head. He caught his balance on the edge of one of the boxes and slowly turned.

The woman's eyes were piercing in the darkness. Tom strained to summon his voice:

"Who—who did you say's in the dark?" he managed at last.

The woman dropped her head to spit in the ground. "Lillia. She who scatters darkness in light. And carries toil in her hand. She left this place to delve the shadows of the Mountain. To summon her hidden children. Soon she will return here with them. The prophet foretold it," the woman clasped her hands in prayer and bowed. "He warned us to keep watch for her here."

Tom dropped to his knees and drew close to the ragger. She wreaked of bile. His hands were trembling as he spoke:

"You said Lillia—I heard you say her name. What do you know about her?"

The woman's eyes rolled as if she were going into a trance. Tom grasped her by the shoulders, pressing his fingers hard into the protruding bones. The woman did not flinch, but her voice hummed.

"Tell me about Lillia!"

She fell into a kind of song that was joined by the others:

"*The darkness she sings. The toil she brings. Save us, oh save us, from the hidden ones. The darkness she sings …*"

Tom let out a loud groan. A barrage of questions, stammering and almost incoherent, followed. How did she know Lillia's name? What happened to her? And over and over: where is she? Where is Lillia?

"*Save us, oh save us, from the hidden ones.*"

He slapped her hard across the face:

"Tell me where she is! Tell me, you bitch!"

"*Darkness she sings …*"

Tom knew this was pointless. Like trying to pry the truth from a startled child. All these raggers could speak was gibberish. And yet …

If you press a gulleystar, sooner or later, it will shed light.

He could press these women. Hard. Hurt them. Wring out what they knew. A rapidly fading part of Tom's consciousness was warning him that he was losing his senses, just as these raggers already had. Tom watched his hard veined hands shaking the ragger by the neck.

"Where is Lillia?! Where is she?! Tell me!"

"Eli … will come again …"

"I'll break your neck—"

The woman's head rattled about, but she only sung louder. Her three companions lifted their hands and joined her.

"*Tell me!*"

Rage had taken over Tom, blinding all his senses, the ones that should have warned him there was movement in the darkness beyond the obelisk, drawing closer, hemming him in.

CHAPTER THIRTY-TWO

J ACK'S FOOT STRUCK a half-buried beam. He was running, and his momentum sent him stumbling headfirst into a pile of ashes, his clerk's sash tumbling off his shoulder. Jack cursed loudly as he picked himself up and wiped his palms clean on the sash. His big toe was throbbing, and when he looked down at his clothes, he noticed he had gotten blood on himself somehow, someone else's.

One of the shadows running ahead stopped long enough to hiss back to him.

"Move your ass, boy. Before they get away."

A smile spread across Jack's dirt-stained face. He started to hobble on his hurt foot to catch up.

"Right behind you, Topher," Jack panted.

It was Jack's first press. The exhilaration of sprinting in an open cavern alongside a troop of sweating, burly, foul-mouthed wardens was ushering back fond memories from all the times he worked with the hands on Prosperity Farm. Only now he was not after goats, but men; and these weren't swarthy, guildsman ranchers he was working with. This was a press crew. The stoutest, boldest wardens in the Crag. And he was part of it. Despite the smoke lingering in the air and the near darkness that surrounded him, Jack felt giddy.

He ducked beneath a burnt awning and tried to keep pace with the press crew's sergeant, Topher, a burly shadow running before him. For a man who must have topped fifteen stone in weight and seemed to sway like an ox with his strides, Topher could be surprisingly swift, and silent, when he needed to be. Spreading out from Topher's flanks, Jack watched an assortment of grizzled fighters begin to sweep across the grounds of the ruined market. It looked like they were aiming for the monument near the center, the one shaped like a giant stylus.

"A good press crew's like a cast net," Topher had explained to Jack before they set out. "You cast it quick, open it wide, then draw it tight fast—so nothing gets away."

Jack bustled after the press crew, nearly tripping once more before he came to the periphery of a lamppost's light where he paused to hide. Hidden in the shadows, he could now make out the quarry that was about to become trapped in Topher's net: a group of Craggies sitting in a circle. There were five in all, bunched up together and trying to conceal themselves behind a ring of crates. The press crew closed in around them undetected, Topher's men hurrying now to close in around the monument and cut off any escape. Jack crept a few feet closer to get a better view of what would happen.

It was strange, but it looked as if the Craggies were fighting among themselves. A man was standing up, arguing with the others about something. Topher was only a few feet from them now. They had no idea what was coming. Jack giggled in his hands and almost failed to notice that Topher was looking straight back at him, jabbing his finger hard in his direction.

"C'mon, sash!" he hissed between his teeth.

It was Jack's cue.

He was so excited, and out of breath, and flummoxed because he had never done anything like this before that he fumbled to open the packet of papers he had brought with him.

"Can't start 'til you read it!" Topher said, his voice an angry whisper. "That's the law."

"Sorry, sorry," Jack said.

Jack spread the paper open and angled it so that it caught some of the lamppost's light. He sucked in a deep breath and started to read the words aloud, like a command, just as Topher had taught him. His voice strained and then cracked, its sound falling without an echo in the marketplace:

"In the name and by the authority of a duly constituted commission of clerks and wardens, all those who can hear these words are ordered to halt and pay heed. I repeat: halt and pay heed. Do not move. Do not speak. Do not resist. This is a call for service."

One of the Craggies, Jack noticed from the corner of his eye, had stopped whatever it was he was doing and was trying to break through the ring of men that now surrounded him. It looked like he was wrestling with one of the crew and getting the better of him until three other men piled on top of him. It was turning into a melee.

"Keep reading, dammit," Topher prompted him. "He's not going anywhere."

"Sorry," Jack found the place where he left off. "This is a call for service" he read, "to those who are able-bodied. Your Commonwealth needs your work to meet a pressing exigency. Your present labor assignment is hereby suspended. Your new assignment will be explained to you once your paperwork has been completed and processed. You have the right to object to this reassignment. You also have the right to receive the fruits of your labors upon commencement thereof. Govern yourself accordingly. As an authorized clerk, I will now process your forms."

Topher nodded at Jack.

"That'll work," Topher grunted. "Come on over here with your papers. Looks like we got one that was worth the trouble."

Jack tried his best to ignore the chaotic scene unfolding beneath the light of the lamppost. Several crates were smashed to pieces, a cloud of ash had been kicked up, and most of Topher's men were still fighting to hold down a half-naked, bearded wild man. The remaining guards were leading four ragger women away, all of whom were singing as loud as they could—something about darkness and toil. Topher did not seem the least concerned with any of it, though. He motioned for Jack to come closer.

"Don't be scared, sash," one of the wardens with the raggers jeered at Jack as he passed by. He twirled a length of rope like a lasso above his head. "We'll get these girls tied up so they won't hurt you."

"Shut up and do your work," Topher growled. With a great sigh, the sergeant set himself down on the only remaining box that could hold his weight. He pulled a leather hood off his head, wiped the sweat from his brow, and waved the hood for Jack to come next to him. Jack tried not to stare at the ear that was missing from the side of Topher's broad, hairless head.

"Not a bad press, Jack. We caught a keeper. I want you to process him as a guard. Under my command, got that? I like the look of him. As for those others," he absently ran a finger across his throat, "needn't bother with that paper work. They're Elites, and I've got *no* use for Elites."

"The ones that pray to a dead porter?" Jack asked.

"Yep," Topher slipped his hood back over his head.

"But …" Jack hesitated to contradict Topher. "Shouldn't I at least take down their names? I mean, so it's official what we—"

A sudden scream rent the air. Out in the darkness, the sound was repeated three more times, and each time it was cut suddenly short.

"Officially, they're now dead," Topher replied. "Just do this one here."

Jack could hardly bring himself to look at the Craggie they had caught. Bloodied, ragged, frantic, dirt and ash spilling from the scraps of cloth that still covered him, he was twisting in every direction, struggling to break free from the four men who each held one of his limbs. The Craggie's head was bowed, a trickle of blood spilling to the ground from his nose, but he did not look at all subdued. The men who grappled him were swearing loudly. They, too, were bruised and bleeding, almost as severely as the man they held captive.

"Go on, then," Topher waved at Jack impatiently, "You've got to do the questions before we can finish pressing him. That's the way of it."

"Oh, right."

Jack flipped his paper over to find the form—this was all so new to him—and squinted at the first question:

"Name?"

One of the press crew holding the man by the arm gave it a hard jerk, causing the man's shoulder to turn. The Craggie grunted in pain.

"Give the sash your name," the guard warned.

"Noman."

"First name?"

At first, the man offered no answer. Another twist of his arm, another moan, and his name came out:

"Norman."

"Norman Noman?" Jack shook his head. "Where are you presently assigned, Noman?"

The man paused, then gave a halting answer:

"Farms."

Jack dropped the paper and for the first time regarded the man more closely.

"Yeah? What plot were you assigned to?"

"What's it matter?" Topher said, his voice a rumble of growing impatience.

"It's just—" Jack started. Cautiously he started to creep closer towards the pile of men writhing on the floor. "I think he might have worked near the counting-house. I think …"

Topher blew his nose in his sleeve and swore at Jack.

"Who cares? He ain't farming anymore. Finish up so we can get back to—hey! Watch him!"

In the lull of Jack and Topher's discourse, the press crew's grip on their quarry had slackened just enough for the man to make a desperate lunge to get away. He wriggled an arm free and pulled a scraper knife from underneath a loincloth. The blade flashed in the lamppost's light, and then it went flying.

One of the guards, the one who had twisted Noman's arm, scurried off, yelping in pain. He curled on the floor and covered his face with his hands. The blade had sliced his nostrils open.

"Bastard!" the wounded guard squealed. His fingers were becoming drenched in his blood. "*Bastard!*"

Topher's roar came loud and fast. "I said, *hold* him!"

Jack leaped out of the way as Topher bounded over and threw himself on top of the pile before Noman could pull himself all the way free. All the men, Noman and the press crew, grunted beneath Topher's great weight, the air forced from their lungs.

"Hold still," Topher ordered.

More shouts, a volley of curses, Noman's body kept flailing, searching for some other escape, but he was growing weaker now. He jerked a few more times from the bottom of a tangled mass of bodies, then slowly grew still.

"That's more like it," said Topher, "no point getting killed over this. You just lie still and let the sash finish his job. Everything's going to turn out fine for you, you'll see."

Topher kept talking, never noticing that the wounded guard had gotten back on his feet and was making straight for the man who had cut him. A knife was in his hands, unsheathed from a hiding place inside his boot. A trail of blood trickled alongside each footstep. There was murder smoldering in the guard's eyes, Jack could see it.

"Hey," Jack pointed at the guard feebly. "I don't think—"

Noman inhaled a ragged breath followed by three gasps:

"Is there—no help—for a worker's son?"

Topher drew up with a start and happened to turn around. And then he too saw what was about to happen: "Hey, Sullivan, what're you doing there with that blade? We can't use blades in a press—you know that."

The knife dropped from the guard's hand with a clatter. Sullivan pointed to his ruined nose as if the stream of blood pouring out of it might not have been obvious for everyone to see:

"Look what that bastard did to me!"

Topher let loose a ringing laugh from the belly. He tapped the side of his hood at the hole of his missing ear.

"That's nothing. Ever seen what happened to me at my pressing? Just leave that knife right there. Clerk'll take it off your hands. Go on, boy."

Haltingly Jack crept over to Sullivan, bent down, and picked up his knife, pinching it between his fingers as if it were a snake coiled to bite him. Sullivan spat on the ground.

Sullivan's face was screwed into a fierce scowl. "I want to pay him back."

"You don't whip a dog for being strong," Topher said. "Our orders were to get fighting men, and this Noman's a fighter. So there ain't going to be any payback. We'll take care of that little scratch of yours back at camp. Here, use this in the meantime," Topher tossed a rag from his pocket over to Sullivan. Then he called down to the pile underneath his bottom. "Hey, Noman. Thought I heard you say something just now. Can you hear me?"

Noman made a sound, something between a grunt and a desperate gasp for air.

"Tell me," said Topher, "where have you come from?"

"From the—base," the man moaned.

"Mm-hm. And, uh, where were you traveling?"

"I—I—dark ..."

Topher stroked his chin.

"He's out sir," one of the other guards reported.

Slowly the pile of men unmade itself and the guards of the press crew stood back up, one by one, stiff and aching. They stared down at the sprawled and battered body of the man they had pressed, now out cold, grumbling to one another about the fuss he had made. A few kicked Noman's ribs in payback for their hurts. Jack tiptoed through the guards to draw closer to him. Something about the Noman's voice had roused Jack's curiosity.

"Better wait 'til we shackle him," Topher warned Jack. "You can finish your papers later. He's a Noman, that's all we need to know for now."

Jack got down on his knees and peered into the man's face. Purple welts covered his cheeks, and both eyes looked like they would remain swollen for a few days. He was an animal. But one that seemed oddly reminiscent of …

"I know this man," Jack's voice broke. He was on his feet now. "He's not a Noman. He's a guildsman. A guildsman named Tanner."

Topher squinted at Jack for an uncomfortably long time, like a boulder staring at a fragile little animal that had wandered beneath its shadow, one that was on the verge of being crushed. At last, he wiped his mouth and the stony lips cracked into a half-smile.

"You don't say?"

Topher leaned back in a chair and draped his arm behind an old well spout. The leather hood had become askew so that the vacant hole of his left ear was peeking out from underneath like a third eye. He was sitting on the edge of a small, octagonal alcove, a place where, once, servants of more prestigious masters could pump their water in private. The well had not given a drop of water in years, and the only light came from a line of mismatched gulleystar lamps strung along a cord across the ceiling. Their incandescence reflected against a bright sheen in two of the walls, polished rose quartz paneling that still shone through, a jarring contrast to the lumps of mortar that had been plastered across the rest of the room. A rusted metal door, the room's only ingress, allowed the rare luxury of privacy. A good place to hold a conversation out of earshot, if one needed to in the Lower Ward. At the moment, the door was shut.

Tom shifted his weight from one foot to the other. He was standing in the room's center dressed in a coarse pair of black pants that were sliding off of his hips and a faded yellow guard's tunic that hung from his shoulders. Tom kept pulling at the tunic under his left arm. Part of the cloth beneath his armpit had been stitched back together around a bloodstain, which made the fit uneven. He rubbed at the line of welts on each of his wrists, where a set of shackles had just been released.

"I'll take that from you," Topher gestured for Tom's document. As Tom approached to hand it to him, Topher grasped onto Tom's hand. "You've got something else for me, I think," he added. Tom gave him the guilds' token, and the sergeant nodded. He fixed his leather hood and then scanned Tom from top to bottom:

"Well, let's have a look at you, Tanner, now that the quartermaster's got you outfitted. Hm. Much better," he said, ignoring the pattern of black welts across Tom's face. "Still could use a shave, but a big improvement overall … Just need to get you fed up a little, and then we'll make a warden's man out of you in no time."

Tom stood mutely and stared straight into Topher's face.

"Lucky break for you, Tanner," Topher said. "Out there, all alone in the shit holes, scavenging. No assignment. No pass. Not doing any work. You might have been taken up. Or worse. You came across a press crew just in time. Now you got some new clothes. You've got proper work and papers. You'll get some food. You're a lucky man, Tanner."

The sound of Topher's heavy breathing, a rasping inhalation followed by a series of guttural noises, filled the span of silence between them. Tom studied the sergeant's face, wondering where the hood ended and the forehead began. From outside, a baby's bawling cry was followed by the peal of a woman's laughter.

"I've done you an enormous turn," Topher locked his dark eyes onto Tom's, "I've pressed you into my personal service, which means no one but an officer can touch you. You don't need to thank me, but you'll damned sure keep your bond by not doing anything foolish—like trying to run away."

Tom swallowed dryness, then gave a curt nod.

"Good. There aren't many of us left. Guildsmen, that is. I'd hate to have to kill a brother."

"Your boy Sullivan seemed eager enough to do that for you," Tom said.

"That was the kid's first press. And you gave him a pretty souvenir to remember it. He'll do as he's told, though. He's a good guard that way."

"Like his sergeant," Tom answered.

Topher's mouth slowly spread like a crack in a foundation:

"Just like me. Since you mention it. See, I got pressed right after I finished my apprenticeship. The sergeant that pressed me, he knew I was a guildsman. Didn't give a damn. All he cared about was that I could out-wrestle any man in the Lower Ward, him included. I could take a blow," he tapped at his missing ear, "and keep right on swinging. You know what he told me then?"

"No."

"Same thing I'm telling you now. You're a lucky man."

Tom set his face like a stone, revealing nothing. Topher leaned forward with a crooked smile.

"You can do as you like as a warden—so long as you can do as you're told. How about it, brother? Can you do as you're told?"

And here was the whole point of this interview, Tom realized. He had put himself in the hands of a brother guildsman; and, in so doing, the man had put himself into Tom's. The time had come to take one another's measure, and to see if a bargain—if a bond—could hold between them. Only once had Tom ever transgressed the bond he had made as a guildsman, for Lillia's sake, when he had denounced a brother—to a warden. Now he would become a warden himself. The irony may have eluded Tom, but the thought did not, and it troubled him. At least this guildsman who had become a guard was laying out plainly what would be required of Tom. And if indeed Tom could 'do as he liked,' as Topher said, perhaps Tom could hope to make his way back to the market—to look—eventually. It was, Tom reflected, a kind of luck, if not the precise kind he would have liked.

Topher was staring at him. At last, Tom drew a long breath:

"Do I have a choice?" Tom asked.

Topher shrugged. "Sure. You know the rules. Everyone has the right to object to being pressed. We'll get you chained right back up and send you onto Craggie Court, so you can make your case—"

Tom shook his head. No one who ever objected to a press assignment left the Tombs. Tom was pressed. He might as well tell this brother what he wanted to hear.

"Nah. I'm your man."

"Good." Topher's attention turned for a moment to the paper Tom had handed him. His eyes glazed over the writing, and then he flicked it to the ground and cracked another smile. "Norman Noman, huh? That the best you could do?"

"It was all I could come up with at the time."

Topher waved at him not to worry about it.

"Everybody tries to give a fake name when they're pressed. Don't know why. Names don't matter for shit. I'll call you 'Mama' if you want me to, so long as you do what you're told. But, uh … I think you'll have to stick with Tanner. Seems our little Jack already knows you. Knows you real good, I gather."

Unsure of what Topher may have been told, Tom gave an indifferent shrug:

"He's a clerk I helped out once."

It was the polite and widely understood way for a worker to identify a sash he had needed to bribe. Topher nodded knowingly.

"Uh-huh. I figured. Listen, don't worry about him. Little bastard practically begged me to press him when we swept up the Farms for men. Clerks would never let that happen, but I got him reassigned to my crew, and now he's as happy as a whore on payday. Don't worry about Jack. He likes it here too much to get sideways with me. He'll do as I tell him. "

"Thanks."

"You'll come to like it, too, Tanner. Even in times like these, being a guard's about as good an assignment as men like us can hope for. And being personally assigned to me ain't a bad draw for a rookie. I take care of my own, you'll see."

Topher let out a knowing laugh which Tom returned with a jagged half-smile. The bruises over his face made it hurt to move his mouth. The sergeant wiped his eye with a dirty finger, and then Topher dropped his voice, indicating a more serious turn.

"You came along at a good time. See, while we're encamped, there's what you might call a, uhm, sensitive task that needs doing. Nothing hard about it—it's just a prisoner detail—but it needs a man who can keep mum about what it is he's doing. Who he's guarding. You might see a couple of things that some of us," here he arched his eyebrow meaningfully to indicate he meant himself and Tom, "may not want the whole camp to know about. As a brother, I can count on you keeping it to yourself. You'll keep your head down, and no one else will ever know where you're assigned or what you're doing. You can keep your mouth shut, eh?"

"Yes," Tom answered, though he had no idea what Topher could be talking about. He was starting to feel light-headed. He needed to eat, then sleep. "I can."

Topher looked pleased and returned to his chair where he made a pretense of studying Tom's orders. "Don't suppose you can read?"

The question stung Tom for some reason, though as a worker he would have had no occasion to have learned how. Tom admitted he couldn't, and Topher nodded with satisfaction.

"All the better," the sergeant said. "So, you'll just do as you're told. As *I* tell you. Nothing more. Even if your orders don't exactly read right. Even if a clerk puts down something different. That won't matter to you. 'Cause you're my man. And you'll do exactly as I'm going to tell you now."

Tom met Jack in front of a lean-to tent not far from Topher's office. The boy was standing behind a high table, scribbling on the back of the paper Topher had told Tom to hand him and seemed singularly intent on ignoring Tom's presence. Behind the clerk Tom saw a workstation of men and women, all sitting cross-legged and busy mending what looked like an enormous fishing net. Torches burning oil-soaked rags shed a wavering orange glow over the gathering. The net's webbing, Tom noticed, seemed to be steaming, as if it had been recently burned. Most of the workers kept their hands bundled in rags or scraps of leather so they could touch the ropes. None of them bothered to look up from their work at Tom.

"So what were you doing in the market, Tanner?"

Tom was startled by the question. Jack was leaning on his elbows, staring at Tom with an insolent expression.

"Not that it matters," Jack continued, "now that I'm off the Farms, I could care less. Just curious what made you leave without getting papers from me."

"I was—I was looking for something."

"In the market?" Jack shook his head. "Pretty stupid of you to—" Jack paused, a thought coming to him. "Lillia was in there, wasn't she."

Tom kept his face steady, a cold, imperturbable façade. Jack folded his arms and sneered:

"If she was in the market when it got sacked, she's dead. The dwarves don't leave survivors. She's a corpse now. Like all the other dumb Craggies in there." He narrowed his eyes into slits and then added icily: "Serves her right."

Tom would not rise to the bait. He stared straight into Jack's pinched, gray eyes and immediately took the boy's measure: a frightened child struggling to face him like a man.

"She was in the market," was all Tom said.

Jack looked away and pursed his lips:

"Figures. She should've worked with me when I gave her the chance."

A spindly old woman carrying a sack appeared from nowhere and shuffled wordlessly past Tom and through the tent. Without prompting, the menders in the workstation dumped refuse they had gathered from the net into her bag. Jack folded the paper he had been writing on in half and motioned for Tom to step closer. Reluctantly, Tom approached the table.

"Listen, Tanner," Jack pointed toward the crimped words scrawled across the page. "Topher left your orders open. It's for me to decide where you're assigned. So, I've put you on a trawling crew ... for now."

There was something wicked lying beneath the cocky little smirk on Jack's mouth.

"I've never worked on a boat before," Tom replied.

Jack thumped the table's surface. "Not a boat, you idiot. Nets are how we fight the dwarves now. Snatch them up, hold them down, then kill them quick as we can before they kill us. It takes a dozen men to handle one of these trawling nets. If we're lucky, a couple might make it home from a fight." His eyes pulled Tom's towards the order lying open on the table between them. "I just wrote your death sentence, Tanner."

Such an impotent little ass, Tom thought to himself. This was tiresome. But Jack might grow suspicious if Tom didn't perform his part. So Tom wrung his hands and darted his eyes while feigning a bluff that even the densest boy would see through:

"Well . . ." Tom licked his lips, "such is life in the Mountain. A clerk's pen sets to write, a warden's sword—"

"Yeah, yeah," Jack nodded. "But *this* clerk's pen," he jabbed his thumb in his chest, "could write something different for *that* warden," he pointed at Tom, "if he wanted to."

It was all Tom could do to keep from rolling his eyes.

"What is it you want?" he sighed, already knowing the answer.

Jack tried to sound plaintive, reasonable, but the greed in his voice came out like drool on his lips:

"Nothing much, really," he said. "Same price as before. What got you on the Farms will get you off a net. You do have more … don't you?"

Tom let the silence fall between them, pretending to be stuck in deep and anxious contemplation. In truth, he was thinking about how annoying it was to have to play this farce and string along this sash when he had promised food waiting for him. Best to play along, though. The boy was still a sash, after all.

"When the market got attacked," Tom made his words come out slowly, "it happened so fast, I-I … I put everything I had in a hiding place. Then I ran."

Jack leaned forward hungrily.

"So that's why you went back to the market."

"Uh-huh. I think I can find it. I just need some time."

Jack regarded Tom closely while the work crew behind him sewed, and cut, and mended the charred and bloodied lines of a fishing net. One of the sewers called out for the woman with the sack to return. She had plucked a couple of fingers from the net and wanted to throw them away.

"Alright, Tanner," Jack smiled. "I can wait a day or two before I stamp your order. Better hurry up and find what you're looking for. I'll be in touch soon."

CHAPTER THIRTY-THREE

TIME TO EAT. He had gotten his papers from the clerk. They weren't stamped, but that didn't matter since Topher had all but told him the clerk's orders would be just for show. Tom's orders—his *real* orders, from Topher—were to get his papers, eat, and then report for his assignment. His actual assignment.

Tom followed the first scent of food he came across. It led him around a corner from the net menders' workstation and then up a short rise in a tunnel that opened up into the Lower Ward. As the cavern mouth widened, Tom felt his breath leave him.

Stretched before him was what looked like a nomad's city. One that seemed to have sprung up from the roots of the Mountain.

Hundreds of tents, huts, piles of rocks with shingles, lengths of rope layered with blankets as makeshift walls—every imaginable kind of shelter—sprouted like mushrooms across the plateaus and basins of a wide grotto in the most random hodge-podge of groupings. As if half of the Crag had been corralled into this honeycomb in the Lower Ward and told to make a place for themselves.

Smoke from countless fires fed a gray smog that hung in the air, making it hard to see beyond a few yards in any direction. Tom tried to get his bearings among the throngs of people walking aimlessly everywhere, but the only signs that had been posted showed obscure pictures with arrows pointing in opposite directions. At last, though, Tom happened into a clearing that, from the litter of broken axles and wheel ruts, was apparently used for moving heavy wares, and there he found the end of a meandering line of workers. They were all waiting for their turn to go into a cave within a far wall, which was glowing orange with fires and spewing out black smoke. A strong waft of burnt cooking oil hovered in the air. The food line, Tom gathered from the murmurings.

Tom sidled into the bustle of sullen, hungry-looking workers. One fellow not far ahead of him was licking his hand furiously. The rest stood melancholically awaiting their turn, the way they had always waited for the allotments in their lives.

As Tom drew closer to the cave, a rusted furnace came into view. It was belching a steady stream of flames and smog into the air and attended by a slew of cooks who had their faces wrapped in rags. At the edge of the cave's entrance, there was a pile of clay plates to pick from.

Tom heard an angry commotion break out ahead of him. The man who had been licking at his palm held one of the plates, apparently waiting to be served, when one of the cooks grabbed his hand, looked at it, and beat the man mercilessly with an iron ladle. The sight of it sent a brief ripple of laughter down the line.

Step. Wait. Shuffle. Wait a little longer. At last, Tom reached the periphery of the cooking cave, and the heat from the furnace already felt sweltering. By the time Tom reached the serving station, his new uniform was sticking to him with sweat. He picked up a plate and followed the motions of the queue. A squat, boil-faced woman sitting next to an open grate in the furnace plunked down Tom's meal—one heavily fried potato, three beets, three soggy mushrooms, and a few leaves of cabbage—while a second woman gestured impatiently for Tom to give her his hand. Before he could ask why, his palm was wet with paint, and the woman's dire warning of what would happen if he so much as tried to wash off his "dinner marker" before tomorrow was ringing in his ears. "You got the fruit-o-yer-labors," she said with an impatient wave, "off you go." Shouts to hurry along rained down on Tom, and the line pushed him forward to the other side of the cave's entrance.

He walked and ate, happily gorging himself on the first food he had had in days. By the time he finished licking the plate, Tom felt the hunger that had been his constant companion finally slink back into its lair. In its place, a warmth began to percolate. His stomach was full and his head was empty, and so Tom found himself wandering the encampment, making sure he remained, as Topher insisted, "inconspicuous."

It was easy melding into the camp's activity, and since Topher had not told him to hurry through his meal, Tom decided he would take his time and perhaps learn the lay of this new place a little better before he reported for duty. As he passed by a row of potato plots and latrines, he spotted someone who looked like a chattering type, a short, wiry, bow-legged man washing a mound of soiled, bloodied jerkins in a scrub bucket. He was plunging one after another into the brown water and paying no mind at how soaked he got. All the while, the man was talking openly to himself and, judging by the occasional bursts of laughter, very much enjoying his own company.

"Ahoy there," the man haled as Tom approached. The little drenched fellow set down a brush next to an almost empty bottle of cragfire long enough to give Tom a friendly wink. "Call me Wag. Everybody does 'cause of how I wag my tongue all the time."

Tom felt himself smile. "Alright, I will. Listen, Wag. Would you trade you a pull for a hand?"

"You've got a bargain!"

To Wag's obvious delight, Tom only took a small sip of gin from his bottle. Tom set himself to work rinsing one of the piles of laundry and quickly found how Wag had earned his moniker. Without uttering a word (he hardly had a chance to), Tom learned more from helping Wag wash and hang a pile of jerseys than he ever could have on his own.

"Fucking dwarves," Wag spat into his bucket. "Vicious, savage, god-spewing bastards. Hit us when we weren't looking. But now we're fighting back. Oh, that we are. They may be tough to kill in all that armor—but not impossible," Wag cackled grimly. "Little bastards are running like rats now. Back to where they came from. No one's heard any of their gongs for days now. But then it's hard to be brave and bold when you're hanging upside down in a trawling net. Ha!" Wag laughed, as he threw a pile of wrung out clothes at Tom for him to hang. "Now it's time to take the fight to them. Put an end to all this, once and for all. Don't know about you, but I'm looking forward to it—not the fight, I'll have no part in that—but getting back to my regular work. I was a laundryman on a crab skiff. It's true. Now that's the life, let me tell you. Nothing better than being out on the open water, talking to the gulls—"

"Who's going to lead this attack?" Tom slipped the question in to keep Wag from straying into a new topic.

"Huh? Oh, whoever's in charge these days ..." Wag made an expression, one familiar to Tom, to indicate he had ventured into a subject above this man's rating and training. Not that Wag refrained from a little more musing:

"Nobody knows *exactly* who's skippering all this," he gestured at the camp around him, a trail of laundry water following his hand, "don't need to know— but I *suspect*, whoever it is, he'll want to press a few more men before he makes his launch. Probably need to get the clerks to fill out some papers, too, make sure they're all on board, that sort of thing."

Tom shook his head and talked aloud without thinking.

"I can't believe the Crest wouldn't—"

Wag suddenly plunged his arms into the water, all the way down to his shoulders, making a loud splash. A warning look told Tom to shush. A bubble of soap quaked under Wag's chin as he shook his head.

"Best not to talk too loud about what's what up *there*," he muttered into his bucket, "if you catch my drift?" Then, leaning closer to Tom and in a hoarse whisper that anyone would have heard, he added: "Maybe you're new, so you haven't got your bearings yet. With all this fighting and commotion, we haven't exactly been keeping up with our allotments to the Crest. I know for a fact there weren't no caravan to cross the Spine yesterday. First time in probably a hundred years. Clerks are real fussed and bothered over it, but they don't want to end up with a dwarf's gaff in their gullet either. So, no one talks about quotas and such, or the Crest, at least for the time being. Not the kind of thing we ought to be discussing over laundry." Wag peered at Tom closely to emphasize the point, and then offered what was meant to be a kindly face. "Just do your part and say, 'Wait 'til the new Plan comes out,' that sort of thing when it comes to the Crest. Do you follow my wake?"

Tom nodded and Wag straightened back up. Glancing about him to see if anyone had been listening, he said loudly with a wink at Tom:

"The new Plan will set everything straight. Yes, it will. Any day now."

There was, Tom discerned, a roughly spun order that had either been imposed or had spontaneously evolved for the camp's layout. More likely the latter. He heard it in the accents of the guards and workers lingering about the smoldering campfires, but he could also see it in how the different groups held themselves. Lower Warders and Farmhands had taken up places on the periphery, dockworkers and porters had settled a little further in the encampment, while the clerks and skilled tiers of laborers had the stations on the higher ground in the center, where Tom was heading.

He walked a long while, slipping in and around the knots of people and dwellings until he came to a rise that gently sloped upwards. At the crest was a wide plateau and a low-roofed building which seemed to serve the sole purpose of fixing in place a massive mast and boom, lashed with a Commonwealth banner as broad as a sail. The sword, pick, and hammer emblem was spread taut, as if it might capture a breeze if one were to ever blow, and the winking lights of gulleystars underneath it played tricks with the amber coloring of the cloth. Just as Topher told him, you couldn't miss it if you tried.

Following the sergeant's directions, Tom veered around the building's left and began walking across the dusty elevation until he found a lector's stand. An irascible looking woman was leaning out from the seat like a perched vulture over a congregation of women, who were mending another net. The lector was spouting a constant stream of escalating numbers—potatoes harvested, pelts cured, tools made—"all of which," the lector practically dared someone to contradict her, "is thanks solely to the guidance and direction of the Stewards during these difficult times. We should be grateful that their new Plan is quelling the temporary disruptions we have been experiencing in the Gutters, which workers are reminded to avoid unless they have a sealed—*wax* sealed, mind you—clerk's warrant to ..." Tom ducked around the stand and went on until he reached another, even more secluded plateau hidden behind a gathering of rock columns where there were no more buildings, or tents, or stations and hardly any lights.

Half-blind in the dark, he shuffled out, a lone insect crossing the expanse of a quiet, stony field, and reached in his pocket for the gulleystars he had brought with him. It felt oppressive, the loneliness; more than once, he caught himself glancing over his shoulder at what sounded like a whisper in the air. But he was supposed to wait until he was certain he was out of anyone else's sight.

Worried that he might be walking in circles, Tom decided he had gone far enough. He squeezed his hand tight, felt the pop and crackle of the mushrooms, and held the glowing mass out before him for light. It made a pitiful glow, the illumination seemed to fall dead before him. His eyes strained, and Tom wondered how he was supposed to find anything at all out here, whether he should violate Topher's command for silence and call out for help. But he pressed on, tiptoeing so that the only noise he made was his teeth chattering in the cold, as he waved his hand slowly from side to side.

His foot found it for him. A small ridge of rock jutted out from the otherwise featureless floor. Tom's little toe stubbed against the side of it. He winced and then crouched down to examine it more closely. As he brought his gulleystars around in an arc, he could see what looked like the tip of a tongue poking through the flatness. Tom scurried around to the other side where he found a hole and a run of spiral stairs descending into the dark.

Carefully, Tom made his way down the long, winding flight until the cramped stairwell suddenly opened up into a low-ceilinged chamber. At its far end was a barred door.

There, in the shadow beneath a sputtering gulleystar lantern, Topher sat with his back against the rock wall, a club straddled across his lap. He eyed Tom warily, and for a moment, Tom was worried that the sergeant didn't recognize him. But then Topher clambered to his feet and tugged the brim of his leather hood.

"You found it," Topher said by way of a greeting. He peered over Tom's shoulder to make sure no one had followed him.

"Yeah." Tom studied the archway carved into the stone and the smooth steps he had just descended. "Odd place to put a room."

"Odd's a good word for it out here. But no one comes here much, so it serves our use." Topher glowered at the darkness around him, as if something in it offended him. "C'mon, let's get you set up."

Topher had a ring of keys clamped around one of his wrists. He felt for the one he needed and unlocked the door. Inside, Tom found a warm, almost welcoming glow. Someone had splurged for oil lanterns along the walls. They were all burning freely on long wicks. As Tom's eyes adjusted to the light, he saw that they were in a long rectangular room. The farthest quarter of the chamber, however, remained shrouded in shadow. A set of jail bars separated the darkness from light. At his side, adjacent to the front door, were the room's only other furnishings: a straw mattress and a blanket, a desk and chair, and a coal stove. Bubbling on top of the stove, a foul-smelling pot of liquid was about to boil over. Topher shoved it aside and then called out into barred off darkness:

"This here's your new guard. He'll look after you now, do your feeding." Topher jutted his chin toward the stove and said to Tom: "There's a spoon and a rag under the desk. He eats through the bars—when he eats. Try not to make a mess, 'cause no one but you'll be here to clean it."

"So," Tom said haltingly, "this is—a jail?"

"Pretty much."

Tom stared hard into what he now realized was a makeshift cell, but he couldn't make out anything within the shadows. Sensing his confusion, Topher continued:

"You'll see him soon enough." He made a face at the cell as if to challenge whoever was in there to come out and show himself. Then he turned back to Tom. "Look here, Tanner. This assignment's real simple. There's one prisoner in that cell. It's your job to guard him. Keep him alive. Keep him safe … And don't breathe a word about what you're doing. If he don't behave, you'll have this," he handed Tom his club, "and if that don't work, you'll have plenty of hot gruel." A leer spread across Topher's scarred face. "Little splash of that'll keep him in line."

"When do I report—?"

"You don't," Topher shook his head. "Like I told you, this ain't something we're going to talk about. No matter what your orders say. You'll stay put in here. You know where you got your food?"

"Yeah."

"I'll make sure the cooks set aside a good allotment for you. You won't even have to stand in line for it. When it's time, you lock up the door, head to the kitchen, get what you need, and come straight back here. That means no more wandering around," he fixed Tom with a knowing look. "Unless you're fetching your allotment, you're to stay put in here. Got it?"

"Yeah," Tom repeated. He was starting to feel a sagging weight bearing down on him. His assignment sounded more like a sentence.

"You're a lucky man, Tanner," said Topher, clapping him on the shoulder. "You got the easiest job there is. You keep him in there, and you keep to yourself. That's all there is to it. I'll come and check in on you later, brother."

With that, Topher dropped his keys unceremoniously onto the desk and shoved the door back open, leaving Tom, seemingly alone, inside the jail.

Tom closed it after Topher, and then he stood quietly by the desk for a long while, wondering what he ought to do. He listened to the sound of his breaths, the crackle of the flame in the stoves, a bubble from the gruel. He moved the broken wooden pen from one side of the desk to the other. He had never had time to himself like this before, where there was no work, no scavenging, and no danger to contend with. It was oddly disorienting. Tom looked around the room, searching for something that needed his attention. The gruel had started to cool so he poked at it absently with a ladle. Then he rearranged the keys on the desk. He neatened the blanket on his bed until, at last, his curiosity nagged at him. He took a few cautious steps towards the cell.

The bars were rusted but bolted fast on all sides to the floor, walls, and low ceiling. The caging felt solid in Tom's grip. A real smith, a guildsman, must have done the work. He stared inside, careful to avoid glancing back at the oil lanterns, and slowly his eyes adjusted to the darkness. Like a dawn break, the cell went from black to charcoal, then, at last, to colorless gray. It was stone inside, and it looked cramped in the long shadows from the lanterns' light. He could see flakes of moldy straw littered across the ground. In a corner, he caught the glint of a metal bucket that had been tipped over, probably the cell's toilet.

Motion stirred in the dark. A shadow roused from one of the corners. Tom let out a sharp breath. He squinted to get a better look at it.

It was a small shape. A man, or maybe a boy, lying on his side. It turned over and moaned a word that Tom could not understand. Tom went back to the desk for one of the lanterns. He brought it down from its hook and held it up to the bars to get a better view.

"Hello?"

The prisoner let out a sharp, pained gasp. He was wincing, flailing a hand at the light, and Tom quickly fumbled to return the lantern to its place.

"Sorry," he said. His voice, though a whisper, rang loud in the darkness.

The shadows settled, and Tom stood before the jail bars, transfixed, listening for the next movement. For a long while, nothing happened. The patch of darkness in the corner played tricks with Tom's eyes again, as if it were oscillating or flickering, the way a candle might if it shed blackness instead of a glow. But it made no other sound or motion.

Tom worried that his prisoner might have died, and how he would have to answer for it when he remembered the food. He tiptoed back to the desk and rummaged for a bowl that he wiped clean with the end of his guard's tunic. The gruel on the stove, a colorless, scentless mix of water and flaccid bits of shape had settled into a lukewarm stew. Tom served some into the bowl and brought it over to the cell.

"Here," Tom clinked the spoon against one of the bars, "got your meal."

The man in the dark remained where he was. Tom thought he heard a sigh.

"I'll, uh, leave it here," Tom bent down and gently set the bowl and spoon on the floor. "If you want to eat in private—"

"Need … help," a strained voice rasped.

The man in the cell was sitting upright now, and though still concealed within the darkness of a shadow, Tom could see that the figure was much shorter than he.

"Alright," Tom called to him, "come over here then."

There was a pause and then a shuffling sound. He was hauling himself across the floor by one bent arm, his legs dragging behind him. As he came into the dim light near the cell's bars, his features came into relief, and Tom stifled a gasp. It was just what Topher told him it would be.

A dwarf.

The sight of him left Tom speechless.

He gaped at the man on the other side of the bars. Wrapped in gauze and scraps of smock, much of the dwarf's face and body were covered, but Tom could see from what little of his flesh showed through, he had been horribly burnt. Cracked, blackened flesh, marred with lesions that were still weeping fluid. His hands were engulfed in bandages that had been wound into stumps. As terrible as his wounds appeared, it was the look fixed upon what remained of his face that struck Tom most, haunted him from the moment he laid eyes on the dwarf: it was like a noble child's face, searching and intelligent, filled with life, but marred.

Tom had never seen a dwarf before, and the sight of this one, broken and disfigured, left Tom feeling a deep sense of melancholy. As if something beautiful had been needlessly ruined. It brought to his mind that wrought iron arch soaring above the pilings of the Docks, a wonder that had been left to crumble into rust.

"You'll not—spit," the dwarf was struggling to form the words from his caked lips. "Last—jailer," he continued, "spit in—spoon."

Tom came back to his senses. He shook his head.

"No, I'd not do that."

The dwarf grunted and then positioned himself up against the bars so that his back was resting. Grimacing in pain from the effort of movement, he was able to incline his head to the side just enough that part of his mouth fit between the bars. Tom spooned small bites of the gruel into the dwarf's waiting mouth, gently blowing on each spoonful before serving it to him. One of the dwarf's eyes was studying Tom as he ate, a glowing amber iris, but slowly, the watchfulness diminished. They went through half the bowl, neither saying a word, until the dwarf turned his head back around to indicate he had had his fill.

For a while, the two sat together, each eyeing the other from opposite sides of the metal bars. It was the dwarf who spoke first, and when he did, a slight smile unwittingly came over Tom because, with the strength of the food, a note of music could now be heard in the dwarf's voice:

"Have you a name, jailer?"

"My name's Tom. Tom Tanner."

The dwarf murmured to himself, and to Tom, it almost seemed like a song. Tom longed to hear more. Tom tried to sound friendly:

"What's your name?"

The dwarf's eyes narrowed. He sat in thought for a long time, and then, as if some unspoken concern had been resolved, the dwarf drew a deep breath and let his words ring like a bell:

"I am Elon."

Tom sat cross-legged before a charcoal fire, a huddled figure beneath the shadow of a small rise of rock, finishing his allotted meal. The fire was low and it shed a meager light in the empty field of darkness that surrounded him.

When he looked up again, he was somewhat surprised to see Topher's shadow plodding towards him from the dark. Tom whistled softly to the sergeant and lifted a fork in a faint wave.

"You call this guard duty?" Topher said as he tromped over the fire. He was out of breath and streaks of sweat coursed from underneath his leather hood. Without a word, Topher grabbed Tom's plate and stuffed the last bit of meat in his mouth.

"It's my mealtime," Tom replied, his voice low. "I'm off duty and enjoying the fruits of my labors."

"You're a warden, you're always on duty."

Topher said it tritely, like the hackneyed slogan it was. Our all for all meant much the same to workers. He handed the empty plate back to Tom and plopped down next to him.

"Why are you eating out here?" Topher asked.

"Can't build a decent fire in there without smoking us out." Tom kept to himself that it was also a kindness to his prisoner, who seemed to dislike open flames. "Been a while since I've seen you," Tom remarked.

"You complaining?"

"Nope. Just wondering what brings my sergeant out here."

Topher made what, for him, would have passed for a worried face.

"Things are stirring up," he sighed.

"More fighting?"

"No. Dwarves haven't come into the Crag for weeks now. This is different. Now it's like we're chasing shadows. Or the shadows are chasing us. You heard the latest?"

Tom gestured at the hidden jail behind them to show it was not a place where news frequently traveled.

"There was an attack in Fellowship Corridor," Topher said. "But it wasn't no dwarves. No gongs, no footprints, not so much as a scratch on any of the bodies. Just," Topher snapped his finger, "dead. Six bodies in the middle of a tunnel, and not a cut or bruise on any of them, all looking like they might have been asleep."

Tom shook his head dismissively. "Sounds like balm."

"I wish it were, brother. But I saw them myself. Got a good look at them all just before the corpses were burnt. It was like—nothing I ever seen before. I ..." his voice trailed off until he recollected himself. "So now the word is, we're going to be moving out of here. The clerks. The wardens. What's left of the guilds. Everyone agrees. It's time to go. Something just ain't—right out here anymore."

Tom murmured in acknowledgment.

"I don't know what that'll mean for our friend," said Topher.

"He's improving," Tom observed. "But I wouldn't try to move him yet."

Topher gave Tom a searching look.

"He ain't *ever* moving, Tanner. What do you think we've got him locked away for? Why the only man I've got guarding him is a guildsman that don't ever speak unless spoken to? If the Craggies knew we had a dwarf within spitting distance of camp, there'd be a mob coming to rip him to pieces. And us along with him ... Nah. That there's his tomb, most likely."

It was a truth Tom had already come to realize, yet hearing it made him sad all the same. A question that had been bothering Tom for some time came out:

"Then why did we bother keeping him?"

Topher smiled:

"I asked the same thing Tanner, when I pulled him from the net. Yeah, it was me that found him. Thought he was dead, like the others we'd caught up, but then he starts to moaning about some lady—probably his missus—and I wasn't sure what to do. So, I called over a brother of ours, and it was him that gave the order to hold him under wraps ... See, some think we ought not to close off all our ties with the dwarves. Despite the troubles they've given us. Keep an inroad to the Quarter, just in case. Maybe strike a new bargain."

"Like a new Plan."

"Something like that."

Tom would not let on that he understood Topher's meaning perfectly, perhaps better than Topher himself. It was an obvious point.

They needed the dwarves. They always had. The Farms, the Docks, the water pipes, the tunnels, even simple tools—anything that needed to last—the dwarves had always been the ones to fashion and fix such things. Without the dwarves, everything in the Mountain would fall into ruin eventually. In a way, wasn't that what was happening around them now? Killing the dwarves was like a long, slow suicide for the Crag.

"So, he's an inroad," Tom said.

Topher shrugged. "I'm told he's got some pull. Enough to make him worth holding onto. Has he talked to you at all?"

"Some," Tom replied.

"Good. Keep him talking if you can. Some good might come of it."

They stared out into the darkness and listened to the sound of cross drafts howling through the hollows and the tunnels off in the distance and the charcoals crackling out the last of their light and heat. Topher grew strangely silent as if something more was vexing him. Tom was unsure whether he ought to disturb the sergeant's reverie. When the fire was little more than red embers, Topher brought out a thumb-sized gulleystar lamp, smaller than Bette's chained orb. A single mushroom crackled between Topher's heavy fingertips, shedding a useless glow, one which did nothing but highlight Topher and Tom's presence within the void that surrounded them. At last, Topher spoke, but his voice sounded flat, drained of his usual vitality. He pointed out ahead in the darkness.

"Look out yonder, Tanner."

Tom's eyes, never very strong, could find nothing to focus upon.

"Don't look straight, but out of the corner of your eye. You'll catch it if you're not looking for it."

"What is it?"

"Something's—stirring out there."

Instinctively, Tom started to rise, but Topher held him in place.

"It ain't dwarves. And it ain't men. Just … a stirring. I've noticed it lately, in the open places … I don't like it."

No matter how hard Tom strained his eyes, he could see nothing ahead but blackness. But Topher remained fixed on whatever it was that troubled him. The breeze died down, and now Tom could hear Topher's guttural breaths. He was leaning forward, hovering over the dying campfire, gritting his teeth. All the while he kept repeating, more to himself, how much he didn't like whatever it was that he sensed.

If Tom could have seen better in the dark, he might have detected a change coming over his sergeant. And it would have seemed familiar to Tom. Like the one he had once noticed in his daughter at the tannery. When she sat, staring long into the darkness of a lake, listening for voices.

The same shadow had slipped into Topher's eyes.

"It only takes you twenty minutes to fetch your dinner," Elon said with a long slurp of his gruel. He wiped the bottom of his lip with one of his bandaged hands. "They must have your plate waiting for you."

"How would you know that?" Tom replied. He fixed his prisoner with a suspicious gaze. "Have you got informants in there? Or did someone sneak you a clock?"

Elon shook his head in exaggerated disbelief.

"Why in all the gods' names would I need a clock to tell me how time passes? You just count it out."

"Right, right, the counting thing. I forgot."

As Elon had tried to explain to Tom before, one could measure time without resorting to watching the sun or the moon. It was a simple matter of counting. Being aware of the space between events. And tracking the longevity. The rhythm of keeping a count in one's head seemed to come as naturally as breathing to Elon's people. Tom tried it briefly but found it was impossible to focus on anything other than keeping the tally of the numbers. He had made it no farther than forty before he gave up.

"You were gone for exactly twenty-two and one-quarter minutes. It took you eleven and a half minutes to eat your plate—thank you again for not cooking it in here—and then it took you seven and a half minutes to make my stew."

Tom chuckled to himself and wedged a bowl in the bars for Elon to feed himself.

"Eight minutes," Elon said as he lifted the first spoonful.

He finished the bowl beneath Tom's bemused gaze.

Since Tom's first arrival as his guard, they had gotten to know each other in these snatches of banter. And in that time (however long it had been, only Elon could say) Elon's condition, if not his appearance, had improved. Remarkably so. Of course, no doctor had ever visited Elon; Tom knew Topher would have never allowed it even if there were one to spare in the camp. There was nothing special in the gruel Tom cooked for him. Yet, Elon could feed himself. And he was walking now, upright and on his own. With a noticeable limp, to be sure, but he could pace the perimeter of his cell three times around before needing to rest. His voice had also grown stronger, and it brought delight to Tom every time he spoke.

Tom suspected, though he couldn't quite put his finger on why, that Elon was drawing this renewal—from Tom, somehow.

The lanterns had been dimmed, and in its closeness, the jail felt almost comfortable from the chill outside. Tom set a second bowl with a fresh spoon on the floor before the bars and then relaxed on his stool, stretching his long legs before him. When Elon finished it, he abruptly stood and began his paces around his cell. It had become a routine between them since Elon had regained his steps. As he walked, the conversation resumed, as if it had never paused.

"Not a bad jail," Elon pronounced, scanning the expanse of bars, "for men's work. Six locks seem a little off, I'd have made it an even seven. Guildsmen built this place?"

Tom watched him turn a corner, smiling.

"Why do you ask?

"Just to make talk. I already know it to be true. I can see those ridiculous guildmarks—they look like eyes staring back at you—stamped on every one of the bars."

"So there are," replied Tom without looking.

"What's the point of those things?"

"The guildmark? It's supposed to show that something's been made by a guildsman. That it's halfway decent."

"Sacrilege," Elon sniffed. "Craft reflects the soul. It should be better than decent. It should be perfect, or not be made. I presume you're a guildsman then?"

For Tom, that had always been a question to be answered with an abstruse reply—"I'm paid the fair fruits for my labor," something of that sort—to be followed with a lie if the inquiry was pushed. Yet he found himself nodding yes to Elon, though it cut against a thousand grains within him.

"I figured," said Elon. He shifted his position to get more comfortable. "When my bards sing of my daring escape from this cell, I'll be sure your brethren are treated respectfully. They'll tell of the fast iron hold buried deep in the men's realm—that no one but Elon could break free from."

"Can't wait to hear it."

"There'll be a verse about my silent, stalwart, gargoyle-faced jailer, as well."

"No songs for me, thanks," Tom said, chuckling. "Make sure to tell them it was Topher who was on guard duty when you broke out."

Elon leaned his head against the iron caging, a film of sweat moistening through his bandages. His breaths were beginning to sound labored. He shut his eyes.

"There'll be no escape for me," Elon murmured. A pained expression passed over his features, and it cut Tom to the quick. "I should have burned with my men in that cursed net. That's a proper way for a warrior to fall. Would have given the bards something to sing about."

The sight of Elon—Tom could no longer think of him as a dwarf—trapped in a cage, wearied and doleful, sent pangs of sorrow through Tom.

"I-I'm sorry," was all Tom could say.

Elon's charred lips curled up into a smile.

"As am I."

Tom held out a hand in between the bars to help guide Elon back to the ground. He lay on the ground before Tom, his chest rising and falling in panted breaths. Tom brought him a skin of water, which he took a long pull from, letting the liquid trickle down his cheeks.

"Thanks, jailer. At least I'll have kind company when my line comes to its end."

Of all the strange threads of conversation he and Elon had shared in the confines of the jail, this was the most intimate. It took Tom by surprise:

"You don't have any other family?"

"Father's passed. Now my cousin's dead—thanks to your people."

"What about a wife, children?"

"My people can't have children," Elon replied. "That has been our Curse. Our punishment. Ever since we made a treaty with your people to end the Overthrow."

"I—I'm sorry. I didn't know."

There was anger in the air, Tom could sense it, but it quickly passed, and Elon lifted a wrapped hand, what was meant to be a wave that he would not hold it against Tom.

"We seldom speak of it, even amongst ourselves." Elon was trying to lighten the tone in his voice. "But what about you, good jailer? Are there little jailers waiting for you when you leave for supper?"

Now it was Tom's face that clouded. He quickly regained his features, but it must not have escaped Elon's notice:

"Have I now caused you a hurt?" Elon asked. "That was not my intent."

"I had two," Tom said, and for some reason, speaking of it aloud, with Elon, felt as if a burden that had long been weighing on his shoulders was slowly being lifted. He realized he had not spoken about his children to anyone since that day in the Farms market. "A girl and a boy."

"Tell me of them."

A distant smile came to Tom's face. He reminisced, a sequence of pleasant scenes flittering before his memory:

"The boy was a good sort," he said. "He was going to be a tanner, like me. But he died in a market."

Elon looked directly into Tom's eyes, held them with an understanding, a sympathy that was unalloyed by pity.

"As for my girl," Tom continued, "now, she was a rare one. Clever. So clever. Could read, and write, and make numbers do tricks—you would have been amazed at all the things she knew."

"Cast from her father's mold, no doubt."

"No. No, she's far beyond her old man."

"Did she fall in the market as well?" Elon asked, his voice rasping with a quiet intensity.

Tom fell silent, and after a pause shook his head hesitantly. "I—I don't think so. I mean, she was there. Right next to Tim. But ... I never found her body. I tried to look. I mean to keep looking for her, only …" He let out a long breath. "I don't think I'll ever find her. She—you won't believe this."

"Tom," Elon laughed sadly, "you would be shocked at what I'll believe. My poor late bodyguard certainly was. I've lost everything, my fortune, my friends," he tapped at the bars of his cell, "my freedom—for what I believe in. I believe in a goddess that no one but a cluster of derelicts and I have ever seen. She's turned out to be a heartless bitch, by the way. But I've gone right on believing in her. She told me to come into the gods-forsaken holes you men live in, and I followed her. Because I believe whatever I'm told." He fell into a burst of pitiable laughter. "You tell me what happened to your girl at the market, friend jailer, and see if I won't believe it."

"You'll think I'm mad."

"Perhaps. But perhaps it's a madness we can share."

Tom stared into Elon's eyes. The spheres in them seemed to steal the lantern's light and shape it into something more lovely, like liquid gems. Elon sat, listening, and beneath his gaze, Tom felt a need begin to overtake him, to delve into himself and bring out what had been sealed off within the reaches of his memory. That day in the market, the horror, it came back to him of its own accord.

Tom told Elon everything that happened.

It must have sounded incoherent, Tom feared, like a gush of impressions. No matter how hard he tried to fit the images into language, what he was trying to express kept slipping away, eluding him; he knew no words that could capture what it was he had seen. For his part, Elon remained quiet, paying close, if guarded, attention, until the point when Tom described the change he saw in Lillia's appearance, the awful shining light that surrounded her just before she disappeared, and then, all of a sudden, Elon rose.

His mouth had dropped open, and he pressed himself hard against the bars as if Tom's every word had become the most precious sound Elon had ever heard.

"And then they were all in front of her, all the warriors," Tom said, "your people, but they were disappearing, and the fire and smoke were everywhere. I couldn't see much, but I could still see her. Shining so bright it almost hurt to look at her. One went up to her … and then she was—was just … gone."

"Tom," Elon croaked. His fingers were outstretched between the bars, trembling, begging Tom to take them in his hand. Tears flowed freely down his ruined cheeks. "You're not mad—you're not. You are *blessed*. Blessed among men."

In his hand, Elon's fingers felt hot to the touch. Tom tried to pull away, but Elon would not let go of him. In his eyes now, Tom could see the flicker of an orange flame.

"Tell me," Elon pressed, "as your daughter shined light in the market, was there one of my people who—saluted her."

Tom's eyes went wide.

"Yes …"

"And laid a trident before her—"

"—he-he had a helmet on, I remember now. It looked like-like clouds or a-a—"

"—a storm."

Tom felt his heart pounding in his ears:

"You were there?"

"It was I who knelt before her."

Tom was struck senseless. Inside his cell, Elon was weeping, but not from pain or sorrow. Still in his grasp, Tom trembled with him, the bars between them nothing more than shadows, wisps of smoke.

"Miserable, faithless worm!" Elon's shoulders shook. "Blasphemy on my lips, and still—still, she calls out to me. Blessed be the Maiden. She's alive! I came at her call, and she's blessed me. Oh, blessed be Lillia! She lives!"

In the days that followed, Elon pressed Tom unceasingly on two topics. Mostly he wanted to learn all he could about Lillia (which Tom gladly indulged). But sometimes, despite Tom's obvious discomfiture, Elon would try to steer Tom into a rambling discourse about Elon's gods (which Tom found both unnerving—gods and priests were, after all, supposed to be abhorred—and more than a little baffling). Their time together became a whirl of words that halted only when Tom could no longer keep his eyes open and had to sleep, or when it was time for Tom to run outside to fetch their food from the encampment's kitchen. On each returning, Elon was waiting to pick up their talks wherever they had left off. Tom, who had never spoken so much in all his life, had grown hoarse, but Elon was unrelenting.

At Elon's urging, Tom shared every detail, every story, no matter how mundane, and every remembrance he had of Lillia's life, her upbringing, her dreams, her foibles. Far from dissuading Elon of the absurd notions he held about his daughter—for, as Tom gathered, Elon was apparently convinced that Lillia was a goddess—the proud recounting of a Crag girl's father somehow buttressed them. To Tom, much of what Elon said was a jumble of nonsense. Elon's joy was no less infectious. He constantly found himself grinning alongside his prisoner.

"Yes, yes," Elon clapped his hands once when Tom had paused to wet his throat, "it all makes sense. Matches perfectly with the old stories—perfectly, you see? If only Nicodemus were here! Even he'd believe. Nord delved in mines; Kaley brewed beer. Amdal scurried about like a lizard under rocks. Lillia's tale is just like all the other stories. Just like them! They're always born humbly, you see? The gods come to us in a low form—so that we can exalt them. Oh, if only Kohath, Merari, and Gershon had lived to bear witness to this …"

Tom, of course, had no idea what his friend (for that was how he thought of Elon now) could be talking about. If anything, Tom suspected that Elon's belief in his gods, or his wounds had begun to leave him touched in the head. Yet, that didn't matter at all to Tom. It was a magnificent madness to be in the presence of.

"She's alive," Elon breathed for what must have been the thousandth time.

Over and over, he had said it. And each time Elon spoke those words, their assurance had taken a firmer hold of Tom. Like warmth that spreads from a hearth's fire. Elon had seen her just as Tom had in the marketplace, saw her disappear, and knew she was alive. Hearing it from Elon was like an affirmation of what Tom had felt.

Of course she was alive.

Lillia was much too clever to be dead. Wasn't that why Tom had been scouring the tunnels and corridors outside the marketplace before he was pressed? Not to find her body but in the hope of finding—her. Even those mad raggers that Topher had killed, even they knew it was true. She was alive. Tom's faith in his daughter—if that was what it could be called—was something far and foreign from Elon's. But they shared a centrality of sorts:

Lillia was alive, somewhere in the Mountain.

They both knew it to be true. And Elon said he knew where she was.

"Maybe I'm going mad, too," Tom said to himself. "Or I already am ..."

But are you mad if you can still question if you're mad?

Tom stared at his feet shuffling beneath him and tried to avoid eye contact with the press of people scurrying about the encampment. The camp, he noticed, was lit with an unusual surplus of gulleystars. Piles of the mushrooms had been swept and bunched together and then pressed into pulsating yellow heaps. Alongside them, dozens of torches burned high from on top of stalks that had been planted in the ground. They melded together, the incandescent glows and the oily fires, which made a jarring visual effect throughout the caverns. The landscape reminded him of a deep wormhole that had suddenly been tilled, a place that was never meant to be seen laid bare. Within the makeshift illumination, pale and anxious men and women were scuttling around like beetles folding up the sheets of their tents, loading stores into boxes, rounding up feral children, and racing after clerks and wardens who cupped their hands to scream for their directions to be heard over all the din. Tom was soon able to gather enough pieces of conversation to learn what was happening.

The order had come down to break camp.

Angry shouts drifted along air that was already charged by the cloud of anxious, frenetic activity. A noise turned Tom's attention. A brawl was breaking out in front of a partially deconstructed stall, something to do with meal allotments. He quickly brushed through a small mob that was gathering to watch the fight and clambered up onto a rock shelf to get a better view. With so many throngs moving in different directions and the camp's landmarks all coming down, he needed to orient himself, to find some point of reference within the scrum.

Three porters were arguing over whose load should go first in a narrow alley between two rock piles. A steady stream of workers eddied around them, carrying bits of luggage along with them. A wailing toddler, probably lost, stood apart in a rutted roadway. A carter almost ran her down. His cart was full of clothes.

Tom spotted what he was looking for.

Just beyond the stalled porters, rising like dingy foothills, Tom saw a line of drab-colored mounds. They were made of shirts, pants, tunics, aprons, and jerkins, and were tottering from the constant weight of clothes being cast onto them from passersby. Underneath the shadow of the laundry, a kettle of frothy water bubbled over a fire. A sweat-drenched old man with wishbone legs was scurrying around it, talking loudly to himself. Tom watched him a moment, drew a long breath, and made up his mind.

"Madness ..." he set off towards the launderer.

Dirty steam hung like a sweltering drape all around the kettle fire, and with it, a powerful stench of mildew, which kept all but those who were dumping their clothes off a respectful distance away. As hard-pressed as he was scrubbing clothes, shaking them out, and hanging them on a line to dry, the man who called himself Wag still managed to keep a lively conversation with himself.

"Twenty to the pot, it's the only way, otherwise them piles ain't ever coming down. Ships will all have sailed if we don't double up the load. And where's the soap? Gone and used up. Well, a soak and a dry is all there'll be. A boiling won't kill the lice, Wag, they'll say. And do you know what I'll say to them?" He had a wet shirt wrapped around the end of a stick and pointed it warningly as Tom approached, "I'll say, you find me one crabber who ever set sail with Wag that had so much as a louse's shit on his clothes, and *then* tell me if a good boil won't do for bugs. That's what I'll say. Just drop off what you've got for me over there on the far pile."

"No, no," Tom held up a scrap of paper he had brought with him. He tried to make it appear nonchalant. "I'm here to take some clothes off your allotment, for another washerman."

Wag's eyebrows nearly leaped off his forehead.

"Since the first day I got pressed here, I have been the only launderer in this here camp."

"Topher's orders," Tom waved the paper, "I'm to take a special load for immediate cleaning. Help speed things along."

The expression of surprise turned into indignation, then virulence:

"You tell that fat-assed, earless son of a bitch that I know what he's playing. Special load, my prick. Don't think I know what's what? Topher's trying to tack one of his guildmates into *my* waters." Wag leaned closer, squinting at Tom. "Hey, I remember you now …" He hocked deep in his throat and spat at Tom's feet. "So it's you, eh?"

"What?"

"You're the one who's after my assignment! Was that why you helped me the other day, just so you can come and elbow me out of my work? Not that you was any help. I had to rewash all you did—"

"No, no, no, that's not it at all."

"Don't think you'll play me a fool. Been at sea most of my life, and I can tell when a gull's about to pounce a man's fish. You're trying to ship me off to the fighting line now that we're moving out. But I ain't going. This work here's mine, I tell you. I'm not sharing it!"

Wag's shriveled hands were bunched into fists, and Tom worried that his plan would fail before it even began, but then he had an idea. Tom smiled knowingly at the panting washerman:

"Alright, Wag," he sighed, "there's no fooling you. I suppose I'll have to let you in."

"Eh? Let me in on what?"

Wag was still tensed, his tongue flickering about his lips. He was watching Tom's every movement. Tom flipped a crate over, sat down on it, and motioned for Wag to come closer. For once the launderer listened, more or less in silence.

"This has nothing to do with your assignment. You can keep it. All I need's some of your delivery. I've got a bargain in the works."

"What kind of bargain?"

Tom made a pretense of making sure no one was eavesdropping:

"You know that there hasn't been a new set of clothes made in months."

"How could there be? Ain't a sheep been sheared or a loom been worked since we started fighting."

"Right. Which means good clothes are getting hard to come by. Some will pay coins for cloth that's in decent shape. Real coins … The kind that'll be worth something, once things get back to normal."

Slowly, a calculating look dawned over Wag. He dropped his voice very low.

"So, a few of the good pieces get, uh, blown off course?"

"I'll deliver them to a tailor," Tom nodded, "who will take care of the other end of the bargain. All you have to do is switch out a few sets of good clothes for some that aren't quite as nice."

Wag, who seemed to like the prospect of a sly bargain almost as much as he enjoyed talking, was bobbing his head and grunting.

"You guildsmen," he said with begrudging respect, "you always find a way to make a coin."

Tom gave a demure nod. "All I need from you is a wagon load of your finest."

"That can be arranged. So long as, uh, I get half of your take."

Inwardly Tom groaned, but he knew this would be necessary. A haggle. One that was going to be wearying and pointless, but for the ruse to work, he would have to finish this business out in the customary way. Otherwise, Wag might grow suspicious.

"A tenth," Tom replied.

"Half, here and now."

And so they haggled while the washing water boiled over, and the pile of dirty clothes grew larger, and the men and women in the Lower Ward slowly packed up their tents and refuse. One of the fires had gone cold when at last they settled on Wag's portion. A third of Tom's payment, once Tom received it, for a wagon load of good, clean clothing.

Their hands shook, and Tom waited as Wag scurried around the other side of the pile and announced (with a conspicuous chuckle) that the laundry was closing early today. Then the launderer began picking over the mounds of clothes, sifting through to find the best pieces to fill up an empty rickshaw wagon he used to make deliveries. Each time he brought one down from a line or out from a pile, he gave Tom a knowing wink, or whispered a comment like "a fine one here," or "this should fetch us a pretty penny," before he folded it carefully. Tom could almost hear the ill-gotten riches being counted in the man's head.

When the wagon was full to the point that it was in danger of toppling over, Tom insisted for Wag to just set aside any other good pieces for the time being. They should not try to move too much at a time.

"Smart, smart," Wag agreed. "Don't want to call out attention, do we?"

Tom lingered over the wagon cart, staring down at the piles of shirts and pants it now held. Beyond the laundry's fires, people and porters, clerks and wardens, were all shouting, arguing, packing—stirring. A cloud of steam blew across Tom's face, and yet he felt a coldness seeping into his bones.

It was not worry, nor his instinct. He was, he reflected, remarkably at peace with what he was about to do. Instead, Tom found himself returning once again to that nagging query.

Was this madness?

He still had no answer. The query kept returning him to the same thought, the same image: Lillia's face, glowing brighter than this fire.

"No," Tom smiled sadly. He turned to face Wag. "We don't want to call out attention."

Wag laughed to himself as he went back to his business. Tom gave the cart a shove. He pushed off in a roundabout direction, a tanner who had become a guard, now a carter carrying his load. He thought he wore his new guise well.

CHAPTER THIRTY-FOUR

"PRESERVE ME, PROTECT me, be my guiding light."

Elon had dozed off murmuring the prayer. As his eyes blinked open, he made certain they were the first words from his lips.

He was alone. Tom had not returned from his errand. Elon expected it would take him some time—maybe the whole day—to locate what they would need. Tom had left behind two full bowls of stew and a flagon of water near the corner of the bars, but Elon was not at all hungry. He settled on the cool hardness of the cell floor, rewrapped a bandage that had become loose, and repeated the prayer. The words were spoken reverently, through a broad and gleaming grin that had spread across his face.

Elon's heart was full to the point of overflowing. He had been blessed. His goddess had heard his prayers, faithless though they were, and sent her father to Elon's aid. It was a blessing to be cherished, and thankful for, whatever might come of it. If he died at this moment, if he were struck down and made to draw his last breath in this dank, smelly, gods-forsaken cage inside a hole, the bliss that was coursing through his soul could sustain him through the rest of his afterlife.

There is no stronger faith than the one forged from broken pieces, Elon reflected. Such was Elon's faith now.

So mote it be.

Elon started to pull himself up from the bars so that he could walk his steps around the cell when he heard a jangle of keys from the other side of the outer door. The lock opened, the door swung inward, and two men crept into the dwelling. Elon laid back down on the floor, pretending to be asleep, and left an eye cracked open.

His nephil sight revealed the men with perfect clarity; neither one was Tom. The men wore hoods to cover their faces. Except for their height, they looked much the same outwardly. Slender, booted, well garbed. As soon as they had passed the jail's transom, the smaller one closed the door softly behind him. The tall one, Elon noticed, had a scabbard dangling from his belt. He spoke low but haughtily, with a faint lisp in his words:

"So, your people made a jail down here," he remarked, "for one prisoner."

"It seemed a wise precaution."

"Indeed. Who takes care of him?"

"One of your sergeants. Who also happens to be one of us. I'm surprised he's not here."

"Well, well," the lisping man sounded impressed. "He's done good work. Since I see this place has not been set ablaze—and our prisoner is still here. Well done, Master Samuel." There was a long silence as both men lingered by the desk until at last the man with the sword broke it with a thinly veiled command:

"Thank you again, Samuel. I believe I can take this matter from here. You may leave now."

"Leave? I-I thought I might—" Samuel's voice was an awkward stammer.

"This kind of work," he replied in a polite, but firm tone, "is a specialty of mine. It requires a rather delicate touch. You understand, of course. If you'll make sure your carter has his preparations in order, I'll join you shortly."

Samuel made a sound as if he might protest his dismissal, but in the end, he yielded without complaint.

"I'll wait for you at the depot then," he said.

"This shan't take long."

When Samuel had left, the man with the sword approached the cell bars and called into the cell:

"I say, no need to keep up the caper. He's gone. And I know you're awake. Elon, that's your name, isn't it? I am Oliver. It's just us now. Why don't you come over and let's have a chat?"

Elon shut his eyes and breathed.

"Her will be done."

Slowly, with the words of his prayer still at the forefront of his mind, Elon sat up and gave his visitor a long, level stare. The lanterns had been left to flicker at the end of their wicks, leaving Oliver to squint in the darkness. Elon grasped onto the side of the wall to pull himself to his feet and then, with exaggerated slowness, limped over to stand before the man on the other side of the bars. Oliver flipped his hood back from his face.

He had a wry, cocky smile beneath the shadow of a long nose and was dressed in a golden tunic and a black-trimmed cloak that would have passed for finery among men. His hair and beard were neat, though he had the appearance of one who was accustomed to leisure but found no time for it lately. Elon addressed him curtly:

"You're the one who's a captain, right?"

Oliver dipped his head.

"Oliver will suffice unless you prefer to stand by formalities. Your Majesty."

"I see no need to. Given the circumstances."

"Neither do I. So … you've recovered wonderfully well, it seems. Since I saw you last."

"My Lady has looked after her child," Elon replied. "I am grateful for her goodness."

"Your—? Ah, yes. I sometimes forget we permitted your people to keep your gods."

It was a barb but Elon refused to respond to it.

"Whatever the source of ministration," Oliver continued, "I'm pleased with the result. Now, at last, you are in a condition where we can talk. Just in time, it seems."

He paused as if waiting for Elon to say something, but Elon's only response was to adjust another of the bandages around his arms. Oliver pressed ahead:

"I'd like to clear the air. Perhaps come to an understanding of what's to be done with you."

"I'm your prisoner. Say what you have to say."

"Alright …" Oliver laid a gloved hand and curled it around one of the cell's bars. "How did it ever come to this?'

A silence fell over the room, broken only by the crackle of a charcoal fire in the stove. Elon let out a labored sigh and shook his head slowly, sadly. Why was he besetting him with pretenses? Get on with the torture, it would be more endurable than this pandering. With a sudden burst of energy, Elon lifted his bandaged face and laughed from behind his clenched teeth.

"What kind of parley is this? Here I sit in a cell as your prisoner. My body's been burnt by your mob, my people slaughtered in their tunnels by your hands, and you have the cheek to ask me how this came to pass?"

"Who said I came here to parley," Oliver said, his eyebrows arching. "I've come to have my questions answered. Foremost of which is to learn why your people breached the Treaty and waged this awful, unprovoked war upon our realm."

"Alright, I'll tell you." Elon squared his shoulders. The glow from his prior prayers was slowly turning into a smolder. Elon held Oliver in the heat of his gaze. "This war," he spoke his words measuredly, his voice mounting like a storm, "has been waging since before you were born. It is the old war. And it has never stopped. Never. Do you hear? Since that day when a godless cult swarmed out of your sewers and overran the Mountain. My father—my people—have never stopped fighting the apostasy of nothingness. *That* is the war that is still being waged. Is it awful? Unprovoked? Yes, indeed. A horrible war your people started—and never ended."

"Never ended?" Oliver said. "Here I was under the impression your late father and our stewards swore an oath together. They signed a Treaty and brought those hostilities to a mutually satisfactory conclusion."

Elon spat on the cell floor. "Godless men make faithless oaths. Whatever worth that pact had, it's been broken. By you," he raised a wrapped hand and pointed it accusingly at Oliver's chest, "when you lured my people into an ambush."

Oliver stood before him passively, seemingly unmoved by the accusation.

"I've no idea what you are talking about," he said.

Elon let out a warning growl, reduced to a caged animal that had just been provoked. Tears were brimming through his bandages and he spoke through gritted teeth:

"My cousin led that delve for the Crest. I sent my kin, my best thane … Abidan, he … He was *butchered* in that mine. He and his delvers. I found their bodies lying in the dirt cut up like hogs."

Oliver took in a sharp breath. "Well, I offer my condolences for your loss."

"Keep your sympathy. It's bile to me."

The two stood quietly in the cell for a time, Elon's rasping breaths and the hissing stove fire the only sounds between them. At last, Oliver spoke very quietly:

"Now that you mention it, I may have heard about the attack you speak of, Elon. The one in your delving tunnel. If it's true, it was ... regrettable. Our reports, though, were that guildsmen may have been responsible for—"

"It was wardens' work," Elon declared. "Hell and death, the ruse was pathetic. A blind Cragman could see it for what it was."

"How do you mean?"

"The weapons you left for us to find by the bodies, all those picks and axes all covered with guildmarks, they were no better than kindling. They couldn't have killed my cousin with those bits of wood and tin. No, my people were hacked to pieces with swords. Steel swords that only wardens have."

Elon had to sit down on a patch of straw to rest a moment. Then he tilted his face up to Oliver.

"So now you've learned what I know, which is why you came here, right? But you've another question, and since I have such little company these days, I'm happy to answer that one, too ... Yes. The nephil *all* know who struck this blow against us. I had the bodies carried through my temple—for all to see. Though my thanes had different counsel on how we should respond. We all know who our enemy is." He pressed his face between the bars and narrowed his eyes at the man standing over him. "It's you."

Oliver bit at his bottom lip for a moment contemplated something, and then made a resigned gesture.

"Alright," he nodded. "There's little point denying it now, I suppose. Yes. My men staged your delvers' bodies to make it appear as if guildsmen had attacked them. They were under orders—the highest orders— to do so. We were told to start a little skirmish between the guilds and the dwarves. The guilds had gained too much clout. Especially with the clerks. Too much money. Too much power. It was thought that the time had come to make a sweep of them. Excise the rot, courtesy of your people. That was the intention, at least." He let out a long breath. "I imagine the Crest was rather surprised to discover the depth of dwarven fury—and perception."

"Men are men, Cragmen, guildsmen, wardens, you're all the same. You were faithless in both your bargains."

"Both—?" Oliver seemed on the cusp of asking Elon something further when he suddenly changed his tack. The captain made a flourish with his hand. "Well, I suppose that's an understandable sentiment, but I want you to know ..." he paused as if to make sure he had Elon's attention, "none of my men killed a single one of yours. It's true. All those poor miners were dead when my guards arrived. Much to everyone's surprise."

Elon's chin fell into his chest. This was becoming absurd. He started laughing.

"I am telling you the truth, Elon. We are innocent. If I told you how we found your men ..." Oliver paused, vexation clouding his face for a moment before he shook his head. "I suppose it doesn't matter. You wouldn't believe me."

Elon was still chuckling:

"You're right about that," he agreed. "I'll believe many things, but nothing you'll ever tell me. You're a liar, warden. There's falsehood in your breath. You wreak of it."

The two stared into the space of the iron rods between them. Mere inches apart, yet a chasm. One that would never be crossed.

"At least," said Oliver at last, "we can agree it's a pity what has come to pass. However, it may have happened."

"A bloody pity."

"There you are. A bloody pity indeed. So why," Oliver said, "are we prolonging it? As they say, once you press a gulleystar, you can't unlight it. We should be looking forward. Elon?"

"Yes."

"We find ourselves strangely aligned in two respects; do you know what they are?"

"You'll tell me, I'm sure."

Oliver leaned as far forward into the bars as he could to convey that he was sharing a most intimate confidence. He spoke very softly, almost caressingly:

"We find ourselves at each other's throats because of the Crest—and yet all of us have been forgotten by the Crest. Isn't that a strange coincidence?"

Elon gave it little thought and simply shrugged.

"In my experience," Oliver said, "there are no strange coincidences."

"I'm sure your masters are drawing up papers that will sort it all out for you."

"You would think they would be, wouldn't you? I mean, here there's a *war* raging inside the Mountain. Not just against the guilds. The Crest's clerks, and wardens, and workers are dying by the hundreds, the tunnels are collapsing, all the Crag's in flames, and do you know what the captain of the Crag's wardens has heard from the Crest?" He snapped a finger in the air. "Nothing! No orders, no summonses, no notes. They don't respond to my letters. I thought when I suspended the allotments, stopped the caravans from delivering any more food to the Crest and Quarter, surely that would bring out the High Guard. That kind of dereliction borders on treason … But no. Only more silence." Oliver paused, thought to himself for a moment, and then continued in what was almost a whisper. "I went to the Citadel, you know. Walked the length of the Spine to the Inner Keep just to try to speak to someone. Do you know how I was greeted when I sought entrance?"

"With a feast."

Oliver shook his head as if he could not believe his recollection.

"They shot arrows at me."

"Pity they missed," Elon answered. "You had nothing to fear, though."

"No?"

"I've seen your people's archery."

That made Oliver laugh aloud:

"I suppose you're right there. The only hurt I suffered was my pride. Still," he wiped his mustache and grew serious again. "It was most disconcerting. Without a word, the Citadel has been shut. *Thought* and *Peace* are locked and barred, and no one, it seems, will be permitted to pass through them. That hasn't happened since the Overthrow. But no one seems to know *why* … Most distressing indeed. Ah, but where one doorway has been closed, perhaps another may be opening up."

Here, at last, Elon could sense a hidden purpose behind Oliver's visit coming into the light, why this preening captain had endured the jibes and grousings of a prisoner who he would otherwise have just as soon killed. He wanted something more than Elon's thoughts then. Elon folded his arms across his chest, a silent prayer running through his mind.

"*Preserve me, protect me …*"

"We've made a truce," Oliver said.

Elon felt a jolt of dread coursing through him at the news.

"Or I suppose armistice would be the more precise word," Oliver continued. "Hard to say without a clerk to work through those particulars, and they're all as scared as rabbits right now, since they have no orders from the Crest. Whatever we'll call it, it's done. We have a new pact with the Quarter. Still a few scuffles breaking out here and there, but otherwise, the peace appears to be holding. There will be no more raids in the Crag and no siege of your realm. We'll even send caravans to the Quarter again, under the promise of safe passage. In return, your people will start to fix what's been broken and leave our realm in peace. That is … the new bargain. If it can hold, we'll avoid another Overthrow." Oliver folded his hands before him and addressed Elon gravely. "It *will* hold, Elon. I promise you. We're going home now. All of us. You as well. I'm going to fetch a special wagon to escort you to your realm. I hope that news pleases you to hear."

"I …" Elon found it hard to reconcile what Oliver had just told him with his mounting apprehension. There was deception lurking in this, he knew it; like every other dealing with men. He tried to sound defiant:

"I made no truce."

Oliver scratched his cheek with two fingers. "No, you didn't. But there are others in your realm who have kept their senses despite all these misunderstandings. Fortunately for us all. I am to deliver you to those wise leaders as our prisoner. With some conditions, of course."

And there it was. Elon scanned his cell, wondering how soon he would come to long for its relative comforts. Its three uneven walls, ten long paces, eleven, then nine to the edge of the bars. The warmth of the straw and lanterns, the food from a kindly jailer—it would become a haunting memory in the days ahead. For there was no doubt, none at all, in Elon's mind but that he was to be delivered to pain and death. That the pretense he had suffered was the prelude to his regicide, in his own realm.

There was nothing for it, but to trust in his Lady's goodness. So, Elon forced himself to smile:

"To whom do I owe my thanks for this ransom?"

"One of your thanes. Can't recall what he goes by. Your people have such odd names."

The cart was too heavy. In his greed, Wag must have loaded a hundred pounds of clothing into a rickshaw that had mismatched wheels. Pushing the bulky weight in a straight line was proving more than Tom could manage. Stooped and winded, he had to stop by the time he reached the lector's chair at the camp's periphery. There were still too many lingerers for him to dump part of his load here. Even the lector seemed to be eyeing Tom with some suspicion. She paused in her reading to address him directly:

"You're not on leave yet, are you?"

Tom grimaced into his shoulder and then smoothed his expression into placidity and shook his head that he was not.

"Then back to your route, carter. Back to it. If your load's not delivered, you've not earned the fruit of refreshment yet. Up you go!" Then, more loudly, she addressed the harried workers who remained within earshot, ignoring the fact that they were completely ignoring her: "Workers are reminded that even in this time of temporary transition, especially now, sloth and indolence cannot be tolerated. Your Commonwealth needs your work. Your clerks will give you your guidance and directions. Follow them! Our all for all."

As the lector prattled through hoarse and breathless reports of the prosperity that awaited them (punctuated by countless recitations of "our all for all"), Tom grudgingly returned to his trek, grateful to leave the last of the noise and notice of the Lower Ward behind him. The light faded as he walked the familiar jagged course of stones. He knew the way across the plateau well enough now to reach the hidden rise and its stairwell, though he still pressed a couple of gulleystars he had brought with him to light the way.

A meager glow washed out what little color there was in the cavern, but with the light, he could at least avoid the worst of the holes. The mismatched wheels of his rickshaw rattled, the clothes inside slumped into a disorganized heap, and Tom pushed forward, one step, then another, his steel eyes scanning the wavering orb of copper light around him. Too small to be noticed, he hoped, in the expanse of subterranean darkness. He pulled the cart for over a mile in nearly total silence.

With each step, he found his thoughts growing more disturbed, as if the darkness of the field was penetrating the little light he made and seeping down into him.

He gave a start when he looked up from the cart's pull bar to see the jail's ridge was before him. Tom hoisted the cart around to the other side of the jut of stone and hurried down the narrow flight of steps to the jail's door. But when he slipped the key into the lock, he was surprised to find he had left the front door unlocked. Cursing himself, he cautiously leaned it open with a shoulder. The lanterns inside had all burned out.

"Elon," Tom's voice was a hiss in the darkness.

"Still here," Elon replied calmly from within his cell.

Tom shuffled across the floor and nearly bumped into the cell's bars where he could make out Elon's slight and bandaged figure sitting, as if at his leisure, with his forefinger extended along the bridge of his nose.

"What are you doing down there?"

"Praying."

Tom instinctively recoiled. When he realized that all this prayer entailed was Elon sitting with his eyes closed in silence and breathing steadily, his discomfiture quickly turned to impatience. Tom crouched down to the floor, the gulleystars in his hand joining the two figures in the aura of their glow. Now that Tom had drawn closer, he could see that Elon's face appeared serene—surprisingly so, given what they were planning to do.

"We've got a problem," Tom whispered.

"Yes, we do."

"The camp's disbanding. Everyone's supposed to report back to their regular assignments. Clerks are issuing new orders, new passes for everyone. Everyone's going home."

"So I've heard."

Tom looked at him incredulously. It took him a moment to regather his thoughts:

"Which means there won't be any way for me—for us—to slip away. Once the clerks and wardens set up their stations again."

"Unless we leave at once. And take the straight route there. The stairwells your people called Forward Way."

Tom nodded.

"That wasn't what we planned, though."

"No," Elon said, "it wasn't."

Tom let out a long sigh. Elon sat before him, still bandaged from head to toe, his arms set at odd angles from splints. He could no more make it up a flight of stairs than Tom's rickshaw could make it through this doorway. The glaring impossibilities—and the foolishness—of their plan, given everything that was happening, were becoming too much for Tom to keep to himself anymore.

"This might not …" Tom started.

He tried to explain, to put his worries into words. As he stammered, Elon regarded him with a kindly expression. For some reason, Elon's scarred face awoke within Tom a deep and painful pang to see Lillia. To watch her proud chin once more, to hear her snap a clever line at a haughty clerk. To see the way people would naturally make way for her wherever she went, like in the old days. As the longing came over him, Tom felt it as a connection to Elon. Each shared the same desire: to see Lillia again. Tom's words faded into a jumble.

"Father of the Maiden," Elon gave him a friendly grasp from between the bars, "I would not ask anything more of you than what you can freely give. I'll face my death alone when they come to take me away."

"No. I've made up my mind, I—wait, what are you talking about? Who's going to take you away?"

"Your wardens. They're going to return me to my realm."

Tom blinked in surprise.

"How do you—?" he started, then his face brightened. "If that's true, that's great news for you. Isn't it? They're just going to—to set you free? So, we don't need to break you out of here."

"No, Tom," Elon smiled even as a note of melancholy entered his voice. "They're going to take me home in chains. They will deliver me to one of my thanes—I think I know which one—who will demand that I renounce my faith. I'd do no such thing, of course. So, your good Captain Oliver will ensure that by torture, or poison, or starvation, or, who knows—ventriloquists perhaps—one way or another, I will say whatever that scheming bastard Reuben wants me to say. To break my people's faith in Lillia as a goddess, and in me as my people's king. Once I've obliged them, I expect they'll lop off my head."

Tom felt his face drain, his stomach turn cold.

"Oliver? You saw him? You-you're sure—?"

There could be no doubt of it, Elon assured him. He told Tom of Oliver's visit while Tom had been out and what he had learned. As Elon spoke, Tom felt his heart pounding in his chest, as if he was already being given chase again. Elon's sad laughter broke through the mounting gloom of Tom's worries.

"My thane did try to warn me," he said, "my head would roll. Never would have guessed it would be at his hand ..." Elon turned his face resolutely. "Don't worry. I fully intend to disappoint them all. That is not how my line will end. Tom, if you no longer wish to follow this through with me," Elon said it without the slightest hint of accusation, "I'll understand and not hold it against you. But I would ask a final kindness of you. If you walk out a way from your people's camp, back towards your market, and look about in some of the wet cracks, anyplace where the Mountain's water drips and holds in one place. There are redcap gulleystars that grow in these parts. It might take a little searching, but you'll find them. Could you bring me one, please?"

It was a baffling request. Tom ignored it. Without a word, he brought out the set of keys Topher had entrusted him with, climbed on top of a stool, and slid each key into the six padlocks along the ceiling and floor that held the bars in place. Elon said nothing, but asked him only once as he worked:

"Are you certain?"

"No," Tom replied. A small part of him was screaming that he had gone mad, as mad as the raggers in the market, while another part held him in a stoic resolve. He could not honestly say which part, if either, was his instinct anymore, but the latter proved to be the stronger. "I—I've made up my mind," Tom said and popped the last of the locks open.

When the last lock clinked free, Tom shoved his shoulder hard into the set of bars. Elon pulled from his side of the cell, and together, with much work, and sweat, and grunting, the two were able to pry the bars from their brackets and guide them down to the ground. The metal gate made a slight rattling noise when it fell. But it was down.

And so, at last the barrier between Tom and Elon was gone.

When Tom took Elon's weight on his shoulder, they each felt a charge coursing between them, like a gulleystar that had been on the cusp of cracking into light, finally pressed all the way. They shared a look, neither one speaking, as Tom helped Elon up the stone steps to the cart that was waiting for him.

A broad smile spread across Elon's face when he realized Tom's plan.

"My throne's become a barrow," he laughed softly. "My raiment dirty laundry. By all the gods, this bard song just keeps getting better, you know that, Tom? We'll have to live, just to hear the song of our story."

Ignoring the jest, Tom began hurriedly scooping out armfuls of clothes, piling them on the ground in front of Elon. When he had nearly reached the bottom of the cart, he took Elon by the arm to help him into the cart:

"In you go."

But Elon held back. He slid his hand into Tom's and then, without explanation, began moving Tom's fingers into an odd gesture.

"What're you—?"

"This is important," Elon replied.

When he had fashioned Tom's hand so that it was a fist with the forefinger extended, Elon guided it to the bridge of Tom's nose and told him to hold it there. Then Elon whispered to him what to say, as he brought his wrapped hand to his bandaged forehead.

"Be it so," Elon breathed.

Though Tom felt a little awkward, he answered, as Elon told him:

"So mote it be."

"Now we are ready to go."

Elon sifted through the clothes until his small body was buried beneath the mound of laundry, his bandages blending with the dingy clothing like a camouflage. When he was settled, Tom grunted and gave the cart a pull to start it rolling. He stooped his shoulders some, let his chin fall to his chest, like all the carters he had ever seen in the Crag. Nothing but a nameless worker bringing out his load. As he moved, Tom paused to make a few adjustments inside the cart, pulled a few shirts and pants from the bottom to better conceal Elon.

As Tom carried his friend across a rocky wilderness within the Lower Ward, something occurred to him. When Elon had taken Tom's hand to shape it like his, the two of them, he and Elon, without realizing it—had briefly shared a guildsman's token.

CHAPTER THIRTY-FIVE

ARKNESS MOVED. STRANDS of shadows were racing across the empty chasm, like pikes darting through a lake on the hunt for prey. It had started as a flurry, now it seemed to be swarming. Entropy in the air.

For the first time, Tom could see what Topher had been trying to show him the last time they had spoken. In the dying light of that campfire, he could still remember the sergeant's face, the hardened leather cracked by some strange anxiety. Tom saw what Topher had seen before, high above in the distant darkness—a stirring, just as Topher said.

Tom did not at all like the look of it.

They had been traveling, Tom pulling the laundry rickshaw with Elon concealed inside, a slow, quiet crawl across the stone strewn plain, heading farther away from the jail and the breaking camp. One gulleystar was all Tom would risk to light his way, and without Elon's eyes to help him, it was almost impossible to find landmarks in these unmapped caverns of the Lower Ward. But by Tom's reckoning, they should have been nearing the corridors outside the market. Perhaps another mile and a half.

He cast another wary glance at the stirring vibrations in the air. He would have sworn that one of them (he knew no other way to think of the shadows he was watching) was trying to break free from the others, pulling itself loose to descend from the heights—to meet him below. Tom had to stifle a gasp. The hairs on his neck were standing on end and his forehead beaded with sweat. At the same time, he felt the air turning colder, as if he was traveling farther down into the Mountain's climes rather than where he truly heading, towards its surface. Something in the stirring seemed to be falling, fluttering to the earth like a leaf, and then Tom heard a sound.

The noise made him leap, though he knew at once it had not come from the darkness. Footsteps were approaching fast from behind.

Whoever it was, he had to have been following Tom for some distance. Far enough behind that Tom hadn't heard his pursuer over the rattling cart.

"Someone's coming," Tom murmured. "Don't make a sound."

He cast another glimpse at the wavering shadows, but now they had receded into the darkness as if the sudden intrusion had frightened them off. Tom spun around in time to see a lantern light making straight for him. A tall, gangly boy with a menacing face held it high.

"Tanner," he snarled, half out of breath.

"Jack," Tom replied with a mixture of relief and vexation. He tried to assume a casual tone, though the boy had the look of a man about to come to blows. "What brings you out here?"

Jack's shirt was stained and ripped around the collar, his sash was on the verge of falling off his hips, and it looked as if it had been some days since he had washed or shaved. But despite his rough appearance, he squared his shoulders and knitted his eyebrows:

"How dare you ask a clerk his business."

Tom dipped his head in apology. "That's not what I—"

"Where've you been hiding, Tanner?" Jack stepped closer to him and held the lantern inches from Tom's nose as if he were interrogating him. "I've been looking for you for days. You never reported to a warden. Never showed up for any assignment. No one's seen you, no one's even heard of you in camp. You're absent without orders."

"I got orders," Tom replied. "They were just never stamped."

Jack's nostrils flared; his cheeks shone a rosy hue in the orange glow of his lantern:

"I didn't seal those because you were supposed to get me something."

Tom straddled his elbow over one of the cart's rails to appear unconcerned. He plucked absently at a loincloth in the barrow, showing it to Jack.

"Do you think I'd be lugging this stuff around if I'd found it yet? I haven't had a chance to look. Topher's kept me too busy. But now that camp's breaking, I can get out from under—"

Jack drew another step closer. There was a turn in his expression that made Tom instinctively clench his fists. The boy had grown taller. He seemed to relish being able to look down upon Tom:

"Don't give me your lies, Craggie. You're not doing any work for Topher. He's gone."

"Topher?" Tom's mouth opened then shut again. In the tumult of the past few days, Tom hadn't thought to wonder what had become of his sergeant since that day he had come out to visit at the jail. Strangely the news did not surprise Tom as much as he thought it should have.

"Yeah, Topher. He disappeared a few days ago. Everyone's saying he's dead. Whatever. He's no good to me—or to you anymore."

"I—I hadn't heard."

"So let's have it, Tanner. Now."

Tom blinked at Jack.

"Have what?"

The base of the lantern came crashing down on Tom's forehead. He crumpled to the ground, clutching at the pain. He lost track of Jack's harangue in the rush of sound that filled his ears, like ocean waves breaking against the rocks.

"—you said you had more," Jack was slapping Tom's face with his open palm. "You said it was hidden in the market. You were supposed to get me more."

"I …"

"More! They're going to put me back on the Farms. I need more coins. Now! Tell me where they are!"

The lantern smashed against the side of Tom's face. He tried to speak, tried to get to his feet, but he was too dizzy. His vision clouded. Tom wiped at his eyes, but they refused to focus. For a moment, it almost seemed that the light had inverted itself around Jack. What had been illuminated was now dark; what had been shadowed now glowed. Two black holes where Jack's eyes had been bored into Tom's, while a burning orifice formed Jack's words:

"I'll kill you if you don't give them to me."

"I already … gave them to somebody."

"You're a liar! Just like your whore daughter."

Jack stood back up and gave Tom a hard kick. Then another. The clerk made a disgusted grimace at the sight of Tom clinging onto the cart.

"Maybe it's time for you to join her, Tanner."

"Lillia …"

Jack unscrewed a cap to his lantern and tipped it at an angle. A line of ochre oil splattered over the barrow's clothes and trickled down to Tom's face and hands. The metal door that hid the lamp's wick squeaked open. A smile stretched across Jack's dirt-smeared face:

"You're going to tell me where your treasure is. If I have to burn it out of you."

The corner of the cart caught fire. A sputtering flame quickly spread across where the oil had soaked into the cloth and wood. A wreath of smoke went scurrying into the air to join the shadows above. Tom screamed Elon's name, and at that moment, the cart's barrow erupted.

"*Infidel! Cragman!*"

As the rickshaw toppled over on its side, smoldering in flames, Elon burst from his hiding place. Wild, shrieking, ringed with smoke, flailing his bandaged arms, kicking his legs, shouting Lillia's name. Tom saw Jack's horror-stricken face turn to him as if hoping for his help. Stunned, the clerk staggered backward, caught his foot, and fell headlong against a crop of jagged rocks. A spray of blood, then his dull blonde hair was soaked red. The boy gaped in silent horror, dazed, his body unmoving. Elon limped to where Jack had fallen and brought one of the burning cloths, flaming in oil, before Jack's face.

"Infidel," Elon's blackened mouth hovered above Jack's, as if on the verge of a kiss. The boy's eyes were rolling, searching for an escape, but his arms and legs were seemingly paralyzed. Tom heard him sputter:

"Help-help me … I can't move. Help me, please. I want Dad …"

Elon drew a symbol in the air with the smoke of the burning bandage:

"Take and eat the Maiden's light … Given to you …"

There was a muffled cry as Elon crammed the fiery rag into the back of Jack's throat. From where he was crouched, Tom could only watch, unable to look away. The boy made a pitiful sound, his body frozen where it had landed, while his head thrashed in convulsions. Elon held him fast.

Fortunately, it didn't take long. Jack stopped fighting, he let out what sounded to Tom like a sigh, and then it was over. What life had been in him departed quietly.

"Elon?"

"I'm unhurt," Elon replied. He was trembling, standing lock-kneed over Jack's still body. "The fire—the cart—so like … the net …" His voice trailed off and then he turned to face Tom, his eyes rimmed with tears. "Were you hurt?"

Tom shook his head and slowly rose to his feet. The ground was still spinning. His head throbbed from the lantern blows and he felt drained, but with Elon's help, they were able to pull Jack's body to the nearest crevasse they could find that was deep enough to conceal the body. Before they rolled him over into the hole, Tom caught a glimpse of the boy's final expression: something between affront and puzzlement.

Tom picked up Jack's lantern, shook it, and then examined the cart. The fire had mostly gone out, but it had done more than a small share of damage. The wagon, which had never been in good repair, was ruined now. The sides had fallen off in charred heaps, and one of the wheels had split in two around the axle.

Elon and Tom stared at the remains of the rickshaw for a while, watched the last of the flames flicker out, and then, without a word, each put his arm around the other's shoulder to bear their weight together, and they began walking.

Darkness lay ahead of him. Shadows. Taunting him. That's what they were doing.

"Bastards," he breathed.

Topher scrambled in the dark, clambered up the endless, winding steps on his hands and knees. The stirrings in the air had come to life. He was chasing them now, the shadowy figures, now that he could see them for what they were. Topher's revulsion had consumed him like a madness.

"Bastards …" Topher let out a labored breath. He was panting uncontrollably, doubled over, long clouds of mist trailing from his mouth and nostrils.

The shadows paused, and though Topher could hear little with his heart thumping so hard, he was certain they were hissing to one another. Whispering. Bad things telling bad secrets. From the rocks below, he shouted his challenge to them:

"You *bastards!*"

These shades floating through the Mountain, stirring out in the open now. They were … abominable. He felt a wild fury at what was there, but should not have been.

"You—should've—STAYED—HID!"

Topher roared so that bloody spittle flew out of his throat. He felt no pain from it.

The shadows scattered at the sound and Topher ran after them.

For a day he had been following the vibrations he had found in the darkness. Chasing the shadows' shadows. Across the crevasses and ruined corridors of the Lower Ward, he trailed them, heedless of the dark and bitter cold that was enveloping him. They led him up the broken tunnels and stairwells of Forward Way. He would follow them to the Gutters, to the top of the Mountain, if there was such a place.

Up he went. Two, three steps at a time. Topher's heavy legs trudged underneath him. Step. Step. Endless, benighted steps. Up, it seemed, would be forever.

But with each new step, he saw the traces of the darkness flitter before him just beyond his reach. His footfalls thudded. They were answered by muted voices in the dark ahead of him. They were taunting him again.

"Fight me, you bastards!"

His voice boomed as it always had, but now in a way that sounded foreign in Topher's ears.

He would kill them all.

Topher's clothes and boots were torn to shreds. Sweat drenched his thick, bare head, trickling down the hole where his ear had once been. It stung his eyes, the freezing air burned his chest, but he felt none of it. All that mattered was catching—and killing—these dark things he had found in the Mountain.

"I'm—coming—for you!"

Another flight of steps, and then he reached a landing on a stairwell, a junction between corridors in the middle reaches of the Crag. The ground here had a layer of frost on it. An old stone fountain in the center of the floor, the water frozen within its broken base, was the room's only feature. At its summit stood a plaster crest of the Commonwealth's sword, pick, and hammer emblem topped by two badly sculpted figures of a man and a woman. Their arms were linked at the elbows and they carried a banner between them while they stared up—not towards the future, but at the cloud of shadows that was stirring above their heads.

The banner the statues held read:

THE WORLD WITHIN IS OURS TO WIN

Topher skidded to a halt and ground his teeth at the shadows hovering above the fountain. The swirling vortex regarded him. A din of rustling noises, like human voices but empty of human words, filled the chamber. Topher straightened himself, brushed off his shirt, and flexed his arms. He would meet his enemy on his feet.

"Come down!" He stabbed his finger into the air. "Come down, you bastards! I know what you are … Come down so I can kill you!"

The shadows paused in their motion, as if in contemplation.

"Come down to me!"

At last, they did as he wished.

Darkness, vast and cold, opened like a maw to swallow the line of twinkling lights that stood idly in its midst. They had left the last of the lampposts and torches in the Lower Ward and the mounds of gulleystars that had temporarily lit the whole encampment behind. A group of wardens, and their wagon, wending into a flat, darkened plain. It was like a regression, back to the native blackness that once dwelled within the Mountain. A void.

Oliver scowled at it.

"Must I grope like a blind man for someone to fetch me a *light* up here!" he called out.

The men with Oliver shifted nervously, unsure of what to do, until one of his aides, a young toady with a humped shoulder, came limping from the rear carrying a torch of bundled rags. As he passed the guards, the sputtering flames illuminated the wagon Oliver's men had been pulling. Four iron-rimmed wheels held a massive, windowless metal box. There were airholes haphazardly drilled on one of its sides around a locked hatch, but otherwise, it looked as solid as a metal block. It took ten men to move its weight.

The hunchbacked boy hurried by the wagon to offer his torch to Oliver, who snatched it from him without a word. The boy scuttled off, as Oliver held the light up.

The stone lip that led down into the guildsman's prison cell was still there. The only feature in this vast, empty plain of stone. The stairwell was still hidden on its other side. Not that it mattered whether his men knew of this place now or what it had held. Not anymore.

They were starting to grumble again; Oliver could hear them. The men were tired, and hungry, and eager to rejoin their families who were, by now, probably well on their way in the return to their homes. No one could remember the last time they had been paid the fruits of their labor. While the men rested in the temporary lull, they resumed grousing among themselves about why the captain had ordered them to lug this contraption out here into the middle of an uncharted field.

A fair question, Oliver had to concede. At the moment, he found himself uncomfortably deprived of an answer.

A man emerged from the stairs, his hooded head poking up from the other side of the rock ridge. He quietly made his way over to Oliver who stood, waiting, in the shadows cast off from his torch's glow. The man was rubbing his hands together hurriedly, whether out of fear or to keep warm in the cold, Oliver couldn't tell.

"They can't have been gone long," Samuel said. "There's no dust on the bars or locks."

"Oh, thank goodness, they kept their escape a clean affair."

Samuel gathered up the hems of a long, billowing cloak he was holding. He made a sour face at Oliver:

"He was your guard."

"He was your brother," Oliver replied.

Samuel let out a long breath.

"Will it matter? Whose man Topher was when he freed Elon. Will they care?"

The guildsman had a point—self-serving, of course, but valid. Their prisoner had vanished, the prisoner they had promised to deliver in exchange for a truce.

Oliver had already gone down into the jail cell to see for himself; briefly, for he did not trust that his men would stay very long in this desolate place without his watching eye. As soon as he had opened the door, he knew something had gone awry. The inside of the jail was dark, the stove felt as cold as the air around it, and the entire wall of gated bars that had kept Elon imprisoned was lying neatly on the floor, every one of its padlocks sprung open. No sign that they had been pried, each one had been unlocked with a key. Prisoner and jailer had both vanished. And now the man who had been responsible for building this cell and guarding its charge had searched the whole place over and had nothing to add.

"No," Oliver said, "I suspect they won't care at all."

They stared past one another, watching the winds shift eddies of dust across the cavern. The men by the wagon continued murmuring under their breath. Their leaders' conversation was just as clipped:

"When were you supposed to deliver him?" Samuel asked.

"Soon."

Samuel seemed annoyed by the enigmatic reply.

"We're allies, Oliver."

"So it seems."

Oliver let the silence stretch before he decided to relent a little:

"We still have time. If we can find him quickly. Were you able to learn anything more down there?"

"I found an order. It was crumpled under the desk and the assignment was left blank. I'm thinking Topher may have pressed another guard to help him with Elon. A newcomer, by the look of it."

Oliver chewed a fingernail.

"But Topher would have kept his keys, surely."

"Surely."

There could be no doubt that the escape was Topher's doing. The troubling question, though, was for what purpose? At the moment, only one possibility presented itself, and Oliver did not wish to think about it. He turned his full gaze onto Samuel, intent on studying the guild master's reaction.

"It's too late to turn back now, you know. Even if I wanted to, I couldn't muster my men again, not without killing half their families. And that would lead to a rebellion. They're on the verge of starving. They all want to go home. Whatever leverage I had with the dwarves vanished the moment we made that pact and broke camp."

"I ..." Samuel paused.

It was an open, candid admission of Oliver's weakness, and it caught the cagey guildsman off guard, just as Oliver intended.

"We-we all agreed, Oliver," Samuel said at last. "Because we had no choice. No one's growing anything, making anything, the corridors are all falling, our people are dropping like rats. There was no way we could keep fighting. I don't know how you were able to hold us all together for so long. Much less win victories over the dwarves—that was a feat."

"Costly victories. Eight of my men for every one of theirs, according to the clerks."

"Even so. It brought the dwarves out to beg for a truce. The thane came to us, remember?"

"He came to you, actually," Oliver pointed his finger towards Samuel's heart. He tapped it against his chest and watched a shade of color drain from the guildsman's face. "His first contact was with the guilds. I didn't come into the parley until later."

"That may be," Samuel's eyes were beginning to dart. "But you played your hand perfectly with him."

"Unless someone else dealt a better card on top of mine."

"You're not suggesting—"

"That your people might have struck a better bargain with the dwarves beneath my notice? Why not? You did it once before."

Samuel scoffed, as if Oliver was joking, but Oliver drew a step closer to him. He leaned his head forward so that he could study every twitch, every blink, every crease in Samuel's face, the way he would interrogate a prisoner.

"Elon mentioned something I found quite interesting during our chat. We men are all the same, he said, faithless in *both* our bargains.

Now I know what bargain the Crest had with the Quarter. I can only wonder who else would have the connections, the pull, to have struck another bargain with the dwarves without the Crest knowing of it." He studied Samuel closely. "Did you also have a pact with our vanished friend? Please don't burden me with having to extract the truth from you—when I can already read it plainly in your face that you did. We're past the point of subterfuges now."

Reluctantly, Samuel nodded.

"You heard there was a sweep coming?"

Samuel's voice croaked: "We only knew there was going to be some kind of trouble for us out of the Gutters. Our friends in the wardens, they were warning us to get ready for something. So, we reached out to the Quarter."

"To buy protection?"

"That was … the idea. Silver in exchange for passage and protection. We put a call upon all our brothers and sisters to raise the funds."

Oliver whistled softly. "What happened to your bargain? You obviously got no protection from the dwarves."

"We lost the silver," Samuel's reply was thick with misery.

Oliver began chuckling to himself. More likely, the guild masters and foremen had skimmed so much off from what they had gathered, there was nothing left to pay.

"Well, well," Oliver said. "You can understand my concern then. If the dwarves are so eager to off their erstwhile king, I could only imagine what they would pay to lay hold of me. I've been leading their most hated enemy, after all. Someone with the right connections could stand to strike a very rich deal if he could deliver both of the dwarves' enemies—their king and our captain—together at the same time."

"That's preposterous," Samuel shook his head vigorously. "I-I would never—never—sell you out. How can you even suggest—? I-I couldn't. We need you, Oliver. The clerks will make a hash of us all without someone to check them. Besides … the bargain the guilds made with the dwarves was broken. I'm sure Elon hates me as much as you."

"Elon does," Oliver agreed. "But would Elon's thane share that opinion? Who can say? *He* might hale you as a friend and toast your good health, for all I would know."

"Look at the corpses, then," Samuel gestured around the cavern as if it were a graveyard, and Oliver noticed his hand was trembling. "My people, your guards, clerks, Craggies, they've all been slaughtered together out here. The dwarves attacked guild markets and clerks' markets. If anything, they hit us even harder. The guilds are broken, Oliver. We're finished. No one would ever deal with us again."

Oliver watched Samuel, who was fidgeting with the buttons of his clothes and swallowing dryness again and again, but it seemed to Oliver, it was all the right kind of fretting. Oliver kept his eyes locked on the guild master until he was certain the man's uneasiness was because he feared for his safety, not because he had been found out in his scheming.

With a pretense of camaraderie, Oliver extended his hand to Samuel's, and gripping it a little tighter than Samuel would find comfortable, gave it a firm shake.

"I suppose you're right there, Samuel. It did turn out to be a rather hard sweep for your people … But," he released his clasp and clapped his hands together, giving Samuel a slight startle, "that's all in the past. We're joined together now. We'll just have to find your prodigal brother, my guard—together. So, we can finish this business with the dwarves. Together."

Samuel smiled, the relief palpable in his face. Oliver took the cloak from him and was about to get his men back in order when he recalled a final point:

"The newcomer you said Topher had guarding Elon. The one in the crumpled press order. What was his name?"

"Oh," Samuel furrowed his eyebrows as he tried to remember how the press order had read. "It was scratched up and blotted pretty bad. Most men give a fake name when they're pressed anyway. I think it said 'Tom' something or other."

Darkness hung above the air, as still as a shroud, and yet alive. Omnipresent, aware—alive. It seemed to have noticed the intrusion of two tiny beings, thought on them for a moment, but then turned to more pressing matters. The silent passage of two gnats within its realm was apparently beneath its notice. For the present.

Tom was huffing. The old Forward Way's bottommost stairwells had always been a hard climb. But now most of the steps were broken, and those that weren't had become overgrown with lichen, and mushrooms, and frost. His feet kept stumbling out from beneath his legs. The air was not simply cold and veiled in blackness, but somehow oppressive. Tom could feel it in his chest. He bore Elon on his shoulders, and though he would have been a light enough burden in ordinary times, the weight left Tom stooped and wearied. Tom had no idea how much farther he had to climb, the passage of time and distance having ceased to hold any meaning for him. It was only step, step, step, each one a fresh shot of pain, as he climbed on blindly up the stairs. Elon clung to Tom's shoulders, rising and falling with the rhythm of Tom's movements. Every so often, he would whisper into Tom's ear. He was their guide.

They were making for the Gutters.

"I could go quicker," Tom rasped over his shoulder, "if I had a gulleystar. See what's in front of me."

Elon said nothing for a few steps. Tom felt Elon's head turning about, scanning the area with a sight that Tom very much wished he possessed. He heard Elon whisper in his ear:

"I don't think that's a good idea. Something about this place, I don't know … It feels like bringing light out here would be … offensive. Unwise."

"Well," Tom half-tripped on a crack, "it would be unwise for us to tumble down this flight."

"What, my eyes aren't good enough for you?"

Tom knew Elon was trying to cheer him. But it did little to lift his spirits:

"I'm just saying—it would help."

"Just as it would help anyone who might be pursuing us. Stop right there, Tom. Veer a little left, the edge here's worn away—a little more. Alright, carry on."

Tom grunted and kept climbing. He had not heard a sound of any pursuit, but with the thud of his footsteps, his heavy panting, and the pounding din of his heartbeat, a troop of wardens could have been on his trail and he wouldn't have known it. Tom had completely lost his bearings in the blackness, and without Elon's count, he had no idea how long they had been climbing:

"How far have we come?"

"Two and a half flights since the last time you asked. We've gone a little over three leagues in all. Two steps to the right now—"

"Need to rest. About to fall."

It wasn't Tom's way to complain. But he knew that his legs were about to give out from under him. And he couldn't get enough air into his chest. Like hot needles had pricked his lungs apart. He would have told Elon this, but somehow Tom knew that Elon felt it with him.

"Soon, Tom," Elon's attempt to sound encouraging fell flat, "just a little farther. If I remember the maps of your realm, there's a junction with a fountain coming up soon. You can get a drink and rest your legs there. A few more steps. Then you get me off your back, eh?"

They trudged onward.

Step, step, step. Tom fell into a kind of waking dream. The endless succession of steps brought back a memory, from when they still lived in Industry Caverns: Lillia scampering down another part of this stairway with her friend Mava in tow. Their academy sashes freshly laundered for their day at the Docks. Just before she rounded a bend, Lillia paused, shot a glance over her shoulder at Tom, and raised her eyebrows in vexation:

"*You've got to keep up with me,*" she said, her voice a sibilant whisper.

"I will …"

"What's that?" Elon asked, thinking Tom had spoken to him.

"Nothing."

"Almost there now. Keep going."

Each step became a battle. Tom shaking uncontrollably, heaving in gulps of air that felt like daggers inside his lungs. The air had grown colder, which Elon declared could only mean they were coming upon an opening. Soon, soon.

Tom made it up one more step when Elon's voice filled his ear with excitement.

"There it is, Tom," he patted him. "The landing. See the archway up there? No, sorry. Of course you don't. Just stay close to the wall. That'll be safest."

Somehow Tom climbed the final two-score steps.

When the floor leveled out beneath him, Tom fell to his hands and knees and curled onto his side, his teeth chattering loudly. He was sweating so hard that, at first, he didn't notice the layer of ice that covered the stone ground. Elon had slid off his back, and though surely stiff from his wounds, was able to help move Tom over to a low granite plinth that rose above the frost. He stretched Tom out on its surface and draped one of the cloaks he had taken from the abandoned cart over him like a blanket. Tom tilted his head up, smiled at Elon, and let it fall gently back.

Darkness reflected across the landing but kept a respectful distance from the nephil king who wandered about the landing. It felt good to walk, and even better now that he could let his companion rest and regain his strength. Elon walked his paces like he had when he was imprisoned in his cell, as he studied the landing.

Not a landing, Elon thought to himself. This was a place that had been designed by one of his people's architects, long ago. A kind of gathering square connecting strands of stairwells, ramps, corridors (little better than caved in tunnels now, Elon reflected sadly), and passages from the Middle Ward, Industry Caverns, and the Gutters. There was a grand fountain in the middle, broken, its statuary toppled over and replaced with an atrocity that had doubtless been sculpted by a talentless Cragman. Someone had carved a banality into a stretch of quartz, the last two words crimped together because he had failed to space the lettering properly:

THE WORLD WITHIN IS OURS TO WIN

The fountain had once been beautiful, Elon could tell; judging from the placement of sconces and grills around its base, there could have been a wondrous backlit reflection of fire that would have shone from underneath its collected waters. Half of the bottom's arc now lay in rubble, and the parts that weren't encased in frost held a thick coat of dust and debris that hid any luster within its quartz. Elon could envision it as it was meant to stand, though, as if clear, flowing waters still cascaded over hidden fires, and the zenith of the vined columns that rose from its center was still graced by a god, not the abomination that someone had carved in its stead. The figures, the man and woman, looked like they had been chiseled with a pickaxe. The ruin, the lost beauty, the barrenness of the fountain sitting dead in the cold brought a feeling of melancholy over Elon.

Such a waste.

Without knowing why, Elon limped over to a cobblestone that was slightly larger than the others around it and with a grimace, hoisted it up from its resting place. Elon stooped over to peer underneath it. Rusted pipes covered in cobwebs, fallen silt, and insects scurrying to hide filled a crevasse beneath where the stone had been. Elon's eyes traced the curves of the joints, not so much studying the mechanics, but feeling their design as something intuited. He ran a finger across a busted valve stem, and at once sensed that the thing could be made to work again, even without any tools.

The fix was easy enough, though it probably would not last for very long. It only needed a little digging in the dirt. He was so entranced with the work, he almost didn't hear Tom approaching from behind.

"You alright?" Tom asked.

"Fine," Elon answered without looking at him.

"What are you doing?"

Elon thought about it for a moment, then answered Tom with a flash of a smile:

"What I was made to."

Elon felt through the sifting dirt for what he knew would be lying underneath the mainline, a master joint, hidden and hopefully protected from the decay around it. The touch of strong metal sent a thrill into Elon's hand as he brought it within his grasp and turned it hard inward. Quickly, with his other hand, Elon pried the broken stem so that air could escape from the lines. A low murmur rumbled underneath the ground, gradually growing louder, like an iron leviathan coming out of hibernation. Bursts of steam sputtered and coughed. Elon covered the hatch with the cobblestone and stood to watch the fountain return to life. A loud, grating whine, a short silence, and then suddenly the spout above the banner that the statues held draped between them burst with liquid.

The middle letters of the word "WITHIN" were soon covered in a blackened slime, until the water gushing up from behind years of accumulated filth could finally begin to trickle out of the spout, running clear once more. It was a pittance of what it should have been, but still—there was water flowing in the fountain.

"Hey ..." Tom breathed, his voice thick with wonder. "That's something."

"I thought we could use a drink."

Elon and Tom searched the rubble for something that could work as a cup when Elon spotted something lying at the bottom of the fountain. He called Tom over. The two stood transfixed, their hands on the edge of the pool, staring into the shadows at the bottom of the fountain.

"What-what is that?" Tom asked, unable to hide his fear.

Elon did not reply. He leaned over the fountain's brim as if he were about to plunge into the little puddle that had accumulated in the bottom. His face was unrevealing of the admixture of wonder and worry that raced through his thoughts.

"Elon?" Tom asked.

In the perfect darkness, a soft light was now glowing. The first light they had seen since they had begun their journey up the stairwell.

Tom's eyes went round. Elon gazed into the fountain, the waters gathering together, and murmured a prayer to the Maiden.

There, in the bottom of the fountain's well, just beneath the columns that held aloft the statue figures, just beneath the surface of the water, a soft yellow halo was shining from the peacefully reposed face of Topher's dead body.

THE QUARTER

CHAPTER THIRTY-SIX

J EMUEL SON OF Jemuel, was widely, if not begrudgingly, regarded by the nephil as an exceptional chamberlain. He surpassed both his father and his father's father when it came to scrupulous observance of the duties of the royal household and court. There was no propriety, or custom, or more beneath his notice. He knew every thane, courtier, merchant, parvenu, up-and-comer, and ne'er-do-well, and their family trees—and secrets—as intimately as he knew his own. In speech, and manners, and fastidious service, Jemuel was beyond reproach.

As a chamberlain, he was also quite at ease with passing a wide array of minor exaggerations when necessary, and he did so frequently in the course of his responsibilities: overly gracious compliments, thin excuses, a mild fib; he could maintain the most stoic, steadfast silence in the hearing of others' blatant falsities, without the least concern that it impugned his sterling integrity one whit. But he had always maintained a demarcation. The tempering of his honesty went only so far as propriety required. To foist an outright deception, to utter a brazen falsehood, to *lie*, that was a transgression he had never stooped to in all his years of faithful service. It would have been beneath him.

But what a lie it was he was participating in now.

After he had recovered from his daze, his Divinity had instructed Jemuel to pick up the lifeless body of Merari from where it laid on the altar and bring it over to the stairwell that led down into the royal family's crypts. The boy was light enough to carry (he had hardly eaten a bite of the sumptuous meals Jemuel had delivered). Jemuel followed Divine Nicodemus down the winding stairwell. And there, at his Divinity's explicit command—and against every grain of propriety that had been etched within Jemuel—they hid the Gutterling's body in the tomb of his Majesty's royal cousin. Blessed Thane Abidan, a royal thane who had just been decreed a saint, would share his grave bed with a common, fatherless, apostate Gutters boy. Jemuel dropped the body, unceremoniously, next to the hallowed skull and bones of Thane Abidan and expressed his unease to his Divinity.

"I'll come back for him," the priest promised, "after things settle down. Give him a proper ceremony."

"And his tomb, of course," Jemuel had said. "In a place more fitting to his station."

"Of course," his Divinity had said, though it seemed to Jemuel it was an afterthought, and he would likely have to remind his Divinity of it.

There, in the crypt, beneath the disapproving gaze of Thane Abidan's skull, Jemuel hid the boy's body while Divine Nicodemus whispered a plan to Jemuel. He had tried to pay attention. It may have been that Jemuel's brain was addled from shock or lack of sleep, but the whole time the priest spoke, Jemuel would have sworn the blessed thane's skull was growling at him. He could well understand the thane's displeasure.

What his Divinity proposed was as straight-forward as it was spectacular. A lie of breathtaking dimensions.

But, as his Divinity had repeated as Jemuel laid a threadbare rug over the boy's cold corpse, they had an intractable problem. Merari was dead. When his vigil ended at dawn and the sanctuary was opened, everyone in the Realm would know it. And would demand an explanation for how it had happened. His Divinity's plan was the only one that presented the chance of avoiding internecine bloodshed.

That it was a complete and total fabrication (a point that left his Divinity surprisingly unperturbed) would be of no consequence—so long as it preserved the peace.

"If this works," Nicodemus said as they ascended the stairs, "we will have saved our Realm from tearing itself apart. I don't like it any more than you. But the gods will judge our hearts justly in this. Ours are noble intentions, Jemuel. That's all that matters."

"I-I suppose your Divinity knows best," had been Jemuel's faltering response. Unwillingly, he would serve as an accomplice in this falsehood—and fervently insist on his Divinity's prayers for his soul's salvation afterward.

So it was that morning broke, and Jemuel found himself scurrying through the halls, still in his clothes from the night before and still without a wink of sleep, wringing his hands and wondering how he could maneuver what he had been asked to undertake into a more palatable kind of transgression.

"Perhaps," he said to himself, as he entered Elon's throne room, "perhaps I'll need not say a thing. Since his Divinity will be present."

He chided himself for his wistfulness. Of course, there would be questions hurtled at him. He was the royal chamberlain, the one responsible for guarding the sanctuary against intrusion during the boy's vigil.

Jemuel struggled to maintain a demeanor of equanimity as he strode through the doorway and made his way into a gathering throng. Gutterlings mostly. Friends of his Majesty and his Majesty's so-called sect. They must have been congregating for the past hour. To Jemuel's horror, some were smoking pipes. The sextons had lit a fire in the hearth and done their best to keep the forum clean, but the presence of all these rough nephil from the Gutters somehow gave his Majesty's throne room the look and feel of a tavern. Jemuel could not hide the shudder and the accompanying scowl.

It was on the tip of his tongue to ask whether any of them had jobs to keep them occupied, but he mastered the urge when he realized he had suddenly become the center of attention. A hush fell across the room, and all the nephils' eyes trained eagerly upon the tall chamberlain striding purposefully across the room in his flowing garb. Some dipped their heads respectively; others glowered; one nasty looking miner blew a ring of smoke directly in Jemuel's path so that Jemuel had to hold up his sleeve to keep from coughing.

Only one addressed. A plain, sturdily built nephil woman with black hair he only vaguely recollected.

"Master Chamberlain."

"Yes, uhm—"

"Rachel."

"Rachel, yes. From the other evening."

Her copper face looked strained and pallid, patinaed with gray, and her dark hair hung limply at her shoulders. As she spoke, she kept having to pause to belch, as if she were on the verge of being sick to her stomach. Probably still drunk from the night before, Jemuel thought to himself. All the same, he deigned to listen to her politely.

"I've brought his Divinity's—er, Master Merari's—mother with me," she said. "May we—may we come with you, please? She wants to be the first to see him when his vigil's broken."

Jemuel bit down hard on his tongue. This was an impertinence. But as she was surrounded by companions, and with no pretense that would possibly work as an excuse, Jemuel could only stretch his thin lips into the resemblance of a smile.

"But of course, Miss Rachel. Nothing would give me greater pleasure."

She thanked him and motioned for an older woman to hurry and join her. Merari's mother, gray-haired and needing a cane though she was a little older than Rachel, shuffled quickly as the crowd parted before her. Jemuel offered her the barest nod and then without another word, spun on his heel, and the three of them made their way to the alcove that led to the sanctuary behind the throne room.

Much to Jemuel's relief, most of the crowd had the sense to stay clear of what was now the temple's doorway.

Since the delvers' funeral, Elon had had all the stored crates removed from the tiny passageway and cleaned it into something more suitable for a sanctuary's entry. The great portrait of his Majesty's father, King Zebulon, had been rehung on a side wall, no longer needed to conceal the doorway. In the painting's place, a lovingly carved arch and door with an iron lock underneath its handle now dominated the far wall. A mosaic of a beatific woman coming down from clouds and sharing rays of light was still drying above it.

Standing before the doorway waiting patiently for Jemuel's arrival, the Divine Nicodemus stood, rocking on his feet and whistling to himself. He let out a delighted sound when he saw the chamberlain enter the hallway and, catching sight of his trailing company, at once embraced both women with the warmest greetings.

"Why, Rachel," Nicodemus said, pulling back from hugging her with a look of concern, "you don't look at all well."

She waved a hand dismissively, but let out a long, rumbling burp from deep in her stomach.

"Long nights at the Copperbottom lately. I always feel better by lunchtime."

"And dear Milkah," Nicodemus leaned over and kissed Merari's mother gently on the cheek. "How happy Merari will be to see his mother again. After his long labor of prayer. I for one cannot wait to see the expression on his face."

She dabbed a handkerchief to her eyes and nodded.

"Are we ready then?" Nicodemus turned to Jemuel with an expectant look. As if nothing whatsoever had transpired between them mere hours ago. The audacity of his Divinity's pretense was staggering, even for Jemuel.

"Yes, your Divinity," Jemuel said.

Nicodemus raised a robed arm in a sign of blessing and then approached the door to trace a symbol with his finger across its boards. Slowly, the crowd from the throne room encroached into the alcove to get a better view of the opening. As if sensing their presence, Nicodemus raised his voice in a solemn proclamation:

"Merari son of Levi swore to keep a vigil at the request of his Majesty, Elon son of Zebulon, for the good fortune and safe return of his Majesty's army. Merari has prayed without ceasing—and without interruption—these past three days. As a called and ordained priest, I declare that Merari has fulfilled his oath and kept his vigil and decree it now ended. Master Chamberlain, will you unlock the door to the temple to relieve our dear brother Merari?"

Jemuel grit his teeth and fumbled about in his pocket to find the key, which suddenly felt heavy and slippery at the same time. At last, he came up with the metal cylinder, nearly dropped it on the floor, but then guided it into the hole, all the while hoping no one detected how badly his fingers were shaking.

"It's time," Nicodemus said.

Jemuel shut his eyes. The lock clicked. A breath of air slipped into the hallway as the door swung open.

Behind it, a blazing light came flooding into the alcove. Squinting and holding his hands out blindly before him, Nicodemus was the first to stumble inside the sanctuary.

Candles, hundreds of them, set within sconces and candelabras or standing upright on the floor were spread across the entire sanctuary and burning with a fierce intensity. As Jemuel entered, he felt his stomach turning to water, and his feet weighted with lead. The priest must have been as shocked as he, for his Divinity was milling about the candelabras, gazing at the flickering lights, as if in a daze.

"H-How—?" Jemuel started to sputter.

His Divinity stole a furtive, fearful glance at Jemuel. While the rest of the nephil filed inside to gape in wonder, Nicodemus lingered back so that he could whisper at the chamberlain:

"Did you—?"

"N-no. How could I possibly? Should-should we—?"

Nicodemus shook his head:

"We follow our plan …"

There was a piercing shriek. Nicodemus turned toward the sound, which was near the bottom of the dais, while Jemuel shrunk back into the doorway. Milkah was on her knees. She had torn her shawl in two:

"Where is my *son*?"

At that, the spell from the candles broke. The cry was taken up in every corner of the sanctuary:

"Merari! Merari!"

"Your Divinity?"

"Where's Merari?"

The initial shock that had seized the crowd quickly turned into panic. Tearful shouts for Merari were followed by the angry murmurs of men as they began flipping over the pews and censers and tearing down the tapestries, which, at least, brought back some of Jemuel's senses. Instinctively, he found himself scurrying after the nephil, trying to tidy up what was becoming a ransacking of his Majesty's sanctuary.

"Merari!" the cry echoed everywhere.

When some of the miners growled that this was "looking mighty foul," Jemuel feared there would be a riot, but, thank the true gods, at that moment, his Divinity took charge. The priest hurried up the dais stairs, where he stood before the altar, spread out his arms, and raised his voice to be heard above the din:

"My children! My children, hear me!"

"Where is Merari?"

"I want my *son*!"

"Listen to me—" Nicodemus' voice broke.

"Merari!"

"What about that chamberlain? Bet you he knows something—"

"By the gods," Nicodemus said, his voice thunderous, "you—will—*listen!*"

There was a moment when Jemuel feared his Divinity may have waited too long, as if the balance between the fear and confusion of a small crowd and the bloodletting of an angry mob had already been tipped. But then the commotion subsided, if only a little.

"Isn't it clear what's happened? Can't you all see?"

His Divinity's eyes were fixed and wide as mirrors reflecting the glow from all the candlelight. One of the candles had been toppled over and was dripping wax onto his foot, but somehow, he ignored the burning. Every nephil in the temple was looking up at him in a collective, vacant stare.

"I am a called and ordained priest," he continued, "but anyone with eyes should be able to see what's happened here."

"Well?" someone shouted back at him. "What is it, priest?"

"Yeah, where's Merari?"

"Tell us plain. None of your sermons."

Such impertinence, Jemuel scowled. He shushed at the one who had said it.

"It's as plain as the light we've been left with, the light *she* has left us." Nicodemus gestured at all the burning candles and his face assumed an enlightened expression that, to Jemuel, appeared as a mimicry of this goddess' believers. Nicodemus was scanning the crowd, and when his eyes alighted on Jemuel, he paused:

"You were tasked with looking after our friend, Jemuel. Tell us. Did Merari ever break his vigil?"

Jemuel gave a start at hearing his name, and as everyone turned to stare, he feared that his face was blanching, or that they would see his shoulders trembling underneath his robes. He swallowed several times, and Divine Nicodemus arched an eyebrow, a subtle prompting. As if his Divinity had given him an unspoken command, Jemuel found himself shaking his head as he croaked:

"No, Divinity."

"Did you guard the door well?"

"I-I guarded it, Divinity."

Jemuel was sure his face was as white as that alabaster idol above the altar, and he knew his legs were swaying. *Please, Great Nord, no more questions.*

"And none but us have passed through this door since this vigil began?"

At least it was a half-truth. Jemuel was able to respond with a little more assurance.

"Yes. Only us, Divinity."

"Then," Nicodemus made a flourish with his hand that became a very slow, meaningful sign of the gods, "we have—a miracle."

There was a long silence as the nephil standing before their realm's ordained priest tried to grasp the full measure of what he had just declared. What Divine Nicodemus had told Jemuel last night he would say when the moment was right. His Divinity was trying to hold them all with his gaze. His face conveyed conviction and power, though Jemuel could not imagine how he managed such a mask. Jemuel glanced around the crowd, unsure if they would believe what they had just been told.

There was a wretched, crippled delver. A shiftless metal trader. A harpist, likely struggling to find proper work. That tavern keeper, Rachel. The dross of the Gutters. They still looked unconvinced to Jemuel.

His Divinity would have to spell out the lie plainly for them. He spread his arms wide and raised his voice to a shout:

"As your priest, I declare a miracle has occurred this day. Merari … His Divinity Merari—" the priest paused dramatically, "—Blessed Merari—has gone before us. He has been taken up by his goddess from her temple. To dwell with her forever. Like one of the prophets of old. Like in the scriptures I've preached. You know the stories. Well, today, at last, we are *living* them. I say unto you, the scriptures have come to life today!"

There was a loud, shared gasp, and, to Jemuel's relief, he heard murmurs of assent. Many of the nephil brought their forefingers to their heads. The clouded, grief-soaked face of Milkah was staring up at the altar, at Divine Nicodemus, framed by the silhouette of that awful idol

behind him. The old woman was beaming with joy. Milkah's torn garment fell and she raised her hands in praise, and everyone in the crowd
followed her example.

As Jemuel watched, Nicodemus closed his eyes and finished his
falsehood, the one that, if his plan worked, only he and Jemuel—and the
gods—would ever know.

"The Maiden is a true goddess," he lied. "And Blessed Gershon,
Kohath, and Merari were her prophets. I declare it to be so. So mote
it be."

Nicodemus hurried down a long and lonely corridor that led out of
the Gutters and back to his home in the Old Mines. The arthritis in his
knees was flaring, his hip was aching, and his head was foggy from missing his bed, and so he found it taxing to think. But he had no choice.
The fallout from what he had done (what he had to do, he reminded
himself) would surely be as swift as it would be strident.

He began rehearsing his answers, working through the arguments
and counter-arguments, bracing himself for the confrontations that
were to come. To some extent, they were past due. His refusal to openly
denounce the Maiden and her sect—always accompanied by his promises that he was praying and scrying over the issue—was already the subject of a long and simmering ire throughout the other thanedoms of the
Inner Realm. In the past weeks, he had endured cold glares from nephil
who had once sought his counsel and overheard more snide remarks
and tisking tongues than he could count. Attendance at his devotions
and services had dwindled. It would be a bitter dose for the faithful to
swallow that he, Nicodemus, the only ordained priest and protector of
the faiths, had just proclaimed Elon's new nameless goddess.

Some would disavow Nicodemus over it.

Huffing for breath, he paused at a corner, leaned against the cool
surface of the wall, and rested for a moment. For some reason, he was
reminded of a very old memory, one that had been locked away for
decades, something his master had told him after he had been initiated
into the first degrees of the temple:

"A good priest will have to spend some time in hell. Just like everybody else."

Nicodemus had been a young acolyte when the old Divinity offered that little piece of wisdom, so offhandedly and with a touch of wistfulness, as if he were commiserating with this overworked, gangly weaver's child who was busily mopping all the temple floors in preparation for some festival. Everything has its cost, and everyone must pay for what they would have. It had irritated Nicodemus at the time, and its memory brought back the same sense of feeling.

So mote it be.

He nearly tripped over his feet as he tried to pick up his pace.

Ever since he had extricated himself from the joyful throng in Elon's sanctuary an ominous mood had taken hold of Nicodemus. It was not simply the enormity of what he had just done and what the repercussions might be. He was a priest, after all; his whole life embraced incertitude and ambiguity. Never before, though, had such—emptiness—threatened to overwhelm him as it did now.

"I am holding this Realm together," he said aloud with a conviction that came nowhere close to fooling his ears. He repeated it in a louder, sterner tone, listened to the echo die against the carved granite stones of the walls and floor.

There was no time for introspection. Plans had to be made. Letters needed to be written. Talks scheduled. He would skip his supper if need be.

Because if he could manage the inevitable swell of opposition to Elon's sect becoming a faith, keep the most vehement opponents from coalescing, tamp down some of the passions, these factions might learn to accept one another, eventually. Given enough time, and a little guidance. The possibility was there, dangling before Nicodemus. It would all depend on the thanes, though. Especially Reuben; he would be the hardest stone to crack. But if Nicodemus could bring the thanes around to see the potential of *corralling* the energy of this new, exciting faith into the traditions of the old. If he could just meld this Maiden into the pantheon with gentle (but no less firm) direction from the one whose avocation was the preservation of the true faiths—then he, the Divine Nicodemus, could bring order to a belief that was still wild in its youth.

And at the same time inject vitality into the older faiths that had become, it had to be allowed, sclerotic, and, to many, little more than a collection of despondent rituals. It would be a revival—a shared revival—and he would be its head. Holding it all together.

The thought brought the first, faint smile to Nicodemus' lips. The smile of one who had, at last, discovered the distant glimmer of an innermost hope, waiting for him, it turned out, in a most unexpected channel.

Nicodemus scurried faster down the empty corridor, unmindful that the trains of his ceremonial robes were brushing along the floor and getting dirtier the further he went. He had reached the outskirt of his neighborhood and was making fast for the courtyard of his doorway. As he walked, he was sounding out the opening lines of the letters he would write, trying to hit upon just the right admixture of religious authority, coaxing, and inflation of the thanes' egos, when he nearly stumbled headlong into a cluster of nephil men spread around the perimeter of the fountain beside his home.

They were broad, nervous-looking for the most part, and armed with swords. The flutter of black and gold capes hung from their shoulders. The colors of the Granite Reach. Reuben's thanedom.

"What have you done?!" Reuben's voice boomed.

Nicodemus could scarcely react before the thane was upon him. Reuben's face, never a particularly pleasant thing, looked a dangerous hue of purple, the blood vessels had burst throughout his nose, as if he had already been engaged in a prolonged and furious rant by the time of Nicodemus' arrival. He yelled in Nicodemus' face, inundating the priest with so much spittle that Nicodemus reached straight into his pocket for a handkerchief to dry himself.

"What in the name of the true gods have you *done*?" he repeated.

Nicodemus, who was not accustomed to startles, much less shows of martial force, surprised himself by the composure he was able to maintain. He dabbed the edge of his handkerchief into the fountain's water and streaked it across his forehead, which, at least, got Reuben to draw back a step.

"I've come home," he replied. Then he managed to smile at the gathering around Reuben and gave them all a friendly, if not somewhat awkward, welcome. They fingered their belts and glared back at him in a poor imitation of their master's temper. One of them, though, dipped his head in a hasty bow but was quickly elbowed by the man standing next to him.

Reuben was not swayed by his outward calm. "This is not a social call."

"No? What a pity. I was just about to pay my respects to your Excellency. We have much to talk about."

He gestured for Reuben to follow him and started to move towards the doorway, but the thane did not budge.

"No," Reuben crossed his arms. "We don't."

The thane flicked his head towards one of his men standing closest to Nicodemus. Very hesitantly, the man took a step closer to Nicodemus and, as gently as a parent guiding a small child, placed his hand around Nicodemus' elbow. The poor fellow was ashen and could not look Nicodemus in the eye, but his grasp remained. The realization came upon Nicodemus in an instant, but he did not panic.

"Oh, I see. Well, if that's the route you've chosen. Take me away." He raised his voice so that it spread across the courtyard, over the bubbling noise of the water fountain. "Allow me to at least bid adieu to all my neighbors whose doors I see are cracked open and who are sure to wonder why his Majesty's thane is absenting his Majesty's priest under armed guard while their king fights in the Crag. These are tense times, and they're sure to worry. As will the congregants with whom I have just shared fellowship. The only remaining priest in the Realm taken at the point of a sword. I only pray they will not respond in kind."

It was a hollow bluff, but it made Reuben hesitate. Nicodemus felt the hand on his arm withdrawing, and in the span of a frozen moment, he knew how to use the leverage he had just gained. He took a step closer to Reuben and propped himself up on his toes to speak in confidence.

"You are a hard thane," Nicodemus said softly, "and a stout warrior. But never bloodthirsty. I can't believe it's a holy war that you're after."

"It's not."

Finally, he heard the first hint of doubt in the Thane's voice.

"Then we are allies."

"We were. But you've made yourself my enemy."

Nicodemus regarded the old thane before him. Proud, erect, shoulders still squared despite his years. There was a note of betrayal, deep and very raw, that Nicodemus would have to contend with. He gave an understanding nod and a wan smile.

"I can understand why you might think that—given recent events. But I can swear by the true gods, there is no enmity between us, Reuben. Or there shouldn't be. I can explain if you'll let me. And if you're not satisfied—then I will go, quietly, as your willing prisoner."

Reuben's face pinched in distrust, but Nicodemus only deepened the confidential measure in his voice:

"We have much to talk about."

Of all the thanes, Reuben could least stand the prospect of losing face once he was resolved. It was as against his nature as the imposition of someone else's faith.

"Wait here," he grunted at his men, who to a one, looked visibly relieved. With his head looming over Nicodemus', he followed the priest inside his home into his study.

Nicodemus led him past the ornate mirror near the foyer and into the private, canopied set of chairs beneath the gaze of his collected idols. The grand statuary soaring above them invoked the anticipated effect on Reuben, though he scarcely showed it beyond a muttered comment. They sat and Nicodemus offered Reuben his pipe, but the thane refused. Now that they were out of hearing, some of his temper could return.

"You proclaimed Elon's blasphemy, Nicodemus. You made his bitch idol, Lunacy, a goddess, right up there to rub elbows with, with—" he paused to search the statues around them, and finding the one with the severed hand, angrily bowed his head and brought a thick finger to his forehead, "—with our father Nord!" he hissed, as if the all-knowing god would not bear to hear it spoken too loudly. "You should have denounced them as blasphemers months ago. And anyone who didn't renounce her," he brought the same finger he had used to make a holy sign in a quick slash across his throat. "Would've nipped this insanity in the bud. But instead, Elon's cult is now a *faith*. It's only going to spread! You've ruined everything! Why'd you do it?"

"Because," Nicodemus replied calmly, "I had no choice."

That nearly brought Reuben to his feet. He flailed his arms about from his chair and almost fell over.

"What do you mean you had no choice? You're the damned priest!"

"Precisely. I'm the priest. And I had just witnessed a miracle."

Reuben let out a howl like a wild animal. Slowly, it became coherent words, each one punctuated by the thane beating his chest:

"Miracle-as-rat-*shit!*"

"Were you there? Did you see?"

"I heard all I needed. A Gutterling vanished, and a bunch of candles were lit inside a sanctuary," he rolled his eyes and shook his fingers as if he were conjuring a spell. "Some miracle!"

"But there was no way to explain—"

"Gods, you could not be that gullible! It was a trick. Any Gutterling with a bribe and a match could have made all that happen."

"Don't you think I considered that possibility? Really. Give my learning credit for something, Reuben." Nicodemus assumed the posture of a teacher explaining the nature of a problem to a somewhat slow student. "The temple has only one door, which was locked. Besides Elon, who's not here, Jemuel had the only other key. And Jemuel kept watch on that door throughout Merari's vigil, just as he was ordered. Jemuel son of Jemuel, who, whatever else may be said for him, is no Gutterling—and certainly no friend of Elon's sect."

"That puffed up butler had some part in this. You watch. I'll wring it out of him."

"I hardly think his Majesty would look kindly on that when he returns. Besides, what would you learn? That Jemuel *despises* this goddess as much as you? That he positively loathes her Gutterling followers? You know that already, Thane. Or do you now think that *that* chamberlain, of all the nephil, went mad, betrayed his master's orders, and foisted the most brazen and elaborate 'trick' in the history of our Realm?"

Reuben's eyes smoldered, as a low growl rumbled in his throat. Nicodemus continued,

"I find this hard, as well. Believe me. I do. But you weren't there. When that sanctuary was opened, there was so much light. I've never seen anything like it. And then, Merari ..." Nicodemus shook his head. "Everything happened so quickly. What happened to him, whatever it was, was—miraculous.

Much as I hate to admit it. It's impossible for me to denounce the Maiden's sect now, after what happened this morning. I would have to deny the obvious, decree most of a thanedom as heretics, and disclaim my king's sincere, if somewhat misguided, faith. No," and here Nicodemus paused for an exaggerated swallow, as if ingesting something he found distasteful, "it was clear to me the only way to hold us together was to bow to the inevitable. As must we all, for the sake of our king and kingdom."

For the first time, Reuben turned away. He seemed unable to meet Nicodemus' gaze, which was odd. It occurred to Nicodemus that perhaps Reuben might also be holding onto something that ought to be explained. Nicodemus decided to venture a little further:

"Foremost on my mind was that his Majesty will be returning from battle any day now. Hot with fervor, no doubt. When he does, when he learns of what happened within his sanctuary during his absence, there must be no strife between his faith and ours—gods forbid, we must not give him or his followers cause to defend their beliefs with swords. Cries of 'We come!' answered with shouts of 'Nord save us!' Think of it: the last of our warriors bleeding out the last of our strength, fighting one another? *That* would be our ruin. Surely, you don't want that to be your greeting to our returning king?"

"You don't understand what's happened …"

Nicodemus rocked forward. A tingling of mounting anxiety was beginning to crawl over him.

"What has happened?"

The thane fixed his eyes hard on Nicodemus and jutted out his chin. Reuben had assumed fully his role as thane now. Resolute, determined, in command. He responded to Nicodemus' question with an announcement.

"There's going to be a change when Elon comes back."

"What kind of change?"

"Elon's fighters are dead. That so-called priest of his, too. There was a battle in the Lower Ward. It went badly. The men remembered their old tactics. Nets and numbers, the way they fought us before."

Nicodemus felt his heart drop within his chest. "And what of Elon?"

"Burnt to a crisp. He's still alive, but only barely. The Cragmen hold him prisoner."

A startled gasp slipped from Nicodemus, and he made the sign of the gods, which Reuben reflexively followed. In the torrent of feelings that immediately followed, the cold, pragmatic impact of this development, how it upended everything, came through with startling clarity. Reuben pressed on in almost a matter-of-fact monotone:

"Arrangements have been made for Elon's return—but on terms. Elon will take responsibility for his part in instigating this stupid war, which, you know, we all begged him not to wage. For the good of the Realm, he'll acknowledge he forswore the oath of the Treaty, he'll renounce this false goddess, he'll abdicate, and then," he paused and shrugged as if he were discussing how the weather was likely to turn out after some nasty spot of rain, "then we'll finally have peace again. We'll trade with the Cragmen, like before."

Nicodemus' head fell into his hands, his blood drained from his fingers. The repercussions of what had happened without his knowledge, and how he had unwittingly positioned himself, were settling on him like the weight of a millstone. He managed to croak:

"And what will happen to Elon?"

"Hopefully, he'll do the honorable thing. Put a noble end to the trouble his capers have caused us."

It was clear what Reuben meant. His hope would be assured: one way or another, Elon was done for. When Nicodemus made no other sound, Reuben continued, still gruff but with at least a pretense of something akin to sympathy.

"Look, I'm sorry I didn't bring you into my plans when they were being negotiated. It all happened—well, as you say, things have happened quickly. You'd been so damned tepid about Elon's faith, I didn't know where you'd stand, what position you might take. I did warn you at the feast—we needed your support. You never gave it."

The floor seemed to be dropping further and faster from beneath Nicodemus' feet. He would not have normally asked it of Reuben, but saw no reason for discursion:

"Are all the thanes joined in this-this bargain?"

Reuben gave a terse nod, his eyes straying off once more. "More or less. Simeon won't like it. But they'll all fall into line."

They had no idea what Reuben had done; Nicodemus was sure of it. But how could they object if it meant their people would have bread again? However Reuben had managed it, he had timed this move of his perfectly. Nicodemus drew his head back up, tried to assume a benign, dignified posture, and came to the point:

"What of me?"

The thane let out a long breath through his nostrils, pulled his jaw tight in what, for him, would have passed for deep, troubled contemplation, and rubbed at a small scar that was hidden just beneath his chin. When at last he spoke, his voice was as low and gravelly as the rock beneath them:

"That's the damnable thing. You've made yourself—well, now you're a, like a—"

"I'm a knot in your plan," Nicodemus came to his aid.

"Right. That's a good way of putting it."

"And now you've got to figure out the best way to deal with the knot."

Rueben was eyeing Nicodemus. His face became hard and he made a quick slashing motion with his hand:

"I could just cut you out … Nothing personal, Divinity, but for the good of the Realm, you know."

Nicodemus struggled to keep his voice from wavering:

"You could. But I don't think you will. Because that would be your worst choice."

"It would be a bad choice," Reuben corrected him, and then added coldly, "for the time being. You still carry some clout. And you made yourself some new friends this morning. I'll grant you that. They don't have much else going for them, but there are a fair number of them and they are a fiery bunch … Maybe the knot could untie itself? Undo what you did this morning?"

Nicodemus shook his head.

"Once decreed, a god is a god for all time. Even if I tried," he held out his hands helplessly.

"The Gutterlings wouldn't accept it. They'd figure I had gotten to you, and they'd be right. I thought as much. So that leaves only one option."

So it did. Nicodemus knew what Reuben's plan would be even before Rueben did because it was the thane's only alternative. And as Nicodemus reflected, given what had transpired, it was the best he could hope for. He looked about his private chamber as if seeing the place for the first time. Large, airy, ornate, even by his people's standards, but would it still feel that way when his eyes beheld nothing else year after year? How many paces could he walk from wall to wall? In which room would he escape the tedium; he had only four to choose from. He would find out in the days ahead. This room, he realized, where he spent so much of his time when he was at home, with its carpets and canopy, pedestal and mirror, and all the gods that had been saved during the Overthrow—it would likely become his tomb. When he emerged from his thoughts, he saw that Reuben was looking at him with his usual hard expression but tempered with the faintest shadow of a sad smile, perhaps one he reserved for old friends who had fallen out with him.

"You've served us well for a long time, Divinity," Reuben said. "You deserve to enjoy the fruits of all your hard work. You should retire, I think. Enjoy the quiet life. We'll see to your every need in here. Guards will make sure no one bothers you. With apartments like this," he waved around, "you'll never need to come outside at all."

Nicodemus nodded and then let his head fall.

"So you'll leave the knot in place," he sighed.

"I'll keep it close and pulled so tight, no one will even know it's there."

CHAPTER THIRTY-SEVEN

I T WAS A SMALL and boisterous crowd that had gathered in the common room of the Copperbottom tavern. What began as supper, turned into a medley of hymns, then libations, then more hymns, and was now an impromptu worship service, albeit one without a priest. Thirty or so of the sect's believers were celebrating Nicodemus' proclamation from three days hence. Many had come, and gone, and then returned (a few more than once). They were the earlier converts mostly, those who had felt the stirring of the faith back when Blessed Gershon had first begun describing the Maiden's dreams. That had been in this very tavern room. As they shared fellowship, their gazes kept returning to the display of colored bottles behind the bar, and every time they looked there, a smile (and, more often than not, a song) would erupt that would set the whole group into a renewed round of cheers. For set just above the scripted letters of the inn and the name of its proprietor, Rachel, a shelf had been cleared, and in its center, a cylindrical roll had been screwed into place. From the roll hung a hoary white silk cloth, one without blemish or sign, about five feet long, what had become an emblem of the Maiden now that they could have one.

There it was. An open statement of their faith. A symbolic proclamation that echoed Nicodemus'—their god was true.

"Our Lady comes," they shouted, "to shine upon us all. Blessed be her Prophets."

One of the nephil at the table, a pipe cleaner, with tears brimming in his eyes, gazed up at the banner affectionately, wobbled to his feet, and lifted his tankard:

"I preposh—," his heavy tongue slurred, so he plunged straight into his toast: "To his Dif-in-ty, Nicodemus. May th' Maiden grant 'im long life. Lots and lots of blessings."

That was met with a thunderous, "Be it so," followed by the clanks of pewter cups coming together. The pipe cleaner swayed from the noise, but Rachel was right behind him to guide him safely back down to his seat.

He would need a cot before the hour was through, she thought kindly.

"Thank you, love," he smiled at her.

"You're welcome, Hiram, but I think you've reached your limit."

The frown that clouded Hiram's face was so disappointed and for-lorn, like a child who had just had his present taken away, that Rachel had to relent. She tilted the jug she was carrying over Hiram's cup and served him a half measure with the warning there would be no more.

Not that it would matter. The beer was already watered down; the only way it would ever last through the tavern's next shift.

"You'll be blessed," Hiram smiled. Another song, one that had become the sect's standard, started up with renewed vigor. "Blessed," Hiram repeated more loudly as their voices rang:

"So let her godlight fall
and fall for endless days.
And let us heed her call
from in the Mountain's maze."

Rachel nodded absently along with the tune as she scanned the tables. The plates were emptying. Nothing but crusts and skins floating in watery sauce remained, but the bellies would stay full. At least for a couple of hours. Filler food. That was what Rachel had been reduced to serving now, something she would have sneered at in any other tavern. But what else was left?

She wiped her forearm across her brow and was surprised at how clammy and sweat-drenched it felt. Her stomach lolled, then started to climb into her throat.

"The dark path she has walked
will shed light in her wake—"

"Rachel?" Hiram was squinting at her, a vaguely worried expression hovering above his stupor. "Y'alright, dear?"

Rachel swallowed hard and made a face:

"I'm alright ... I-I just need a little air. Stuffy. Excuse me ..."

"I'll make sure the ale gets served!" Hiram called after her.

As if on their own, Rachel's legs were carrying her swiftly to the tavern door. With each step, she prayed she would make it outside before she was sick. Fortunately, the nephil were more intent on their celebration than on the hasty exit of their hostess.

Once Rachel was in the courtyard and the cool, open air of the cavern, she felt the queasiness that had seized her slowly begin to subside. She found the closest bench on the patio and promptly collapsed. Her muscles were throbbing in protest, but no matter how she sat, or slouched, or laid herself out, she simply couldn't get comfortable.

All these strange pains, her stomach turning weak, the constant aching in her back and legs, these were all new sensations for Rachel. New and puzzling. The work of keeping a table was something she had been happily doing without the slightest hitch since she was tall enough to reach a tabletop. It was as if she had suddenly aged a century in the span of a few weeks. Rachel pulled her old shawl higher up on her shoulders, wondering if she was beginning to grow—old.

"Nonsense," she chided herself, "Mother could still brew a keg and hang shingles at twice my age."

The memory of her mother bustling about the tavern brought a smile to Rachel, but no relief. Her joints were still groaning in pain. A shiver went down her body. She reached for the shawl's clasp and tried to tie it around her chest. Odd, she thought to herself. It was her favorite cloak, one she had worn comfortably for years, but now it no longer seemed to fit.

"Button must be broke," she muttered to herself. She sniffed, stretched her legs, and decided to try a short walkabout, to see if it might work through some of the knots in her muscles.

She set out across the tavern's patio, walking briskly beneath the hanging bronze cauldron while trying to avoid any patrons who might be loitering around. Just beyond the patio's edge, there was another broken stone bench that was both secluded and well hidden beneath the shadow of a tall granite spire. Her feet were already beginning to feel sore, and since the bench was empty, Rachel sat down again and let out a long, exhausted sigh.

She slumped to rest her back against an outcrop of stone and tried to blink the tiredness out of her eyes, but another yawn came out all the same. The breakfast crowd would be arriving soon, she had little more than scraps to serve them, and all Rachel wanted was to curl into her bed. She stuffed her hands into her apron pockets. One of her fingers brushed against a piece of cloth that felt smooth and very soft. She brought her hand back out and let fall a tiny pouch that dangled from a length of silk cord. She watched it twist in a slow pirouette. A whiff of fragrance escaped, and Rachel felt her pain easing ever so slightly.

Hops and spice. Jacob's last payment to her.

Her eyes closed at a distant remembrance.

That had been—how long ago was it now? Little matter. She could no longer recall, any more than she could remember the features of the warden's face—they were nothing memorable, she was sure—but she could still picture that evening with him in the backroom of the tavern vividly. The barrel she had brewed with his gifts was still there, tucked beneath a drop cloth in a corner. The tavern's kegs were all running dry, but for some reason, Rachel could not bring herself to tap that last barrel. There was something … special within it.

The sharp churning came over her stomach again, and Rachel hunched in pain. Her dinner was coming. She let out a long groan, which was followed by a sputtering as she tried to catch her breath. When she was sure the nausea had passed, Rachel looked up and saw that someone had approached her.

"Miss Rachel, do you need help?"

There was a very old man, leaning on a cane in the shadows. His intrusion was so kindly and well-meaning, Rachel's initial annoyance at his appearance at once dissipated.

"I'm fine, Mr. Peleth," she tried to smile, still feeling light-headed, but then added more firmly: "Really, I'm alright."

He did not look at all satisfied with Rachel's answer, and told her so, followed by a string of warnings, injunctions, and scattered anecdotes of health advice he had, no doubt, heard countless times from his wife.

"And where's Mrs. Peleth," Rachel interrupted. It just occurred to her that she had not seen either of these regular customers for two, three weeks now.

"Eh? Oh, her," Mr. Peleth's face blushed slightly and he glanced over his shoulder, as if she might have snuck up from behind him. "She, uhm, couldn't make it. Not, uh—well, it's like this. She's religious. Always has been. And, uh, well. Much as she likes you—and she thinks you're the finest girl in all the Gutters—she's got it in her head that, uh, what with what's happening in the Realm, and certain folks believing in certain gods that others may not believe in, and you believing what you believe—not that there's nothing wrong with that, mind you. But, uhm. She's got the notion that it wouldn't be right for us to come 'round here anymore, and I can't talk her out of it. She can be a stubborn ass when it comes to the gods." He lapsed into a mocking, but quite passable, imitation of Mrs. Peleth: "'There's proprieties we have to take into account,' she says. Whatever the hell that means. Bottom line is we can't be seen coming into your tavern 'til things simmer down some."

Rachel gave a slow nod.

"I understand."

"Good." He seemed relieved that he would not have to explain himself any further. Unbidden, he sat down next to Rachel.

"But you didn't come all the way out from the Granite Reach just to tell me you can't eat at the Copperbottom anymore."

"Gods, but you are sharp for a Gutterling," Peleth shook his head. "You got me. There is something else. We figured, me and the missus, that living down here, you may not always catch wind of what's happening elsewhere in the Realm."

The way he spoke, Rachel felt a nervous lurch in the pit of her stomach.

"What's the news?"

Mr. Peleth let out a long breath:

"Our thane's fallen out with Nicodemus. No other way to put it. He says Nicodemus—" Mr. Peleth's hand hesitated in its motion to make the sign of the gods, "—His Divinity has gone past his time as our priest. There's some law or rule about it. Sounds an awful lot like a Crest shenanigan if you ask me, but Reuben's holding firm. Says it's an ancient temple law that Nicodemus should've been replaced years ago … So now he's been replaced."

"Wha—? *Replace* Nicodemus?"

Peleth nodded, unable to believe it himself.

"By who?"

"Thane Phannias."

"You're joking."

He shook his head.

"But he's a *poet*. You have to be joking."

"Miss Rachel, I wish I was. I wish to Nord, wish to Amdal, wish to every god, demigod, and power in the pantheon, hell I wish to your Maiden goddess, that this was all some silly lark. But it ain't."

The air went out from Rachel. For a long while, she could only stare at her bare feet, scraping helplessly against the dirt. A floating sensation came over her. It was as if she were looking down at someone else's legs, someone else's hands clenched nervously on someone else's lap; there had never been a time in her life when the Divine Nicodemus had not been her people's priest.

"What-what did Nicodemus have to say about all this?" she managed at last.

Peleth opened his palms wide in a display of emptiness.

"Nothing. Not one damned thing. And he won't so much as set foot outside that palace of his. Supposedly he wrote a letter, which Reuben and Phannias read out loud yesterday, wishing Phannias the blessings of Nord in his new role. It's rubbish. No one believes Nicodemus wrote it. Weren't a flowery word in the whole thing. But truth is … most folk in our thanedom don't care one way or another. Not after what he—well, you know what he did in the sanctuary."

Rachel nodded. In the distance behind her, she could hear the sounds of reverie from the Copperbottom. Someone must have made another toast.

"Anyway," Peleth angled one of his legs to give his backside a scratch, "thought you should know where things stand. What'll be coming."

Flustered as she was, Rachel thanked Peleth for his concern for her and for having walked so far to deliver this news. Her thoughts kept returning to the tavern for some reason. She would have to tell the others. But then she felt exhaustion weighing on her shoulders like a heavy blanket. She had to shake it off. Rachel stood abruptly, apologized that she had to get back to her people—her customers. She had almost taken her leave when Peleth suddenly remembered something:

"Don't know how I forgot, since I nearly broke my back carrying it. Wait here for just a moment." He winked at Rachel, then ambled off to where he must have been waiting. When he returned, he was lugging a heavy wicker basket, which he dropped at her feet.

"For you," he said, flipping open the lid with his toe, "for all you done for me and Miriam over the years."

Inside was a packed but perfectly sorted collection of foodstuffs: loaves of hard bread, dried sausages, raisins, potatoes (a score at least, Rachel reckoned), a block of salt.

"Where did you—?" Rachel began.

"Reuben. Don't know how he's managed it—probably best not to know—but he's got the Crag sending us food again. Barely a trickle, but thank the gods, we're getting something. Now I know you'll want to just serve this out to your friends, and nothing I can say'll stop you from doing it, but listen here." He fixed her with a stern fatherly gaze, which Rachel duly returned as if she were a dutiful, attentive child, instead of a barkeep. "Half's for you," he said. "And you only. I don't care what your sect says about sharing. You need to take care of yourself."

"Alright," she smiled, "I will." She took Peleth's callused, wrinkled hands in her own and teased him: "Sharing food with heretics? That can't be a propriety. What would Mrs. Peleth say?"

Peleth's mouth slowly stretched into a sly grin. He squeezed Rachel's hands firmly and with a seditious gleam in his eye he replied:

"Who do you think made the damned basket?"

Phannias read over the report he had been handed a final time, folded it back up, and tucked it away into the pocket of his new priest's robes. The paper brushed against his sermon.

Not a poem. Not a sonnet. A sermon.

He smiled at the thought of that, and at once forgot the dour tone of Reuben's officer's account. It struck Phannias as somewhat presumptuous of Thane Reuben to have a report made for him; after all, Thane Phannias—*no*, he reminded himself with another rush of pleasure, *The Divine Phannias*—was coming to the Gutters to preach to his flock. Surely the lowly nephil would welcome him to their bosoms as one of their own. The art of his words would bridge their divisions.

Still, the news had been rather more somber than he had expected.

A trickle of bread and potatoes, the report said, had finally wound its way into the Gutters. Carried in by Reuben's soldiers. At every junction throughout the thanedom, his warriors had announced greetings on behalf of "the High Thane Reuben." They had come to "preserve the peace" and "extend a helping hand" to their suffering brothers and sisters. Every soldier carried a heavy sack filled with food in one hand and a weapon in the other. It did not take long for the cohort to multiply into a heavily armed garrison.

The food, at least, was welcomed.

While more of Reuben's soldiers poured into the Gutters, the white banners of the Maiden's sect, which in the few days' time after Nicodemus' proclamation had festooned almost every home and shop, had all but disappeared. Many were burned in bonfires.

All of which had been met with a great deal of angry murmuring on the part of the Gutters' residents, but only one, a half-mad old baker named Kanai, dared to openly defy Reuben's troops. One day around noontime, this poor old fool came screaming in the middle of a corridor wrapped in a white sheet, wielding a kitchen knife, and vowing to defend his Lady to the death. To their credit, Reuben's guards tried to talk some sense into him, but he only grew more agitated, and when Kanai lunged at one of Reuben's sergeants, the soldier calmly ran him through with a dagger. Lest the bloodstained banner becomes some sort of holy relic, the sergeant ordered his men to take Kanai and discretely burn both body and banner on a pyre in some remote place.

According to the report, there had been a few more scuffles, some acts of vandalism, but it seemed Kanai's fate had taken the fight out of the sect's adherents for the time being.

While the images of the Maiden were withdrawn and her faith reduced once again to a cult, images of Nord had been carefully placed in the hopes of returning the heretics to the true faith. In squares and at the junctions of every tunnel and corridor, sconces were fastened onto walls to display sculpted molds of Nord's severed hand. Everywhere one looked, open palms were braced above them, reminders that they were all now in Reuben's reach.

"Helping hands," the locals called them.

But whoever had written the report seemed intent on dousing Phannias' enthusiasm. For its final paragraph was nothing but a long, tedious warning that, despite the return of order to this poorest corner of the Inner Realm, neither High Thane Reuben, nor Phannias, nor Nord himself, would be welcomed in the Gutters.

"Such stuff," Phannias sniffed to himself. He patted his sermon fondly and rehearsed its opening lines over again as he rounded a bend in a tunnel that would take him to the very heart of his new congregation.

Knowing that the Copperbottom had been a favorite gathering spot for the false goddess' 's believers, Phannias decided to make his first priestly address from the humble patio outside the tavern, a show of goodwill to the Gutters' erstwhile flock of believers. As he approached, he saw a ring of soldiers around the small platform that had been built for the occasion. The cuir-bouilli armor and heavy spears seemed a trifle out of place, especially among such a small gathering of onlookers.

We should have posted more handbills.

Annoyed by the meager turnout, Phannias nevertheless gave a cheerful wave, but he tripped on portable wooden steps by the platform, and only his soldiers made any effort to stifle their laughter. Phannias smiled self-effacingly, straightened his robes that were so newly made the train still stood stiffly, almost straight out from behind his legs, and held the podium within his fingers.

My audience.

"Greetings, my children," he began keeping his voice cheerful, but his chosen introduction did not have quite the effect he had hoped for. A pool of smudged, sullen, silent faces glared back at him.

"I am Phannias, son of Ithamar, formerly Thane of the New Mines. No doubt you've heard of me. In the Name of our All-Knowing Father, bringer of order and virtue, most Blessed Nord, I wish you grace and peace. What a joy it is to be among those whose faith and fervor have long been a sustaining force within our great Realm. Here in this pious country of the Gutters. For from the earliest days, the realm of the Gutters has tended and nurtured our kingdom's spiritual life. Countless prophets came from this small corner of the Mountain, heeding the call of our ordained gods to lead our people in the ways the gods would have us follow. And who can count the number of priests these humble tunnels have produced? Truly, we in the other thanedoms, who have long enjoyed the warmth and light your people so freely shared, owe you a great debt.

"Today we shall repay our obligation to you. We come to share both our material and spiritual nourishment with you, as dear brothers and sisters."

Some of the Copperbottom patrons nearby scowled at that, and Phannias thought he heard someone mutter, "You can keep the latter." It was loud enough to be answered with a rumble of assent. Phannias smiled and pressed on reading from his notes:

"These have been dark days for us all, but especially here in the Gutters. Trapped between the constant gnaw of poverty and the apostasy of men on your borders, it is no wonder that some in this realm would begin to question the true faith and to wander from the true gods. Without an ordained shepherd to tend to this flock, how could it be otherwise? Truly, dark days indeed. But I bring good news. Your wandering is over. As a called priest of the Order of—"

A defiant shout came from the crowd, "We already got us a shepherd."

Phannias felt his face tighten. He tried to carry on in his speech, but now he heard his voice crack. "—I, that is myself, who shall be consecrated for ordination in ten days' time, have been called to minister to you—I mean, to us—"

"But we want Divine Nicodemus!"

The call was soon picked up by others. The nephil guarding the stage gripped their spear shafts more tightly.

"Where is Nicodemus?!"

"He preached the truth! You know he did!"

"Our Lady has been proclaimed!"

"Give us Divine Nicodemus!"

Phannias swallowed hard and held out his hands above the podium to plead for order.

"His Divinity," Phannias explained, "had longed for retirement. Besides, he could no longer serve as priest. He was too old for the work and should have stepped down a long time ago. The Canon of Cohanim prohibits anyone over the age of—"

A blind, bent over blacksmith, his head and features as smooth and weathered as an old piece of flint, had wobbled up on top of a chair and hollered back at Phannias:

"Who're you saying's too old to work? Look here, boy, I'm forty years older than Nicodemus. You don't think I still got plenty of fire in my furnace?"

A wave of laughter and cheers erupted from the crowd.

"But you see," Phannias struggled to make himself heard, "the canon doesn't allow for clerics—"

"Who gives a shit about cannons? Damn things always blow up. That's why we don't make 'em anymore! Which you'd know if you were a little older!"

More laughing, but now a rebellious edge was beginning to come through. For such a little crowd, they were making a tremendous noise, and much of it was beginning to veer into the obscene. Eventually, their cries coalesced into a chant, which the whole gathering took up, jabbing their fingers toward the platform:

"You're a poet, not a priest! A poet, *not* a priest!"

Phannias strained to raise his voice, to make himself heard, but it was hopeless. He felt rooted where he stood, unable to decide what he should do. Reuben had ordered him to make a conciliatory but decisive introduction. To stand tall, for he was the people's new spiritual leader. Reuben's guards were urging him to get off the stage so they could hurry him back to his lodgings before a riot broke out.

A poem, that's what we need, for I am both poet and *priest.*

"I am reminded of a verse—"

And then something broke, like the first thunderclap of a gathering storm.

One of the women in the throng hurled her shoe at him.

Phannias watched with an oddly detached fascination as a laced sandal sailed through the air, tumbling end over end, straight for his head.

He watched its trajectory as if he were studying a line of literature until the poignancy of its meaning hit him squarely in his temple.

He fell to his knees, dazed, his ears ringing over the jeers of the crowd. A tiny trickle of blood stained one of the newly laid planks of the platform. Phannias stared at it in disbelief. He heard a hard baritone shout, the sergeant:

"Form up! Form up!"

Reuben's soldiers came together into a single line bristling with spearheads.

"In the name of the High Thane," the leader bellowed, "you are ordered to disperse. Clear out, now!"

As Phannias watched, a torrent of shoes and sandals came raining down over the platform. When they ran out of footwear, the Gutter-lings turned to throwing stones. Sharp and jagged, they pelted Phannias mercilessly.

Nord, will these brutes not protect their priest?

As if in answer, Phannias heard a terrified shriek from beneath the podium as the line of Reuben's warriors surged forward. Spears set, they let out a loud grunt, one step, then another. The Gutterlings closest to the platform turned and tried to flee. In their panic, some were trampled over, while others were cut down from behind. The spears thrust at any-thing standing before them. A steady, merciless advance, leaving bodies in the wake, so awful not even the poet could make a metaphor for it.

From the doorway of the Copperbottom, Rachel watched it all unfold—first the riot, then the massacre. Like witnessing an avalanche from afar, one that was swallowing her friends. The suddenness of the violence, and the strange awkwardness she felt at watching it, left her numb.

But it was over quickly. By the time she realized what was happen-ing, the killing was done.

Her sect now had its martyrs, the first of many.

CHAPTER THIRTY-EIGHT

IT BEGAN AS a whisper, something faint and distant. Okran tilted his head to catch the noise. It reminded him of the sound of exhaling a deep breath, only more sustained.

Okran came to a halt at a junction of six tunnels and set his pack down against the corridor wall, craning to the left and then to the right to try to hear it better. The work crew of nephil that was following him stopped. There were ten of them in all and other than Okran they were all from the Granite Reach. Thane Reuben's men.

"Hey, Gutterling," one of the nephil snapped. His name was Gilead, but he went by Gil, a ruddy, quartz-skinned mechanic stooped from his years of work, who had a habit of keeping his hands slightly clenched all the time, and made no secret of how little he regarded the nephil of the Gutters. Okran didn't answer him.

"I'm talking to you, traitor," he thumped one of his knuckles against Okran's shoulder, "Why are you stopping?"

Another voice hissed from the crowd: "scared he'll run into a Cragman that'll take him up again."

"Yeah," a third voice rang, "and he's run out of friends to sell out."

The group of nephil fell into snickering. Okran ground his jaw and kept listening.

Since his return to the Gutters, the lies about Okran had become such common gossip in the Inner Realm even the new arrivals from the Granite Reach had heard it. According to the rumors, at the height of the troubles, Okran had been taken up to the Cragmen's prison on the orders of the warden Jacob. It was rare but not unheard of that someone from the Realm would be taken up. But Okran was the first to ever return. Roadworn, underfed, and weary, Okran refused to say what had happened during his short absence. All he wanted was to be left alone and return to his kiln. But the wagging tongues had filled in his silence with lies. The whispers were that he betrayed another nephil—perhaps Jacob, perhaps King Elon himself—in exchange for his freedom. No matter who it was, Okran was a betrayer. How a lowly Gutterling potter could have sold a warden, much less a king, to anyone was a point no one discussed, for the truth of the rumor quickly became both accepted and unassailable.

Okran was a pariah. From the moment he set foot out of his home, he felt it keenly.

"Look here," Gil continued, "my job's big and my time's short. If you're too scared to see us into the Pipes, give me back my money and I'll hire another guide—"

"Shut up," Okran responded, his voice flat. The work crew fell silent.

Okran was uncommonly large for a Gutterling, and if anything good could be said to have come from the false stories that swirled about him, it was this: behind all the sneers, and murmurings, and sour faces, there was also the tiniest grain of fear, fear that he had some power with the hated Cragmen. Gil snarled to himself but said nothing as Okran peered down the tunnel.

Okran had no idea what he was even looking for. As if he might catch a glimpse of whatever the source was of this strange noise. It was coming from this tunnel, though, he did not doubt it. But he had never heard such a sound coming from the Pipes. Something about it troubled him.

"This way," he said at last, heaving his pack back on.

As the group clambered down a series of sloping corridors behind Okran, more and more rusted metal piping appeared, jutting out at odd angles from the ceiling and walls, or rising from the floor to bar their way. The farther they went, the wider the pipe works spread, an elaborate, steaming system of metal joints and tubes that enveloped all but a narrow walkway in the tunnel. The noise that had given Okran pause was growing louder and more distinct.

"So-so what is that?" Gil had to raise his voice to be heard over the sound.

"No idea," Okran replied without looking at him.

The corridor narrowed and the way ahead became completely cluttered with the labyrinth of pipes that lent this place its name. The metal was all flaked and rusted, and in places, where the joints were breaking, a slimy black mold was spreading prolifically. Their feet splashed through puddles of water, and a cloud of mist settled down from the ceiling. The noise in the tunnel was becoming deafening now; they could only talk by shouting at one another. Okran would have sworn that what he was hearing was water falling—but, no. That was impossible. There were no fountains anywhere in the Pipes.

By the time they reached the final run of steps, everyone was soaked to the skin and holding their hands to cover their ears from the thunderous noise. Orkan led the crew down a curving stairwell. He had pulled far ahead but now had to come to a halt. Slowly the rest of the crew filed in behind him, straining to see past his bulk at what was barring his way. Okran almost reached for the Nord amulet that he used to wear around his neck, but remembered it was gone now. Like so many things.

Like the Pipes.

Beneath Okran's feet, the edge of a massive, icy black lake lapped against the stone surface of the remaining flight of steps. It was so broad, he couldn't make out the far side. High above the water's surface, a piercing roar echoed, and the source of the sound was now as plain as his nose. Waterfalls. Scores of waterfalls were casting torrents of water down from the blackness above into the depths below. As Okran's gaze went higher, he saw hundreds of feet overhead, like broken strands of a spiderweb that had been pulled asunder, the remnants of the pipes. They hung limply from the cavern's ceiling, swaying from their weight in broken brackets. Great arcs of frothing water spewed from where the pipes had burst, falling from the heights, down through the void as streams, or falls, or mist to be gathered together again on the cavern's floor. Silver lines and white curves hurtling across nothingness, then falling. Far below, the capstones of a few pillars broke through the surface of the lake here and there as scattered islets. Otherwise, there was no trace of what had been a crowning feat of building at the height of the priests' power—the channeling of the Mountain's deepest springs.

Orkan, Gilead, and the crew of workers propping on their tiptoes behind them could only stare in awe at what they beheld.

The elements were loose. Air, water, and stone, unbounded, crashing savagely upon each other, striving for dominance. It was like standing in the presence of gods, as they made war.

Tom picked up a small, flat rock, fitted it snugly in the arch between his thumb and forefinger, and let it fly. It sailed far into the darkness before it plunked against the surface of the water. The stone skipped along seven more bounces before it sank quietly.

It was something he had learned as a boy, though he couldn't remember when. Probably back in the days when he had scavenged around the Docks. Skipping stones was what it was called. Tom had been staring absently at the waters from a balustrade rail when the memory suddenly returned to him.

No sooner had the stone disappeared, then another unexpected remembrance came from perhaps a year ago, just a scene of quiet domesticity: Timothy, coming into manhood, bent over a table and scraping a goat hide by the soft luminescence of a gulleystar pot. In the shadows behind him, Tom's wife, Bette, sewing a pouch of leather and watching over her son in a rare moment of content. They were talking together and something she said had made Tim smile.

Tom had never taught Timothy how to skip stones, though they had gone down to the Docks plenty of times together.

He felt a pang of regret. Tom bent over, picked up a piece of broken tile, and flung it as hard as he could. It flew in much the same direction as the rock had, but bounced only once in the churning waters before it vanished.

Tom was standing on edge of a balcony in a cavern on the farthest border of the Crag. Beneath him, stretching out as vast as a horizon, a turgid, black lake filled what had once been a massive octagonal chamber that housed a suite of clerks' stations. The only furnishing in the balcony had been an elevated chair; apparently, the place had served as a lector's station, one of some eminence. Tom had used the chair wood to make a fire. A few orange embers still glowed from the bottom of the pile.

Tom watched as the waves churned beneath him, listening to the faint echo of falling water from far out in the void. The waves, the ripples, the cascades, were in constant motion, a random flux, like his thoughts. He tried to summon one that could hold off the weariness that was overtaking him.

Unbidden, his reflections turned to Topher. Tom shuddered at the recollection of his former sergeant and guild brother. Lying dead in the basin of a broken old fountain on the stairwell landing, his burly body was glowing like a pressed gulleystar. A hard, earthy man, Topher; but in death, his face held the most serene expression, one as unsuited and unnatural as the light that surrounded his corpse. It seemed wrong to leave a brother's body lying like that, drenched in the cold waters. Yet it seemed far worse to disturb him.

Tom and Elon had pushed on from the fountain and finally reached the top of the Forward Way stairwell, where they found every tunnel, and chamber, and cavern that could have taken them on into the Gutters had become impassable. Flooded. For three days they had searched for a way, poking into hidden cracks and crevasses, but they found the same thing at every turn. Floodwaters. Icy, dark, omnipresent. It was as if the ocean had decided to take up a residence deep inside the Mountain where the Pipes once were.

Tom's eyes drifted to where the stones he had thrown had disappeared. If he was expecting an answer as to where these waters were coming from, the elements had nothing to say to him.

"That's a neat trick," Elon yawned behind him. "How you made those sandstones dance across the water like that."

Tom turned around. Elon was propped up on his elbow beneath his blanket. He was a light sleeper, Tom had learned, what little he slept. Tom took a few aimless steps around the ashes of their campfire. He kicked at a plank of the chair, causing a small stir of sparks, and then sank across from Elon.

Elon had regained more of his strength; he could move about on his own now, without leaning on Tom, so long as the ground was level. His arms and torso were still bandaged with strips of cloth, but the wounds on his head were no longer weeping, and so for the first time he left his face fully uncovered. What remained of his features were as seared as what was left of their firewood. Yet even disfigured, Tom still found himself struck by the beauty that seemed to cling to Elon: like a masterful piece of statuary, its surface disfigured, but its figure still intact after being pulled from the flames.

"Any change?" Elon inquired.

Tom shook his head. The waters were not rising; nor were they receding.

"That's it then," Elon declared. "The Pipes have burst."

At any other time, Tom would have been horrified at that news; like learning that a quarter of the world had just come to an end. But all it elicited now was the mumbled question:

"Will it drain?"

Elon's eyes fluttered as if he were trying to remember a story:

"My great-grandfather used to talk about what the Gutters were like before my people built the Pipes. Back when he was a young nephil boy." Elon lifted himself higher to peer over the railing. "This is just as he described it. A big lake. Flooded grottoes. Before the Pipes, our people— yours and mine—ran ferries back and forth between the Gutters and the Crag. Long flatboats, he said, like what you'd see around the Docks, but with oars instead of sails."

Tom brooded in silence.

"The water's not going anywhere," Elon said.

Only the sound of breaking waves and the faraway echo of falling water broke the stillness between them. Tom brought his knees up to his chin and stared straight ahead, seemingly fixated on a scorched piece of armrest.

"We need to decide where we go from here," Elon continued. "Oliver will send men to come look for me. Likely he already has. We have to keep moving …"

Tom hardly heard his name being repeated.

"Tom," Elon was nudging Tom's shoulder as if trying to wake him.

"Hm?"

"I'd ask what's on your mind, but I know the answer."

That brought Tom around. He craned his head slightly.

"You were thinking of your children just now," Elon smiled. "Both of them."

Inwardly Tom cringed. This had happened more than once in the days they had spent together. They might be hurrying down a tunnel, or squeezing through some crack to get into a cave, and Elon would casually speak Tom's innermost thoughts aloud, with no more compunction than if he had read a clerk's order or an items list. It unnerved Tom every time he did it.

"Yeah," Tom said.

"We'll find Lillia—once we find a way into my Realm."

"Unless she's already dead. Like my boy."

Tom got up and silently worked on gathering up their meager belongings. He would not look at Elon, and his every movement felt taut, as if his body and limbs were about to snap.

"You know she's not."

Tom froze.

An onslaught of impressions flooded his mind. Within them, the same image kept repeating itself. From far away, Lillia's shining face in the market, poised as if about to tell him something, then vanishing without a trace. Snatched away. An unrequited loss, if that were possible: one that was both keenly felt and questioned at the same time.

When he finally spoke, Tom's voice was barely a murmur: "I don't know—what I know."

Elon reached out to him:

"That's when faith is at its strongest. She promised she would come to my people with light. She said that in her dreams. She's in my Realm, Tom. I know she is. We just have to keep our faith."

Tom gritted his teeth, but he could no longer hold back what came out:

"Stop *saying* that," he hissed, and the viciousness of the anger he felt surprised him. "I've had to listen to it for days now, this-this dream faith of yours, I *hate* it. Shit and lies, that's all it is." He stooped down so that he was within inches of Elon. "I don't believe in any of your-your—"

"—madness?"

"—yeah, madness. Lillia's not a-a—whatever it is you think she is. She's a girl, you understand? That's all. A beautiful, clever girl who read lots of books and was going to become a commissar. *That* was *her* dream."

"To you, she may have been a clever girl," Elon said, maintaining his calm, "but I believe she is more than that. I know it ... You'll see. I know that, too."

Tom pulled the strands of his hair back from his forehead. The veins in his temples were throbbing:

"The only thing I see is an idiot—and you know what? She'd tell you that. If she were here, she'd say that to your face. Anyone who believes in gods is stupid. Because it's all made-up, what all the priests said, and it-it's all—hubris—that's what she'd say, and then she'd, she'd—" Tom started choking up. He found it hard to swallow and had to turn away from Elon's unrelenting stare. A sob wracked through his frame, but he regained his composure quickly:

"You don't know anything about her."

Elon narrowed his eyes.

"Do you?"

That hit Tom like a blow. His lip curled, and he would have lashed out at Elon, but Elon got to his feet, held out his hands, and spoke in a soothing, almost melodic timbre. Somehow the sound of Elon's voice quelled Tom's anger, shaped it into something more ordered, like channeling an angry fissure into a flowing fountain.

"Calm down, Tom. Calm down and listen to me for a moment. I'm not mad. I just see something in a different way than you. Look here. My dad once told me this; the only thing he ever said to me about the gods. Why we have so many of them. It always stuck with me for some reason."

He leaned down and picked up a piece of quartz lying nearby, a long shard from a broken lamp, and turned it so that the flecks buried in the stone sparkled in the light.

"You can look at a stone more than one way," Elon said. "Now you might see how sharp this is," Elon slid his fingertip carefully across a jagged point. "Which it is. But someone else might see its hardness. Me, I'm looking at the luster, what we call the stone's soul."

Holding the broken piece of lamp in the space between them, Elon fixed Tom with that curious gaze he had first greeted Tom within his prison cell, at once both intimate and domineering. All the while, the glittering stone hovered before Tom's eyes.

"This is Lillia. Understand? You see her one way, as her father. Me? I see her in another way. You know what you're looking at. So do I. I'm telling you: we're looking at the same thing. It doesn't bother me that my goddess was born in a ditch to a Cragman tanner who probably strapped her divine backside with a belt whenever she talked back—which it sounds like she did quite a bit."

That brought a trace of a smile to Tom's mouth, the first one he had had in days:

"That was her mother's job," he replied. "She did all the whippings. I never had the heart to punish Lillia."

Elon's smile was slow and hinted at what lay beneath the surface. "There you go. My point is: she can be your girl and my goddess at the same time. So stop thinking I'm mad, alright?"

Tom was still struggling with what Elon was telling him, but at least his anger was spent. Elon's words had poured water over it. Besides, it was pointless to argue further. There was nowhere else for him to turn. Whether Elon was mad or not—and Tom was still convinced he was—he had cast his lot with him; he would have to see it through. Tom let out a long, resigned sigh:

"Fine."

"Fine," Elon nodded.

"So ... a way into the Quarter."

Elon rubbed at a small remnant of his ruined chin.

"There are three," he said. "Or were. The easiest, and safest, would have been to walk through the Pipes into the Gutters." He turned as a wave lapped up through the railings, sending a small puddle of water spreading across the balcony floor. "That's gone. There's the caravan route along the Chasm's edge. Which would take us right up to the front halls of the Granite Reach."

Tom shook his head.

"If what you said about Oliver making a truce is true, that'll be swarming with porters. Wardens, too. And there's nowhere to hide on the route."

"True," Elon said. "Even if we could slip past your people, we'd be no safer once we reached the Realm—that's Reuben's thanedom, and he's not likely to throw a welcome feast for me at the Goat's Groat. So that way's shut, too. Which leaves us with only one choice."

Tom shook his head. He knew what Elon's decision would be—what their decision had to be—because it was the only choice they had left. Tom stole another glance at the flooded chamber beneath them. Elon spoke for him:

"Granda always said the ferry boats were a wonderful ride."

That was it, then. They would cross the waters.

"We'll have to try to build—" he scanned the clutter of the balcony and felt a sinking weight seize his stomach, "—something that floats. It won't be a ferry."

Elon laughed, and took Tom by the shoulders and in that still, calm voice, said to him:

"Let's just see what a guild-trained tanner and a forge-working nephil can come up with."

Nicodemus held his palm open above the calm, clear water in the marble pedestal and studied his fingers. Knobs around the knuckles protruding at odd angles, a proliferation of brown spots spreading over his silt-hewed skin, lined with purpled, varicose veins. An old man's hand, he reflected. He brushed the fingertips gently across the surface of the pool, skimming the wetness, which he flecked into the guttering flame of a candle to put it out. It hissed, the little yellow arc of light tethered to the wick fluttered a moment, but then it returned as it was before. Stubbornly clinging onto its tiny life.

He frowned at his reflection staring back at him from the pedestal's bowl. A pool that remained clear, empty, just as it had since … since he first began this practice. He let out a long breath that sent a ripple across the water. His scrying was nothing more than the shell of a habit now, a pretense. A ritual that brought him no comfort. He had stopped praying some time ago and had already learned that he didn't miss its absence.

Nicodemus sighed again, more loudly than he realized, for it brought his house servant from the kitchen. She was as waspish looking as ever, the perpetual trace of a scowl still fixed across her thin Gutterling lips. As she stomped into the canopied section of his private chamber, she gripped a heavy ladle as if it were a battle mace. She, too, heaved a sigh, but it was to signal her presence and her annoyance.

"You're gasping again," she said.

"I wasn't," Nicodemus reached over to the candle and, mindful how she could not tolerate blowing out candles (for the wax that gets wasted), he snuffed out the flame between his fingers.

"You were. Could hear you in the kitchen, even with a fire and three pots boiling."

Nicodemus wanted only to be left alone:

"Then I'm sorry for breathing."

The woman scrunched her face to study Nicodemus. She started to say something but seemed to catch her tongue right as her mouth opened. In the eleven days since her master's arrest, the old servant had finally learned to sugar her pestering.

"Is it too stuffy in here?" she asked.

"I am comfortable, thank you."

"You don't look good."

"I'm fine."

Another, shorter sigh, this one indicating she did not accept his assessment of his health. She swirled her lips thoughtfully, sucking on her teeth while she watched him, then, apparently having made up her mind, shook her head.

"No, you're not."

Unbidden, the servant sat down in the chair beside him, and to Nicodemus' utter irritation took his wrist in her hand to feel for his heart. As a priest, Nicodemus had learned to endure every kind of inanity and idiocy with the same well-worn thoughtful expression—but he simply could not muster it now.

"Now, this is uncalled for—"

"Quiet."

The servant tightened her grip and shushed him, and Nicodemus fell into an obedient silence.

"Hardly ticking anymore."

This was too much.

"If I needed a doctor, I'd—" he started.

"You don't. You need company." She let go of his wrist and the smallest trace of sadness seemed to pass her perpetually harried face. "You need people to talk with. Like you need food. What they're doing to you is cruel. Keeping you locked away in here. It's like starving someone."

Her words, spoken bluntly and in her plain, Gutterling drawl, stuck sharp in Nicodemus. All the more so because what she said was undeniably true.

"Well, thank the gods I have you to keep me fed," he replied, "in both regards."

She tilted her head and barked a single rasping laugh.

"I can keep your belly full, but I'm no good to you for conversation. Though that's more your fault than mine. No, you need crowds to sermonize to, and the high and mighty to come and whisper in your ear and ask for your advice. Nothing else is going to satisfy you."

Nicodemus shut his eyes and turned away from her. It was a redounding mark of the woman's virtue that she hadn't hesitated when the choice of remaining with him in his arrest had been given to her. She was his Divinity's servant, and if that meant she spent the rest of her days shut up inside his home with him, well—at least, the place would be tidy. But, he wondered for the dozenth time, were these apartments so small that his only companion couldn't leave him in solitude? No, she was still here with him, talking:

"And I'll tell you, it's a shame, Divinity," she continued, "'cause if you had learned how to talk with the common folk, not just preach at them, you might have—"

She was about to say, "put a stop to all this," but thankfully caught herself. For all her brusqueness and years of familiarity, there were certain boundaries that she still honored, and one had been reached here. She would never disparage his priestly service, any more than she would ever admit to a shortcoming in how she kept his house. Not that it would have mattered if she had. Nicodemus was hardly listening to her, drifting once more into the gloom of his ruminating.

"Well," she said rising from her chair, "I suppose it's not your fault what you weren't taught how to do. Here I've been so chatty, the pots are probably boiling over."

Before she could leave a room, though, she had to tidy the place. A scroll canister tucked back into a drawer, the canopy ropes straightened, a quick brush at the cushions of the chairs so the dust would fall to the ground. When she finished, she sniffed at the air.

"Too gloomy in here," she said, and with a small metal tinderbox she always carried in her apron pocket, brought the wax candle's flame back to life once more. It cast the marble pedestal in a soft orange hue. Nicodemus sat sullenly in his chair, brooding at it while his shoulders rose and fell slowly with his breathing.

No sooner had the light steadied, there was a light knock on the door of the entrance. Three short raps. In the first days of his arrest, that would have excited Nicodemus, but he recognized the familiar sound and scarcely stirred. It was one of his guards. Probably delivering their food.

"He's early to be bringing supper," she said.

"Go and see what he wants," Nicodemus waved at her.

His servant lingered a moment, as if to make sure he would stay alive in her absence, and then bustled out of the chamber. When she returned a minute later, her face was contorting through a strange vacillation that looked like something between gratefulness and disdain.

She held a letter.

Nicodemus felt his heart flutter.

It would be the first letter allowed to reach him. She no sooner told him what it was, when Nicodemus, dropping every propriety, jumped up from his chair and seized it eagerly from her outstretched hand, as greedily as a child on his birthday.

Its black and gold seal had already been broken. Still, even if his jailers had read it before him, it was news, and he ripped the paper free from its envelope as something to be devoured. He felt light and giddy for the first time in days, but as soon as his eyes reached the salutation he had to pause. His eyebrows arched high.

The letter was from Jemuel. Nicodemus read it aloud:

To Nicodemus son of Gurion
Jemuel son of Jemuel
Chamberlain Designate to
The Right Excellent Reuben,
Regent of the Inner Realm and High Thane of the Granite Reach

Nicodemus pursed his lips, but as soon as he reread the letter's opening, he felt a renewed vigor steel his voice. He began thumping the paper with his free hand:

"It hasn't even been two weeks," he said, "and already I've lost my only honorific, while Reuben's added to his. A Right Excellent Regent, eh?" He chuckled. "That's a clever dodge."

The servant woman only blinked at him.

"You see," he continued, "only a priest can consecrate a king, and Reuben does not have a priest. Not yet, at least. Ah, but a regent—no need for a priest's hands at all to call yourself a regent, or 'high thane,' for that matter, whatever that means. Though it does seem to carry a more benevolent ring to it than usurper."

"Why's it matter what he calls himself? He's taken over."

"Oh, it matters," Nicodemus wagged a finger emphatically, "the same way it matters to a rich nephil that his cloak is silk embroidered and not plain wool, or that his torque is real gold, not brass plated. We wear our titles like we wear our clothes, for others to behold. They're very dear to us, our little stations and honorifics, so we weave them with the finest sophistry. Rueben still needs to be regarded to hold his power, and he knows it." Nicodemus clicked his tongue against the roof of his mouth as he reread the opening of the letter. "At least, Jemuel's managed to keep his title intact. Good for him."

"I never liked that shifty butler," the servant screwed her face into a scowl. "He's not plumb if you ask me."

"He's a chamberlain," Nicodemus waved his hand dismissively, but as his eyes fluttered down the page, his expression quickly turned into a reflection of his servant's. "Listen to this …"

Good Sir,

On behalf of the Court of the Right Excellent Regent Reuben, we send you greetings. It gives us great joy to hear how fulfilling you have found your retirement, that the pension you have been receiving meets your every need, and that you remain in good health and high spirits. Indeed, our reports of your well-being are uniformly glowing and lend us a small measure of gladness to counter the grief we all feel at your absence. No one has earned the seclusion from public affairs that you requested more than you, good sir, and his Right Excellency will continue to honor your wish to be left alone, though he misses you more than any other in the Realm.

Nevertheless, we hope that you will suffer the small intrusion of this letter. His Right Excellency wishes to apprise you of the health and well-being of our Realm. As one who dedicated himself to its service for many years, you'll be pleased to know that all is well. Food and supplies are making their way to refill our empty cupboards. A modicum of trade, and even some discourse, has now resumed with the men in spite of the late conflicts instigated by a certain erstwhile thane. Perhaps most welcome of all, there is a resurgence of fervor for our old, tried and true traditions. This rekindled Flame of faith is a testament to the pastoral care of the Divine Phannias, who is carrying on the True Words that you so eloquently proclaimed during your priestly service. May our father Nord continue to bless us in the true faith.

Throughout this time of change, his Right Excellency's thoughts and prayers have remained with you; as, he trusts, yours have remained with him. He hopes you find this news pleasing. We will not deign to intrude any further into your justly deserved retirement by asking for the favor of a reply, certain that the knowledge of the Realm's renewed prosperity can only add to the satisfaction and comfort you already hold.

Wishing your continued health, prosperity, and blessings, I remain

Your humble servant,
Jemuel

"Very, very strange," Nicodemus said aloud.

No doubt if she had been asked, his servant would have growled that she couldn't understand one in four of the words Nicodemus had just read. Likely, she would have complained about the "airs" of learned men, and why couldn't they just write the way folk talked. But he was primed for conversation, and, knowing her duty, the servant sighed, played her part, and begrudgingly asked him what was strange about it.

"Well, as a powdery showpiece of propaganda," Nicodemus replied, "it's serviceable enough. Apparently, it was my wish all along to be placed under arrest in my own home. Retirement, indeed! No doubt copies of this self-serving drivel have already been delivered to the other thanes and their courtiers. But why send it on to me? I'm under lock and guard. I couldn't speak out against Reuben, even if I wanted to."

"You're the priest," she answered, her voice quite matter-of-fact.

"No, Phannias's the priest now. I ceased to be a cleric six and a half years ago thanks to a very warped interpretation of the Cohanim Canon. They don't even extend the common courtesy of calling me "Divinity" anymore, see? Because I'm nothing now. And there is absolutely nothing I can do to Reuben ... So why would Jemuel bother writing out another copy of this letter to send to me?"

They both looked at the folded parchment in the candlelight. The silence of the statues and idols in Nicodemus' chamber enveloped them until the servant blurted out something most unexpected:

"You'd think he could have written it from somewhere other than a tavern."

"What?"

She pointed accusingly toward the paper with her ladle. "The paper wreaks of wine. Where he's managed to find a bottle is a wonder, but he spilled his drink all over the page. Can't you smell it? It's cheap stuff."

Nicodemus brought the paper up to just beneath his nostrils and inhaled deeply. Sure enough, there was a faint, vinegary smell clinging to the parchment. He regarded the folds before him thoughtfully and then, with a burst of surprise, his eyes flew wide open:

"By the gods, what a wonderfully cunning fellow!"

"Eh?"

Nicodemus fumbled for the candle, and to his servant's horror held the paper no more than an inch above the top of its flame. The page quivered in his grip and started to brown along the edges.

"What the damn—" she could not help but swear, "y-you'll make a *mess!*"

A broad, beaming smile was creasing across Nicodemus' face as he swept the smoldering letter before his servant.

"Look here ..."

Along one of the margins, a series of beige, shadowy letters, hastily written, but obviously from the same hand that had fashioned the more formal, flowing ink script in the letter's body, had now appeared. Though she could not read the scratch of beige words, the servant knew they had not been there before.

"M-magic l-letters," she hastily made a sign of the gods.

"No, no, no, my dear. Just an old trick of us learned men. Something we learn as students so we can write nasty messages about our teachers without getting caught. Ha! Ha!" He let out a long, mirthful laugh and then clapped his servant fondly on the elbow. "Which you discovered thanks to that penetrating nose of yours. I should have puzzled it out eventually. '*Flame* of faith,' 'carrying on the *True Words* …' Awfully purple prose for a shifty old butler, don't you think? Hah! He even capitalized the clues for me. I must be getting slow."

"What does it say?"

He turned the letter sideways to read it, and the bright glow that had subsumed Nicodemus at once dimmed. His jaw drew tight, and he let out a long breath as he gently laid the letter aside on the table. The paper stayed open along one of its folds and with the candle flame casting its glow behind it, the word "blood" blazed with a peculiar intensity.

"It's a private message from Jemuel," he said flatly, "he's telling me what's happening in the Realm." Without looking again at the letter, he repeated the words Jemuel had hidden for him:

> *The Pipes have burst.*
> *The Gutters run with blood.*
> *The nephil are at each other's throats.*
> *We need a priest.*
> *Save us.*

CHAPTER THIRTY-NINE

"I'M PRAYING FOR you," Rachel whispered.

She watched the old nephil woman strangle on her breath and hold it for what felt like an eternity. The woman's face had changed rapidly from a flushed golden hue to white, and now, at last, into mortar colored gray. A stone to match the tiles beneath her, her eyes, two lusterless gems gazing at nothing from within their setting. A long gash, caked in dried blood, had bit into the woman's forehead.

She let out a great groan of air, impossibly long it seemed because it was her last breath. A cloud of fog hovered above her parted lips, then slowly dissipated in the cold air.

Her name had been Esther.

"Is that it?"

The guard had been watching from the doorway. Rachel turned to glare at him. He was middle-aged, with a hard angular face colored like sandstone, and broad, strong shoulders covered in a fur cape. His hands were clapped inside of a black and gold tunic to keep warm. Since the day of Phannias' Farce (as Rachel's people now called it) and the slaughter that ensued on the Copperbottom's porch, the guard had been posted here. The only guard that could be spared, for fights were breaking out at every turn in the Gutters, it seemed. He ate only what he needed, kept out of her way, and sometimes even tried to help. She hated him all the same.

Rachel gave a curt nod, too angry and exhausted to say any more, and drew her cloak tighter around her shoulders to fight the chill.

"She was the last one, huh?"

She nodded again. Rachel had had eighteen wounded nephil spread throughout the Copperbottom on makeshift beds and in the booths. Stabbed, trampled, and in shock that their own people had turned so mercilessly upon them. In the days of fighting that followed, Rachel's tavern had become a hospital—and then a place of mourning. The sect's believers had ministered to the wounded with bandages, medicines, and prayers. With Esther's passing, all but two had died.

"You, uh," the guard hesitated, "you want me to fetch the priest to say some words?"

Her voice rose within her throat. "Do you want another riot?"

"Nah," he shook his head. "Guess you're right. I'll, uh—I'll just go and stoke up the fire some." He shook his head and left for the tavern's main room.

Rachel was beyond shedding tears. She had never known Esther very well, only that the woman had been orphaned at a young age and had a talent for organizing lavish wedding banquets. Her passing would be celebrated, in secret, like all the other martyrs of the faith. Perhaps tonight they would light candles in some hidden basement and whisper their hymns for the Maiden to receive another one of her own.

Another saint. Another dwindling of the remnant.

It would fall to Rachel to bring the news of Esther's death to the sect tonight.

She glanced around the back room for a cloth to cover the body, and her gaze fell on the beer barrel beneath the drop cloth. She tucked at the dust-covered blanket and when it came down, a wave of spice and herb smells at once rolled through the air. It brought a sad smile to her. Without realizing it, Rachel's fingers traced along the barrel's lid and then, just as absently, came down to her stomach. Her chin dropped and she looked down at her hands, which were gently cradling the shirt and apron around her belly.

Strange, she thought, that despite the short rations they had been under, her middle was stretching her apron strings to their ends.

"Getting old," she muttered.

And then Rachel felt a fluttering within her stomach.

Not sickness this time—it was as if something had stirred. Like a little moth, flittering about a lamp light before settling onto a wall. Rachel clutched her stomach closely. Her heart was racing, and a warm rush came over her cheeks. Tenderly, Rachel's fingers massaged around her stomach, probing after the sensation again. But whatever it was, it had hidden itself, tucked deep down inside.

Or she had only imagined it.

A flush of anger, and then, for some reason, Rachel's eyes began brimming with tears. She grit her teeth in frustration.

"It was nothing."

Rachel brushed an arm across her eyes and hurried through the back door of the Copperbottom. She had no desire to entertain the few customers that still came. There was a prayer meeting tonight, and she desperately wanted to pray. She set out at once.

The corridors were empty; they always seemed to be these days. A nephil with a shovel wandering, not knowing what he should be working on, a woman carrying an armful of baskets, and, at one junction, a knot of Reuben's warriors. Whether by order or by instinct, the guards were always clumped together in groups whenever they were outside, loitering beneath one of the hands of Nord that festooned the Gutters' common areas, as if for protection.

Rachel kept to herself. She took a circuitous route past a series of vacant rooms, warrens, and winding arcades that, though familiar, all held a haunted feel about them. With every step, she could hear the constant, soft whisper of the waterfalls that had conquered the Pipes, a sound broken only by the lonely tread of her tiny footfalls in the empty space. Everywhere, a bitter, biting cold hung in the air. Ushered in with the floodwaters she had overheard an engineer in the tavern explain it one evening with a limerick:

> "*Water and air,*
> *hot, cold, or fair.*
> *The two are like brothers:*
> *what one is, so's the other.*"

The floodwaters were rumored to have icecaps floating in them. Rachel wondered if she would live to see snow in the Mountain. Like in the legends.

She walked through the afternoon until she came at last to a small, circular stairwell of winding steps that led her to a passageway that ended in a cavern. The walls were smooth and unadorned except for a cluster of humble doorways. A slurry of ice and mud had been shoveled up against either side of the cavern's walls, and most of the doors had a path cleared for them. Rachel made for the only one that didn't, a simple, planked square in a darkened corner.

As if someone had been watching for her, the door swung quietly inward just as Rachel walked up the front step. A furtive whispered exchange, and Rachel was ushered quickly inside.

It was a long, windowless room. A small cooking fire burned in a hearth, which, along with the press of the small crowd of people kept the inside of the house relatively warm. When the door closed, everyone inside spoke more freely. Hannah, who had first greeted Rachel in the doorway, showed Rachel to a cushioned chair next to the fire, which looked like it had been specially set aside since several of the believers had to stand. Rachel was too tired, and her feet ached too much, to object to the indulgence.

There were about twenty nephil in number, men and women, and they greeted Rachel warmly, relishing the chance to express their faith aloud, if not openly:

"May the light of our Lady reflect within you."

"Until she shines upon us all," Rachel smiled.

"The prayers of Merari, Gershon, and Kohath are with us, Miss Rachel."

"Blessed be the Prophets."

Rachel made her talk with them as light as she could under the circumstances. Young Hannah, Abram, Korah (the poor old fellow could hardly hear a word anymore), Matred, Esau (grooming that long mane of red hair of his, as always), Laban—good common, simple folk. Thankfully, they were in fair health and spirits. When the pleasantries were finished, Rachel shared the news of Esther's passing as gently as she could. There were tears, some weeping, but the mourning was subdued, for truthfully, most were relieved that the Maiden had decided to call Esther to the light. Of all those who fell from Phannias's sermon, Esther had lingered in her suffering the longest. Much too long was the consensus.

Throughout their prayers and conversation, Rachel noticed Hannah glancing from face to face, particularly Esau's. The girl had never been able to mask her feelings, but Rachel could almost hear within the anxious looks, some silent message being passed among her friends.

More bad news most likely. Someone else had died or disappeared. She decided she might as well hear it out now.

"I can tell," Rachel said, "there's some news I haven't heard."

Hannah and the others slowly trained on Esau who, with a curt nod, stood up. At full height, he was a giant in the Inner Realm, almost as tall as a Crag man, with flaming red hair and eyes as dark as onyx, and a voice that always seemed to convey a veiled threat of force at any moment:

"Yesterday I was *approached*," he said the last word in a way that was meant to convey some dark or hidden meaning.

"I'm sorry," Rachel replied. "We're all being watched. And you worked in Elon's forge. Just stay clear of the guards, and we'll all—"

"What? No, I wasn't talking about them," he screwed his face as if he would spit on the floor and raised his voice to near bellowing: "Reuben's little pricks don't have enough balls between them to come up to me. Hell, they won't so much as push a fart in my direction. Too scared I'd smell it."

Some of the women blushed, but not Rachel. Esau's friends enjoyed a hearty chuckle.

"No," he continued, "I got approached by my old boss. Tubalcain. Damned good blacksmith. Plumb and level as a line. He's from the Old Mines, Simeon's man."

A visitor from another thanedom was unheard of in the Gutters these days. Indeed, Rachel could not remember the last time she had come across anyone other than a Gutterling or a warrior from the Granite Reach.

"What did he want?" Rachel asked.

A fearsome light reflected in Esau's black eyes, and his bottom lip jutted out in defiance.

"To show me something."

Esau scanned the entirety of the room as if someone might have stolen inside the hovel, and then he pulled his coat aside to reveal a satchel. He reached inside, jumbling around what wounded like metal and stones, and brought forth what he had been given. Rachel found herself leaning forward in her chair.

In his broad, callused hands, Esau held up two objects. The first one immediately seized Rachel's attention and sent a slight shiver down her spine.

It was a dagger. Even to Rachel's untrained eyes, its purpose was plain: it was made for war. Esau's eyes narrowed, a wolfish smile spreading across his face.

"Simeon's taken Elon's forge weapons. Snuck in and stole them right out from under Reuben's nose as soon as he heard what Reuben was doing down here. Now he's got a whole cellar full of armor and arms."

The color drained from Rachel's face as the implication dawned on her.

"He means to fight Reuben," she concluded.

"That he does," Esau nodded, unable to conceal his delight. Rachel noticed that most in the room seemed to be sharing his expression. "Simeon may not know our Lady," Esau said, "but he knows a coup when he sees one. He's had a lot to say lately: 'At least Elon took his warring to the men,' that's what Simeon's been saying, 'but Reuben— he does his killing in our homes.' Shunting Nicodemus off in favor of that little pisser, Phannias, was the last straw. Tubalcain says Simeon's not having it. He won't kneel to Reuben, and he'll never ask for Phannias's prayers. He ain't the only one of this mind either."

Esau flexed his massive forearms and drew closer to Rachel. "Tubalcain says *lots* of folks are whispering—they say Reuben's brought down a new curse. They say the Pipes have busted because of what he's done; that he betrayed the king. The gods are punishing us because of him. And so now something's got to be done about it. That's the general feeling." He started to draw the dagger from its sheath, and a silver flash reflected from its blade onto Rachel's lined face. He brought the blade home with a loud clink. "There's going to be a fight, Miss Rachel. Whether we like it or not, we need to get ready."

Rachel felt her head becoming heavy, the weight of this news pressing down on her. Her answer, when it came, was soft. "I don't like it at all." Rachel lifted her face just as a tear escaped down the length of her cheek. It clung to her chin like a jewel, quivering while she spoke. "I've just come from laying a shroud on Esther. The only fight she ever had was over table decorations and fork placements. But she's the one that got her skull run through. I don't want to see any more killing. I can't. Tell Simeon to leave us alone. Tell him … we have enough martyrs."

"They've got weapons now, Rachel. And they don't mean to become martyrs with them, if you know what I mean."

Rachel's eyes heaved in her head.

"Oh, of course they don't. Because that's all war is to you men—it's banners, and marches, and pipes and drums, and flags, and, and—" she pointed at the dagger Esau was holding, her voice dripping with sarcasm, "swords to wave around like it's your prick for everyone to ogle." Esau stifled a laugh, but Rachel's anger was burning now. "You'll leave it to someone else to clean up all the blood and bury the corpses when your war's done because no one ever *meant* to die. Fools. Simeon. Reuben. Elon, too. You're all fools. You have to have a war just because you're armed."

"We do when we're the ones being slaughtered."

Rachel started to open her mouth but found herself stuck. A grain of truth, or a kind of truth, cut through Esau's words. Rachel recognized it; so did her brothers and sisters in the sect, apparently. They were all nodding with Esau. Only Rachel, though, sensed that this particular truth was shadowed by a greater lie. She could feel the duality like a trap. Once sprung, it would hold you, forever.

A priest would have known how to explain it.

The others were waiting for her guidance—they could still be persuaded to turn from whatever course Esau would drive them down, she was certain of it—but the words would not come to her. So instead she floundered and replied with the worst question she could have asked:

"So what if Simeon was able to steal some weapons out of Elon's forge? Reuben will just make more. He has the forge. Remember? Or have you even thought about that?"

That brought a grim smile to Esau's face. From within his eyes, Rachel swore she could see the bellow fires of the forge, stoking up to a white heat. Whatever chance she had was lost; the sect was with him. Throughout the room, she could hear the gathering's whispers turning into grim murmurs of Elon's battle cry: "We come."

In response to her question, Esau held out his other hand to show her what else he had brought with him. It was a small, perfectly clear crystalline sphere connected to a metallic post. Almost like a doorknob, but one made of diamond.

"It's a valve cap," Esau explained as he turned the wondrous device over to catch the light. "What holds the forge's magma channels in balance. I've got a satchel full of them. All the caps that Blessed Merari found."

Esau leaned forward and told Rachel in a determined voice:

"We've taken care of the forge."

The bottom of Jemuel's coattails brushed against the stone floor as he hurried around a bend of a corridor. The hems were already graying from the grime and dust, which bothered Jemuel, but he had no time to fret for his attire. He was moving at a good pace despite an awkward gait and a constant creak in his knees. When he came to a small run of stairs, he descended them two at a time.

A muffled echo of a voice calling down curses could still be heard. Elon's throne room was at least a half-mile behind him now, but Reuben's bellowing still shook the walls. It was as if the thane had tapped a vein in the Mountain to carry his wrath. Jemuel shuddered. A second voice, much closer and far milder, called out to Jemuel from the top of the stairs:

"A moment, Master Chamberlain. Just a moment, please."

It was Phannias. The Divine Phannias, Jemuel quickly reminded himself. For some reason, Jemeul found it difficult to remember the young thane's new station in the Realm.

Though younger than Jemuel and longer limbed, Phannias was finding it a challenge to keep up with Jemuel. Perhaps, Jemuel thought, it was his newly made Divinity's decision to wear the full raiment of the priestly robes he had acquired from his predecessor. Marvelously woven clothing, to be sure, golden and bejeweled, but they looked cumbersome. Likely why his Divinity Nicodemus only wore the garb for high ceremonies.

Jemuel came to a stop at the bottom of the stairs and waited:

"My apologies, Excellency."

"Divinity."

Jemuel blinked a fraction of a second longer than he should have, but then dipped his head.

"Your Divinity. Yes. I am still becoming accustomed to your new salutation. Pray forgive my habit, and my haste."

"Of course," Phannias made a sign of blessing as he descended the steps. "We all have had adjustments to make." At the bottom of the stairwell, Phannias leaned against the corridor wall to catch his breath and looked back over his shoulder. A repeated volley of "thieving, god-damned lunatics!" rolled over him. Phannias cringed at the noise. "The Regent," he said, lowering his voice, "will appreciate our haste. He's quite, uhm—"

Unhinged? That would have been Jemuel's assessment. He had been privileged to serve two kings, Elon and his father, Zebulon, and had navigated through their many moods and tempers, and with respect to the late King Elon, the zealotry of a cockeyed faith. But Reuben's wrath was something of another magnitude. Where Zebulon and Elon were storms—slow in gathering and easy to spot from a distance—Reuben was a volcano. Sudden, explosive, a cataclysm to everyone around, including himself. Jemuel had just come from Elon's throne room, which Reuben was using to hold his court, and only felt it safe to exit because Reuben was engrossed in biting the cloth of a tapestry. He looked like a wild dog bent on tearing it to pieces. It had been one of Jemuel's favorite hangings. The Regent had lost his mind, but Jemuel knew better than to share such a thought with Phannias.

"He is concerned," Jemuel offered.

"Yes," Phannias agreed, "that's exactly it. He's terribly concerned."

"Understandably so. Given what's transpired."

"Yes indeed."

"All the more reason for us to hurry to our task. If you're ready, Divinity?"

Phannias tried to smile, but it was obvious the nephil was even more ill-suited for prolonged exertion than Jemuel, who, though by no means a stout walker, could at least manage the outer halls of his Majesty's chambers without falling into a swoon. The bookish looking priest was sweating profusely, and the slate tone in his cheeks was appled from the strain. But he nodded at the chamberlain that he was ready.

"It's only a bit farther," Jemuel tried to sound reassuring.

They walked in silence through a long stretch of the Gutters that was, thankfully, empty of nephil. They came to a connecting passage where Jemuel had to halt once more so that the thane (… the priest, Jemuel chided himself) could catch his breath again. A few feet farther, and a waft came belching out from an archway, rippling the air with heat and carrying a sickening stench of sulfur. A faint orange glow pulsated from within its depths. Jemuel tried to crane his neck to peer into the passage, but the air scorched his face and he had to draw back. Phannias was pointing dumbly at the doorway.

"Is-is that it?"

"Yes," Jemuel replied quietly. "His Majesty's—I should say, Elon's— forge is down that way. Or rather, it was." Jemuel's head dropped, while Phannias shook his in wonder.

"It is—gone then," Phannias declared. "All that work, that craft."

"It is … a shame."

An inadequate assessment, Jemuel thought, but what else could be said? Though personally, he had never cared much for the forge floor, or the vulgar brutes who had worked it, like all of nephil of the Inner Realm, he held a deeply ingrained respect for what a forge represented. No other place captured art and elements and so closely bound them together. Elon's forge, the first to be rebuilt since the Overthrow, had been a triumph for all.

"And the magma," Phannias waved his hand as if to cool the hotness that brushed along the wind, "it flooded everything?"

The answer seemed self-evident:

"So I have been told. Apparently, its spread will seal off this corridor before the day's out."

Phannias shook his head again. "A terrible accident."

"I have it from a knowledgeable source that it was nothing of the sort. It was sabotage. Someone—spiked, I believe is the word he used—the forge's channels. Some sort of contraptions that ought to have remained in place were surreptitiously removed. His Right Excellency understands the mechanics better than I, which is why, I suspect, he is so incensed by this event."

And frightened, Jemuel could have added. He needed that forge to help keep his grip on the Gutters. Reuben was isolated here in Elon's throne room, his soldiers were few, and they were poorly armed. Fights between guards and Gutterlings were breaking out daily. Reuben had good reason to be scared. Which was why he had commanded his priest and chamberlain to deliver his orders to his soldiers, rather than come himself. He needed his forces to regroup at once so that he could consolidate what strength he still had.

Another blast of hot air escaped from the passage.

"We had better cross quickly," Jemuel said, "before it becomes impassable."

Jemuel took three bounding leaps, suffering no more than a slight singe on his cheek. It took a few halting attempts, but Phannias followed him, crossing the space of the entrance and whimpering with every step. When he made it to the safety of the other side, he patted down his clerical vestments as if they might have caught fire, clucking worriedly to himself as he did so.

Once the priest had composed himself, he thought it worthwhile to share something that occurred to him.

"Tally-ho! Traverse the transoms of hell," he rolled each of the r's as if he were delivering a recital, "sally bold Hero, heed not the toll'd bell."

Jemuel was almost dumbstruck:

"I-I beg your pardon?"

Phannias was smiling as he explained:

"The final couplet to a sonnet I once wrote. *Fidessa* was the name of it. It struck me as apropos."

"Ah."

"Lead on, good Chamberlain. Our brave soldiers await us."

Jemuel suppressed the urge to roll his eyes as he set out, following the wending tunnel until it sloped sharply down and then opened into a grand, arched hallway. It was a meeting square that held a scattering of booths, platforms, and stages, all filled with wares—and Gutterlings. Scores of people, shabbily dressed, mingling out in the open. Sullen, resentful faces, all turning as one to see who had joined them.

Phannias blanched. He hissed at Jemuel:

"Wha-what are they doing outside? I-I thought there was a curfew."

"There is," Jemuel answered from the corner of his mouth. He noticed one group erecting a flagstaff. Strung to it was a banner of pure white silk. Some of the men standing around it noticed Phannias in his robes and stared back at him.

"Look there, Jemuel," Phannias pointed, "they're displaying the symbol of that false goddess. Openly!"

"Yes—" Jemuel began. He recognized several in the crowd from Elon's court. These were not simply Elon's wide-eyed sect friends fomenting some kind of a protest. Those were warriors, stolid Nord worshipers, down there. And some were with them that Jemuel had never seen before, dressed as if they were from …

The realization struck Jemuel like a block of ice and his whisper was no less insistent: "We need to go."

"Nonsense, the guards must—"

"*Now!*"

Jemuel tried to grasp Phannias by the arm, but the idiot was wandering haplessly into the crowd, making signs of blessing every few feet, and calling out for Reuben's guards who, he must have thought, would be close at hand for his protection. The fool truly believed Reuben's promise that he would be in no danger out here. He had learned nothing from his welcome at the Copperbottom.

"My-my children," Phannias stammered. "You should not be out without the Regent's protection. Guards, ho!"

The nephil slid down from the stages, and out from behind tables, and, without a word amongst them, enveloped the priest. Slowly, the harlequin draped in gold and jewels found himself swallowed within a mass of undulating gray. Phannias kept calling for guards, even as the silent throng tightened around him. Jemuel took a cautious, backward step, trying his best not to appear as if he was about to flee.

"Phannias," Jemuel heard the pleading in his voice.

Something struck Jemuel hard in the middle of his back. His ears rang loud, and he fell with a thud to the ground, the breath knocked out of him. The room lurched. He heard a familiar voice:

"Wait, wait. Not the chamberlain."

"Why not the chamberlain?" a second voice directly above him challenged. The nephil who had asked sounded very intent on killing him. "He ain't in your sect, is he?"

"Nah, but—" the first voice paused and made a musing noise. Now Jemuel recognized who it was. One of Elon's forge workers. The tall, surly red-headed fellow.

"He was Elon's man," Esau continued. "Elon wouldn't want him hurt. We can always get him later if we need to."

An irritated growl, and then a foot prodded Jemuel hard in the ribs.

"Off you go, chamberlain."

He felt a face pressing close to his ear and a hot, ale-soaked breath pierced through the fog of Jemuel's senses. Like the waft of magma:

"Go tell that traitor he's not our king. The gods—goddesses—whatever, they're not having him. An' neither are we."

Hands grasped Jemuel's arms and torso. He felt himself hoisted to his feet, and a stabbing pain raced down his chest. He winced and struggled for air, but as he was forced out of the room, he was able to turn his head just enough to see the surplice of Phannias's robes being pulled free and passed over the heads in the crowd. A great roar went up. The gleam of metal blades bristled everywhere, burning hungrily in the light. Long, beautiful sword blades.

"Phannias," Jemuel coughed.

There was a joyless chuckle.

"Keep his Divinity in your prayers, Jemuel—whoever you pray to."

Nicodemus bowed his head and shut his eyes. He let his breathing slow, felt his heart becalming in his chest. His slippered feet were planted firmly on either side of his chair legs. Back straight, face up, in open expectation. The tiny noises of his empty chamber emerged: a whisper of air from a crack high up in the ceiling; the ripple of his candle's flame; his stomach growling; outside, one of the guards pacing in front of his door (they had grown more and more agitated lately, it seemed), his servant snoring from inside the alcove she used as her bedroom; his stomach rumbling again.

The cacophony within the quiet.

Another favorite saying of his old master. Nicodemus, a restless, easily risible novice, had always struggled with the meditative part of priestly life, like most of the young, restless nephil in the temples. His mentor had laid a kindly hand on his shoulder and explained that one's thoughts, one's senses, will always find something to fill the silent void we strive for to commune with the gods. He said it as a profound truth and a challenge to overcome his mind; but to Nicodemus, it only confirmed what he had always suspected: there is no such thing as quiet. Not in the Mountain.

He tried to return his mind to the clear surface of the great mirror that stood before him. The scrollwork frame held a silver plane that covered most of a wall, and if he let his eyes unfocus, it almost looked like a doorway, into the divine. He stood awash in its unblemished reflection. The union of depth and plane. It should have been a sacred space.

He clenched his hand in frustration. A strand of pearl beads, separated by alternating platinum emblems of outstretched hands and goat heads, rattled in his fingers. His thumb and forefinger were still pressed hard against the first one.

The priest could not pray.

No matter how he tried.

"Because I am," he looked at his reflection in the mirror, "alone."

An old man in rumpled house robes blinked within the great silver framed mirror. He had nothing to say to Nicodemus.

Nicodemus sunk back in a chair and let his arm dangle from the side rest. His hand brushed against another letter he had received that morning. It held another hidden message from Jemuel—more detailed, and dire than the first. The chamberlain had sent it under the pretext that the newly ordained Divine Phannias required any remaining priestly vestments in Nicodemus's possession to be surrendered immediately so that his Divinity could discharge his duties (a comical request since the only "vestment" Nicodemus owned were the ceremonial robes that the guards had already pried from his servant at spear point). The secret lettering, once again written in diluted wine and revealed by Nicodemus' candle flame, had been interwoven between the chamberlain's scripted lines.

The news was bleak.

Fighting was spreading throughout the Gutters, and into the other thanedoms. Reuben still had his soldiers, and the only food coming into the Realm was under his control, but his enemies were multiplying by the hour. And coalescing.

Nicodemus let the parchment fall to the ground.

A fine job I've done holding the Realm together.

His eyelids fluttered. From between the slits he caught another glimpse of his mirror.

Such an ostentatious thing, he thought angrily, as big as an idol. Something about the temple relic grated on him. It was too big, he decided, too greedy for attention. Rather than spreading light, the mirror seemed to swallow it.

"I'm just tired," Nicodemus sighed, as fatigue took hold of him again. His head felt as heavy as a stone.

It had become a companion of his lately, this feeling of sudden inexplicable exhaustion, and he seldom fought it any more. He pinched the bridge of his nose, nestled his head back into his seat cushion, and let his eyes shut all the way.

Without trying, quiet finally came to the priest, the only quiet he had ever known, in sleep.

CHAPTER FORTY

S HE AWOKE.

Though she had never fallen asleep, not truly. Amidst the fall, the bite of the air tearing at her skin, the darkness that had swallowed her very thoughts, the empty blank page that had become her memory. But she was certain she had been awake all along, throughout, before and now.

Now was different, though.

She was sensing things she hadn't before. A tingling awareness was emerging. Waking was the only experience she could liken it to.

Lillia blinked at her surroundings.

It was a strange place she found herself, utterly silent, cloaked in a heavy cold. And dark. Except for a curious penumbra that extended three feet around her. She turned and craned to try to find the source of the marble light. There were no gulleystar pots or lanterns, no torches anywhere. Nothing that would cast any light, and yet, light was here. A flickering illumination, no brighter than a candle's. Lillia slowly turned a full circle and watched the soft light raining down, falling over the rugged surface of stone covered in sediment and a level, dusty floor. The ceiling was held high overhead by wooden beams.

She looked down at her hands. She was holding a pouch. Fragments of memory seemed to hover about it. It was worn at the seams, its draw-string frayed, but still sturdy. A well-stitched little bag. In the light, she could make out the tiny swirled oval of a guildmark in the thread pattern. There were coins inside, she knew without looking.

A memory. Her father's muddied face smeared in dirt and blood, his pale eyes burning as bright as stars; he had pressed the pouch so hard into her palm it had hurt. His lips had moved, but she couldn't hear what he had said. Her brother, Tim, and his woman—Enid, was her name, Lillia thought—they were all running from something. There was a crowd of people, a great surge ...

A fire. Fear. Then darkness. The last of the memories sputtered and receded. She was left with a blank page once more.

Lillia drew a deep breath. The frigid air stung in her chest, so she pulled the rags of clothes closer around her shoulders, fixed her sash, and wiped her eyes. At that moment, she felt an urge, a compulsion, to curl up on the ground and cry, to sob until she had no more breath in her until she was as broken as the stones beneath her toes. Moisture lapped at her eyelashes. She blinked it away angrily. Her mind was roaring its disapproval.

"I am in a tunnel," she declared. She repeated it, more firmly, and felt pleased to hear her voice against the side of a wall. There was a solidity in it, and that was soothing.

"If I am in a tunnel, then I am on a point of a line, or maybe a curve," she continued. Recollections of her earliest classes began falling into place in rapid succession, like bricks and mortar. "Which I could only have arrived at by way of another line or curve. An intersection of points."

This was working. Her breathing slowed.

"All lines and curves terminate at endpoints. For each such segment, there can be only two conclusions ... There must be an ending."

She adjusted her sash again and, having decided that either direction was just as likely to bring her to where she had come from, walked methodically down the tunnel, a slow, steady trod across a sandy ground that sloped imperceptibly down. As she walked, she recited a series of postulates she had memorized in her first year at the academy in a monotone murmur. It became a kind of tantric cadence.

"... and if from equal things, equal things should be taken away, the remaining things are equal. And things fitted to one another are equal to one another. And the whole is greater than the part ..."

Something lying in the dust nearby glinted and caught her attention.

In the glow that accompanied her, a bit of metal gleamed. Lillia paused. Cautiously, she crept towards the thing and stooped down to take a closer look.

Strange how the light seemed to become more intense whenever she neared anything solid. The surface of the wall, the floor, they were almost glowing as she drew close to them. The metal object she had seen was half buried, but she could make it out as plainly as if it were lying outside in the sun.

It was a tiny fastener. She poked at it a few times, wondering what it could have been, then pulled, and up it came, a slender belt of leather attached to a proportionately sized glove. The glove was exquisitely made with clips, a belt strap, a decorative strand of pearls, and a fastener around its base. It had special padding, like vellum but stronger, sewn tight over the palms. Not even her father's tannery could have made anything near its equal.

Why, then, did it look like it had been made for a child's hands—for no one else could have fit into it—and what was it doing here, lying on the ground in an empty tunnel? Lillia started to open the glove. The light pierced into the darkness of its recesses.

She let out a terrified gasp. The glove fell back to the floor with a thud. Her heart was racing. The tears she had held back flowed freely down her cheeks.

Inside of it was a cold, dry severed hand.

A sound, like a voice, seemed to stir within the glove. But before it could form a word, Lillia was fleeing down the tunnel, the tears now brimming in her eyes and trailing down her cheeks, the light following her every step, farther and farther down a tunnel that seemed to defy her learning, for it surely had no end or beginning.

Lillia fell to her hands and knees panting. Her hair hung in loose strands, effervescent in the strange light that still followed her so faithfully. The tears had finally stopped flowing in the panic of her run and the medley of scenes that had raced by her: the walls of the tunnel drawing closer, the rugged ground rising, then falling, the frosted ice on the stones, the sense of hope when she came across a great collection of metal-flecked stalactites that she knew she had seen somewhere before. And the bitter disappointment when she realized they were nothing more than a figment of familiarity; that she was still hopelessly lost. She was freezing, and thirsty, and her sight was closing in around the periphery; she was losing consciousness.

Lillia's legs buckled underneath her, and she collapsed in the dirt. Lillia looked at her hands. Caked in dirt, but still holding the pouch, her father's pouch. For some reason, it reminded her of the hand in the child's glove. The terror she had felt before surged anew inside of her.

But this time when she lifted her head again, she drew no comfort. Instead, she sensed a presence.

The aura of white light remained about her, but just beyond it, the darkness was stirring. The walls, she could now see, were made of polished onyx—and they were moving. Along with the air. A surge of motion, like a current, closing in around her—from above, from below, from the glistening blackness of the walls.

She knew what it was even before she heard the first of the voices. It was what she had been running from since that day at the Docks, what she had dreamed of, what had tormented her all these days from afar was here in the tunnel with her. Coming to engulf her.

When the sound finally came, she could hear the words plainly for the first time, and the voice was deep, and booming, and beguilingly familiar.

"*We are*—"

"—in the Mountain," she pinched her eyes shut tightly. "I know."

Her thin body was trembling. Against her will, Lillia's eyelids creaked back open. Faint flickers of amber, orange, yellow, and white—all the colors of flame—glimmered from within the depth of the swirling shadows above her. No, not flickering. They were blinking. Thousands and thousands of eyes, glaring at her in hunger. The shadows from all her dreams gathered together. Now they were descending, moving closer, and the first of their shapes came into focus.

Lillia's heart stopped. She felt her breath freeze within her neck. It was the first time she had seen her shadows clearly, and she was at once petrified and overcome with loathing.

Dragons. And snakes. Spiders. Demons. Krakens and pikes. Calling out to one another and to her. A mass of flying shades that seemed to change, one into the other and then back again, if she tried to stare at any one of them for too long. Like flipping the pages of a picture book, one that was filled with nightmares.

How?

They roamed in an orbit around her, heedless of the walls or the floor, vanishing through the solid lines and planes of the rocks only to reappear somewhere else, or in two places at once, as if unbounded from any order. Their strange noise grew steadily louder, into a roar, until at last, one broke off. It fell softly to the ground in front of Lillia, like a dark stalactite stretching to free itself of its anchor to reach the ground where it rose and floated in the air over her, a thin strand of silver fluttering behind its form. Lillia watched as its shape came into being above her. A spindly leg covered in bristling black hair, like an insect's but as long as a tree limb, it hovered lazily overhead and then reached out towards Lillia.

It seemed to be a toying gesture, a playful grasp but malevolent: a predator's curiosity. Another, then two more, followed. The fangs and orbed eyes of an animal, something like a spider, emerged. Its face stayed shrouded in darkness that not even the light around her could penetrate, but she sensed its expression all too clearly.

Lillia could hear its thoughts, mingling with her own, how it wanted to bite her, to eat her skin and pull out her bones, to take her life—no, to keep taking her life again, and again, and again …

The thing ventured within the aura of Lillia's light and waited there, watching her, its legs twitching greedily. Then the legs slowly closed around her skull in a horrible embrace.

She tried to scream; her words choked:

"Don't-don't … don't," was all she could manage.

The creature's face, somehow still hidden by shadows, came to within an inch of the side of her head. A scentless, hot breath struck her cheek, as two curved, scarlet-colored fangs caressed the nape of her neck.

Lillia's thoughts were a torrent.

Run!

But her legs and arms would not move. Her head darted around, scraping her face against the gravel, searching for an escape. She was trapped. Invisibly chained, pinned to the ground. The fangs lolled about her skin.

"Hate you," her mouth formed the words.

"*Hate you,*" it answered.

A deeper feeling grasped Lillia. An animal desire, to kill this awful thing with her hands. To bite it herself. To tear it apart. She had always hated this thing, this dream. She felt her face flush. Still frozen to the ground, Lillia curled her hands into fists and bared her teeth.

The spider tightened its grasp. A fang gently pricked the surface of her skin.

Lillia's mind went blank. All of her thoughts, the fear, the rage, and the last piece of ration that had held them together, all came tumbling out of her head. She could no longer be sure whose voice she heard:

"Fight."

"*Yield.*"

"Run."

"*Hide.*"

A moment, an instant, of peace came upon her. Lillia was ready to die. The creature came into her, and Lillia's eyes went wide.

She looked for it, but it had disappeared.

She listened, but it made no more sound.

She flailed about for the thing, grasping for it, clutching after it, but there was nothing there for her to touch.

Nothing at all.

The tunnel was gone, the dreams, the awful shadows. Vanished. All that remained was her light. And a mirror reflecting it back at her.

Slowly Lillia got to her feet. She felt lightheaded, but there was nothing to take hold of, so she had to crouch back down a moment until the dizziness passed. When she looked up again, she saw before her a sprawling plane bordered by an ornate and gilded frame. Its surface was smoky in color, but gradually the sediments within it settled and it grew clear, a perfect reflection of her face—thin, hollow-eyed, haunted—staring back at her. In the reflection, she was alone. Only Lillia. The figure in the mirror, Lillia, regarded her closely and blinked.

And then, that sublime sensation of dawning clarity—of awakening—came upon Lillia once again. She became aware that she was looking at herself in a mirror—while looking back at herself from within the mirror—at the same moment. Both beings, the one inside and outside were conscious, both aware of themselves and the other.

Then, like a breeze wafting through ashes, the reflection in the mirror waivered and dissipated. Lillia's narrow face, her pale eyes, were reformed. A middle-aged woman, stout, flat-nosed, with flaked, callused skin, and rust-colored hair, scowled back at her.

It was Bette. Her mother.

"You hurt me. Made me sick the moment you got in me, then you tore me up for nine months. Should've got rid of you for the trouble you were. Always trouble. Bled out all my other babies 'cause of you. 'Cause of you! You cut my womb when you crawled out of me, you little bitch, 'cause after that, there weren't no others that lived!"

Lillia stared back at her reflection, uncomprehending.

"And what've you done now? Got my only other baby killed. Took my husband from me."

This wasn't a memory. Bette was real, right here, talking to her, a part of her.

"You know what you are? Trouble. And what does Trouble got in her hands there?"

Lillia glanced down at the pouch that somehow was still dangling from her fingertips.

"Why it's toil! A whole bag full of toil. Every one of them coins. The sweat and blood of workers. All their hardship. In your soft little hands. Trouble and toil. It's going to weigh you down. But you don't know anything about that, do you? 'Cause you're so smart. Hate you …"

Bette shook her head and receded, and in her place, came a thinner, younger figure. He looked like he had before the Farms, when he was the apparent successor to Prosperity Farm's chief clerk, his hair unshorn, sauntering against a wall with an academy sash slung loosely over his shoulder and a bemused expression fixed on his face.

"Lil," he whispered into her ear.

"Jack."

"So, what's at the bottom of the Chasm?"

Lillia swallowed hard. She knew the answer, and she felt a deep longing, a need, to tell him what he wanted to hear. But this wasn't a question; it was a riddle, and she couldn't guess its meaning. She tried to chase her thoughts down, to force them to work out the problem.

"Rocks?"

"That-that's what I read."

He looked disappointed.

"You're such a little liar."

Watching him, his body, in the mirror from where she stood, somehow Lillia could feel his presence as if he were there with her, his arms intertwining with hers, clutching her tightly, grasping her, inside of her. The scent of the ranch, the dust and manure, the smell of his sweat, filled her nostrils. He was on top of her, like in the counting-house.

"Lil."

The sound of his voice saying her name echoed in Lillia's head. She wanted to seize onto him, to stay with him, to embrace the wave that was crashing over her. But the water was already flowing back out to sea.

Two new figures appeared before her. Her brother Tim, smiling faintly, and her father, Tom. Tom was searching frantically behind Tim for something.

"Dad!" Lillia blushed and scrambled to get off her back. She waved at the mirror and held up the pouch. "Dad! Here I am! Dad—"

He paused, but not because he had heard anything. He was crouching on his hands and knees, digging intently in a spot, looking everywhere and into every place, but never at her.

"I'm right here," Lillia's voice trailed off.

Her father and brother fell back into the shade, and Lillia lost her bearings. The box before her was wavering violently. A plane, collapsing around a point, even as it expanded again. Still a box full of shadows, but one that she was both within and without. And that held her in the same regard.

As if in answer to that realization, a myriad of images flashed before her from the mirror's surface, and though she sensed a familiarity around them, as if these were retellings or echoes of stories she once knew, they were utterly confounding. The visions came pouring into her, filling her skull, driving everything before them as relentless and merciless as a changing tide: Madame Teacher furiously scrubbing at a word on the chalkboard that would not erase, then dousing it with blood. A lector singing from the top of his stand while flames licked about his feet; one by one, he was pulling out his teeth and scattering them like seeds. Craggies digging graves in potato fields. A gulleystar—that red and black one that Victor had told her to step on at the fire—it flashed brightly and then became a spider that scurried up a writing desk and slowly wove a web around a well-dressed man from the Crest who seemed oblivious to it.

Then she saw three young men, not much taller than her—they must have been dwarves—all shielding their eyes, while an older, more muscular dwarf, waved at her. The old one was dressed in leather and covered in dangling, metal hooks, and he was pointing towards some-place with a pick and trying to mouth something to her at the same time. But Lillia could not get his meaning. He faded away, still smiling, still silently calling to her.

Hawks and gulls. An octopus stretching out its tentacles to show itself, only to hide within a cloud of ink. A horned demon napping behind its wings. A ram leaping off a cliff, followed by a thousand goats. The ocean's spray rose to greet them in their fall. The droplets reflected a segment of a rainbow's arc, and when the first goat dropped through it, they all turned into statues—enormous idols draped with flowers, and burning candles, and offerings. One of them looked just like that mad porter, Eli. His marble face glared at her accusingly before it faded into the depth of a cloud. Lillia was falling with him.

The last thing she saw was the Mountain, but from afar, as if she were on a ship heading fast out to sea, and then she was plunged into the icy blackness of the water. An undertow seized her, yanking her body down; it was a crushing weight that both pushed from above and pulled from below. The air drained out of her lungs. She heard a voice, harsh but with a lilt to it that, somehow, she knew was the dwarf's that had been trying to speak to her before.

"*You must give before you take,*" he told her. "*It's a hard lesson. But the cost must be paid.*"

She was plummeting down, faster and farther down, to the bot-tom of the Chasm, for that was what she now knew she had fallen into. Falling again, as before. Flailing her arms, but going nowhere. Any moment, the waters of this new darkness would flood into her chest and crush her life out.

"*Open your hand. And then you can take.*"

It only then occurred to Lillia that she was still holding fast to the pouch of coins. Her father's coins. The treasure he had pressed so tightly into her palm, what he must have hoped could save her. Even drowning, she had not given it up. And even though she knew she must, Lillia found it a hard thing to let it go.

But her fingers twitched, then opened all the way, and the pouch slipped from her grasp. It disappeared into the nothingness beneath her, and at once she came sputtering up through the ocean's surface, the tunnel's cold air filling her lungs once more.

Now there was a mighty figure standing before her. Another dwarf, only tall and great. Bathed in dusky light, he looked ancient, and when he grimaced at Lillia, his eyes creased and twitched in spasms of pain. As he held up an arm in salute, she saw that his wrist ended in a bloody stump.

His image scattered like a dissipating mist and Lillia was gazing at her reflection once more. Clouds of smoke, the shifting shadows, percolated behind her image, settling here and there into their familiar forms, some of them right on top of her reflection's head and shoulders— a little dragon stretched its mouth wide into a yawn, a spider bustled from inside her ear and busied itself building webs in fanciful shapes before discarding them into the air, an eel swished its tail and disappeared within one of her reflected eyes. A perfect orb revolving about her pupil radiating shadow from its perfect center.

The mirror spoke, and as it did, so did Lillia:

"I am in the Mountain."

"Be it so."

"Forever."

Lillia was standing erect. The light that had been her guide was dimming, but she could see what was before her plainly. It saw her, too. They took a halting step to come closer together, and then all the voices, thousands of them from all the shadows and shapes that had gathered together, in her and all about her, together with Lillia, they spoke as one.

"We come."

Her eyes closed for a moment, no more than the span of a blink, and when they opened, she awoke for the third and final time. The aura of soft light that had been her companion was gone. The Mountain and the sea were gone. The voices, the shadows, gone. Their memory felt oddly distant.

All there was now was Lillia, standing barefoot on a tiled floor in soiled clothes, her academy sash in tatters and slipping from her shoulder. One pair of pale, hollow eyes within a lined face. Almost a stranger's face. They blinked from within the surface of a mirror.

It was tall, made of silver, perhaps twenty feet in height, and its surface was perfectly smooth without a trace of any dust or blemish. A frame of bronze, cunningly carved in geometric patterns, surrounded its edges. Lillia leaned forward, studying her image and staring hard at herself, wondering why there seemed to be something missing. She was so focused in her puzzlement, that it was some time before she noticed the rest of what lay within the mirror's reflection.

A legion of statues towered within the shadows behind her. They were marble, granite, alabaster, quartz, jade—stones she had never seen before, and they looked so real and fearsome, Lillia spun around with a start, her hand jerking to her chest.

One of the reflections in the corner of the mirror had stirred.

The littlest one. Closer than all the others, so small and dim it was almost veiled within the darkness. It stood before her. Within a silt-colored face, two eyelids blinked.

Not a statue after all.

She met his eyes and beheld the terrified face of yet another dwarf, slight and stooped, and standing no taller than her chest. He was old, dressed in his house robes, and staring straight at her.

THE SPINE

CHAPTER FORTY-ONE

GREGORY SQUINTED INTO the burning sunlight. He buried his head behind his arms, scrambling into the back of the covered wagon in a feeble attempt to ward off the stabbing brightness. The manacles around his wrists shook loudly. A woman's hand reached out from the aura of whiteness spilling inside and gently took Gregory's in her own.

"This way, Mister Gables."

Her voice was firm but respectful, and the note of deference sounded so pleasing to Gregory that he could not help but follow where she led him. "Just come forward a little," she said soothingly, "there's a step, but I'll help you with it."

As he moved, a painful jolt shot through his groin, but once it had passed, he was able to stretch his legs before him and sidle out of a small iron doorway in the rear of the cart. Not a cage, but solid metal sheets, formed a half-dome over the wagon that had carried Gregory out from the Tombs. A row of air holes in the bottom had been his only source of light or sound for—however long he had been locked inside. It had been dark and suffocating.

With the woman grasping him around his waist with one arm and guiding his head so that it would not bump against the door frame with the other, Gregory came outside. His foot reached out, his toes probing for the ground. He heard the sound of wood creaking, a wave of dizziness came over him, his knees started to buckle, and Gregory let out a frightened whimper.

Her arm was there to steady him. A firm, wiry arm, sleeved in yellow.

"Your eyes will adjust shortly," she assured him.

So they did. As he took his first stiff and halting steps, his chained hands leaning on her shoulders, the sights, the sounds, and the smells around him gradually settled into forms he recognized. They were in a wide place with a polished, tile floor, and almost nothing to hide the sky from view. It was still hotter than Gregory would have preferred, dry, with a warm, steady breeze blowing out of the north. He thought it likely to be around midday. He heard a small crowd mingling in the near distance, chattering as mindlessly as seagulls.

Gregory's nose crinkled. He paused midstep and craned his head searchingly:

"That-that would be the Kadosh Tavern, yes?"

The commissar glanced to her left and acknowledged it was.

"I ate there on a recent occasion, a removal if I recall correctly. Wonderful fare." His mouth stretched into an unctuous smile, and he blinked rapidly. "I don't suppose there could be any chance for a brief diversion—?"

"That is quite impossible," she replied.

He examined the woman closely, now that his eyes could make out her features. A lined, weathered commissar of middle years and uncommonly tall height, she looked vaguely familiar. In the crook of her arm, she had a file of parchments carefully balanced.

"I know people there, you see," Gregory explained. He tried to maneuver himself closer towards where he had smelled garlic and hops. "Important people. There's sure to be someone inside—we could clear up this whole, unfortunate nonsense. I have friends—"

The woman's grip around his arm became as tight as another manacle. Gregory squealed in pain.

"I have papers, Mister Gable." She paused. "I hope we will not need to call on a guard again?"

Gregory's mouth quivered at the recollection. When he had finally been taken out of his cell, he had made a small, pittance of a request— he simply wished to speak with Jonathan again—which the jailer had denied most haughtily. When Gregory insisted, the jailer had called for the guards. New ones dressed in High Guard uniform had burst into his cell to "take care of him." They were ... rough. The stain of his urine was still stiff on the crotch of Gregory's pants. Hearing the commissar's warning, Gregory felt a knot turning taut inside of his neck.

He tried to draw a deep breath, to protest to the commissar, but a wet, gulping noise was all he could manage.

"Come along, then," she said, resuming their walk, "we're almost there."

They went down a worn path along the tiled plaza beneath the filtered shade of the Great Dome outside of the Citadel, and now Gregory could see and hear everything clearly. People bartering, arguing, a few along the way stopped to glare at him. Once, he could hear a woman tisking her tongue as they passed her by, and Gregory was tempted to tisk right back at her for being out in a dated dress and in a color that washed out her features—but the commissar was tugging him along. He walked after her past a row of pavilions, some cages filled with birds, amphorae piled high, and in the middle, his wine merchant, Marcus, haggling with an old woman. The old fellow broke off from his negotiating for the briefest moment, cast a furtive, almost apologetic look in Gregory's direction, and then resumed his trading where he had left off. He seemed quite intent at avoiding Gregory's attempts to catch his attention.

Around a cluster of tables and a set of benches, they came to a pipe that broke off from a long wooden stage, which concealed the set of steps that led up to the back of the stage. Another commissar, a tall, muscular man, was sitting on the bottom stair waiting for them. She showed him a form from her file, and he hoisted himself up from his seat without a word. The man had dead, slate-colored eyes, and Gregory saw he was carrying a yellow, felt hood in one hand and a long folded cloth in the other.

They had only gotten up the first step, Gregory flanked by the two commissars, when Gregory halted. He turned from one to the other, and having decided that the man was probably dense, he decided to address the woman one more time. He squared his shoulders, trying to appear dignified:

"Madam Commissar, I must order you to stand down. My being here—this, this whole *proceeding*—is all highly, highly improper. I dare say illegal. I've been acquitted. Don't you understand? What you are doing is illegal," he said warningly, "and you will have to answer for it. I'll make sure of that." Seeing that had no effect on her whatsoever, Gregory quickly changed tack: "How can this even be in order? As a citizen of the Crest, I am entitled to challenge the particulars of any commissar's papers—"

At that, she cut him off. The commissar never raised her voice, but spoke like a merciless bureaucrat that was confident in her documents:

"I have a judgment from the Court of Common Corrections— which was suspended by an opinion from the Supreme Court of Appeals in Jachin. I also have a Magistrate's Order finding you in violation of four civil offenses, an affirmance of that order by the Supreme Court, a countersigned warrant from the Board of Wardens, your order of transfer, my acknowledgment of receipt of that order, and a final order of disposition that will be signed when we are concluded." She stared hard into his face, an unrelenting mask of certitude that forced Gregory to turn away. "My papers," she said, "are in proper order."

There was nothing more to be said. They went up the last of the steps.

There Gregory stood, hapless, annoyed, confused, looking out from the precipice of a stage he had once watched for his entertainment, and found he could not move any further. It was not resistance—he was no longer capable of that—but he could not willingly go any farther on his own volition. He was frozen. He needed help.

Her hand again, the commissar's strong, reassuring hand, the Commonwealth's hand, took Gregory one last time and led him to his place. A few more feet. Now he was where he was supposed to be. It brought a small measure of comfort to him that for once, he had been *ushered* to the center of a stage.

But now he felt disappointed, for it was a pitifully small gathering. Perhaps thirty? No more than forty, even if you counted the commissars working the grounds. The male commissar had put his hood on, set his folded cloth on the stage floor, and ambled back behind Gregory. It sent a cold shiver down Gregory's spine, but that quickly passed once the proceeding began. With the sun cascading on his face, Gregory heard the woman commissar begin reading in a loud, official voice:

"Ladies and gentlemen of the Crest. I humbly pray you to give heed, draw close, and bear witness to the justice of our Commonwealth ..."

She droned on. It was some long, tedious legal text that she had no doubt blathered a thousand times. Gregory's mind quickly wandered, and he began examining the little gathering before him to see if he recognized anyone. Some young up-and-comers sharing a joke. Merchants. Someone he thought might have been a solicitor. Very few women. If Regina, or even Elaine, were out there ... but no, if they had come, they would be in Regina's carriage on a hot day like this. His audience, the few there were, were all standing, milling about ... looking bored. How was that possible? Gregory felt vexed as he scanned the whole of the crowd, picking each face out one at a time, assessing who and what they were. At least, he had a good view up here.

Gregory's heart fluttered, and without thinking, he raised his hand in greeting. For a brief moment, his eyes had met Dr. Karl's, standing but a few feet below him. The old professor scowled and turned his head away to resume some conversation with a companion standing at his side, but made a point to raise his voice so that Gregory would have to overhear him:

"I wish they'd get on with it already."

"Looks like the commissar's reading through her forms," Karl's companion mused. "I heard this Gables fellow was in Regina Acacia's retinue. Did you know him?"

"I knew *of* him," Karl answered. He cast a sidelong sneer up at Gregory. "A hanger-on, a parvenu. You know the kind, Miles."

"And now he's being removed for—well, I didn't quite catch what the commissar said he did."

"I'm told the legalities were complicated. I suspect that's why it's taking her so long to read his warrant."

"It sounded like he was tried in Craggie Court?"

"At first."

Miles gave a distasteful shudder.

"I'm not a lawyer," Karl said, "but it was explained to me that he didn't commit any crime, per se—"

"I had heard he was acquitted."

"Indeed. That was what the criminal court had held. However, that ruling was suspended so that the Magistrates Board could investigate what turned out to be a most egregious civil infraction on Gables' part. Concerning his public advocacy."

"Oh?"

"The man did not hold a single license or credential."

"None?"

"Not one. He's nothing more than a run-of-the-mill Master of Arts. From a Boaz school of all things."

"And he held himself out as an expert?"

"Worse." Karl sniffed with indignation. "He deigned to urge policy—to the Stewards. The man forced an audience with Steward Temple to proselytize his unvetted opinions, which as civil transgressions go, was intolerable."

Miles clicked his tongue with disproval.

"People must know their place," he said, "leave the matters of expertise to the experts."

Karl agreed whole-heartedly, and Gregory would have given anything to have marched down the steps and slap that fat grin from his jowly face. As if sensing Gregory's thoughts, Karl drew himself taller and assumed that arrogant pose Gregory so loathed, the one that always preceded one of Karl's interminable lectures:

"According to my friends in the juridical sciences," Karl intoned, "the legal controversy here was not so much about *what* Gables professed—which was nothing but puerile drivel, believe me—but that he was ever heard to profess *anything* at all. He had no right to foist his inflammatory views upon us, you see. Because he was not an expert in anything. However, since licensure is a matter vested within the Crest, Gables' offense was confined to the Crest, which was why, in the end, it fell to the Magistrate's Board to pronounce his guilt, not the criminal court."

Miles shook his head in wonder.

"Like you said, a complicated case."

"Technically speaking, his removal will not be from the Commonwealth, but only from the Crest. You will note," Karl gestured toward the stage, "only the sword is presented."

"So it is. Well, that should give him some comfort."

"As will the fact that Gables' case shall become a minor point of legal citation for years to come. At least, that's what I've been told. It seems someone will finally have to read about him."

"Pity the poor lawyers."

From the stage, Gregory watched the two men, Miles and Karl, and the smattering of people within earshot of them, sharing a pithy laugh. His fat, bloated pedant's sneer seemed to spread among the tiny crowd ... Gregory's eyes narrowed enviously.

He was lost in imagining a perfect repartee, a cut that would have left Karl as flummoxed and sniveling as he had been in the coffeehouse with Judge Cloud so that he did not notice that the crowd had grown quiet as the commissar came to the end of her reading:

"... of these so-called theses. And so to ensure that no one else need ever be subjected to the intolerable, divisive invective of this citizen, to preserve the peace, tranquility, and diversity of this Commonwealth, and to vouchsafe the governance of our Stewards for the good of the people, particularly the citizens of the Crest, the execution of this Warrant shall commence forthwith."

There was a slight murmur, and Gregory noticed a shadow fall over him. He glanced around his shoulder and saw that the hooded commissar had hoisted a rusted broadsword high above Gregory's head. Gregory shuddered and quickly turned to the crowd again, as if the instrument of his impending demise might disappear if he didn't look at it. But there was no escaping it. The long line of the blade's shadow, poised to strike, bent at an angle and hit the stage floor in front of his feet. He decided it would be best if he shut his eyes. He didn't hear his executioner's deep, flinty voice:

"For the Crest."

A thought had just come to Gregory, and it troubled him terribly. The last thing to pass through Gregory's mind—just as the edge of a sword cleaved it free from his body—was that he had never sought a copyright for his master work, and so none of his ninety-five propositions would ever be attributed to him.

Elaine pressed her face against the beveled glass of a window. It felt warm against her cheek, and the afternoon sun filled its angled edges with a harsh white hue. In the center pane, though it was smeared with grease and dust, she could make out the plaza four stories beneath the Outer Keep's wall. The shops were doing small trade. The warbled images of carters and drovers coming and going. Near the center, the stage had a small crowd mingling about its front. Like Elaine, they had been watching a yellow swordsman plunge his blade into a slow, steady succession of prisoners. The last one, a rotund pale figure, had been Gregory. It was hard to see anything clearly through the old glass, but Elaine was certain it was him. Her eyes widened a fraction of an inch as the man's head toppled down from his body.

The people in the plaza didn't even bother to cheer anymore, she reflected.

"We're almost done, I think," Michael whispered from a stool next to hers. He was still in his parade uniform, his legs stretched out before him, and had apparently just woken from a nap. Elaine turned from the window, looked at him, and said nothing.

She and Michael had been relegated to the far wall of the chamber. It was the usual place for the betrothed, while the lawyers finalized their marriage. While the two of them passed the hours in silence, a small phalanx of sharply dressed men and women were murmuring, arguing, writing, and revising sets of documents that seemed to have no begin-ning or end. The lawyers were seated around a great polished table in the center of the room, with piles of folios and papers stretched across it like a rolling mountain range.

Amidst the washing noise of papers being shuffled from point to point across the tabletop, two alone sat in stillness. On one end, Regina was glowering at a pile of documents that had recently been thrust before her. Her knuckles had gone from pink to white from gripping her pen so tightly. At the other side of the table, Elaine's uncle lounged in his high-backed chair, exuding bored diffidence. Regina cleared her throat and at once, all the commotion was stifled.

"I can't accept this," the words slipped like bile from between Regina's teeth. "There's nothing here for my other son. Nothing. You breached our agreement."

Steward Temple let out a long sigh and appeared on the verge of responding sharply, but the lawyer at his right stood quickly. He had been negotiating all morning and much of the night before, but somehow Solomon Waters still looked rested, meticulous, and as always, prepared.

"Madam Acacia," he replied in an apologetic tone, "that particular provision which was the subject of your former agreement, has, unfortunately, become impossible to perform in light of—well, not to put it indelicately—your son's recent job performance—"

"He made a mistake," she hissed. "One mistake. And it didn't even matter. You've had all those wretches removed, haven't you?"

The lawyer bobbed his head with a pained expression.

"True enough, Madam. But that, uhm, mistake, as you put it, has made it impossible for my client to advance your son's nomination in Jachin." At that, Waters glanced at the Steward who held up his hands as if they were bound and helpless. "The Council of Stewards was so terribly dismayed to learn that Judge Acacia refused to render an appropriate adjudication in that Article Two case. Speaking personally, I can tell you his decision came as a complete shock. It greatly complicated matters for the Council and the Board—and it left my client in a particularly bad light."

"Terrible light," the Steward agreed.

"None of the Stewards will entertain your son's nomination now," the lawyer continued. "It is, as I said, quite impossible. And as I'm sure your learned counsel has advised you, impossibility of performance is a complete defense to a breach of a bargain."

"So long as the impossibility was not the result of the breaching party's actions," a woman sitting on Regina's end added. There were mutterings and more papers moved about.

"Yes," he said, "I will admit that is a fair clarification, but we've already covered that point thoroughly. Steward Temple had no involvement with the cases that went before Judge Acacia."

"Other than bringing them about," Regina's lawyer countered.

"The *verdict* was Judge Acacia's and Judge Acacia's alone," Waters raised his voice ever so slightly, but quickly regained the calm, droning composure that had marked his mannerisms throughout the day's long negotiations. He straightened the hem of his coat. "With all due respect, there is no point belaboring this further. As they say, what is done is done, and such is life in the Mountain. You cannot expect us to secure an appointment that can no longer be had. We've done all we can for Judge Acacia—his present position in the Court of Common Corrections is secure, which you'll see," he gestured toward the papers before Regina, "is guaranteed in no uncertain terms."

"For all the good that will be," Regina scoffed. "What can he do for me in the Crag under this new Plan of yours?"

The woman shot a challenging glare across the table to which Waters answered with a polite, but uncomfortable cough. From the way she was smiling, it was obvious to Elaine that Regina had gotten a hold of something—or someone—and made herself privy to a document she should not have. For the first time, she saw her uncle's face cracked with a hint of vexation. Waters quickly moved on:

"We're not here to speculate about what the Plan might or might not contain with respect to the Crag. What we do have before us, what we can discuss, should be our only concern. If you'll turn your attention to the addendum we now propose—it begins on page twenty-seven—you will see we have also endeavored to compensate you most generously for this change in circumstances. We are prepared to give back a thirtieth part of the southwest vineyard's production for the fall season—"

"—when the vines are barren," Regina quipped.

The lawyer shared a look with the Steward and pulled his lips into a tightened smile:

"We can change it to reflect the winter."

"Gross or net?"

Another silent conversation between attorney and client. Steward Temple twirled a finger to indicate he wished to conclude this.

"Gross," Waters agreed.

"I didn't hear you."

"A thirtieth of the gross production," he said more firmly.

"And Michael's promotion is expedited," she demanded. "One year in this facility, no more."

"Madam," Waters pleaded, "my client has a measure of authority, to be sure, but he cannot direct how the Board of Wardens implements their commissions. They have lists, seniority, protocols—"

"I will arrange it," Steward Temple cut him off. "Assuming he doesn't do anything embarrassing like his brother, he'll have his promotion within the year. Let's be done with this already."

From the far side of the room, Michael smiled with satisfaction.

"Looks like I'll be coming to Jachin sooner than we thought," he murmured to Elaine.

She glanced over her shoulder, away from Michael. It was mid-afternoon in the plaza. The sun was making the flagstones shimmer in its heat. The little crowd had dispersed; everyone was going back about their business. It looked like a commissar might have been mopping the stage.

"Your brother will be thrilled to hear it."

Michael's face soured.

"Why are you bringing him up?"

"They're leaving Jonathan in the Crag. Doesn't that bother you at all?"

Michael only shrugged.

"It's sad. For him. But not surprising. Jon never could follow a straight path, in anything; he's always been a little—off. He cut his own throat with that stupid ruling. So Mother had to cut her losses."

It took every bit of her effort and will but somehow Elaine managed to hold her tongue.

The attorneys, however, had more to talk about, more ink to spill, and paper to mark. They dragged on, half-heartedly, for another quarter-hour, but the negotiations were, at long last, over. Regina Acacia and Steward Temple were finally relaxing in their chairs, drinking from wine glasses, and even sharing light comments directly with one another. The tension that had hung so heavily over the chamber all day was already dispersing. There came a point where the lawyers were satisfied, too, and then Waters called over to Michael and Elaine to join them at the table.

"No, no," he smiled when they started toward their family's respective sides, "you stand together now. Right here, if you please. If you'll each sign your names here, here, and once more here," a succession of particularly large, ornately written parchments were put before them. Each one held a wax seal with a bit of yellow ribbon. And to Elaine, who had been so well trained to read closely before making her mark, signing them felt like something incorporeal, almost unreal. Her eyes lingered only on the numbers, the exchange that she (and, to a degree, her uncle) would receive for marrying into this vintner family from Boaz, and as large as those sums were, she could not help comparing them to what lay on the surface of the page adjacent to the figures: a cheap hunk of wax, a fragment of silk; tokens that lent some official imprimatur. She wrote the cursive letters to spell her name, next to her husband's, on the last document and dropped the pen quietly on the table.

"There we are," Waters declared brightly, "the bride and groom."

Waters clapped his hands once, and a solemn chorus of congratulations duly followed from all around the table. Regina did not bother looking at either her son or daughter-in-law, as she was relishing a long draught of wine. Her former rival, the Steward, was already out of his chair. He breezed past Elaine, pausing only to kiss the air by her cheek and give a nod of farewell to Regina. And then he left the room, to his next appointment.

As the rest of the gathering dissipated, Michael brought his arm around Elaine's waist, and his fingers felt, every one of them, like fetters on a chain. He held her the way one would hold a newly won trophy.

To Elaine's credit, she did not recoil.

By the time Elaine reached the doorway to Tower Sixteen, the muscles in her calves had gone into knots. Each step brought a stabbing pain to her knees. She had no idea how high she had climbed, how many flights of stairs, only that it had grown colder, and darker, despite the burning torches in the brackets along the walls of the stairwell.

It was a dreary place, the half of the Citadel inside the Mountain. With no sun to light or warm its walls, and Cowan's Chasm no more than a stone's throw from the outer parapets, the Inner Keep had always had an ominous air about it, and the upper towers were especially desolate. The moaning winds from the Chasm cut straight through the stone ramparts, the hallways were always covered in blackened mold, and the light inside the high battlements never seemed sufficient, though the builders had provided ample plenty hearths and sconces for fires. The few who dwelled up here—a collection of commissars and clerks, some layabouts from Boaz who had given up looking for paying work, a brothel of men and women, and the keep's lone battalion of guards—all shared a sullen, withdrawn spirit that came over them within a few weeks of life in the most forlorn reaches of the Inner Keep.

It had been two days since her marriage, and Elaine needed to see her husband. She had spent the better part of the first day trying to track down his whereabouts. Surely it was a feat that a man so prominent could make himself disappear inside a building, even one as vast as the Inner Keep; but, at last, she had found his logbook, the real one. Michael reported he was on "reconnaissance inspection—16," one of the top-most bartizans.

Elaine's hand came up to the planked door to knock, but then she decided she would just open it. It took a hard shove for the door to push inward.

"Hey, who's there?" Michael's hard voice challenged.

She slipped inside, holding up the palms of her hands.

"Just me. Don't shoot."

In the white sphere of a lantern's glow, she saw Michael jolt his head around.

"Shit—what the? Wha-what are *you* doing here?"

There was a flurry of movement just beyond the light, but Elaine could see the shape of a half-dressed girl fleeing into the shadows by the wall, and Michael hurriedly adjusting his belt. It was a silly subterfuge; the room inside the tower was not much bigger than a closet. He spun his legs around and Elaine could see he had been straddling a cob-webbed, rusted iron tube, about four-to-five feet in length, some long-disused instrument of war fallen to disrepair. The girl was trying to press herself against the far wall, as if she might slip in between the cracks of the mortar. After a painfully long silence, Michael repeated his question:

"What are you doing here, Elaine? You're supposed to be in Jachin."

So many barbs raced through her mind, so many ways she could unman him, but she settled on the one least likely to prolong this encounter any longer than it needed:

"Did she pass inspection?"

Michael's face went crimson. He curled his fists, cracking his knuckles, turned around, and motioned for the girl to come out from her hiding and leave. She was younger than Elaine, very thin, and as gangly and flat-chested as a teenaged boy. In such close quarters, the girl could not possibly make a discrete exit. Her short hair was tousled and as she approached Elaine, a smell of very bad perfume mixed with the scent of mold that clung to the cheap and tawdry house robe she wore. One of the Keep girls, as they were called. To Elaine's bemused surprise, the girl smiled at her as she passed through the doorway, as if they were two patrons passing in line at the same crowded coffee shop.

When the sounds of her footsteps had vanished down the stairwell, Elaine came straight to her point:

"I need a pass."

That caught Michael completely by surprise.

"You can leave whenever you like. I thought you already had."

She shook her head.

"I want to go over the Spine."

Michael's face turned to astonishment.

"That's impossible. The Spine is shut."

"You're the second-in-command. You can get me a pass."

He shifted his seat on the metal pipe and ran his fingers through his hair to collect his thoughts.

"I could ... but, but—why?"

Elaine closed her eyes to draw a deep breath. It was impossible to explain; she wasn't certain she understood herself. He started to rise, gathering his uniform about him, his composure quickly coming back to him.

"Look, if this is about that girl, I'm within my—"

She flicked her hand dismissively.

"I know. The marriage papers say we can bed whoever we like." She studied him a moment. "I thought you'd at least wait—" Then she stopped herself short and shook her head again. "No, it doesn't matter. It doesn't. I don't care about that, Michael. Just get me a pass."

"I can't send any men with you. You'd be alone ... You could get hurt."

"So gallant of you. But don't worry. I'm not going any farther than the courthouse. And I've been there plenty of times. I can fend for myself."

Michael stood before her, apparently no longer embarrassed, but still visibly perplexed. He seldom grappled with inquiring about the concerns of others, Elaine knew well; and it was obvious from his features that he would rather not bother with it now. He brought out a pen and notebook from his vest, scribbled on one of the pages, and tore it out, leaving it for her on the far edge of the pipe. Elaine took it quietly.

Perhaps it was some inchoate sense of duty that made Michael ask: "Why?"

Why indeed? She had asked herself that question over and over. Ever since the wedding day, when Elaine learned that Jonathan's elevation had been scuttled, that he would have to remain in the Court of Common Corrections, she had been haunted by an unrelenting image. It was almost like a vision that kept coming unbidden into her mind, and it would not leave her alone. The thought of Jonathan, tied and bound in the dark fast of the Crag, pleading for mercy. He was trying to speak to her, imploring Elaine for help, but his mouth was gagged with long strands—of silver webbing. The more he struggled to make a noise, the more webs enveloped him. Until, at last, he vanished, pulled down into a void.

"He's been left behind," she said at last. "He's trapped, and he has no idea. He doesn't know what's going to happen. What the plan is. No one's told him anything."

"Who—Jonathan?"

"Yes."

Michael gave a pitiless laugh. He began fixing his clothes, straightening his belt, as if he were getting dressed in his bedroom, and as he did so, he launched into the colloquy he had at hand whenever the subject of his wayward brother was broached. Elaine knew it, almost verbatim. It was necessary, unfortunate but inalterably necessary, for the family to "move beyond" the controversy Jonathan created. Jonathan had made himself a pariah. There was nothing to be done for him. A platitude about service and sacrifice, a reminder about the wealth and esteem that was at stake, and the dollop that Michael really would miss his "odd little brother—but such is life in the Mountain."

"So it is," Elaine agreed.

Michael's heartlessness steeled her resolve. She decided she might as well be completely honest with him—he was her husband after all.

"I have to go," she said. "I have to."

Elaine turned to leave, and moved to close the door behind her, with Michael still fixing his clothes by the far wall, the Commonwealth seal on his uniform slightly askew.

"You need to straighten your pants." Then, though Michael had not pressed the question, she added as an afterthought. "Someone has to love your brother."

CHAPTER FORTY-TWO

A FREEZING WIND BLEW across the Spine, never from any one direction. It stirred a thrill within Elaine. In one arm, she straddled
a parcel of two documents. The other was curled up before
her and ended in her fist, with new money from her marriage jingling
against her breast. A determined smile was fixed fast across her lips.

Had Elaine thought on it, the excitement she felt on this walk
might have struck her as peculiar, so different from the last time, when
she had needed a tonic to sleep through the passage. Lately, the passage
across Cowan's Chasm had left her with a sinking despair. But this time
the desire to see Jonathan—and to help him, if she could—seemed to
restrain the dark, foreboding loneliness that surrounded her. It did nothing to keep out the cold, however, any more than the fashionable linen
clothes she was wearing. In her haste, she had not thought to bring a
lined wool cloak.

Elaine shivered and hurried her stride. The gulleystar lanterns, the
ones still lit, grew farther and farther apart, so that by the time she
reached the final approach to the Crag, the Spine was almost completely
benighted. One forlorn gulleystar lantern hung from a rusted bracket on
the outer wall of the fort of the Court of Common Corrections. It cast
an impotent glow against the bricks behind it. The caravan doors within
the gatehouse were shut, and from the dust that had piled around the
transom, it appeared they had not been opened for some days. Tall, silent,
the doors stood like two vigils, sworn to keep whatever secrets they now
held within. It was much quieter than Elaine had ever remembered the
courthouse fort being.

Tentatively, she reached out and knocked on the door. She waited,
then tried again, a little louder.

The breeze picked up, her hair fluttered in her ears, but nothing stirred.

She tried slapping the door with her open palm, so hard that it stung, and at that, a sliding iron arrow slit set high upon on the side of the doorway thrust open to reveal a guard's startled face. The man was coming out of a stupor, she could tell at once, and surprised to have been woken.

"Who're you?"

"Elaine Temple."

"Where—where'd you come from?"

"The Citadel. Open the door, please."

The man's face disappeared long enough for him to turn about and hurl a tremendous glob of spit from the back of his throat. When he returned, his bloodshot eyes bobbled in the space of the little crack, as if searching for the lines he recited to Elaine:

"Per the, uhm," he cleared his throat again, "the ad hoc committee, the, the—whatever they're called—the Captain said to tell all travelers that under the current, uhm, circumstances, being what they are …" Clearly, the man had taxed his sotted head beyond its limits. He gave up on the speech and said:

"Look, if you're here about the caravan, it's out of commission. 'Til we get some help from the Crest. That's the bottom line."

The metal started to slide back into place.

"Wait, no," Elaine raised her voice, "you don't understand. I want to come inside. That's why I'm here. I need to get into the courthouse."

Slowly the slit reopened, and the moment his puzzled, bulbous nose appeared within, Elaine explained her purpose. But first, she showed him a coin, which seemed to penetrate the man's inebriation almost instantaneously, as if the silver gleam of the metal pierced through his fog like a ray of sunlight. He was able to understand Elaine's proposition perfectly well.

Of course he could open the gate for her. And he'd be honored to escort her to wherever she needed to go—he couldn't set foot inside the courthouse, unfortunately (a boundary that the guard's hurried and varying excuses did nothing to explain), but he could take her up to its back door, practically to the judge's chambers. No need for passes, he assured her. So long as she could pay him a small fee, not much more than what she was showing him now—just enough to cover "the fruit of his labor" for the walk—and he would see her safely there and back to the gatehouse whenever her business was concluded.

"It's gone a bit dodgy in the courtyard," he said, "but no one knows his way around there better than me. I'll keep you safe. I've seen a thing or two since I put on a warden's tunic."

Elaine nodded.

"I'm sure you have." Then a peculiar notion came to Elaine that she might have seen this man once before in a different place. She asked him for his name.

"Tye, ma'am," he smiled. "Just Tye."

The chandelier above the courtroom's bench had long since burnt out its last candle. The torches had all been taken away. A few gulleystar lamps still smoldered, surreal blots of amber light scattered across a darkened canvass of disorder. Mixed among the rushes on the floor, torn pages from past dockets, clerk's notes, pleadings, motions, dispositions, reports, a carpet of papers laid scattered and unread. The pens in the clerk's stations were broken and stilled. No prisoners were there to learn their fate; no bailiffs to guard them. A ruined courtroom, empty. Except for the judge.

Jonathan drifted through the rows of the gallery, a solitary phantom in his magistrate's robe. Though it was cold inside, the neck of his shirt was wide open. He walked with his book spread open in one hand, while his other hand was furiously dashing a pen across its paper. The book was open to its final pages, and he was writing in a frenzy, as if, seeing a finish line, the time had come for him to sprint the final leg of the race to its completion. Jonathan only stopped his walking and writing to find an inkwell every so often. Outside the walls, there was an occasional hum of distant murmurs, of whispers. Inside, nothing but the comforting sounds of the tread of Jonathan's shoes and the scratching of a feather tip across book paper.

"*Brilliant*," the voice within his head decreed.

Jonathan smiled at the compliment. He halted long enough to flip back through the last few pages approvingly, nodded to himself, and then resumed his work.

"A bit more description in the last part, over here, would flesh out the dénouement, don't you think?"

Jonathan bit the end of his pen.

"Just so," he agreed and resumed his scratching with renewed fervor. But then he came to a sticking point, a thought on the page that struck him as out of place, and before long he and his "Muse" (as he had taken to calling this inner voice) were engaged in a deep, at times profound, discourse about the resolution of conflict within a character.

"I will not tie a gaudy bow or hang a bell about the neck of my magnum opus," Jonathan protested, "just so the reader can feel satisfied with the ending."

"You're drowning your reader in allegory. All I suggest is a lifeline, a resolution for this one, minor part that you've left unresolved—"

"—it's resolved. Right here."

"What, a death? I suppose that is a kind of resolution … But it hardly satisfies."

Jonathan raised a triumphant finger.

"Precisely its point."

The Muse fell silent for a moment, as, in truth, it was not a terribly important part of the work. At last, begrudgingly, it allowed that if an inconsequential death was how Jonathan desired to end this chapter of his story, then that was his affair. In the heat of the discussion, however, Jonathan did not hear the entrance of a figure, a real one, slipping through the back doorway that led to his chambers.

"Who are you talking to?" Elaine inquired.

Jonathan spun around in surprise and slammed his book shut with an echoing thud. Why was she here? He felt his face flush with anger, not at being disturbed, but that his affair, his private affair, might have been spied. That was the whole point of staying here in the Crag, to keep far from the prying eyes. And now here they were, coming after him. Elaine was tiptoeing around the dais towards Jonathan, but when she came within the penumbra of a lantern, she came to a halt:

"Jonathan—" she started, "what-what's happened to you?"

"Huh?"

Elaine's eyes were blinking rapidly as if something had frightened her.

"You look like—" she started to reach out to him, but her fingers recoiled. "You don't look well," she finished.

"Oh." He ran his palm over the coldness of his cheeks and felt something sharp pricking into his skin. Stubble, no doubt. "I've been very busy. No time. No time."

As he spoke, his first conversation with another human being in almost three days, a heavy weariness settled over Jonathan. Here he had been so devoted, so enraptured with his work, and making such wonderful progress that its ending was literally within the grasp of his fingertips, and along comes this intrusion.

"Jonathan, are you listening to me?" Elaine glanced furtively around the courtroom. "I said, what happened here?"

Vaguely, he was aware that Elaine was pressing him with questions. But the more she spoke to him, the more Jonathan could sense that all those lovely, poignant thoughts, what he had been on the verge of pouring out into his book's completion, were in danger of slipping away. This woman was jeopardizing his great finale.

Jonathan looked down and saw that his fingers were beginning to twitch. He set down his pen and reached for the silver flask in his pocket. He took a drink, his stomach roiling slightly from the redcaps that were dissolved in the liquid, and at once felt the exhaustion begin to lift. He noticed a scowl spreading across Elaine's lips:

"It's just water," Jonathan said, a distinct edge to his voice. "See? Not to worry. Mother's little wine blockade's holding fast."

"*Get rid of her, Jonathan.*"

"What did you say?"

Elaine was staring at him, as if confused, and for a horrifying moment, Jonathan thought that she had somehow heard his Muse.

"Jonathan?"

"*I must go. Make her leave. Then I'll return.*"

"Sorry. Sorry, Elaine. All this work. I-I think I've been talking to myself lately. It's fine."

Slowly, she seemed to relax. Jonathan tried to smile, while Elaine leaned against the back of a pew.

"So ..." she said. "Why did you do it?"

Jonathan looked about for a seat, and as what would have been Elaine's chair at defense counsel's table was the only one that looked comfortable, he slumped into it. The drink made the room waiver a little, the contrast between shadow and light came into sharper focus, and, though his stomach still felt queasy, Jonathan felt more at ease, more himself. He leaned back and propped his feet up.

"Do what?" he asked with exaggerated innocence.

"Don't be dense. What in the world possessed you to adjudicate Gregory and that so-called guild of his not guilty?"

Jonathan raised a mocking eyebrow.

"Counsel, I am shocked that you of all people would question that ruling. Fifty-five innocent men and women were prosecuted for the crime of being louts and making too much noise in coffeehouses. Their only offense was vulgarity. I ask you. How would it have been cognitive justice to find them guilty? That's one of the legs on the stool of justice, you know. Social, economic, cognitive. They don't make for very comfortable sitting, but if you would do the job of a judge, you must be willing to lose your job as a judge. I think it was Cloud who liked to say that. Best advice he ever had to give. Until he came down here and suggested I have all those innocent men and women removed. Our all for all, I suppose."

It was so wonderful, the way the words would just sprout and bloom, Jonathan thought as he spoke. Quick and sharp, like the point of a pen. Though part of him fretted, the way Elaine was looking at him, that his clarity was being mistaken for lunacy; she was eying him the way she had watched balm addicts ramble on in court, even as they were carted off into the Tombs. But what if those poor defendants hadn't been mad at all? What if they were enlightened, while she was mired in ignorance? Whose shortcoming would the misunderstanding be? Jonathan was on the verge of sharing that insight with Elaine when she drew closer to him and crouched on a knee to face him fully.

"Listen, Jonathan. I don't know what you're on about with Cloud, but Gregory ... all those people—they were dead the moment they got taken up. The Stewards had them marked and noted. You had to know that. So why stick a pen in the Stewards' eye and find them not guilty? It was completely pointless."

"I respectfully disagree."

"You threw away everything, Jonathan. Jachin. The Supreme Court. That's all gone. Your own mother's disowned you."

"So I'm free at last," Jonathan lifted his pale, stick arms in a gesture of jubilation.

"No. They're leaving you in the Crag. You'll be cut off. Forever."

She said it with such severity, and for the first time, Jonathan noticed a small parcel of papers underneath her arm. Held tight like a child's blanket. Such a lawyer, he thought.

"Why are you smiling, Jonathan? Don't you understand? That ruling cost you everything. You should have just done what they told you, whatever the justice."

Jonathan tisked at her:

"Look who's a cynic now?"

Elaine fell silent as if stung by the venom that laced his words. Jonathan rose from his chair and slowly circled around her. Something in him reveled at how he could make her cringe, even as another, fading part of him recoiled at it.

"I used to enjoy our talks, Elaine," he said. "In law school. After court. All those lofty ideals of yours—economic justice, solidarity with the workers, unity in diversity. I always thought you were smart. Much too smart for Michael. But now that I'm seeing you in a clearer light, I think I may have given you too much credit."

A tear formed in Elaine's eyes:

"What's that supposed to mean?"

Jonathan regarded her. He trimmed his voice to the measured clip he assumed when he cross-examined a witness:

"You knew what was going to happen to Gregory. You knew no other lawyer would touch his case. Why didn't you come to defend him?"

"I ..."

"You're down here all the time to defend Craggies."

"Yes. Those cases are different—"

"Because those are cases no one cares about. No question there. Still, it's peculiar, don't you think? How you'll cross the Spine for a total stranger in the Crag, but when your own neighbors, people you've known for years, are run into the dock on trumped-up charges … you won't lift a finger."

"Gregory," she wiped her eyes, "his, his prosecution—"

Jonathan threw his hands in the air:

"—wasn't even for a crime! A violation of Article Two? It's impossible! Unless upsetting others is a crime. In which case, everyone is a criminal." Jonathan shook his head in disgust. "The analysis was absurd, and the proceeding was a farce. You'd have cut the Commonwealth's case to ribbons. So why weren't you here to defend him, counselor?"

"My uncle said—I didn't want to—" she faltered.

"Because you're a hypocrite," Jonathan answered for her. He held her with an icy look of satisfaction. "If you had made an appearance for any of those fools, it would have *cost* you something. Your station. Your pull. Maybe your marriage to a preening, empty-headed cock. My mother's fortune. You're not willing to *pay* for what you believe in, Elaine. All you're good for is talk—talk, talk, talk—" he made a yapping gesture with his fingers. "A belief is supposed to cost you something. Something more than just words. But you won't pay that price. Which makes you a hypocrite."

Elaine's hand jolted as if she was about to claw his face. But she held it. Her brown eyes flooded with tears, as she gazed at Jonathan.

She looks at me like a stranger now. Good.

Jonathan walked over to where his book lay. His hand stroked the ornate, leather cover.

"Scratch a hypocrite and you'll find a cynic," Jonathan said softly. He studied his flask, the warbled, frowning reflection of a man in a cloak gazing back at him from its metallic surface. His eyes seemed too hollow. He took another drink. With a sudden flurry of motion, Jonathan rounded on her.

"Why are you still here?"

Elaine let out a hurt gasp:

"I came—I came to see you—to tell you I …"

"No," he waved her off, "leave me alone. The show's over. Don't come around here to relieve your boredom anymore. Find someone else to entertain you. Leave me alone."

"*Boredom*—?" her voice tremored. Jonathan had never seen Elaine struggle with what to say before. Her mouth opened and closed, and then at last she gave up the effort, let out a long breath, and narrowed her eyes: "I crossed the Spine for you. I came because—I wanted to help you. I stole … Here."

She dropped two folded documents unceremoniously on the table-top between them. One was thin, a single page, and stamped with a seal for a pass into the Citadel. The other was a small sheaf, three or four pages, what appeared to be an official copy.

"This cost me … more than you deserve," she said.

"Well, thank you," Jonathan quipped. "I can never have enough papers."

"You should read them, your Honor." She turned her back on him and began walking back the way she came. Jonathan watched her leave, a vague apprehension now nibbling at the edge of his redcap bliss. He reached for his flask and heard her last words echo against the dull, grime-stained walls. She had already left by the time Jonathan lifted his head to acknowledge them: "And govern yourself accordingly."

CHAPTER FORTY-THREE

ONATHAN LAY ON the courtroom floor beaming. Like a child marveling at a new toy, he had himself propped up on elbows, his legs spread lazily behind him, his feet swishing contentedly in circles. The final page of his book lay open before him.

The ink that he had so carefully plotted across its surface had at last dried. He breathed deep of the musty air but smelled only the tannin aroma from the ink and the crisp parchment paper. And magnificence. Dangling from his grip, a quill pen, its tip gleaming like an onyx, floated just above the paper. He let it hang there, relishing the moment that its presence created, the conflict between whether there was anything more to add—or whether this was truly the conclusion. His eyes darted back and forth from corner to corner of the page, unable to satiate their greed, to bask in what he had made.

"It is finished."

He set the feather aside, and the dab of ink it had held spilled into some mortice of the floor. Jonathan's forehead dipped to touch the page in a silent, intimate embrace. Then he rose with a flourish, holding his finished book aloft as if presenting a newly named child to the world. Soiled rushes fell from his robes.

"It's finished!"

Jonathan heard his laughter ring loud across the empty courtroom. From the shadows that loomed in the farthest corner, a friendly voice answered him:

"*Well done, Jonathan. Very. Well. Done.*"

The Muse had never sounded so clear to Jonathan, or so affectionate with his praise. He looked over at it and grinned.

"It is, isn't it?"

It seemed to shift as if drawing a little closer to Jonathan. Behind an overturned bench, right above the portal door that led down into the Tombs, Jonathan could see some of the darkness vibrate.

"And you've brought me around to that ending of yours. It's masterful. I wouldn't have it any other way."

"Yes," Jonathan nodded. He glided over to the only table that was still upright and sat down on it, clutching his knees close to his chest, the smile still shining from his lips. The papers Elaine had left behind were next to him, still unopened and unread. Jonathan hoisted his flask and drained the last of its contents with a toast.

The spot of shade that hovered above the Tombs quivered around its edges. To Jonathan, it seemed like a friend returning a salutation.

"You're going to publish it, of course."

"I will not," Jonathan answered emphatically. He wiped his mouth with the back of his sleeve. His eyes lingered over his manuscript. "This is mine. Mine alone."

"Really? No soirees, no coffee shop appearances? No critical acclaim? Your mother will be disappointed."

"It will torment her. When I tell her I've completed a magnum opus that would dwarf all of Surefoot's doorstops, but that it shall be kept in my private papers—that she'll never be able to boast about it—the old bitch will keel over."

"So you're denying the world your creation to spite your mother?"

"Yes."

"Bravo."

"It's not just that, mind you," Jonathan added. "I've been giving this some thought. Sure, when I began working on this, I had hoped to one day see it in binding, read the critics' reviews, perhaps earn a coin or two, but—let's be honest."

"Let's."

"Who will grasp this?"

"Ah …"

"You see? You see, don't you? The metaphors we have woven in here, that we've stitched just so into this," Jonathan made a sewing motion with his hand, "only two could ever hope to grasp the allegories in all their majesty. Why should we hand something so sublime over to men like Dr. Karl, or-or Gregory? Troglodytes! They couldn't possibly comprehend the depths we've plumbed here! This is as far beyond their reach as-as the sky is beyond a spider's."

"*Well put.*"

"The way I see it—why should I throw the fruits of my labor before the goats?"

The Muse thought on that and was quick in its reply:

"*You're quite right. Best to keep it close.*"

A warm grin spread across Jonathan's face, for he had feared his Muse, although it always seemed to grasp Jonathan's thoughts, might not understand the complexity behind the certitude Jonathan felt about not sharing his book. But of course it had understood. The Muse always knew what lay within Jonathan, sometimes in ways Jonathan himself could not reach.

He and the shadow fell into a friendly discourse that, at times, resembled the banter between siblings. They spoke more on Jonathan's book, the parts they had slogged through, the bits that had seemed to float unbidden from pen to paper, and relived the highs and lows of crafting a work that spanned almost a thousand pages. The reverie only dimmed when Jonathan once brought his hand down to rest at his side. His fingers brushed up against one of the two parcels of paper from Elaine. Jonathan glanced over at it with an annoyed expression.

"I suppose I ought to have a look at this," he sighed. "Now that I've finished the book."

"*It won't bring you pleasure.*"

"No. You're probably right."

"*So. Burn it.*"

"I—I … That seems a bit—I mean, I will … after I look at it. I at least owe her that."

"*Why?*"

"She—she was a friend of mine."

No sound came from the Muse for a long while. At last, it answered coldly:

"*Some friend. She was trying to drag you back, before you could even finish your book. That's why she came. To take you away from here. From me.*"

"I know …"

Jonathan's fingers quivered, unsure whether he should even touch the packet Elaine had carried with her from the Crest. He swallowed and faced the far corner of the room. The gray dull walls smeared with body stains, the broken furniture, the wooden portal in the floor were fading before his eyes. Only the shadow floating there remained vivid, watching him intently. If it had a body, it might have been folding its arms across its chest.

"Fine. Read her lies. And then let's be done with her."

Jonathan released the breath he had been holding and nodded. He brought the collection of papers over to his lap and was surprised to find it bound with silk. A rare extravagance for what looked like nothing more than an expensive handbill. He unfolded the pages across his knee, one of them, a heavy seal on its bottom, nearly slipping away from the others. It had been unbroken, unread, until this moment.

Jonathan's eyes burst wide with astonishment. The first lines of the page held him fast; he read and re-read them over and over, unable to believe what it was he held. But as he hastily fingered through the rest of the pages, there was no doubt that what Elaine had brought was a true copy—one of but thirty-two that would have been made. Stolen from her own uncle, a Steward.

It was a document that should have spanned hundreds of pages, with tabs alongside its reams and volume covers, but was here no more than four folded notebook-sized pieces of paper. A fully grown leviathan that fit in the span of Jonathan's palms. And within its body, one darkened spot, the bolded word "sever," stared back at Jonathan like a tiny, probing eye.

He fluttered back through the papers to start at the beginning. As he read, the lines of text, the honey-colored wax seals, the creases where the pages had been folded, took on an ominous luminosity. Slowly, carefully, echoing the precision with which the document was drawn, Jonathan's voice whispered its words aloud …

The First Day of the First Year of the Tenth Plan of the Commonwealth

In the Name and by the authority of the Commonwealth of the Crest, Crag & Quarter, We the Council of Stewards, hereby Promulgate this, the Tenth Plan, for the common Good and Governance of our Resources, our Labors, and our Lives.

Elaine scanned the darkness of the courtyard's alley from the back door of the courthouse. A line of rats scurried noisily through a long puddle of filthy water. A box that had been teetering atop of small hill of litter inexplicably tumbled down with a crash. From somewhere (it was hard orienting herself in the blackness that spread before her), she thought she heard an ox braying, but that couldn't be right. It must have been one of the voices out there. The constant, guttural hum of idle, drunken men. Lurking around scattered, smoldering fires of burning crates and garbage, men on the verge of lawlessness. Men her escort had been able to steer her clear of by taking a ponderously long and wending route from the gatehouse, across the unlit spaces between seemingly endless mounds and piles of smoldering rubbish, behind empty shacks, and underneath fences, until they had finally reached the back of the courthouse.

She should have traced all those steps.

Elaine kept hidden in the shadows, staring long into an oily darkness, and arguing with herself whether it would be worth trying to call out to Tye. No. The moment she creaked open the back door and saw no one outside, Elaine knew she was alone. The guard who had taken her safely through the labyrinth of rubble and clear of all the "riff-raff," as he called the denizens that remained in the court's keep, was gone. The man Elaine had paid a year's wages to wait for her—was nowhere to be found.

In truth, she was not surprised. Besides his drunkenness, her escort's persistent refusal to come anywhere close to the courthouse was almost laughable:

"… We're all, uh, under orders to stay clear of the Tombs, ma'am," he had told her. "Besides, better I keep an eye out for you here. Don't you worry, though. I'll be right outside while you're doing your business. You can count on old Tye."

"Bastard," Elaine breathed as she scanned the empty courtyard one more time.

The gatehouse that guarded the entrance to the Spine was probably no more than a hundred yards from this very doorway. She had a rough idea of the direction—but not how to navigate her way through the maze of clutter to reach it. Not without running headlong into some of those voices.

Her attention returned to the only other building she could see, one that was still illuminated with a faint, grayish light, the last gulley-star lamp that seemed to have remained lit in the courtyard. At least, it was close. No one was around. Elaine watched it a long while. A low shingled roof, shuddered windows, double doors in the entryway. One of them was opened, a bar of hazy light spilled out into the courtyard, illuminating an overlarge circular sign with the Commonwealth symbol painted in its middle.

"The clerks' pub," she said softly to herself.

There is but one constant in man's being: to consume. To be is to devour. The stomach must be fed. The worn-out must be replaced. The mind must be occupied. Every part of the body craves for more, and more, and more.

Yet, in the clamor to fulfill these never-ending needs, we contend against another constant: what the Mountain can yield is finite. There is only so much iron in the Mountain's veins, so much land upon its surface, so much water running through its rocks and stones, and then its bounty of commodities will be exhausted forever, the extent of our life's larders.

From time immemorial, this has stood as the intractable dilemma of our existence. Our needs are many. Our resources are few. We scurry to fulfill what we can, while we can, as fast as we can. As has been observed in every Plan since the Founding of our Commonwealth, it must fall to the Will—the conscious direction of the people's force and motion—to mediate between these two antithetical poles.

The Council of Stewards, the repository of the Commonwealth's Will, has labored long to resolve this problem. Indeed, it has been our aim since the beginning of the Commonwealth. In the Three Articles of the Commonwealth, what we consider the First and Primary Plan of our Governance, we declared our guiding principles:

Article I: There is no god, and none shall be proclaimed.

Article II: There is no turmoil, and none shall be sustained.

Article III: There is no right, only will; and none, but our all's, shall be allayed.

Bold and aspirational, true, but having fought and bled for these shining principles in the Overthrow, that glorious event, could we do any less but take up this challenge, headlong, to bring the Three Articles into reality?

Elaine was certain she could make it to the pub unnoticed if she hurried. Inside she might find another bailiff, or a clerk, maybe even a commissar. Someone who could help her. The pub was quiet, like an island of relative calm amidst the noises of fighting and bawling that echoed all around her. It was the only place to try, since Jonathan …

Elaine's face darkened at the memory of their meeting. She glanced one last time over her shoulder into the empty hallway in the courthouse. A small flutter of hope, and then Elaine cursed herself for being a fool; of course, he hadn't followed her. He was where he wanted to be.

Alone with his book, with his court, with his madness. And the copy of the Plan she had brought to him.

Another cry carried across the darkness, someone screaming about "the eyes," and then the place fell quiet again. She made up her mind.

Elaine took a deep breath, lifted the ends of her skirt to her knees, and ran from the doorway.

No sooner had the dust settled from the Overthrow (and the parasitic drain of the priesthood excised) when the Council of Stewards convened the first panel of experts to commence this most monumental of labors. Their work spanned five years. What resulted was nothing less than the Second Plan ("Our Great Leap Forward"). That venerable document heralded the collective ownership over all the productive sectors of the Crag, the abolishment of profit, the establishment of

a currency founded on labor, not hoarded accumulation, fair and just quotas, and an equitable rationing of all prosperity.

In the years since then, the Council of Stewards, employing the finest credentialed minds at its disposal, has rendered successive—and increasingly more exacting—Plans for the governance of our Commonwealth's resources. Our Third Plan ("Solidarity Working in Diversity") created the Board of Wardens and its functionaries, formalized the separate offices of clerks and commissars, and defined, for the first time, the tiers and classifications of labor roles that have remained enshrined within our Commonwealth's guidelines. Our Fourth Plan ("Ever More") approved the use of lectors to proclaim laudatory and instructive commentary on the Commonwealth's undertakings and counter discursive speech among the workers. The Fifth ("We Shall"), Sixth ("Forward"), Seventh ("Arise"), and Eighth ("Awake") Plans were each a marvel of progress, each a tremendous stride, that would eventually bring us to the summit of the Commonwealth's governance, our Ninth Plan, "Our All for All."

Throughout the past twelve years under the Ninth Plan, we have continued to refine the metrics of analysis to such a honed precision that we have, at last, reached omniscience over the affairs of the Mountain. In every corridor of the Crag on every day of the calendar, we can tally exactly how many will be born, and how many will die. We have calculated to the twelfth decimal guidelines and quotas for the distribution of our scarce resources. We have measured, assessed, assigned, and allocated every gram of useful material and service that can be wrung from our Mountain. Under the directions so thoughtfully compiled by our experts in this Plan, not a single grain would fall where it shouldn't, not a moment of a man's life would ever be wasted.

And yet … despite this benevolent direction, somehow, the problem we set out to solve seems to have worsened. Far too much is now consumed by far, far too many for the Mountain to sustain us.

Her shoes clacked loudly against the stones. They made a great plunk when she plunged through a puddle, and Elaine cursed herself a second time for not having thought to take them off. She was flanked on either side by two makeshift stockade fences, which seemed to serve no other purpose than to provide a way through the detritus that had been piled

behind them. It stank of vinegar poured to mask the stench of shit. The
ground was wet and uneven, and a crack in a flagstone caught one of her
heels fast. She nearly rolled her ankle, but Elaine grasped onto one of the
fences and held her balance. She was already panting, and her feet were
soaked in cold, muddy wetness.

But the pub was closer now. She started hopping, trying to unlace
the thongs around her ankles while moving to reach the door. But she
was making far too much noise.

From behind a long stretch of planks behind her came a shuffling
noise. She looked over her shoulder and dimly she saw the outline of a
man jutting his head over the top board. He slurred at Elaine:

"Hey, where you off to now?"

Elaine did not slow her gait or look back.

"I been waitin' for you. Found a jar. Make you feel good …"

The man staggered over the barrier, landing with a thud and swearing loudly. He started plodding after her, swaying wildly, but moving
with surprising swiftness.

"Hey, I went and bought this for the both of us. You owe me. Bitch!"

Elaine's heart raced. Still keeping her eyes fixed ahead, she reached
down and fumbled at her ankles, her fingers numb from the cold and the
panic that was gripping her, but finally the straps of her shoes came loose.
She surged forward on her bare feet, but the man was already behind her.

A hand groped at her waist and took a hold of her skirt, dragging her
down like a dead weight. Elaine refused to turn around, even as she sank
to her knees. The pub, the doorway, it was so close now …

*Meanwhile, the Crag's population burgeons. With each new baby, a new mouth is
made to devour more of what little remains of our precious stores.*

*Early in the Eleventh Year of the Ninth Plan, the Crag's population had effec-
tively grown beyond the clerks' capability to manage. Faced with underemployment
and lax oversight, the workers grew idle in their occupations and profligate in their
vice; incidents of assault, homicide, rape, and shirking have reached levels that would,
if enforced, require incarceration of the majority of the populace. Even among those
we might characterize as the "elite" of the various strata of laborers, there is marked*

gravitation toward guilds, which constitutes arguably the greatest drain on productive resources in all the Crag. The Crag, to borrow one of its colloquialisms, is eating its own seed corn.

"That's better," the man tightened his hold on Elaine.

A waft of balm assaulted Elaine's nose. She could read the pub's sign hanging from its doorway now—*Fruits*—it was close enough that if she shouted someone would have to hear her. But would anyone come? And who would they help?

She was spinning in her numbness. Her strength and her senses drained away like a rivulet of water. Flowing out. Over the stones and underneath the doorway. She was inside the pub, seated at a barstool and sipping a glass of burgundy, and watching what was happening to her. From afar.

This was all just a play. She could even remember the opening lines of the act. Michael sneering from the other side of the tower door as she hurried down the stairs:

"By all means, go get yourself raped and killed for my brother. My commission goes forward with or without you. I'll make a fine widower ..."

The pub building blurred, replaced by the darkness of the open air. A sequence of odors: shit, vinegar, balm, sweat. The man was twisting Elaine onto her back. He thrust his weight on her. Another blast of balm. Elaine's eyes fluttered at it, and it made her finally look at her attacker, his face a hand's breadth above hers. He was trying to pry her legs apart and loosen his pants in the same motion.

The conflagration has spread. In the Dwarven Quarter—a realm that, it must be said, has always posed something of a challenge for the Council—the skilled labor and engineering work that we had long relied upon (and that was required of our dwarven colleagues under the terms of the Treaty) has been gradually withdrawn. To be sure, some of this reduction is likely due to the anomalous fertility condition in the Quarter. But in many sectors, the minimal work we had expected to

be forthcoming has been absent. Thoroughfare tunnels are collapsing outright; over fifty percent of our interior waterworks are nonfunctioning; the roads and bridges are in dire condition from lack of maintenance. But instead of performing their agreed-upon work, our compatriots have, unfortunately, spent their time reviving religious and tribal passions.

We now have incontrovertible reports that our Quarter denizens are arming themselves. Whether out of misguided allegiance to their leaders or slavish fealty to their idols, they are forging weapons—and colluding with hostile, revolutionary factions among the workers, most notably the guilds. They have broken the Treaty. In our indulgence of this realm's diverse peculiarities, we unwittingly succored treason.

Thus, our present condition: workers multiply like roaches; a realm foments war and religion; fallow fields; empty mines; ignorance; violence; disorder.

Let us be candid. We have failed, despite our best efforts, to solve the problem of our existence on the Mountain. That failure now portends our destruction.

A specter is haunting the Crest. A storm has gathered around us. A growing, agitated population on the one hand, neighboring a martial and fervent population on the other. Each is starving, desperate, and ungovernable. The Crag and Quarter look to the Crest no longer with trusting hope for guidance, but with resentment—and envy. All that stands between these restless realms and ours is a bridge and a force of nine score High Guard. Should the elements of the Crag and Quarter unite, the Crest would assuredly fall. Unending hordes of workers, armed with dwarven weaponry and spurred by dwarven zealotry, pouring across the Chasm like ravenous animals—it is a threat that is all too real and already looms at the gates of our Citadel. Our end is knocking upon our door.

So what is to be done?

Elaine's hands scrambled the ground for something to grasp. Stone, silt, grout cut into her palms, and then she felt something cool and solid. It was glass. A heavy jar half full of liquid.

He had brought his balm with him, she realized through the haze of what was happening to her. He couldn't part with his drink, not even for this. It truly was a disease.

Tye's head came closer and he mouthed something in her ear, a whispered voice that was not his own:

"It's not a disease."

Elaine let out a horrified scream and brought the jar hard around, smashing it against the side of Tye's skull. A splay of blood, a look of vague disbelief, and the guard crumpled to the ground.

Elaine turned over on her side, panting, but Tye's hairy fingers still held the hem of her skirt. She scrambled to her feet and pulled at it, tearing the stitching in the cloth.

She was free. Her knees warbled beneath her. She tried to fix her hair, to stand erect, but her head was spinning too fast.

She doubled over and threw up.

The bangs of Elaine's hair hung like a curtain before her eyes. Frozen sweat beaded and then flowed down her forehead and cheeks, mingling with her tears. The air had stuck in her throat. She was gagging, trying to swallow, to force herself to breathe, and finally what had been trapped came out. A sob.

For too long we have sat idly before the maw of our oblivion. We pondered, we issued reports, we dithered—but did nothing. Now there is only one solution left to us, and so we have no choice but to embrace it.

We must become fewer. A fewer, and better, people …

We must sever the Spine.

We will cut ourselves off from the rest of the Mountain. For those who are the head, who by nature are endowed with the immutable traits of cognitive excellence, must live apart. That which remains must follow its natural course. Apart, not a part; that has always been our destiny on the Mountain.

The severance will occur in three degrees.

First: It is imperative we prevent an alliance between the lower realms from coalescing while we effectuate our severance. Embargos and blockades between the Crag and the Quarter have had only marginal success in this regard. Thus, a casus belli was recently arranged, a provocation designed to stir animosity, which, we are pleased to note, succeeded well beyond our aspirations. An undeclared state of war presently exists between workers and dwarves. While they fight amongst themselves, we will consolidate unto ourselves. The Board of Wardens is to be commended for the success of this degree's accomplishment.

Second: We will withdraw our presence from within the Crag. Caravan imports are no longer necessary. All commissars stationed in the Crag have been reassigned to menial tasks in the Crest to support our population (Crag wardens, who have no suitable occupational equivalence in the Crest, will not be reassigned). No further guidelines or directives will issue into the Crag. The Court of Common Corrections shall be abolished.

Third: We will shut the gates of the Inner Keep forever. On pain of removal from the Crest, no one shall open Knowledge *and* Peace *again. Nor shall anyone be permitted to approach them.*

What we propose is the preservation of those, who by just merit, have earned the right to the fruits of this Mountain—the fulfillment of all that which economic, cognitive, and social justice demand. What we propose is progress—the inexorable manifestation of Our Will. We have the land and labor to sustain ourselves in the Crest; so that is what we will do. Our separateness shall be our salvation.

The cost of this separation will be great—in lives and in treasure—it may well prove incalculable. But we are prepared to pay it, whatever price the achievement of our goal may carry. What choice do we have? The price of progress must be paid.

Therefore, We, the Council of Stewards, who have affixed our seals below, resolve ourselves firmly, steadfastly, and unanimously to this Plan, our final Plan for the governance of the Commonwealth—final because, henceforth, we shall never again have to face the question that has vexed us for far too long, what is to be done?

CHAPTER FORTY-FOUR

T HE SCENT OF blood and burning refuse mingled in Elaine's nostrils. Her legs were shaking violently. She watched them quivering with that odd disconnection again; as if they were miles away underneath her, detached, the long scrape on the side of her knee bleeding freely registered as nothing more than a dab of paint. Elaine brought her hand down to cover the wound and then, turning her back on Tye's body, she shuffled in the direction of the pub.

Within a few steps, her pain reemerged. Biting, stinging scrapes up and down her limbs, and what felt like needles plunging in her chest with each breath. But she made it to the doorway. From habit, Elaine fixed her hair, tucking it behind her ears, and tried to straighten her clothes so that the tear wouldn't show too prominently. She brushed some of the dirt from her arms and walked through the front door, tilting her chin with a patrician air.

The pub inside was a long, open hall, perhaps half-filled, and to Elaine's immediate relief, yellow sashes prevailed everywhere she looked. Even the odor—unwashed bodies, cheap ale, tobacco, but not a whiff of balm—felt welcomed after what she had been through. There was a gulleystar chandelier made from a rusted, spoked wheel that hung from the ceiling and cast the middle part of the room in a steady light. Only one fire was going, a soup kettle simmering over it.

Elaine shut the door behind her and looked for a place to sit where she might keep hidden and still have a good view of the pub's interior. A booth. A table in a corner. Even a stool, as long as it was outside the light of the chandelier. Someplace she could slip into the shadows and gather herself. She looked around, but all the tables seemed to have customers.

Sensing some of the eyes in the room were beginning to linger on her, Elaine decided to keep moving. She brought her head down to her chest and walked, slowly but with an air of purposefulness, towards the bar. A collection of greasy court clerks seated along a table watched her with something between sullenness and indifference. But she could hear their whispers trailing as she passed.

"Look at that pretty bronze skin; she's been in the Crest."

"Commissar?"

"Nah, too well dressed. Looks like some of the rats already gave her a tumble, though, I think."

"If not yet, soon enough …"

Elaine's pulse quickened. Were they getting out of their chairs?

"Miss Temple?"

Elaine spun around. She had been so focused on listening to the conversations, she had not noticed the man's approach. A slight, serious-looking fellow stood before her. Whatever else could be said for his appearance—he had not shaved in some time, and his clerk's sash required laundering—the deference that must have been thoroughly instilled in his training still shone through. His gaze darted between Elaine and the other patrons.

"Yes," she said.

"You shouldn't be here," the clerk gently took her by her elbow and, without any resistance from Elaine, led her past the bar, into a hallway that led to a barricaded door. He was so assured in how he guided her; Elaine only halted once when she dimly recognized him for who he was.

"You're the—the court clerk."

"Nicholas, yes ma'am," he fidgeted with a crossbar until he finally pulled it aside and shoved the door open. "Inside. Quickly, please."

The moment Elaine had crossed the transom, he shut the door and barred it again.

There was a lingering pungent odor inside, but it was a tidy chamber, the first orderly place she had come across since she had crossed the Spine. The walls were rounded with matching curved shelves that spanned from the floor up to a low ceiling. A few wooden crates filled with potatoes, some spice racks, and a dozen keg barrels were the only furnishings. A small stove was burning rubbish for warmth, the acrid smoke funneled outside through a pipe in the wall. Elaine found one of the smaller kegs nearby and stuck her feet as close to the heated iron as she could, while Nicholas kept his ear pressed against the surface of the door. He held a finger up for her to keep still, but eventually, he pried himself away and joined her by the stove.

"You shouldn't be here, Miss Temple."

"I know," Elaine nodded.

Sitting in this walled-off room, bricks and firelight separating her from the shadows outside, with the warmth coming off the stove beginning to seep into her toes, all Elaine wanted to do was sleep. She brought up her hand to cover a yawn and rested her chin on it.

"I'm afraid the courtyard has become a dangerous place," Nicholas continued, "filled with dangerous people. Brigands, loiterers, layabouts. Even the guards—the ones that are still here—can't be trusted."

Elaine smiled wanly.

"So I've learned."

"I can extend you a measure of protection while you're in the Fruits, but—oh! But you're *hurt*." He pointed to the blood oozing from her knee. "Oh, that needs tending, counselor. I can tell it does, and I'm not authorized to administer medicine ... Would bandaging run afoul of any licensure—?"

"You're within guidelines," Elaine assured him.

"Alright. Alright, let me see if I can't find some clean cloth somewhere. I'm sure we've got something ..."

While Nicholas fretted and poked around the shelves, Elaine asked him what had happened since she had last been here.

"We've been at war, Miss Temple," he rummaged through a small cloth bag but finding nothing inside other than peppercorns, cast it aside.

"With who?"

Nicholas paused from scouring the shelves long enough to give Elaine a baffled expression:

"With the dwarves. Surely ... surely the news must have reached the Crest?"

"It may have," Elaine replied, her voice languid in her ears. Her eyelids were beginning to settle upon themselves. "I've been so busy lately, though."

"Yes, well. We've had quite a time of it, too." The tone of resentment—and reproach—was unmistakable. But the clerk quickly recollected himself. "Forgive me. This war has touched us all, myself included. You see, the dwarves did not just attack workers, they assaulted clerks, too. My comrades. Slaughtered like goats." He lifted his chin a degree higher. "Many of them stayed at their posts so that they could fall in service to the Commonwealth."

"My ... goodness" was all Elaine could say. Hadn't she heard rumors about violence in the Crag or some kind of trouble in the Dwarven Quarter? Something her uncle may have mentioned once. It rang familiar, but she hadn't given it much thought. In the fog that was settling over her, she had no desire to do so now, but she would not want to seem unconcerned.

"That must have been terrible," she said at last.

"Indeed it was, ma'am. The violence has been most obscene, most terrible indeed. And it's touched every part of the Crag. Even our far corner out here in the courthouse—this very tavern, in fact," he pointed towards the door. "A dwarf spy was able to slip into one of our rooms. The scoundrel was chased out, but who knows what he could have done to us while we slept in our beds? Ah, here we are."

He brought down a gray cloth from one of the top shelves. It had once been used as a sign banner, and on one side was a painted cluster of purple circles, supposedly grapes, and the pub's name *Fruits* in crude cursive. Nicholas tore a strip off the end and wrapped it carefully around Elaine's knee, each fold at precisely the same overlap:

"I'm afraid good order's gone to pieces now. All the wardens were mustered. They took everyone. First our guards, then our auxiliaries, and then even our workers got pressed to fight the dwarves. Every man in this fort that could push a cart or hold a weapon was taken. Not one of those press crews was authorized, mind you. Never seen such shabby papers. But the only ones left here now are us clerks," he jabbed a thumb at the storeroom's outer wall, "and the ones the press crews wouldn't have. It's been days since we've had word from the wardens—from anyone. No one's come back or told us what to do. We can't get that new plan from the Crest soon enough."

Nicholas tied the bandage off in a perfect double knot.

"How does that feel?"

Elaine folded and extended her bandaged knee and smiled at him gratefully:

"Good. Very good. Thank you, Nicholas."

They sat in the quiet of the storeroom for a while, Elaine's head dropping as the warmth from the fire enveloped her. Nicholas quietly tended the stove, sifting through what was at hand for a more suitable fuel than the food scraps that were smoldering inside its hollow. He went about his work so quietly Elaine might have dozed off. But then her eyes blinked open again:

"I saw him," she said with a sudden waking. "In the courthouse."

Nicholas cast her a dark, foreboding expression.

"Judge Acacia?"

"Yes."

It was a subject the clerk did not wish to discuss, not even in the seclusion of a locked storeroom.

"I'm surprised," he said at last.

"He's all alone in there."

"Yes, well … I tried to convince his Honor to leave. Early on. I practically begged him. He could have gained entry into the Citadel, surely. Do you know what he said to me?"

She shook her head.

"He said, 'I rather like it inside the Mountain these days.' He said it's finally become 'an interesting place.' I'm afraid, he's—"

"He's sick. Something with his mind, it … It's a sickness, that's all."

Nicholas studied Elaine for a moment.

"Perhaps," Nicholas' answer carried little conviction. "Only … I do not think that his Honor's malady is entirely of the mind. It's also the place. Where he's locked himself in …" Nicholas tossed a broken cask head into the fire and quietly watched its pale timber turn brown, then black, and then finally combust. Once it had lit, he continued in a grave voice: "The courthouse has become a bad place."

The way Nicholas uttered "bad," was so guarded and with such trepidation, Elaine looked at him curiously. Nicholas explained:

"You see after the wardens pressed our prison guards from the Tombs, we didn't know what we should do with—with the prisoners. How were we supposed to feed and water them and such? The press sergeants told us not to bother; that the press would only be for a little while. They said we ought to just … leave the prisoners in their cells, for the time being, until the guards could come back …" Nicholas buried his chin within his knees, the lines in his face furrowing in the orange glow of the stove. His voice dropped so low Elaine could scarcely hear him. "Of course, they never came back. The prisoners … You could—you could hear their wailing all the way to the Spine. The sound from the Tombs. It was … It was like a song. Almost. A horrible song. Ever since then …"

The clerk shuddered.

"What?"

Nicholas would not look at her, his lips, his hands, the entirety of his thin body, had drawn tight upon himself.

"Nicholas?"

He shivered, but his reticence eventually yielded to his training: a Crest citizen had posed a request upon a clerk. Slowly, his held breath escaping through clenched teeth, Nicholas uncoiled himself from before the fire and motioned for Elaine to follow him over to the wall at the opposite end of the door. Between two shelves there was a rectangular metal grate, what looked like a vent for air to circulate into the closed-off room. Nicholas' fingers worked a latch and he silently pulled the grate out of its frame so that in the grate's place was now a small window into the outside. Elaine's eyes were slow to adjust to the darkness again, but soon she could make out the piles of effects in the courtyard, the wending alley between the fences she had run, and beyond it, the shadow of the courthouse.

"Look up," he whispered to her, "above the roof. But do not stare."

Elaine did as she was told, and for a long while saw nothing other than wisps of fire and smoke and ashes floating across the dark air. Her eyes squinted and she wondered if the same madness that afflicted Jonathan might have also touched his clerk when suddenly she spied something. It drew her breath. Nicholas gently pulled her back and put the grate into its place once more.

"We try not to talk about it. Or look at it for too long. But, yes, you saw right. It appeared the moment the last cry inside the Tombs went still. It has been there ever since. Do you see now why the courthouse is a … a bad place? Why it should be avoided?"

Elaine's heart was racing, the panic of what she had been through outside replaced by what she had just seen.

In the span of a breath, there had been a cloud of black fog, deeper than the darkness that surrounded it, hovering purposely in the air above the roof of the courthouse. It was small, shifting, very hard to spot at first. Like smoke untethered from any fire. If she hadn't caught the glimpse from the corner of her eye, she would never have known it was there. Even now, she couldn't be sure that her eyes had beheld anything at all. But the cold that had crept into her chest, the prickling in her skin, the hairs on her neck, her ragged heartbeat, all confirmed—a presence. A malevolent presence had perched itself above the courthouse, and it was watching the degradation below.

In the center of the cloud, she had seen two flecks of yellow light, poised like eyes. Watching until Elaine had blinked her own, and then they were gone again.

It was late. The exact time was impossible to tell. The water clock by the clerk's stations had long since been drained of its contents. But for the first time in days, Jonathan was beginning to feel the lateness of the hours. It must have been well past midnight.

He stretched his arms and let out a loud yawn. The sound of his voice carried to the front doors of the courthouse.

The Tenth Plan still laid open on the table next to him. The little bundle caught his eye. With its phalanx of officious looking seals embedded in gold-colored wax, tiny black lines of hammers, swords, and picks, all queued up across the bottom of a page. Like a row of diminutive soldiers, awaiting their orders. The initial thrill he had felt when he realized what Elaine had delivered to him had faded. He had read it twice now and was already bored with it. Another yawn slipped out.

On some level, Jonathan marveled at his lack of—what was it he lacked here? Outrage? Shock? Concern? After all, what this Plan proposed was nothing short of cataclysm.

He felt none of these things, though. What was there to be surprised about? The Crag was overcrowded, underfed, and careening toward anarchy. The dwarves were wild, irrational, untamable creatures, the same as they were before the Overthrow. What else could be expected from the Crest, but that it would eventually remove itself from the other two? It was a sound Plan. Brief (for a welcomed change) and logical. Jonathan could find little within it with which he had not readily assented. Indeed, there was a pragmatism there, one that was sorely lacking in any other Plan he had read before—much in the sense of a writer concluding he might as well crumple up a paper and start afresh than continue scratching through lines to cram in more edits that could no longer be read. No, the Crest *should* go its own way; and the other realms should go theirs, even if that meant their eventual destruction. Just part of the inevitable sorting that nature seems to so adore.

None of it mattered to him. Because Jonathan had found a special place in the dark fastness of this courthouse. He could not be concerned, because at last, he was by himself, as he had always felt. He had become a group of one, akin to no other, in a way that both set him apart and wrapped him in security.

Whatever purpose Elaine may have held in secreting this copy over the Spine, whatever frightened effect she thought it would engender once he read it, was entirely lost. Out of propriety, or acknowledging the risk Elaine had taken, he did try, for a moment, to produce some sincere feeling of concern, of caring about what the Crest was unleashing in the realms, but found he could summon nothing more than a wistful sigh of resignation.

Jonathan simply could not make himself care anymore. It was probably best that Elaine had left him while he was reading through the Plan; had Jonathan shared any of these thoughts with her, the tedium of her reaction would have been unbearable.

Jonathan rose from the desk stiffly, his knees creaking as they straightened. His head felt a little wobbly from sitting for so long. One gulleystar mushroom was sparkling the last atoms of its life in light from a sconce nearby. The air was freezing and filled with the smells of moldy rushes and burnt wood. Jonathan pulled at the end of the ceremonial belt of his robe but had run out of holes to tighten it, so he tied it into a loose knot. Quietly, he drifted across the floor to pick up his book again. He opened it tenderly and glanced over the final pages, a smile creaking across the taut skin on his face.

This was all that mattered.

Clutching the binding close to his chest, he breathed deep the heady smell of dried ink and parchment. A little sleep to rest his eyes, and then he would read his book, from beginning to end. With a lazy grin still on his face, Jonathan searched about until he found an old blanket that the bailiffs used to keep on hand for prisoners whose rags had left them indecent. It would do for a pillow. Just a short nap was all he required. He started to reach down to pick it up.

Jonathan gave a full-throated gasp, and then he shrieked. He was clawing backward, away from the stained beige cloth on the floor. His hand flew as if it had touched a lit furnace. His heart beat madly in his head, and his lips curled back in fear, the last vestige of warmth in his face drained away.

Just as his fingertips had touched the frayed threads of the blanket, an enormous black spider scuttled over them. The thing had been hiding within a fold. Its movement felt like the brush of a feather.

Jonathan brought his fingers before his eyes, unable to control their quivering, their flailing about from the protruding bones of his knuckles. For a terrifying moment, he thought his hand had become the spider, and then he let out another, much longer scream.

A cluster of shadows skirted between the wooden pillars that guarded the portico and front doorway of the courthouse. One of the shadows, bearing a stump of a flickering torch, tarried a few steps behind its companions. It was limping. The torch's flame sputtered bright for a brief moment, enough to illuminate a haggard middle-aged woman's face, wincing with pain.

"Here, Molly," a shadow near her whispered, handing the limping woman a flagon to drink from.

She took it without a word, gulping deeply, and then sank to the ground.

The rest of the shadows huddled around her at the transom of the court's doors, each figure instinctively burrowing as far into the darkness as it could, pressing against the heavy planks of the doors or the chipping plaster wall. They were five in all. Bundled in rags, shivering, and panting.

The mist from their breaths rose like smoke through the cloths they wore as scarves. They had been on the run, attacked by the others in the courtyard, once again.

"You-you think it—think it saw us?" One of the figures stammered.

Molly stirred enough to shake her head. Her eyes pressed closed, and she answered in a strained, but solemn voice:

"Eli's light will protect us. He has promised. This presence," she waved her torch to point to the air above the building, "will soon be cast back into the darkness. It will return to the hidden ones. We'll be safe here."

"Be it so," the others murmured, though each could not help but glance worriedly around, as if expecting the yellow eyes above the courthouse to reopen and train upon them at any moment. No one had dared come so close to the courthouse since the cloud and its eyes had first appeared.

"Well," the one who had given Molly the water breathed after a while, "at least there's plenty of fuel here for a fire." Loose papers had spilled out from underneath the doorway, covering much of the tiles of the entryway. He tapped one of the columns on the portico lightly and nodded with satisfaction. The wood was still intact. "And we're well clear of the others. Do you think it's safe to—I mean, can we—?"

"Go ahead, Ellis," she said. "The warmth will speed our prayers."

While Ellis got up to search around the portico, the others linked hands. Molly began whispering a soft litany while her companions sometimes joined in refrains, or muttered a quiet, made-up babble, what they called a secret prayer language. It was a calming noise amidst the crackle of shouts and scuffles farther out in the courtyard. As the newest convert, it fell to Ellis to build their fire. He went about the portico, stooped over at his waist, scooping up bundles of paper, and then placed them all in a pile beneath the base of one of the columns. An upturned clerk's table on one of the steps was a rare find, so he hurried to drag it over. When he had finished his scouring, a small pile for a fire was in place.

Ellis took Molly's torch and began setting a succession of papers alight—warrants, lectors' notes, posters, receipts, clerk's orders—until the wood in one of the table legs finally caught fire. It was a pitiful blaze, but its warmth was welcomed. The group shuffled closer to it, making a ring. They had between them a few pilfered stores and an ox's tail, and so they began cooking a meal by passing a quill pen stripped of its feathering back and forth to use as a roasting stick. There was little conversation, and not a single argument, as they shared out their food equally. Before they ate, Molly lifted her hands:

"Bless this food, You who are Over the Mountain, let it give sustenance to your children that we may sing your praises. May we one day rise again from the rocks at the call of your Servant Eli, he who fell and rose again, when we shall break bread together, as one, forever. Drive from us this present darkness—"

Molly's invocation was suddenly rent by an inhuman cry from within the Courthouse. It pierced through the walls, an awful wail of fright and despair that the whole of the courtyard must have heard. While the others cowered, Molly turned to face the sound, rising on her injured leg with a determined expression.

"The eyes!" Ellis let out a sharp cry. He held his arms over his head for protection, and leaped over the fire, and ran off into the darkness, screaming "They're coming! Darkness scatters light!" The rest of the group broke in different directions, kicking the fire over in their haste to escape from the sound. Flaming papers shot up behind them and flew off into the air like a covey of birds. The table leg rolled to the side, the orange tendril of its fire writhing higher and higher up the face of the courthouse column.

Molly braced her shoulders and held her head defiantly. Her voice cracked as she raised a ragged hand aloft:

"In the name of Eli, I cast you out. I defy your darkness. Behold the light and despair! Creature of darkness, flee from this place! I cast you out! In the name of Eli. Go!"

The doors stood shut before her, watching her in silence. It was as if the whole of the courtyard and the very air around it was intent on the spectacle of this bedraggled woman standing before a doorway and the challenge she had issued. No sound but a faint, crackling noise, and Molly's breaths broke the stillness of the portico. Slowly, the side of Molly's mouth creaked into a triumphant smile. In the grayness of her watery eyes, a flame was shining. A reflection of a fire that was spreading fast around her.

Jonathan had drained the last bottle of redcap water he had on hand, a glass beaker he had hidden away for emergencies. It was gone in a single pull. The mixture had done nothing to calm him, though. The remembrance he had of a part of his body—his hand—waving its appendages on its volition, like a spider descending from a web; it had seared into his thoughts, and now it haunted him. Like a picture, he was forced to gaze upon because the eyelids within his mind had been sewn open. He stumbled into a row of chairs of the courtroom's gallery, gurgling like a cornered animal.

He was waving his hand through the air. The spider—if that was what it was—had gone, replaced by the familiar pale, knobby fingers that were his own. He shook them hard all the same, as if to ward off the return of what he had seen.

"S-s-so horrible … Horrible …"

He repeated the word over and over, rubbing the top and palm of his hand until it hurt. Stinging tears misted beneath his eyes. He brushed at them angrily and fell into a fit of coughing.

In his panic, Jonathan had not noticed the haze gathering around him. Acrid, gray, wiping out the clarity that the drink should have provided. The Commonwealth banner above his bench was being blotted out of view, the walls around it receding into a gray fog. Jonathan hacked again.

"*We have to go.*"

The Muse was right by him. Jonathan would have let out a relieved sigh, but it turned in his throat into a fit of wheezing.

"Where have you been? There was a spider—and then it became my hand … Oh, shit and death," he tried to clear his throat, "you should have seen my poor hand—"

"*We have to go. Can't you see what's around you?*"

Jonathan's head warbled haplessly.

"I can't see anything. Am I—am I going blind?"

"Look with your eyes, Jonathan. Your real eyes."

The tables, the chairs, the witness stand, the words on the wall—
"OUR ALL FOR ALL"—had become draped with a gray curtain, smearing everything beneath its obscurity. Bits and pieces of familiar objects
peeked through the miasma, like actors peering out at a gathering crowd
from backstage, but the entire gallery was slowly becoming subsumed.
The litter strewn across the floor was the only thing Jonathan could
make out plainly. His eyes and nose were burning.

A red glow pulsed from underneath the court's front doors.

"What—what's that?"

Jonathan squinted. A moment later, the first coil of flame slipped
between the doors' wooden boards. He gaped at it, the bottom of his
jaw-dropping in affront at what he beheld; as if the presence of fire were
an especially personal intrusion upon the comfort of his darkness. Jonathan was coughing again. The doorway had become in inferno.

"Flee from here, Jonathan."

"My book—"

"There's no time."

Jonathan staggered in different directions, the smoke blinding him.
The light from the blaze stabbed hard in his eyes.

"No!" he spat. "I can't leave my book …"

He had dropped it when the spider startled him. Jonathan remembered now. It had to be on the floor somewhere.

He fell to his hands and knees, rooting through the debris on the
ground. Transfer orders, case notes, clerk's orders, guilty judgments,
rolls of names—hundreds, thousands of names, arranged in neat columns—more clerk's forms, the pass Elaine had left him. He swept
them all aside. More paper—a tide of papers—floating in ebbs through
his outstretched fingers. One by one, they would be caught up in
the flames. Jonathan plowed across the floor, grasping everything he
could touch. A surge of black smoke roiled past him. But the book was
nowhere to be found.

Tears fell freely and mixed with the soot on Jonathan's cheeks.

"Lost …"

He let out a long wail keening with heartbreak. If it weren't for the
roaring noise of the fire that had now engulfed an entire wall, Jonathan

might have heard from the other side of the doorway a woman shouting back at him in answer, a cheer of victory.

Something took him by the arm and pulled him upright.

"*Go. Take these and go.*"

His pouch of redcap mushrooms slipped into his palm. As he felt their weight settle in his hand, some of his senses returned. The anguish subsided into a dull throb. The disappointment burned, like a cut, but now he felt the heat of the flames nearby. Not bothering to look to see who had brought him his hidden store of mushrooms, Jonathan began groping around a table.

"Wa-water—" Jonathan's throat felt as if it had caught fire. He seized over coughing. "Need—water."

"*No time.*"

A gentle shove had him on his way. His fingers let go of what they had been searching for and tightened around the pouch, which, he knew, was all he truly needed.

"*Go!*"

Without realizing it, Jonathan's feet obeyed. They were carrying him through a wall of smoke, feeling for a way around the witness dais, past the bar that separated the gallery from the clerks and lawyers, past the clerk's stations and the judge's bench, they only halted when the burning cloth of the Commonwealth flag came down before him. He hopped over the smoldering pile to reach the door to his chambers.

It was already open.

The fire engulfed the Court of Common Corrections. The building's old plaster and termite riddled framing ignited like kindling, and with no one to cast water to put it out, the blaze was soon reaching high into the air. A terrible noise of burning flames, falling boards, timber cracking, and the skirl of paper igniting filled the courtyard. What life there still was within the courthouse had fled. Except for one.

From beneath a blanket, the orbed eyes of a spider gazed blankly at the pages of a book that had fallen open nearby. Its legs were twitching, for the thing was already dying. Yet it sat, as if waiting. A set of rafters crashed to the ground, sending the book's pages fluttering in sequence.

They were sketches.

The first was of a spider, not unlike the one that was about to die in the folds of the blanket. Each page that followed held a new angle, a variation on the first. The spider's head, then its face, its bloated torso, its legs, its fangs poised to bite; each drawing was a study of its being, part by deadly part. They were vibrant and perfectly detailed. One by one, the papers curled and then turned in the billowing smoke, and in the middle of the book, suddenly, the sketches shifted focus to a man. He was pallid and gaunt, his stare always fixed upon some part of himself. Looking down at his feet, into his chest, staring at his hand.

A stray cinder landed on the corner, and the page was set alight. As the book burned, the final drawings twisted in the agony of the flame, in imitation of their subject: the man, seemingly unaware of his book's companion, had become caught in the spider's web, a prey to be devoured.

CHAPTER FORTY-FIVE

I N THE MOUNTAIN, in a place high and deep, a light burned, scattering the darkness.

The outpost at the end of the Spine, the crude fortress that had long guarded marked the boundary of the Crag, was wreathed in flames. Tongues of yellow and orange danced across the roofs of a courthouse, a shed, and the outpost's broken keep, while mountains of detritus that had been rotting in its courtyard burned freely. Veins of smoke billowed high into the void above, rising higher and higher, floating forever into the cold, vacant air of the Mountain's hollow, drifting, but never meeting resistance, like lost thoughts. Every so often, a wave of embers would cast out from the outpost walls into the empty gulf of the Chasm. Their glow would linger in the air some long minutes as if taunting the emptiness.

Jonathan saw none of this.

Blinded with smoke and panic, the once dignified robes of his magisterium soiled, ripped at their seams, and stuck to his sweat-soaked body, the judge's skeletal legs propelled him forward, an inward sense guiding his direction. He was groping his way to the gatehouse. And then on to the Spine. His mouth was filled with the taste of blood hocked from his lungs and mixed with the harsh tang of burning filth. It felt as if his tongue had been painted with ashes. He was too thirsty to spit. Jonathan fell to his knees, wheezing, then pulled himself up to resume his benighted trudging.

He swiveled his head, scanning the plumes of smoke and burning heaps with the hope that his searching might somehow summon the Muse. But his companion's voice had fallen silent since Jonathan staggered out of the courthouse's back door. Or perhaps Jonathan simply couldn't hear him in the maelstrom he now found himself in. The sounds of a roaring holocaust and the throes of its victims filled Jonathan's ears:

The steady, washing drone of the fire consuming its fuel. Its heat scalding to breathe.

The shriek of rats, fleeing into the dark.

Shouts ringing out for "water," or to "stop," or "run," and, here and there, to "Eli," reverberating from every direction.

In a momentary break in the smoke, Jonathan spotted a guard, one of his bailiffs he thought, stumbling by. The man was holding his bloodied scalp with one hand and with the other gulping down a jar of balm. Something in his expression kept Jonathan from calling out to him. He watched the bailiff trip in a pothole and fall headlong into a pile of burning sackcloth where he lay, burning, and not a grunt of disapproval.

Jonathan hobbled a few halting steps across the courtyard. Bent almost down to his ankles—there was no air above the ground—he was joined in his odd, waddling flight by a small throng of people scurrying in different directions, who clambered around or underneath the smoking piles of debris in the courtyard.

Jonathan's eyes darted from side to side as he held his sleeve up to hide his face; though he knew if he crossed anyone's path it would be impossible to conceal who he was. Strangely, despite the bustle and bumping in the mayhem of the burning outpost, only one man seemed to notice Jonathan at all. A bald and hunchbacked latrine cleaner who used to greet Jonathan with a respectful bow whenever their paths crossed. The man was busy prying a backpack free from the clutch of a much heavier man's corpse when his head spun at the sound of Jonathan's approach. The cleaner squinted at him but was suddenly overcome with terror. He fled, screaming, leaving his prize in the dead man's grasp.

The encounter was unnerving, but Jonathan had no time to dwell on it. Just beyond a long trench fire, in a clearing between the burnt-out husks of a line of carts, the doorway to the gatehouse loomed, beckoning him to pass through it.

Passages floated past him, unending, ethereal. Bone colored walls melted into black, a hue so deep it shimmered. Corpses stared up at him from the dust, longingly—or perhaps expectantly. A doorway opened before him.

Jonathan staggered out onto the flagstones of the Spine, wisps of smoke still falling from his ruined clothes. He was shaking. Not from the cold, though he could see his breath trailing off into the air around him. Every inch of his limbs was tingling as if millions of barbed needles were wriggling into his skin. And a twisting, wringing sensation had laid hold of him, like his whole being had become a broken tree limb, still clinging to a trunk, being turned and turned over upon itself, not quite ready to break.

"Water ..." the word slipped from his cracked lips.

There was only wind. A cloud of ashes and silt blew along its currents. Jonathan clasped onto the pouch of redcap mushrooms in his pocket.

With no real plan or direction other than to find water, Jonathan shuffled across the bridge. He hugged himself for warmth and to try to massage the stinging from underneath his skin. Even breathing hurt. The dry, frigid air cut like a knife into his scarred lungs. He coughed and hacked, and a dry rattling shook in his chest, but eventually the last of the smoke came out, and Jonathan could draw short gasps without wracking himself in pain.

One step, then another. Jonathan tread as carefully as he could, gingerly because of his hurts, but also from a sense that the stillness of Cowan's Chasm ought not to be disturbed more than it already had been. A succession of steps, halting and unsteady, but in a straight direction.

In all the times he had come and gone between the Citadel and the court, Jonathan had never walked the bridge before. The solitude was jarring. As was the feeling of his diminishment. Alone, except for a suffused presence of emptiness. And the remnant of a fire's light. The blocks of granite rails and the smoothed flagstones beneath him still reflected a rust-colored glow from the burning fortress at his back.

Earth. Air. Fire.

But not a drop of water.

Jonathan pushed farther out into the darkness.

Time passed, a great length or a short length, he couldn't say. He abandoned trying to reckon it anymore. Minutes, hours, days ... What did they matter? What were they made of, anyway? These markings layered onto life. These contrived silos of existence. A stone in the sky oscillates between brightness and darkness, and all of one's affairs must be governed accordingly? Might as well measure life out in heartbeats. Or footfalls. And mark the increments between them by the span of one's pain. It would be just as arbitrary.

His thoughts became bleaker and bleaker. He started to reach into the pouch of redcaps, but then jerked his hand free. Jonathan shook his head, hoping to clear his senses. There was water in the Mountain, oceans of water within and around it. He would come across some—and then he could partake of what he needed.

He kept moving, hurrying now, a slow running gait over the Spine. The bridge, he noticed, somehow remained lit before him, even though the gatehouse was far behind him now. He gave it no further thought but remained intent on searching the vast darkness of the Chasm, or the cracks in the flagstones he came across, or the occasional litter he came across on the bridge's roadside. Bits of rag, a broken ruler, a goat's horn, shattered bits of pottery.

Once he rushed over to an empty pedestal along the railing's edge, one that had once held an idol. A pair of marble booted feet were all that remained of the statute. But beyond the pedestal, Jonathan thought he had spotted one of those rainclouds the Chasm churned every so often. He draped himself against the cold plinth, holding onto the broken remains of one of the statue's feet, and leaned out as far as he could into the cold void. He stared hard into the space before him. The darkness seemed to be receding unto itself. In the center, a point of blackness was collapsing into a smaller and smaller spot, its motion sending angry ripples of movement in its wake. But there was no cloud. No water.

Jonathan slumped back down to the ground, his back resting against a balustrade. The pouch was in his hand again.

"No, no, no, no, no," he whispered to his fingers.

They held for a moment, unsure whether to obey him, and then reluctantly withdrew. All Jonathan could think on, all that he desired, was the respite of his redcaps. His beloved spice. It would silence the pounding in his head, still all the hurts in his body, mollify his troubles. Oh, how he hurt. Had there ever been a time when he needed this tonic more than now? Or that he had more deserved it? After all he had been through …

His palm brushed down what remained of his clothing, emptying out the pockets, as if a flask of water might have crept into them unnoticed. If only he had some piss or enough spit in his mouth, he could dissolve his mushrooms that way; but no—every part of Jonathan's body was parched. Surely that was why he was shaking so violently.

The fingers of his right hand traipsed back down the length of a hem in his robe into the pocket that held his redcaps. They were loosening the drawstrings to the pouch. Tenderly a fingertip caressed the smooth, polished head of one of the mushrooms. It felt firm, as if inviting his touch.

"One," he said.

"*Just one,*" his Muse agreed.

Jonathan had missed his Muse terribly in the time of its absence, and yet he was not in the least surprised that it should choose this place, this moment, to return to him. That calm, familiar voice. The welcome sound seemed to carry along the breeze blowing out across the Chasm beyond the bridge, and yet still as close as the words of a lover, sharing the same pillow. Jonathan trembled, but now with excitement.

"Just one," he said, "couldn't—it couldn't be as bad as all that. What-what's he know anyway?"

"*That so-called apothecary?*" the Muse said. "*Man's a charlatan.*"

"Did he even ever test it, I wonder—ever see it poison anyone—for himself?"

"*Of course not. He as much as admitted he had no experience with what he sold you.*"

"Yeah—" Jonathan nodded uncertainly. He rubbed at the stiffness in his neck, the grit in his fingernails irritating the skin. "But if I … If I were to … You know. Take it straight. Without anything to cut it … There's got to be *some* risk in that. I would think …"

"*Everything has a cost. It's a hard lesson. But such is life in the Mountain.*"

Jonathan couldn't deny it. Then he reflected:

"But if it's just a small one. Like a half-portion. That'd be alright. For someone like me … Wouldn't it?"

A momentary pause. It stretched the tautness within Jonathan beyond anything he had ever endured; another twist, and he would break.

"*Govern yourself, Jonathan.*"

The quiet assurance of his Muse's response unleashed a flood of emotions within Jonathan. Feelings he had thought boxed up, locked away, and long ago buried, came rushing forth like a bursting dam, with the ardor of when they were first felt. Faces, his family's—always dour and disappointed. Wishes he had forgotten he once made. A slurry of images from his childhood, his school days, the court; in all of them, Jonathan standing far out on the periphery, peering in.

He had no tears to cry.

"Why must I lose everything...? Everything! My book ... M-Mother ... Liam ... Everything's lost. Oh, I hate this ..."

Jonathan doubled over, swooning with grief. Memories were piercing him like blades; the ones he had thought had grown dull could still draw blood. "It hurts ..." he groaned. "Hurts so bad ..."

"*You've paid the cost ... ten-fold.*"

"I-I hate this."

"*So stop fighting it.*"

"I need this."

"*Then quit running.*"

A scarlet dappled mushroom floating in the space between Jonathan's thumb and fingers appeared. Tiny. Beckoning. Pregnant with light.

"Just one."

"*Just one.*"

His fingers clenched, like jaws pinching shut. A burst of red light in the darkness. The light floated down, down, straight toward Jonathan's waiting tongue.

Even before it touched, in the moment before it landed, in that hair's breadth of space between what he had chosen and what he had done, Jonathan knew he made a terrible mistake. It touched him and froze within his mouth. Jonathan started to turn.

In the vast void of the Chasm, the darkness had vanished. And in its stead, Jonathan saw eyes, hundreds of bodiless, amber eyes glowering at him, pulling closer from an immeasurable distance. A terrible weight settled over him, smothering his senses, his pain, his being. He had strength enough to turn his head one last time, where he saw a figure.

The Muse.

A loud, clear voice, one that rang up and down the length of the Spine, all the way to ends of the void, to the bottom of Cowan's Chasm, greeted Jonathan:

"At last ..."

In the center of the bridge's road, bathed in his own light, a man stood, stretching, as if waking from a deep slumber. His dark, thin limbs hung lazily at his side; they were impossibly long, and yet, as he craned his body to its full height, the man's arms and legs seemed to extend even further from his torso, as if there were no ending to them, as if they would swallow the world. Straightening his back, he must have stood seven feet in height. And still, he seemed to grow taller.

Set deep within a small, pale head and a face that was at once familiar and abhorrent, two eyes burned like candles in the dark. They trained into Jonathan's, burning him with their intensity.

"At last," the man repeated, and a smile spread across his thin lips.

"Who ...?" The thought died before it could reach Jonathan's throat.

"Govern yourself," the man chuckled. His voice faded into a joyless cadence: "Govern yourself, govern yourself, govern yourself ..."

A tremor shook inside Jonathan. Something had changed. As quickly as the heaviness had come upon him, now it had dissipated, replaced by a peculiar lightness beyond any he had ever known. In his body, in his senses, his thoughts, there was now a weightlessness. Almost like sleep. It soon spread to all that surrounded him. The firmaments of his world—the stone in the bridge, the arc of its span, the depth of his own body—they were all falling away, like the contrivances they were. Like time.

He was like the air now. Like darkness. Jonathan.

It only vaguely occurred to him, scarcely as an afterthought, that he was no longer breathing.

The man looked around his surroundings for a bit, seeming very pleased with everything he saw before he drew closer to Jonathan. A finger, as sharp and lustered as onyx, beckoned Jonathan to come closer.

Jonathan came.

Not by steps, or by crawling; the man had summoned Jonathan's presence—and Jonathan's presence came at his bidding, without countenancing an idea that it could be otherwise. Jonathan could only come. And that horrified him all the more. For if he had legs, he would have run away, screaming, as far and fast as he could. Had he arms, he would have grappled his body, held it fast, to keep it away from this awful being. But he had none of these things, not anymore. Jonathan cried softly, even as he came into the stranger's presence.

"Please—" Jonathan begged, "Please. Go away. Please."

The man threw his head back and laughed.

"Of course we'll go. At once. Come."

Jonathan tried to keep from looking, but he had no eyes to shut.

He pulled closer to the man as if by some long, unbreakable thread, drawing him nearer and nearer, and it filled him with revulsion. And yet at the same time, Jonathan's being was reaching out longingly for this creature, like an infant grasping for its mother's breast. He clasped onto the man tight, with eagerness, and heaved himself up higher onto its back, and the loathing he felt with each pull was unbearable.

The man was scentless, which was as repulsive as the sensation of his skin, which, Jonathan could see, was like a mushroom's. Like a redcap's. The spider hairs that protruded from his neck and his shoulders were sharp, glossy. They pierced into Jonathan. But Jonathan burrowed closer, the tightest embrace he had ever given anyone.

Tears and blood flowed freely now; a hidden well had been struck.

Jonathan managed a single word. "Where—?"

"Where we've always been."

With that, the thing loped atop the stone pedestal of the Spine's railing. They stood there together to gaze down, as still as a statue, a grotesquery poised upon a plinth on top of the world. A whistle of wind called to them, and the man laughed a final time.

And then Jonathan was hurtling into Cowan's Chasm, leaving the last vestige of his body slumped in the dust, a soft, gentle glow slowly settling upon it.

Jonathan fell.

At first, he tried to shake himself free, but the barbs were set. They would never break. Nor would this embrace. Ever. Bleeding him to a death he knew he would never reach. As he fell, farther and farther, to a bottom he would never find. And with that realization, a whispering came upon Jonathan to answer the only question that had ever mattered.

"We are in the Mountain."

THE END

ACKNOWLEDGEMENTS

To my late parents, the Rev. Norman and Dolores Lucas, who venerated the written word like a sacrament, thank you. For everything. I love and miss you both.

To my wife, Alexis, and our boys, James and William, an enormous, bear-hug of a thank you for all your loving encouragement (and gracious indulgence) while I wrote this book.

I owe a special debt of gratitude to John Rak, an extraordinary editor who has truly been a pleasure to work with. Thank you, John, Charlie, Rick, Amit, and all the team at Montag Press for taking a chance on a doorstop of a manuscript and turning it into something special.

Thanks are also in order to these fine souls: Clayton Bricklemyer (for the helpful suggestions), Mrs. Bryce (for the note of encouragement), and the late Judy Candice (for the writing advice).

Finally, thank you, dear reader, for taking a chance on this story. If you liked it, I'd be honored if you would leave a favorable review wherever you can.

AUTHOR BIO

Matthew C. ("Matt") Lucas was born and raised in Tampa, Florida and lives there now with his wife and their two sons. He's the author of the historical fantasy novel, *Yonder & Far*, as well as short stories that have appeared in *Bards & Sages Quarterly*, *The Society of Misfit Stories*, *Collective Realms*, and *Swords & Sorcery Magazine*. Find out more about Matt's work at www.matthewclucas.com.

www.ingramcontent.com/pod-product-compliance
Lightning Source LLC
Chambersburg PA
CBHW030737030726
47497CB00001B/16